The Turning

Book Two in the Medici Warrior Series

by Emily Bex

Foundations Publishing Company
Brandon, MS 39047
www.foundationsbooks.net

The Turning
Book Two in the Medici Warrior Series
By: Emily Bex

Cover by Dawne Dominique
Edited by Laura Ranger
Copyright 2019© Emily Bex

Published in the United States of America
Worldwide Electronic & Digital Rights
Worldwide English Language Print Rights

ISBN: 978-1-64583-013-9

The Medici Warrior book series is dedicated to all the dreamers, the hopeless romantics, and to my partner in crime, Johanna Morisette.

Acknowledgements

This book could not have been written without the help of my collaborator, Johanna Morisette. She dragged me reluctantly into a world of vampires and inspired me to write. She had the initial vision for Shade and was instrumental in the development of his character. Throughout the seven years it took to write this series, she remained my sounding board for the development of the storyline. These characters, and this saga, would not exist if not for her constant support and input which kept me motivated to keep pushing forward.

Table of Reference

Italian to English Translations

Alzati guerriero
Stand-up warriors

Amica
Friend

Amore
Love

Bambino(s)
Baby/babies

Bastardo
Bastard

Bel
Beautiful

Beleeza
Beauty

Bellissimo
Very beautiful

Bravado
Brave

Buonasera
Good evening

Cazzo
Generic curse word (typically interpreted as fuck)

Dipendenzo
Addiction

Dolce
Sweet

Dormire guerrieri
Sleeping warrior

Familia
Family

Figlia/Figlio
Daughter/Son

Fino ad allora
Until then

Fratello
Brother

Grazie
Thanks

Guerrieri
Warriors

Impavido
Fearless

Lei e il mio vero amore
She is my true love

Madre
Mother

Meile
Honey

Mi/Mio/Mia
My (based on gender)

Moltobella
Very beautiful

Nostra Figlia
Our daughter

Padre
Father

Per Favore
Please

Per Sempre
Forever

Rosso
Red

Scusi
Excuse me

Si
Yes

Signorina
Young Lady

Sorella
Sister

Stupido
Stupid

Ti Amo
I Love You

Recap of Book One: The Blood Covenant

The Medici Warrior Series is a series meant to be read in sequence. The Turning is book two of the sagas. What follows is a refresher of book one, The Blood Covenant.

THIS RE-CAP CONTAINS SPOILERS OF THE BLOOD COVENANT

Shade Medici, a vampire warrior king, takes up residence in the United States from his native Florence, Italy, hired by another master vampire, Alec Canton, to provide protection to him and his mate, Larissa (Rissa). Alec and Rissa are day-walkers who live freely among mortals. Alec entered the world of mortal politics and holds a seat in the U.S. Senate. His goal is to eventually seek the Presidency.

A vampire of impressive power, Shade has made a lucrative career training and supplying warriors to other masters. He also owns a string of vineyards in Italy, France and Greece where he produces fine wines for both the mortal and vampire communities. As payment for overseeing the mercenary warriors Alec hired, Shade is paid with two additional vineyards. One in Central Virginia, and another in Napa Valley. Unbeknownst to Shade or Alec, there is a double agent amongst the mercenaries, who's agenda has yet to be revealed.

In the midst of setting up protection for Alec, Shade meets and falls in love with a mortal woman, Kate Reese. As a vamp of royal blood, and the sole surviving member of the Medici dynasty, he is expected to mate and produce an heir to ensure the longevity of the Medici coven. Cross species breeding is strictly forbidden. Mortals are viewed as playthings, never acceptable mates. Driven by his passion for her, Shade shuns the rules and pursues her. For them to stand a chance at all, he feels she needs to fall in love with him before discovering he is a vampire. Gradually, she lets her defenses down, and learns his secret. The two move to his newly acquired estate in Virginia together.

Despite the depth of their feelings for each other, Kate struggles to adapt to the changes of vampire culture. To protect her from the more violent aspects of his world, Shade tries to keep her secluded at Bel Rosso, his Virginia manor. The passion that sizzles between them is worked into a frenzy when Shade invites Kate to drink from him and seal a blood covenant between them. With this covenant bond, they bind themselves as eternal mates. While Kate remains mortal, she must continue to feed from Shade in preparation of being turned.

The world they're building together is shattered with the arrival of Sabine, Shade's ex-lover. Believing a mortal female is undeserving of a vampire king, Sabine tries to kill Kate. To protect his love, Shade submerges her further into his culture by introducing her to the Medici warriors. From their ranks, a vampire by the name of Luca is chosen as her protector for life.

It should be a time of great joy when Kate and Shade discover she's pregnant. Instead, it unleashes a fresh wave of complications since a half-breed can never inherit the Medici dynasty. Alec and Rissa see the pregnancy as an opportunity to achieve their own twisted goals and devise a scheme that will kill the infant... and possibly Kate along with it. For now, their underhanded deception has yet to be discovered.

Unfortunately, Kate indeed miscarries. Overcome by grief, sorrow drives a wedge between her and Shade. While he unleashes his sadness in a fury of rage and violence, she retreats within herself. It falls to Luca to try to pull the two back together where they belong. But Shade isn't the only one plagued by anger from their loss. Kate seeks an outlet to unleash and goes against Shade's wishes by asking Luca to train her as a warrior. As book one draws to a close, he reluctantly agrees, knowing they will have no choice but to work behind the back of vampire King Shade Medici.

The
Turning

1

Larissa, or Rissa as her friends called her, made an appointment to meet with a competitor at noon. They occasionally worked together on large projects, although technically, she was a rival to her business, taking more middle-class clientele than Rissa did. She had called and wanted to speak with Rissa about a specific florist she used on a regular basis. Rissa didn't normally share information on her business, but she knew this client could not possibly afford her services, so Rissa thought she would throw her competitor a bone. Besides, she was feeling generous. She was still basking in the glow of Alec's approval of the role she played in Shade and Kate's loss of that half-breed thing she was carrying around.

Rissa didn't deal with middle-class clientele if she could help it. She was above that now. Her business had grown leaps and bounds, and she was determined to keep it there, as the event planner for the elite. One false move in this town could wreak havoc with her reputation, putting her on the blacklist, so every client was screened and chosen to meet her select criteria.

Driving up to her friend's business, she felt nervous, the Capital Hill district had some great attractions, like the Eastern Market, but it wasn't the upscale neighborhood of Georgetown, or G-town as the locals called it.

As the meeting progressed, her rival was most appreciative, but then everyone was when they need her. All in all, it was entertaining to see how her competition operated and Rissa enjoyed intimidating her as much as she could. Rissa wrapped up the meeting as soon as possible. She had a huge gala for the foundation tonight, and she wanted to get home and relax before the event. She and Alec attended every year, and all the right people would be there.

Excusing herself to use the restroom before leaving, she freshened her make-up, said her goodbyes and left. Eager to get back on familiar turf, she hurried to her car, threw her designer tote bag on the seat next to her, and noticed a scrolled note lying on the passenger seat. *What in the hell is this?* Picking up the note, she unrolled it and began to read…

Rissie,

My angel I let you go once.

It is not a mistake I will make twice.

Max

"Max." His name was out of her mouth before she could think. Her head was spinning, her heart racing, and her blood began to pound in her head. She threw her head back on the seat and took some deep breaths. If Alec ever knew! She had to control this, Alec would feel her turmoil. *What is Max's purpose? And why now?*

Firing up the engine and putting her foot to the pedal, she sped out as her thoughts churned in her head. The memories she had of them together, how he smelled, how she felt in his arms, his kiss. *Stop it, Rissa. Stop it!*

Slamming on the breaks, she ripped the note to shreds and flung it out the window. *Max! Why, why, why?*

Taking the longest route home, she stewed about this unexpected intrusion and tried to get him out of her head before returning home to Alec. *Alec can never know...*

2

The sun was not up yet, but it would be soon. Shade teleported onto the patio behind their house, after spending another night on the streets of D.C. He was still reeling from the loss of their child. His *bel* appeared to be healing, letting go of the pain, but his seemed to be building. He looked down at his blood-stained leathers. Killing rogues helped, but it didn't provide the release he thought would come, and perhaps, it never would. He would always carry the guilt of changing the pills to save her life and give up the life of their *bambino*. That decision would haunt him until he died. Kate would never have agreed to stop taking the pills, and she would never forgive him if she knew. Lighting up a smoke, he walked down the path to the grave marker. He wanted to say goodnight to him, sit in the quiet of the garden, and get himself together before entering the house to be with *bel*. He must be strong for her.

Walking down the winding garden path, he came to the bench and sat down, staring at the marker. His mind rolled over and over with so many things. His heart bled for the mess he had made of his family, his mate and the loss of something so dear to them both. He wondered if he would ever be able to get their lives back to where they once were. Would they ever be the same? Could they get back what they had? He held her through her tears, remained the strong one. It was his duty, as her mate to take that pain from her, store it inside himself, and keep her from finding out he hurt more than she could ever fathom. He knew he should go back to the house and be with her. She grieved as well, and neither of them could ever go through this again.

He needed to turn her but wondered when he would find the time. He would have to take her to Florence for the turning, it would take days, and things were getting more out of control in the city. The rogues just kept coming. It took all his warriors to get rid of the bodies every night before the mortals noticed anything. Hunting them seemed endless, and he shook his head to lock it out of his mind. *Shut it down, Shade. Shut it the fuck down! You are home.*

He was startled as Gi sat down beside him. He knew it had been too long a night that he didn't even hear him coming.

"Master."

"Gi? What is wrong? Fuck, is it *bel*?" Shade quickly stood and turned to run to the house.

"Sit, master, all is fine with my lady. She does well, but I cannot say the same for you."

Shade sighed and sat back down beside his faithful manservant. "You know me too well. Does it show that much?" Shade hung his head, propping his elbows on his knees and stared at the cherub marking the grave.

"Master, you are so much like your *padre* at times. You remind me of him, in more instances than you can imagine."

Grunting, Shade rolled his eyes to him, "I don't know if that is a compliment or a kick in my ribs. You want to explain before I decide to pop you, old one?"

Shade felt Gi slap him on the back and chuckle. "Master Shade, it is quite a compliment. I recall a time, before you were born, your *padre* was young like you. It is a story which you know nothing of. I was told by your *padre* to never speak of it, but I do believe, if he were here at this moment, he would tell you."

Shade slid off the bench and sat on the ground beside the marker, lit up a cigarette and eyed him. "Go on, you have my full attention."

"Your *madre* was a beautiful woman, and her heart was even more beautiful and giving, much like the one who has stolen your heart. She most certainly stole your *padre*'s heart. He was a warrior of great standing, proud and stern. And I know you think you cannot compare, but you have far surpassed what he achieved. He would be so proud of you, your mate as well. He would not like that she is mortal, but I do believe the love your *madre* would have for her, would have made him think differently over time. He did all for her, lived for her and fought for her. She was his life and in that, you are much like him, for you are the same way. In the early years, before you were even thought of, your *madre* came with child."

Shade's head snapped up, as he looked at the old one with furrowed brow. "What? Have you gone mad in the head? I never heard of such. I am an only child."

Gi nodded, "Of course you never heard, it was a secret we pledged to your *padre* to take to our graves. Your *madre* was with child. It was early in her pregnancy and had not been announced to the coven. One day, her feet tangled in her gown and she fell down the marble stairs. I found her unconscious and bleeding internally. We called for your *padre*. He came home. We were all afraid of his anger. We thought he might slay us where we stood. He never wanted the coven to know the future King of their coven had not survived, and we were sworn to secrecy.

"None of the staff was home that night, it was our night of rest and he had left her alone, while he tended to the territories, something he rarely did. I cannot begin to tell you what we went through, but we suffered in our hearts for your *madre*, we loved her as we do, my lady.

"Her heart was broken. He took it all for her, he took it and never let her know how much he suffered for not being there for her. She eventually healed, but your *padre* almost went mad over the loss, never letting her in. He tried to shut her out, so she would not see how much he grieved. But, of course, your *madre* saw his pain, she took him to her heart and healed him, she led him back to where they both needed to be. Her strength healed him, and she protected her great warrior. Your *padre* fought this for a long time, pushing her away, but she never gave up, their love so great for each other. If he were here, master, he would tell you to let my lady heal you. Let her take the reins, let her show you nothing can destroy the love you have for one another.

"She may be a small bit of beauty, but my lady has a strong heart, and she would die for you, as you would for her. Don't be so stubborn, like your *padre*. Heal each other, for the sake of what is to come. For they took a long journey of many years before he would once again touch her, give her another child. That child was you, and no other came after. He may have been tough on you. I saw that, but learn from him. Do not make the same mistakes he did, for he would want you to thrive with children around you and honor the love of your eternal mate."

As Gi stood, he laid his hand on Shade's shoulder and turned, walking back into the house.

Shade sat quietly by the grave marker, his tears streamed down his face. As he looked at the marker, he knew this place was where he needed to leave his pain, and here it would stay. He looked up at the house that held the love he would have for the rest of his life. He couldn't wallow in the past for it would hamper the future he craved with his *bel rosso*. Wiping away the tears, he realized he looked as though he had been through a war. With Gi's words still ringing in his head, it was time to put away the pain and the guilt and give her all he had. Standing, he walked back to the house, entered, and saw Gi nod to him as he took the stairs three at a time.

Walking past the nursery, he stopped dead in his tracks. The room was completely bare. He stepped inside and stood in the stark emptiness. It no longer felt hollow to him, but simply still and quiet. It was again an empty canvas ready to be painted with their story... his *bel rosso* and her savage lover.

Kate heard him bounding up the stairs. Her heart skipped a beat knowing he was home. She waited expectantly for him to enter their bedroom, but he didn't appear. It was quiet. She no longer heard him. It took her a minute to realize he had probably seen the nursery. She went to him. He was standing in the middle of the empty room. "Lover, please don't be angry, but I couldn't bear to look at his things, to walk past his room every day. I should have asked you first, but the pain it brought... it kept pulling me away from you."

With his back to her, he listened to her words, feeling her pain was less now. This was *her* final step. He turned to her. He couldn't hold his own guilt and agony in any longer. In painful humility he pled, "*Mi amore*, I am so sorry for all of this, I am torn in half by it. Please forgive me, just say the words." He looked at her and held out one of his blood encrusted hands. "Please..."

She stared at him, covered in blood and knew this was how he came home every morning. This was what he washed away before coming to her, what he tried to shield her from. Did he think she didn't know? Did he still not understand she loved everything about him? That she was drawn to the beast in him? That she made no distinction, as he did, between Shade and the beast. To her, they were one and the same. She walked to him and stroked his blood-stained face.

"Shade, I am a warrior too. We fight different battles. You fight with weapons to protect us. I fight for you... only you."

He looked at her, this small woman who stole all of him. Taking her in his arms, he kissed her with so much love and let go of his pain. He brought forth music from thin air as Lifehouse sang *You and Me,* and they swayed to the rhythm in this empty room where they would now begin again.

She couldn't remember when they last listened to music in this house. She felt the darkness lift from him, felt him let go of the pain, and knew they would heal together, they had found their way back to each other. "Come, lover, you need a shower... we need a shower."

Smiling at her, he hugged her close to his chest and held her there. After the song ended, he threw her over his shoulder, smacked her ass lightly and chuckled. "I think there might be enough soap and water for two warriors in that waterfall."

She giggled as she kicked her feet and wiggled. He knew he had his *bel* back, and she had her savage lover.

3

Taking a last look in the mirror, Rissa made sure everything was perfect with her gown. The Fashion Fights Poverty Gala was one of the biggest events of the year. Her heart was saddened Alec was not attending with her tonight, but he seemed to be in his own hell with the rival coven. This gala was one of the few times she got him out. He was very different in public than behind closed doors. Taking a deep breath, she pushed away the thought of the note she found in her car and walked out to find Alec. She wanted his opinion of her dress and to see if he wished for her to do anything for him tonight while at the gala.

Alec heard the soft swish of her gown as she entered the room and picked up the scent of her exotic perfume. He looked up to see her in a floor-length blue gown that accentuated her eyes. He gave her a smile of appreciation as he looked at her from head to toe. "My darling, you look good enough to eat." He smiled wickedly. "I do regret I will not be able to join you, but I know you understand."

Her smile was genuine, she had his approval, and she lived and breathed for a compliment from him. "Of course, I understand. And I'll make your excuses. Everyone will be disappointed, and I'll miss being on your arm. This rival coven, is there any news? I'm not worried for myself, I can take care of myself and besides, the gala will be teeming with people."

Alec frowned, "Plenty of news about the rogues, my darling, and none of it good. But Shade is on top of things... thanks to you." he gave her a wink. "And I don't worry about you. I worry about anyone with the misfortune to cross your path." He smiled at her.

She laughed out loud. "No one would attack me. Who has that kind of balls? They know they would have to face your wrath. I must get on my way. I don't want to be late." She grabbed her invite from the table, turned and smiled at him. "I'll miss you."

"I hope the gala is successful, Rissa. Have a wonderful evening, and I'll miss you as well. I expect to be busy, but call if you need me."

She gathered her clutch and pulled on her gloves, "I should think I would not have to call you, but I promise to be alert and on guard for anything unusual."

Picking up the edges of her gown, she tucked her evening clutch under her arm and made her way to the door. Turning, she looked at him and they locked eyes, his stare so blue and wicked it made her shiver with want of him. "Please Alec, try to relax some. I know it is useless to tell you, but I do worry about you, I am not totally heartless." Blowing him a kiss, she was on her way.

Walking into the event, Rissa found her table, but it took her a long time to work her way through the throngs of people milling about as she smiled and waved, kissing cheeks and issuing the required hugs. She put on her best Larissa face and made the most of it. As she made it to her table and sat down, she began to chat with several of those around her, mostly Alec's contacts. She and Alec had been a staple at this annual fundraiser and were major contributors. This was the first year he had not been able to attend with her, and she felt a bit lost without him. Alec was usually the one who entertained the crowd with conversation and she politely smiled her way through it.

As the entertainment and awards began, she tried to pay attention, but her mind was on Max. She rolled it over and over in her head, and wondered how he found her and why, and it both excited and scared her at the same time. Alec literally stole her right from under Max's nose, and she never once looked back.

Finally, the meal was finished, and people began to walk around and mingle. Several of her top clients stopped by the table and sat opposite her. Rissa took in all the gossip, it was so vital for her job and occasionally, she even picked up a tidbit that was helpful to Alec. She had to be his eyes and ears tonight. The juice always flowed at these events, which was why it was rare for him to miss it.

As the evening progressed, her feet were hurting in her designer heels and she wished she could leave, but knew she had to put in a strong appearance. It would be rude to leave so soon. An orchestra began to play, and she watched as some of the couples started to dance. She sat quietly at the table, observing the crowd as they drank, danced, and chatted about Washington politics, who's doing who and making those all-important contacts. She kept her ears open but heard nothing she didn't already know. When Alec took this town, they would see a rush of power like never before, and she intended to be by his side.

Max watched her from the edge of the crowd. He had been a fool to ever let her go. He had refused to turn her. Turning a mortal was a huge responsibility, and he had not been ready to take that on at the time. And now look at her, she was vampire, and with one of the most powerful vampires in the States, holding her own among these mortals who didn't have a clue. Alec was his arch-rival, and he had no idea it was Max's Aries coven that wreaked havoc on his town and kept him too busy to look after his mate.

Max and Alec had maintained a civil relationship over the years. They understood a war between them would ultimately benefit neither of them, and they had always negotiated a peaceful settlement around their issues. Then Rissa left him for Alec. Max thought he could get over her, had tried to get over her. He was a master and a warrior with lots of options when it came to females. Rissa was the first mortal he ever fell in love with. Mortal-immortal relationships were still looked upon with skepticism in their world. She wished to be turned, he refused, and it cost him. He would not make her his mate, and it was a decision he came to regret. Even after all this time, he wanted her back. He decided he would do whatever it took.

He steered clear of her all evening, watching her. He knew her, she was bored, putting up a front. As the evening wore on, she was seated at the table as couples took to the dance floor. He approached her from behind. Her gold locks were swept up on top of her head, and her neck was bare and tempting. He ran his finger down the curve of her neck and onto her bare back. "Have you missed me, my angel?"

She felt the light touch of his finger glide across her skin, her body shivered from the contact, and his voice thrilled her, bringing with it a flood of memories. *Max*. She should be frightened, but she wasn't the Rissie he once knew. He would soon find that out. Without looking at him, she responded. "You should watch your tongue. Someone may cut it out for you."

Max slid into the empty chair beside her, keeping his arm across the back of her chair. His body turned to face her.

"Watch my tongue? What an interesting choice of words, my angel. I would love for you to watch my tongue, as it slides across your plump white breasts and those rosy pink nipples, across that tight belly and into that sweet nectar." He leaned in close to her ear, so she could feel his breath as he spoke, "Don't tell me you don't remember. I remember... I remember how you moved beneath me when I bathed you with my tongue, my sweet angel."

She felt his arm as it rested on the back of the chair and she shivered again, as he leaned so close his breath felt hot against her skin. The images rolled through her mind of how his arms held her all night long, his body so attuned to hers. It was always her needs before his, and she had forgotten how incredible that once felt. *Rissa, snap out of this!*

When he called her 'angel', his voice changed, like it always did, such a soft and loving tone. *Why now? Why the hell didn't you fight for me when he took me?* She turned her head to glare at him but looking into his eyes brought other emotions instead. He was here beside her, close enough to touch, and it slammed her hard to look into his eyes. His eyes stunned her. He was dressed in a tux that made him look both elegant and rugged. His dark brown hair was still long, but neatly tied back, and her hands itched to run them through his hair. She remembered Maximus far too well. She fought for control of her voice as she responded to him. "I need to remind you I belong to Alec now. You cannot touch me. Nor do I wish you to. If you will excuse me, I'm leaving for the evening."

Standing, she wanted to run, she couldn't stay here one moment longer.

Max grabbed her wrist hard and pulled her back to her seat.

"Not this time, Rissie, and I suggest you not struggle, wouldn't want to draw the attention of the mortals, now would we? I let you go once. I didn't want to turn you, but I see my old friend Alec had no problem with that. I should never have let you walk out. And unlike Alec, who doesn't like to get his hands dirty, I am both master and warrior, and I'll fight for what I want. And what I want, my angel, is you. I know you. And I know Alec. He can't possibly give you what I can. He can't love you the way I loved you, still love you. Do you want me to fight for you? Is that what you need to see? Because if that is what you need, I will gladly provide it."

His words shocked her to the core. She wanted to scream for Alec, make him come and show Max he loved her, and he would fight for her. But he spoke of love and that simple word turned her upside down. His grip on her hand was hard and forceful, and somehow, it reached straight into her heart. She fought through it, and yet, there was a part of her that didn't want to.

"Lower your voice, please. You know nothing about Alec or me! Fight for me? Love me? Where was that Maximus when I wanted and needed him? You didn't have the balls then and I don't believe you have them now. Alec will eat you alive. He owns me, and you couldn't out fuck him if you tried. You are wasting your time."

Rissa felt a hand on her shoulder and she jumped. "Miss Benneteau, is there a problem? You seem upset. May I be of assistance?"

As Rissa turned her head, she saw Senator Winston, a junior Senator and she smiled at him. "Oh, Senator Winston, it's wonderful to see you here tonight. I'm quite fine, thank you, just in a political disagreement with one of Alec's old friends. Nothing to be alarmed about, but I do thank you."

She sat with her nerves jangled, not having any clue how Max would respond to this. He could make a huge scene.

Max locked eyes with her and smiled wickedly and waited for the mortal to walk away. "Owns you, does he? Oh, I have no doubt about that, my angel. I know Alec well. What kind of warrior would I be if I didn't know my rival? Let me see if I've got this right. My friend Alec is all about control, he controls you, yes? He makes you wait for his affection. He makes you beg for his affection. And as I recall, he was very much into the delivery of pain. He has turned your heart, so it is cold and hard. Is that how you wish to be loved? Or is that what you are willing to settle for? A woman like you should never have to beg for love. And I have the balls, my angel. If you need me to take him down and clear the path for us, consider it done."

Her breathing became ragged, strangled. Every word he spoke hurt her, made her see Alec in a different light. She felt as though her whole world was crashing around her, and she could feel the tears as she fought hard to hold them back, her voice a whisper. "Stop, please."

He saw her emotions rise to the surface, so he softened his voice as he ran the back of his hand across her cheek. "Rissie, I did not come here to hurt you. Don't cry, my angel, shh. I want you back, and I am willing to do whatever it takes. I made a mistake letting you go. I have to own that. I hurt you, and for that, I apologize. My actions probably drove you right into his arms, so I feel responsible. But I'm back now, for good. I know this is a lot to lie at your feet. I don't expect an answer tonight. I know you need time, but we are vampire, we have all the time in the world. I'm not going anywhere. You can expect to see me regularly. I won't come around when he's with you. I'll not put you in jeopardy. But I'll be close and waiting."

She could feel her chest heaving for breath. She wanted to lean into him, but she couldn't. She felt like she was losing her mind. *Oh, Max, why do you put me in this place? A choice, no, no, no!* His voice was gentle, loving, and she closed her eyes and fought the impulse to give in to him so hard her body ached. She needed to get to Alec. "I'm not your angel. Don't follow me. Please Maximus, stop this."

Standing, she rushed headlong for the doors, she didn't care who she bumped into. She just needed to be away from him, away from the temptation, and back home to her Alec.

Max watched her flee and felt her turmoil. *Run home, my angel. I have all the time in the world.*

4

Alec had been on the phone with Shade on and off most of the night. There had been random attacks on mortals all over the outskirts of the city, but every night, the attacks moved closer to Georgetown. Shade said the coven was much larger than they originally expected. Alec was in between calls when he tuned into Rissa. She was flustered, excited and sexually aroused. Alec could feel her body respond to whoever it was and his beast roared. Whoever she felt drawn to, she did not leave with him, but she was leaving in a hurry. *This will not do!* He checked the time. She would be home shortly, and he would be waiting. He slid on a pair of black leather gloves.

On the drive home, it took all she had to calm herself, relax and walk inside that door. She just wanted to be with Alec. Opening the door, she felt his anger hit her like a ton of bricks and she stopped in her tracks, her hand still on the doorknob. She had forgotten to block her emotions when she saw Max. She locked eyes with him. He could kill her where she stood.

"Meet someone interesting, baby girl? Did you think I wouldn't notice? Get over here. Now!"

His voice was so cold her heart damn near stopped from fright, and she immediately blocked all thoughts from her head and concentrated only on his words. She walked to him, her eyes still locked with his. "Yes, daddy."

He gripped her throat with his gloved hand as he stepped up to her, their bodies touching, and he put his lips to her ear as he spoke in a whisper of barely controlled rage, "You have two options. Either you remove the dress quickly, or I will do it for you."

As he went for her throat, Rissa knew this was no game. He had felt her with Max and his beast had surfaced. She must move carefully. Alec could easily kill her. She quickly reached around her back but struggled with the zipper, as he had such a hold around her neck. She saw his rage flare up when she didn't move fast enough to please him and before she could blink, he ripped the gown to shreds.

She stood before him in her bra and panties, garter belt and stockings. He could see the fear in her eyes and it fed his beast. His fangs were bared as he spoke through clenched teeth. "Get. Upstairs. Now. Face down on the bed."

She ran fast, and she didn't know if it was from fear or excitement of him, but she needed him to take her hard. She lay across the bed face down and her body shivered, waiting, never knowing what the beast would lavish on her.

Alec followed her up the steps. She was already on the bed when he roughly grabbed each ankle and tied them to the bedpost.

"Would you like to tell me who sparked your interest tonight, baby girl?"

She winced as the restraints were so tight, she felt the rope cutting into her skin through her stockings. "A colleague of yours, daddy."

Alec stalked her as he walked slowly around the bed, like a predator sizing up his prey. "Ah, a colleague of mine, and you found him attractive, did you? Did he make you wet? And what was this colleague's name, baby girl?" He ran his gloved hand along the back of her calf, up her thigh, and across her ass, where he delivered a hard pinch that would leave a bruise by tomorrow. He felt her flinch in both pain and pleasure.

"He was trying to seduce me, daddy. Baby girl was bad, so wet."

His beast was angered as his eyes fired red and he roared, "What is his name, Rissa! I'm not fucking playing games here."

She jumped at his words and whimpered, "He whispered nasty, dirty things into my ear. Winston."

Alec creased his brow. "Winston? Are you fucking kidding me? That little candy ass mortal made you wet? Is that all it takes? I think you need a little reminder of who owns this ass. Now, what will it be? Hmmm? Paddle? Belt? Whip?" He leaned onto the bed, his lips by her ear, "Tell daddy which one you want."

"Whip, please. I have been so naughty."

He coiled the whip around his hand, felt the braided leather. "Now, how did I know this is the one you would choose?" He swung his hand back and with the quick snap of his wrist, brought the whip down across her ass. The sheer material of her panties tore away with the strike, and the red welt appeared immediately on her tender skin. The mere sight of it fueled the beast.

Rissa made the mistake of clenching and tightening her muscles in anticipation of the whip. As it ripped into her skin, she screamed in pain. She immediately felt the blood and Max's words rang in her ears. *No, no, no!*

For Alec, her screams only fed his beast, and he wanted more. He ripped the clothes from his body and climbed on top of her, his cock large and throbbing, and ran his tongue across the bleeding welts the whip created. The beast was crouched over her, sniffing, looking for a scent. Vampire. He smelled vampire, and he released a roar that shattered the glass in the windows. Alec fought to regain control. He knew she had no idea about the rival coven. They had been close enough to leave their scent on her. He dropped the whip from his hand, slid his legs between hers, spreading her open. *They think they will take Rissa? No fucking way will they claim her.* He slid his hand up her back, and put pressure on her shoulders, pushing her head to the mattress, while he lifted her ass in the air.

"Remember who you belong to, baby girl." He entered her from behind in one quick thrust.

He felt her respond, as she lifted her ass to receive him as he fucked her hard. He slid his free hand beneath her hips and pulled her against him, feeling the curve of her ass fit perfectly against his hips as he thrust into her, claiming her, marking her, leaving his scent on her.

He heard her growl, as she looked back at him over her shoulder, and saliva dripped from her fangs. He fucked her harder, and he could feel the bed shift forward with each thrust, her legs pulling free from the bindings. As her feet were freed, she raised up on her knees, ass high in the air, and head down for her master, giving him greater access to pound away at her, his cock throbbing to release. He grabbed a fistful of her hair, pulling her head back as he came inside her, and the beast roared once more, echoing into the night, letting every vampire know she was his.

He felt her body quiver as he came in her, poured into her, but she held back her own pleasure, waiting for his permission, which he didn't give. He pulled his cock from her, hot and wet and slid it across her ass as he listened to her groan. With one swift move, he flipped her over, so she was lying on her back. He slid his hands down her body, across her breasts, to her narrow waist and grasped her hips, lifting them once more as his mouth covered her sex, already hot and dripping wet with his cum. He licked at her slowly and watched her squirm, tempting her with his tongue, probing, teasing, until he heard her beg, "Daddy, please."

He covered her sex with his mouth and sucked hard at her clit, and felt her raise her hips against his mouth. He looked up at her from between her legs. "Cum for me, baby girl. Show me you know who you belong to."

He lowered his mouth to her once again and flicked his tongue over her clit before sucking at her hard, drawing her clit into his mouth, teasing it with his teeth. He felt her release as she thrust her hips hard against his mouth, and he probed her to the depths with his tongue, letting her ride out every sensation that washed over her.

As she collapsed limply on the bed, he sat upright on his knees, and pulled her to him like a doll and held her to his chest. He stood and picked her up, holding her against him as he pulled back the sheets, and lay her back down on the bed, and climbed in beside her, pulling the blankets over them. He curled his body around her, she was his. "Sleep. I will take care of you."

* * *

Max returned home from the Gala, refreshed and alive. He had talked to Rissa. She had been startled to see him at first, but in a good way. He could see it in her eyes. She was conflicted, torn. All good signs, because she didn't reject him outright, and her initial move to leave the table was motivated more by fear of Alec. He knew his angel, and she was no longer his angel, Alec had made her heart cold. Max knew he could win her back from his arch-rival with time and patience. He watched as she finally left the Gala, rushing home to him. Max stayed close, as he had for some time now. He watched her, always watching her. It was not a long wait before Max heard the mating howl that shattered the glass, and he knew Alec's beast had picked up his scent. Max had hoped the potion would block it. *I am so sorry angel... so sorry.* He could only imagine the pain and torment Alec inflicted upon her tender skin in retribution. Max would need to be more careful. Rissa would need to take the potion as well. The next time he saw her. *Oh yes, my angel, there will be a next time.* He would convince her she must also take the potion, so they could meet undetected, even from Alec's beast.

5

Rissa woke slowly, reaching across the bed for the warmth of him, but he wasn't there. She sat up and moaned as her body ached from last night and his claiming. She could feel Alec in the house. She slowly pulled the sheet around her, as she slid to the edge of the bed, the wounds from the whip healing but still tender. She could already feel the bruises forming. Sitting would be hell throughout the day. Always his reminder, he owned her.

She sat on the side of the bed, not wanting to move, her mind tortured with the thought of Maximus. Even after Alec had taken her, she didn't feel whole. She felt the hollowness building inside her. She felt she was missing something vital. She had lived with Alec for so long. She knew he loved her, of that she had no doubt, but he rarely showed her tenderness, at least not in a normal sense. He wasn't capable.

She remembered Max's gentle touch across her cheek, his concern for her, and not a false concern based on what she was able to give him later, lying naked under him. It tore at her, that simple touch, how it stole through her body and landed directly inside her heart. Max knew there was a side of her that occasionally craved a gentle touch, arms that held her protectively, arms that cradled her in the night. Rissa was tired of being the strong one, never letting go of her emotions. It took Maximus to remind her of what she was missing.

She moved with an aching slowness to the shower and let the hot water wash away the soreness. She dried off and wrapped the towel around her, walking to her sitting room. She pulled out her schedule book and saw there wasn't much on the calendar for today, and the few appointments she did have, could easily be rescheduled. Making the calls, she begged off and rescheduled everything, deciding she needed to be alone and think this through. Dressing casually, she gathered a few things, and decided she would tell Alec she's heading out for her appointments. She convinced herself this was what she needed, some time to think, and get away from it all. Grabbing her gym bag, she knew by this evening she would need the gym to restore mind and body. It was her only release when he withheld from her and wouldn't give her what she craved. Heading downstairs, she knew she would encounter him and cleared her mind, blocking her thoughts.

Alec heard when she came down the stairs. He needed to tell her what he knew about this rogue coven. She needed to understand the danger.

"Rissa, where are you going? We need to talk before you leave this house."

She closed her eyes, took a deep breath, laid down her bags, and went to his study. "Right here Alec, just going out for some appointments, then the gym afterward."

"Come in, my darling. Sit down, we need to talk." He took a seat, lit up and offered her a drag, but she shook her head no.

She sat down gingerly, trying not to wince. "What is it?"

Alec noticed her guarded movements. He inhaled deeply from the cigarette, laying his head back on the chair cushion and releasing the smoke slowly, letting it relax him. "Are you okay? I don't usually allow the beast to ravage you, but you provoked me last night."

She waved her hand. "I just have a few aches. I'm familiar with the beast, and I can take it. I'm sorry. I didn't mean to provoke you. I didn't start the provocation, Winston did. Is this what you wanted to speak to me about?"

"No, my darling, Winston is of no consequence, and I'll deal with that situation myself. But my beast picked up a scent on you... vampire, and not of our coven. Not of Shade's warriors. It can only mean someone from the rogue coven was close enough to you to leave their scent. I can only assume you had no idea they were there. They masked their presence from you. They were stalking you. You need to be more alert, my darling. If I think they are stalking you, I will need to find you a protector. I know you don't like it, but I can't have you at risk, Rissa."

As his words spilled forth, she gasped and her heart felt squeezed in a vice. The last thing she wanted was a protector.

"Alec, no vampires were there." Standing, she began to pace. "I would have known. You can't be serious. And why would they be stalking me? I was alert the entire night. I would have picked up their scent immediately."

Flinging her hair over her shoulder, her anger kicked in. "And I want no protector. I'm no weak mortal. I can take care of myself!"

Alec issued a low growl, it was a warning. "Watch your tone with me. I have no doubt you can take care of yourself, but clearly, you missed something. I assure you, the beast was not wrong. If I pick up that scent again, you will have a protector, whether you like it or not. I'm going to alert Shade as to how close they got to you. I'm not at all happy about that. Why didn't his warriors pick up on it? He will have to answer for that little breach in security. In the meantime, you are to be on your guard. We're not fooling around here, my darling. This coven is dangerous. Don't take it lightly."

She spun on him like a feral cat ready to strike and his warning went unheeded. "How dare you! You created me, Alec. Your blood runs in my veins. You taught me to take care of myself, and then you accuse me of missing something? Tells me a lot about how little you think of my skills." Growling, she took off like a bat out of hell straight for the front door.

Her words defied him, angered him, and he released the beast as she stormed out of the room. The beast teleported to the front door, reaching the door before her. He grabbed her throat and forced her to her knees. "I'm glad you remember who created you. Now, remember you also obey me. I'll not take insubordination from you. I decide your fate... I do, not you. Now put your head to the floor. Bow down and remember your station. You're my mate, and I'll protect you as I see fit. And yes, I trained you, but you are young, and way too cocky and sure of yourself. You think another vamp could not deceive you? Do you honestly think your fighting skills are superior to that of a trained warrior? Don't be ridiculous, Rissa. And never speak to me in that tone again. What I do, I do for your own safety and mine. We can't afford a breach of security."

He grasped her by her hair and yanked hard, pulling her to a standing position. His eyes glowed red and his fangs exposed, he put his face to hers, so they went nose to nose. "Now, tell me you understand. You will follow my commands, or you will not leave the house. Not today or any other day."

"Yes, master, I understand." Her breath was shallow and her body shook under his hand.

He released the hold on her hair and dropped his hand. "Rissa, you have never lived to see rival vampire covens battle. You have no concept of it, the amount of carnage and killing. It's out of control. We're on the brink of it now and I need to avoid it if at all possible. You don't seem to understand the scope of what's going on here. It's what I'm trying to explain. I'll not apologize for my actions. You needed a wake-up call, my darling. And I suggest you heed to it, if you expect both of us to be alive on the other side of this thing."

She stood perfectly still, not moving a muscle. She didn't even blink. "I understand, master. I have disappointed you, and I am weak. It will never happen again. May I be excused?"

He shook his head in frustration. "No, Rissa, you don't understand. My message is not that you are weak and disappointing. My message is, you must be alert and on guard to the dangers that threaten us both. If Shade's warriors missed it, then there is no way you would have picked it up. That is my point, Rissa! We are being stalked by something powerful and dangerous, and I need you to keep your head in the game."

'm no warrior, but I'm yours. And I'll not let anything take me from you. If you don't wish for me to leave, I won't. If you think I need a protector, then assign one to me. I understand you do this for us, for our survival."

He stared at her for a minute, pondering her words and weighing the risk. Rissa was strong, and she knew how to fight, but she was no match for a warrior. Whatever happened last night that exposed her to the rogue, she felt no threat, so he was probably just scoping her out. "You can go. But I'm going to talk to Shade. I'll let you know my decision about a protector. I need to think about it."

"I understand. I have some clients to visit and then I'm going to the gym. I'll call you if I sense anything."

She opened the door and walked out. She needed to get away! She needed to think.

6

Waking early from his slumber, Shade watched her sleeping soundly, curled into his side. He smiled down at her and knew they were on their way to recovery, and he was thankful. He cannot function without his *bel rosso*. He felt more at ease leaving at night, knowing she was doing better, moving forward, and leaving behind the darkness that had consumed her. He slipped out of bed quietly, wanting her to sleep as much as possible. Her sleep had been restless and uneasy. Dressing in his leathers for the night, he left their bedroom and headed downstairs to pack a bag with extra weapons and ammo. He could hear her stir, followed by the sound of her bounding down the stairs to find him. He stood in the doorway of his office and watched as she rounded the corner, crimson hair flying.

"I was hoping you were going to give your warrior a kiss before he left you for the evening."

"You promised me, lover. Never again would you leave me without a kiss, without saying goodbye. Do you think I don't feel your absence from our bed immediately?"

"Whoa, you saucy minx, slow down, will you? I was on my way up to wake you, but you came bounding down those stairs like your ass was on fire. Do you think I would ever leave here without having you in my arms? Not going to happen, *mi amore*, and I am still waiting for my kiss."

She ran into his arms full force, throwing herself at him as she wrapped her arms around his neck. He was forced to drop his bag of weapons to the floor to grab hold of her and return the kiss she placed so forcefully on his lips.

"Damn, *bel*, you do know I have to leave, right? You keep this up, my ass will be in a sling with Alec, because I sure as hell won't be leaving!"

He slapped her ass lightly. "Now listen to me, I have something I want you to think about tonight, please? Things are heating up in D.C. It may not be as easy for me to stay home for the night. So, I want us to have some time together before I leave each night. This is how it is going to be for a while, until we get control over the city. We can wake early and feed, play, whatever you wish. Just some time together for the two of us each night before I leave, *si*?"

"Of course. I'll always make time for you. I just want my warrior to remember what he's fighting for, and it's not Alec."

She tilted her head and nipped at the skin on his neck as she listened to the sharp intake of his breath.

Cazzo! She had him stirred up, his cock hard and already straining against the leathers.

"Woman!" Leaning back, he looked deep into those dark pools. "*Bel*, do you need to feed? Tell me."

"Tonight, lover, I will save it for tonight."

Hugging her to his chest, he laid his hand on her head. "I love you so much, *mi amore*. I don't want to leave, you know that. I have to. Luca is here. You don't worry for me, *si*? I will be fine, hell, most nights I am in the Dead House and not even on the streets. I want you to keep busy, with the houses and the gardens, like before. But here are my conditions and you need to follow them. You do not leave this house without Luca, you don't go into D.C. for any reason. If you two need to teleport someplace, that's fine, but it has to be far from D.C. Luca knows my conditions, and if he thinks something is wrong, you follow him without question. Understood?"

"I'll follow Luca's instructions. Please, I'm fine now, and I don't want you distracted with worrying about me. Now go, my warrior. I'll be waiting for you."

Kissing her with passion, he made the kiss last and felt her melt into him, her body like putty. That was what he needed to send his ass off to battle. He tipped her chin up and smiled.

"*Ti amo, mi amore, per sempre*." His hand slid along her cheek, as he grabbed his bag and headed out the side door, yelling as he went, "I'm out, Luca!"

As he left the house, Kate ran back upstairs and put on jeans, a t-shirt and sneakers and headed back downstairs. She had asked Luca to train her to fight, to give her an outlet for her anger over the loss of the baby. She knew he had reservations about agreeing to help her. She walked to the door of Luca's suite and was about to knock when he opened the door. Her closed fist was suspended in the air, ready to knock. He raised his own hand and covered hers.

He asked, "Are you ready?" She nodded her head once, and he liked the determination he saw in her eyes. "Then follow me."

He took her to the bunker where all the weapons were stored. He needed to figure out what she already knew and what skills she possessed that may be helpful in her training. Determination would not be enough. Determination would get her killed. He unlocked the door to the bunker. He better do this right, or Shade would have his balls on a platter. He pushed the door open and stepped aside for her to enter.

The walls were lined with weapons, and Kate knew there were even more stored behind these walls. There were enough weapons here to supply an army.

Luca watched her face, as she scanned the walls and he already doubted his decision to help her. They were starting at zero... maybe, if he was lucky, they were starting at zero.

"Sit down, Kate. First, I need to figure out what skills you already have." He pulled out a chair for her, then sat down next to her at the conference table.

Kate thought to herself, *Skills? Well, this will be a short conversation.*

Luca took out a piece of paper and a pen and looked at her. "What weapons have you used in the past, what have you been exposed to or taught?"

Kate thought a minute, then responded, "Uh... you know about the shotgun, right?"

"Yes, the night you fired the shotgun at Sabine. I know about that. And it knocked you on your ass."

Kate shrugged. "Yeah, well... that's about all I know about weapons."

Luca rubbed his hand across his face, and wrote on the paper, 'Weapons Skills: None.' *Really, Luca, you have stepped in it big time.* "Okay, what other skills. Growing up, did you play sports? Soccer? Run track? Anything like that?"

She tilted her head and looked at him. "Do I look like a girl who plays soccer?"

He shook his head. "No, I was hoping." He ran both hands over his face and then wrote, 'Athletic Skills: None.' *What the fuck have I gotten myself into?*

She looked at the frustration on his face, but she wasn't willing to give up. She didn't know if it mattered, but she decided to share the things she did know how to do.

"I was a cheerleader. And dance, I studied dance, and a little gymnastics. Does that help? I can ride a horse. I took horseback riding. Do vampires ride horses? I never heard of a vampire on a horse."

Luca lowered his hands from his face, as he looked at her again when a light bulb went off in his head. *Gymnast? Fuck yeah. Gymnastics will work just fine.*

"I don't think we need dancing or cheerleading, but we can definitely work with gymnast, and let's leave the horses in the barn, shall we? Now let's figure out what you're comfortable with. Come with me. We're going to look at the weapons."

He slid the useless piece of paper away, sensing it would be a very short skills assessment list, and stood up, taking her hand, and leading her around the room, so she could look at everything.

Kate took in the display of weapons on the walls and inside the cabinets, looking at everything. She didn't even know what some of this stuff did. She didn't like the guns. She walked past all of the firearms displayed on the wall. She looked at the swords, and she ran her hand down the long blade. At least she knew what it was, and how it was used. Would she be strong enough? She couldn't imagine herself fighting with a sword. There were bows, she knew about bows. Could she shoot a bow? Who walked around with a bow and arrow, besides that Oliver guy on that TV show *The Arrow*? Then there was another weapon, something like a bow... but not. She ran her hand over it. It intrigued her. "What is this, Luca? What is this called?"

"That's a crossbow. It's an ancient weapon, but it has been modernized and is still used today."

She turned and looked at him. "This is the one. This is the one I want." He started to pull a crossbow down from the wall and she stopped him.

"No, not that one... this one. I want this one, this black metal one with the scope thing on top."

Luca took the crossbow down from the wall and handed it to Kate. It was heavier than she expected, and she looked up to see a slight smirk on his face. He knew this was more weapon than she could handle.

He watched as she juggled the weight of the crossbow. "It's a long race, Kate, and you don't start at the finish line. A warrior trains a lifetime to master these skills. Your body is soft. You have led a life of leisure, yes? Before you learn to master any weapon, we must first build up your strength. We will start every day with a run to build your stamina and endurance. And then we will work with swords. I wouldn't suggest you fight with swords, as a sword battle is a close encounter battle, and you will never hold your own in that fight."

Luca watched as a look of annoyance flashed across her face. *Good. She will need some of that spitfire temper to motivate her, if she is going to tackle this task.*

"Working with swords will help build your upper body strength, give you the power and control you need if you want to use that crossbow. But let me make one thing clear, Kate." He needed her to hear him, hear his message loud and clear, so he grasped her chin in his hand and locked eyes with her. "This is not a game. These are not toys. I'm going against master's direct orders to train you, and the first day you don't follow my direction, the first day I feel you're not taking this seriously, will be the last day we train... Are we clear?"

She was startled when he took her chin and his eyes bored into her. He was deadly serious, and she nodded her head yes. She wanted to do this, and she would play by his rules. She understood she had placed him at odds with Shade by her very request.

He took the crossbow from her hands and hung it back up on the wall. "You won't need this for a while, that is a lesson for another day. Right now, we run. Five miles."

He took her hand and led her outside, where he had her stretch before they started a run. He would push her five miles today, and perhaps, by tomorrow, she would already tire of this game.

Kate thought, *Five miles? I haven't run five miles since... ever! Maybe we should start with one mile. I don't dare say that, even as a joke, he made it clear this was no game. So, run.*

They ran together, he matched his pace to hers. Kate knew he could finish five miles in a blink of an eye, but he ran alongside her. He coached her on her posture, her breathing. *Seriously? Who knew there were rules on how to run?* Her lungs were burning, and she was gasping for breath. Her feet felt heavy when she turned to him and asked. "How far... have we... run?" She had to pace her words to her gasping breath.

He shook his head and smiled, and she was crushed by his answer. "About a mile, just four more to go."

He was testing her. He wanted to see if she was serious, if she was up for the task or would she cave.

Okay, Luca. Bring it. I will not back away. She went inside her head, got focused. She concentrated on one step at a time, just focusing on the next. She tried to modulate her breathing, kept her eyes on the horizon, and got into the zone. She blocked out everything, except the next step... and the next step... and the next.

He thought she was going to throw in the towel, but then he saw her make a turning point, resolving to push past the discomfort. *Good. That ability to go inside her head and ignore the pain in her body will be necessary at every part of training.* He pushed her until they completed the full five-mile loop, and they were back at the house. She stopped, bent over, breathing hard, hands on her knees, red hair wet from sweat and falling forward around her face.

Luca directed her, "Keep moving. Walk it off. Don't stop suddenly. Let your body cool-down."

He made her drink water, and lots of it. She would feel this tomorrow, and they were just getting started with what he needed her to accomplish today.

"Take a break. Catch your breath, and we will start again in thirty minutes."

She was already thinking about how great it would feel to stand under the steaming hot water of a shower when he said something about starting again. *Wait! What?*

She opened her mouth to speak and had to bite her tongue to keep the words 'you're kidding, right' from being uttered. One look at his eyes told her he wasn't kidding, and the first time she complained, this little adventure would come to an end. She finished off the bottled water and continued to pace the yard, as he entered the house and returned with two swords. *Holy Mother of God... what have I gotten myself into?*

He returned with the swords. Learning to hold and swing the sword, to defend herself against an opposing sword, would teach her speed, improve her reflexes, build the strength in her arms and shoulders, so she would be able to handle a crossbow. *Make 'em or break 'em. Is that not master's mantra? Find out fast who will stand and fight, and who will fold.*

The swords were heavy. He stood before her with a sword held upright in each hand. Without speaking, without warning, he tossed one of the swords to her. Would she grab it, or jump back from it? He watched the startled look on her face, but her eyes never left the sword and she reached out and grabbed the handle. *Good instincts. Good eye to hand coordination.* He nodded his approval.

"Now get ready to fight, warrior."

He moved slowly around her, holding the sword with both hands, his arms raised at shoulder level. She tried to mimic his pose. *Fuck, this sword is heavy.* He took mock swings at her, and she moved her sword to block him. Her shoulders ached already. He kept moving in a circle around her, forcing her to constantly turn so she was always facing him as they parry, back and forth, blade to blade, in a slow dance that was measured out in the clanking of their two blades meeting.

She had to focus so hard on his movements—where he would go next, how he would swing his blade toward her—which didn't give her time to focus on the pain in her shoulders, her neck, and down her back. He spoke to her in a soft, low voice.

"Watch my eyes and my blade, warrior. My eyes will tell you my intent before I ever move the blade. Focus. Focus."

They continued this dance for what felt like hours until her muscles were screaming and she wanted to cry out, 'enough!' But she knew he was looking for her breaking point, and she wouldn't give in.

She stood her ground as he circled her, turning to meet him head on, and never once taking a step back. Master would be proud of her. Luca kept pushing, forcing her to bear the weight of the sword, watching her hold the blade high, knowing her muscles must be screaming for relief, crying out to drop her arms, to drop her guard. Not once did her eyes leave his. Not once did her face betray the pain he knew she felt.

He finally stopped circling her and lowered his sword, planting the point into the soil. She remained poised, blade held high for several beats as she considered his movements. Luca had to smile. She had a warrior's instincts, trust no one, and expect anything. She waited to see if his move was a ruse.

"At ease, warrior. You're done for the day. We'll start again tomorrow with a run, seven miles this time. And more swords, bigger and heavier. Assuming you can even move tomorrow."

She slowly lowered the sword and felt the cramping in her shoulders. She ached from head to toe. She handed him the sword and turned to walk toward the house, every muscle screaming in pain and she couldn't wait to get under the hot water of the shower. Her head was screaming 'Forget it!' But she looked at him over her shoulder, as she walked away and issued the challenge, "Bring it!"

7

Teleporting into the Dead House, Shade climbed the stairs to what was now their command center, and settled down for one long ass night. *Bel* was much better, and he felt ready and anxious to get out there and kick some fucking rogue ass. Checking out the grids, he marked each new site where they had spotted rogue activity, and still, there was no rhyme or reason to their pattern. He sent out his teams every night and he was maxed out with warriors. They were getting tired, and soon, he may have to bring some of his own into this nightmare. *Son of a bitch, why can't I figure this out?*

Flopping down in the chair, he picked up the local newspaper, going over it, looking for any report of activity that could be related to the rogues, making sure nothing had been left to be discovered by the mortals, when the front page headlines caught his full attention.

'Senator Winston Dies in Mysterious Car Accident.' *What the fuck?* He quickly skimmed over the article and flipped the page to see a photograph of a very twisted looking vehicle, so destroyed the reader couldn't identify the make or model of the car. Shade focused on a few details no mortal would see, and knew this was no accident, this was a vampire strike, a revengeful kill. *Cazzo, Alec is going to blow a fucking fang on this. I don't need this shit right now!*

His gut began to churn, and his brain was clicking with the possibilities. Something wasn't right. He read the article again, checking the time of the accident, and thought he saw Alec's hand in this. He decided he should find out. Picking up his cell, he called Alec.

Alec pulled his cell from his jacket pocket and saw Shade on caller ID. "Glad you called, Shade... got something on my mind..."

"I bet you do. Have you seen the fucking papers today?"

"Yeah, I've seen it. That particular Senator got in my way, a little too friendly with Rissa, so don't get distracted by that. But what I'm worried about is when Rissa got home from the gala last night, my beast picked up the scent of vampire, and she had no clue. So, one or more of them were stalking her. Got close enough to leave their scent and she wasn't even aware. I talked to her today, tried to make her aware of the danger. She says she understands, but she's never seen a battle between covens.

She has no idea the scope of the danger. I've never used a protector with her, and she doesn't want one, but what do you think? "

Shade laughed out loud, "*Cazzo*, if you do give her a protector, he will have to be one smart, slick bastard to outwit her. She won't go down without a fight. If she were mine, her ass would be covered whether she liked it or not. She had no clue she was being stalked? Something is not adding up here. You don't need anyone fucking up right now, especially Rissa. This is your life at stake and one fuck up could be your demise. This damn rogue coven is not fucking around, and they are getting more brazen every single night. I got everyone I have out there, and they have shaped up pretty well. There are no slackers in our crew and we can't tag 'em, brother. The rogues are all over the damn grid."

"You're right about a protector. I think I'll keep an eye on it. See if I pick up the scent again. If I put someone on her now, I'm afraid she'll spend more energy trying to dump the protector than she will trying to look out for herself. Get them both killed. Look, if you need to add more warriors, then do it. If you need more money, let me know. I want this thing brought to an end. I'll try to keep a rein on Rissa, as much as possible."

"Well, you and I think differently, but in the end, our goals are the same, what is ours remains ours. I am going to figure this out if it kills me. No fucking coven is going to outsmart me. And if I need my own warriors, I will bring them in. One thing I want to know, where on the grid was this gala event located last night?"

"Rissa was at The Kennedy Center for that fashion fundraiser." He checked his copy of the grid map to find The Kennedy Center. "Section 5, I think. Locale Point 11."

"Got it. Fuck, Alec, that's moving inside your personal perimeter. Too damn close."

"They're not in the outskirts anymore, brother. They're in our backyard. You understand that is just blocks from Georgetown? Too close for comfort. We need Intel, the kind of Intel we're only going to get from a hostage. What's it going to take to bring back a live one?"

"You want one, I will have to be the one that brings the slime in. Half of our warriors are disposing of bodies and the other half fighting off the random outbreaks. I can do this if that is what you want. I'm the only master in this group and my skills far outweigh what any of them can accomplish."

"If that's what it takes, Shade, then do it. I knew I could count on my brother-in-arms."

Shade held back the phone and stared at it. *You fucking bastard. I am only your brother when things get bad. God fucking forbid you get your hands dirty.* "I will call you at the end of the night, before sunrise to let you know the details."

Hanging up, he decided it was time to get his ass on the streets. He had an area to check out and a live body to bring in. Letting the music blare, he loaded up with weapons and slid on his gloves. Checking his boots, he pulled on his knit cap, tucking his hair up inside. He turned up the music, as the sounds of Disturbed singing *Animal* played loudly in the Dead House, while he prepared to hit the streets.

The night was crisp and clear and Shade breathed it in, he felt alive inside. His *bel* was with him in his heart, and he could conquer the world. She kept all his senses more alert and focused. Hovering above the Kennedy Center he saw nothing unusual, people milling about as they left a performance. Checking the time, it was close to midnight and this was about the time this rogue coven began its most active killing spree.

They lay in wait for the mortals to separate and spread out, and then struck without provocation. They killed their prey, drained them, and left them to be found. Shade skipped over a few blocks, keeping his eyes peeled to the ground as he ventured out a little further. There were questions running through his mind. Rissa had detected no scent, had no awareness of these vamps on her heels. Alec didn't pick up a scent either, but he said his beast did. Could this be how the rogues were getting through their defenses? No scent? How the hell was that possible? If that was the case, a rogue could be right beside them and they would have no clue. If these rogues were able to mask their scent, then this was a brilliant tactic. It would make finding them nearly impossible, and Shade focused even harder. He took some comfort in knowing the deepest, truest part of the vampire, the beast, was still able to detect the rogue's scent. At least nothing got past that black bastard.

After an hour of hunting, Shade had seen nothing, and he was restless and ready to strike at anything. Dropping down to street level, he decided it was time to walk the streets as the crowds thinned out, but they would fill soon with the second wave of mortals. The drunks who always closed down the bars and other venues would emerge in inebriated states, stupid and unaware of their surroundings and easy prey for the rogues. The rogues had no preference of target, old or young, male or female.

They just took and took. Before he could even think, he was surrounded on all sides by four rogues, dropping down on him from the rooftops and Shade picked up no fucking scent whatsoever. In an area populated by mortals, he couldn't use a noisy weapon and immediately crouched, fangs bared and ready, sword in one hand, shuriken in the other.

"Bring it, you fuckers, bring it good because you've just been dealt the death card!"

The first one came at him with no fear, just young and stupid, and Shade backflipped over his head, using his feet to hit the brick wall of the building behind him, bouncing over the rogue and snapping his neck. Quick kill. His adrenaline was pumping, and he relished the feel of it. This was what he was born to do. The dead rogue lay at his feet and he felt another coming at his back. Shade spun around, delivering a round kick, hitting the rogue in the throat, then flinging the shuriken to pierce his heart and it's another dead rogue down. Two down, two more stupid rogues to go, and he remembered he needed to bring one in alive. Neither of the other two rogues knew what to do. Both were confused by how quickly their brothers had been dispatched. They were deciding whether to attack together or separately, and Shade knew they were being put out on the streets without much training. They were just pawns in some masters' game, too young and hungry to even know they were nothing more than bait.

"Which one of you bags of shit wants to die next? Picked the wrong target tonight. Show me what you have. Come on, bring it, bad boys!"

Shade was counting on the taunt to fire them up and they both came at him at the same time. He twisted and lifted his body, rolled through the air, gliding like a kite, and they had no damn clue where he was. Shade landed on the smallest one and sliced his head clean off with one stroke of his sword. He looked at the remaining rogue, fear blazing in his eyes as Shade raised the sword and licked the blood from the blade then spit it in the rogue's face.

"You can fuck with me and I'll kill you now or you can just fucking come with me, but either way, you belong to me now."

Shade's eyes glowed a bright red, and he bared his fangs and growled, tempting the rogue to take him on. The rogue dropped to his knees in surrender and Shade had the bastard. With lightning speed, Shade blindfolded him, bound his arms behind his back and tied his legs before he teleported them the hell out of there. He let his warriors know the location of the mess he had just left on the streets and for them to get out there to clean it up immediately.

Getting back to the Dead House, Shade felt so alive he could howl all night. He was beside himself to torture this fucker until he knew everything, but he knew that wasn't how Alec would want this to play out. Shade chained the rogue in the soundproof basement and kept stalking him, watching his fear build.

"Don't worry, I am not the boss, just his henchman, you will know when he gets here. And you will pay for all your brothers' deeds, and the deeds of that mysterious master of yours."

Shade went to call Alec when his warriors started filing in and surrounding the bastard, as he hung from the ceiling in chains. The word was getting out they had a live one. Shade issued an order to the warriors, "No one touches him, no one!"

Walking out of the dungeon and upstairs to the command center, he called Alec as he lit up a smoke. *Fuck, I need a damn drink!*

Alec grabbed his cell phone and saw Shade on caller ID, "What news do you have for me, brother?"

"The rogue is hanging in chains, waiting for you. Get here before I decide to fuck him up good."

Alec smirked, "I'm impressed. But don't do anything until I get there. I would hate to miss any of the fun. Give me a few minutes."

He ran upstairs to let Rissa know he was going out and signaled Alto to have the car brought around. Rissa was already in bed. He went to her side and leaned down close to her ear.

"Rissa, I need to go out for a while. Don't know how long this will take."

She responded, her head still cloudy from sleep, "Alec?" She reached for his hand. "Where, Alec?"

"I have to see Shade at the Dead House. They caught a rogue, alive. We need to see what we can find out. I don't want you to leave this house under any circumstances, is that clear?"

She sat straight up in bed, pushing the hair from her face, "I won't leave, I promise." She squeezed his hand. "Please be careful, I beg you." Laying her head back down, she was glad that something was moving on this rogue front. She could feel his blood surging and pumping.

He leaned down and kissed her lightly. "Sleep, I'll be back when I can."

He left the room, down the stairs and out the door to where Alto had the car running, holding the door open for him. He jumped in and they were off to the Dead House, arriving in about fifteen minutes. He asked Alto to park and wait. He entered the old Victorian house, and into the gutted parlor which had been converted into their command center.

Shade felt him coming and it was about fucking time. Why the hell didn't he teleport like a normal fucking vampire was beyond him. Watching as he strolled in, Alec was all business. Shade gave him a fist bump and led him in, providing him details as they went. "Alec, I was on the streets, blocks from the Kennedy Center, and they dropped out of the sky. I smelled nothing whatsoever."

He led him downstairs to the dungeon where the rogue was chained and manacled, fear burning in his eyes. The warriors backed against the walls when the two masters entered.

"No scent?" Alec frowned. "That could explain why Rissa never knew they were close to her. But how the fuck is that even possible?"

Shade shrugged. "I have no idea, but I can confirm Rissa would not have smelled anything. I had no warning, they just dropped from the rooftops. But I sure as fuck will be finding out how they do it." Shade pointed to the rogue who was chained. "He is a punk rogue. All of them were, this master is using anything he can find, turning them and letting them loose with no skills, they are starving and have no direction, no training, no discipline."

Alec walked around the rogue. "Well, that explains the chaos, and the bodies left on the street." He sniffed at him, nothing. He continued the slow predatory circling, and he could feel the rogue's fear.

Alec got in his face. "We're going to have a little talk now. Or rather, you're going to talk. If I don't like your answers, or if I don't get answers, this one," he pointed to Shade, "will start to peel the skin from your body, one strip at a time. Understood?"

The rogue nodded, his eyes wide with fear.

Shade grinned, walking up to the slime and sliding the hooked blade across the rogue's abdomen, letting him bleed just a little, holding the blade in front of his eyes, he showed his fangs and smiled. "Ever see one of these? This is a skin skimmer, and every inch of yours belongs to me now." Shade spun the blade in his hand as the honed edge of the blade caught the light. "Tell the master why you have no stench, speak clear and loud."

Shade was waiting for the rogue to make some response, but this was taking too fucking long and he was already impatient and punched him in the gut with the blade handle. "Fucking speak, you slime!"

As the rogue doubled over, coughing and groaning in pain, he whispered out a response. Shade thought he heard the word potion. *Potion?* He turned his head to Alec with a questioning look.

Alec stepped in closer, so he could hear the rogue, "What do you mean, potion?"

Shade's eyes never left the rogue, as he spun the blade unconsciously in his hand, the rogue answered that his master had made a potion to hide their scent, and Shade couldn't believe his ears, a fucking potion?

Shade got in his face, "How do you take this potion? And I suggest you fucking tell the truth, or start praying, because you will think the devil took your soul."

As the rogue answered you drink it, Shade looked to another warrior, and said, "Search him."

They stripped the rogue and found nothing.

Shade was frustrated and angry, as he paced in front of the rogue. "Fuck! I have had enough of this bullshit, Alec. Let me take the rogue out strip by strip, my hands are itching."

Alec shouted, "No! We need to find out who controls them." He stepped up close to the rogue. "They are itching to strip your skin, do you understand? They have been chasing your ass all over this city, and now they want payback. I'm the only thing standing between you and a room full of highly trained, bloodthirsty warriors, so listen closely. Who is your master?"

The rogue hesitated, did not answer and Shade watched as the warriors circled, ready for the kill. Alec nodded and this fucker belonged to them. The rogue's fear spiked as he was surrounded, and he spat on Alec and said, "Angel."

Alec's beast emerged as the young rogue spit at him. Eyes red and fangs bared, he screamed to the heavens, "There is no master named Angel. Kill him!" He watched as a frenzy of warriors tore into him, ripping his limbs free, tearing his head from his body, and leaving nothing recognizable when they were done. *Angel. Who the fuck was Angel? And what hell was about to rain down on us now?*

Shade watched as the blood spattered, and he turned his back and walked outside for a smoke. He was done for the night and ready to get the hell home to a shower and his woman.

Alec saw the warriors ripping the rogue to shreds and followed Shade outside to find him leaning against the wall, smoking a cigarette. "I know every vampire master on every continent. There is no master named Angel. Does Angel mean anything to you?"

Shade scuffed his heavy boots against the pavement, "Nope. And if you don't know..." He turned his head to look at Alec, Shade's bloodied hair and face in such a contrast to Alec's. "...then we got more hell than either of us could imagine, brother."

8

Leaving Alec, Shade teleported home, feeling good after a night of killing rogues and getting info, even though the Intel made no fucking sense. It was still better than being cooped up in the damn Dead House all night. Coming in, he looked like fucking hell. He went upstairs to let *bel* know her warrior was home, and to see if he could coax her into joining him for a long bath. He entered their bedroom to find her asleep, sprawled across the bed. *Well, hell, no welcome home this morning, warrior*. Reaching down, he pulled back the sheet that barely covered her and admired her lily-white skin, her curves and how her softness called to his hand like a lover's caress. He smacked her ass and she groaned, burying her face in the pillow as he chuckled again. "Wake up, *mi amore*, your warrior is home."

She felt the sting of his slap and startled awake, as he roared he was home. She had returned to their bedroom after her workout with Luca and had only lain down for a second before planning to take a shower. She must have dozed off. *Good grief! How long have I been asleep?* She started to sit up and felt her muscles scream in protest. "Lover, are you home early? I must have dozed off."

"Early? It is almost sunrise, *mi amore*. Are you all right, you look tired?" He watched as she sat up slowly in the bed and he began to undress. "*Mi amore*, I need your assistance, can you help this waning old vampire with something?"

She pushed herself upright, confused from such a deep sleep, trying to clear her head and ignore the pain in her muscles. "Of course, what do you need?"

Standing as naked as the day he was born, he grinned at her and winked. "Will you wash my hair? I love your hands in my hair."

He had stripped the soiled leathers from his skin and stood there looking, for all the world, as if chiseled from marble. She ran her eyes from head to toe, as she heard his request to wash his hair. *Oh, I will do more than wash your hair.* She threw back the last of the blankets and jumped to her feet, her muscles regretting her quick movements immediately. Grabbing his hand, she led him to their bathroom.

"What're you gonna do, little minx?"

He wanted to play. They needed to play. Ignoring the ache in her muscles, she raised her hands and ran them through her hair, lifting her arms high in the air above her head, as she rolled her hips to the slow rhythm in her head. Her hands slid down her breasts, across her flat stomach, and between her legs, as she rolled her hips in a slow turn so her ass was to him. She tossed her hair back, as she looked over her shoulder at him. "Fight that, warrior."

Fuck! This woman will kill me. He picked her up, crushing her to his chest. He nuzzled his face into her neck and sank his fangs deep and felt her instantly melt into him. He drew deep, just a hit, and then licked the wound. She moaned, and he could feel her need for sex, as he whispered in her ear, "That will teach you to mess with this warrior, you minx."

Carrying her to the bathroom, he had their bath waiting, and the scent of roses intoxicated him as he stepped in, pulling her into the deep warm water with him. He willed the fire to burn in the gas fireplace behind the glass wall.

They both sank into the hot sudsy water. It had been so long since they had been playful. She loved the feel of his wet skin against hers, the slickness as they glided against each other in the water. His hands washing her and hers washing him. She sat with her back against the tub and had him lean his head against her breasts. She scooped the water over his hair and then poured the shampoo into her palm, and began the slow, sensual massage on his head and those dark tangled locks. She felt him relax into her and moan. She continued to massage his head and move down to his neck, his muscles tense and tight, as she massaged away whatever burdens he carried. When she had washed his hair clean, she used her hands to scoop up the water to rinse the suds away, but it was not enough to remove all the shampoo. She playfully slapped her hand on the surface of the water, creating a big splash soaking them both.

He felt the water splash his face and he was sputtering. "You wicked little minx." Chuckling, he turned in the tub, pulled her into him and slid her straight onto his cock, already aching to be inside her. Nuzzling his head between her breasts, he suckled her nipples, so taunt and sweet, and pulled them gently with his teeth. He felt her head fall back, her body ready and willing to ride him. He moved his hips, thrusting them upward, filling her completely, as she began that sweet ride on his cock. He slid one hand up her back and into her wet hair, pulling her into his neck.

"*Mi amore*, feed, make us cum together. I need you, *bel*... as you need me."

She bit him hard and felt his blood flow into her mouth, hot and salty, as she felt the explosion of heat between her legs. She gripped his shoulders with her hands, and rode him harder, feeling his cock throbbing inside her, as the water flowed like a waterfall over the side of the tub.

He felt her muscles tighten, gripping him hard as she unlatched and threw back her head. The blood trickled from her mouth, and it was the most sensual thing he had ever seen. He realized he had lived his whole life just to find the one who was his. He came hard, rocking her body, his voice raised to the heavens as he roared.

She felt his release, his cock throbbed and he filled her with his cum, pushing her to follow. She sank her nails into his shoulders, as she clung to him and rocked her hips hard against him, her body craved to feel him deep inside of her. She cried out with pleasure, but her cries were drowned out by his loud roar, his claiming.

9

Alec had his driver, Alto, return him to their home. He sat in the back seat, pondering the information he had just received. *A potion they drink that blocks their scent. Brilliant!* Wouldn't he love to get his hands on that? The real question remained, who the fuck was Angel? The masters were a close-knit community, even if they were not all allies, and there were no masters named Angel. Must be a code name... angel of death maybe? Whatever. There would be more rogues and more clues. They would find this master who had decided to make Alec's life hell, and they would wipe the floor with him. They arrived back at the house and Alec entered to find Rissa asleep. He sat next to her on the bed and ran his hand through her golden hair. She needed to know about the potion. "Rissa, wake up, my darling."

Moaning softly, she opened her eyes. She could tell from his expression he had something to tell her. "Alec, what happened? I was certain I felt your beast emerge."

"I got a call from Shade. They caught a live rogue. They were holding him at the Dead House, so I went down to interrogate him. There is something you need to be aware of. Seems our rival has developed some kind of potion that blocks the vampire's scent. That explains how one of them was able to get so close to you at the gala without your knowledge. This is crucial, Rissa. You must be on guard. This master is turning mortals fast and letting them loose. He is going for quantity, not quality. They don't have the training or the discipline of trained warriors, but they are deadly nonetheless. So, I know you get your back up when I tell you to be careful, but I mean it. Be careful."

Rissa took in the information about a potion. *Was Max using a potion?* "Yes, I need to be on guard and I promise I will be."

He stood to leave her side, but then remembered the strange name and paused, looking back at her. It was not likely she would know the answer, but it was worth a shot. "By the way, when we asked the rogue the name of the master, he replied 'Angel,' does that mean anything to you?"

His question made her head spin. *Angel? Oh my god, it is Max!* She tried to hide any reaction on her face. "Did you say... Angel?"

Alec nodded, "Yes, mean anything?"

She shook her head. "Never heard of it. And what a ridiculous name for a master." She flopped back on the bed, responding dismissively, praying he walked out that door before she completely cracked.

Alec shrugged. "Yeah... has me befuddled too. But it doesn't matter. We'll find him. Shade will track him. It is just a matter of time. In the meantime, heed my warnings... be careful."

He left the room and returned to his study. She stared at his back as he left, and her body began to shake from head to toe. How could this be happening? Alec's territory was under attack and now she knew who it was. But it wasn't Alec they wanted, it was her! *Oh Rissa, what have you done, you stupid bitch. You have to fix this immediately, and Alec can never know.*

Pulling herself together, she quickly showered. It was Sunday and she could spend the whole day in the gym, so she could think, and work this out. But she needed to find Max and find him soon. He had a lot to answer for, and Rissa would set his ass straight. *He better gather these asshole rogues and get the fuck out of our town!* Picking up her gym bag, she headed to the study to let Alec know she was leaving. "Alec, please may I go to the gym?"

"Yeah sure, just be alert, Rissa. If I start to feel you are at risk, I will have Alto drive you everywhere, so let me know if you have any problems."

Rissa fluttered her hand at him. "I'll be fine, I'll be more alert now based on what you've shared. I won't be too long, but you know how I am, once I get there, I lose track of time." Spinning on her heels, she tried not to run out the door. *Where the fuck are you, Max?*

Working out seemed to center her, and today, Rissa needed to be centered more than ever. She had felt so confused about Alec, Max and all the chaos of recent events. She had never had anything bother her like this, she was always focused and on her game. But the appearance of Max had definitely taken her off center and she didn't like it.

She needed to talk to Max, she needed to know if he was the one behind this rogue coven ravaging the city, and turning her vampire into a maniac with his uncontrolled beast. Her body still ached from the rough sex he bestowed on her, and although she loved every bit of his attention, craved it even, when Alec's beast came out, it was something to be feared.

The more she was putting the pieces of this puzzle together, the clearer the picture became. Max wanted her back, and she knew he would stop at nothing. Unless she decided to go back to him, Max would try to take Alec down, and rule this territory with her at his side.

She knew Max might be able to pull this off, but she still had her reservations. Alec held equal power, even if he wasn't a warrior. Was Max's desire for her enough to make him push harder in his quest for her? His words from the gala rang in her head and rattled her heart strings. Max still loved her, never stopped loving her, and he wanted her back. He was willing to fight for her, taking Alec down and giving Rissa everything she ever dreamed of. But Max had forgotten one small thing. He had given up his chance once before, refusing to turn her from mortal to immortal when she was with him.

Alec protected her now. He taught her to be all he ever wanted in a mate, and she willingly gave that to him. No one could love her like Alec, and he knew she loved the unique type of love they shared. She was proud to be his mate. They were far from conventional, and it was best no one knew what Senator Canton did behind closed doors to the Darling of G-town. She knew Alec's goals and knew she was part of them. But Max, what the hell did he have for a goal? Where did he think he was going? That was something she needed to find out, for her own benefit and sanity.

And this potion? How brilliant and diabolically evil was that? Did Max know the beast could still detect the scent? Rissa was even more curious to figure out how the potion was made, what was in it, and how to get her hands on some. Wouldn't she love to be the one to hand that to Alec? But she needed a foolproof plan that would not expose her. Getting to Max would be easy, but explaining how she got the potion, that was another story. Those were minor details, and Rissa was sure she would find her way through. Alec would be so overwhelmed and proud of her accomplishment he would probably not be overly concerned for details. *Oh yes, Maximus, I will play your little game and lure you in. Hell, you are already on my heels with a fire you can't put out, and you will give your angel all the tools she needs to take your ass out. Alec has taught me a thing or two, Max. You may think I am cold-hearted, but you have seen nothing yet, for this angel loves her mate and will never betray him. You want war, Max, you will have a war!*

* * *

10

Leaving the house tonight was a bitch, Shade didn't want to leave Kate, but she seemed anxious, in a strange way, for him to leave. He shook it off. She was probably working on decorating another damn room. He didn't care, whatever the hell made her happy was fine with him.

It felt good to come home now, she was back to his normal sweet *bel*, and peppering him with questions and making him laugh. He no longer felt the need to hide everything from her. He wasn't to the point where he would tell her the details of what went on in the Dead House, though. She may never understand the brutality of his world and he didn't want her to. She was his soft *bel* and he wanted to keep her that way. If she ever turned into a fucking Rissa, he thought he would kill her himself.

Taking the last puff on his smoke, Shade walked back into the Dead House and wandered through the halls to the makeshift command post. There was nothing fancy here and he liked that, there was a place for comfort and this was not the place. This was where the beast was allowed to rule, and he wanted all the warrior's beast to come out and play here, uninhibited.

Walking into the command center, he found Skelk sitting on the metal stairs, crossbow in hand, and Shade shook his head. That was one crazy mother fucking killing machine. Skelk nodded, he wasn't the talkative type, so just his presence here had Shade on alert. Something was rattling around inside his head, and Shade had a feeling he was about to find out what it was. Sitting down in the chair, Shade propped his feet up on the desk and grabbed the grid map, looking it over.

"You know, Skelk, that's an odd weapon of choice, but a damn good one. I know you rarely go street level, you would look like some fucked up coke addict gone mad walking in G-town with that thing." Chuckling, Shade lowered the grid map and looked at him.

Skelk answered, his voice low and gruff, "I don't need no streets under these boots to kill. My aim is good, and these arrows work just fine. I do my share of laying those bastards low. I don't give a rat's ass what mortals think, either. Master Alec gives his orders and I just follow them."

Tossing the grid map down on the desk, Shade spun in his chair and looked at him, face on. "I have no doubt about your skill, I respect that. And rooftop level is one place I need you. So, what's going on, brother? Your ass isn't here to suck up to me, so give it to me straight."

Skelk eyed him slowly, he liked this master, he knew warriors, he was warrior, and Skelk knew he could trust him. He had seen Master Alec take his word and extend his trust, and if that powerful bastard trusted him, then Skelk could too.

"I was here last night. Listened to that rogue tell his tale of potions and bullshit. I ain't so sure I believe all that, Shade. And it doesn't matter. I can take care of business, scent or no scent. But I been noticing something, and it ain't my place to tell Master Alec what the fuck I see and know. So, I'm telling you."

Shade furrowed his brow and got a gut-wrenching feeling. He didn't know where the hell Alec found this piece of work, but basically, it didn't matter. Skelk was an artist with the crossbow, and he knew how to take down whatever he was told. He followed orders and knew Shade gave them under Alec's command. Skelk's presence here tonight told Shade whatever he knew was important. He wasn't exactly the social butterfly in this league of brothers. Shade lowered his boots to the floor and they hit with a resounding echo across the empty room, his signal to Skelk he had his full attention.

"Speak your mind, Skelk, I'm listening. Anything, as far as I am concerned, is vital to this operation. Your eyes and ears are my radar on the streets. Go on."

Skelk drew slowly on his cigarette. "I don't spend my time walking around them rogues. I stay up high, that's my skill. Other warriors keep telling me they ain't smelling shit. But I am. I ain't saying I'm different or better. I got eyes like a fucking hawk. And last two nights, something ain't fucking right. I smell them. And when I find them, they ain't rogues, Shade. They are mortals been turned. Not drained but turned. And just let loose to fend for themselves. They ain't no warriors or coven mongers."

Shade's brain was churning. *What the fuck?* "So, you're telling me Aries is turning mortals, not just killing them, and leaving them to fend for themselves? Turning them into killing machines from hunger?" Standing up, he began to pace, running his hands through his hair.

"That's what the fuck I just said. They ain't bearing no tats, they women, men, teenagers. They ain't fucking picky what they turn. They just go round making newborns now. Just thought you should know. Heading out, I ain't sitting in this hellhole all fucking night. I ain't born to do that shit, makes my ass lazy." He strapped the bow on his back, stood up, waiting for his dismissal. He knew better than to walk out of here like he owned the fucking place.

Shade was processing the information. This fucking Master of Aries had taken this to another level. This was going to be a son of a bitch to control. *Cazzo! Like I need more fucking chaos to deal with.* He slammed his fist on the desk and watched the crack spread across the table. "Good job, Skelk. Fucking good eye, brother." Shade picked up the grid map and pointed out Skelk's assignment from the previous night, tossing the map across the table to Skelk. "Is this the grid where you saw them last night?"

Skelk nodded as he looked at the map.

"Get out there and let me know if you see more, or if they move."

Watching as Skelk stalked out, Shade let out a long breath. *Another fucking long night trying to figure out what the living hell this bastard Angel was up to.*

* * *

Alec was getting home later than usual. He'd be glad when this session of Congress was over, and he could have more time to focus on this mess with the rogues. He walked into the study and poured himself a Midnight, then pulled out his cell phone and hit Shade on speed dial. He needed to see if there was anything new since the Intel they got from the rogue last night.

Shade was barking out orders and recording locales of sightings and hits when he heard his phone buzz. He didn't even have to look. Who else would be buzzing his ass at this time of night? "Shade."

Alec could hear the rustle of paper on the old table set up in the command center, and had a visual of Shade shuffling through the clutter. "Just checking in, brother. Anything new I need to know about?"

"Yeah, something you need to know, but you sure as hell won't like it. Sit the fuck down, brother, don't bang a fang, but one of your warriors picked up something the last two nights. Where the hell did you find that Skelk character? He is a piece of work!" Shade lit up a cigarette, waiting for Alec's response.

Alec laughed under his breath. "Skelk... yes. He was kicked out of another coven. He worked independently for a while until he realized even his bad ass needed some backup. He's not much for rules, but then, neither am I, so I recruited him. He can be a wild card, but he has come in handy more than once. So, I'm sitting. What bomb are you going to drop tonight?"

Shade shook his head. "He wanders around this damn place like Robin fucking Hood with that crossbow. Tonight, he tells me these rogues are attacking mortals, turning them, and letting them go, unattended. So, now you have rogue warriors from the Aries coven and a bunch of fucking mortals being turned into zombie immortals overnight with no damn place to go, no guidance, no fucking nothing. They are wreaking havoc, uncontrolled bloodlust and the need to feed, and who the hell knows how many there are. This fucking master just upped the game, brother."

Alec jumped to his feet, pacing the floor. "Jesus fucking Christ, Shade! How the hell do we keep a lid on this? How many warriors have I lost? Do we need to bring in yours? This is completely out of control. This won't go unnoticed by the mortals for very long. It will be on the front page of the *Washington Post*. Then every reporter in town will be snooping around."

Shade suppressed his laugh, because suddenly, Mr. Fucking Bad Ass Master sat up and paid attention. *Well, son of a bitch, took your prissy high and mighty ass long enough!* "Casso Alec, I am no untrained master, I got this. I don't want your beast going ape shit on me. I got enough of them to deal with now. I need to bring in my own. I'm done with this playing. It's time I showed you what the fuck a real warrior does. I'm tired of this fucking hell hole and being stuck here with no real progress. I'm going to Florence, I need to get my boys in here, get this fucking nightmare on the right course or we are both going to be looking for another place to live. I need to talk to Kate, I need to have a place to house them and they sure as fucking hell can't shack up in the Dead House."

Alec was half listening to him rant on about his warriors and Kate. *What the fuck is he talking about?* "You lost me, brother. I understand bringing in your warriors, bring in whatever you need. But who is Kate?"

Shade squeezed the phone in his hand, almost to the point of popping it apart. *How fucking dare you not even know my mate, you bastard!* He should go over there and rip his fucking head off. His beast rose up and Shade had to tap him down.

"Damn Alec, sometimes I wonder how the fuck you got where you are. Don't worry, you don't fucking need to be concerned about my woman, just like I don't give a fuck how you deal with yours. I will line this up, leave soon and bring back what I need, be gone two nights, tops. I'll leave Tomas in charge while I'm gone."

Alec felt his anger through the phone. *Fuck! That fucking mortal is still causing me problems. What master takes a fucking mortal for a mate, anyway? At least I turned Rissa before making her my mate.* Alec's temper flared at Shade's tone, but he needed his head in the game right now, so he let his comment about Rissa pass. Alec swallowed down his anger before he answered him. "Oh, Kate! Of course, no, I remember. You confused me with the reference to your warriors. Yes, by all means, do whatever is necessary. If you need to go to Florence, then go. Let me know when you leave. Just get this under control, brother. For both of us." Alec ended the call, downing the glass of Midnight in one gulp.

Shade sat there seething. *Damn right, I will go. You don't own my ass, Alec, and you never will.* Shouting out a few commands, he headed out. Time to get the hell out of here and go home to some peace and quiet, but he was afraid it wouldn't be quiet for long. He needed to talk to Kate about Florence.

11

Kate got up when Shade woke and waited for him to leave before getting dressed to go downstairs to Luca. She put on jeans, t-shirt, sneakers, and a jacket. The weather was cold, but he worked her so hard, she would be shedding any clothing heavier than this anyway. Luca said they would run seven miles tonight. She stopped off in the kitchen and had Reynaldo fix a big high protein breakfast. He seemed delighted, but if Luca worked her like yesterday, she would burn this off by midnight.

Kate walked to Luca's suite where the door was closed. The message was clear. While he was still her protector, when they are training, he was in charge, he would call the shots. She knew if she ever skipped a single day, if she didn't take this seriously, he would end it.

Luca waited in his suite for her. He would never go looking for her. She would come of her own free will or not at all. She seemed hell bent on issuing him a challenge when she left yesterday, but let's see where she was today after a full day of sore muscles. He was pleased with her performance so far, and a little surprised. She was still soft and had a long way to go, but she never backed down. Still, the swordplay was mock and slowly paced. He would push her further until the swordplay was real. He was beginning to think she had changed her mind when there was a light tap on his door.

Without speaking, he stepped out and started walking outside, and she followed him. "Warm up, stretch," he barked at her, and she complied.

Yikes! Where did my gentle Luca go?

After a few minutes of warm-up, he started to run, and she ran beside him. He reminded her of posture and breathing. He took her on a longer loop, and he had increased the pace. Yesterday, he had let her set the pace. Today, she was forced to keep up with him. Her lungs were burning still, and her muscles ached, but there was something in this physical demand on her body that was cathartic, and it was the release she had been looking for. She let him push her the entire seven miles. As they ended up back at the house, he instructed her, again, to cool down and drink water.

Luca had purposefully pushed her harder today, forcing her to dig deeper. She kept up with him as he watched her go inside her head, finding the runner's zone that allowed her to block out burning lungs, the pounding heart, and the screaming muscles. That was both good and bad. As they returned to the house and she was cooling down, he asked her, "What did you notice?"

She paced the yard, letting her breathing return to normal. He asked a question that confused her. "What did I notice?" She stopped and looked at him. "About what?"

"What did you notice as we ran? Did you hear the owl in the tall pine tree? Did you know there was a coyote in the brush, as we came around the large bend? Did you see the house cat that chased down the mouse in the field?"

Kate stared at him for a second. *Is he kidding me?* His eyes told her no. "Uh... you know it's dark out, right? And I'm not sure I would have noticed those things in broad daylight."

Luca nodded, "And that is exactly what your enemy is counting on, Kate."

Kate looked up at him, "I have enemies?"

"Was Sabine not an enemy? Had you not been drinking master's blood, and he from you, your bond would not have been as strong, he may not have heard your call and responded as quickly."

"Well, yes, but... that was an isolated incident."

"Not so isolated. I watched you go after the feeder. That was not exactly a warm welcome you gave her."

"Yes but... she was..."

"Another isolated incidence? You are mate to a master, Kate. And a master will have many enemies. Every master rules over a coven. Some of these covens cover vast territories, and multiple countries. And all masters will fight to defend, and sometimes expand, their territory."

"Shade has a coven?" As she asked the question, Luca looked at her like she had three heads.

Luca could only shake his head at her response. "Were you not at Castello? Did you not see the warriors? Master's coven is centered in Florence but extends across all of Tuscany. It is the second largest coven in Italy. Here, he commands the warriors in Master Alec's coven, because he is a Master Warrior, the best. Master has smaller covens in California, Greece, and France, where he has vineyards, to protect his business interest. And all of us here at Bel Rosso, we're a part of his coven. Doesn't talk to you of these things?"

Kate kicked at the dirt. "No. He talks around them. I didn't understand the warriors at Castello were his. I mean, a coven, I guess I thought it was just a school. You know, like anybody could go there. And when you graduate, you just... go back home or wherever."

Her innocence of their world took him aback. No wonder master worried about turning her. Her innocence could get her killed. It wasn't his place to judge his master, but he should have started training her earlier. His love for her and his desire to protect her from all that was evil in their world, wasn't doing her any favors. Luca was more resolved now than before to train her. He knew she was seeking an outlet for her pain over the loss of the baby, but he had a different mission in mind. She must learn to kill. He wondered if Kate could kill. Could she take the life of another? And then he remembered the look in her eyes when she attacked the feeder. "You have much to learn, Kate. Take a break, and then we begin again with swords."

She watched Luca as he walked inside, and she let his words sink in. Her own capacity for denial was hitting home. *I mean, I watch Shade come home covered in blood. Whose blood and why, I never question. I have a freakin' vampire warrior as a personal twenty-four-hour bodyguard. Why would I not consider the idea that Shade has enemies, and his enemies are my enemies? How could I have lived in such a bubble?*

She knew the answer. It was because she didn't want to acknowledge it. She didn't want to see it. She only wanted to see Shade and the life they had here inside these four walls. She watched as Luca returned with not two swords, but four. With his words still ringing in her ears, she resolved to handle whatever it was he threw at her.

He would make her parry with a sword in each hand. He placed the larger sword in her right hand and the smaller in her left as he explained, "I know you are right-handed, but you must be able to fight with both hands. You must build your strength in both arms, and be able to respond equally as quick, regardless of which direction your attacker approaches you from."

He stepped back and assumed a confrontational position in front of her. She lifted both swords, and her eyes were piercing his. She heard his words, and she had come to fight.

* * *

Kate left Luca as the sun began to rise, knowing Shade would be home soon. Her arms and shoulders ached, even more than yesterday, if possible. She headed for their bathroom and sank into the bath of hot water, her head resting against the back of the tub, neck deep in the sudsy water. She felt herself relaxing and drifting into sleep when she heard his voice.

"*Mi amore*, you did not wait for me?"

She looked up to see him standing by the bathtub, already undressed, and smiling down at her as he stepped into the hot water, sitting opposite her. She smiled at him. "I am always waiting for you, Shade." She watched as he slid his own body beneath the water and laid his head back against the rim of the tub, closing his eyes. She teased him, "Rough day at the office, dear?"

She watched as he slowly opened his eyes and looked at her, just before splashing her with the water that drenched her face and hair.

"Yes, my little smart-ass minx, rough day at the office. Now climb over here and remind me why I come home to you."

12

Alec was taken immediately to their table at CitiZen. Rissa had not arrived yet. He checked his watch as he sat down. It wasn't like her to be late or to keep him waiting. The waiter brought him a Midnight without having to be asked, and he lit up a cigarette, while he waited for her.

As the cab dropped her off, she checked the time. *Damn! I'm late. He'll give me hell for that.* Rissa had had a long day and spent way too much time at the gym this morning, making her late for every appointment. As she rushed inside, she smiled at the staff. They recognized her and told her Alec was already seated at their table. Walking up behind him, she slid her hand across his shoulders, walking to the seat opposite him. "Good evening, Alec, apologies for the time. Busy day."

"No problems, my darling. It gave me a few minutes to collect my thoughts. Sounds like both of us had a busy day." He flagged the waiter to bring her a Midnight.

Sighing, she placed her hand on top of his. "Thank you." The waiter brought her drink and she sipped it, trying not to gulp it down. "And what thoughts have you gathered together? Anything you wish to share with me?"

"You mean thoughts like why you might be spending so much time at the gym lately? I know that's where you go when you have things on your mind. Anything you care to share, my darling?"

Oh, I have things on my mind all right, but not anything I want to share. Looking down, she adjusted her dress and crossed her legs. "A few things, yes. The rogues bother me some, this potion business has me on guard constantly, wears on me a bit. So, I tend to lose myself in the gym. It's just an outlet for things, Alec, nothing to be concerned over, I assure you." Reaching over, she took the gold cigarette case with his initials, flipped it open, slid out a cigarette and lit it. Taking a small drag, she handed it to him. "Have you made a decision on a protector?"

He made a note of her actions. She never smoked in public. Something had her rattled. He took the cigarette from her hand and inhaled deeply, releasing the smoke before handing it back to her. "You tell me. If the rogues concern you that much, wouldn't you prefer a protector?"

She casually waved the cigarette away. "I don't think it's so much about the rogues, but more the issue of why this situation isn't over with already. Why is this taking so long? What's that warrior of yours doing night after night? I don't feel threatened in the least, and I don't feel as though I need a protector. I can defend myself. I know you're busy, Alec, I am just trying to stay out of your way."

"It is not over with, my darling, because this master is turning mortals and just leaving them on the street, with no maker to guide them. He is converting mortals to warriors as fast as he can, so there is a never-ending supply. They aren't trained. It's stupid and careless, but dangerous nonetheless. And they have the added advantage of being able to block their scent. The verdict is still out on your protector. Shade thinks I should assign one to you now. But I know how much you will resist it. So I'll wait a while and see how this plays out. Shade is heading to Florence for a few days, to bring back some of his own warriors, so hopefully, we can wrap this up soon. But until we discover who this master is... this Angel... until then, I'm afraid we are stuck in this standoff."

She watched him carefully, trying to figure out if he had any clues whatsoever about Max, and found he didn't, but when he said the word Angel, it sent a small shiver up her spine. "What does that warrior know about me needing a protector, he's with a mortal. But you forget one thing, Alec, I already have the most powerful protector possible... you."

"I'm flattered. But I'm not with you twenty-four hours a day. And you're not the little homebody. You're out and about all the time. One of these rogues could be walking right beside you and you wouldn't know it. And I can't exactly teleport myself off the floor of Congress in front of every Senator and the ever-present press, now, could I? So, the issue of a protector is still on the table. And while we're on the subject, any reason why you have been blocking me from your thoughts so much, my darling? What is going on inside that head that you need to keep from me?"

She felt her heartbeat accelerate and she calmed it down quickly. *Have I been blocking him that much? I must watch that.* "I didn't realize I was blocking you that much. I apologize. Forgive me, please? I think I'm so focused on my surroundings. I'm trying to be alert and aware, just as you asked of me."

Smiling, she reached for her glass and sipped at the Midnight. She couldn't keep up this charade much longer. He was way too smart for that.

"Don't get overconfident, darling," he warned her. "We are immortal only in we do not age and die. That doesn't mean we can't be destroyed. And that includes me. Don't misunderstand my words. This is a battle I intend to win. I have not lived this long without learning how to outsmart my adversaries. But my power to protect you only extends so far. A clever master would use you to get to me, just as we used the mortal to try to break Shade's attachment and distraction. Ah, speaking of the mortal, I forgot her name when talking with Shade." He chuckled through his words, "That was a conversation that did not end well."

"Well, I'm sure that phone no longer exists." She laughed softly, "Why he would ever want her is beyond me." She crinkled her nose. Leaning in close, she licked her lips and whispered low and sexy, "Daddy, baby girl just wants to go home and relax with you. May we please?"

"Of course, but you know I don't like it when you call me daddy in public, or when you refer to yourself as baby girl. There's a place for that, and you know where that is." He stood up and pulled out her chair, threw some bills on the table and sent a message to Alto to have the car at the front door for them, taking her arm and leading her out.

Rissa gritted her teeth as he led her from the restaurant. *So many rules!*

13

Kate's precious hours with him passed, as night slid into day and he rose from his death slumber, put on his leathers, kissed her goodbye and left for the Dead House. The very name of it sent chills up her spine. She didn't ask him what the name meant, and he offered no explanation. As he left her, once again, she dressed quickly, putting her hair in braids to keep it out of her face. She ate another power breakfast and headed to Luca's suite to see what torture he had devised for her today.

Luca prepared for her arrival. He thought they were making good progress. While she was mortal, she had the advantage of having fed from master now for half a year. She didn't even realize the changes made to her body when it came to her strength, speed and endurance. Her determination and focus helped as well. Still, there was much to learn. He heard her light tap at his door. He opened it and led the way outside.

"Tonight, we will run ten miles. And I want you to control your breathing, quiet your breath and quiet your mind. You have been escaping into what mortals call 'the runner's zone'. It allows you to block out what is around you and just focus on the run. Listen, even if you do not understand what it is you are hearing. The recognition of what the sounds mean will come with time. You must learn to be aware of your surroundings always. You'll learn to feel your enemy long before you hear or see him. And you start with hearing the small rabbit by the road or the birds that roost in the dense shrubs. Pay attention to scents. Tonight, you focus on your senses. Pay attention to what you see, what you hear, what you smell, and eventually, what you intuitively feel. Ready?"

She nodded her head as she stretched her muscles and took in his instructions. She didn't feel the soreness in her muscles now. She felt ready and eager to start this run. She realized she was actually looking forward to the session tonight, as her body adjusted to this new routine. *Look, listen, smell, and feel. Got it.*

Luca led and set the pace, faster than yesterday. Kate did as he asked and tried to control her breathing. She tried not to make so much noise by panting and gasping for air by taking in slower controlled breaths through her mouth. They ran side by side in the silence of the night. She looked and listened. She heard a rustle in the tall grass and noticed a raccoon, it moved slowly away from them. She pointed it out to Luca who only nodded at her. They ran further, and she saw the glint of moonlight reflected back in a deer's eyes and pointed to the deer as Luca smiled in approval. As they completed the loop and returned to the house, she started the cool-down without being directed. She waited for his praise, but he said nothing.

"So, how did I do?"

"Good. You did well for the first time. You picked up two out of ten."

Kate was dumbstruck. "Ten? I missed eight things?"

He smiled at her look of surprise. "Yeah, well, I thought the black bear was pretty obvious, but you'll get it in time."

"A bear? There was a bear? You're kidding, right?" *How could I miss a bear?*

"He wasn't close, and I picked up his scent. Like I said, you will get it with time. Before we're done, and after you're turned, you'll hear the ant that crosses your path. You will then have to learn a new skill, what to block out, and what to pay attention to. But that's for the future. Today, we fight for real. I'm going to give you sabers, lighter weight so you can manage them more easily, more swiftly. And we will fight. No more mock fighting. I want you to defend yourself and if you see an opening, I want you to take it, because if I see an opening, I plan to take it."

Luca wouldn't actually fight her. If he left a single scratch on her with his blade, master would have his head. Plus, her skills were still far too amateur, but she must think he would attack her. She must start reacting as if her life depended on it.

Kate looked surprised. "What do you mean if I see an opening I must take it? You mean, actually strike you with the blade. For real?"

Luca had to suppress his laugh. He was amused that she seemed concerned for him, but not for herself. As if she could actually land a strike.

"That is exactly what I mean. You can't hurt me, Kate. And any strike of the blade from you will heal before the sun rises, so don't hold back, assuming you can even land a strike that is." Luca smiled at her in a way that reinforced his challenge, as if to say, I dare you, mortal.

Kate stood with her hands on her hips. "Are you implying... You're laughing at me, Luca!"

Luca smirked, "I think you should be more concerned about me landing a strike, my lady."

He taunted her in a mocking tone and watched as her face reddened. She had acquired master's temper from her feeding and her own red-haired temperament, and it was a volatile combination. He could only shake his head to think of them together once he turned her. He handed her the sabers and they began to parry. He landed several early strikes, calling out each time he broke through her defenses to let her know, in a real battle, she would be dead or injured by now. He watched as she got more frustrated. "Channel that, Kate. Channel your frustration into action. Don't let it defeat you. Anticipate me. Look, listen, smell, feel... remember your lessons."

Luca came at her quickly with his sabers, and even still, she knew he was not moving as fast as he was capable of. He landed strike after strike. She felt inadequate and frustrated, which only allowed him to penetrate her weak defenses even easier. He was directing her to channel her anger and frustration. She settled her mind, released the frustration and focused her attention. Anticipate him, he said. Look, listen, smell, and feel. She watched his eyes, watched how he moved, learned to read his body movements so she could tell in advance, when he would strike, and finally began a pattern of being able to block his strikes consistently. She saw a lapse in his attention to her, and she flicked the saber upwards and nicked his face, watching as a small trickle of blood ran down his cheek. She stopped and stared as a look of surprise washed across both of their faces, and then he smiled.

"Well done, warrior, well done."

14

Teleporting home, Shade was in one bad ass hurry to get this trip to Florence underway and he needed to talk to the most important person in his life before he went. As he strolled in through Luca's entrance and saw Luca waiting for him, standing there with his arms across his chest, looking all cocky. *What the fuck is going on?* "What?"

Luca laughed at him. "What? That's it? I can feel you coming in like a bull with his ass sideways in a race. I know something is going on, master, you trained me well."

Shade laughed, "You are too astute sometimes, smart ass. Upstairs, now. I need to talk to you and *bel* together. I might need back up here." He winked at him. "And I better fucking get it."

Luca followed him up the stairs and he could tell Shade was anxious about something. He knew it wasn't about him training Kate. If that had been the issue, Shade wouldn't talk, he would fucking kill him, then ask questions later. Getting to the bedroom door, Luca hung back as Shade rapped on the door.

"*Bel?* Are you decent, I have company." He turned to smile at Luca and noticed a slash mark on his cheek, small but deep enough to draw blood. *What in the hell?* "You want to explain that mark on your face?"

Luca shrugged it off. "Weapon got out of control, jumped off the wall at me, and I wasn't paying attention. A slew of the sabers fell, I was grabbing them, trying to make it a swift game, but one of them won."

Shade stared at him. "Well, if you have so much time on your hands, perhaps I need to give you more to keep you occupied while I am out, *si*?" Banging on the door again. "Damn it, *bel*, wake up!"

Kate had rushed upstairs and showered after her lessons with Luca, removed her braids and washed her hair before Shade returned, but he was already banging on the door. She slipped into her robe and rushed to pull the door open. "Lover, I was in the shower. What's wrong?"

"Well, I would think when your warrior comes home he would be greeted without having to beat the damn fucking door down, woman! Now give me a proper welcome home."

She saw Luca standing in the hallway as she slipped her arms around Shade's waist and leaned into him, planting teasing kisses on his neck. "What has you so riled up? Do you need more bathtub therapy?"

"Do not tempt me. Luca is here, and we would not want him to see such exploitations, *mi amore*." He slapped her ass softly. "Now, be good."

He led her to the chair by the window and pulled her into his lap and nodded for Luca to take the seat across from him. "I have some things to discuss, and it is important both of you are here, *si*?"

Kate was confused by the fact he had asked Luca to join them. Her heartbeat picked up as she felt nervous about whatever news he was about to share. "I'm listening, lover."

Shade pushed a still damp strip of crimson behind her ear and smiled. He looked at Luca who nodded. "There have been some changes on the rogue front, not good ones. I have decided to go to Castello, bring some of my warriors here." Shade saw Luca's eyes light up. "I will be gone maybe two nights, three at the most. This is not a pleasure trip, I have a lot of work to do there, decide who stays to protect Castello and the Tuscan coven, and who I need here. I will make that decision once there. I am not even sure how many I will bring back with me, at least six, perhaps as many as ten. They will need housing. So, this is where a few things come into play for you both. *Bel*, I need to know you will be okay here alone with Luca for that amount of time. If not, I will take you with me, leave Luca behind to keep watch on things. Also, I need you to prepare for having that many warriors around the house. I wish for them to stay in the staff quarters temporarily, but long term we need to plan accommodations for them. *Bel*, you can assist Gi in handling all their needs. I need you to be all right with this. I don't want you to feel uncomfortable."

Shade directed his attention to Luca, "I need you to get more weapons prepared while I am gone. You know what I will need, what they will need. And I am relying on you, if *bel* chooses to stay here, you are to be by her side every second. You will sleep outside that door to protect her. Both of you need to give me your thoughts, I need to know very quickly, we need to make this decision together, we are family."

Kate was torn by his request, three days without him? Three days he would not sleep by her side? She felt his energy, his need to go, and she knew once they were there, she wouldn't see him. He would be with his warriors and she would wander through that massive castle with nothing to occupy her nights except thoughts of their lost baby. She would stay here and wait for him.

"Something in your voice tells me you'll have much to do once you're there. And I doubt there will be time for me. I'll stay here. I feel safe with Luca. And, of course, I'm comfortable with your warriors. Whatever you need, Shade."

He hugged her tight and kissed her softly. "*Grazie, mi amore*." He looked at Luca and watched his face. "Luca?"

Luca had been hoping for a different message. He had been hoping Shade would take both of them back to Florence.

"Of course, master. You know I'll be at her side every minute. You can rest assured of her safety."

Shade saw his disappointment, and could feel that he missed home. But Luca needed to learn, he was warrior and sometimes, home was not an option.

"Luca, when all of this is done, and things go back to normal, I promise you can go back home for some time. This is not easy for me. I don't like leaving either of you. It will be hell for me. I can barely make it through one night without aching to be home with *bel*, but I need you both to be strong, take care of each other, and I am just a call away. Any other concerns?"

Kate looked at the floor. *Concerns? He comes home some nights covered in blood from a place called the Dead House, and now he has to go to Florence to get more warriors and he wants to know if I have concerns?* "No, lover, I have no concerns."

Shade responded to her by telepathy, **"You lie well, *mi amore*, but I feel it... I feel it hard."** Shade lifted Kate off his lap and went to Luca. He gave him a hug and slapped his back. "Luca, you can go. I need you to protect the only thing I love more than my own life. I am proud of you, so damn proud of you."

Luca said nothing but held his gaze and the hearts of two warriors locked and understood. Shade waited until Luca left the room, then turned to Kate. "Now tell me what you really think, *bel*."

Kate cast her eyes downward. He hated when she told him to be careful, she didn't want to give voice to her concerns and make him angry before he left her for a few days. "If I ask you to be careful, you get angry. I can't help that I worry for you always. You think my worrying is somehow about me doubting your strength as a warrior. It isn't. I'll always worry. I love you and I'll always worry when you're away from me.

You shield me and I let you because there are elements of your world I know I'm still not ready to accept, and those things scare me. I fear what I don't understand, lover. So, when you tell me there are changes on the rogue front, and I don't really know what that means, and you need more warriors, yes, I have concerns. But I have faith in you. I believe in you. So, if you are asking me if I'm okay with you going to Florence, the answer is yes. But when you ask me if I have concerns... the answer is always, Shade, always."

Walking to her, Shade took her hands and pulled her up from the chair, sliding the robe from her shoulders. It fell with a soft whisper to the floor and she stood before him, naked and clean from her shower, smelling like heaven, her hair still damp, and her eyes so soulful, showing concern for him. He slid his hands softly up and down her arms, up her neck, and into her hair, tilting her face up so their eyes met. She was so damn small, and he towered over her, it made him feel like he must always protect her from all the evil and corruption in the world.

"*Mi amore*, there is so much in this world I never wish for you to see. And yes, I do shield you from much. I keep you here, isolated from everything because I am selfish in that I want you to remain as you are, my soft *bel rosso*. I escape here to you. I escape all that is evil when I come home to you. So, that is why I do not share my life away from you. But the rogues are doing things that are making a mess in the vampire world. They are bringing in the mortal world as they do, and it could easily get out of control, forcing us all to leave in order to not be exposed. I am not ready to give up all I have fought for. I will fight to keep what I have here. This is our home now and I won't let that go without a fight. I love you, I love this house. I need my warriors here to help, to wrap this up and then we can move forward with our lives. We deserve that, *si*?"

He pulled her into his arms. "I will miss you. I know you will be okay with Luca, but it doesn't mean either of us has to like it. You will be surrounded by warriors now. They will flow in and out of this house for a time, for weapons, for talks. If you can, I need for you to accept them like you have the rest of my family, welcome them, and make them feel at home here. I have no doubt you can do that, I just worry it is too much for you at this time. Tell me you are okay with this. That I can bring them here. That you will welcome them in your heart as I do."

Her skin tingled at his touch, and her heart calmed at the sound of his voice. She could deny him nothing. "Of course, they are welcome here.

And I'll be fine. Now, put this away, if this is my last night with you for a while, I don't want to talk any more about rogues and warriors."

He lifted her in his arms and carried her to their bed.

15

As Shade woke from his death slumber, Kate had to fight back her disappointment, knowing when he left her, tonight, she wouldn't see him for a few days. She was torn with her decision to go or stay, but she sensed his relief when she decided to stay here. She knew he would be preoccupied in Florence. Not having to worry about her would be one less thing for him to deal with. Since she had moved here with him, he had always come home to her to sleep, and she had always lain beside him. This would be the longest time they had been apart, and her heart already ached for him.

She clung to him as they said their goodbyes, and he kissed her with such deep passion and longing. She fought back her tears, as she didn't want him to see her cry.

Shade never anticipated leaving this home in Virginia would be so difficult. But this was home now and leaving was like nothing he had ever felt. He always thought the first time he left Castello was one of his most difficult moments, but this was far more heart-wrenching because he was leaving her behind. He trusted his staff implicitly to look after her, and they understood his duty, as their master extended far beyond these four walls. She sheds no tears, brave little minx that she was, but he saw her struggle and tried not to make their goodbye a drawn-out affair that would leave them both emotionally drained.

Hopefully, this trip would be over quickly, and they would have their homecoming. He still wasn't sure Kate could handle warriors stomping about all over the place, and keeping them shacked up in the staff quarters might be difficult on his warriors. They would all need to make the best of it.

Looking for Luca, he gave him the last-minute instructions, and knew in his heart Luca would carry them through without fail. With his hand on the doorknob to leave the side entrance, he heard a familiar voice, quiet and timid, and he turned to find Theresa.

Theresa had followed in her master's footsteps this evening, waiting for a moment when he wasn't preoccupied with preparing for this trip. She wished to speak to him alone, without prying eyes, before he ventured back home to Florence. She was hoping he would understand

and not feel her request was an inconvenience. Finally, she saw him wrapping up with Luca and getting ready to go when she spoke softly. "Master Shade, please, may I have a few moments before you leave us?"

Letting go of the doorknob, he smiled at her. Theresa had been with his family through generations, and she was so sweet and obliging. He could feel her nervous tension. He laid his hand softly along her cheek. "You may have as much time as you need. What is bothering you? Speak your mind."

Reaching into her apron pocket, she pulled out a small package, wrapped in fabric and tied with a ribbon from her hair. She held it out to him. "Since you are going home, might I beg for a favor? Would you please make sure Marco gets this?"

Shade raised his eyebrows. *Marco? Hmm, wonder how long that has been going on and how the hell did I not notice it?* He took the package, tucking it in his leather coat pocket and smiled down at her. "Marco, huh? Keeping secrets from the master, are we?" He watched her blush and he chuckled. "Do not worry, Theresa, I will deliver it into his hands. You must miss him, *si*?"

"*Si*, Master Shade, but it is his life, and this... just a small token to remind him he is missed. Thank you, master." She bowed her head to him and quickly returned to her duties.

Shade watched as she scurried away. He was totally befuddled he had never noticed any attraction between Marco and Theresa. *Cazzo, where the hell have I been? In a fog, warrior, in a fucking fog!* Teleporting out, he was eager to see Castello again, but his heart and soul remained at Bel Rosso with Kate.

Kate's tears fell as she dressed to meet Luca. She wiped them away and walked downstairs. She stopped in the kitchen for another breakfast from Reynaldo. As she sat and ate, she contemplated the people in this house. They were part of Shade's coven, they were loyal to him. Yet, all of them watched after her as she hid away for days in the nursery, after the loss of the baby, and not one of them betrayed her secret. They helped her drag everything from the nursery, destroy it and kept silent. And now, as she trained with Luca, once again, they protected her. She knew if Shade were to ask outright, they would not deceive him. But she had such respect for them, and her love for them grew every day.

They served through loyalty and honor, and she felt humbled by them. It was a comfort to have them here. As she finished eating, she walked to the closed door of Luca's suite and tapped lightly.

Luca was wondering if she would come tonight. How she would respond to master's absence? Would she continue to fight through her pain? Or would she retreat back into it? Shade had stopped in earlier to give Luca his orders before leaving. Telling him what weapons he needed to procure in anticipation of the arrival of the new warriors, and her... 'Don't let her out of your sight, not even for a minute.' Luca could see the concern in Shade's eyes for her. He didn't like leaving her. Luca assured him she would be safe with him, he would remain at her side until he returned. As he prepared to go upstairs to take his station outside her bedroom he heard her tap at the door. He had to smile at her resolve. He opened the door and silently stepped out, and she followed him outside once more. She started warming up without prompting.

She looked over at him. "How many miles will we run tonight?"

"You will run only ten miles, little warrior, the same as last night. I'll be adding some new exercises to your routine. Are you ready? Just like yesterday, I want you to look, listen, smell, and feel. You'll pick up more every night. Let's go, we have much to accomplish tonight."

He started their run, pushing the pace a little harder, watching as she monitored her breath. "Listen to the sound of your feet as you run. Listen to how far that sound carries in the night. You will have new skills when you are turned, but you need to think, now, about how to move without detection. Because just as you are listening to the sounds around you, your enemy is also listening for you. Move with more ease and more lightness."

Kate took in the instructions. Breathe, posture, look, listen, smell, feel, and now run with lightness? Who knew running had so many instructions. She tried to change how her feet hit the ground. How do you run with lightness? In her head, she saw a flash of the Native Americans, and how they were moving with quiet stealth through the forest. She saw it, and she tried to mimic that motion and spirit, tried to find that space in her head.

Luca noticed the improvement. "Good... much better. It will improve with time and practice, Kate. Now, focus." They completed the run and returned to the house. She was able to identify four of the eight animals that were in their path this night. She seemed disappointed in herself, that she didn't pick up on all of them. Her impatience matched that of Shade.

"Kate, last night you only got two out of ten. Tonight, you picked half. Don't be so hard on yourself. That's my job. Speaking of which, we're adding some things to your routine, just regular exercises to build your core strength. The running helps with your endurance and builds strength in your legs. The swords are building strength in your arms and shoulders. Now, we add core. Nothing fancy here, just push-ups and sit-ups. So, drop down and give me twenty, and I want your body to be as straight as a board. And no, you can't do girl push-ups on your knees... full plank. Move it."

Kate hated sit-ups, and the only thing she hated more than sit-ups were push-ups. She sighed and dropped to the ground and got in position.

He was immediately correcting her, "Arms straight, under your shoulders, flatten your back, get your butt out of the air, straight line, straight line, weight on your toes," as he counted off the twenty repetitions. She dropped flat on the ground at the end of the twenty count, only to hear him say, "Good... now give me twenty more."

After putting her through the forty push-ups, Luca had her do sit-ups with a weighted ball, forty of them. And then he had her walk it off and hydrate. "Are you ready for swords?"

Still breathing heavily, she looked at him, "You want me to cut your face again?"

Ha! Master is right. She is a smart-ass. He had to suppress his smile. "That was a lucky break."

She shot back, "Not so lucky for you. I should be more careful, though. Wouldn't want to scar that face and scare the girls away."

"Yeah, well, don't you worry about me and the girls. Let's focus on you, right now." He walked to her and tied a scarf around her eyes.

She put her hands out in front of her. "Hide and seek?"

He backed away from her, leaving her standing isolated. "You wish! Tonight, you will fight me blindfolded. You respond with your sword based solely on what you hear, smell, feel."

"Are you kidding? How is that even possible? Are you blindfolded?"

Luca was fighting hard not to laugh, she was standing with her hands on her hips and he could feel her agitation. "Oh, it is more than possible. And no, I'm not blindfolded." He placed a sword in each of her hands and stepped back from her, picking up his own swords. "Now listen... feel... block out everything else. You'll be surprised at what you pick up."

She felt him place the swords in her hands, and she heard him step back from her. She heard him pick up his own swords from the ground. She was already amazed she could tell what his actions were, even with the blindfold in place. She listened as he moved around her, and she turned her body accordingly. She could hear the soft whisper in the air, as he swung his sword. She could tell if it is coming from the right or the left, and was able to respond. He was moving slowly, letting her get the feel of it, and gradually picked up the pace. She was not able to strike him, to go on the offense, but she was able to block most of his strikes.

Once he stepped away from her, she got quiet, and Luca saw her level of concentration. She responded quickly to the sounds, she had good instincts. She wasn't able to attack, and wisely, didn't even try. Her posture was one of pure defense, listening, feeling, and responding to block the strikes. They parried for a good hour before he stopped the exercise. "Drop your swords, warrior. I'm going to remove your blindfold now."

She dropped her arms to her side, as he stepped in and removed the scarf from her eyes. "Good job, I'm pleased with your progress, warrior."

She looked down at her feet, "Warrior? I am hardly a warrior."

"Excuse me? Were you not the one telling me warriors are born not trained? That a warrior is one who chooses to stand between his enemy and all that he loves and holds sacred? Trust me, little one, you are a warrior."

He dismissed her for the night, and she headed back to her bedroom to shower. She ran her hands over the empty bed, and took her shower alone. She put on fresh clothes. The sun was starting to rise, and the electronic blinds started their soft whir, as they closed over all the windows, blocking out the light of day. Normally, she would be sliding into bed with Shade now, but the bed looked cold and uninviting and only reminded her of his absence. How would she get through these next few days? She walked through the house, but there was nothing that needed to be done. The staff took care of everything.

She plopped down on the sofa in the living room, grabbed the remote and opened all the electronic blinds, watching how the natural light warmed all the colors in the room. She missed the beauty of the sun. She pulled her cell phone out of her jeans pocket and started scrolling through her contacts. As she looked at the names of friends and family members, it hit her how much she had cut herself off from everyone she knew in the mortal world. She would give them up all over again to be with Shade... but she did miss her girlfriends. When was the last time she just sat and talked with the girls? The only female vamp she knew was Rissa, and she worked during the day and spent her nights with Alec.

As she scrolled, she saw her name... Shannon, her bestie. They had spoken a few times on the phone since she moved in with Shade, but like everyone else in her life, Kate felt she had to keep Shannon in the dark, for Shade's protection. Besides, how do you tell someone you're engaged to a vampire? On a whim, she hit dial.

16

Kate held her breath as she listened to her phone ring. A part of her was even hoping it rolled to voicemail. She had no idea how to approach Shannon after all this time, to invite her here to Bel Rosso, to explain where she had really been for the last six months, and then she heard Shannon's voice.

"Well, hello, stranger."

"Shannon! Oh my god, it's so good to hear your voice. I have so much to tell you... and so much to apologize for."

As she rambled on, Kate realized she didn't just want to talk to her, she wanted to see her. She knew she could arrange to meet her somewhere, and Luca would follow, remaining in the background. But, on impulse, she decided to ask if she'd come for a visit. Kate could always tell Shannon it was Shade's house, and she was just here in the States for a few days, or maybe she would come clean, at least as much as she was able to share.

"Shannon, you remember Shade? I told you he had a place in Virginia, and he said I could stay here whenever I came to the States. Well, I'm here, and I was wondering if you'd like to drive down for a visit? I have a free day."

"Of course," she answered. "I would love to! Give me a couple of hours and I'll be there."

Kate gave her directions, ended the call and started pacing. Cripes! She had never invited mortals to the house. But this was different, this was Shannon. Kate had always told her everything, well, except for this. She headed to the kitchen to let Reynaldo know they would have a guest for lunch, and maybe dinner. He seemed delighted and was immediately in a flurry of preparation. Kate let Gi and Theresa know to expect a guest. She was giddy with the anticipation of seeing her old friend again.

She ran upstairs to change clothes and put on some make-up. Shannon always looked gorgeous, even on her worst days, and Kate had adopted a daily costume of jeans and a sweater. She found something a little more feminine to wear. It was still a little cool outside, but she pulled a spring dress from her closet and a light shrug in a pale coral that accented her coloring. She brushed out her hair and spritzed on her rose fragrance. She heard the doorbell, and before she could get downstairs, Gi was at the door, welcoming her. *Yikes! Well, now I'll have to explain house staff. Wow! Right out of the gate.*

As Kate entered the foyer, she saw Shannon at the door and ran to her. They both grabbed each other in a hug and start giggling like school girls. Kate watched the expression of amusement on Gi's face as he carried her coat away.

Shannon stepped back, looking at her, "A butler? Shade has a butler? Oh, you have so much explaining to do!"

Kate laughed and shook her head, "Shannon, you have no idea. Do you want to see the house first?"

"Absolutely! The grounds are beautiful. At least what I could see coming up that long drive, and this house is a delight."

Kate gave her a quick tour of the first floor, introducing her to Reynaldo where Shannon gave her a sideways glance and mouthed the words 'a chef' as they left the kitchen. They headed up the stairs and ran into Theresa, who was coming down, and Kate introduced the two of them. Kate showed her the many bedrooms, walking quickly past the empty nursery, ending up in the master bedroom.

Shannon stood in the bedroom, taking it all in, this house, the staff, and she looked at Kate's face. She was glowing, and Shannon knew she was in love. She was happy for her, but she had known Kate long enough to know she wasn't getting the whole story, and she decided she wouldn't be leaving here today until she knew everything.

Shannon noticed the two separate his and hers walk-in closets, both filled with clothes. Kate was here for longer than a few days.

"So, this house..." She paced around the room, taking in the details, noticing the oil painting of Kate on the wall. "You're telling me Shade lives in Florence and only travels here on occasion, and you just pop in when you're in the States, but there just happens to be a butler, a chef, and a housekeeper who keep things running on the off chance someone pops in?"

Kate wrestled with how much to share. She was never good at lies, and this one was too convoluted to carry on for long. "Shannon, the truth is, I never went to London. I moved here, with him."

Shannon seemed surprised. "But why would you hide that? I knew you were seeing him. Why did you feel like you had to make up this big story about a job in London?"

Kate flopped down on the bed. "Because it happened so fast. Because he asked me to quit my job and sell my condo, and it sounded insane even to me. I had just broken it off with Ethan, and then I met Shade. I mean, my head was telling me it was a crazy thing to do, but my heart... I just wanted him. I was afraid of your judgment."

Shannon joined her on the bed. "Girl, we have both made stupid choices when it comes to men. I wouldn't have judged you, but you're right, I probably would have tried to talk you out of it. I mean, you took a big risk, quitting your job and selling your place. What if... you know?"

"Yeah, I do know. I thought of that. And he knew I'd think of that, which is why he signed the deed over to me."

Shannon sat upright on the bed. "He did what? You own this?"

"Well, technically, yes. But really, I don't think of it as mine, it's ours, our home. I know he did it, so I'd have no excuse."

Shannon shook her head. "And where is the man of the house, Mr. Tall, Dark and Dangerous? I want to officially meet the man who has kept you so busy for the last six months that you haven't had time for your best friend."

Kate took both of Shannon's hands in hers. It felt so good to have her here, and to tell her the truth, well, almost the truth. "He's in Italy right now... on business. You know he owns several vineyards, in the United States, Italy and France."

As Kate shared this with her, she knew she wanted Shannon to meet him. She must still be guarded with what she shared, but of everyone she knew, Shannon would be the most likely to understand.

"When he gets home, and things settle down a bit, I'll have you come again to meet him. I know you saw him that one evening at the restaurant, but I want you to get to know him."

"Kate, I can tell you love him. You light up when you even speak of him. I'm so happy for you, really, I am. And you look so happy. I forgive you for ignoring me for the last six months. Now tell me everything!"

Kate took her hand and led her from their bedroom and back down the stairs. She shared what information she could about Shade, and she was wondering if she wanted to tell Shannon about the baby. Did she even want to open up that box of pain? As they hit the bottom of the stairs, Luca emerged from his suite into the corridor.

Luca looked at Kate and then shifted his eyes to Shannon, and Kate watched the expression on his face, as he seemed mesmerized by her.

Kate turned to Shannon and noticed she had seen him as well. They were both just staring at each other.

"Oh... uh, Luca, this is my best friend, Shannon. Shannon, this is Luca my pro... my, uh, trainer. My personal trainer."

Shannon couldn't take her eyes off this man, "Your trainer? Your trainer lives here?"

Kate's mind was running a mile a minute. *Fuck! I almost called him my protector. But trainer is not a good option, either. Now she wants to know why he lives here.*

Kate was trying to come up with an explanation, as she watched Luca walk slowly across the corridor, never taking his eyes off Shannon. He extended his hand, not for a handshake but palm up. Shannon laid her hand in his palm as Luca slowly lifted her hand to his lips, kissing the back of her hand, and saying, "It is my pleasure to meet you, Shannon," in that glorious Italian accent, never letting his eyes leave hers.

Kate looked at Shannon. Shannon had her eyes locked to his, her mouth slightly open. *Well, well, well... what have we here?* She smiled to herself, as she witnessed the little love connection. And then it hit her, *Fuck! She is mortal... and he... Fuck! Oh Shannon, I really hope you have an open mind, sister.*

Shannon practically purred her response, "The pleasure is all mine, I assure you, Luca."

Luca was still holding her hand, and they were both just standing, eyes locked on each other. Kate cleared her throat. "Uh... Shannon... lunch is probably ready, would you like to follow me?"

Shannon stood with her hand still in Luca's. "And will Luca be joining us for lunch?"

Luca responded, "Sadly no, *mia bellezza*, I have much to do for the master of the house." He let go of her hand with reluctance. A mortal! He had never felt such an attraction for a mortal before, and she took his breath away. But she was a distraction, and he had much to do before master returned. He turned to go to the bunker when he heard her call after him.

"I hope I'll see you again, Luca." She watched him as he walked away, the loosely tossed hair, his broad shoulders and narrow hips, his stride, and she was spellbound.

Luca looked over his shoulder at her and replied, "I will make a point of it, *mia bellezza*," as he disappeared behind the door.

Shannon turned to Kate. "What does '*mia bellezza*' mean?"

Kate shrugged, "Beats the hell out of me. Shade speaks to me in Italian all the time. I have to look it up on Google."

Shannon pulled her cell phone from her purse and googled the phrase. "My beauty. He called me his beauty! *His* beauty. Oh my god!"

Watching her brought back a rush of memories for Kate, of when she first met Shade and hearing him call her '*mi amore*', and '*bel rosso*'. How she loved the sound of those words on his lips and feeling how special they were. He only spoke those names to her. She knew a lightning strike when she saw one. *Oh, brother... I didn't see this one coming.*

Kate dragged Shannon away from Luca and they headed to the dining room where lunch had been laid out for them. They sat down to eat and talk. Kate was trying to fill her in, telling her what she could about Shade buying this house for the vineyards, bringing his staff over from Italy, the California house in Napa Valley, the Medici Vineyards there, as well as his home and vineyards in Florence. She decided to leave out the part about it being a freakin' castle. She told her she had been working on renovations here at Bel Rosso, as well as decorating the California house, giving her as much detail about the events of the last six months as she felt safe sharing. As she was talking, Shannon grabbed her hand, noticing the ring, like she could miss it, and nodded at it.

With a mouth full of fettuccini, Shannon almost choked. "So you're engaged then. You're going to marry this man? Can I assume I'll be your Maid of Honor?"

Kate was momentarily stumped. Wow. Every conversation was a minefield. She was already mated to Shade, and there would be some kind of ceremony among the vampires that would take place in Florence when she was turned, but she really didn't understand the details.

She stammered her reply, "Well... uh... of course!" Now she would have to figure out another lie when the time came.

Shannon pushed the subject. "And have you set a date?"

"No, not yet. Shade has been very busy. We haven't actually talked about a date. But I have to tell you, I feel married to him already. I don't know what else I could possibly ask for in a man."

"You look really happy, Kate, and I can't wait to get to know him. And by the way, it didn't slip my attention that you didn't answer the question about why your personal trainer lives here."

Kate smiled to herself that Shannon had found a way to work Luca back into the conversation. "He also works for Shade, as a personal assistant and bodyguard, so he has his own private suite here at the house."

"Wow, a bodyguard. How hot is that? And he lives here. Does that mean he's single?"

Kate laughed at her inquiry, "Yes, he's single."

"Seriously? You're telling me that guy doesn't have a girlfriend? How is that possible, unless he's a complete asshole?"

Kate shook her head. "He has just moved here from Florence, he hasn't been in the States for very long. He works hard, and no, he's not an asshole. He is probably the kindest person you will ever meet. Do you want to know what he does in his free time?"

"Of course!"

"He paints. That portrait of me, the one that hangs in our bedroom that you made comments on? Luca painted that. How poetic is that?"

Shannon pushed her plate away, "Okay, seriously? Can I go out with this guy?"

Kate twisted the pasta around her fork, avoiding Shannon's eyes. *Do I tell her?* Rissa had told her Shade was a vamp before she invited him home with her after that party, but she didn't believe her. Besides, Kate didn't even know if Luca would go out with her. She thought it best to keep that vamp information to herself for now.

"Shannon, that's a decision for Luca, don't you think? I mean, he stays really busy. But yes, I saw the sparks fly. If you're asking me if I mind, the answer is no. But I think the ball's in his court, so to speak."

Shannon leaned across the table, "But if he asks about me, you would tell me, right?"

Kate laughed out loud. "Oh girl, you got it bad. But yes, if he asks about you, I'll let you know."

They spent the rest of the afternoon chatting away about people they both worked with, trading stories, sharing memories, and laughing till they cried. It felt so good to be with her, and the time for her to leave came too quickly. But Kate needed to catch a few hours of sleep before nightfall and she and Luca started training again. Shannon had the drive back to D.C., so they both got up from the table and walked to the door. Kate called to Gi to bring Shannon's coat, but it was Luca who appeared. Kate watched as Shannon's face lit up.

Luca stood behind this mortal girl, and the scent of her perfume assailed his senses. Vampire women did not usually wear perfume. He helped her with her coat, as he slid it up over her shoulders. He wanted to bury his hands in her dark brown locks.

He stood so close to her she could feel the heat from him, feel his breath on the side of her face as he spoke, and felt his hands as they brushed against her hair.

He pulled the coat more tightly around her, as he stood close to her back and spoke softly into her ear, "I told you we would meet again, *mia belleza*, and a gentleman always keeps his word."

"I... it... uh... it was so good to meet you, Luca." She turned to him as she spoke, and almost wished she hadn't. She was at a loss for words. She was stammering, and she felt her face turning red. "Will I see you again?"

"Is that your wish, *mia bellezza*?"

Luca was captivated by her eyes. She was not as small as Kate, she was taller, maybe five-foot-seven, but slender, delicate looking. Her eyes were a brilliant blue and looked huge in her face, and he couldn't turn away from her.

"It is my wish, Luca."

He responded to her with a smile and a nod, and she turned back to give Kate a hug, and whispered to her, "Be sure you give him my number," before breaking the hug and saying her final goodbyes.

As Shannon walked back to her car, she kept repeating in her head, Oh my god, Oh my god, Oh my god!

Kate stood with Luca as they watched her car drive away, and then he turned to her. "Does she know what I am?"

"No, of course not." As she spoke the words, she watched him drop his head. "Luca, don't assume what her response will be."

Luca looked away. "In Italy, we never saw unions between mortals and vampires, we kept to our own. When we heard master was with a mortal, we didn't believe it until he brought you back with him to Castello. Until then, I had never seen a vampire with a mortal... except to feed, that is. But to take a mortal as a mate? It was unheard of. Master says things are different here in the States, and I have seen that for myself, to some degree. But I'm not so naive to think that all mortal women will accept a vampire."

"But Luca... if you give her time to know you... really get to know you, then the vampire thing, it doesn't matter. At least it didn't matter to me. I was so in love with Shade, there was nothing he could have said that would have changed my mind... then, or now."

He nodded his head. "It is a risk."

"Love is always a risk, Luca... mortal or immortal. Trust me, I've been in love with both. But when you find the right person, it's all worth it." Kate watched as he stood still, staring at the floor.

"I'm not sure my life will accommodate her. I cannot do for her what master does for you. I can't provide the things for her that master provides."

"Love is not about things, Luca. Can you love her like Shade loves me? Can you show her that kind of love?"

"You know I can. But you make it sound simple. I live here. I am expected to be here. This is my life as a warrior. This is what I was trained for, and we enter that life knowing there may be no room for a mate. That is why we have feeders."

Kate cringed at the word 'feeders', but before she could respond, he turned and walked away, closing the door to his suite behind him. Kate sighed. What was it with these men? They walk away when they are done with the conversation!

17

Teleporting inside Castello, it felt somewhat odd to be here. It was his ancestral home, where he was born, where he grew up. He still had the warrior camp here, his coven throughout Tuscany, his largest vineyards, and yet, home was now on the other side of the world, not this grand castle, but a villa in the foothills of Virginia. Still, he loved these people. He called out in the grand foyer, as his voice echoed through the halls, "Master is home!"

People came scurrying from everywhere, with smiles and happiness to greet him. Many were looking for Kate. He answered all their questions, informing them it would be a short stay with much to do, and his *bel* was fine. He would be returning with her soon to be turned, which brought many more smiles. Some of the housemaids clapped and giggled, and it made his heart beam that they already loved her.

He spent his first hours meeting with his house staff, going over their needs and getting updated on all the maintenance issues for Castello, since his last visit. He would save the primary reason for his trip for tomorrow, when he was rested.

Strolling through the long halls, he was tired. His death slumber was calling. He must rest, for he didn't wish to stay here longer than he had to. Making it into his old bedroom, he recalled the last time he stood here, remembering how beautiful, how loving, and sexy she was when they were here, where she fed from him for the first time. She owned him, body, and soul. The sun rose as the electronic blinds started to close, and he sat on the side of the bed.

He daydreamed of little *bambinos*, scurrying around his feet, calling him *padre*, and his heart broke again, remembering the little one they lost. He felt the soft touch of a small hand upon his shoulder, *Madre*, he thought. He knew she would be here, he knew she would come to him. He felt her hand, as she softly caressed his hair. He lay down on the bed and fell into his death slumber, calmed by his *madre*, but dreaming of *bel*.

Hours passed and from deep in his slumber, he sensed her, hearing her laughter, he woke immediately. He lay quietly and focused his senses on her, feeling what she felt, letting her happiness consume him, and he felt bereft that he was not the one giving her such joy. He sat up quickly, who the fuck was with her? *"**Mi amore**, **you are so joyous, who is with you?"***

Kate was laughing with Shannon as they talked about old times and she heard his voice in her head. She answered him. **"It is my friend, my mortal girlfriend, Shannon. You remember her? I invited her to the house today to help pass the time. I miss you so, lover."**

He sent her his love and drifted back into his slumber, aware of her absence in his arms.

As night hovered on the horizon, Shade woke and went in search of his Second-In-Command. In addition to deciding which warriors should come back to the States with him, he had a small present he promised to deliver. Smiling as he passed several warriors and house staff, he realized he missed being in his own territory, not answering to a damn soul but himself. As he walked across the training field, he stopped one of the warriors and asked where he might find Marco. The warrior told him Marco was doing his usual gym workout. Shade headed out to find the man he considered his true brother. Marco knew he was coming, and they had much to discuss.

Walking into the gym inside the warrior camp, he found Marco working out alone. Marco spied him and a huge grin spreads across his face.

Marco shouted, "You old dog!"

As they both laughed, Shade looked at him and shook his head. "When will you learn, Marco, no matter what you do, you will never be able to keep up with the young pups."

Marco had picked up his scent long before he heard him. Shade was closer than any blood family had ever been. Most of the time, they needed no words to communicate. They had saved each other's asses more than once, and had the scars to prove it. As Shade strolled in, Marco detected the changes in him, not physical but emotional. Things in the States had improved for him in many ways, but something was stressing his brother out far more than he would ever say. If he told anyone his woes, it would be Marco.

Marco had stayed in contact with his Theresa. He knew some of the hell Shade had been through with the rogues. Shade was one crazy-ass vampire, and his temper flared at the drop of a hat, but Theresa told him since he had met this mortal and mated her, he was different in so many ways and changing every day. Marco was glad to see him, he needed to come home more, leave this mortal mate behind and reconnect with his roots and his brothers.

Marco hugged him and slapped his back. "I may not be able to keep up with their young cocks, but I can strike 'em low like the dogs they are, brother!" Marco looked at him closely. "So, tell me, Alec got your balls in a twist and shoving 'em up your ass? Or is that new mate of yours running your ass in the ground fucking your brains out? You aren't young either, Shade." Throwing back his head, laughing, Marco walked to the rings and looked at him.

"You never mind about my mate. But fuck if I don't miss her already, and I'm thinking you are missing someone yourself."

Grinning, Shade liked the growl he got out of him. "So, how long has that been going on? I would have never guessed, *fratello*."

Pulling the package out of his coat, he handed it to Marco. "Small gift I promised to hand-deliver from your *bella* in the States."

As Marco took the package, he could smell her, he closed his eyes and calmed the beating of his heart, laying the gift inside his gym bag.

"Yeah, brother, you're fucking getting old, losing your damn senses as well. My connection with Theresa happened long before your ass got tied up by a mortal. Fucking hell, Shade, you walked past us a few times, and once you came barging in my room and she was moving that fine sweet ass under a pile of blankets and you never spotted her."

Marco bent over laughing as they both reminisced about the old times.

Shade laughed with his old friend, but he had not missed the tone of dislike in Marco's voice when he spoke of *bel*. He got serious. "About Kate, she isn't going anywhere, I love her. She is my mate and that is all there is to it. So, speak your mind. No hard feelings. We are brothers and it stays between us. But you will give her your pledge the next time she is here."

His face became deadly serious and his tone let Marco know where he stood.

Marco grunted, knowing he meant business, but he had never withheld anything on his mind with Shade, including when he felt a lot of his actions were questionable and could have been handled better. As Shade's tone became serious, so did his own. They didn't stand on ceremony.

"She will get my pledge when she is immortal and not before. So, I suggest the next time you bring her here, it should be for the turning.

And I am not alone in my thoughts. The others won't have the balls to tell you, they love you too damn much, but you need to turn her soon. Her mere appearance here the last time stirred up a lot of controversy. I didn't want to bother you with such. You have enough hell with Alec. But it is something you need to consider seriously. She will be much more accepted here, and your fucking heirs better be pure immortals if they are to be taken seriously."

Marco watched him and saw his temper flare and held up his hand. "Don't let that beast loose on me. I have one of my own just itching to beat the living fuck out of something. "

Marco grinned at him and watched Shade's smirk appear. "It is what it is. I'm just telling you, as a brother, the minds of the others. Nothing new, but this is serious, and I know you love her. That is obvious. I have no qualms about your love for her, and Theresa adores her. You've been a warrior a long time, and it's time you settled down, produced heirs to inherit your legacy. Your brothers were just surprised is all, as was the Council, to hear you mated a mortal. The quicker you get her turned, the better."

His words struck him deep, and Shade wanted to reach out and wrap his hands around Marco's neck until his life was gone, and not for the first time. But he listened to him talk, and he wasn't surprised at his words, he knew in his heart Marco was right. Shade had a momentary flash of their lost *bambino*, and the knowledge that he would have been born a half-breed had he survived, and he knew that son would never have been acknowledged, could never have inherited his legacy to continue to run this camp or the coven.

"Marco, I have every damn intention of making her immortal, but things have happened, she had a setback in her strength. I can't turn her until she gains that back and once she does, and I settle this fucking bullshit in the States, she will be turned. The main reason I am here is to get this hell over with in a hurry. Grab your fucking gear. We need to have one long ass talk about who is coming back with me and who stays. Let's walk, brother, I need to hear and see my warriors, and I need you to give me the details on their training and who has made improvements."

As Marco grabbed his gym bag, he threw his arm over Shade's shoulder. Shade knew deep in his heart, he had to leave Marco behind here in Florence. Shade trusted no one else with his warriors, his land and his home, but his brother, Marco.

* * *

18

Kate headed upstairs to get a few hours' sleep before nightfall. She slipped into a gown and climbed beneath the covers. She pulled Shade's pillow to her chest and buried her face in the soft down and inhaled his scent. She slid into the space he usually occupied. This bed felt so empty and cold without him. This whole house felt empty without him. Her body was tired, but her mind wouldn't shut off with thoughts of him. She tossed and turned in the bed, trying to find a comfortable spot, but her comfortable spot was lying with her head on his chest and his arms surrounding her. **"Lover...can you hear me? Can you feel me?"**

She waited to hear his voice in her head, and then he came to her. **"Si, mi amore. I feel you always. I love you always. Sleep now, bel rosso, I will be home soon."** His voice soothed her, calmed her and she fell asleep.

She had set her cell phone alarm to go off after nightfall, and she awoke in the darkened room to the sound of its beeping. She dressed and opened her door to head downstairs, only to find Luca just outside her door. He had been there the entire time she slept, and she realized that Shade probably instructed him as such. She asked him to join her for breakfast and he followed her to the kitchen, where Reynaldo had breakfast waiting. Luca sat with her while she ate.

"So, when do you sleep, Luca?"

"I'm a day-walker. I don't require the same sleep. We can go for days without sleep, if necessary. But if Master is here with you, I will use some of that time to sleep."

Kate stopped eating and looked over at him. "Some of that time? I would think you would use all of that time to sleep."

"My body does not require it. That is my free time. I may paint... or I may leave the house to feed."

Feeders. There it was again. This was a concept she was finding difficult to accept. "May I ask... Sorry, if this is too personal just say so, but do you see the same person?"

Luca leaned his elbows on the counter, "In Florence, I saw the same person, I was with the same person for years. But here, not yet."

Kate knew she was prying, but she wanted to understand the feeder relationship. "Do you love her? The feeder? The one in Florence?"

"Love? No, I wouldn't call it love. Affection, yes. There is a bond you establish with your feeder when you remain together."

"Do you miss her?"

"Yes... I do. But I'm sure I will find someone I connect with in time."

Kate nudged. "But if you had a girlfriend..."

Luca flashed her a look that said 'don't go there.'

Kate paused a second before continuing. "Why are you resisting this idea, Luca? I'm mortal, not blind! Do you think I didn't see the sparks fly between you and Shannon yesterday?"

"You don't understand. A relationship with a mortal brings a lot of complications."

"Uh... Hello! Mortal here! If there is a complication to be found, trust me, I will find it. But I would not change anything. I wouldn't. Everything that Shade and I have been through, and everything we have yet to go through, whatever it is, it's worth it. Don't you understand?"

"Oh, I understand plenty. I was born a warrior. It's my station in life and it requires certain sacrifices."

Kate grabbed his arm, "Love? It requires you sacrifice love? That makes no sense to me. Shade is a warrior."

Luca shook his head, "Shade is a master."

Kate sounded exasperated, "What difference does that make? Love is love, I'm sure he would never expect you to go through life without love. Luca, I will talk to him..."

"No! Kate... You understand so little of our world. I work for Shade, I am a part of his coven and I have a sworn loyalty to him. I have been chosen as your protector, and there is no greater honor as a warrior. He entrusts me with your life... Me! You are his most precious gift, and he entrusts me! Do you understand that?"

"I do understand that! But what does that have to do with you and Shannon?"

Luca ran his hands through his hair, "I have nothing to offer Shannon. I have no home to take her to. My first loyalty must always be to Shade and to you."

"Oh my god, if it is just a home... I mean, Luca, if you needed a separate house on the property or something. All these problems are just logistics. They can all be solved."

She watched as he closed his eyes, lowered his head and answered her in a soft voice, "Kate, do you understand if this house were under siege, if the lives of every person in this house were at stake, my duty is to you. To protect you. And if I had a mate, my obligation is still to protect you first, she would be second. And that is why warriors frequently choose not to be mated. They cannot choose between duty and love. There can be no conflict."

She watched as he slipped off the bar stool and walked from the room, as the impact of his words hit her in the chest like a sledgehammer. Must he endure a life of loneliness out of some code of loyalty? And she was the reason? Kate looked up to see Reynaldo looking at her as little puzzle pieces fell into place. They lived in a hierarchy. Their stations were defined at birth, master, warrior, worker bees. She saw Reynaldo nod his head, as he read that recognition in her face.

Kate left the kitchen and headed for Luca's suite. The door was closed. *Is he angry with me?* Her heart was breaking for him, and she didn't want to leave things this way. She tapped on the door and he opened it to her.

"Are we training tonight?"

Luca replied, his face showing nothing, "Of course, my lady, why would you think differently."

My lady... we are back to that. "Please don't call me that, Luca. If I upset you, I'm sorry. It is never my intention. I care deeply for you. You must know that."

He didn't give an inch, "I think it might be easier if I remember my station, my lady. You did nothing wrong. The problem is mine. It was wrong of me to even lay it at your feet."

She stood and looked at him. How did she get past centuries of tradition? "Am I more than a job to you?"

He looked up at her, startled by her question. "How can you ask that? Of course, you are more than a job to me. I love Shade like a father... like a brother. And I have come to love you. I watch the two of you together, and I see what joy you have brought into his life."

"Then please, dispense with the 'my lady' crap, and call me Kate. Please!"

He nodded his head and led her outside to begin their training. They ran the ten miles and she found the run that was once so challenging, came easier now. She remembered her lessons from previous runs and focused on picking up the sounds. She was still not great on scents, but Luca told her it would come. As they returned to the house, he had her go through the routine of push-ups and sit-ups, adding more repetitions. She was beginning to notice a physical change in her body, more definition. She wondered if Shade would notice it, and then immediately heard herself respond, 'Of course, he will notice it!' She needed to make sure she made some comment to him soon about working out.

As they wrapped up the core exercises, Luca had been quieter than usual tonight. She turned to him and asked, "What next? Blind man's bluff again?"

He shook his head. "Rock climbing. Have you ever used a rock climbing wall?"

Kate put her hands on her hips as she glared at him, "Okay, is this a punishment? Because I said I was really, really sorry."

For the first time tonight, she saw the slightest smile on his face.

Despite his mood, he couldn't help but smile at her. "Not a punishment. We'll start with a rock climbing wall in a gym, but before we are done, you will climb real walls. Now, come with me. I'll teleport us to the gym."

Kate had only teleported with Luca a few times. It still felt strange to her, as she stepped in and he held her close. He didn't take them into D.C., heeding Shade's warning to steer clear, but took them to Charlottesville instead. They landed in the parking lot of a gym. It was dark and there were not a lot of cars about. He led her inside where he paid for time on the rock climbing wall. He helped her into the harness, but didn't strap one on himself, he didn't need one. They climbed side by side at first, with him instructing her where to put her hands, how to grip with the tips of her fingers, and where to move her feet. He dropped down to the floor and then instructed her from there. He made her climb up the wall over and over, from different angles. And finally, he made her remove the harness. They worked for hours before he called it quits and they teleported back home.

When they got back to Bel Rosso she asked, "No swords tonight?"

"Not tonight. There is more to being a warrior than just weapons. We will add the skills I think will be most useful to you. You're making good progress, I'm pleased, Kate."

He was wrapping up their session as the day broke. Though he was in a somewhat lighter mood than when they started, he was quieter than usual. Their conversation from earlier that night still rang in her ears. His loneliness was the price he paid to protect her, and that seemed like too steep a price. She walked back to the bedroom to shower and pulled the phone out of her jeans pocket as she undressed, scrolling through the contacts. Shannon. *Should I call her? Invite her back?* No, this needed to be his choice. She wrote her number on a piece of paper, put her clothes back on and walked back to his door. She tapped lightly, and he answered, his brow furrowed.

"Is something wrong?"

She caught his gaze and held it. "There is a lot wrong, but nothing that can't be fixed." She put the piece of paper in his hand. "Shannon. That's her number. Call her."

She turned and walked away, back up the stairs, with her fingers crossed.

He took the paper she placed in his hand, as he looked at the phone number written there. He closed the door again. That was one stubborn woman. He started to throw the paper in the trash, but then he looked at it again, folded it, and slid it into his pocket. Shannon, he could see her face in his head. He could still smell her perfume. *Maybe.*

19

As Shade stood on the field watching the warriors, he was impressed. They were learning rapidly, he saw a few new recruits and it pleased him that their ranks were growing. It did his heart good to know his people would be so well protected. He had begun to worry about this master named 'Angel.' He was one mysterious fucker and that bugged him. He did a little investigating while here and found no one who seemed to know who the hell he was.

As Marco and he discussed which warriors would be returning with him to Virginia, Shade was busy from sunset to sunrise, making sure the warriors he had chosen had time to prepare. He got no resistance. Most of the warriors had been with him a long time and were eager for a new assignment. He left behind his most trusted and strongest leaders. They must remain here to keep the home front safe and protected and continue the education of the young warriors in his legion. He knew the camp would feel the loss of the warriors he took back with him, but it would help develop them as new leaders as well. He had always tried to move the most promising warriors up in the ranks, giving them a chance to advance, and prove their worth. Marco was the best person to help him make those choices.

As the two old friends sat, Marco was restless to get outside and move. Hell, they might be the oldest of the lot here, but they were still warriors to the bone.

Marco watched as Shade stood and paced. "Marco, I have chosen seven, but I want eight warriors. I had a particular warrior in mind, but I have not seen him in the camp. I need to know where he is and what he's up to. I will make my final choice once I have had the chance to review his skills. Where is Marcello?"

"So, you fucking bastard, you take Luca out of our ranks, and now you want his cousin as well? Son of a bitch, you will end up with our army over there instead of here! I promoted Marcello. He is out on the Siena border. He's not Luca, but he's getting there. He needs some discipline, but if you want some muscle, Marcello is your boy. You need to watch him with the women, boy likes to hunt a bit, one of the reasons I sent him out there. He isn't into the feeders like Luca. Wildcard that one is, a bit like his master. But he has calmed down since being out there. He's doing well leading the others and I have had no problems. You want your boy, take him. I will change it up here and send someone else to cover Siena. Now get the fuck out of my sight, I got some pup ass to bust!"

Shade had one more stop to make in the camp before heading out to Siena. He walked down the long row of barracks to the last building and tapped lightly on the door. Cory jumped up to answer, expecting one of the warriors seeking custom leathers. His face lit up when he saw his master.

"Cory, all right if I come in?"

He eagerly swung the door wide, welcoming Shade into his workshop. Shade walked in to find the room even more crowded than his last visit. Patterns tacked to the walls, a large workbench with leather being cut, and stacks of fresh, new leather waiting to be crafted. Cory cleared away a stack of leathers waiting for repair to make a seat for Shade.

"Of course! I heard you were in the camp. Is there something I can do for you? Would you like me to make a set of leathers for you?"

Shade smiled at his enthusiasm for his work. He had only heard good things about Cory.

"Maybe later. This is a quick trip for me, so I don't have time for a fitting. Besides, looks like you have your hands full."

Cory beamed at him. "In the beginning, it was just the young warriors who came to me. Luca, before he went to Virginia with you, Marcello and of course, Raven." Cory laughed. "I think Raven is my best customer. But then they all started coming. The older ones just came for repairs at first, and now they all seek me out for new leathers."

Shade smiled back at him, he looked healthy. Shade slapped him on the back. "You look better, not so damn scrawny. So, you're eating... And still not letting anyone feed from you?"

"No master, no one feeds from me. I eat human food, and I go to the feeders. The warriors let me work out with them sometimes. I'm no match for them, of course, but it has helped build my strength, helped me to maximize the vampire skills I do have. I went with the young warriors to hunt once, but I don't have the speed or skills, so I'll stick with the feeders. Besides, I don't have the instincts for the hunt."

Shade heard the pride in Cory's voice, but inside his head, he realized this would have been the kind of life his *bambino* would have been limited to, had he lived. And while he, too, took pride in the path Cory had taken and what he had achieved in such a short period of time, he knew this was not the life he envisioned for his own son. The decision to switch out *bel's* pills flashed through his head, and he knew the choice was made to save her life. But in doing so, he destroyed that tiny life inside her. He destroyed the *bambino* that would have always been 'less than.' His baby would not have been fully vampire, nor fully human, and not capable of inheriting and managing the Medici legacy.

Shade chatted a while with Cory before standing, giving him a big hug, clapping him hard on the back before leaving. "As long as there is a Medici coven, Cory, you will have a home. You are welcome here, son and you have made me proud. Marco speaks highly of you, and trust me that fucker speaks highly of very few."

Cory accepted the embrace, surprised at how much it meant to him. Surprised at how much he craved this man's approval. "I won't let you down, master."

"Of that, I have no doubt."

Shade left the workshop and headed back across the training field as Cory watched him walk away, wondering where he would be by now, if Shade Medici had not intervened in his life. *Easy question*, he thought to himself. He had been close to being dead and he knew it. Shade Medici gave him his life back, and one with a future.

* * *

Shade teleported to the ancient walled city of Siena, unchanged in centuries. It was one of the many Medici outposts in Tuscany. He had his outposts located throughout his territory. The outposts provided maximum protection for his coven, and gave his warriors an opportunity to learn additional leadership skills. He rotated them around, giving them some experience and independence. He wasn't surprised Marcello made it here quickly. He was slightly younger than Luca, and Shade didn't have the pleasure of training him personally, but if Marco had assigned him to Siena, he was more than worth Shade's time to check him out. Shade also had an ulterior motive. He wanted to surprise Luca. He deserved to have someone at home, his only surviving blood family, and near his own age. Maybe loosen him up a bit. Luca had fit so well into their life, and he could tell the bond between Luca and *bel* was building. He entered the central Piazza del Campo and went to the post, seeking out his warrior.

Shade stood in the narrow ally that opened onto the courtyard, and watched as Marcello led the small league of warriors. He shadowed his presence, wanting to watch without intimidating any of them, and he liked what he saw. Marcello was forceful yet respectful in commanding the warriors and the warriors responded well to him, respected him. His fucking sword skills astounded Shade. *Yeah, I can use you well, my warrior, very well indeed.*

Unshadowing himself, he walked out onto the courtyard and immediately, warriors stood at attention in his presence. They weren't expecting to see him way out here. As he walked among them, he shouted, "At ease." And let them relax. Shade pointed out a few things he was impressed with to each warrior. As a master, he must always reward growing warriors. He was stern on discipline but recognized theirs was a lonely life, and he must always give them reason to strive for perfection. He left Marcello till last. As he approached him, he nodded and gave him a fist bump. "Marcello! Kicking some ass out here. I like what I see."

Shade pulled him aside, and they walked and talked well into the night. Marcello said he was anxious to go abroad. Shade had to remind him of the conditions and differences in the States, but was convinced Marcello would do well there. Damn, he reminded him so much of Luca in many ways.

As Shade headed back to Castello, he had a good feeling about his selections. He felt confident now that he had his eight and they would be kicking some ass in D.C. He wanted this damn hell over with. He wanted to spend his fucking nights with *bel*, not a bunch of damn warriors. Although it had been his life, at some point, every warrior must find something more meaningful that makes all the hell they had been through worth the struggle. Otherwise, a warriors' life was nothing more than a series of battles, gaining territory, losing territory, and racking up kills.

That had certainly been his life, and then *she* came into it. He realized with clarity, he would live out his life now with *bel*, in Virginia, and if he had anything to do with it, surrounded by *bambinos* at his feet.

Teleporting inside his bedroom at Castello, he showered and laid naked in the bed, sunrise was soon upon him. There was only one thing on his mind now, his minx, and he moaned thinking about that crimson hair surrounding his face as he nuzzled into her neck. *Soon, mi amore.*

20

Kate returned to her room, feeling tired from the new exercises Luca had thrown at her. This was the time of day Shade would be coming home. But not today. And there would be no distractions to take her mind off him, like yesterday. She stood under the hot shower, then slid between the sheets, holding Shade's pillow. She had asked Theresa not to change his pillowcase when she changed the sheets, so she could still pick up his scent. It was a poor substitute, but she would take whatever comfort she could find. She tossed and turned in their bed, sleeping fitfully. She slept, she woke, she read, she fell back to sleep. She felt lost without him. She had stayed on his schedule, sleeping during the day and being awake at night, so their routine would not be interrupted when he returned.

The day passed slowly, and she felt agitated and wanted to get up, get going, and do anything that would make the time pass. As soon as the sun started to fade, she was out of the bed and getting dressed. She opened the door to head downstairs and almost tripped over Luca's legs, as he sat on the floor with his long legs stretched across the hallway.

"Luca, really... you don't have to stay right outside my door. I hate that you spend your day here."

He jumped to his feet as she stepped from the room and walked with her, as they headed down the stairs and into the kitchen.

"It is what master instructed. And that is what I will do."

His words reminded her that despite the bond between them, Shade was still his master, and he would be careful as to how far he pushed the boundaries. "And yet, you have pushed the boundaries with me. You kept my secret when I was hiding away in the nursery, and when you helped me burn everything."

"Yes, I did. But you hid away to deal with your pain. He had his own pain and his own way of coping. It didn't serve any purpose to burden either of you with more pain. And your actions were not putting you at risk. So, I felt I was meeting my obligations to you as your protector, and I was not betraying master. If he had asked me, if he had seen something that raised his suspicion and asked me outright, I would have told him. I will not lie to him."

She gave him a sideways glance. "And the training?"

"The same. I know why you seek this. It's an outlet for your anger, your frustration over the loss of your baby. Losing the baby was a situation where you had no control. The training gives you control. It occupies your mind, it tires your body, there is no room left for grief. But like I said, if he asks me, I'll tell him. I'll tell him why, but I don't kid myself. He will not approve. Not about what you are learning... that is not the issue. He'll be angry because he wanted to train you, and he'll be angry because I went against his order."

"And Shannon?"

Luca sighed. In his head, he could hear Shade shout 'woman!' at her. It's what he called her when she pushed too far, when he felt frustrated with her, and Luca had to bite his tongue not to use it now. He took a deep breath and considered his words. "I understand your intention, Kate. I do. Your heart is in the right place, but that's a line I won't cross. Not without talking to him."

"And what do you think he will say?" There was no sarcasm in her voice. She was asking the question openly.

"I think he will say no, Kate."

She grabbed his arm and pleaded, "But if I talk to him..."

"Please, don't. I'll ask him. I'll talk to him. But his decision has to be his own. I have to know he reached it on his own and not because he felt pressured to do so. Otherwise, he'll always doubt his choice. If I'm to have a mate, then he must approve it and feel it's the right thing for all of us. I know you don't understand that right now, but I'm asking you to respect it, please."

They entered the kitchen where Reynaldo had breakfast laid out for her. "You're right, I don't understand it. And I think you're wrong, I think he will approve. But I'll respect your request." She sat down at the counter to eat and Luca sat next to her.

Luca looked at all the food Reynaldo had laid out for her. Eggs, steak, fresh fruit, toast, juice, coffee, and he shook his head as she consumed it all. "I don't understand how such a little person can consume so much food."

"Trust me, you'll burn it all off me by midnight. And I'm not gaining weight. But look, muscle!" She flexed her arm for him.

He reached over and felt her bicep, and yes, there was muscle in her slender arm. He had to hold back a laugh. "Yes, you're a regular powerhouse."

Laughing as he mocked her, she punched him in the shoulder. They both stood and walked from the kitchen. She shouted her thanks to Reynaldo, as they headed outside.

"So, what torture have you devised for me tonight?"

"Run first, then exercise. Then torture. You'll just have to wait and see."

She was glad to have her happy Luca back. They warmed up in the chill night air before they started their run, listening to his instructions again, trying to run more quietly, and learning to hone her skills of observation. The ten miles that seemed so tortuous before, now went by quickly, painlessly. They completed the loop and after a short cool-down, he had her doing the sit-ups and push-ups again. He increased the size of the weighted ball and made her keep her heels off the ground as she sat on her butt, shifting the weight from left to right. She could feel the burning in her abs, as he directed her to do more reps. When she thought she had reached her limit, he pushed her with just ten more.

She collapsed flat on her back when he took the weighted ball from her. She was trying to catch her breath when she heard him barking out more orders. "On your feet, warrior. Tonight, we climb."

"Climb? That's what we did last night."

"That was play... for practice. Tonight, we will really climb. You'll learn to scale real rock walls, not play toys like at the gym. You'll learn to climb the sides of buildings. You'll see hand holds and foot holds where you never saw them before. No ropes. No harness. No pitons. Free climbing. Now, let's go."

She could feel her heart rate pick up, as he described his plan for the rest of the night. She would say, 'Are you kidding me?' But clearly, he was not. Climbing the rock wall at the gym was fun. But there were padded mats on the floor. Climbing real rock walls... if she fell...

"Are you sure I'm ready?"

He looked at her with a smirk. "Your enemy doesn't ask if you're ready. Your enemy looks for your weakness... and your fear. Are you afraid, warrior?" His question was issued as a challenge. He was trying to push her, and she wouldn't give in to him.

"No... I'm not afraid. Bring it." *Oh yes, I am very afraid!*

Little one, I can hear your heart beat faster, I can smell your fear, but I love your defiance! He smiled to himself and shook his head. He wouldn't let her fall. He could reach her before she ever hit the ground. But she wouldn't know this. She would need to climb unassisted, and rely on her own wits and strength, overcome her fear of heights and falling. Once she was turned, the falling would be a non-issue.

As they walked through the wooded area, he walked silently, and she was getting better. She was still too noisy, her footfalls still too easily detected by the wildlife, and certainly, easily detected by vampires, but at least she was able to move with enough stealth that most humans would not detect her. *Progress, little warrior.* They reached a sheer cliff wall that scaled the side of the mountain and he stopped. She halted beside him and looked up.

They had been walking through the woods for some time, headed in the direction of the mountains. She was trying to block out the fear that he was actually going to make her climb the mountain. She knew where he was taking her. It was a popular spot for climbers, but they used ropes and pitons, and he said she would free climb. She swallowed hard and turned to look at him. He smiled at her and nodded his head in the direction of the wall and said, "Go."

Go? That's it? Go?

Luca prodded her to start her climb, as she stood immobile. "The first step is the hardest, little warrior... just go. Start climbing."

She stared straight up the cliff wall, as she answered, "Actually, I think the missed step might be the hardest."

He smiled at her joke, but he could hear her heart pounding. She would have to push past the fear. "Go. Trust in your skills, warrior."

She walked to the wall and began to climb, feeling carefully for each finger hold, testing each crack before she let it bear her full weight. Hand over hand, foot over foot, she moved slowly, deliberately. Every cell in her body was alert, and she was totally focused on the wall. *Don't look down... just look up and keep moving.*

Her wrists burned, her fingertips hurt, but there was only one way out, and it was up, so she continued. She paused only once, releasing one hand to shake it out, and then the other hand. She rested her head against the rock face, got control of her breathing and moved on. She could finally see the crest of the wall. It was only a few feet away now. *Don't mess up, don't mess up, it's a long way down!*

As she reached the top, she saw him standing there, waiting for her. He extended his hand to pull her up over the edge, and they stood together at the summit, looking back over the Bel Rosso estate in the distance.

"How high are we? How high did I climb?"

He stood looking out, arms crossed over his chest. "About a thousand feet."

"A thousand feet! Seriously? I climbed a thousand feet?"

He smiled at her. "Master's blood serves you well, yes?"

"*Si.*"

He laughed out loud as she used Shade's words. "*Si,* now let's head home, warrior."

She was on an adrenaline high. "Oh my god, I can't believe I did that! I can't believe I climbed that high. It was awesome, Luca! I've never climbed before... except the gym exercise, but real climbing. You are just so... focused... so in the zone. I mean... intense! It is so intense. I feel so alive, so energized. My mind is clear and yet, I'm concentrating so hard."

He was stifling his desire to laugh. "Are you going to talk like this nonstop all the way back? If so, I'm going to teleport ahead."

She punched his shoulder again. "Yes, I am. I'm so excited! And you better not leave me out here, either."

He couldn't help but laugh at her. She always made him laugh. She made him want this in his own life, what she had with Shade, and he thought of Shannon. *Not my choice to make. I will talk to him, but master decides my future... not me.* They walked the long walk back to the house, where they both headed for their showers.

Kate finished her shower and changed into fresh clothes. The sun was coming up on another day she would spend without him. She felt too restless to climb into that empty bed, so she headed back downstairs. The house was empty without Gi, Theresa, and Reynaldo. She wandered about the empty house. This was the time she and Shade would normally be together, just before his death slumber. Maybe this was when the staff slept as well. She walked back to Luca's suite to find his door was open. He was painting, but the canvas was not visible from the door. He paused and looked up at her.

"Where is everybody?"

Luca stopped painting, wiping his hands on a towel. "In the staff quarters. They're getting everything ready for the warriors master will be bringing back with him."

Kate threw up her hands. "Why didn't they tell me? I could help. I'm going there now to see if there is anything I can do."

Luca covered the canvas with a tarp and left the room with her, walking toward the staff quarters.

"I don't think they need any decorating skills."

She punched him in the arm again. "You know, I can do things besides decorate. I... can climb mountains."

He smiled at her. "That you can, little warrior. I hope you know what you're getting into. Shade is bringing eight warriors back with him. They're a pretty rowdy bunch. This isn't a tea party he's throwing."

She shrugged. "They will all be like you."

"They will be nothing like me." He chuckled to himself, as he ran through the possibilities of all the warriors Shade might return with.

As they entered the staff quarters, Gi was directing like a traffic cop. Furniture was being moved out of Luciano's room to make room for four single beds. There was a discussion about Gi moving into Reynaldo's room, so they could free up another bedroom.

Kate spoke out, "Why don't we have Theresa stay in the main house? I can't imagine she would want to stay here with a house full of men."

Theresa looked at Kate with relief as Gi responded, "We would never impose, my lady. This is the staff quarters and this is where master directed us to prepare for the warriors."

Kate shook her head. "Nonsense... decision made. Theresa, you'll stay in one of the guest rooms for however long the warriors are here. And it's no imposition."

Theresa looked at her with a quiet smile and said, "Thank you, my lady. That is very gracious of you."

Gi took over and directed both Luca and Reynaldo in removing the furniture from Theresa's room. Luca flashed Kate a look that said, 'Thanks a lot.'

Theresa spoke up and said, "Let me get my personal things out first, to take to the main house before you move the furniture out of the room."

Kate clapped her hands together, "Good idea... I will help you."

She followed Theresa into her private bedroom. She hadn't been in the staff quarters since she completed the renovations and decorating. Theresa and Kate grabbed some boxes and started emptying drawers, putting her clothes and personal items into the boxes. Kate stood and moved to the closet, and noticed a blanket draped over some items on the floor. She pulled back the blanket to discover a painting. She recognized the artist. It was Luca's work, but the subject was unfamiliar to her. "Theresa, who is this?"

Theresa stopped packing the box and looked up to see Kate pulling a canvas from the closet. Her face reddened as she looked at the face of the handsome man in the portrait.

"Oh... my lady, he is one of Shade's warriors."

Kate smirked. "Really? What a handsome man. And would you, by any chance, know this handsome warrior?"

Theresa's blush deepened as she answered, "Yes, his name is Marco."

Kate held the canvas up in front of her face to examine it closely and to obscure her smile. She lowered the canvas so she could look over the top of it at Theresa. "And is there some reason why you have a portrait of Marco in your closet?"

Theresa tucked her head even further.

Kate dropped the portrait from in front of her face. "You love him! You love him, don't you?"

Theresa jumped up and ran to the bedroom door, closing it. "Shh, don't tell the others. We have kept it quiet. No one knows. Well, now master knows because I gave him a gift to take back to Marco when he went to Florence."

"Wait... this man loves you as well? You love each other, and you don't tell anyone? And now you are living here? Is Shade bringing him back with him? Is he one of the warriors that will be coming back? Because Theresa, you don't have to hide. He can stay with you."

"My lady, there is so much about our world you don't understand. Marco is a warrior. Many warriors never take a mate, and if they do, it is only with their master's approval. Marco is Shade's warrior, and I am his housemaid. This is our station in life. Please don't misunderstand. I love master, and I love working for him, and for you. You have shown us all such great kindness and we all feel at home here. We speak of it often, Gi, Reynaldo and I. But I go where I am assigned to go, as does Marco. Marco will not be coming back with Master Shade. He is Second-in-Command to master, so he will be left in Florence to manage the warriors that remain there and to oversee all the activity in Tuscany."

Kate set the canvas down and looked out the window. She felt like she was listening to a replay of Luca's explanations about Shannon. This felt so unfair to her.

"This is a very personal question... and you have no obligation to answer me, so please, tell me to bug off if you don't want to answer. But this Marco... when you were living in Florence... you were... together? As in... together?"

"I understand your meaning, my lady. And yes, we were together. Exclusively. We weren't mated. I had not fed from him. He fed from me, and I would only feed from a feeder's wrist. So, as exclusive as we could be without being mated."

Kate didn't need to ask her what Marco did now, or where he went for feeding and sex. She knew the answer.

"I'm so sorry, Theresa. I had no idea."

"Please do not apologize, my lady. It is our culture, our way of life. It is what we were born into and what we have all grown to accept."

Kate turned to face her. "But you love him. You still love him? And you would be with him if you could?"

"Of course, my lady. I am not sure Marco would ever settle down enough to commit to mating, but yes, we would be together."

"Then I'll say something to Shade."

Theresa held up her hand, "No! Please do not. That would imply discontent with my station. That I am not grateful for what I have been given! Please. I will see Marco again... in time."

Kate sighed and returned to the closet, finding two more pieces of art, another oil painting of Marco, and one sketched in charcoal that showed him as a warrior. Kate tried to imagine not being able to be with Shade. Her mortal culture rejected their union. Her mortal culture would be horrified by him. Just as she knew there were many in his culture who objected to her. And yet, they had come together anyway. She couldn't let this go. Not for Luca, and not for Theresa.

"Let's take all of these to the main house, Theresa. And don't hide them in the closet. Hang them up on the wall where you can look at him, and don't be afraid to declare your love for him."

"Yes, my lady." Theresa smiled to herself, knowing that Kate understood a woman's heart. And she knew she had asked her not to intervene, but Theresa had watched her in that house now, and seen her stubbornness. She knew Kate would approach master anyway, in her own time, and she knew he would fight her on this. It may not be a battle she could win, but Theresa was beginning to see she could hold her own with master.

They finished packing all her things and carried them to the main house, getting her settled into one of the guest rooms. When they returned, the men had removed all the furnishings from her room and replaced them with four more beds. The two bedrooms looked like a military barracks, functional but comfortable. She hoped Shade would be pleased. Luca said it was luxury compared to what they were used to.

Kate helped Theresa make all the beds, placing extra blankets folded across the foot of each bed, and lots of extra towels.

"You do not need to help me, my lady. I am used to the work."

Kate laughed, "Believe it or not, Theresa, I'm used to the work as well. And I need something to do."

There were lockers for the men to store their clothes and gear. Luca had brought in the additional weapons Shade requested and had them stored in the bunker. **"Everything is ready, lover."**

Shade heard her voice in his head. **"*Mi amore*. We shall return tomorrow night. I bring with me eight of the finest of my legion. Prepare yourself, woman, you will have more protection than you can handle. I am anxious to be home. I am in need of you, *bel*, desperately in need of you! *Ti amo, mi amore*."**

Kate left the staff quarters to return to her own bedroom. She had stayed up long into the day hours, trying to tire herself out to the point of exhaustion, so she could sleep. This was the longest period of time they had been separated, and she missed him in her bed, his booming voice in the house, and his undeniable presence.

Kate climbed into their bed, pulling the sheets over her, grasping his pillow and holding it to her chest.

He sent a small warm whisper to blow across her neck. **"Soon, *mi amore*, I will be there, holding you, loving you, with all my heart. Sleep, *mi amore*. Feel me there, my arms around you, protecting you."** He let her feel the strength of his arms surrounding her. He sent his scent to her, letting her know he was there.

She felt a light breeze across her neck and then felt his arms around her, inhaled his scent. She relaxed into him, quieted her mind. **"I can feel you, lover."**

"Rest, *mi amore*. It will not be long now. Lay your hand across your heart and feel me there. We beat as one, *bel*, always and forever as one. *Ti amo*." He surrounded her with his scent, with his presence and she heard his soft voice in her head. **"And I love you."**

She felt herself drift into sleep.

21

Walking to the conference room, Shade could hear the low rumble of the warriors, as they prepared to leave. He had asked Marco to gather them all before they headed to the States. There were a few things he needed to make damn sure they were aware of, before they got there. He stood outside the door and closed his eyes, feeling the presence of his *padre*, and knew he had walked this road many times before him. Entering, his warriors stood at attention and he bid them all sit down.

Marco passed out an agenda to all the warriors. Shade remained standing as he browsed through the material, until all eyes were on him. He was their leader, their master, ultimate commander, and their lives were in his hands.

"You have been given the maps with the coordinates for arriving at my property in Virginia. My home there is situated directly in front of the staff quarters where you will be housed. The property is large, not as big as Castello, but you will be away from mortals. Arrangements have been made to accommodate you in the staff quarters. If you have issues, don't go bitching to Gi, or any of my staff there, you will bring them to me or Luca. Is that clear?"

He looked at some of his warriors for acknowledgment.

"There is a well-equipped bunker and conference room in the main house below ground, you will need to access it through the first floor. The upper floors of my home are off limits. I have a mate, most of you know she is mortal. You will show her respect, honor, and try to act like gentlemen and not a pack of gorillas, for hell's sake."

Hearing a few chuckles, he kept his face stoic, letting them know the fun ended in this room tonight. Looking up and staring at a few, he saw they understood his message damn clear.

"There will be grounds to practice on within the confines of my estate. We do not wander, nor leave, without distinct permission. You do, your ass belongs to me, and you just bought yourself a one-way ticket home, disgraced. This is business, warriors, not a fucking vacation."

Glancing at one warrior in particular, Shade knew he heard him loud and clear.

"The battle we fight is not my own, but one I was hired to manage and therefore reflects on me, personally. You have in front of you, folders containing graphs, grid layouts, and maps of D.C. This is where the battleground lies. I expect results and visible ones. I am master here in Florence, but we fight in another's territory and domain, while protecting my own as well." Looking up, he scanned the room. "Don't fucking get your swords in a twist, you will take all orders from me and report to me only.

"As I said, I have a fully supplied bunker, filled to the brim with every weapon we could possibly want. Use whatever you need. My weapons are yours, brothers, but I will command them to be cleaned and put inside in the bunker in their proper place before each sunrise. No weapons are to be left lying around. If you are bringing your own swords, as most of you will, do not carry them with you when you are not on duty. You may leave them in your living quarters. Do not strut your bad ass selves in my home, carrying a sword bigger than the fucking Excalibur itself. That does not happen in my house. Understood?"

Shade could feel how restless they were, and he knew they were pumped and ready, wondering what lay ahead for them.

"And along those same damn fucking lines... wear some fucking clothes. You look like a bunch of damn barbarians. You are not in the warrior camp. Keep your cocks in your pants and your fucking attitudes locked down. That's a fucking order!

"My rules are the same there as here, females are off limits in the quarters. You are warriors of the highest level, act like it. I do not expect angels, and believe me when I tell you, your sorry asses will be too damn tired by sunrise to even think about screwing anything but that fucking bed. One simple thing, warrior, do your job, do it Medici style and we rule the night. You know the situation we fly into. Use every damn thing I or Marco has taught you, concentrate on the job at hand. All I can ask of you."

Shade stood tall. He was the ultimate alpha male in a room full of alphas, proud as hell at what he saw before him. *My warriors! Born and bred right here.*

"I chose each of you, hand-picked. Give me what I need, and you will be rewarded highly. I am a master of my word, and you know I am good for it. Show me who you are, show me what you have learned, put it to use. Give me a reason to walk proud. We leave in an hour. Be in the courtyard, I wait for no warrior. I am anxious to be home with my mate, and I do not like keeping her waiting. Are there any questions before we leave?"

Shade watched as Marcello stood to speak. *Now how the hell did I know he would be the one to speak for this mob?*

"Marcello, speak. It appears you are the representative for this group, brother?"

"I am, master. We have held council and I have been chosen."

Marcello waited as the master nodded to him, his signal to speak his mind on behalf of his brothers.

"I have one question that plagues our minds. If we're not allowed to leave the grounds, and we're on duty in the city through the night, will there be feeders provided for us?"

Smiling, he looked at all of them, knowing this would be central.

"I knew that would trouble you. You will find the feeders in the States a little different from our homeland. There is a feeder compound near D.C. It is where Luca, Gi and the rest of the house staff already go to feed, and I have made arrangements for your arrival. You will be allowed to feed from them at the compound. I cannot stress this strongly enough. Feeders do not come on my grounds. I find one and your balls are gonna be shoved up your ass so far, you will be eating them."

Shade held up his hand, "I know some of you have established feeders here, you will have to change your routine a bit, but American feeders will fit your taste quite well, I assure you. I have no doubts. We will do a nightly run. You will be taken to the compound and given a specific amount of time to spend there. We will split the group into two. You will go every other night. I will allow you to leave the hunt in the city on your chosen night to feed. For now, that is how we are going to roll with feeders. And let me tell you one thing, and hear me well brothers, my mate hates feeders. If she so much as sniffs one out, you will deal with the hell she unleashes, not me. She may look small, but she is a powerhouse when her temper is flared. Be off then. One hour, we fly!"

The warriors filed out, heading back to the camp and their barracks to pack up their gear. Shade felt there were things left unsaid between him and Marco. He seemed to have left the meeting quickly, and Shade knew it must be hard for Marco to see Shade go without him. Shade headed to the camp and found him in his quarters with the door ajar.

Marco knew he would come.

Walking in, Shade drew on his strength, and suddenly, this wasn't as easy as he thought it would be. "Marco..."

Marco looked up. "Took you long enough, old man. Losing your mind as well as your senses?" Giving Shade a quick smile, he couldn't let him see how hard this was for him. "Listen, you are a hard nose son of a bitch, and the best warrior I ever met, and I need to ask you to take care of her, Shade. She is all I have in this life. Work and being a warrior doesn't come close to what she gives me and I'm not going to lie, brother, I want to strike down those eight going back with you and just come along. It is a comfort to know she is with you. She is so soft and gentle, and I would fucking go out of my head, if she were with anyone else, *si*?"

Shade felt his pain. He gave him a brotherly hug and they stood there, like old fools in a piss pot of misery. No one but a warrior would understand the depth of their feelings.

"*Si,* Marco, *si*. We are two miserable old fucks in love. You can say whatever you want, but I understand it better than I ever thought I would be capable of. She is in good health, brother, well taken care of, she is happy. But damn it, why the hell didn't you fucking tell me about the two of you? I would have fucking brought someone else to the States with me. I promise you, once I get this settled, you are coming for a visit, or we will all come back home for a long while. I promise you, as master and as your best friend."

Releasing him, Shade turned to walk to the door and halfway out, he heard Marco's response. "Fly brother, take out the hell that plagues you and come home. Turn her, train her to be the mate she should be, the mate you deserve and bring her home to Florence. Your *bambinos* need to be born here, trained here, and live in the legend that is Medici. *Per sempre*, Medici!"

Marco watched him walk out, and his heart ached for the woman he left in Shade's care.

22

Kate had her cell phone alarm set for sunset. She awoke to the sound of the alarm, and put on her uniform of jeans, t-shirt and running shoes. She opened the door of her bedroom carefully, to find Luca sitting outside her door once again.

"Well, at least Shade will be home soon, and you can actually get some sleep."

As Luca stood up and started to walk with her down the stairs, he responded, "That may depend on which warriors he brings back with him, and what time they arrive. I'm pretty sure master will need to sleep, and someone... as in me... will need to get these warriors settled in."

Luca followed her into the kitchen where Reynaldo had a huge breakfast prepared. She ate quickly, then followed Luca outside for a warm-up and their nightly run. She had improved her observation skills, so she rarely missed any of the things Luca detected. And like he had said, she wasn't always able to identify what it was, but she knew something was there. She still didn't have the skills to pick up scent like he did, and he said that would probably not come until she was turned.

Turned... he used that phrase often during their training time. Kate had no idea when Shade would turn her. He did not speak of it often, and said he would know when it was time. They completed the ten-mile loop and returned to the house where she began the cool-down. He walked inside to bring out the equipment he would use tonight, and directed her to start push-ups and sit-ups. He began setting up a bench while she continued her reps.

Luca turned to her once he had the bench assembled. "This is a weight bench. I want you to lift free weights. I have a weight bench in my room. I use it all the time. You might want to think about putting a small gym in the house. Maybe you could use the nurs... uh, the spare room?" He had almost said the nursery.

The nursery... could she ever hear that word again without feeling the pain wash over her? "Yeah... I'll think about it."

She saw the expression on his face, the frown, he was angry with himself for bringing it up. Kate wanted to say it was okay, but it really wasn't, and talking about it brought it all back anyway, so she let it go. "So, show me how to do this."

He showed her and then instructed her on how he wanted her to use the weight bench, and silently cursed himself for mentioning that room. She had come such a long way, but her pain was still just below the surface. He gave her 30 pound weights. They were a lot to start, but she had been working with the swords and climbing, and he thought she could manage it. He would increase the weight as she built her strength.

He pushed her through the weightlifting. Here was an exercise that would allow her to escape inside her head. Count the repetitions, let her mind go blank. As they wrapped up, she turned to him, and was almost afraid to ask what exercise he had planned next. But there was another question in her head, and those were the words she spoke instead. "Luca, what's it like to be turned?"

He stopped in the middle of taking the weight bench back inside, as he heard her question. "I have no idea, Kate. I was born vampire. It's the only existence I know. And I've never turned anyone. We are taught that turning a mortal is not to be taken lightly. It is a huge responsibly. Have you asked Shade?"

"I... he talked about it briefly, not in detail. I mean, I sort of know what he has to do, but I don't know what I will feel... the experience, you know? Has he turned others?"

Luca looked at the ground. This was not a conversation she should be having with him. "I don't know for sure whether he has turned others or not. You'll need to discuss that with him. I can't help you with how the experience of being turned feels. I can tell you that once you are turned, you will be stronger, your senses enhanced. All the skills you have been learning with me will be escalated, heightened. You will still have things to learn, like how to teleport. I doubt you will be taught to hunt, since you will only feed from master. But teaching you how to survive as a vampire, how to navigate our world, that is your maker's responsibility.

"I will tell you not all maker's do that, honor their responsibility to the mortal they have turned. And then we have rogues, they are created by vampires who turn humans and then give them little if any support. This is different from a turning in that the mortal never feeds from the vampire prior to being drained. And they do not feed from their maker after they are drained. The rogues are looked down upon in our culture. They shame us all by their actions. They are frequently the vampires we battle, as well as the vampires they themselves then create."

He watched the concern on her face and thought he had shared too much, or confused her with this explanation. "Are you afraid, Kate?"

"I'm not afraid. But it's a huge decision. I must leave behind my mortal friends and family because they will age, and I won't. And there's still so much I don't know. But I have no choice, do I? To not be turned would mean I would have to leave Shade, and that's not an option. I can't live without him."

"Talk to him. He'll answer your questions as best he can. None of us, including Shade, may be able to tell you exactly what the experience is like... what it feels like, since none of us have had to go through it. But I do know Shade will be with you every step of the process. Now come, we have a lot to do tonight before Shade gets back. Tonight, we are back to weapons training."

"Swords again?" she asked.

Luca shook his head, "No, tonight, we advance to bows. Not the crossbow yet. We will start with a longbow."

He gathered up the bow and arrows and showed her how to mount the quiver for the arrows on her shoulder, how to reach back and withdraw the arrows quickly. He set up a target for her, and had her practice shooting the arrows. The exercises with her arms and shoulders had improved her strength, and she was able to easily retract the bowstring. She hit the target board every time. At least she was on the board. Now with time, they would improve her aim.

Kate felt frustrated that she couldn't land a strike near the center, let alone hit the actual bull's eye. She dropped the bow down in front of her and growled.

He laughed at her frustration and especially her growling. "Patience, little warrior. You expect to master everything with your first attempt? Warriors train for a lifetime. It will come."

He let her practice for about an hour and then wrapped up. He was not sure exactly what time master would get back, and he sure as hell didn't need Shade landing right in the middle of their training session, pissed off, with eight warriors right behind him to kill Luca's ass.

"That's enough for tonight, Kate. We'll start again tomorrow night. We'll need to be more careful... of Shade... and the other warriors on the property."

She watched as he gathered the weapons and carried them back into the house. She followed and headed for the stairs and straight to the shower to get ready for Shade's return. She made sure to use her rose scented bath gel in the shower, and in her hair. When she emerged from the shower, she slipped on a clean gown, and slid into their bed, and waited, and waited. Maybe he wasn't coming? Maybe he was delayed? Luca would know.

She put on her robe and walked back down the stairs to Luca's suite. His door was ajar, and she tapped at the door and looked inside. She didn't see him anywhere. She called his name, but he didn't answer. There was a canvas on his easel, uncovered but angled so she couldn't see it. She shouldn't enter. This was his space, but her curiosity about the canvas drew her in. She walked quietly into his room over to the easel, and gasped at what she saw.

It was her, dressed in leather armor and on bended knee with her head bowed. She held a sword and a rose.

Luca had walked outside to have a smoke. He had some things that were heavy on his mind. He had stepped so far over the boundaries with Shade when he chose to train her. Walking back in, he instantly picked up her scent. He looked to see her standing in front of the canvas. "Kate, is everything all right?"

She was spellbound by the painting on the canvas. "Luca... is this... me? Did you paint me as a warrior?"

He sighed softly. "Yes. You've come so far, you've worked hard. It has been on my mind, and when that happens, my fingers leak the images to the canvas. I wanted to give this to Shade, as a gift, once you are trained and he knows you can handle much more than he thinks. Do you like it?"

Kate ran her fingers lightly over the canvas, "I do like it, but what I really like is that you see me as a warrior. I know you have called me little warrior, but I didn't really think that, in your eyes, I could live up to that. I know I've put you in a difficult position. It's never far from my mind. I need you to know how much I appreciate what you're doing for me. And this... This is an honor, and I'm not sure I deserve it."

Pacing further into the room, he faced her. "You can't train just anyone to be a warrior. It takes heart to become one. You have the heart of a warrior. It drew you to master, one warrior's heart to another. You're a fighter, a survivor, and I tried to incorporate all the things I see in you within the canvas."

His words touched her heart, as they always did when he shared what he saw in his paintings. "I saw the paintings you did of Marco, for Theresa. They were beautiful, Luca. You have so much talent. And what's this... this other canvas?"

She reached for a canvas that was propped against the leg of the easel, the back of the canvas exposed. Luca started to reach for her hand, as if to stop her, but she had turned the canvas over and was looking at the image. This one needed no explanation, she knew what he was trying to portray.

"Luca," was all she could manage before the silent tears flowed.

It was another portrait of her, more abstract, but the imagery was clear. Her head was bowed in grief, her expression filled with pain as her hand partially covered her face. Her hair surrounded her head and ran like blood off the bottom of the canvas.

"Kate, I am so sorry, I never meant for you..." Taking her in his arms, he held her softly, knowing he shouldn't, but he needed to comfort her. "Please, forgive me. I shouldn't have been so careless to leave it here. You must be strong, remember our lessons, be strong for master. He returns tonight. He wouldn't want to come home to see you sad. He has missed you. Come, let me take you back to your room, he'll be a few hours yet and you need to rest for his return."

Kate wiped away her tears. "I'm glad you painted it. It's exactly like I felt, like I was being pulled down into the blackness. You saw that. You understood that. It's why you sat with me and ultimately, why you trained me. I don't regret seeing it. It's everything I went through, captured in one image. You have the heart of a warrior, but the soul of a poet. That's how I see you, Luca. I'm fine. I'll be fine. It just caught me off guard. Please, don't worry. But I will ask... please don't destroy it, but don't display it either. It holds my pain on the canvas. Let's leave it there."

He walked with her up the stairs, returning her to her bedroom. Kate turned and kissed him on the cheek. "You have been the best of friends. I don't have the words to express how much you have helped me." She entered the bedroom, closing the door behind her.

Her words went to his heart like a sister, when she kissed his cheek. Spinning on his heels, he headed down to the staff quarters to check for the tenth time that all was prepared and ready for master's return.

23

Teleporting into the staff quarters, Shade waited until all the warriors made it inside. Watching them was hilarious. They couldn't believe the staff actually lived here. He was pleased that the trip had gone without event, and everyone had made it here without a problem. "Please, gather around and have a seat, I have a few things to go over before I leave you." As they gathered around in the central room of the staff quarters, he sent a message to *bel* telepathically, **"*Mi amore*, are you awake?"**

Almost immediately, Luca strolled in and it was like a party. The warriors hugged, exchanged fist bumps and started joking with each other, and they hadn't been there fifteen minutes. Luca spotted Marcello and his response was as Shade expected. They went to each other and united in a big bear hug, accompanied by several hearty slams on each other's backs.

Then he heard her soft voice in his head, **"Lover, I'm awake. I've been waiting for you."**

"*Mi amore*, I am home. Please come to the staff quarters."

She jumped out of bed. This was not the welcome home she expected. What do you wear to meet warriors? She brushed out her hair and applied some make-up to her pale skin, adding a touch of crimson lipstick. She pulled on a pair of jeans, a pair of knee high black boots, and a soft red sweater. He liked her in red. She headed out in the direction of the staff quarters.

She could hear them before she got close to the building. They were laughing and talking loudly, some in English but most in Italian. Did they all even speak English? She hadn't even thought of that. She wasn't expecting to meet them right away. She felt ill prepared and nervous.

She opened the door and stepped into the room that had been set up to serve as Gi's central room for meeting with the staff. There was Shade, and Luca and eight other tall, burly, loud, imposing, intimidating men. On closer inspection, she made that seven tall, burly men, and one shorter, more lanky built man, with hair longer than hers. They all fell silent as she entered.

Shade had picked up her scent and turned slowly, as the warriors fell silent in her presence. "*Mi amore!*" He held out his arms. She ran and jumped into them, straddling him, wrapping her legs around his waist. He covered her face with kisses and nuzzled into her neck. He loved that she made no mind to hide her affections in front of this mob of warriors. "I have missed you, *bel*, so damn much. I have a few warriors to introduce you to. Don't be frightened. They are all from my coven. God, you feel so good in my arms!"

She released her legs from around his hips and stood next to him, ready to meet his warriors. Shade turned to address his warriors, "Some of you have met Kate, and some of you haven't. We were only at Castello a brief time. You are welcomed now to our home and you will act accordingly."

They went down on one knee and lowered their heads. "*Alzati guerrieri di Medici!*"

As they stood, he introduced them to her, and they each expressed their gratitude and honor to be here.

"*Bel*, I have saved the best for last. Marcello, Luca... come.

Mi amore, may I present Marcello, he is Luca's cousin. He has been chosen by the battalion to be their representative while they are residing here."

Kate looked at Luca's face, and she could see his joy at having his cousin here. She wanted to kiss Shade for bringing him here, knowing how much this would mean to Luca. "Marcello, I'm so happy to meet you. It is my honor to have you in our home." Kate looked at all the warriors. "To have all of you in our home. We have tried to accommodate these quarters to hold eight warriors, so I hope you'll find everything you need."

As they all gave her a nod, and some smiled, Shade told Luca to coordinate the sleeping arrangements and get things settled down for the sunrise that was quickly approaching.

"Luca will direct you to your sleeping quarters, get some rest. Sunrise is upon us. We will meet here at sunset and head out together this night. As for me, I have my own sleeping arrangements."

Picking Kate up in his arms, he cradled her to his chest. "Come, woman, your warrior is home."

Heading out the door, he carried her back to the main house, up the stairs into their bedroom and dove for the bed. He rolled on his back, pulling her onto his chest, his nose immediately in her neck and hair as it covered his face. Her scent drove him wild. He wanted to ravage her until the moon rose again.

"Miss me did you, my minx? *Cazzo*, you feel incredible in my arms."

"Lover, I have missed you so. I hope to never be away from you for that long again. This bed... this house... feels so empty without you."

She loved the feel of him. She lay across his chest, his arms around her, his hands exploring. She had missed the feel of him, his touch, his kiss, the sound of his voice.

They lay together, re-exploring all the things they had missed about each other. He slid his calloused hands across her arms and shoulders and felt definition in her muscles. He ran his hands along her sides and could feel her abdomen was harder and her thighs were firmer and he wondered what the hell she had done those nights he had been gone. Rolling her over, he looked down into her dark eyes flecked with amber, and kissed her passionately, long and soft, then harder and more intense. Before he knew what was happening, they lay naked on the bed, still entwined, kissing and teasing, and he was in heaven.

"I need to leave you more often if this is the welcome home I get. *Bel*, have you been running? Your body is more defined. I can tell you are building muscle. What the hell have you been doing, *mi amore*?"

She had known he would notice the change. He knew every inch of her body, and she could see the changes herself when she looked in the mirror.

"Running, yes, and I have been working out. I started before you left, actually, when you were going into D.C. every night. It has helped me to not focus so much... to take my mind off of..." There was no getting around it. She had to say the words, "To take my mind off of the baby."

His heart lurched. He didn't want this to be a sad reunion for them. He could see she had come a long way, but still, the emotions were right under the surface.

"*Bel*, please. I know we will never forget, and before I leave tonight, we will visit our sleeping warrior together, *si*?" He nuzzled into her hair and moaned so loudly. "*Mi amore*, I need you."

"And I'm here for you, lover. I think I have waited patiently enough, *si*?"

She bit at his shoulder and neck, playful nips that teased at him, as she slid her hand along his firm chest. She bit at his ear, and kissed his cheek, and sought out his mouth with hers. How she had missed the taste of him.

"Woman! You will drive me mad with passion and want of you." Grabbing a fistful of that crimson, he pulled her into his neck and slid his hand between her legs, dipping his fingers into her moist honey, then placing his fingers in his mouth, sucking loudly and moaning, "Christ *bel*, I can't take this, please feed, I need to be inside you now!"

She craved his blood as much as she craved his body, and she slid her lips across his neck, pushing his tangled hair aside with her hand, and bit hard into him. The flow of blood hit her tongue and it felt electric, her need for him building with each swallow and she gripped him with her hands and felt the fire between her legs. She heard his moan, and felt his arms tighten their hold on her as his cock throbbed against her belly. She needed to feel him inside her, and she slid her hips forward, feeling his cock as it slid between her legs.

His hands moved to her hips as he thrust forward, penetrating her in a single stroke that made her cry out in pleasure. Her mouth temporarily left his neck to release the cry, and then returned to the fountain to drink more. She rode the long shaft of his cock, and felt his hands gripping her tightly, pulling her down hard against his hips. Then she felt the sharp sting of his fangs as he bit into her shoulder, drinking from her as she drank from him.

The explosion of sensations that rolled over them, as they drank from each other was explosive. They rocked and drank in a rhythmic dance, together as one. His body hard and heated, and her blood a nourishing rush to his soul. The taste of her was the biggest high, and it belonged to him alone. He thrusts deep and hard, his fingers clung to her hips, and he felt his passion build as he gorged on her bounty. With each draw she took, he was elevated to another level of erotic passion and he could no longer hold back. He withdrew his fangs and felt her sex spasm and tighten around his cock. "*Mi amore*, cum with me."

He thrusts hard and the world spun, their bodies rode the waves of their orgasm together. Throwing back his head, he roared into the night, "*Ti amo, per sempre!*"

Collapsing, he fell to her side and pulled her to his chest, as she struggled to catch her breath.

She laid her head on his chest, and felt his arms surround her. "This is how I sleep, lover."

She felt his body relax as he slipped into his death slumber, '*Ti amo*' on his lips in a soft whisper.

24

Kate slid back beneath the sheets as he left the room, pulling the sheets to her face and inhaling his scent. She was so happy to have him back. She would wait here until she heard them leave, as he asked her to. It wasn't long before she heard Shade and all his warriors tramping through the house on the way to the bunker, and it sounded like a herd of elephants. She realized these were warriors used to living in barracks and on the battlefield or clambering up the walls of an urban jungle, not living in a house of fine antiques. She giggled to herself at the image she had of them walking through the house, dressed to conquer, carrying weapons, and trying not to knock over a lamp on the way. She made a mental note to check with Theresa and help her out with the laundry. The washer and dryer in the staff quarters would be running non-stop with linens and towels for all these men. As the house finally got quiet, she felt him leave. She could always feel Shade's absence from the house.

She jumped out of bed and put on her jeans and running shoes. It was her warrior uniform. She headed downstairs where Reynaldo had breakfast laid out.

"Good evening, my lady. You look very happy this evening."

She beamed at him, "Because I am very happy. Shade is home and that always makes me happy."

"Yes, my lady, we're all glad to have him back under our roof."

She finished up breakfast and headed for Luca's suite, tapping at his door.

He answered and stepped outside, pulling the door closed behind him. She was jumping up and down with glee. "Luca, your cousin Marcello. Aren't you excited? I was so happy Shade brought him back, you must be so happy to see him!"

He had to laugh at her enthusiasm. "Yes, I'm very happy to see my cousin. He's my only blood relative. I didn't know when I would ever see him again. Now, let's see if I can't work off some of that energy for you."

They headed into the yard and began her warm-up before they started their run. He could tell she ran with ease now, and she picked up all the visible and audible clues as to what moved around them. He would have to stay alert to the warriors' schedule, and keep track of when they came and went. Luca couldn't afford for one of the warriors to see him training her. They completed their ten-mile run and she cooled down as he set up the weight bench. Push-ups, sit-ups with the weight ball, and now, free weights. She was working through the reps with relative ease now.

He thought it was time to mix it up a bit. "Remember when you said you trained in gymnastics?"

"Gymnastics? Yes, of course. But that was in high school and college, so it has been a few years."

He teased her, "So, are you too old to do a back handspring?"

She put both hands on her hips and looked back at him, answering with indignation, "Too old?"

He smiled. He knew that would spark a reaction. Mortals were so concerned with their age.

"Just asking...cause I'm gonna need to see one."

Good Lord. I really haven't done gymnastics in years. And a back handspring... Wow. Does he have to start with one of the hardest moves? She stretched out first, warming up her back. She hadn't pulled off one of those in a long time. If this didn't work out, she would have a lot of explaining to do to Shade. She did some forward flips first, just to loosen her back muscles, and some handstands to re-check her balance before she stood up and decided she was ready. *Okay then, here goes nothing!* She ran through the steps in her head and then took the leap of faith.

He watched her warming up and could tell she was nervous. But then she threw herself into the backflip, and repeated four in a row, and landed on her feet. He was standing with his arms across his chest as she landed, and smiled at her.

"Good job. You won't win any gold medals, but it will serve the purpose."

He was mocking her again, and she put her hands on her hips and glared at him. "Oh, like you could do better?"

Luca laughed at her taunt. "Well, yeah, actually, I can."

Kate watched as he effortlessly executed the back handspring, repeating ten reps, and realizing he could probably go on forever. As he walked back toward her, she just stuck her tongue out at him. "Show off! Is there some point to this lesson? Or were you just looking for a chance to strut your stuff?"

"Oh, there is a point, little warrior. There is always a point. Tonight, we are going to work on skills of stealth, how to move among your enemy without being detected. You're getting good at moving through your run with almost no noise, but you'll need to learn to not be seen or heard. And when you are detected, you need to be able to escape your enemy. Here, put this on."

He handed her the black pants and robe of a ninja. She held them up against her body. "Seriously, you want me to wear this?"

"For now," he answered, "you'll have your own leathers eventually, and they will shield your presence in the dark. For now, we'll work with these."

She stepped back inside the house and shed her jeans and t-shirt, and pulled on the loose black pants, and put on the robe, cinching the belt tightly. When she stepped back outside, he lifted the hood of the robe to cover her hair and placed a black veil across the lower part of her face, leaving only her eyes exposed.

Stepping back to admire her, he was struck by how small she was. The loose robe and pants covered her feminine curves, and the hood and veil covered her long red hair and her face, but then that was what he was looking for. He wanted a way for her to move about without being seen, or to avoid being recognized if she was seen.

"Now, run the wall and catapult yourself into your back handspring."

She creased her brow. "Run the wall? What do you mean, run the wall?"

He nodded toward the house. "Run toward the side of the house, start running up the wall, and then push off into your back handspring. You only need to get up a few feet. You can do this."

Run toward the side of the house? Run up the wall? Every road-runner cartoon she has ever seen flashed through her head, and all she saw was the imprint of a flattened Wile E. Coyote smashed against the side of the building, before he slowly slid to the ground. She shook her head and stepped back several steps to get a running start. She gauged her distance then stepped back a little more.

Luca was watching her hesitancy. He picked up the image in her head of a coyote flattened against the wall. It had no meaning to him, but it made him smile, nonetheless. He watched her as she continued to back up. "You keep backing up, you will be in China soon. Just run, Kate. Now! Run!"

She took a deep breath and said a silent prayer, *Heaven help me*, as she ran toward the wall. As she approached, she ran up the wall several steps then used it to push off and do a back flip. Her first attempt landed her hard on the ground, flat on her back and Luca stepped over, reached his hand down and pulled her to her feet.

"Again," he said, as she got upright, rubbing her back before running at the wall again, this time landing on her feet. "Again," he repeated... and over and over until it became one seamless motion.

Once she had mastered the skill, he tossed her a sword. It had been a few weeks since she held one, as they had practiced other skills. It was important she not forget her first lessons.

"Now fight me, warrior, and use the skills you have learned to climb, to run the wall, to evade me. Use your senses to hear, to feel, and anticipate. Put it all together now."

He tossed her a single sword and they fought. She knew he still moved slower for her, and yet, he pushed her mortal limits. If she dropped her guard, he would tap her with the sword and call out 'strike' just to remind her that if this were a real battle, she would be dead by now. Their mock fighting led them into the wooded area, where he used trees to hide, jump, disappear from her, and then spring out again, catching her unaware. She realized how unprepared she was. *Focus Kate, focus. Use what he has taught you!*

She started to use the trees as he did. Running the tree was no different from running the wall. Using the darkness of the night and her dark clothing to hide from him, she was finally able to maneuver herself behind him. She watched without moving, knowing his sense of hearing would give her away. He was standing with his back to her, looking forward. She had managed to get behind him without him knowing it. She knew she couldn't charge him without being heard, but this was as close as she would ever get to an ambush. She squatted down in the brush and called to him, "Strike!"

Luca was startled to hear her behind him, and turned to see her crouched, the hood fallen from her head and her red hair glowing in the moonlight. He smiled at her progress. "Good job, warrior."

She stood up and walked toward him, and they headed back to the house. "Don't you mean, little warrior?"

He looked sideways at her as they walked back. "Not tonight."

* * *

In D.C., Shade was getting everyone familiar with one another, warrior to warrior, and things were going better than expected. Alec's boys sure as fuck sat up and took notice when they saw Shade's warriors, and he could not have been prouder. This was what a warrior looked like, and all hell was about to be unleashed on these rogue mother-fuckers.

Shade created teams of four, three from Alec's old crew with one of his warriors. He assigned every team to a different grid and sent them out, then sat down to track the activity and record the kills as they rolled in. Once settled, he picked up the phone. He knew he needed to let Alec know that Medici were on his streets. Shade hit speed dial.

Alec was working later than he cared to, but trying to get this bill passed had been more of a problem than he anticipated. Still shy the votes he needed, he was spending every last minute before the vote lobbying and bargaining. He heard his cell phone buzz and saw Shade on the caller ID. *Good, I hope this means he's back.* "Shade, please tell me you're back from Florence, brother."

Shade had his feet propped on the desk when Alec answered his call. "That's right, brother. Sitting in the Dead House, ready to take the kill count as they come in, and they will come in. Medici is on your streets, bro. Get ready to rock this fucking town."

Alec chuckled, "That's what I want to hear. How many did you bring back with you?"

"I got eight of my top boys out there showing your lot what the hell to do with a rogue."

Alec shrugged. "Eight? I would have thought you would bring more. But hey, this is your area of expertise, not mine. You call the shots here. What about Angel? Did you hear anything about that in Florence? Anybody know anything?"

"I got more contacts there than here, and no one has heard a damn thing about this Angel bastard. I got Council working on it, brother, and when they work on something, you can bet your ass it will get investigated, you know how they roll. Don't be alarmed if Council contacts you. Don't be giving them shit, they are on our side so far. If I need more warriors, I will bring them in. I don't plan on this taking long, but I will switch them in and out as I feel the need to keep the troops fresh."

"I like what I hear, sounds like it's under control. If I pick up any more info on this Angel, you'll be the first call. That's the part that really bugs the shit out of me. How can there be a master we don't know? And the reality is, there can't be. So, this is some kind of code name, for somebody we do know. So, think on that, his M.O., if this type of attack, turning humans, leaving their dead... if that fits anybody we know. It's in my head every day, brother, and all I can say is, when we find him..."

"Don't think I haven't thought about it, Alec. Try explaining to your warriors you have no damn clue who their enemy is. I feel you. You need to let me know, right now, what you want done to him when we find him because my warriors are hungry for a kill. If you want him alive, I need to know."

"If you catch him, kill him. We can't risk having him escape. I would like to do it myself, and if the opportunity presents, I will take it. Whoever delivers the blow... he will know where it came from. He knows he's being hunted as we speak."

Shade felt the smile spread across his face. Yeah, now that was what he wanted to hear.

"Works for me, brother. I'm out, I want to take in a few grids myself tonight and see how things are rolling. We got four kills already since we've been on duty tonight, so we got this. Nobody fucking messes with Medici warriors!"

25

Waking hours before sunset, Shade lay in their bed. His sweet *bel* had rolled off her usual perch on his chest and was curled up next to him. Her hair was spread across the pillows, encasing her head like a fiery halo. He lay and stared at her, his mind already filling with the many things he needed to attend to, but he didn't let it steal him away from this quiet time alone with her, to just look at her and absorb all the beauty that was truly his.

He had so much to ask her, and some of those questions floated through his mind. She was running now? His eyes slid across her body, observing the changes. She was doing much more than running. Though, whatever it was she was doing, he rather liked the results. Not to mention, this physical conditioning would assist her through the turning when the time came.

Now she had brought Shannon into their lives. He had met her only briefly, and he knew how close Kate was to her. He felt bad she had separated herself from all she knew in the mortal world. But there was always a risk, and she had brought another mortal into this house. He preferred knowing ahead of time and being present. He didn't trust all mortals. He would need to talk to her and find out how much Shannon knew, and if he needed to do some damage control. *Yes, mi amore, we need to have a talk before I walk out that door tonight with my warriors.* "*Mi amore...* wake up. We need to talk, and I need a kiss. If you don't wake up, I shall take it."

She opened her eyes to see him staring back at her.

"*Buonasera, mi amore.* Sleep well, I assume?" He smiled softly at her. "Do I get a kiss, or do I have to seize it?"

She leaned in and kissed him. She loved his lips, and the feel of his beard growing in, rough against her skin. "I think you should do both and that way I get two kisses."

"Smart woman you are, minx." His hand slid through her crimson hair and pulled her on top of him, kissing her thoroughly, letting their tongues play, sucking her tongue into his mouth, then nipping her lower lip. His hands dropped across her ass and he left them there. "We need to talk."

"What would you like to talk about? I have missed your voice, so talk to me."

He chuckled. "So, I have been gone three nights and all you miss is my voice?"

He felt her wiggle beneath his hand and heard her soft laugh.

"Seriously, there are a few things I want to check on. First of all, if you have any problems with the warriors being disrespectful, you come to me, *si*?" He slapped her ass lightly for effect.

"Of course. But I don't anticipate any problems. And Marcello! Luca was so happy to see him. Did you see that? Did you plan that?"

"*Si,* in a manner. I checked on Marcello's progress and he had gained skills as a leader since last I was home. Had he not been ready, I would not have chosen him. But Luca needs family here. I know it's hard when nothing is familiar." He skimmed his hands over her back and up her shoulders, as he cradled her face in his hands and looked into her eyes.

"Did you have issues with Luca while I was gone? Anything happen you want to tell me about?"

What is he implying? Does he know about the training? "Issues? With Luca? Luca has been nothing but helpful to me. He stayed right outside my door when I slept, just as you asked him to. I couldn't ask for a better protector. Why do you ask?"

"Good, I am counting on Luca when I'm away. This was my first time away for any period of time, and I want to make sure you got along. And another damn thing, what is with the running? You need to tell me more about this, *mi amore.*"

She knew these changes would not go unnoticed, not to his eyes, and certainly not to his hands. "Lover, we don't talk about it much and I don't want to talk about it, but I needed to do something after the baby. At first, I was just so sad... so broken. But then I was angry, and I started running. Luca runs with me, he never leaves me unattended. He would never let me run, even on the property, without being there. I do other exercises as well, not just running. At first, it was just an outlet, somewhere to put all the anger. But now, I just like the way it feels."

"I like it, *mi amore.*" His tongue slid along her collarbone, nipping her shoulder. "I am proud of you, *bel*. You take anger and grief and make it work for you, not against you." His hands continued to explore between her legs, as he nuzzled into her hair. "Now, tell me about the visit from Shannon."

Listening to the sound of his voice was seduction enough. But his roving hands created an even bigger distraction. **"Now, lover? You want to talk about that now?"** She pushed his hand away, so she could think, and he chuckled.

"Shannon? You remember her. You met her briefly at the restaurant that night in D.C. We worked together at the Brunswick Agency. We went to college together. She was my best friend. You know I've shut myself off from my mortal friends and family. I've only spoken to her on the phone since moving here, and she thought I lived in London. While you were gone, it felt so lonely here. The house feels so empty with you not in it. I just called her on a whim. I had her come here because I knew if I left I would have to take Luca, and I didn't know how to explain that. So, she came here. Originally, I told her I was in town on business, and you let me stay at your house, but she noticed the ring on my finger and I confessed we were engaged. I acknowledged I live here with you. She met the staff. Reynaldo fixed us lunch. We laughed and talked all day. I hadn't realized how much I had missed her."

He lay still as she spoke. "You invited a mortal into our home. Okay, I can handle that, *bel*. Did you tell her anything?"

"Nothing. I told her you were out of town on business, that you owned vineyards in Europe. She saw or heard nothing she would think unusual. I was very careful."

Closing his eyes, he let out a deep breath. He couldn't lock her away forever, but he didn't like this at all, and he knew she had little time left to be with mortals before she was immortal herself.

"*Bel*, just explain something to me, make me understand this because it confuses the fuck out of me. Why would you do this when I am not here? And tell me Luca was around because I will bust his ass good if he left you alone for one second!"

"Lover, I don't understand. You never told me I couldn't invite mortals here. I would never have invited her if I thought, for one minute, you didn't want her here. I invited her because I was lonely. And of course, Luca was here. Luca never left the entire time you were gone. He met her, along with all the staff. Please, I never wanted to make you angry."

Realizing he was raising his voice, he leaned in and cuddled her to his chest and stroked her hair. "*Bel*, shh, I am sorry. We rarely share our world with mortals. I am simply being protective."

"Would you like to meet Shannon again? Maybe you would feel better about her if you got to know her."

"Of course, I want to meet her, *mi amore*, if she is this important in your life, I would like that. And perhaps once I meet her, and you wish her to be here when I am away, I will feel more comfortable about it."

He saw the sky darken and knew his new warriors were waiting when he heard Luca in his head, **"Retract those fangs and put your cock back in your pants. I got eight warriors ready to rip the fuck out of anything that moves. I suggest you get a move on if you don't want them bombarding the house, master. Marcello and I are in the staff quarters."**

Damn! What time is it? "*Cazzo, bel* I need to get moving. The warriors are ready, and their leader is lying about. You stay on this floor until we leave, *si*? That is an order, minx."

"Am I not safe with them here?"

"*Bel*, listen to me please." Shade got dressed while he talked. She sat naked on the bed and listened, her hair tousled, and the bed sheets pulled to her bare breasts. He hated he had to leave her there. "Until these warriors are settled, I don't want you out before I leave. They will never harm you. Hell, they would lay down their lives for you, *mi amore*. But they are hungry for the hunt and that attitude in a group can be dangerous."

"I understand, lover."

"I'm late, can you tie back my hair?"

He sat on the side of the bed and she ran her fingers through his hair, pulled his locks back into a loose ponytail, and secured it with a leather cord. She kissed his exposed neck, and inhaled deeply, relishing in the scent of him.

"There... go now. I can tell you're itching to get moving. I'm so glad you're home, and that you return to me at sunrise. So go, warrior, and be sure you take my love with you."

Her words gave him all he needed, as he kissed her hard. "*Ti amo, mi amore*. Luca will be here, and this warrior of yours will return to you, as I have always promised. And tonight, your heart goes with me, your soul protects me, and nothing will ever make me stop loving you... ever!"

Walking out the door, he teleported to the staff quarters. His warriors were fired up and ready to take out the rogue population of the most powerful city in America... Washington fucking D.C.

26

As the winter weather began to ease in D.C., the spring had started to fight its way in, and the days were warmer now. Rissa's schedule was light for the day, so she decided to go for a run instead of being cooped up inside the gym. All the things Alec had spoken to her about remained ever-present in her mind. She needed to stop blocking him so much, watch her time away from home, and to be mindful of how much time she spent at the gym. These were all clues to him. But she did remember his warning to keep constantly alert.

She was feeling a bit restless, and she hated passing up this nice weather, so she made a quick decision and drove about an hour outside of D.C. and the surrounding gridlock into the Virginia countryside. On a whim, she took the Occoquan exit off of I-95, a small village on the Occoquan River. It would be safe to run here, no one would recognize her, and there would be no damn press and flashing cameras in her face. She could run along the river, concentrate and think, and maybe clear her head for a few hours. Pulling into a parking lot, she got out and stretched before she started.

She began slow, at a walking pace, and then blasted it for miles, going full out, non-stop down a narrow footpath that ran through the wooded area along the river bank. She felt such freedom to run without caution, to go without someone constantly following her. She got lost in her thoughts as she jogged. She looped back toward the village, slowing her pace as she re-entered the quaint town, and began to walk through the streets to cool down. She looked at all the small shops and art galleries, the restaurants where mortals mingled, and no one noticed her. No one noticed Senator Alec Canton's fiancée, the Darling of G-town, event planner to the royalty of D.C., Larissa Benneteau. She was just some woman in a tracksuit, out for a stroll, and that made her laugh out loud. *If they only knew!*

Glancing at her watch, she realized she had been gone far too long and should be heading back. She had a ways to drive and traffic would be picking up in D.C. Jogging back to the car, she got back on the interstate, but she could feel her body slowing, her heart rate sluggish and she stepped on the gas. She knew what this meant. She hadn't fed for a while and her body had used up too much energy, with the heavy gym workouts and now the run. *Damn it, Rissa!*

Slamming her hand down on the steering wheel, her foot on the gas pedal, she moved as fast as she could, but she had to maneuver through the never-ending gridlock of traffic around D.C. It took almost two hours to get home and she felt weaker by the minute. She parked the car and saw Alec wasn't home yet and for that, she was grateful. Getting into the house, she fumbled with the key in the lock, her coordination affected by her waning energy.

Finally getting inside, she went straight for the Midnight. Her hand began to shake as she tried to pour the glass full but spilled the Midnight on the bar. Giving up, she put the bottle to her mouth and began to drink, hoping it would give her enough strength before Alec returned home.

She headed upstairs, walking to the bathroom. She could feel the small jolt from the Midnight as it began to work, but her system was so depleted the effects were short-lived. In her head, she knew she should signal Alec. Let him know she needed him, needed to feed, but she feared his anger. By the end of her shower, she was feeling light-headed and sluggish once more.

Lying across the bed to rest, hoping for the Midnight to sustain her, her eyes began to droop, and she thought she may have waited too late. She tried to reach out to Alec. She desperately needed to feed from him. She felt the death slumber drag her down, and she could no longer fight to stay awake and wait for him. She had waited too long without feeding.

* * *

Alec left the Senate office building after Shade's call, feeling like they might, at last, be able to get this situation under control, and had Alto drive him home. He knew Rissa was already home. He saw her car when they pulled up, but the house was eerily quiet. Maybe she was resting. She had been working out every day. He headed to the study for a drink and a smoke and to maybe check the news. The local TV news had all the D.C. political gossip. As he walked into the study, he saw the open bottle of Midnight on the bar, the half-empty glass, and the Midnight spilled on the counter.

Alarm bells went off in his head. Rissa never left a thing out of place in the house. A speck of lint on the carpet was a freakin' emergency. She would never leave this mess, something was wrong here. He headed through the house looking for her, calling her name, but didn't get an answer. The rogues flashed through his head. He ran up the stairs and into the bedroom. She was draped across the bed, deathly pale, and it hit him. She had not fed, and she had been pushing herself in the gym. Expending energy, but not replenishing it. He shook her, called her name. "Rissa, Rissa, wake up so you can feed."

She was too depleted to pull out of the death slumber. He couldn't arouse her. He removed his cufflink and pushed back his shirt sleeve, biting into the skin of his wrist and holding it to her lips, holding her lips apart with his other hand, sliding his fingers into her mouth to force her mouth open, and letting the blood flow into her. "Drink, Rissa, swallow!"

Moaning softly, she felt a single drop of life hit her tongue and it was an explosion. She let it slide down her throat and felt more blood, slowly dripping into her mouth. Her body responded, and her heart jump started. More! Her fangs punched through and she grabbed his wrist, sinking her teeth into him, taking his blood, gulping like a starved animal. She felt him surround her, fill her, flow inside her and she took more.

Alec was relieved to finally see her respond, and to drink heavily from him, but he was angry she had allowed this to happen. He would deal with that later. Right now, she needed to feed. "Take what you need, Rissa. Take all you need."

His voice rang loud inside her head and she sighed, her body alive but still slow. She retracted her fangs, licked his wound lovingly and curled into him, ashamed of her actions, her need of him so desperate. "Master."

Alec ran his hands through her silky blonde hair as she curled against him. "Rissa, what were you thinking? We just had a conversation about the rogues and being tracked and how careful you need to be, and you let this happen? I know we play games. I withhold and control. It's what I like, what we both like. But I expect you to be responsible. You have increased your activity, going to the gym every day. If your body needs to feed, then you must tell me. If I can't trust you to make good decisions, then the protector is the only solution. I can't have you vulnerable right now. You know what's going on."

Her heart wept, he was so upset with her, yet his touch conveyed what was truly in his heart, worry for her safety. Wrapping her hands around his waist, she laid her head on his lap. "Alec, please, I'm begging. I'm careful. I need an outlet. I ran today and I shouldn't have done so." Shaking her head. "I will do whatever you wish. If I need you, I will tell you. I have been pushing the exercise to build my strength. I haven't forgotten that, I cannot handle these rogues. I'm not trained to fight at their skill level. "

Alec sighed in frustration. "I have no issues with you working out, Rissa. But you understand how this works. When you expend more energy, it must be replenished. You were careless, not careful. My age allows me to go longer without feeding. I sometimes forget the needs of a young vampire. Are you so afraid of me, you fear approaching me?"

She lifted her head and locked eyes with him, "No, master, no!"

"Then I expect you to behave more responsibly. You walk in the shadow of my power, but you are centuries away from having my power. You are far too confident for your own good, and I say that knowing your confidence is one of the things that attracted me. But you push too far as a young vampire, my darling. There are those among us who would cut you down in a heartbeat. So, I will not say it again, be careful, or you will find yourself with a protector. This is your last warning. I can't deal with pulling off my role as a mortal in this power-hungry city and battling this rogue master who seems intent on taking this territory, and worrying about your safety all at the same time."

Rissa sat up, pulling her legs under her and laid her head on his shoulder. "Thank you, master. I will follow your guidance and know I must listen. I'll do as you request and ask to feed when I need it. I'll be on my guard always. Thank you. I love you, Alec."

As she laid her head on his shoulder, he turned his head and exposed his neck to her. "Do you need more? Drink your fill if you need it."

Letting her fangs punch through, she breathed on his neck softly, traced his vein with her nail and licked it gently, then sank her teeth deep, drawing his nectar into her mouth. Her hand slid up his chest as she held onto his shoulder and fed. It was heaven to have him so near her, to feed from him at leisure, she had been too depleted to feel the sexual pull from this feeding. This was a master giving his progeny what she needed, out of love and protection.

27

Shade made his way home with the warriors, leaving them in the staff quarters and directing Luca to get them settled in. He laughed to himself, yeah, his warriors had stamina, but working inside the confines of a warrior camp was nothing like running the streets the entire night, your senses on high alert, knowing all hell could break loose any minute. He knew that lot would be in their slumber before too long.

Climbing the stairs to get to *bel*, he walked past the guest bedroom and noticed a light on. He took two steps backwards and realized Theresa was in the room. Tapping on the half open door with his knuckles, she timidly peeped around the door and smiled. He smiled back and asked, "May I enter? I suppose you felt a bit out of place in the staff quarters?"

Theresa smiled shyly, knowing master had recently been with Marco and hoping he brought word from him. "*Si,* it was my lady's insistence. I do not want to cause any problems, I can return there if you wish, master."

Shade shook his head. "Return there? No, *bel* is right, this will be a much better place for you."

He chuckled as he saw her blush and then he noticed a painting of Marco on the wall. Walking toward it, he stood and stared. "Damn, the old codger looks young in this one. Luca, I presume? That boy can sure capture images on canvas, brings back many memories for me of Marco."

Theresa sighed with relief, knowing she would stay in the main house and near my lady. They were the only females about, and while she was happy to help out with the warriors, she didn't want to live among them. "*Si,* Luca is gifted, master. He favored me with several portraits." Looking down and twisting her hands, she hesitantly asked him, "Is he well, Master Shade?"

"Marco is well, and ornery as ever. He misses you. And I might add, was quite impressed with that gift. You have my word as master, once this chaos is over with, I will be going to Castello with *bel*, and you will be coming along."

Theresa gave him a nod and a soft smile as he exited to the hallway and called out to his mate, "*Bel!*"

From their bedroom, she could hear his booming voice. It always made her smile. "Lover, you are home."

He entered the room and was assaulted by her as she covered him with kisses. "Slow down woman! Hell, you damn near knocked me over, and that is no easy task." Smiling, he nuzzled into her neck and growled. "Miss me, did you?"

"I always miss you. You saw Theresa? You don't mind, do you? I just couldn't imagine her being the only woman among all those men."

"*Si,* I saw her. She is used to the warriors, but she is also used to having her own space. I like the idea. I feel better knowing she is here. Thank you, *mi amore*, for taking care of things for me. I promise to make it up to you." He nipped her neck gently.

"And the paintings... the paintings Luca did of Marco. Did you see those?"

Pulling back from her, he gave her a serious look. "You know of Marco?"

"I don't remember if I met him when we were in Florence. There were so many warriors, so no, I don't think I know him. But when I was helping her move to the guest room, I found the canvases covered with a blanket in her closet. I asked who he was and she told me. They love each other, but she was afraid to display the paintings. I told her to hang them on the wall. Love should never be hidden away. Why would she hide them?"

He stood tall in front of her. "To begin with, I had no idea of this love until she came to me before I left, and asked me to take a gift to him. How the hell did I not know this? I spoke to Marco. They had kept it hidden. *Bel*, you need to understand, warriors are not always meant to find love, they are meant for war. It is custom, it is how it is done, and females are a great distraction, especially for young warriors. Once out of camp, they need to explore the world for a very long time, to practice their skills in the streets, to learn to live among mortals. Leaving females behind is a struggle and a great weight to bear on them. Marco and Theresa know the rules, they were raised on them, abide by them, as is my wish. But I would have made exceptions for them both. They are both dear to me."

Kate looked at him with a puzzled expression. "But you are a warrior. And we found love. I'm not arguing with you, I'm only trying to understand."

"I am also a master, and royalty. I am expected to find a mate and carry on the bloodline, so that is different. I have made exceptions for my warriors. I look at their circumstances. Marco trains now, he is rarely in battle himself. He stays at Castello, so I would have made an exception. *Bel*, I need to shower quickly, I told Luca I wanted to go over some things with him, then I will return to you. He is waiting on me, *mi amore*. Can you find me some jeans and a t-shirt?"

Kate looked about confused. "I, yes, okay, I'll get your clothes ready. But you're leaving already? You just got home."

He answered impatiently, "Woman! I am master here, I have warriors housed, and I have to get some things worked out, *si*? Please, do not argue with me, I am having this meeting with Luca in my office, not leaving the house, so I can be with you later... without interruption. May I have your permission, my lady?"

Undressing, he flung his clothes across the room, his boots tossed to the corner.

She watched his temper flare as he reminded her who was master, and mockingly called her 'my lady.' Her own redheaded temper flared, as she answered him. "Since when have you ever needed my permission to do anything, Shade Medici? Please, don't let me stand in your way."

Whipping his head around to her, he growled. "Don't you even think about copping an attitude with me, woman! I will spank that tight ass of yours red, and make you beg for the master of this house, his cock and kisses! Do you not understand, I am doing this for you, so I can be with you the rest of the night? Making love, and lavishing you with all my incredible charms."

She stood with her hands on her hips, "From where I stand, you seem to have lost some of that incredible charm. Maybe you should find it before you come back to me. Are your warriors rubbing off on you already?"

Holding up his hand, he roared, "Enough! As you wish, *bel rosso*, I won't return to you until my charm has returned." Walking to the shower, he spun on his heels to face her. "I do not wish, my lady, to inconvenience you any further, so I will retrieve my own clothing."

He went to the armoire, whipped out a pair of jeans, went to the shower and slammed the door shut. *Cazzo, why doesn't she understand I'm overwhelmed right now, and I'm doing this for her?* He took his shower quickly, then dressed and teleported to his office, seeking out Luca.

Kate was fuming mad. *He turns his back on me? And then he teleports away? Well, isn't that just fucking handy?* She stormed out of the bedroom, stood at the top of the stairs and screamed at the top of her lungs, "This isn't over, Shade Medici!"

Shade heard her shout, and before he could tap him down, the beast ripped to the surface, his fangs punched and his eyes flared like flames, as he walked to the bottom of the stairs, and stared at her. Shade heard Luca behind him, and without turning his head, he issued a low growl. "This is between Kate and me." He heard Luca turn to leave and he saw Kate glance at her protector. "He won't save you. You are mine."

The beast began to climb the stairs, growling, his eyes never leaving hers, locked tight onto her, holding her there. Reaching the top of the stairs, he circled her once, then twice before he picked her up, threw her over his shoulder and made his way to the bedroom, kicking the door closed behind him. He pitched her onto the bed and hovered over her, as he roared back at her. "Then *make* it over!"

Kate saw the beast emerge, and her instincts told her to stand still as he slowly climbed the stairs toward her, circling her, before throwing her over his shoulder. She swallowed hard as she looked into his eyes, glowing red with anger, not lust. Her heart was pounding, and as much as she wanted to look away, she locked eyes with him, responding in a soft voice. "You always walk away... always."

Leaning down, he touched noses with her and growled in a lowered tone. "And you always push and push. What do you want from me? Tell me."

Her voice trembled, "You, I want you, I always want you. I'm sorry, I know there is a lot going on, and I'm trying to be understanding. But I see less and less of you. That is what I want, lover... your time."

Sliding his hands up her face and into her hair, he gripped two fists full and closed his eyes. He felt his body tremble, fighting for control, as he pushed back the beast and fought to say the right words. "My time is precious right now. I do not want to fight with you. I do not want this, *mi amore*. I am doing all I can to be here. I have responsibilities beyond your belief. I do all of this for us. Can you not be patient with me? I want to run away with you and leave this all behind, but I cannot. I am master. These warriors, these people around you, they depend on me, just as you do." Lowering his head, he laid it on her chest. "Forgive me, but I am doing the best I can, just be here for me, do not test my emotions more. I am fighting to protect you, and make you proud."

"You always make me proud, Shade. I don't even know how we got here. One minute talking, the next minute fighting. Our time together is precious, and fighting is not how I want to spend my time with you." She placed her hand in his hair. "I'm sorry."

Leaning down, he kissed her long and soft. "Please, I need to see Luca and then I'll return, *mi amore*. I want to come to you, all of it done for the night, so you may have me, body and soul, with nothing on my mind. Can you please give me that?"

"Yes, go, and I promise there will be no more screaming from the top of the stairs."

Looking at her longingly, the master of the house had decided to change his plans. "Oh, you will be screaming, *mi amore!*"

Hooking his hands on each side of her jeans, he ripped them free, yanking her to the edge of the bed, and dropping to his knees. His kisses began slowly at her abdomen and then to each hip, his tongue leaving a trail of wet kisses. Nuzzling into those gorgeous curls, he growled and willed the music of Van Morrison singing *Tupelo Honey* to play loudly, as he slid his tongue deep inside her, pulling her legs over his shoulders.

It was a night of passion, a passionate argument followed by passionate love, before he slipped into his death slumber, and she slept soundly, sated, curled against him.

* * *

Kate felt him as he woke and slid from their bed, slipping out from under her arm and leg thrown casually across him as she slept. She stretched out, hands overhead, toes pointed, feeling the pull on all the muscles in her body as she shook herself awake. Shade was right about one thing, he did have her screaming at the top of her lungs in their bed. She watched him as he dressed, the leathers conforming to his shape. He looked up at her from beneath his dark hair, still tossed from sleep.

"*Buongiorno, mi amore*. Has my crimson spitfire settled down this evening?"

She smiled back at him, "*Si,* lover, I have no energy left for anything except calm."

He softly chuckled, as she reached out from their bed and took his hand. "Shade... I should never have yelled at you like that. I was just so..."

He placed one finger on her lips, indicating he didn't want her to speak.

"Not now, *bel rosso*. We will speak of it later. You needed time, and I did not give it, you were angry. I had obligations to others in the house, with every intention of returning to you. Somewhere, we got our wires crossed, *si*? But right now, I need to be in D.C. I do not want to start another conversation we don't have time to finish." He leaned down and kissed her goodbye. "Stay in this room until you hear me leave with all the warriors. Clear?"

"Clear, lover."

"*Ti amo, mi amore.*"

"I love you more."

She listened to his feet on the stairs, boot heels clicking against the tiles as he headed for the bunker, followed shortly by the sound of that thundering herd of warriors, laughing, speaking rapidly to each other in Italian. Within minutes, she heard them all leave the house, and she got up to dress for the night when she heard her cell phone buzzing. Kate scrambled around, trying to pinpoint the sound, and found the phone still in the pocket of the jeans he had hastily removed from her. She pulled the phone from her jeans pocket and saw Shannon on her caller ID. "Hello?"

Shannon was practically shouting into the phone, "Kate! Did you give him my number?"

Kate giggled. "Well, good evening to you too."

"Oh... sorry... I was just so certain he would call me. He pretty much said as much when he was helping me with my coat. I have felt like an idiot walking around for the last few days with my phone in my hand, afraid I would miss his call. I mean, did I read him wrong? Because I really thought he was interested."

"No Shannon, you didn't read him wrong, and I assure you, he's interested. But Shade is back home, and there are several of his... uh... business associates staying here at the house. Luca has been really busy. Just give him some time, okay?"

"Okay... okay, but like, how much time? A week? A month? I'm going crazy here!"

"Cool your jets, girl. I assure you, there is no one else in the picture, and however long it takes, you'll find he's worth the wait."

Shannon sighed. "Oh, he looks more than worth the wait, girlfriend. Did you see his eyes? That man could start a fire with those eyes!"

Kate was still laughing. "Do you need me to hose you down?"

"Maybe, I'll let you know. In the meantime, I've worn out two sets of batteries on my vibrator."

Kate screamed. "Shannon! TMI...please! And I want a good girl for Luca."

Shannon practically growled out her response, "Oh I'll be good, I promise."

"Okay, I am ending this conversation now." Kate was giggling uncontrollably. "Seriously, be patient, he will call. And in the meantime, behave yourself."

"No promises. And I'm calling back if I don't hear from him. Or... you could give me his number and I could call him?"

Kate shouted, "No! He has to keep his line clear for emergencies. I can see you texting him nude photos all day."

"Hey, a girl's gotta do what a girl's gotta do. And don't tell me you captured your Italian Stallion by playing goody two shoes."

"Okay, seriously Shannon, I'm hanging up now. This conversation is not about me."

Shannon pledged, "Three days, four max, and then I'm calling you again."

Kate ended the call. She had no idea if Luca had talked to Shade yet. But after last night, she would have to walk on eggshells with this one. She finished getting dressed and headed out for her evening breakfast and to meet Luca for training and torture.

28

Kate headed to Luca's suite and tapped on the door, he answered immediately, giving her a raised eyebrow look as he led her out of the house to start her warm-up. As she stretched, she looked up at him. "What was that look about?"

He chuckled lightly. "After yesterday, I wasn't sure I'd see you here tonight."

"Why would you think that?"

"Kate, I have known Shade my entire life. And I can tell you the only people to raise their voice to him in anger like that are masters from rival covens, and some of them aren't around to tell the story. We have all heard his beast emerge with you before, but never in anger. I was afraid for you."

"Yeah, that was a little over the top. But Luca!" She balled both hands into fists, "He made me so mad! And then he just teleported away and left me standing there. I wanted to scream."

He nodded his head in the direction of the footpath and they began their run together. Only a few weeks ago, this could not have happened, running and talking, she was just struggling to breathe.

"Yeah... we heard. We all heard. As a master, you shamed him, Kate, in front of his coven. I mean, I don't know what it is you do to calm the beast." He laughed and shook his head. "And you probably shouldn't tell me, but let's just say, that's a skill you better not lose."

"Well, first of all, he's not my master. And secondly, the beast and I... we got a thing going on." She giggled. "But I did think I had pushed him too far yesterday. That was the first time the beast scared me. I saw you start to intervene, Luca. Please, don't ever put yourself in that position again."

"Okay, well, let's break this down. First of all, he *is* your master. You are mated to him. You are a part of his coven, and more than any of us, you belong to him. We are a male-dominated culture. And if you don't feel it now, you will when you are turned. He gives you free rein in most things. Very unusual by the way. But you might want to figure out which lines not to cross."

"Like screaming at him from the top of the stairs?"

Luca laughed. "Exactly. And you need to understand the beast. Every vampire fights for control over their beast nature. Learning to control and direct the beast comes with age, but no vampire ever has full control. There is always a point of no return with the beast. That's a dangerous game to play. And most protectors, like me, have a very long list of don'ts they are monitoring for their master's mate. Shade has only given me one, and that is, when he is absent don't ever leave you alone."

"But I wasn't arguing with the beast, I was arguing with Shade. Seems unfair, doesn't it? Two against one and the beast always wins?"

He laughed at her again. "Did the beast win? I think not, or you wouldn't be here running with me tonight."

"Well... I think it was a draw. And you intervening, what were you thinking?"

"It's just instinct now. As your protector, and with the bond we have, my response is automatic when you're in danger, even if the danger is from him. And trust me, you were in danger. It's not my place to ask, but what set you off?"

"I don't know, it all seems so stupid now, in hindsight. We were just talking. I was asking him questions about Theresa and Marco? Trying to understand why they weren't together? And he was answering me, and then, just like that, 'okay, well, I'm done talking' and he was walking away. When I said something he yelled, "Woman!" And I know what that means."

Luca laughed. "We all know what that means."

"But then he started reminding me that he is my master..."

"Which he is."

"And then he asked my permission to take a shower or something and addressed me as 'my lady,' and that was it. I don't even remember what I said after that, but he stormed into the shower and then teleported out of the bedroom. That is the part that pushed me over the edge. He always just... walks away."

Luca looked over at her. "Part of that is Shade and his own stubbornness, and part of it is to protect you, and him, because he doesn't want the beast to confront you."

Kate looked back at him as she ran. "I know this might be hard to understand, but I would rather confront the beast than be left standing there. I hate that. I hate when he walks away."

"Then tell him. Tell him what you have just shared with me."

"Well, that's easier said than done. He's so busy now, with whatever is going on in D.C. I'm lucky to have five minutes with him for a conversation. That's how this whole thing started last night. He was walking away in the middle of a conversation."

"Talk to him. Find the time."

"You're right. I know you're right. Speaking of which, have you talked to him about Shannon? She called this evening. Right before I came down, she said she hadn't heard from you."

"No... not yet. I'm pretty sure I know the answer anyway. But I'll talk to him."

"Don't give up, Luca. I haven't said anything to him because you asked me not to. And I won't bring it up. And don't worry... If the beast shows up, I'll save you."

Luca laughed out loud. "And why do I not doubt that statement one bit?"

They ended their run back at the house, and he put her through her paces again with sit-ups and push-ups and free weights. Then he tore down the weight bench and returned with the bow. He set up a target for her again and they practiced for hours until all of her shots were landing in the target circle, and half her shots were in the bull's eye.

"What's your goal here? Do you want me to have every arrow in the bull's eye?"

"My goal? First of all, it is not my goal, it's your goal, little warrior. And your goal is to split the first arrow with the second arrow. To have such control over the arrow you can hit your target exactly where you want it, every time, or what is the point? The difference in a kill shot and an inconvenient wound can be a mere inch."

"Kill shot? But I'm not planning on killing anything, Luca. This was just... an exercise... sort of. I mean, I'm not a real warrior."

"Really? Because I only train real warriors, even little ones."

He took the bow from her hand and slid the quiver of arrows over his own shoulder. Pulling one arrow out, he shot it into a tree. Then he pulled a second arrow and shot it. Kate watched as it split the first arrow and it dropped to the ground. His third arrow split the second arrow, and he repeated it, time after time, landing his arrows in the exact same spot.

"Just like that. Just like master taught me. And now I teach you. That is your goal."

"But... I'll never be able to do that!"

"I think I said those same words to master when he was teaching me. Time and patience, little warrior. We will get there. Time, we have plenty of, but patience?" Luca just looked at her and shook his head, "That is another story. Now go, we are finished for the night."

Kate headed back inside and upstairs to shower, just as the sky was starting to lighten. He would be home soon.

29

Shade was happy to be getting home a little early. It had been a good night, the kills increased every night and they were starting to feel like they were getting ahead of the rogues, finally. He hadn't left the Dead House, working the command post all night, so he was more mentally than physically tired, and decided to have a smoke before heading inside to *bel*. She knew he was here, and knew he would soon join her. After their blow-up earlier, he needed to figure out how to manage his time and be with her more. He didn't want to have his beast flaring up every time she wanted her way, but he got the message, and so did the beast. Lighting up, he saw Luca approaching.

Luca stepped outside on the patio. "Mind if I join you?"

Shade threw him the pack of smokes. "Nope. You don't need to ask. You're probably cranking for a smoke. Everything go well tonight?"

Luca caught the pack of cigarettes, tapping one free and removing it with his teeth before lighting up and tossing the pack back to him. He sat down across from Shade.

"All good. No problems." Luca thought he seemed calm, so this was probably as good a chance as any to bring up this topic. "You got a minute?"

Shade watched him closely, something was on his mind, and he wondered immediately if it was about *bel*. Chuckling. "Well, after this morning, I'm not so sure anymore, but I always have time for you. Give it up."

Luca didn't know where to start. He reached into his pocket and pulled out the folded piece of paper that held the number for her cell phone, no name. He handed the crumpled paper to Shade.

Shade creased his brow as he accepted the piece of paper that looked like it had seen better days. He saw it held a phone number, but not one he recognized. Wracking his brain, he couldn't imagine what the hell this meant. Raising his eyes slowly to Luca, he leaned back in the chair, crossed his leg over his knee as he twirled the paper between fingers. "Female?"

Luca nodded. "Yes, Shannon, I want to call her. I haven't. And I won't, unless you give me your permission."

Shannon? Am I supposed to know who the fuck... Oh, Shannon, bel's friend. What the fuck? "Let me get this straight, I'm holding Kate's friend, Shannon's phone number in my hand? You have some explaining to do, get talking."

"I'm not sure what to explain. I mean, my lady invited her over when you were in Florence. I met her, briefly, and I don't know how to explain this because it has never happened to me before, but I liked her. I mean, I really liked her, a lot. And I think the feeling is mutual. She asked me to call. Like I said, I haven't, but I want to."

Shade sighed. "Luca, I'm not going to get upset, I'm not going to take you down, but there are a few things you need to consider here." Uncrossing his leg and throwing both feet on the ground, he leaned his elbows on his knees and lit up another one. "She know you're vampire?"

Luca shook his head. "No. I only spent a short time with her and all of it in my lady's presence. And my lady says she has not told Shannon that any of us are vampire."

Shade stood up, ran his fingers through his hair, and tossed the unfinished cigarette to the ground as he stomped out the butt.

"Well, let me get this off my chest first. You didn't tell me there was a mortal female in the house with my mate. I was away, and I already spoke to *bel* about this, I didn't like it. Still don't. Two things that are dangerous, females and mortals. *Bel* doesn't fully understand the consequences, but Luca, you do. I know you were with her the whole time, but you made a mistake. You should have told me. Last night, you came out to challenge my beast for *bel's* safety. That also was a mistake, so let me ask you this." He turned and looked at him. "I want you to bond with *bel*, but if you're getting so close to her that you can't think clearly, protect her properly, you need to tell me, *si*?"

"Master, I understand my obligation to my lady. I never lose sight of it. It remains my honor. And yes, I overstepped my boundaries yesterday, but it is now instinctive for me to try to protect her, even from your beast."

Shade chuckled softly. "I understand. *Bel* is hard not to love. But it is what it is, she is mortal, and I will remind you, so is this Shannon. Believe me, I fought it a long time before I realized I couldn't fight it any longer. Being with Kate was my destiny. So, there is something I need to bring to the table here about Shannon. What is your intention with her? Feed? Fuck? What? Tell me honestly, I need to understand what the hell attracted you to a mortal female? Is it curiosity?"

"It's more than a sexual connection. I can get that with a feeder. And I don't think it has anything to do with her being mortal. I mean, from the moment I saw her, believe me, it doesn't make sense to me either. Like I said, this has never happened before. I've never, you know, I've only been with feeders, and I had a strong affection for the one in Florence, but this is something else. I want to use the word love, but I know I don't even know her, so it just sounds crazy to me. But she's in my head all the time."

Shade threw back his head, roaring with laughter, and slapped Luca on the back. "Welcome to the world of females, Luca. They will fucking absorb your damn mind and make your cock like steel. But this reinforces my point for several reasons, so hear me out. You know my damn rules, warrior. Females are off limits for a reason. You are telling me one of those reasons right now, you can't get her out of your head, and once you get some attention from her for that sword between your legs, it only gets worse. If you think it's bad now, wait till you get a taste of her, feel her wrapped around your cock and you make her moan, a sound you won't ever forget easily. So, that brings me to another point. You protect my mate, how the hell do you expect me to trust you can do this when all you think about is this female in your head? Think about that.

"I never let you go, Luca, I was selfish. I didn't give you the chance to explore what was out there, and I cheated you. I have to live with that for the rest of my life. If you think you need to leave here and explore, like your brothers have done, tell me, because it's done. I won't like it, but it is for your own good. Damn it, Luca!"

Shade paced. "You saw and felt the hell *bel* and I went through with the loss of the *bambino*, how I fucking struggle every day to make her understand this world. It's hell sometimes, and I still have to make her immortal, put her through that change, bring her back to me and I could lose her doing it, is that what you want? Do you want to live through this pain and hell? You haven't even gotten to know this female yet. I'm just putting it out there."

"Master, I have watched that struggle between you and my lady. We all have. We have lived it firsthand. We watched your pain and hers, and even shared in that pain. We have watched your battles. And all I can tell you is, my lady always says she would change nothing, that her love for you surpasses all. And so, I ask you, would you change it? Do you regret you fell in love with a mortal?"

Shade hung his head, kicking the dirt softly with his boot. "No, Luca. I love Kate. I will love her till I die. But I fought with myself a long time about her being mortal. I didn't just follow an impulse. I thought long and hard. You are young, Luca, I am not. I had given up finding my mate, and believe me when I tell you, I never thought she would be mortal and I have been with many. Something inside me, my beast, screamed for her, wanted her like no other female ever. I just don't want you to take this lightly. Don't go too fast, think about it before you jump. That is all I'm asking. In our world, love is a serious matter, mating is for life, forever. If you ever doubt me, walk to that grave marker and feel that sorrow and brokenness, and remember the love that brought us through it together. Is she capable of that kind of love? Is she capable of giving up everything for you? Can you still protect the life of my mate and give your life for my mate over hers?"

Luca put his head in his hands. "I did not seek this out. And I honestly don't know where it will go. But my heart says to follow. Maybe it will be nothing. Maybe she'll run in the other direction when she discovers what I am."

He looked back up at Shade. "And I understand my obligation as my lady's protector. It is something I also wrestle with. I understand I must respond to my lady's safety above all others, and I'm prepared to do so. That is my honor as a warrior. If I fail at that, I fail as a warrior, I fail as *your* warrior, and I will never fail you."

Shade walked to him, sat down beside him. He felt his angst, the hell he was fighting. Shade had been there.

"You are far from a failure, Luca. You are my *familia*, my warrior, and you make me proud every single day. I am not going to say yes." With a sigh he continued, "and I'm not going to say no. I need to think about this, talk to *bel*."

He slid the paper into Luca's hands. "Call her, get to know her some. But here is my rule, you don't stalk her or watch her. You do not meet her. Make it a phone call, hear her voice, see what's inside her a bit. By then, I will have my answer and you will know if you still wish to continue with Shannon. I would never let another do this, but I have discovered lately, too many people I love have hidden their love from me, and if you do that, it will kill me. Be honorable, be a Medici warrior, make me proud. Just come to me before you make any decision." Standing, Shade hugged him to his chest.

Luca tucked the folded paper back into his pocket. This was not the answer he had expected. He was prepared to have him say no. At least he got a maybe. Luca returned the hug to the man who was the only real family he had ever known. As Shade released him, Luca watched him return to the house, and to her.

Luca walked back to his room and picked up his cell phone, then set it back down. Now that he had Shade's permission to talk to her, he had no idea what to say. He didn't need to have a conversation with a feeder. He talked to his feeder in Florence, but since he had been in the States, he had not been with the same feeder twice, and there was little, if any, conversation. It was a business transaction. But this was a mortal girl. What did he talk about with her? He would ask Kate, but he knew she was with master now. Besides, Shade would say if he couldn't figure this part out how the hell did he expect to be with her? He paced the room before picking up the phone again and pulling the paper from his pocket, quickly dialing the number before he could change his mind.

Shannon pulled her phone from her pocket but didn't recognize the number. She was almost ready to discard the call but decided to answer. "Hello?"

He heard her voice and could see an image of her again, as clearly as if she were standing in front of him. He could visualize her blue eyes looking up at him, and feel her hair against the back of his hands, and the smell of her perfume. It all came rushing back and he caught his breath. "*Mia bellezza.*"

Shannon heard his voice and almost dropped the phone. "Oh... Luca, I'm so glad you called!"

"So, you remember me, *mia bellezza*?"

"Remember you? I have thought of little else. I thought maybe you had forgotten me."

"That would be impossible. And I have thought often of you as well. I've been very busy. It's a poor excuse, I know, but my work here... my obligations..."

"Yes, Kate told me Shade was home from Florence and he had brought some business associates back with him."

Luca thought for a minute. *Business associates? Ah, the warriors.* "Yes, business associates. I'm not sure how long they will be here, but we have all been very busy."

Trying to dance around the truth was giving him a headache. He had never been around mortals in this capacity, having to shield what he was, think about his words before he spoke them, and consider what information he might accidentally share.

Shannon questioned him, "That seems unusual, doesn't it? To have them at the house? I mean, why don't they just all go stay in a hotel?"

Fuck! This was so much harder than he thought. "They have meeting rooms here. They can meet whenever they like. And Shade likes to extend his hospitality."

"Yeah, well, I look forward to officially meeting the Italian Stallion. I saw him once, briefly, when he and Kate first met."

"The Ital... oh, you mean Shade?" He suppressed a chuckle. Not sure master would appreciate being called the Italian Stallion. "Might I suggest you not call him that when you meet him?"

Shannon laughed. "Oh god, no! I would never do that. I was just teasing Kate about him, since she disappeared from the face of the earth after she met him. You know, like, what's going on with you two that you can't find five minutes to call me? So, will that happen to me?"

"*Scusi*? Will what happen to you?"

"If we go out... will I disappear for six months too? Will all my friends wonder what happened to me after one date with Luca?"

"*Mia bellezza*, I work for Shade. I'm not Shade. I live in this house, I don't own it. I'm afraid I don't have the ability to sweep you off your feet in that way."

"Oh, Luca... I've got news for you. You have swept me off my feet already."

His heart skipped a beat at her words. "But you understand. I work here."

"Yes, I understand. We all have to work somewhere, and being a personal trainer slash personal assistant slash bodyguard for the rich and famous sounds like a pretty good gig to me."

Luca thought to himself, he was none of those things. Well, maybe protector could translate as a bodyguard in the mortal world. "Yes, I love my, what did you call it? Gig?"

"And I look forward to hearing more about it, and hearing more about you. So, are you asking?"

"Asking, *mia bellezza*?"

"A date, Luca. Are you asking me on a date?"

"I... there is nothing I would like better, but right now, my schedule is not flexible. If I call again..."

Shannon corrected him. "*When* you call again."

"*Si,* when I call again, when things quiet down here, and if I were to ask you on a date, your answer would be?"

"My answer would be yes."

"Until then, *mia bellezza.*"

"Until then, Luca."

As he ended the call, he realized his heart was pounding, and he wiped the sweat from his hands onto his jeans. He took a deep breath. *How can one small mortal woman make me feel this tied up in knots?*

30

It had been some time since Kate heard Shade arrive. He'd let her know he needed to talk to Luca first. She was hoping he wasn't avoiding her over that stupid fight. She finally heard his footsteps on the stairs and he entered their bedroom. "Shade? Is everything okay?"

"*Si, mi amore*. I just needed to talk to Luca." He flopped down on the chaise and patted his lap. "Come, *bel*, I need to feel you."

She didn't want a repeat of yesterday's misunderstanding. "Are we okay? The two of us? I should never have screamed at you like that. I'm sorry. But I just go crazy when you walk away. Can we start over?"

He sighed as she slid into his lap, all soft and warm and smelling like heaven, and laid her head on his shoulder. He laid his hand on her head and slid his arm around her tiny waist. She was so damn small in his arms. "*Si, mi amore*, we are fine. I'm sorry as well. I lost my temper with you. Something I shouldn't have done, and I understand now, I need to pay more attention to you and spend more time together. I am trying to work on the walking away. I do it because I have to control myself, my beast. It's to protect you. Are you okay?"

She nuzzled her face into his neck, inhaled his scent, and felt his arms around her. "I am, lover. We have such little time together lately, I hate when we spend any of it fighting. And I know you have a lot going on in D.C. That it takes you away from me. I'll try to be more patient. Not my strong suit, as you have already figured out." She kissed his neck. "But even in the middle of my screaming fit, you know I still love you, right?"

Moaning and closing his eyes, he let his head fall back on the chaise and enjoyed the feel of her lips against his neck. "*Si, mi amore*, I always know you love me, I feel that so deeply, no one will ever take it out of me. Listen, we need to talk seriously about something. Can you sit with me a bit and talk about this? I need your input. I won't do this without conferring with you."

"Of course. Is something wrong?"

"Well, not wrong, but I need to make a decision. It concerns Shannon."

"Shannon? I... you met her? I don't understand, lover."

He shook his head, "No, I haven't met her, that's half the problem. Look, Luca came to me on his own accord. He wants to see her, he thinks he loves her. He does, he just doesn't know it yet. And I am torn, *bel*. I don't want this for him yet. I wanted him to explore more, experience more, before he even thinks about love and females... And mortal ones especially."

She sat up in his lap, "You don't want him to be in love? Or feel loved? Please don't get angry with my questions. I heard what you said about Theresa and Marco, and warriors. But just because I heard your words doesn't mean I understand. I don't understand. And mortal? I'm mortal. Do you have regrets about us?"

"*Cazzo*, you sound worse than Luca! I think he is hanging around you too damn much. He fires questions faster than you do now!" He sighed, "Kate, can you just listen to me. Listen, stop your brain box a moment and listen. Luca is young for a vampire. He has the whole world to discover. Marco and I have done it all. I don't want Luca to jump into something before he thinks of all the things a mortal woman entails. I have no regrets about us, none. But *bel*, I watched you a long damn time, and struggled with the fact you were mortal before I jumped. Luca doesn't even know this Shannon. He is warrior! Females mess with a vamp's head, *mi amore*, they consume us, we live to cherish them for all eternity. So, you better damn well make sure you have sown all your wild oats, explored it all before you make that call. Can he turn her? Can he leave her side under an attack to save you? Because he will have to, and he is not going to have time to think about it before it happens. He is a dead warrior if he does. There are so many fucking things in my head, *bel*. Help me."

"Lover, you know I struggle to understand everything in your world. But mortals have soldiers, and that's something like a warrior. They train. They fight. And they must leave their wives and children behind to do so. They often give up their lives for their country, for a cause, but most will say they give their life for their brother-in-arms. Soldiers... warriors... mortal or immortal, they have both decided to make sacrifices, including their lives, for something or someone other than their mate. For a cause they see as being greater than themselves, for honor or duty. Those are things I understand. Is that not the same? You think Luca can only be a good warrior if he is solitary. That love will only be a distraction. But I see a man without love, and nothing to fight for. I just see loneliness and darkness, like I saw in you. Are you less of a warrior since you met me?

I'm in no position to judge what came before, but I think you fight harder to make sure you come home to me."

"You are the reason I fight, *mi amore*. I will be honest with you, I would have told Alec to go fuck himself a long time ago if you were not here. I would have gone back the hell home. But now, this is my home. I made Luca a deal."

"And what is the deal?"

"He has her phone number. He promised me he has not seen her since the day she was here. So, I told him I would make a decision, yes or no. He knows he needs my permission, he is honorable. I told him to call her, get to know her by phone only, and if he was still interested, I would have my decision by then." He hugged her tighter to his chest, "Now I need to ask a favor of you, *si*?"

"Of course, Shade. Anything."

"Well, before I ask you this, tell me all you know about this Shannon. Because other than the brief time I saw her with you, I don't know shit and neither does he. That bothers me."

"I've known her for a long time. We went to college together at Georgetown, and were roommates a couple of years, and became close friends. We both did the internships at the ad agency and got job offers there, so we worked together. We've traveled together. She's a good person...a kind person...a loyal friend. She's not the type of girl who will lead him on. Toy with his heart. I don't know what the future holds for them. Is she the one? I hear what you say when you say Luca is young and he hasn't been out in the world. I can read between the lines. But if she's not the one for him, shouldn't he be the one to figure that out? Otherwise, he spends his whole life wondering about what might have been. If you would feel better to meet her yourself, I'd be happy to introduce you. She has already asked me several times when she'll be able to officially meet you."

"Me? She wants to meet me?"

"Of course. We're good friends. She wants to meet the man who stole my heart away. Who, as she puts it, made me disappear from the face of the earth. And I did disappear from my mortal friends and family. I walked away from everything I've ever known to be with you, and I would do it again. People will sacrifice anything for love. Life hardly feels worth living without it. I know this, and you know it as well. Shannon knows it. And so does Luca. Love is what we all seek...mortal or immortal."

"*Si*. I guess I never thought about seeking it, until my eyes saw you, and I fought so hard against something that would win no matter how hard I fought. Okay, so we shall have a small gathering, the four of us. I will make time to do this one evening. But now, I need a favor from you. I know Rissa warned you I was vampire, you did not believe her. Do you think it best to fill Shannon in first that we are not mortal males, we are vampire? Tell me your opinion on this? I do not wish to scare the living hell out of her and scare her away. It is Luca's job to tell her, but if you told her, how do you think she would react?"

"That's a good question. I don't know how she'll react. I was told that you were vampire, and I didn't believe it. If I told Shannon... if I tell her, then I think I have to tell her all. By that, I mean, it's not just Luca who is vampire, but you as well... and Gi, Theresa, and Reynaldo. You know mortals have very different views of vampires, some think they are evil, wicked, controlled by the devil, the walking dead. Others think they are simply myth. And others believe and are attracted to them. She came here during the day, she saw everyone, met everyone except you. I assure you, she had no clue she was surrounded by vampires. And if I tell her now, and she has already had the experience, then I think she will be accepting. That's always a risk, isn't it? Telling a mortal? But you took that risk with me. Shannon wouldn't do anything that would hurt me. If she decides to walk away, she would not betray me, or us."

He creased his brow, "Hmm, well, I don't know her, *mi amore*, so I leave that to you. I am putting my trust in you. I know you would never betray us, so I have to trust you know her well enough to judge. You pick the evening and arrange things with Luca and Shannon. I will make my decision that night. But you think I should let him do this, do you not, *mi amore*?"

"I will arrange it, lover. But I think they will both be very nervous. Luca will be nervous around this girl he is getting to know, and she'll be nervous around him. Luca knows she is mortal, but she will be seeing him through different eyes for the first time, and they'll both be nervous about you, and your impression. But I'll arrange it if that is what you wish. And yes, I do think you need to let Luca explore his own life... Even if she's not the one. He needs to find his own way through this."

"Then let us gather them together, and see if there are fireworks or sparklers. I need a damn haircut! Where are the scissors?"

"Fireworks or sparklers. That's a good analogy. I think we were a nuclear explosion. Let me get the scissors and cut your hair, please? The last time you cut too much away. And while I have your attention, I have another question. Unrelated, about the warriors?"

"Well, you better ask me before you get scissors in your hands," he smacked her ass and laughed. "What is it that you wish to ask me?"

"I know you've asked me to stay inside when the warriors are about, and I have. But they seem rather, uh...rowdy? Maybe restless? Anyway, I sense they feel caged up in the staff quarters. I was going to ask if I could show Marcello the property, with Luca, of course. Show him where the warriors could roam and let off some steam? And I was thinking I could have some workers come and make a fire pit area behind the staff quarters? Then they could hang out there at night when you don't have them assigned to go into D.C.? Maybe being outdoors will feel more natural to them? Is that okay?"

She never ceased to amaze him with the love she showed every single person he brought from his world into hers. "*Bel*, do you know how much I love you? Any idea?"

"Lover, yes, I do know. It fills me up every day. And I only hope you feel it all back in return."

"More than you could ever imagine, *mi amore*. I believe the warriors are restless and they are used to the outdoors when they are in the camp. I like that idea of a fire pit. It will give them a chance to settle down before going to slumber when they return at night. You know, *mi amore*, I thought about buying a fleet of four wheelers and dirt bikes, even for you, something maybe we could do together. What do you think?"

"Me? On a dirt bike? I never pictured myself as a dirt bike kind of girl, but if you are going to do it, then I'll give it a try."

He laughed. "You do know Luca rides. Would you like hitting the road on a bike, hanging onto your vampire while we let the night air surround us?"

"Now that I would love!"

"Really? Then that is our next date, because I've been thinking about what you said, about spending time together. Things are coming together in D.C., it will free my time up a bit. Now get the scissors, you minx, or would you prefer Gi do it?"

She ran her hands through his hair, "The only person touching your hair from now on will be me. Let me get the scissors."

"*Si,* I love your hands in my hair!"

31

Max was pacing the floor of his rented condo. Taking out Alec's band of rag-tag warriors had not been such a piece of cake. He had been able to create chaos and confusion, but now Tomas had called and said they needed to talk. He had Tomas infiltrate Alec's warriors when he first arrived. Alec's warriors had no formal training and were mostly a collection of undisciplined hoodlums other masters had discarded. Alec was never much for taking it to the streets. He brought Shade in, and he had at least brought some discipline and direction, but let's face it, there was only so much even Shade could do with that bunch. Having Tomas on the inside had been invaluable. Max knew what they planned to do before they did, and it had made picking them off easy. And, of course, Tomas had been invaluable to Shade, since he was the only warrior there with any real skills for Shade to rely on. But there was urgency in Tomas' voice when he called, so he was not expecting good news.

As Tomas arrived at his condo, he found the door open as always and walked in, finding him pacing the floors."Maximus."

"Tomas, pour yourself a drink, brother. I'm sure you could use it. Have a seat. What's on your mind?" Max took a seat on the large sofa, anxious to hear what Tomas had to share.

Tomas poured himself a tall Midnight and remained standing, strolling around the condo, he was far from relaxed. He liked his role as a spy within the ranks, but he knew all of this was for a woman. He knew Maximus could be trusted, paid handsomely and had success on his mind. Skill and brains were needed here, and Shade just upped the ante.

"Shade is the man you need to pay attention to, Max. He is running this war on the streets. The good Senator could care less about what goes on as long as he is not exposed. Shade is lethal and wherever he goes, he takes care of business cleanly and quickly. He has no patience for this petty game, but he remains in the dark as it relates to Aries, you and the coven. Your plan is working well," draining his glass as he sat across from him and rolls his eyes to Max, "but you now have some serious trouble."

Max watched him pace the floor. and he knew he had something on his mind. "This doesn't sound good, brother. What's going down?"

Sitting back in the leather chair, Tomas crossed one leg over the other and figured it would be to his benefit to let him know everything, but Tomas still remained hesitant over Max's purpose...immortal pussy. Tomas had had seen bigger men go down for it and he would be damned if he did.

"Look Max, Shade left me in charge of this fucked up bunch of so-called warriors while he went to Florence, and he returned with eight of his finest. He doesn't need an army, he is known as the Warrior of Warriors. His job is training them, making them into fighting machines, and if he only brings back eight of them for this entire city, you can bet your ass he will own it before long. I know of his past, his rep, and the reputations of the ones he returned with. He will literally put whatever you have on the streets out of commission in a short period of time. He doesn't take his profession lightly, Max. This brother knows how to kill and does so without thinking, and his warriors...the same. He has full authority from Alec to take out Angel when he finds him, and I have seen what he did with one of your captured rogues. This bastard has centuries of warrior blood in his veins. Two of his warriors, Raven and Marcello, can knock out three or four warriors single handedly, without losing one ounce of blood. So you need a plan, Max, a damn fucking good one if you intend to dip that cock permanently into Canton's honey hole!"

Max knew his words about Shade's reputation were true. Every warrior knew him and feared him, so he would need to rethink his strategy, but Tomas' words angered him and his beast roared back at him.

"My reasons for staging this insurgence are my own, warrior, and none of your fucking business! You work for me! And whenever that becomes a problem for you, you just let me know!"

Tomas thought to himself, *Well that must be some divine damn cunt to make his beast rock.* Holding up his hand, he growled. "Don't threaten me, Maximus, I'm here to help you, not hinder you, for fuck's sake. Relax. A few things you need to know. My theory is this, you take out Shade, and we're done. This is well over. Alec may be a master, a wealthy one with clout, but he'll not get his hands dirty, so you need to focus on Shade. He lives far out of town, in the Virginia mountain sides. And a wise piece of info, his mate is mortal, and one meek little bag of bones at that. There is a hitch. Shade has assigned her a protector. I hear his warriors talk, he hides the wench inside, and she rarely leaves the house. If you can get past the protector, she's an easy kill. Keep that in mind. Pull back the activity on the streets, it will confuse him. He's used to conflict. He's a street fighter. He has brought in his own, and is ready to amp up the volume, so I think you counter that by going quiet for a while. At any rate, switch your focus from Alec to Shade."

Max got his beast under control. He listened to Tomas. He had been a trusted warrior for him for many years, and he had good instincts. He took a deep breath and chugged down what remained in his glass of the Midnight. They still had the potion. That had given them a distinct advantage so far, but Tomas was right. Eliminate Shade and this game was over. And he was smart enough to know they would never take Shade, but they could take him out of the game if they eliminated his mate.

"Okay, brother, I hear you. But any attack on Shade's mate will get his attention immediately. We'll have Shade, the protector and all of hell's army on our backs. We need something that will keep him tied up, something that has him isolated and so overwhelmed he can't respond. Is he in D.C. with his warriors every night? How do we get him isolated from his fucking warriors?"

Tomas grinned, stood up and pulled out the local area maps he had drawn up of Shade's estate and the surrounding grounds. He threw them down on the table in front of Max.

"Let me handle that, Maximus. Pull your warriors back until I give you the word. Let's see what he does. He is stuck in that fucking Dead House night after night, when he would rather be home with his new mate. If he thinks things are quiet on the streets, his aching cock will draw him home. His patience is running thin, brother.

"Be prepared, when I give the word, to roll with all you have. I can keep all his warriors preoccupied on the streets and leave Shade at home. Since I am running the fucking show from the inside, we can make sure his warriors stay busy that night while he is banging his wench unaware of what is coming straight to him. Take the war to him, and once you take him, his mate, and the protector out, the others will fall, unguided, without a master to lead them. Shade is the sole heir, Maximus, the sole heir to the Medici. It all falls apart when he is gone, and Alec is left wide open for taking whatever the fuck is your fancy. Be patient...plan. Be ready."

Max smacked Tomas on the back. "I like the way you think, warrior. And you've never let me down. Pull back our warriors and let things go quiet for a while. Don't let them totally disappear. I want them to know we're still around, but just enough to be an aggravation. Then I'll leave the rest up to you. When you see the opportunity to stage an ambush, just take it."

"You'll know when I'm ready, Max. I'll stay in close touch. I need to head there now. Starve the root and the mighty oak falls, brother."

Giving Max a back-slapping hug, he let himself out and headed straight into the night, with a plan straight to the target that would make him rich before he moved on to the next fool master.

Max picked up the map of Shade's estate, as well as a copy of the D.C. grid Shade had used to plot out his attacks on his warriors. He even had photos of Shade's house, from every angle, every window, and every door. He had a floor plan that identifieds every room. The house was isolated, situated in the middle of a large piece of property, so they wouldn't have to worry about the noise or the interference of any do-gooder mortals calling 911. All they needed was one night, one night when Shade decided to stay home while his warriors were all in D.C.

If Max made it quiet on the streets in D.C. but staged just enough activity that they had to keep on guard, maybe he could lure Shade into feeling confident enough he could leave his warriors in charge while he took a night off to spend with his mate. After all, nobody understood the allure of a mate more than Max. If he could bring Shade down, then Alec was next to fall. And without power and influence, Rissa would leave him in a heartbeat. Max loved Rissa, but he was no fool. He knew what attracted her. It was power, money, and influence. And she was just a heartbeat away from belonging to him.

32

Kate felt so happy to have him back, to talk, to cut his hair, and play in the shower before climbing into their bed. There was a lot to be said for makeup sex, but not having to make up in the first place, even better. She lay here next to him, as the sun set and knew he would awake from his death slumber soon. Then he would dress in black leather and leave her for the night. He still shared little about what he did. He didn't speak of what happened when he was away from her, and she let him keep those secrets, because there was a part of her that preferred not to know the details. She felt him stir beside her, and watched as he opened his eyes to see her propped on one elbow, looking at him.

"*Mi amore*, you are watching me sleep?"

"I love watching you sleep, lover."

She touched his face, ran her fingers down the stubble on his cheek, and touched his lips with her fingertips before lowering her mouth to his. He returned the kiss, lifting his hand to slide it through her hair.

"Do not get me too distracted, *bel rosso*, I must leave soon."

"I know I lose you to the night, but I hope I never get used to it."

He gave her a sad smile. "*Si, bel rosso*, and I hope you never get used to it as well."

She watched him as he slipped from their bed, and she slid into the spot he had vacated, her head on his pillow. She watched him until he was ready to leave, and he warned her again to not come downstairs until he had left with all the warriors.

When the house was quiet again, and she felt him leave, she got up and got ready to meet Luca. She tapped on his door and he answered right away, stepping out and leading her outdoors. "Do you see the warriors, Luca?"

He looked at her with a question. "Of course, I see them every day."

"Shade tells me to stay upstairs until I hear them leave, and then I hear them every morning when they all head for the barracks when they return. They're a noisy bunch."

Laughing. "Well, I think that's an understatement. Start warming up while you talk."

She stretched in preparation for their nightly run. "Shade said I could meet with Marcello and show him the property where the warriors could get outside a bit. Would you set that up please, since I don't think he wants me going to the barracks? I prefer day hours if he can. I understand he is a day-walker, like you."

"He would love that, Kate. I'll take care of it. He said they were getting a little stir crazy. They love the fight, and being on the streets, but they were feeling a little cooped up here. So that will be great for them."

They started their run, and she let Luca set the pace for her. She gave him a sideways glance. "And is there anything you want to tell me?"

Luca looked at her. "About the warriors?"

"No! About Shannon. Shade said you talked to him, and he said you could call her. Luca, we talked a long time... he wants to meet her... I think he's going to say yes."

Luca scrunched up his face. "Shade wants to meet her? Well that won't be too intimidating."

She laughed softly. "Stop it. But I know what you mean. He can be threatening. But did you call her?"

"I did call."

She stopped running and put her hands on her hips. "Seriously? Am I going to have to pry every word from you?"

"I don't know what to tell you. She said she was excited to hear from me. She wanted me to ask her on a date, which of course, I couldn't do until Shade made his decision. She said I swept her off her feet."

"And what did you say?"

"I honestly can't remember what I said. I mean, when I hung up, my heart was pounding, and I had been holding my breath and my palms were all sweaty. What is that?"

She started running again, laughing as she ran, and looked back over her shoulder at him as he stood there. "That's love, Luca... that's love kicking your ass, and isn't it wonderful?"

He ran to catch up with her, setting the pace once again, as he shook his head. "Wonderful? I'm not sure I would describe it as wonderful, confusing maybe."

"Well, hang on, Luca. I promise you never learned anything like this in warrior camp. We all need to get the shit kicked out of us by love."

He laughed. "You make it sound like a battle."

"A battle for your sanity maybe. Are you upside down or right side up? Does he love me back? Will he call? Does he feel the way I feel? Did

I make him mad? Sad? Happy? Will he like this dress? Or does he prefer me in jeans. What about my hair? Up or down? Am I talking too much? Or too little? Does he like my laugh? Torture. Beautiful, delicious torture."

He looked over at her as she gestured while she ran. "Can I just say if this is supposed to be a pep talk, you are doing a lousy job?"

"All I can say is life is hardly worth living without love. To love and be loved... and it will turn your whole world upside down. And you will be angry sometimes, and you will cry sometimes, but mostly, you just feel this overwhelming joy for life, and this person. This one person who makes your heart pound, and your breath stop, and your palms sweat. Suddenly, you wonder how you ever made it this far in life without them because you know you can't go forward if they aren't with you. I can't describe it, you will just have to dive head first into this madness and experience it for yourself."

"No wonder master warned me..."

Kate glared at him. "Don't you dare back out now, warrior. Don't you dare!"

She was issuing him a challenge as difficult as any he had put before her. "I'm not backing down, I was just..."

She interrupted him, "Thinking? Well, don't. I bet Shade told you to think about it, consider all the ramifications. Love isn't about thinking. Love is about feeling. Just follow your heart. If any of us sat down and thought about it, none of us would ever fall in love. Love is illogical, and messy. I mean look at me. Look at Shade and me. Could it be any more illogical? I followed my heart when I chose him, not my head. You have a good heart, a pure heart. Just trust where it leads. I don't know if Shannon will be the girl for you, but I do know that right now, your heart says she is, and you owe it to yourself to find out."

Luca looked over at her as they ran. "But she'll need master's approval. I still need to wait for his decision."

"You know what? You leave that part to me. I'll think of something that will make this introduction work."

They were closing the ten-mile loop and returning to the house, as they ended this conversation. She started her cool-down while he went back inside and returned with the bow and the quiver full of arrows.

"No sit-ups? No push-ups?"

Luca shook his head no. "Not tonight, we have some ground to cover. Tonight, we hunt."

Looking confused, Kate answered, "Hunt? Hunt what?"

"There are all kinds of wildlife in the woods. You hear them every night when we run. Tonight, we will hunt them. Use your skills of stealth to move in as close as you can, without their detection. Their hearing, their sense of smell is much greater than humans, but still not as good as vampire. If you can approach the wildlife without detection, then you are one step closer to tracking a vampire."

She looked at him confused, "Uh... okay, but just for the record, I'm not planning a career as Buffy the Vampire Slayer, so not really sure why I need this skill."

"Who's this Buffy?"

"No one... not a real person... a TV show."

"The things in your head confuse me, Kate."

She followed him across the open fields and into the woods, where he reminded her to watch where she placed her feet, step lightly, determine the direction of the wind, and how to stand downwind from the wildlife they saw.

Luca watched her as they moved through the woods, letting her spot the wildlife. He moved with her, letting her lead, to get as close as they could to the animal before they were detected, and they scurried away. As they stepped into a clearing, he saw the large buck and realized she had spotted it as well. He handed her the bow, and whispered, "Take him down." She turned her face to him, her eyes large as saucers, and shook her head no. He pulled an arrow from the quiver and put it in her hand and whispered again, "Take him down."

She saw the magnificent buck across the clearing. He wanted her to shoot the deer? No! She couldn't. She heard him instruct her again to take him down. She placed the arrow across the bow and pulled back the bow string as Luca stepped behind her.

"Line up your sights. Feel the wind. Control your breathing. Hold your breath right before you release the arrow."

He was whispering to her. She did as he instructed and as she released the arrow, she felt a tear run down her face. She watched as the arrow struck the deer in the chest and the majestic animal dropped first to his front knees, before dropping to the ground. Luca responded with, "Kill shot!" and started walking towards the deer. She followed him silently, tears falling.

Luca reached the slayed deer and removed the arrow, turning to Kate and saw her tear stained face. "What's wrong? It was a clean shot? A kill shot. He never felt anything."

"I have never killed anything. I don't believe in hunting for sport. Do you know the Native Americans believe all life is sacred and there is a spiritual relationship between people and wildlife? They believe all animals contain spiritual power. To sacrifice an animal for your own survival, you have to honor that animal. You take his spirit into your own. To sacrifice an animal for sport, for no reason... that is a sin against nature."

She knelt next to the deer, and ran her fingers through the warm, pooled blood, marking her forehead and each cheek.

"I honor you," she whispered to the still warm carcass.

He heard her words, but her emotions about the wildlife were something he had never seen before and only confused him. He wondered if her gentle spirit would ever let her take another shot at a living creature.

She stood and started to walk way, but she couldn't. "I can't leave him here. That would be a dishonor. We have to take him back."

"You want to take the deer back to the house?"

"That's exactly what I'm saying. I'll call a soup kitchen. They can pick him up. Reynaldo can prepare him. The deer will be food for the homeless, and at least then his death has meaning and honor."

Luca lifted the deer across his shoulders, as if the large animal weighed nothing, and they walked back to the house. She was silent on the walk back.

Mortals... what was he getting himself into?

33

Shade decided to have a smoke while he waited for Marcello to come back in off the streets. He walked down into the dungeon area of the Dead House and had a look around. He wondered how many dead had travelled through this house. The place was a wreck but fitting for the deeds that were done here. Lighting up, he wondered what the fuck he was doing here. He didn't need to be here every night. He mostly sat for hours at the command center, monitoring their whereabouts, letting his boys take care of business. Things had calmed down some and they seemed to have a good handle on this damn Aries Coven. The attacks on mortals seemed to have died off. The new rogues out there were easy to track and whoever was running this damn show didn't have the brains to hand out this potion to everyone.

Hearing the ruckus coming from upstairs, it sounded like the herd of warriors had come in for the night. It usually took a few hours to get them all back in as they straggled in a few at a time. No one left the Dead House until they all checked in and were accounted for.

His thoughts went to *bel*, and her idea of giving the warriors some running space at the house. He liked the idea but damn, he didn't think she had any fucking idea how wild these warriors were. You let them loose and it would be hell reining them back in. But she had this mothering instinct that made him adore her all the more, and he knew she was bored out of her head lately with him being gone so damn much, so maybe he would let her roll with it and worry about how to crack down on the warriors later.

Walking upstairs, Shade found the lot of them all pissing and moaning about a hot shower and a soft bed. He laughed to himself, they'd been here a week and the sons of bitches had gone soft already. Too damn much good living was what that was.

"Listen up. Now! I'm splitting my warriors down into two packs tonight, first four are going feeding. You teleport, feed, do your business and teleport back to Bel Rosso within two hours. That's an order. You know the fucking rules. You break 'em, your ass goes home. I don't care how you do the split... get it done, now. The rest of us are going home. I'm calling Alec, so keep it down."

Walking back to the piles of grids and kill sheets stacked at the command center desk, he decided to give Alec a quick call, give him the details and then head home to *bel*.

Hitting speed dial, he lit up another smoke and put his booted feet up on the table.

Alec was lying in bed with Rissa curled against him when he woke up a little early. He was waiting for the alarm when he heard the buzz of the cell phone. He grabbed it from the nightstand, saw Shade on the caller ID and sat up in the bed. "Hey, brother. Problems?"

"You are talking to Medici here, we don't have problems, brother, we solve them. Just giving you a heads up. The rogues that were turning mortals have been eliminated for now. Easy as hell, brother. No hocus pocus potion to hide them. Easy targets. But this is far from over. We haven't gotten to the actual Aries Coven rogues yet and there seems to be fewer attacks. Something is about to come, I can feel it. They know we are here, so they backed off and are planning, you can bet your solid gold cufflinks on it."

Alec sighed. "Well, at least you got those walking zombies off the street. That would have been a nightmare if it had gone on long enough for the press to pick up on a pattern. And the attacks are down, that's good. But I agree. This is far from over and they're probably just regrouping at this point to plan a counter strategy. I still haven't heard anything about this Angel... so, that really bothers me. That's just too fucking weird that a master could plan something like this, and nobody else knows anything."

Shade took a deep drag from his cigarette. "He is one big ass master for this bullshit to go down and me not get wind of it, but give me more time and I will hand his head to you, no doubts. You heard anything from Council?"

Alec shook his head. "Nothing, not a word."

"Well, don't fucking panic, they're probably doing some deep snooping themselves. It's a good sign, brother. I'm out. We'll be back out there at sunset. I have a few day-walkers now in our legion, so you want some protection for the house, or Rissa, let me know."

"I'll think about it, thanks, brother."

"No problems. We got it."

As he hung up the phone, Shade headed out and rounded up his crew. The pack had narrowed, and he was left with the strongest four that didn't need to feed, Marcello among them. "Let's roll, warriors! My mate and my bed are calling me."

Coming home from the Dead House, Shade made sure all the warriors were bunked down at the staff quarters. Marcello walked back to the main house with him, and Shade noticed he went right to Luca's door. He was glad to see Luca had some company. Heading upstairs, Shade walked into their bedroom, emptied his pockets on his dresser and yelled out, "*Bel rosso!*"

Kate giggled as she heard his booming voice. "Lover, you make such a quiet entrance. Full of energy today?"

"*Si,* I am. I'm tired of sitting on my ass in the Dead House, directing my warriors from a chair, makes me restless. What have you been up to, you minx?"

Wow. How do I answer that one? Other than killing a deer. "Nothing. I've just been waiting for you. But I was thinking about your request to have Shannon over, so you could meet her. Instead of just the four of us sitting in a room feeling awkward, and you know both she and Luca will be nervous, why don't we all go out? You mentioned the bikes that Luca rides as well, why don't you and Luca take us into town? It will be a nice drive, we can walk around, and they have a live band on the open mall in the evenings. What do you think?"

Propping his boot up on the stool, he unlaced them as he turned to look at her. "The mall? Like shopping, you mean?"

"No, the open-air mall in Charlottesville. They have shops, but also little bistros with alfresco dining. I'm sure we could arrange for one to hold Midnight for you. And the band is outside as well. People just walk and talk, enjoy the night air, and dance and sing along. It's very casual."

"You ever heard me sing, *mi amore.* Because if you did, you would never ask me to sing along, especially after having some Midnight." He threw back his head laughing. "But I like this idea and who the hell am I to give up a night on the bike with your arms around me, hanging on for dear life. Yeah, that works really well, in my opinion."

"You know…" she walked up to him from behind and slid her arms around his waist, leaning her upper body against his strong back, "…I've never ridden with you on the bike before. It sounds very sexy. The vibrations of the bike…"

He turned his head to the side to look at her, his hair falling over his face and he growled. "Oh, I got vibrations for you, *mi amore,* and I don't need a bike to do it."

Spinning around, he grabbed her up, threw her over his shoulder and headed for the shower. "Come along, woman, we need to get real dirty and then we need to shower."

Their shower was pleasure and play as promised, and then he carried her to their bed, where the death slumber pulled him under. She lay with her head on his chest and fell into her own dreamless sleep.

Kate had planned to meet Luca later today to show Marcello the grounds, so she had set her cell phone on vibrate and put it under her pillow. After a few hours of sleep, the alarm went off, waking her, and she slipped from Shade's side, getting dressed in jeans and boots, so they could walk the property.

She closed the bedroom door softly behind her and walked downstairs to Luca's suite. As she approached, she could hear two voices in his room speaking rapidly in Italian, with sporadic bursts of laughter. She recognized Luca's voice, and she assumed the other was Marcello. Kate almost hated to break up this happy reunion.

She tapped on the door lightly and Luca flung the door open, a huge smile on his face. Marcello stepped up behind him.

Kate asked, "Are you two ready?"

"Ready when you are. Marcello, I think you already met Kate... I mean Shade's mate, my lady." *Fuck! I knew that would happen eventually.*

Kate watched as Marcello looked sideways at Luca when he called her Kate, raising his eyebrows, but saying nothing. Kate quickly reached out to shake hands with Marcello to try to cover the moment.

"I've heard a lot about you, Marcello. I'm happy to have you here with us." She was expecting a handshake, but he lifted her hand to his lips and kissed the back of it gently.

"What is this American tradition of shaking a lady's hand? Not in my country. We shake a man's hand. We kiss a lady's hand." Marcello lifted her hand to his lips and watched the surprise in her eyes. "And maybe you should not be too surprised, my lady. I just heard my cousin call you Kate. I have heard a lot about you, but perhaps not enough?" Marcello glanced at his cousin, Luca.

Luca couldn't believe how forward Marcello was behaving and he elbowed him hard when he made the comment. "We're ready to walk the property, my lady. Pay my cousin no mind and please, lead the way."

Kate observed the interplay between them. They were close and teased each other like brothers. But Luca's slip didn't go unnoticed. The less made of it the better.

"Right. So, come with me, please. I'd like to show you the property, where the warriors can roam, and how far, as well as areas that will be off-limits." She led them outdoors into the bright sunlight and walked past the staff quarters into the vast property behind the house.

"There are about 3,000 acres here, altogether. The property is fenced, as you can see, so all these open fields, all the way to the mountain range, belong to Shade. Feel free to do whatever you want here."

Marcello walked with her and Luca through the rolling green hills.

"And my lady, we can fight here? Practice with swords?"

"Of course. Our nearest neighbors are miles away. So, get as loud as you want. Well... maybe not as loud as you want, but loud. And all this land on the other side of the road, you can go there as well. The land here has been plowed and may be converted into vineyards, but that hasn't been decided yet. So, feel free."

Marcello took in the view of rolling pastures as far as the eye could see, with a mountain range in the background. "Master owns all this?"

She stopped walking to allow him time to survey the landscape. "Shade owns much more than this. Do you want to walk with me? It's a long walk."

"Yes, show me everything." Marcello turned to his cousin Luca. "Do you come out here on the property?" He saw Luca glance quickly at my lady before he answered him. *What's up with these two?*

Luca answered, "Yes, I run here, practice with guns or bows. Hunt."

Marcello laughed at his cousin. "You run? You know we can teleport, right cousin? No need for running?"

Luca laughed uncomfortably. "Yes, it is just, uh, exercise."

They had walked several miles. As they approached the wooded area that sat in the foothills of the mountains, Kate pointed out the perimeters of their property.

"Shade's property extends into the woods, but the mountains are part of the National Park, so you can enter them freely. But you understand, there may be mortals there. You need to be aware of that. You can't hunt them, or feed from them. You can't do anything that might draw attention to you... to us."

Marcello nodded. "*Si*, mortals... I will make sure the warriors understand."

Kate motioned for him to follow her as they continued walking. "There is a great mountain stream over here, it's on our property. I like it here because the water sounds so peaceful, but somehow, I don't think your warriors are interested in peaceful."

They both watched her as she walked across the stream, stepping carefully from rock to rock to keep her feet dry. Marcello and Luca just looked at each other and then leapt to the other side of the stream, getting there well before her, laughing as they landed.

"Unfair advantage," she shouted and laughed at them. As they walked through the wooded area, they suddenly came upon two does, and Kate stopped in her tracks. The memory of shooting the buck came back to her.

She spoke to Marcello, but she looked at Luca. "It's illegal to hunt here without a license, so no hunting please."

Marcello looked at his cousin. *Is she speaking to both of us?* Her words seemed to be for him, and yet, she looked at his cousin. Perhaps he was hunting without permission and it was a reprimand? There was something in her voice that sounded like a warning.

"*Si,* my lady. We have restrictions in our country as well, around hunting. The warriors will understand."

Kate motioned for them to follow as they continued in the direction of the mountains.

"This footpath leads into the mountains. When the path ends, you are no longer on Shade's property. You are on government land, but it's open to the people to enjoy. Do you understand? You can go there if you want, but you must be cautious. Mortals may be camping there, or hiking." Kate led them up the path and into the mountains.

As they climbed, the path got steeper, and eventually, ended. "All of this, everything beyond here, I would say use with caution."

Marcello nodded. "*Si,* I understand, my lady. But it looks like the warriors will have plenty of room to burn off steam. We should not have to leave the property."

"Let's walk back then, and I'll show you the vineyards. You'll need to steer clear of the vineyards, or Shade will kill all of us."

They turned and walked back down the footpath and back across the stream and into the open fields toward the main house. One good thing about all this training with Luca, she could walk for miles without getting winded. As they approached the vineyards, she pointed out the expanse of the fields, and the distinct look of the vines suspended on stakes and twine.

Kate swept her arm out across the expanse of the vineyards. "It takes years to establish these plants for the grapes to mature and reach the quality needed to produce wine, so please, make sure the warriors don't disturb these fields. Or he'll send you all back to Italy... myself included."

"*Si,* understood." Marcello stood and looked at the rows of grapes, extending all the way to the mountains. It made him proud to be a Medici warrior. To be a part of this master's coven who had so much power and wealth.

Kate watched him as he took in the view. It was breathtaking, and she got to see it every day. "Do you want to see where the wine is made?"

"*Si,* my lady. I have seen the vineyards from afar in Italy. The fields are everywhere in Tuscany. But I have never seen them make the wine."

Kate led them into the winery and the cool dark room that held the large oak barrels for fermenting. "After the grapes are harvested, they are sorted by hand, removing the grapes that are too ripe, and discarding any remaining leaves or twigs. Then they are crushed in these barrels with a large press, and Luciano decides how much yeast to add, and what kind. Then the wine is transferred to the large oak barrels and left to age and ferment into wine. The aging process varies, depending on the type of grape, but could be six months or three years. The workers here will take samples, test it, taste it, and then Luciano will decide when it is ready to be bottled."

They walked through the fermenting rooms and into the cellars. "While it is fermenting, the wine is stored here in the cellars. Once it is bottled, it is sent to distribution. I'm really a novice, I only understand the basics. Perhaps Shade can give you a more enlightened tour someday. Of course, the Midnight is produced here as well. At all his vineyards, actually, about half the production goes to Midnight, and the other half is wine produced for mortal consumption, so the vineyards don't draw undue attention. No one is allowed into the areas used to produce Midnight. The migrant workers aren't allowed inside either. Just Luciano, and a select group of vampire vintners. I haven't seen it."

Marcello knew Master owned vineyards in Italy, Greece and France, but he hadn't visited any of them. To see how large the property was and how vast the vineyards were left him speechless. And Luca had said he owned vineyards in California as well, even larger than the vineyards here. Marcello took pride in knowing he was a part of this, and this was only a small part of what he protected for Master.

"Thank you, my lady, for showing me this." He bowed his head to her.

"You're welcome, Marcello." Kate led them from the cellars back into the sunlight and headed back toward the main house. The two of them were walking a few steps behind her. She turned and looked at Marcello, his long, light brown locks streaked by the sun hung to his shoulders. His eyes were a brilliant blue and rimmed by long lashes.

"You don't fool me, you know. You've got trouble written all over you."

Luca laughed out loud as he heard her words, and he bumped against Marcello and thought to himself, *you have no idea how much trouble.*

34

The evening was coming quickly, and Shade rolled out of the house early. He decided to head over to the staff quarters to see what this group of warriors was up to, and make sure the group he was sending in was ripping to kick some ass tonight. As he walked in, he could hear a conversation going down. He recognized Marcello's voice, and all he heard on the other end was grunts. He peered around the corner, shadowing his presence and he should have known... Raven. His name suited him perfectly with his long, raven black hair. He was a hell of a warrior but one damn handful. And why was he not surprised he was hanging with the other wild card in this group?

He tuned into their conversation. He was their master, and with this mob, he needed to be one fucking step ahead of them. He heard Raven say he went to the feeders the night before. He was explaining to Marcello what it was like and Shade tried not to laugh.

Marcello was probing for answers. His long brown hair hung in waves to his shoulders, and his baby blues sparkled. His looks were always a hit with the ladies, mortal or immortal.

"Come on, Raven! What do you mean they aren't like our feeders? You fed, didn't you? Come on *fratello*, give up the details. I need to know what the hell to expect."

Raven walked in long strides around the room, his build more slender than the typical warrior, his black hair hanging straight to his waist and his dark brown eyes always looking like he was two seconds from bedlam. He shook his head and his long hair swayed.

"Bro, it is not like at home. Feeders here are more aggressive, like all the fuck over you the second you walk in. They loved my long hair. Bitch almost took out handfuls!"

Shade was holding his sides, trying not to roar with laughter. *Oh yeah boys, welcome to America. They like Italian boys with long hair and hard bodies.*

Marcello followed Raven with his eyes, as his nervous energy kept him on the move. "Sounds like you had a good time. You don't look worse for wear, so I assume you let them know Medici can take it hard?" Marcello punched Raven in the arm as he walked past him.

Raven stopped his pacing and faced Marcello. "Bro, at home, the feeders are trained to be subservient. They are so meek, quiet. They don't speak unless spoken to, they take commands, do as they are told, like a female is supposed to. But here, no way in fucking hell does that shit happen. They are aggressive and they take control from the start. Feeders at home know their place, know their duty, it's just different. I chose one I liked. They have their own places, like little bungalow houses at the compound. You go to their private living quarters. You know my preference is for men, but these feeders are hot. They talk to you, want to know about you and ask a lot of questions. I don't go to talk, I want to feed, fuck, and get the hell out. It's different!"

Marcello was rubbing his chin. "Sounds to me like this might be a good time. So, are you keeping the one you fed from?"

Raven shook his head. "Too soon to tell. And not all of them do that either. I asked her, and she told me some of the girls will do just one on one, but most just get assigned when you come in. So, I guess the next time I go, I can choose another just to experiment. And if master chose this place, it has to be okay. We can't hunt here, so we don't have a choice."

Marcello leaned forward. "Well, what do they taste like? Was it the same or different? I'm going tonight, so I need to know, Raven."

"Bro, the blood isn't the same. It has its own appeal, it definitely sets you on fire, but it is different from the European feeders. And ass? Hell, rocked my fucking saber just fine."

Shade had heard enough, it was time to bust up this little party. The warriors were learning, American feeders didn't take your shit. Unshadowing, he stepped around the corner and nodded. "Let's rock D.C. tonight, get your asses in gear. Round-up time, now!"

As he kept moving through the staff quarters, rounding up the other warriors, he chuckled, *Yeah, welcome to Virginia, boys!*

35

Max watched her every day. He had seen her with Alec at the restaurant they frequented, her daily trips to the gym, even her run in the Virginia countryside. He knew where she was even when Alec didn't. Alec had threatened her with a protector, so perhaps his plan to pull back the activity with his warriors would benefit her as well. Not to mention they were getting slaughtered out there. Alec was away, as usual, leaving Rissa unattended. Max would never leave her unattended. That was not a mistake he would make a second time.

He knew she remembered them together, she would come to him. He dialed her cell phone. It had been weeks since their last meeting, and he read her thoughts. He overheard their conversations. He knew she thought of him.

"Benneteau Beautiful, Larissa speaking."

"Beautiful, indeed, my angel. Am I in your thoughts today as much as you're in mine?"

She gasped and quickly looked about to see if anyone was near and could hear her. *Max? Damn, how did he get this number?* Her heart rushed and her mind was reeling. "What are you doing calling me?"

His voice was deep and seductive in her ear. "Aren't you glad to hear from me? I expected a warmer welcome than that, my angel. I call because I miss you, miss the sound of your voice soft against my ear, the feel of your skin against mine, the taste of your lips, do I need to go on? Don't tell me you don't remember us together."

His voice melted her, made her weep for his soft touch, how he always knew when to hold her, comfort her, his kisses deep and long. *No Rissa, no!* "I remember. We need to talk."

"Oh, my sweet angel, we need to do much more than talk. But I guess we have to start somewhere. Come to me. I think I have been patient long enough, don't you?"

Come to him? Don't even go there, Rissa. Alec will know, and if he senses Max, he will kill you dead! "Max, I can't meet you. I can't get anywhere near you. The last time Alec picked up your scent, so the phone will have to do." Biting her lip, she wished there was a way she could meet him.

"My angel, do you think I wasn't aware of what happened the last time we met? I thought I had protected you, and I'm sorry to say my efforts were not enough. That's why I've kept my distance from you for so long. But I know what I have to do now for us to meet in a way that won't put you at risk, and you know I would never knowingly put you at risk. You must trust me. Do you remember what it's like to lie beneath me? Feel my weight on you? Your legs wrapped around me as you cried out in ecstasy? I remember it, in searing detail, and it eats away at me."

"Max, please don't." Her heart beat so fast, she went weak. She had forgotten, she had made herself forget and she thought it was all behind her, but that night at the gala, and now his words, how they rolled through her. She felt herself wanting him. "He'll kill me, Max, he'll kill me. I can't!"

"Oh, my angel, do you think I would let that happen? He'll never harm you, not as long as I breathe. And I promise you, he'll not detect my scent on you this time. My body craves you. Please don't torture me further. Come to me."

Taking a shaking breath, she made a quick decision before she could change her mind. "Where?"

"I'm living in the condo down by the harbor in Georgetown, in the penthouse. I'll be waiting, my angel."

"Yes, give me forty minutes."

Hanging up, she sat down as her legs wouldn't hold her any longer. She must be losing her mind, but she couldn't resist, she needed to know. Was he Angel? Did he have this potion? And if so, where the hell was the potion kept? Wrapping things up quickly, she said her goodbyes to the staff she was leaving behind with tasks to complete for the spring benefit. She headed out to the G-town penthouse harbor side and wondered the whole way how the hell she was going to manage to hide this from Alec and keep Max at bay?

Arriving, she looked quickly for his parking area under the condo, found the space reserved for the penthouse and parked, sitting in the car for a moment, she took a few deep breaths. She knew she could do this, get what she needed and get the hell out of there. Taking the elevator from the garage to the top floor, she made sure no one saw her. Straightening her skirt, making sure her hair was in place, she reached to ring the bell.

Max heard the elevator doors open and her footsteps in the hall as she approached the door. When she rang the bell, he slowly opened it to her. "Rissie. My angel, I knew you would come. Look at you, as beautiful as I remember. Please, come in, have a seat on the sofa. I have some Midnight for you on the table. I've added a potion to it, my angel. Drink it down. I've already taken mine. Together, it will block our scent. That is where I failed you last time, I took the potion, but you didn't. Come, my angel, sit."

Max, her rugged sweet Max, his dark brown hair was down, and she loved it down, long, and lying in waves. His eyes were deep, dark and magical. He looked better than she remembered. He was the opposite of Alec in every regard. Alec was always polished, clean-shaven, his hair cut short. Max was rugged and careless about his looks. She looked at the couch, then the table with the Midnight. Was he referring to the potion used by the rogues?

"Max, a potion? It blocks the scent? Are you so sure?" She bit her lip, and tried to remain calm, but she couldn't take her eyes off of him.

"A potion, my angel, which blocks a vampire's scent. What I, unfortunately, didn't discover until you, is it doesn't block the scent from the beast. While I had taken the potion, you had not. So, drink it down"

He sat next to her on the couch, sliding his arms behind her on the back of the couch, placing his hand on her bare thigh. He leaned into her, his lips close to her ear. "And if you are thirsty for something more, my angel... you know you can always drink from me."

Her heart almost broke. She took the drink in one gulp as she felt his hand on her bare thigh, and it was like fire on her skin. He was nothing like Alec. Max was a warrior. "Max, please, I belong to Alec."

Quickly standing, she sat the glass on the table, her hand shaking as she turned to him. "He will know! Alec will know if I feed from you. He's no fool. And neither am I. And how do you know that your scent can be hidden from his beast?"

"My angel, please know when you went to him after the gala, and he beat your tender skin with a whip before mounting you and picking up my scent that I didn't realize the weakness of the potion."

He reached up and took her wrist, pulling her back down to the couch, where he slid one arm around her shoulder, and placed the other back on her bare skin, sliding it higher up her thigh, under the hem of her short skirt.

"I have tested it since then, the strength, the dosage, and discovered if both vampires use the potion, then their scent is blocked from the beast in us all. If you drink from me, he won't be able to taste me in your blood. That's how I know, my angel. And he won't kill me, nor you. That's not in my plans."

He lifted his hand from her shoulder and ran it through her golden hair as he looked into those blue eyes. She was afraid but tempted. He could smell her desire. He leaned in and kissed her softly on her face right in front of her ear and whispered, "My angel."

Rissa felt a flash of panic. He knew too much! He had been watching her like a hawk, and no one knew, not Alec, not Shade's warriors, because he was taking that damn potion. She was distracted by the feel of his hands on her, his body so close, too close. *Oh, Max, you don't know, he will kill me!*

Suddenly, her fear spiked high and her emotions boiled over and she couldn't think. She had to leave. He looked into her eyes and she couldn't look away. They were the deepest brown, and so intensely beautiful. They saw into her heart and he knew what she desired. If she asked, he would give it to her, he always did. Before she could think further, she felt his breath hot across her skin and his lips touched her face. His words were soft, calling her his angel, she moaned softly and closed her eyes, and leaned into him. She wanted to fight this, but she still yearned for him.

Her voice was barely a whisper, "Max. Please, I can't do this. I don't belong to you, I belong to Alec... he loves me, he takes care of me, protects me, and gives me everything I need. I lack nothing."

Max slid his lips down across her jaw and onto her neck where he licked her sweet skin and allowed her to feel his hot breath, before sliding his lips to her shoulder. "Oh, my angel, if only that were true. You lack much. You lack tenderness. Do you think I'm blind to how he treats you? I remember the feel of you beneath me, how your body moved with mine."

He slid his hand between her legs to find her panties were already soaked through, as he slipped his fingers under the delicate elastic and into her sweet sex. His mouth moved back to her neck where he nipped at her once more before covering her mouth with his and sliding his tongue into her mouth to tangle with her tongue, tasting her sweetness for the first time in years.

Rissa didn't resist and in seconds she had gone too far. She had taken a fatal leap from which she couldn't climb back. She ached to have someone hold her, touch her like this, with gentleness, need and want, not of power or pain. But she felt the incredible betrayal to her master ripping through her and feared she would never be able to hide this from him, no matter how much she blocked him. She feared Alec would feel this, and he would know. He would hunt her and kill her dead. She will have lost him. She raised her arm and pushed hard against Max and raced to the door. "No, Max! Please, I can't do this."

Max immediately teleported to the door, blocking her path, catching her as she ran headlong into his arms. Her face was stained with her blood tears, and he gently licked them away. "Oh angel, my sweet angel. I feel your anguish. I feel your fear. He can't hurt you now. He will never hurt you again. Let me remind you of what love feels like."

He gently lifted her in his arms and carried her to his bedroom, laying her on the bed.

She curled into him, torn between her fear and her desire. She convinced herself he could protect her. He could love her.

She raised her hand to his face and begged, "Max, please listen to me, just hold me, I want to talk to you. I am begging you, don't make me hurt anymore. I'm breaking inside."

He lay down beside her and pulled her close, as she snuggled into his chest. "I'm listening."

"If I belonged to you, if you had turned me, spent years to make me your own, it would be different. I'm his progeny, Max. He made me. He'll never forgive. This is my death sentence. Think of what you would do if I was yours and did this to you. Please don't tempt me further, just hold me."

"Of course, I'll hold you, my angel." He could feel her heartbeat against his chest. "But don't you understand. He'll never know of this. You don't need to fear him. You owe this to yourself. Do you want an eternity with him just because he's your maker? Or would you prefer an eternity with me, making your body scream with pleasure, not pain? You should be worshipped. He'll never give you that."

He slid his hand slowly down her back and onto the curve of her ass, pulling her hard against his hips, so she could feel the heat and steel of his cock, as he kissed her neck and watched her face respond with passion.

She heard her own moans and turned to him in his arms, gripping his hair and kissed him deep and strong. There was tenderness, but also an aching need of something she couldn't explain. He responded with deep longing and she felt it in her heart. How, in such a short time, could he make her want this, make her ache for him? She bit her lip and scrambled off the bed. "Max, I need to go, I can't do this. I can't make love with you, not now, please let me go!"

"My angel, I love you. I have always loved you. I didn't turn you and I'll forever have to carry the burden of that. I didn't think I would lose you. I won't force you. I want you in my bed, lying beneath me, with your legs wrapped around me and your hands tangled in my hair. I want to feel your body ride the rhythms of my own again. And I will, my angel. I'll take you there. We have time. We have plenty of time. If you need to go, if you need time, I understand. But we'll be together again."

She went to him so fast she didn't even know what propelled her and hugged him tight. "Max, let me go for now. I'm confused, I'm scared. I don't like being scared. I need to go. I can't think when you're so close to me."

Snuggling her face into his hair, smelling the musky scent of him, she almost changed her mind. He was giving her a choice. She let go of him and ran to the door, rushed out and teleported to her car. Her hands were shaking, her body weak with want, but she could handle that, she was used to that. *Control, get control!* Racing out of the garage, she drove away, and his voice reached to her.

"You're safe, my angel, I watch over you always. I am your protector. You will need no other. And we have time. We have an eternity of time."

Rissa drove straight to the gym. It was still early, and Alec would think nothing of her being there. She was still scared. Did this damn potion work? Would Alec smell him? Would he know her fear? Things were so confused. She worked out for two hours, hard, letting it all go.

Going to the showers, she scrubbed her body raw, doing all she could to remove any signs of him from her skin. Driving home, she saw Alec's car in the drive and knew he was home. Rissa drove around the block twice, trying to calm herself before she finally pulled into the driveway. *This is it, Rissa, let go of the blocking, be calm, act as if nothing has happened.*

Walking into the house, she went straight to their bedroom and began her normal routine of putting her soiled gym clothes in the laundry and changing into something relaxing.

Alec was working in the study when he heard her come in and immediately headed up the stairs. "Darling, why don't you join me once you change?" He called to her.

Rissa felt a moment of panic. *Oh hell, he knows!* But his voice sounded normal, no hint of anger. "Be right down, Alec, let me get changed."

Scurrying quickly to change, she didn't want to anger him. She went downstairs and found him in the study. "How was your day, Alec?"

He poured a glass of Midnight for both of them, handing one filled glass to her. "The kind of day that makes me want a drink, my darling. Arguing with mortals is so much more difficult than just killing them." He took a large gulp from his own glass before sitting down and patting the sofa for her to sit next to him. "You know, I think it was easier gaining power over other vampires than trying to gain power over the mortals. The game playing wears thin, my darling. It wears very thin." He lit a cigarette and inhaled deeply before passing it to her.

Rissa was trying to gauge his mood. He seemed fine, but exuded an air of weariness. Taking the glass of Midnight, she sipped it slowly, trying to act normal and sat next to him on the sofa, curling her feet up under her and sliding her hand along his cheek. "I have no doubts you can handle them." Taking the cigarette, she took two long drags and worked to keep her hands relaxed, her body relaxed, her voice normal. She handed the cigarette back to him. "I sometimes wish there was no such thing as mortals. But then again, I would have no entertainment if that were true."

Alec threw his head back against the sofa as he laughed. "My darling, how quickly you forget. If not for mortals, there would be no Rissa. No, I think we need mortals. They can just be more troublesome than I care to deal with, some days. But we'll achieve our goal, we always do."

Smiling wickedly at him, she laid her head on his shoulder. "Well, I think being called First Lady might be quite powerful. I can hear it now. President Canton has a most musical sound to it, don't you think?"

He took a deep drag from the cigarette. "Indeed it does, my darling, indeed it does."

Rissa relaxed. *Nothing, he smells nothing.* She couldn't believe it! She breathed easily for the first time since getting to the gym. "I think I'm going upstairs to rest." She snuggled into his neck, "Join me?"

"Go ahead, darling. I'll be up shortly. I still have some work to do here."

Rissa absorbed the disappointment. *Of course, you do, Alec, and I'll be asleep long before you get there. I'll fall asleep alone, as always.* Standing up, she leaned in and kissed him softly on the cheek. "Try not to let them get to you, after all, Alec, they're just mortals." Letting her hand slide down his arm, she walked to the study door and turned to him. "I love you, Alec. Good night."

Already preoccupied with the House bill that went to vote next week, his mind was elsewhere. "What, darling? Oh... yes, I love you too. Get some sleep."

* * *

Max had monitored her since she had left his place, stayed tuned into her. Felt her fear and anxiety as she approached Alec for the first time, and now felt her disappointment. **"You would not sleep alone, my angel, if you were in my bed."**

Rissa ignored his message to her, as she curled up on her side in the large bed she shared with Alec. She wept softly. The cold bed which never bothered her before seemed like a cavernous lonely pit to her.

Max felt her sorrow and her loneliness, and he wished he could pick her up and carry her back to his bed. He sent a light caress across her cheek. **"My angel."**

Moaning softly, Rissa felt the softest, most tender caress on her cheek. Max had no idea his torture was far worse than any Alec could bestow on her body. Hearing Alec's footsteps coming up the stairs, she quickly wiped her tears and settled into her pillow as if she were sleeping. **"No more, Max, Alec is coming... please, no more."**

36

Kate woke before him, heard the soft whir of the electronic blinds and knew he would awaken soon and return to the streets. He seemed less stressed with his own warriors here, and she had heard him tell Luca things were going better... whatever that meant. The warriors seemed to have settled into their own routines here as well. But sunset came too quickly, and he rose from the bed, donning leathers once more and leaving her to join them all in the bunker before he went back into the night.

Kate dressed and went to find Luca so they could begin whatever he had in store for her this evening. They had not spoken all the way back from the woods after killing the deer. And she had not brought it up, while she had walked with him and Marcello during their tour of the property. Killing the deer still weighed heavily on her, and she would tell him she wouldn't kill another animal again. She tapped at his door and he responded, leading her outside for their run.

As they started their loop, she finally said to him, "Luca, about the deer..."

Luca answered, "I know, Kate."

She responded apologetically, "I'm sorry, I know you don't understand it, but I just can't."

"I won't force you. And it's not my place to say, but I think master shields you too much from our world. There is much violence there."

She looked over at him as they ran. "There is violence in the mortal world too."

Luca smiled sadly at her. "It's not the same... not even close. And some of the violence you see in the mortal world is carried out by vampires."

She was taken aback by this admission. "Do you attack mortals, Luca?"

"No, not me. Not anyone from master's coven, unless a mortal presents as a direct threat to us. But there are other covens, which see mortals as nothing but easy prey. The coven our master fights against currently thinks nothing of killing mortals or turning them and leaving them on the streets."

"What do you mean? Just leaving them on the streets?"

"Kate, I've never turned a mortal, but every vampire is taught how, and what a huge responsibility it is. A maker must stay with the mortal through the turning, first to make sure they survive it, and then, once they are turned, to train them to survive in our world, how to hunt, to feed. I know how you feel about feeders, but they actually keep the vampire from feeding on the mortal population. They're not always available, and when there's no access to feeders, and a vamp is not mated, it's not uncommon to seek out mortals. Vampires seek to feed from them, not to kill them or turn them. Some vamps will find mortals who come very willingly... like..."

She looked at him. "Me? Like me?"

"Yes, like you. But vampires don't normally fall in love with the mortals they feed from. And usually, the feeding is exclusively one way. The vamp feeds from the mortal only. And the relationship is a temporary one. It's only when the vamp falls in love with the mortal, wants to mate with the mortal and they plan to eventually turn them that they allow the mortal to also feed from them. It helps to strengthen the mortal, bonds them to their maker, and prepares them for the turn. But the rogues... They hunt the mortal as prey, turn them, and don't allow them to feed from them, leave them on the streets. The mortal is then just a machine for killing and draining other mortals. That's what's happening in D.C. now, what master is fighting." Luca watched as her expression changed to that of horror.

Kate asked, "But... why don't I see this in the news? There is no report of it. If these turned mortals were just roaming the streets... and killing..."

"Because they aren't roaming the streets. Those rogues must be destroyed, and quickly, before they can be detected. The rogue vamps choose wisely, selecting the homeless, the addicts, and the displaced. The mortals that have lost their way and won't be missed, and not much energy invested in the investigation of their deaths when they're found... if they're found."

She creased her brow. "And Shade... does this?"

"Destroying the turned and abandoned rogues? Yes. But that's not his main target. He is after the rogues who created the problem in the first place. That kind of behavior risks exposing us all to the mortal world, and they must be eliminated."

"And do rogue vampires attack other vampires?"

"Absolutely. And that's where the skill of the warrior comes into play. It's a fight to the death, always."

She felt her blood run cold, and the color drained from her face. *Shade, in a fight to the death?* She thought of the mornings he came home covered in blood or injured. He shared nothing. She asked nothing.

Luca watched her expression change and her face went pale. "You understand, Kate, master is the best. He's the one the other master's seek when they need a strong defense. Master, and the warriors he trains, they have no equal in the vampire world. And that's why I train you. He is a target. He'll always be a target, as will every warrior he trains. Right now, you're mortal, and no threat to any vampire, but once you're turned, they will assume you have been trained by him, and you'll also be a threat, or at least perceived as one. And if you can't kill a deer, then how will you kill something that looks mortal to you?"

"But the deer meant me no harm, Luca. The deer was an innocent sacrifice. There is a difference. I mean, I pulled the trigger on Sabine."

Luca asked, "Did you hit her?"

She shrugged, "I have no idea. The kick of the shotgun knocked me down, and I think I closed my eyes and by the time I looked up, Shade was there... and, well, you saw what the room looked like afterward."

"My point, Kate, is you must look your opponent in the eye. You must pull the trigger, or swing the blade... you must take that life. That is where you have to go."

He watched her nod her head yes, but she didn't speak.

Kate's mind was in such turmoil with the information he shared. And yet, on some level, didn't she know this already? Her capacity for denial never ceased to amaze her. They were ending their run, completing their loop back to the house. She began her cool-down routine while Luca set up the weight bench, and then put her through her exercises.

"So, what do you have planned for tonight?"

Luca responded, "More work with the bow."

"No deer?"

"No. I won't push you there. Not until you're ready."

She stated defiantly, "I'll never be ready. That won't happen again, Luca, not ever. I think I would defend myself. I know I would defend myself, and those I love. But I'll not take another innocent life. Not again."

There was something in her tone, in the set of her jaw, that he knew she was speaking her truth. Luca brought out the bow and set up targets for her. Her aim was dead on in every shot. She couldn't split an arrow yet, but he was more than pleased with her progress. After about an hour with the bow, he interrupted her.

"Let's try something new. The shuriken's."

"The what?"

"The shur... the shiny star thingies?" Luca brought out the smaller star-shaped shurikens and set up a pumpkin for her as a target. He handed her a star and asked her to throw it. She threw overhand and watched as it came up short of the target, falling in an arch toward the ground.

Luca frowned. "You throw like a girl."

"Uh... in case you didn't notice, I am a girl."

He chuckled at her. "I noticed. But you're also warrior. Let's work on your throw."

He stood behind her and directed her how to use her arm as an extension of her arrow, or her blade, how to aim for her target, how to throw sidearm, use her wrist to add speed and spin on the shuriken. Within an hour, she was consistently hitting the target.

As Kate finally got the hang of it, she shouted, "I get it! It's like a Frisbee!"

Luca frowned. "Is that a weapon?"

"No... a toy... you throw at each other. And try to catch it, you know?"

"No, I don't know." *A Frisbee?* It was just another mortal thing that made no sense to him. Luca shook his head. *Catching a shuriken? Not a good idea.* He turned his attention back to her. "Good job, little warrior. I think we're done here for the night."

He gathered up the equipment and returned it to the house and she made her way upstairs to wait for master.

"Thanks, Luca!" she shouted back to him as she ran upstairs to change and wait for Shade. The sun would be coming up soon and he would be returning home, and Kate had a surprise for him today.

37

Outside the Dead House, the warriors were on the streets, the night was cold but crystal clear, a full moon beamed down and it was way too fucking quiet. The rogues weren't out as much as before, and their activity progressively tended to dwindle every night, making Shade nervous. The attacks had decelerated too quickly. If there was an objective, and there was always an objective, then why pull back your forces? A smart master would never do such, and this one was slick, whoever the fuck he was. Shade decided he should head in the vicinity of Alec's and make his nightly check. He walked back in the Dead House and strapped his sword to his back. Ready to teleport out, Marcello sent him something interesting and his mind was peaked.

"**Master, I got three live ones. They're walking northeast in quad six heading into seven. They're street level, and they're in one bad ass hurry to get there. I'm keeping my eye on them, tailing them from the rooftops.**"

Shade answered him, "**Good job Marcello, who is with you? I'm heading in to quad seven, street level, shadowed.**"

Marcello looked across the rooftop and stared at the sorry fucking excuse of a warrior he had been assigned as his partner tonight. What the fuck was his name? Will? Bill? One of Alec's clowns. "**I think it's Will or Bill, that one with the scar on his face. Not much help to me, master, get over here. I feel something, and it's not good. My instincts tell me they're up to something.**"

Shade laughed out loud. "**His name is Richard, but they call him Dick. I'm heading in, Marcello.**"

"**Sounds about right to me, master. He is one walking, talking dick, if I do say so myself.**"

He heard master laugh and looked across the rooftop and the dick was gone, but what he saw wasn't pretty, and it was show time! "**Master... fuck!**"

The rogue swooped down before he could think. Marcello drew his sword, the sword flashed, swinging through the night air and catching the light of the moon, reflecting it back into the night sky. Marcello leapt from rooftop to rooftop, he could hear the scuffle on the street below. It was a fucking setup, and they knew he was alone.

Shade had been laughing at his comment when he heard the change in the tone of Marcello's voice and knew he was in trouble. Swooping in on the rooftop, Shade had no difficulty finding them, the flashing of swords and the clanging of steel against steel was like music to his ears, and he could see it going down. Marcello had his hands full, and before Shade could tell him to keep it to the rooftops, Marcello dropped to the street and right into the middle of the shit pile waiting for him. Fucking bastards! **"Raven! Quad seven! Get your ass to seven now!"**

Marcello had been backed to the rooftop edge. This rogue knew his sword and even Marcello's skills were taking a beating, as he dropped to street level to bring his attacker down with him and landed right into the hell of hells. Six of them surrounded him and he held them at bay. One at a time, they tried to take him, but they couldn't get close.

One approached, tried to penetrate Marcello's defense, but Marcello swung his sword and nailed him straight through the head, retracting the sword as the rogue dropped. Before he could turn, another rogue attacked him from the back and Marcello spun fast and jabbed hard, staking him through the heart. *Fucking die! Dirty bastard!*

Pulling back his sword for the next kill, he felt the pain scream through his wrist as a booted foot slammed into it and his sword hurdled, in slow motion, through the air, flipping end over end, endlessly into the night. Keeping all his senses honed, he pulled the knife sheathed at his waist and reached for the rogue nearest him as they both fell to the ground wrestling and Marcello struck him across the throat and rolled away from the body, as he could sense another rogue ready to strike him down.

Shade saw Marcello's sword hurdle into the air, and knew he had lost his weapon. It was time to slice and dice these low life motherfuckers. *No one fucks with my boys!*

Shade watched as Marcello quickly made three kills, but the others had him surrounded. Shade felt Raven as he teleported in, landing next to him. Looking up, Shade nodded to him. **"Take the two at his feet, Raven, I got the other one."** Both Raven and Shade dropped street level and the rogues never knew what hit them.

Shade kept his eyes to the knife at Marcello's throat. **"Marcello, don't move!"**

Shade landed behind the rogue, slammed his sword into the rogue's back deep and hard as he heaved the rogue up in the air, skewered on the sword, and Marcello rolled away unharmed. Shade looked into the eyes of the dying rogue. Shade's eyes were ablaze and his fangs hung low as he snarled at him. "Fucking do not mess with Medici. You die by my sword, fucking scum!"

Twisting the sword as it protruded from the rogue's chest, Shade flung him off of it hard, hearing his body, as it slammed into the brick wall and crumbled lifelessly to the ground. Shade spun around to see Raven standing there casually, leaning on his sword.

Raven acted bored. "Took you long enough. Can we go home now, master?"

Shade looked at the two dead rogues at his feet, and then at that damn smirk on Raven's face and he burst out laughing. He couldn't get mad at his warriors. It had been a great night of kills.

"You smart ass little punk, get your ass back home, clean up your weapons and we'll be right behind you. Move it!"

Shade watched him teleport out, laughing his ass off as he twirled his blade over his head like a true Medici warrior.

Shade called in some of Alec's warriors and directed them to come clean up this mess and be quick about it. Sunrise was only an hour away. He looked for Marcello and couldn't find him. What the fucking hell? Shade turned and saw him strolling back toward him, Marcello had retrieved his sword. "How's the wrist? That had to hurt, warrior."

Marcello swirled his sword in his hand and winced as the pain streaked up his arm. "Fine, nothing I can't handle, not the first time and won't be the last with these backstabbing bastards. I am Medici."

Shade chuckled to himself. *Yeah, that fucking injury hurts all the way to the shoulder, warrior.* He slapped him on the back.

"Come on, time to fucking head home. Theresa will have some medicinal magic to take that ache away, just like back in Florence. By tomorrow night, you will be right as rain, but I still don't want you to come out. You missed your feeding, so go feed tomorrow and relax. Not a punishment Marcello, a reward. I want that sword arm ready to slice and dice next time we hit the streets."

As Marcello nodded, they teleported home and Shade's pride was bursting. Marco was doing a fucking slam up job with his warriors.

Teleporting back to the house, Shade grabbed Marcello before he could make his way to the staff quarters. "No way warrior, you need to come inside with me. You need some of Theresa's salve to rub that arm down. Come on."

Marcello nodded at him but looked like he wasn't so sure. They both looked the worse for wear.

Shade chuckled and walked into Luca's suite, "*Bel rosso*! Your warrior is home. Come, *mi amore*!" He sent Theresa a message that he needed her salve, and to please bring it to Luca's suite.

Kate heard him call her from the bedroom to come join him. She had tried to stay upstairs when the warriors were coming and going, as he had requested. But she headed down the stairs to find both he and Marcello in leathers, dirt and blood. Marcello looked injured, and everything Luca talked about came rushing back to her about fighting to the death.

"Lover, are you okay? Is Marcello okay?"

Shade smiled at her. "Your warrior is fine. No worries, *mi amore*."

Walking to her, he leaned in and kissed her softly. "I won't touch you, I am a bit of a mess, but I need your help. Marcello has a minor injury."

Theresa appeared, after rummaging through her assortment of jars, bottles and tubes, to find the salve in the dark brown jar. Looking at Marcello as he rubbed his wrist, she handed the salve to her master. "Should I stay?"

"We have it from here, thank you." Theresa nodded as she left the room, and he turned his attention to Marcello, directing him to Luca's shower, telling him to clean up. Shade heard Luca and Marcello talking and laughing and he knew Marcello would be fine. He would be sore and achy until the salve worked its magic. Medici warriors healed quickly. Shade shrugged off his own leather duster, kicked off his boots, and poured a huge glass of Midnight, gulped it down and poured one for Marcello for when he got out of the shower.

He turned back to *bel*, who was watching wide-eyed. Holding out his arms for her, he caught her as she glided into them, a perfect fit. Leaning down, he squeezed her tight.

"See, I am fine, *mi amore*. I will make sure Marcello gets the salve. This is nothing he can't manage, just a muscle strain. It is his sword arm, and I want it healed."

Still holding the jar, he led *bel* to the living room while Marcello was in the shower. He got the fire going in the fireplace just as Marcello walked in wearing a pair of Luca's lounging pants. His hair was still wet but at least he looked better. "Come in Marcello, sit down." Shade handed him the glass of Midnight. "Drink it, all of it. And if you need more, help yourself."

Marcello downed the wine, and then reached for the jar of salve that Shade held out to him, but he struggled with the jar top. Twisting the top clearly caused him pain.

Kate noticed his struggle. "Marcello, let me help you."

She moved to him and opened the jar, dipping her fingers into the foul-smelling salve. She could feel a tingling sensation in her hand already from the exposure to the salve. She took his arm and started to massage the thick substance into the muscles, starting from wrist to shoulder.

Shade smiled at *bel* as her mothering instincts kicked in. He fucking loved this woman. Leaning down, he kissed the top of her head. "Easy, *mi amore*, he has much pain, and the hard head won't tell you such. I am going to shower and change, I will return shortly."

Marcello gave Shade a disgruntled and shocked look.

"Yeah that's right, warrior, I am leaving you alone with my mate."

Taking the second glass of Midnight, Marcello drained it in one gulp. He had used too much energy and not fed, but the Midnight took the edge off and eased the pain. Flexing his arm, he could feel it stiffen and tighten. Fuck! He hated looking like a damn weakling in front of my lady.

"My lady, I can do this on my own, or the other warriors can attend to this. Please, I am most honored, but this is not your place."

Kate sensed his discomfort as he tried to dissuade her from helping him. "Marcello, it is exactly my place. You're Shade's warrior, and you're living in our home. We're all family here. Tell me what you need. Where is the pain? Am I applying too much pressure? Or not enough? You're like Shade, I have to drag every word out of you."

Marcello tried not to laugh, but she was correct. He could only imagine her trying to persuade the master to give her details on anything. "My lady, you're not hurting me. I got kicked in the wrist, but I can manage from here."

Kate massaged more deeply into the tissue of his biceps. "I can manage from here as well, Marcello."

Returning downstairs, Shade could hear Marcello talking to *bel* and felt how ill at ease he was. Shade's jeans hung low on his hips. He wore a loose V-neck sweater over his chest and his feet were bare. He felt better after a quick shower and a change of clothes. It was a great damn night of kills, and he loved when he could get out there and see some action. He watched for a moment more, as *bel* tended to Marcello. He wasn't used to women attending to him, at least not anyone of her status.

Feeders and house staff usually attended to the warriors at home, but most times, they tended to each other.

"Relax Marcello, *bel* likes taking care of me, and she likes taking care of those I love, so that includes you. I am not going to lop your head off. If I didn't trust you, I wouldn't have left you here alone with her. I can smell that salve working. I forgot how bad it smelled. Get your ass to your slumber, take a bottle of Midnight with you and tomorrow... you feed. Go!"

Watching him thank Kate, he grabbed the salve and the Midnight, and headed out the door.

"Damn *bel*, now you smell like hell!"

Kate held her hands out away from her body, "Oh my god... what's in this stuff? It smells like something died! Let me go wash my hands first, and then I have a surprise for you. Quick before the sun is up."

He laughed at the look on her face, as she described the smell of the salve. "Best you don't know what's in it, *mi amore.*"

She ran to the powder room and washed her hands with soap several times before she could remove the salve and the smell, then returned to him. She eyed him from head to toe, standing there in those jeans, hanging low on his hips, and his bare feet. She was tempted to forgo the surprise and take him straight to the bedroom. "Ready for the surprise?"

Shade watched her as she took him in, reading her thoughts and winking at her. "A surprise? Does this include rooms of furniture? Because seriously, *mi amore*, I don't intend to spend what time I have left with you tonight looking at rooms of furniture unless they are filled with beds."

Grabbing his hands and laughing as she led him outside. "No rooms. Outside, please. I have been watching the warriors, how restless they are, cramped in the bunk rooms inside the staff quarters. And I remembered, in Florence, how big that training field was. I took Marcello out yesterday to show him the property, where the warriors could roam, but I told you I had some other ideas as well."

She led him outside to the staff quarters and around behind the structure.

"You have opened Pandora's Box, *mi amore*, showing them where to roam. If they get out of control, I am making you reel them in. Where in the hell are you taking me?"

She led him behind the staff quarters onto the open patio.

"Well, don't underestimate my ability to reel them in. They all seem quite timid when they're around me. Look... they always seem to want to drink when they return, and they all like being together, so I set up this area outside on the patio for them to sit. A long table, with lots of chairs, and I hung lights in the trees. The rest of the staff can use it as well, Gi, and the others, when the warriors aren't here."

"Whoa, *mi amore!* Look at this. Did you do this on your own?" His eyes scanned the table and chairs, and the lights strung overtop. "You will spoil them, *bel*, thank you."

"Come with me. I think they will like this even better. It's another place for them to sit if they are here at night... a fire pit. What do you think?"

She had had builders create a stone and concrete fire pit that was in an open field, and then leveled the ground and laid a gravel surface around the pit, and surrounded the fire pit with heavy Adirondack chairs.

"Damn! Look at that! They are going to love this, *mi amore.* Now that will push me to get those dirt bikes for them." Picking her up, he spun her around in his arms and kissed her face. "*Grazie, mi amore, grazie!* You do so much for me, for my family, my warriors. What can I do for you, anything you wish, it is yours."

"Anything I wish, lover?"

"*Si!*"

"Then take me back to our room and let me peel those jeans off you."

Throwing his head back with laughter, he pulled her into him and her legs wrapped around his waist and he snuggled into her hair.

"*Si, mi amore*, you do not have to ask me twice... done!" Teleporting into the bedroom, he laid her on the bed and leaned over top of her. "Now what were you saying about peeling?"

"Oh, in a playful mood this morning, are we?" She slid her hands slowly up his thighs, over the tight fabric of his jeans until they met at his crotch. She slid one hand between his legs where she cupped his balls, as the other hand reached to undo the snap and pull at his zipper. She could already see the increasing outline of his cock, as it stretched against the denim. "I'm good at peeling, lover, one of my many talents."

He moaned, shaking his mane as he pulled his sweater over his head, flinging it across the room. "*Si,* you have many talents, show them all to me, *mi amore.*"

Kate sat upright between his legs as he stood spread leg before her and slid her hand along the outline of his cock trapped inside those jeans, feeling his heat through the fabric, before covering his cock with her mouth. She slowly lowered the zipper–commando, as always–and peeled back both sides of the jeans then slid them down his hips, freeing his erection from that cage. She ran her tongue from the base of his cock to the head, before circling the tip, then sliding the head of his manhood into her mouth.

For Shade, watching her was erotic foreplay, her lips making love to his cock, tempting him, as she took him deeper into her throat. He slid his hands through her crimson locks, he massaged her head before gripping the silky red into his fists. His hips gyrated forward to push his penis further into her mouth, and he moaned with deep pleasure. "*Cazzo, mi amore*, your mouth, so hot, so soft. Please, *mi amore*, more..."

"Oh, lover, I will give you more." She pulled her lips from his erection long enough to drag him down on the bed beside her, and watched as he slid his jeans off and kicked them free. She started to remove her blouse and he hastily started helping with the buttons. They both laughed at their own eagerness.

She slid her own jeans over her hips, and he pulled at them until they were free and tossed them to the floor. She felt his teeth at the string of her panties as he removed them with a bite. He grabbed at her bra and with one quick snap of his wrist, the fabric tore away, and they both lay nude, in each other's arms, skin on skin, as his lips came down hard on hers.

He kissed her hard, pushing his tongue deep into her throat where his cock had just been. He broke the kiss and nipped her chin, nipped her neck, and slid his stubbled face over her already erect nipples, teasing them more. Letting his tongue circle one nipple, he pinched and pulled the other, playing her like a fine instrument, and felt her body respond, her hips moving, and her moans calling to his beast. She wanted more, and they needed no words. He suckled the taut nipple before moving to the other and buried his face in those glorious soft orbs. She had no idea how he craved her softness. Growling, his hand slid down her curvaceous body, and lay on her hip. *Fuck, she is so beautiful.* He slid his hand over the curve of her ass, then found his way to that patch of soft curls between her legs. He slid two fingers inside her. She was so wet for him, always needing him as much as he needed her. "*Mi amore*, I need to fuck you, deep, hard, feel you surround my cock."

With her lips against his, she begged him, "Fuck me, lover, please, fuck me hard."

She knew what he wanted, she always knew, and he wasted no time satisfying their needs. Sliding his hands under her head, he cradled it and felt her hips lift, as he slid between her legs, letting his rocket tease her sweet jewel. He shifted his hands to her hips and lifted her up slightly and she moved to accommodate him, like instinct, and wrapped her legs around his waist. He slid his cock in hard, in one stroke, looking deep into her eyes. He licked his lips, then hers. Sliding his hands under her back, he cradled that sweet ass and started thrusting into her slowly, watching as she threw back that beautiful head of crimson, spread across the white sheets and he started slamming into her harder and harder. She whipped her head up and gripped handfuls of his hair, and he turned his neck to expose to her what she needed, his blood, her life. "Drink, *mi amore*, drink and cum for your savage lover. Let me make you cum when you take of me."

Kate matched his rhythm, lifting her hips to meet him, taking all of him. She felt his weight on her, and his hands beneath her, pulling her against him so they molded together into one. She had begged him to fuck her hard, and he was giving her what she asked for. He was pushing her to the edge when he exposed his neck and asked her to drink. She nuzzled her face into his neck and bit hard, feeling that jolt of electric current hit her body as his blood ran across her tongue, followed by the explosion of heat between her legs that pushed her hips hard into him, and right over that cliff into the free-fall of an orgasm that rode over her in wave after wave, with each swallow of his blood as it trickled down her throat.

He felt his own release he had been holding back and let go, as he growled so loudly the bed rumbled beneath them. He released his grip on her and felt her body relax as he slid down her figure, leaving a hot, wet trail with his tongue, circling her belly button, burying his face into that now soaked patch of curls, he moaned and growled. **"Far from done, *mi amore*."**

Her body felt like it was in a free-fall back to earth after spiraling out of control, and she was trying to catch her breath when she felt his tongue burning a path between her breasts, across her belly and between her legs.

Nuzzling his nose down further, he sucked hard on her clit, curling his tongue inside her and feeling her squirm, her body still tingling from the last orgasm. His tongue circled her clit, teasing and playing and hearing her scream his name, that's all he needed. His tongue explored deep inside her once more, then withdrew and quickly moved to the inside of her thigh and sank his fangs deep into her tender white flesh and drank as she came again.

Her back was arched, legs locked around his shoulders, one hand gripping the sheets and one hand gripping his hair, before collapsing, their bodies both covered in sweat, gasping for breath, listening to their pounding hearts.

He laid his head on her thigh, catching his breath. *Cazzo*, she was all he had ever wanted or needed. "*Mi amore*, I love you." Rolling over, he moved back up beside her and pulled her into his arms, across his chest as his hands rubbed her back. He kissed the top of her head. She was like a rag doll and he smiled. "I think we both will have no trouble slumbering this day, *si?*"

She heard him speaking but his words didn't register in her brain. All she could think was, *Is it possible to be fucked stupid?*

Chuckling softly, he closed his eyes. "No, *mi amore*, not stupid, sated. Sleep, my minx. I am here, surrounding and protecting you."

Drifting off, he felt her even rhythm of breathing, soft and warm across his chest, and nothing in this world felt more real to him than this moment.

38

Luca paced in his suite. Master wanted to meet Shannon before he made his final decision, and Kate had suggested they all go out together on the bikes. At least it would not be the four of them sitting in a room while master interrogated her. Luca was sure he would never see her again after that. Not to mention, trying to explain to her why his 'employer' was putting her through the wringer. Kate said to call her and set it up for this weekend, and to not leave it until the last minute because Shannon would think it was a 'booty call'. When he asked her what that meant, she laughed and said, "Call early." Learning to navigate this world of mortals seemed loaded with minefields. No wonder they relied on feeders. As he picked up his cell phone, his palms were already sweating again, and he dialed her number.

Shannon heard the familiar sound and pulled the buzzing phone from her jeans pocket and saw the number... Him! Her heart skipped a beat and she took a deep breath as she answered, "Hello, Luca."

"*Ciao, mia bellazza*. You said I could call again for a date. Well, this is that call. Are you still interested?"

"Of course, I'm still interested. I was getting worried. It's been a few days since I heard from you. I thought maybe you'd changed your mind."

"No, I think of you often, but as I explained, my schedule is not my own. If you are free this Saturday evening, we were planning to take the bikes out... mas, uh, Shade and me. And we thought you and Kate would like to ride along? Kate suggested we go into Charlottesville, walk the mall and listen to the band. How does that sound to you?"

"Wow... that's... that sounds great. Bikes? I mean, like what kind of bike are we talking about?"

"Uh, Harley's probably."

"Probably? You don't know what we'll be riding?"

Luca laughed. "Well, there are many to choose from, but Shade will probably want the Harley's."

"Well, yes! My answer is yes, Luca. I would love to go out with you. So, I'll see you Saturday?"

"Saturday, *mia bellazza*. *Fino ad allora*." He ended the call and dropped the phone back onto the table. Done. He took a deep breath. No turning back.

Shannon looked at the phone as she ran his last words through her head. *Fino ad allora*. She immediately entered the phrase into Google to translate, 'until then.' She sighed and wore a smile that covered her face.

39

Max had been counting the days since Rissa was here. It had been three days. He knew she was torn, but most of her resistance was from fear. Fear of what Alec would do if he found out. By now, she knew that with both of them taking the potion, Max's scent was not detectable, and she was safe to come back. He had watched her every day, and she knew he was watching. It was time. He picked up the cell and called her.

Hearing her cell buzz she grabbed her phone, saw it was Max and her heart skipped a beat. "Max."

"Free schedule, my angel?"

She almost laughed, he paid more attention to what the hell she did than Alec. "You knew that before you called, you have eyes everywhere, do you not, Max?"

"Only for you, my angel. I know everything about you."

She sighed. "You know too much. I was just heading to the gym. What are you calling about?"

Max smiled to himself. "The gym? Oh, I think not, my angel. Come see me. If it's exercise you need, I have an activity in mind that is guaranteed to get your heart racing."

She laughed out loud. "I'm sure you do! I don't have... do you have more potion? I can't..." She sounded like an idiot blabbering in incomplete sentences. *Get it together, Rissa!* "Just for a little while, Max. I could use a break, and a drink, but only if you have the potion."

"Of course, my angel. I would never risk seeing you without the potion. Yes, come for a drink, or two. And you let me worry about the potion."

Biting her lip she said, "I'm not driving, Max, I'm teleporting. It's easier and not such a risk. I'm leaving the car at the gym. If anyone sees my car there, they won't think twice about it." Hanging up, she added a few touches to her make-up and headed to the gym, going to the private underground parking. She looked around, locked the car and teleported to Max's penthouse. She landed outside his door and watched as the door was flung open and she smiled. "Max."

"Well, my angel, what a pleasant surprise. Your speedy arrival didn't allow me time to dress. But that will just save us a few steps. Come in, Rissie. I have the Midnight waiting for you on the table."

She checked him out from his toes to the top of his head. He was bare-chested, muscled and those damn jeans, hanging low on his hips, delectable. Walking past him, she went to the table and picked up the decanter and filled the glass to the very brim and drank it down, feeling safe.

Max followed her. She wasn't so timid this time. No fear. Good. He sat next to her on the couch, turned slightly toward her. His knee touched her leg as his arm slid behind her, his fingers playing in her hair.

"Yes, my angel. You're safe." He leaned his forehead against the side of her face, nuzzled his nose to her ear, and let her feel his breath against her skin. "Drink up. You're always safe with me."

She took another sip and tried to relax. Carefully setting the glass on the side table, she turned, and he was right there, his nose against her ear. She shivered as his facial hair tickled her face, something she wasn't used to with clean-shaven Alec. They were eye to eye, their lips almost touching, and she whispered softly. "It is you... you're Angel. You're the one."

Her eyes held him captive, and he could almost taste her lips, she was so close. He brushed the hair back from her face, then slid the backs of his fingers down her cheek, and under her chin. Lifting her face slightly to his, he placed a gentle kiss on her lips, followed by another, and another, the taste of the wine still on her tongue. "Are you asking me, Rissie? Or only stating the obvious? Yes. It is me. My warriors know me only as Angel. And I'm here for you."

She stayed perfectly still, and his kisses melted her. She couldn't breathe. She suspected it all along, but she needed to hear him say it. He had come for her. He would take her away from Alec, he would protect her, love her, and all of this was for her. "For me, Max? All this hell you have brought down on the city is for me? I know you say you love me."

"It's all for you, my angel. I could care less about a power grab from the mortals. That's Alec's game. Is that the life you want? Living in constant hiding among mortals? Your every move examined and open for interpretation? Do you have any idea of the kind of restraints he will keep you under as First Lady? Oh yes, I know his intention. I know what his goal is. Nothing will interfere with his plans, my angel. And that includes you. You have a role to play. He needs to appear as a mortal man, with a mortal wife, and he has chosen you to play that role. That is all you are to him, and never forget it. I want you as my mate, and you will not have to hide it. You will not have to pretend to be something you are not. You will live as a vampire, among vampires, and be recognized as my mate."

He kissed her lips again, before sliding his hand to the back of her head and shifting his lips to her neck where he nipped at her, licked and sucked at the soft skin, and watched as the goose-bumps appeared and he felt the shiver run through her body.

Rissa processes his words. *Would Alec really do that to* me? *Use me? No! Alec loves me... in his own way.* But here she sat, betraying him with another master. She told herself she was doing this for Alec, getting the potion for Alec. Feeling his nip at her neck, her body shivered, responding to her need for attention. Her hand slid up behind his head and grasped that beautiful mane of hair, those long soft brown locks. Somewhere deep inside of her, the craving couldn't be denied and the sound that erupted from her was half moan, half whisper, "Max."

He felt her conflict, but he also felt her desire. She was his. He would make her his. He slid his hand down the front of her blouse, letting the backs of his fingers brush against her breasts lightly, and he felt her nipples respond to the touch. He covered her mouth with his and he kissed her slowly, deeply, letting their tongues play. His hand drifted to her hips, where he grabbed her tightly, squeezing, then releasing and letting his hand drift to her thighs, where he slid his hands along that firm, smooth skin, upward, under the hem of her skirt and stopping short of her panties.

She slid her hand across his tight muscled abdomen, and ran her fingers through his chest hair. Alec's chest was smooth. She snuggled into his neck, his smell musky and male. Sliding her tongue down the pulsing vein in his neck, her body rumbled in remembrance of his taste. She nipped hard at his neck, and a bead of blood pooled there. She ran her tongue over it and moaned, not able to stop herself as she committed the ultimate betrayal. His blood was like sheer fire to her veins.

"My angel." He slid his arm under the backs of her knees and around her shoulders and lifted her as he stood, carrying her to his bedroom. He set her on her feet at his bedside, where he ran both hands through her hair before sliding them down her neck and to the front of her blouse, where he unbuttoned each button, and pulled the blouse free from her waistband, sliding it over her shoulders and letting it drop to the floor.

He gently kissed each shoulder before he reached behind her to unbutton and unzip the skirt, and let it slide to the floor where she stepped out of it. "You are beautiful. This is like opening a present. A long wished for present."

He unhooked her bra and slid it off her shoulders to expose her beautiful breasts. He kissed each nipple, ran his tongue around them, sucked at them, and blew his breath across them before moving to her panties. He slid both hands down her side, and onto her hips, pushing her panties downward until they dropped to the floor, letting her step from them. He picked her up again and laid her gently on his bed and stepped back and looked at her. "My angel."

Rissa couldn't believe she was letting things go so far, but she - wanted and needed something beyond Alec. She could no longer resist him. She craved just once to have someone hold her like this. This was what she longed to feel; wanted, safe, loved. She remembered all the times they had been together like this, and she wanted it again, now, just this once, she promised herself. Sitting up, she slid her hands around his waist and pulled him to the edge of the bed, flinging her hair back as she stared up at him. "Max, I'm still afraid. I can't feed from you or you from me. There is no way Alec won't know."

Sliding her hands up his broad chest, she gripped his hair and pulled his face to hers and licked his lips, then kissed him hard and long. Her body aching and in need of release and the sweet gentle pleasures he could give her.

He unbuttoned his jeans and slid the zipper down, pushing them over his hips. As he did, her hands reached out and helped him push them down, where he stepped free. Her hands were on his black briefs, stroking, turning him to steel.

"My angel. I will drink from you and you from me, just like we used to. And I'll make you feel it all. You're safe, Rissie, he'll know nothing. I promise you, I'll never place you in harm's way. Now lay back on the bed."

He watched as she lay on her back, her hair pooled on the pillow, her skin smooth, her body toned. He slid off his briefs and set his cock free, as he watched her eyes move to take him in. He lay down on his side beside her. "Close your eyes, my angel, close your eyes and feel."

As she lay with her eyes closed, he took a feather in his hand, and ran it across her forehead and down her nose, where he watched her crinkle her nose slightly and he smiled at her. He continued the journey with the feather across her lips and watched as she gently parted them. He ran the feather down her neck, and between her breasts, and then to each nipple. He saw her back arch upwards and listened to the soft moan escape her lips. He let the feather travel down across her tight belly and gently brushed the feather across her sex and heard her whisper his name.

Her hand gripped his upper thigh and she squeezed, then slid her hand to his hardened cock and took him in her hand, hard and erect. She stroked him several times, his rod long and thick in her hand and she remembered how it glided deep and hard inside her, filling her full.

Max chuckled when she grabbed his cock and slid her hand along its shaft. He dropped the feather and slid his fingers between her legs, sliding easily between the moist petals of her sex and finding her clit, before slipping his fingers deep inside her, watching as her hips rose off the bed. His mouth sought out a nipple, and he sucked and bit it gently. He knew she was used to pain as a substitute for pleasure, but she would feel only pleasure from him. He moved to the other breast, as he slid his body on top of hers. He wanted her to feel the weight of him on top of her. He had watched as Alec mounted her from behind, denying her even the intimacy of full body contact. His mouth covered hers and he plunged his tongue deep into her throat. He slid his arm beneath her back and lifted her breasts into his chest, increasing the arch in her back. He felt her legs lift to wrap around his waist, but he slide his hands along the backs of her thighs, and pushed her knees to her shoulders, as he penetrated her, sliding his cock deep into her. **"You will feel me, angel, you will feel me in the deepest part of you."**

He thrust into her, moving slowly at first, giving her time to adjust her movements to his before he fucked her hard, pushing deep, pounding her, claiming her as his.

Rissa relished in the feel of his body on top of her, the weight and smell of him, able to see his face. She could feel the moment he went from making love to fucking, and she was well aware of the difference. It felt good to watch his face, his eyes closed and his hair hanging in his eyes, that shaggy mane swaying with his movements, his lips parted, and she was lost to him. "Yes, Max, your angel."

She bit into his chest and then his bicep and gripped his hair hard. Throwing her head back, she screamed as she tried to hold back the orgasm building inside.

He felt her body respond, arching, hips thrusting to meet his, and he could feel the tension in her body increase, as she was pushed to the edge of orgasm. Alec made her wait. Alec made her ask permission. But Max would take her there, he wouldn't make her beg and he never would. "Drink from me, my angel, now, as I drink from you."

He raised his face to her and bared his fangs, growled from deep in his chest before lowering his mouth to her neck and biting deep and hard, drawing her blood into his mouth. He felt her mouth seek out his neck and the sting of her fangs as they sank into him. The release of blood into his mouth released his beast. His growl deepened as his eyes glowed red and he felt his cock throbbing deep inside her, as he felt her sex tighten around him, pulling, pulsing. He heard her feral growl as she drank from him, raw and animal, hungry for what she was too frequently denied. Her body bucked beneath him, and her growl turned into a scream of pleasure long denied.

He fucked her harder, cumming inside her, letting his hot cum fill her, as she thrusts hard to receive every inch of him. He denied her nothing. He gave her everything. His growl rumbled through the room as he unlatched his jaw from her and threw his head back, feeling his own release into her, and watching her face contort with pleasure, mouth open, gasping, hands gripping his ass, nails piercing his skin as she pulled him deep inside of her. He rode her hard until the last wave of ecstasy washed over both of them, and then he collapsed on top of her, letting her legs drop down before pulling her to his chest. "My angel. My angel. You are mine."

She felt herself let go of something that had been held back for way too long, and she collapsed from the intense sweetness of everything at once. Her body shook as he held her, claiming her as his angel, and she didn't know how she would ever go home. Her arms wrapped around him tight and she cried into his shoulder, feeling vulnerable.

Max felt her tears flow, and he knew she was his. He held her to his chest, ran his hands through her hair and comforted her. "Shh, my angel. You are home."

She shook her head, her hair whipping across her face. "No, Max, no! I have to go home. I have to go back."

Scrambling from his bed, she was so torn. Stumbling, she gathered her clothes and the tears were still streaming.

He rose from the bed and stood before her, still naked and covered in the sweat of their passion. He would not stop her. He knew she would return to him. He saw her conflict, but he knew this woman. "My angel? So soon? There is so much more. So much more pleasure I need to share." He slid his arms around her, as she dressed hastily and licked away her tears. "Don't cry, my angel. It will all fall into place. I promise you. We'll get past all this confusion and you'll know in your heart what you need to do."

He released her to leave, or stay, the choice would be hers. It must be hers. She must come to him willingly.

She closed her eyes as his arms surrounded her, his beautiful soft lips and beard brushed across her face as he removed her tears. And then he let go. She turned to him, her heart ripping in two, her soul screaming and broken, torn between two mighty masters, both of whom she loved, and she realized she controlled their fate. It lay within her hands, one would die, and one would claim her, and it felt more than she could bear. "I'll return, but now, I have to think." Walking to him, she slid her hand across his face and whispered in his ear, "Thank you."

She teleported from his sight instantly and felt the world she once thought she knew crash around her with this life-altering decision she must make.

40

As the sun set, Kate felt him stir beside her as he awoke, stretched and slowly turned his face to her. She was already awake and watching him. He smiled and slid his arms around her, as she leaned her head against his chest.

"*Ti amo, mi amore*," he whispered.

"I love you more," she answered.

He got up and dressed in leathers, prepared to leave their bedroom, kissing her softly on the lips, and asking her once again to stay upstairs until the warriors left.

"Lover, you protect me from so much."

She waited until she heard him leave, with the warriors in tow, before dressing and going to find Luca. She tapped at his door to found him ready as always.

Luca led her outside and she started warming up without being told, then they began their nightly run.

"The warriors love the fire pit area, we'll need to be sure we steer clear of it during our run, or they'll see us. Since the activity in the streets has slowed down some, master has been rotating their shifts, so they're not on every night. I guarantee, if they're off, once they have been to the feeders, they'll be outside around the fire pit."

Luca modified the direction of their running loop to keep them further away from the staff quarters. Master would not question why he ran with her, he would expect that, but he must be careful they didn't observe him training her.

They ran in silence for a few minutes as she waited for him to give her an update on Shannon, but none was forthcoming. "Have you called Shannon?"

Luca looked over at her. "Now, how did I know that question would be coming?"

"Well... did you?"

"Yes, I called her. She sounded very excited to join us. And thank you for suggesting we all go out together. When master said he wanted to meet her... well... he can be intimidating."

She had to laugh at his observation. "Intimidating, that's an understatement."

Luca asked, "Did you find him intimidating? When you first met him?"

"Actually, I did. But I don't think I found him intimidating in the way you mean. I think I felt overwhelmed by him, like I was out of my league. Do you understand that phrase?"

She looked to see him nod his head yes.

"You know I met him through Rissa. I saw him at Alec and Rissa's parties several times soon after he had moved here from Florence, when he had just come here to do some work for Alec. At least, that is how Rissa explained it. Shade approached me several times, tried to start a conversation, but I would just come undone and make up some excuse to leave. I was intrigued by him, really fascinated by him, but I would get tongue-tied and make up some stupid excuse about having to leave. He started showing up at the places I went with my friends after work. He always left me flustered."

"And you knew he was vampire?"

"No, I didn't know at first. And then Rissa invited me to her Halloween party, the one she holds every year for her clients and I only occasionally attend, but I suspected he would be there. Rissa was trying to warn me off for some reason. She told me, 'You know he's a vampire, right?' I just looked at her like she had two heads and said I didn't believe in vampires. Then she laughed and said, 'Well you know I'm a vampire, right? And Alec. Alec turned me.' I really thought she was kidding, you know, just part of her Halloween party plans or something. I mean, I knew Rissa was mortal, we went to college together, and I knew she was mortal then... but now she was saying Alec turned her? It was just a little too Twilight Zone for me."

Luca creased his brow. "Twilight Zone?"

"Oh... an old TV show... weird science fiction stories. Anyway, we had seen each other a few times before Halloween, and I was starting to really feel attracted to him, and then Rissa told me the whole vamp thing. I said I wasn't buying it, and then she started telling me about feeders... and other stuff... that, you know, goes with feeding. She had already been telling me what a player he was, so I'm thinking, you know, maybe I needed to back off here. Why is she trying so hard to warn me off of this guy? I went to the party, and I was determined to ignore him, to sort of put an end to things, but well, he's a little hard to ignore. The party was really fun. They had great music, and everyone was in costume and dancing, I was drinking tequila shots, and the next thing you know, I was leaving the party with him."

"So, you knew then? That he was vampire?"

"No! Still no. I mean, he was dressed all in black leather... but I guess when I thought of a vampire I was thinking, black cape and white skin with fangs exposed, not some hot dark-skinned Italian guy dressed in tight leather pants."

He chuckled at her mortal image of a vampire. "A cape... really?"

"Yes, the cape... turning into a bat..."

She saw him throw his head back laughing.

"I know, right? So, we're at my condo, and he's telling me, you know, that he's a vampire and I was just blowing it off. But I kissed him, and he did the fang thing. I mean, I didn't know you guys could retract them. I just assumed if you have fangs they're always there. So, I kissed him and I could feel them with my tongue and I jumped off the sofa. I was totally freaked. I think I just paced around the room, while he talked to me. He told me Rissa and Alec were both vamps as well. I eventually sat back down. I don't know... curiosity? But I was drawn to him. I had always been drawn to him. And, what can I say?"

"So, Shannon... does she know yet?"

"No. I haven't told her. I mean, I haven't told any of my mortal friends or family. Shade needed me to keep it quiet, so he's not exposed, and well, seriously, who would believe me anyway? And with Shannon, at first, there was no need to divulge that. I mean, I never want to put Shade at risk, you know? But then you two, one look and just... wow! So, then all that started to happen, but you were insistent Shade had to make the decision, I thought, well, I can't tell her now! What if Shade says no?"

Luca looked to her. "Should I tell her? Before we go out?"

"I've been thinking about that. I mean, I'm not sure what Shade is looking for. He feels strongly about meeting her, and he has said he won't decide until then. I can't imagine he will say no, Luca. I just can't. But what if? So, I just keep thinking we should wait. Let Shannon spend time with you, and get to know you, and then you will both know if this is something you want to pursue. And then hear Shade's final decision. And if he says yes, and the two of you want to move forward together, then I would say that would be the time to tell her."

"How do you think she'll react?"

"Honestly, I have no idea. I mean, I have to tell you, this isn't a conversation mortals sit around having... 'So, you go out with a guy and then you find out he's a vampire, would you go on a second date?' I mean, Shannon is my wild child girlfriend. She's the friend who always got me into trouble, but this one... this is just so far out there, I really can't predict it."

He looked dejected. "So she could say no..."

"Well... yes, that is a possibility. But a risk I think is worth taking."

"But if she says no, and she tells others, then we are exposed."

Kate laughed. "Well, here's the beauty of that situation. Most mortals are like me, or like I used to be, in that we don't believe in vampires. So, if she says she went out with a vampire, they will think she's the crazy one. So, no, I don't worry about being exposed. But don't worry about that. Just have fun, be yourself, let her see you. If that happens, the vampire stuff doesn't matter."

"Will you tell her? If Shade approves, and she wants to see me again... Will you tell her? Maybe if she knows Shade is a vampire, and you are with him, then she won't be afraid to say yes."

She stopped running to look at him, and he stopped as well as they stood together on the wooded footpath. "Yes, if Shade says yes, and she's falling for you, then yes, I'll tell her."

As they stood there, they both heard a rustling in the underbrush and looked to the woods. She saw Luca pick up the scent, and then he said, "Coyote." They were standing downwind, so the animal had not picked up their scent as she saw it emerge from the brush into a clearing. The coyote sensed them at last and lifted his head and stared at her. She held his stare for a few minutes, and then started to walk toward him. She felt Luca grab her arm and he whispered, "Kate."

"It's all right," she answered and continued to move in the direction of the coyote. As she approached him, the coyote sat and waited for her. She knelt in front of him and he nuzzled her with his head. She rubbed between his ears and spoke softly to him, and then he turned and walked away, looking back at her before disappearing into the woods.

"Fuck!" He watched as she walked to the animal, to pet him like a dog so many mortals keep as pets. "What the fuck was that?"

She shrugged. "I have no idea."

"But Kate, why did you approach him?"

She looked at him, his face a question mark. "Luca, I have no idea. But... never mind."

"No. You don't pet a wild coyote and then say never mind. Finish the sentence."

"He... spoke to me. Not in words. It was telepathic, like the way Shade communicates with me sometimes. I don't know. I can't really explain it. He called to me, and I knew he wouldn't hurt me."

She shrugged her shoulders and they finished the run back to the house. His mind was racing. She had master's blood, but she had not yet been turned. There were very rare vampires who could communicate with animals... control them... call them to do their bidding. Luca had never met another vampire with this gift. It was only a story that had been shared as their history, passed down through the generations. But Kate was not yet vampire. And the vampires with those skills were born vampire, not turned. They were always masters of pure blood.

He remembered her shooting the deer, and talking about honoring his spirit, something about the Native Americans absorbing the spirit of the animals they killed and watching her mark her face with the deer's blood. Was it the combination? Was it the combination of master's blood and her ritual? If that was the case, if that was what he had witnessed, then she would have the rarest gift of all, Animalism... vamps who communicate with animals. If that was her gift and she was yet to be turned... fuck! The power she would have once she was turned. Master would be so... fuck! He couldn't tell master without letting him know he had been training her. *Fuck, Luca! What have you gotten yourself into?*

She ran back to the house with him in silence, his face in a frown as if deep in thought. As they reached the house, she started her cool-down routine, walking the yard to allow her heartbeat to resume its normal pace.

"So, what's next? The weight bench?"

The impact of what he had witnessed, of what she did not realize about herself, and what he couldn't share had his head in a spin. "What? Oh, weight bench, yes."

He assembled the bench and let her complete her exercises of free weights, push-ups, and sit-ups with the weight ball. He had been gradually increasing the weights, both the ones she lifted on the weight bench and the weight ball. She barely noticed the change anymore as he had increased the weight incrementally. He brought out the bow and let her practice. He knew she was ready to move to the crossbow. That had been her goal, her weapon of choice. He would start training her on that soon. She hit the bull's eye now consistently. Her motions were becoming automatic, remove the bow from the quiver, position it, draw back the string, feel the wind, calculate her aim, hold her breath, release the arrow between heartbeats and hit the target. Of course, the target was stationary, and it posed no threat. He had no way to test her skills under pressure. Could she perform the same? But then, that was his job, and Shade's, to make sure she never had to. "Enough training for tonight, little warrior. The sun will be up soon."

He watched her as she walked back into the house, and he was torn with what to do with the information in his head.

Kate headed back to their bedroom and took a quick shower, jumping into bed to read until Shade got there, but her eyes felt heavy. She set her book aside and thought she would take a short nap before he got home.

* * *

Shade teleported into the house. Gi was bringing Midnight up from the wine cellar. Gi looked at him and nodded, telling him the lady of the house was asleep in their room. Smiling wickedly, Shade loved waking her up. Quickly banging on Luca's door, he called out to Luca. "I know she's asleep, let me use your shower. I want to sneak into the bedroom and not wake her."

Luca nodded and returned to his easel, as Shade took a hot shower. Exiting the shower, slicking back his hair, he was still wet and naked when he teleported into their bedroom. He stopped dead in his tracks as he took in her beauty. Her crimson waves lay across the crisp white linens, her body soft and sweet. He reached out his hand to slide it along the elegant curve of her back, and over that sweet ass. Looking at her mouth, her lips were slightly parted.

Grinning, he grabbed one of the chairs and moved it beside the bed. He sat his naked ass down, lit up a smoke and stared at her. Propping his feet up on the mattress, he laid his head back and took a few drags from the cigarette, waiting for her to open her eyes.

She felt his presence, heard him moving a chair and then picked up the scent of his cigarette. He so rarely smoked inside. She pulled herself up from a deep sleep, groggy and confused, opening her eyes to see him sitting across from her, naked, skin and hair still damp from his shower, slowly inhaling on the cigarette, his cock already rigid and waiting. She smiled at him and reached out her hand, palm up as it lay on the bed. "Lover, finish that cigarette and come join me."

He watched her eyes flutter, feeling her struggle to wake, and he knew she could feel him near. He sat and watched as those big, beautiful, dark eyes opened and scanned him from head to toe. "*Si, mi amore*, all yours."

He saw that sleepy smile spread across those lips and his cock lurched. He could tell she was not yet fully awake, and that turned him on. As he put out the cigarette, her eyes closed once again. *Oh yes, my minx, you want to play that game, we can play it.*

Standing beside the bed, he slid his hands on either side of that gorgeous head and pulled her to the edge of the bed, as she laid on her back, allowing her head to hang over the edge, her hair hanging freely. He felt her moan and he wasn't sure she was moaning from waking or wanting and at that point, he didn't care. His beast saw what he was hungry for and Shade let him have her. Her back was arched, and her firm breasts displayed those sweet nipples, puckered tight and pleasing, pointed to the ceiling and his mouth watered. He felt his cock slide through that crimson and he moaned, the silky softness on his hard steeled, throbbing dick made him insane. He could cum hard in that hair right now. Grabbing his member in his hand, he slid it through her hair and along her cheek, back and forth. He lowered his head to her breasts and sucked her nipple into his mouth, swirling his tongue round and round that sweet bud.

She reached her hands over her head, and slid them along the backs of his thighs, gently raking his skin with her nails. "Lover, I never know what to expect with you."

Feeling her hands raking his skin, made his beast come alive and he was hungry. He loved his *bel*, sleepy, sexy and naked. Pulling hard on her nipple, he stretched it and then popped it out of his mouth. He knew it was a pleasurable pain, one that sent streaks of erotic pleasure straight to her sweet sex. Her back arched more from the absence of his warm mouth and her head nestled deeper into his crotch, her hair tangled around his cock and balls and his growl was loud and guttural.

Bending further over her body, he nuzzled into her soft mound of red curls and blew his hot breath across her clit. Gripping the inside of her thighs, he spread her wide and looked at the soft, moist, pink lips and slid the tip of his tongue along them, just barely touching them and feeling her body writhe. Sliding his thumbs to either side of the hooded gem, he pulled it wide and circled his tongue over that sweet bud, then sucked hard.

Her hips arched to meet him, as she slid her hands up his thighs and grabbed his ass as he moved his hips, thrusting his cock into her hair. She brought her hands around the front of his hips and gripped his cock, wrapping her hair around it and sliding that red silk up and down the steeled hard shaft.

He lifted his head and roared. His fangs elongated, and his eyes lit the room in a crimson red as bright as *bel*'s hair. He grazed his fangs along her thigh and slid his fingers into her sweet honey and thrust into her as she stroked him. He felt his balls tighten and he held on as long as he could, being pushed over the edge from his obsessive fantasy of fucking her hair, cumming hard into the crimson silk. That beautiful red mane that had called to his soul since the moment he laid eyes on her. He roared as he came into her hair, no longer able to hold back the beast, as he bellowed, "*Bel! Ti amo!*"

Removing his fingers from her sweet honey pot, he drove his tongue deep and sucked every single drop of her sweetness his tongue could find, sucking and probing like a hungry beast and feeling her body tense, ready to cum. Pulling his tongue from her, he nuzzled and sucked her clit and felt her wanting him inside her deep, but his beast wouldn't let her have that, teasing her, making her want more from him. "Cum!"

She released her hands from his cock and her tangled hair and slid them into his hair, gripping tightly as she held his mouth to her sex and thrusts her hips upward.

Feeling her body writhing for release, he sucked her clit and drove his fingers deep into her, and felt her body shake with release, his fingers soaked with the sweetest honey he had ever tasted. As her body relaxed, and the spasms of her orgasm faded, he didn't let her rest long as he slid his wet fingers into her mouth and watched as she sucked her own juices from them. He kisses her hard on the lips, plunging his tongue deep inside her mouth, savoring the taste of her honey from her own lips.

He stood upright by the bed, her head still hanging over the edge and her hair tangled and wet from his orgasm and she looks ravaged and sexy. "Roll over."

She rolled over onto her stomach, and he took two steps back as she reached out for him and he smiled wickedly. "Ah, no, sweet *bel*, I am not done."

Walking around to the other side of the bed, he grasped her ankles and slid her on her tummy to the edge of the bed and leaned over her back, his lips next to her ear.

"Stand on the floor, my beautiful minx, and bend over the bed. Tell me," nipping at her neck, he gripped a handful of her hair and turned her head to the side, "do you still love your beast?"

"I crave the beast. Please, lover."

Her voice fed the beast and he was out of control, Shade no longer reined him in. The beast loved her and would never harm her, and she returned that love, giving him what he needed. No other mortal could love him as she did, without fear, but unreservedly with her heart and soul. He stood upright, releasing her hair and slid his hands down her arms, grabbing her wrist and pulling them above her head, stretching out her beautiful back to the fullest, as he admired the curve of her spine, the narrow waist, her slender hips, and the delicious curve of her ass. He leaned forward and slid his cock between her beautiful chiseled ass cheeks and heard the moan of her want.

He stood upright as she remained bent over the bed, her hands stretched over her head, a goddess for his taking. Flipping her hair up over her head, he breathed heavy and hot on the back of her exposed neck and grazed his fangs slowly down her spine, letting them score her precious white skin, but not bringing forth blood.

His hands gripped her ass cheeks as he squeezed and released that soft yet firm flesh over and over. He dragged his face with his scruffy facial hair over her back, kissing the tracks made by his fangs. Squeezing her ass tight, he lifted her hips and watched her balance herself with her hands. His mouth sought out her sex once more, sucking at her, his tongue teasing her again, thrusting and flicking his tongue in and out. He moaned, letting her feel the vibrations of his desire through her body.

He pulled his mouth from her and thrust his cock hard into her, throwing back his head and roaring, his penis buried deep. He felt her muscles clench and grip him tight, taking every thick, hard inch of him inside her. Slapping her ass hard, he let his hand glide up her back and grip her hair like a bridle on a horse and wrapped that red around his hand.

He began a slow, deep penetrating thrust, pulling out, watching her sweet pink lips suck him right back in and he began to fuck her hard and deep, thrusting into her and feeling her respond, her hips bucking back into him, her head thrashing as she felt him deep inside her. Sliding his other hand under her, he fondled one of her breasts and squeezed it hard, pulling her up and nuzzling into her neck. He drove harder inside that ocean of sweetness, scorching his raging cock. "Cum for your beast, feel how much I want you, how much I need you!"

Sinking his fangs into her neck, he drew deep and erupted deep inside her, feeling their heat combine, as they went over the edge together.

They came together, and his primal growl echoed through the house. He felt her collapse over the bed, and he crawled in beside her, turning to her, pulling her close into his chest, and letting her catch her breath.

"I love you, Kate. I love you so much." He kissed her forehead softly, then her nose and finally, her mouth, as the beast retreated. "Do you need to feed, *mi amore*?"

"No, lover. Hold me close, sleep next to me, don't let go."

Wrapping her tight in his embrace, his legs entangled within hers, his arms holding her in safety, he felt her tuck her head under his chin and slip softly into sleep.

"I will always protect you, *mi amore*. Sleep. I am here for all eternity."

Closing his eyes, he felt the death slumber carry him to her.

41

Teleporting back from Max's to her car in the gym garage, Rissa just sat there, trying to compose herself. She stared into nothingness, feeling much more for Max than she wanted to acknowledge and knowing Alec could smell nothing, know nothing. Alec thought she had been to the gym. Besides that, Alec seemed to be off on his own successful endeavors at the moment. Although he had never been in the habit of touching base with her, lately, he seemed oblivious to much of her activity. As long as she appeared to keep to her normal routine, she thought she would be safe.

Pulling into the drive, she saw he was home. She took a deep breath. *Keep everything normal and light, Rissa. He won't have a suspicion.* How would she face him, and block all these feelings tearing her in half? She must continue to block all thoughts of Max once she got out of this car, and keep her wits about her. Walking into the house, it was quiet, and she listened and heard nothing. Biting her lip, she headed straight for the stairs, carrying her gym bag, wondering what he was up to.

Alec heard her come in and head for the stairs, another long session at the gym no doubt. He stepped out of the family room and called to her, "Rissa, could you join me, we need to talk."

She was halfway up the stairs. Closing her eyes, taking a deep breath, she turned around and jogged back down the stairs and to the family room. *Just relax Rissa, just relax.* Walking in, she smiled. "Hi. You're home early. Is everything all right, Alec?"

"Everything is fine, darling. Fix us a drink, will you? And come sit down, please. This discussion is long overdue."

Trying to second-guess him, she tried to figure out what could be on his mind. "Of course, Alec."

Walking over to pour the Midnight, she stood in front of the small bar, so he couldn't see her hands tremble as she fought to keep her thoughts guarded. She laid her hands flat on the marble surface to steady them. *Long overdue. What does that mean?* She controlled her heart rate, poured two Midnights, and turned around with a soft smile. "Long overdue? Please tell me this isn't about the protector, Alec." *Be careful Rissa. Be positive.* She handed him the glass and sat down across from him, taking a small sip of the Midnight before looking up at him with questioning eyes.

"The protector?" He chuckled to himself. "No, my darling, this isn't about the protector. You know I love you. I expect much and take a lot for granted and never see the need for conventional displays of affection. You know that about me."

Looking down at her glass, she ran her finger over the rim. "Yes, Alec, I know you love me in your own way." She looked up at him and those icy blue eyes, sharp and cold, always scheming and planning, not the warm intensity of love that beamed at her from Max.

He took a drink of the Midnight before proceeding, "Well, I think I may have an event planning job for you. That is, if you want it."

She looked away, thinking to herself, *Of course you do, something to benefit your climb to the top. Something to make you look incredible and the woman behind you will always help you get there*. She turned back to him as she answered, "I'm always open to helping you, Alec, in every way I can. Anyone I know?"

Alec chuckled. "Oh, I think you know her well."

Her curiosity was piqued and her heart raced, wondering what he was up to. "What's going on, Alec?"

"Can you plan a wedding, my darling, an extravagant wedding? Something the likes of which D.C. has never seen?"

Watching his face, hearing his chuckle, he seemed quite amused at her curiosity. She ran through her head the vast list of contacts, trying to recall any recent engagement announcements but could think of nothing. "Alec, I know I've been busy, but if someone of importance were getting married, and in need of such an elaborate event, I'd be the first person they'd call." She flipped her hair back and sat up straighter in her chair. "But of course, I can handle it, It's what I do best."

He sat his drink down as he walked to her. "Good, then I think you need to get busy planning our wedding."

He slipped the large 20-karat pear-shaped diamond ring out of his pocket and placed it on her hand. "I know marriage is not conventional for vampires, my darling, but we live in a mortal world and in a mortal world, you would not be my mate, but my wife. Can I assume you have no objections?"

As the words rolled from him, she couldn't believe what he was saying, marriage? A wedding? She knew her face showed her surprise, and her heart was screaming. *Isn't this what you wanted, Rissa? Isn't this how you wanted your vampire to be?* Her mind whirled as she recalled the afternoon spent in Max's arms, the kisses that burned her skin, the words he spoke, always loving, caring, and kind. She looked at the ring and its meaning felt empty to her. It was just a facade, an act he performed for the mortal world. *Oh Alec, why can't you understand how much I want this? I want this moment to be special.* "It's beautiful, Alec. I... a wedding... I'm sorry. I'm so taken off guard. I had no idea you wanted this. You never mentioned it, but of course, it's for the mortals. No objections, none."

She looked to him, praying to see something soft, something more than the cold blood that ran in his veins. *Please, Alec, give me something!*

"My darling, you're already my mate, and there's no greater show of love for a male to claim a female as his mate, in our world. But we straddle both worlds, and I'm afraid that explanation will never fly in an interview, now, will it? We are both asked constantly about our status, when will we marry? How do I tell them their conventional marriage doesn't compare to a vampire mating? Mortals divorce like it's nothing, their marriage vows mean nothing. But a mate? A mate is for all eternity, my darling. I've already committed that to you, so this pales in comparison, in my eyes. But you were a mortal girl once, maybe you see it differently? At any rate, I guess I'm asking in the most unconventional way, and trust me, in 750 years, these are words I've never uttered, but will you be my wife?"

He said all the right words, and she knew he loved her in his own way, and her blood tears streamed softly down her face, unable to stop the emotional roller coaster of this day. "I love you, Alec. Yes, yes, yes!"

He kissed away her blood tears. "My darling, I had no idea this would mean so much to you. Plan something impressive for us. You'll be on the front page of the society section of every newspaper in the U.S., so find that perfect dress."

"Alec! I won't let you down. This is for us... both of us. It'll be perfect, and this country and the world will know I'm yours."

Kissing him, she suddenly felt so alive, as though he truly had understood she needed him in so many different ways and she would never let him down. *No Rissa, don't think about him! Don't!* Then Max's words rang in her ears. Her mind was torn. This should be the happiest day in her life, and yet, she had doubts.

"I didn't mean to get so emotional, I'm sorry, but I had no idea this was going to happen, and I'm overwhelmed."

"Don't apologize, my darling. It pleases me to see you happy. And, of course, spare no expense. Make this the most extravagant and yet elegant event you have ever planned. It will be good for your business as well. Everyone will know Larissa Benneteau Canton before we're done. And you'll be America's Lady Di, and ready to become First Lady."

Smiling, she threw back her head and laughed, breaking the hell she felt inside and the mixed emotions that needed to be released. "Larissa Benneteau Canton, oh, I like the sound of that."

She wanted so much to reach out and dance with him, kiss him, but he would never respond to that type of affectionate display, and her heart fell at the thought.

"Do you wish to have your press agent handle this? We'll need a photo to be circulated with the announcement, one that we choose. You know how the Press is. They will publish a file photo."

Alec chuckled. "Planning already are we, Miss Benneteau? I'll leave all those details to you, my darling. Whatever you want will be fine."

She looked at him and saw the look on his face, and it had softened, his laugh told her he was happy. She kissed him on the lips and slid her hand along his clean-shaven face, so different from the last face she touched with such passion. She shook the image from her head before she whispered in his ear, "Whatever I want?"

He knew that look. She was up to something already. "Whatever you want, my darling."

"You know, sometimes you totally catch me off guard, and I would have thought by now, I could no longer be surprised by you. I think I rather like it."

She let her breath slide along his neck and her hand trailed down his collarbone and along his arm before she pulled back and turned to leave the room. "I think I need a hot bath, and some candlelight and music, but," turning, she held out her left hand and admired the rock on her finger, "I would be missing one vital thing."

Alec smiled his crooked smile, as if he didn't know where this was headed. "And what would that be, my darling?"

"Oh, I don't know, my fiancé, perhaps? The choice is yours. I know you have much to do." She headed from the family room, strolled upstairs and hoped he followed.

Taking the hint, he caught up with her on the stairs. "You know, I'm not much for baths, but if you're willing to compromise on a shower, I will join you."

"I'll make all the compromises you like, no candles, no music, no bath. Just my fiancé, under the steamy water, and whatever else might happen."

Giggling, she took off running up the stairs, stripping as she went, running shoes and sports clothes dropping to the floor behind her. He kicked off his dress shoes and socks as he followed her into the bathroom, laughing at her trail of discarded clothes.

As he reached the bathroom, she was already naked and had lit the room in red candles. Walking to the large semi-circular shower stall, she turned on the water and stood just outside, letting her hair down and shaking it out. Reaching out to him, she took his hand and pulled him to her. Sliding her hands up his starched dress shirt, she pulled against the fabric and watched the buttons pop and fall to the floor. She pushed the shirt off his broad shoulders and let her hands glide along his arms, removing the shirt as she went, letting it drop to the floor. She slipped her hands inside his dress slacks and unbuckled his belt and lowered the zipper. Pulling his slacks down, she knelt in front of him. He stepped out of the slacks, as she helped him, and he kicked them to the side. She ran her hand over the fabric of his briefs, outlining the shape of his hardened cock, before she stripped them down, and licked the throbbing head of his erection. "I love you, Alec."

She stood and took his hand, leading him into the shower where the water fell over both of them. She gently pushed him to sit down on the bench, as she knelt between his legs. Without using her hands, she slid her tongue over the head of his hardened cock and moaned from the sweet bead of semen that lay there. Swirling her tongue over the head, she sucked him slowly into her throat. Rolling her eyes up to his, she saw his beast on the edge, but still held at bay, and she knew this was a rare opportunity, where she led, and Alec followed, but it wouldn't last long.

Alec laid his head back against the shower wall and concentrated on the feel of her hot, wet mouth as he felt her tongue teasing the head of his hardened member. He reached down and slid his hands under her arms and lifted her upright in the shower, walking her backward until she was pressed against the wall. He slid his hands down her wet body, past her hips until he was cupping her ass, when he lifted her enough for his cock to penetrate her. He felt her slide her legs around his hips, as he pushed into her, pressing her hard against the wall, thrusting his penis into the depths of her. He watched her face contort in pleasure and listened to her moans as she gripped his back. **"Vanilla sex, my darling. Not really my thing."**

He slid his hands around her ass, supporting her weight with one hand while the other started to explore. The water cascaded over them, as he slid his hand between the crack in her ass and probed at that puckered opening, sliding his finger inside of her, followed by two, then three. He matched the thrusting of his fingers to the thrusts of his cock.

Her nails clawed at his back, and her fangs elongated. One hand gripped his wet hair, as she swirled her tongue over his fangs. She felt his roar vibrate through her.

He was lost in the pleasure her body brought, thrusting hard into her and pressed his lips to hers, their tongues probing and pushing at each other. He slammed her hard against the shower wall. He removed his fingers from her ass, so he could grip her harder, pushing his dick deep into her, filling her with his cum as the sound of his growl filled the house.

She felt him cum inside her, filling her and her body responded as she came in spasms around him, over and over, as she screamed his name. Tossing her head to the side, exposing her neck to him, she slid her hand down the back of his head and pulled him to her. "Take me, Alec."

It was an act he would normally punish her for, taking the lead, asking him to feed from her, but he would give her what she wanted this night. He sank his fangs deep into the soft skin of her neck and felt the rush of sexual power that came with her blood, causing his cock to continue to throb and release inside her, another wave of orgasm washing over him, as he slammed her against the wall.

Following the spasms of his orgasm, he stood still, catching his breath, as he leaned his body against her in the shower. He felt her legs relax and released her to the floor, as she held onto his shoulders. "Rissa." He picked her up in his arms and carried her to their bed, both of them wet and dripping. He laid her across their bed, crawling across the bed beside her, pulling her across him so she lay on his chest. "Feed, my darling."

She covered his neck in little feather light kisses until she sank her fangs into his flesh, drawing deep and moaning. His blood was heavy with power. Her hand slid up to his neck and to his strong jaw, laying there softly as she fed. Feeling full, his blood singing in her veins, she unlatched her fangs. Laying her head on his shoulder, she kissed him softly on the neck, licking at the wound. "You spoil me, Alec."

He pulled the blankets around them, wrapping them up from both sides in a cocoon, letting the blankets absorb the moisture from their skin. He wrapped his arms around her and felt her head on his shoulder. "Sleep now, baby girl. Daddy's got you."

42

Kate felt Shade wake shortly before sunset. He had so little time with her now. He was at the Dead House every night and returned home for his death slumber. She wished she could share with him what she was learning from Luca, but she knew he wanted to teach her those things himself, so she remained quiet about it. They shared a few minutes of cuddle time before he dressed and left to meet with his warriors. As soon as he was gone, she dressed to meet Luca.

Her body felt strong, and she found her mind didn't immediately wander to thoughts of their lost baby every time she had a quiet moment. She had wanted to train as an outlet for all these emotions, but clearly, Luca had another agenda. She never expected to be challenged with as much as he had thrown at her. Still, she had enjoyed it, and shed surprised herself with what she'd been able to accomplish.

She tapped on Luca's door and he responded right away, ready to go. They warmed up and began their run. She was thinking about the upcoming double date with Luca and Shannon, and how Shannon would react when she learned he was a vamp. Kate was so intrigued with Shade by the time she discovered the truth of what he was that it didn't matter to her. Rissa was the only other mortal girl she knew who fell in love with a vamp, but she'd never discussed how Rissa met Alec. Kate had no idea how Shannon would respond. "Luca, can I ask a personal question? Don't answer if you don't feel comfortable."

Luca wondered what was in her head already today. "Sure, ask whatever you want."

"So... you've said you go to a feeder, right?"

Wow, she is really stuck on this whole thing with the feeders. "Yes, I use the feeders."

"So, if this thing with Shannon goes well, if the two of you hit it off, would you feed from her instead?"

Luca was taken aback. "Wow."

She shook her head. "You don't have to answer that... I shouldn't have asked."

"No, I'll answer. I think the question is just premature. I mean, we haven't even gone out yet, so I don't know where this relationship will go with us, or even if she'll stick around once she discovers what I am. But to answer your question, if she doesn't run in the other direction when she discovers what I am, and if we find we have a connection and it feels like it might last a while, and if she's agreeable to me feeding from her, then yes. I mean, I've never been with a mortal girl, Kate. I've only been with feeders. They know what I'm there for, you know? So, in the beginning, I would still need the feeders. That bothers you, doesn't it?"

"Yeah, it does. I'm sorry, I'm not judging, really, I'm not. I mean, I understand the need. And I think if the feeding didn't have such sexual overtones, I might feel differently... maybe... not sure, because even without the sex, the feeding itself feels very intimate. I know I'm looking at the situation through the eyes of a mortal and I keep placing some kind of moral judgment on it, and I shouldn't. But I can't separate them in my head... the feeding and the sex. It feels like betrayal to me, to have the person you love go to a feeder. I mean, I know Shade came to you, that was different, and I'm grateful. It's just confusing to me."

Luca understood her confusion, even though it was accepted tradition in their world. "Have you thought about how Shannon will respond? When she finds out?"

"Yes, I've thought about it. But I can't predict it. I mean, I think she'll go for it, but... wow. It's really complicated, isn't it? That's what made me start thinking of the feeders again. I mean, when I was first seeing Shade, I didn't know anything about feeders. I think it would have really freaked me out to know that."

"So, let me ask *you* a personal question."

"Okay... that's fair."

"How long were you seeing Shade before he fed from you?"

"Oh... well, there was a block of time between when I first met him and when I actually started seeing him. I mean, I kept running into him, we had a few brief encounters, and he would approach me, and I would get flustered. So, it took a while before we were... uh... together. But once we were, I would say maybe two weeks? It wasn't long."

"And you discussed it first? That he would start feeding from you?"

Kate laughed at the early memory of them together. "He explained the feeding in advance. But when he did feed, I don't think there was any discussion. I think it just happened."

Luca continued to inquire, "So, he fed exclusively from you after that?"

"We talked about that. I asked that he not feed from another. He did talk about how long he was able to go between feedings. And he did explain if a vampire was injured, bleeding severely and not able to get to their mate, they might feed from another to save their life. He didn't bring up the pregnancy thing. That was a shock."

Luca slowed his run and looked at her. "Knowing what you know now... if you had it to do over again..."

Kate interrupted him. "You don't even need to finish the sentence. The answer is yes. Absolutely yes. I can't imagine my life without him. All couples have crap to get through. This just happens to be our crap. But it's worth it, Luca, so worth it. And Shannon will be worth it... you'll see. It will all work out."

He raised his eyebrows in question. "I hope so."

Kate asked, "Would you turn her?"

"Again... you're moving way too fast here. Would she want that? And if she did, that's another decision I think I would need to make with Shade. Do you think about being turned?"

"Not really. I mean, will it make much difference? I already feed from him."

He had to laugh. "Oh, it will make a difference, in everything. You feed from him, but you don't rely on him for food. You still consume human food. Your thirst for his blood will intensify. All your senses are intensified, your sight, your hearing, your sense of smell. Your strength is amplified. And you will have your own beast to tame."

"Oh my god... I never think about that! Shade's hot temper and mine?"

Luca laughed. "Oh, I think about it! Every time his beast emerges, I think about it."

"Do you have a beast?"

"Of course, every vampire has an inner beast. My temper doesn't flair like Shade's, so I usually only deal with the beast when I'm in a battle, and then I want him to emerge."

"Gi has a beast? And Theresa? Gentle Theresa?"

"All vampires have a beast. And the beast varies with each vampire, based on their own personalities. But if Gi or Theresa were threatened, you would see their beast. They are not warriors, their beast would not be as strong or as violent, but you would see their beast emerge."

"I wonder what my beast will be like."

He threw his head back laughing. "Oh, I have a very good idea of what your beast will be like. And let's just say, master will have his hands full."

She punched him in the arm as they completed the loop and returned back to the house. He set up the weight bench and let her complete her exercises while he went inside and got the weapon ready for tonight. He knew she didn't want to learn to shoot a gun, because she feared guns. So, for that reason, he would make her learn to shoot, if for no other reason than to get over her fear. He was setting up the targets as she finished up. "Ready?"

She wiped the sweat from her brow. "Yes, the bow?"

"No bow tonight." He handed her the rifle, and she took a step back.

"I... I don't like guns."

"I know, that's why you're going to learn to shoot one."

She hesitated another minute before taking the rifle from his hand. She held her arm stiff, holding the weapon away from her body. Having alerted the warriors ahead of time that he would be target practicing tonight, so the sounds of the gunshots would not draw their attention, he stepped behind her and placed the butt of the rifle against her shoulder, showing her proper hand placement, how to use the scope, how to release the safety.

"Everything you learned about the bow still applies. Sight in on your target, hold your breath, and when you are ready to shoot, gently squeeze the trigger."

He stood behind her as she fired several rounds, helping her absorb the recoil. Her aim was good. But she flinched every time she fired the gun. "Relax, Kate."

He made her fire numerous rounds, standing behind her, making suggestions and corrections. She jumped every time she heard the blast and didn't like the feel of the recoil against her shoulder. Finally, he took the rifle from her hands. "Good job. You shredded those targets."

Her face looked cross. "I don't like it."

"I know you don't. But you may not always be in a situation where you can choose the weapon. You may have to use what's available. So, you need to, at least, be comfortable with guns."

"Okay, well, I'm comfortable enough. I don't want to do anymore."

He bit his lip so as not to smile, as he watched her hand over the rifle and turn to walk back inside the house. *And she wonders what her beast will be like.* He shook his head... her beast and Shade's... immovable object, meet unstoppable force.

43

That beautiful face, Kate never tired of looking at his handsome face while he slept. She brushed a lock of hair from his eyes and ran the tips of her fingers down the stubble on his cheek and watched as he slowly opened his eyes, those piercing blue eyes. He locked her in his gaze and she watched the smile spread across his lips. An eternity of days and she would never tire of looking at that face. She leaned over him and kissed him lightly. She felt his hands in her hair, and then he chuckled.

"*Mi amore*, your hair is a tangled mess this morning."

She gave him a look. "Oh really? And I wonder whose fault that is?"

He chuckled again. "Are you complaining, *bel rosso*?"

She kissed his lips again. "Never, I love that you love my hair."

She felt his arms around her as he pulled her to his chest and deepened the kiss. She responded to his lips and felt the sharp sting of his slap on her ass.

"And you are distracting me too much, *mi amore*."

She laughed out loud. "Me? Distracting you?"

He laughed as he slipped from their bed and she looked at the strong muscles in his back and legs as he dragged on fresh leathers, and ran his hand over his face and through his hair.

He looked up as he spoke, "Things are getting quieter at the Dead House, *mi amore*. Perhaps, one night soon, I will take some time off... stay home with my *bel*."

She smiled up at him as she wrapped the sheets around her. "I'd love that. I feel like I have so little time with you. And don't forget we have a double-date with Luca and Shannon this week-end."

He smiled and shook his head. "Oh, I haven't forgotten."

He leaned over and kissed her good-bye. She entwined her fingers in his, and held his hand, stretching out her arm as he walked away from the bed, letting go at the last minute. She listened to him as he went down the stairs and headed to the bunker, and heard the warriors trample through the house, followed by the sudden silence as they all exited.

She left their bed and headed for the shower to wash away the remnants of last night's lovemaking, dressed in her jeans, and headed out to meet Luca.

Luca heard her as she approached his door, and he got up to meet her. It was time to move her to her final objective, the crossbow. He opened the door to greet her and they headed outside.

They walked outside together, and the night air was not as chilled as they were moving into spring. She finished her warm-up and they started their nightly run. She had come to love this run. She loved the fresh air, the way the exercise made her body feel, and his company. It was hard to imagine life before Luca. He was such a permanent fixture in her everyday routine. She wondered about his life and how he lived before he joined them.

"So, can I ask, how long have you known Shade? How did you meet?"

"I feel like I have known him all my life. My father really wanted me to go to Shade's warrior camp. My father and Shade were old friends. When I was ten years old, my father took me to the camp to try out. Not all applicants to the camp are accepted. But I passed all the admissions requirements and I think it was my father's proudest day. My father was also a warrior, and he held Shade in the highest regard. So, to be accepted there was a great honor for my family. Of course, I had to leave my family and move to the camp, to live there permanently. And then, when I was about fourteen, my father was killed in a battle. He was fighting alongside Shade. Shade got to him, but it was too late. Shade tried to have my father feed from him, but he'd already lost too much blood. My father asked him to look after me, take care of me and to raise me to be a man he would be proud of. So, Shade took me under his wing after that. I mean, as a student, I was always being taught by him. But after my father died, well, Shade became my mentor. Maybe that helps you to understand our bond. He's my master in that he is my teacher, and I'm a part of his coven, but he has also been my family and my brother-in-arms. And now, to be selected to be the protector of his mate. I think you understand that for a warrior, there is no higher honor. We are connected on so many levels. I never want to do anything that will disappoint him or let him down."

Kate looked over at him as he talked. "That explains so much. I'm so sorry... about your father. And I can't imagine Shade would ever be disappointed in you. He beams with pride when he speaks of you." She watched as the smile spread across his face. "But living in the camp, was that hard?"

Luca shrugged. "I'm not sure what you mean by hard. It was hard work. We trained every day, sometimes on the field and sometimes in the classroom. We lived in barracks with other warriors in training. We were kept in barracks by age groups, so we grew up with other vampires who were going through the same thing. To be there was an honor, and every student wanted to work hard to win the respect of their teachers, but especially Shade's respect. I can remember how all the students worked so hard just to win his approval. A simple nod from him, or his hand on your head was all it took. The simplest acknowledgment that he was pleased was enough to make you push harder, work harder."

Kate smiled. It was interesting to hear this perspective of Shade through someone else's eyes, to view him in a different light.

"When I was pregnant..." She paused a second and realized she could say those words without the searing emotional pain she once felt. "When I was pregnant, and we both felt sure it was a boy, Shade said he would be sent to the camp when he was ten, and I have to admit, I was a little horrified. Ten seems so young... still a baby in my eyes and sending him away was unthinkable. I wasn't sure that was something I wanted for my child. But hearing you speak of it... I don't know, I have a different opinion now."

"You're still looking at it through the eyes of a mortal, Kate. You know we age differently, and our world is filled with violence, much more than you're aware of or have been exposed to. Even after you're turned, my gut tells me Shade will continue to protect you from much of that side of our life."

"So, do all vampires fight?"

"Well, no. All vampires must be able to defend themselves, if they are attacked. There are mortals who would do us harm, as well as immortals. But not all vampires are warriors, so their fighting skills are limited. That's the role of the warrior. The warrior protects everyone in the coven, and also fights for the master in acquiring new territory or defending existing territory against rival masters."

"So, what's a rogue then? You explained once before, but I'm still not sure I understand. I've heard Shade refer to rogues in D.C."

"Rogues are vampires that don't appear to belong to a specific coven. They may be acting independently, or they may temporarily join forces with a master's coven just for the money. I think, in your culture, you would call them mercenaries, soldiers for hire. But rogues may also be mortals who were turned and abandoned, left to fend for themselves. All of Shade's warriors belong to Shade. They were recruited by him, trained by him, their loyalty is to him. Those that come from his own coven will stay with him, while others who were recruited from other covens will go back to their master or may choose to work for another master who is an ally of Shade's. It sounds like all of Alec's warriors were recruited from rogues, which means some of them are self-trained, or they were released by their previous master, or they just struck out on their own. They're usually not as skilled, and never as disciplined. There are no warriors in the vampire world that compare to a Medici warrior."

Kate tried to make a comparison in her head. "So, you're like Seal Team Six."

Luca looked confused. "Is this another Buffy the Vampire Slayer?"

She laughed. "Well, no... Buffy isn't real, but Seal Team Six is very real. Among mortal soldiers, they are considered the best, the elite fighting force. When everything else fails, or when you have a mission that has impossible odds, you call in Seal Team Six."

"Then, yes, a Medici Warrior is like Seal Team Six."

Strange, Kate learned more about Shade from Luca than she learned from Shade, and it only reinforced how little time she had with him. But she could feel Luca's pride as he talked about being a Medici Warrior, and she felt so much pride in Shade that he had created this legacy of warriors. She also thought about everything Luca had taught her in these past few months, and realized he'd trained for years, and just how much knowledge he had stored away in that brain, and that he'd shared only a very small amount of it with her. They returned to the house as they finished up their ten-mile loop, and she cooled down while Luca stepped inside the house.

Luca brought out the crossbow. She had the strength now to manage it, and her aim with the bow and the gun, would help her master this weapon as well. He would not give her the weapon she took from the wall when they started this journey. That one was too sophisticated to start with. They would begin with a basic crossbow. He grabbed up the quiver of crossbow arrows and returned outside.

She saw him return with the quiver in one hand and a bow in the other. As he stepped out the door, she could see his silhouette against the light that spilled from inside, and she saw the shape of the crossbow.

He approached and wordlessly handed her the weapon. She looked up at him. "Am I ready?"

He nodded yes. "You're ready, little warrior."

She held the bow in her hands, turning it over, looking at its design. "This is not the same one I picked, though."

"No, it isn't. You'll have to work up to that one. Let's start with the basics. It's similar to the longbow you have been training on, the string must still be retracted, but you hold it and aim more like the rifle you trained on last night."

He stepped behind her and positioned the weapon correctly in her hands. "It's heavier than a standard bow, that's why I trained you on swords, to build the strength in your arms, plus any warrior worth his salt knows how to handle a blade."

He reached around her, placing her hands on the crossbow as she lifted it to shoulder height. She could feel its heftiness. It was much thicker and heavier than the standard longbow she had been using. She must hold the weapon differently than the standard bow and it felt awkward in her hands.

He watched as she adjusted to the weight of the bow, then he pulled an arrow from the quiver and showed her how to load it. He gently lifted her arms higher, so they were positioned correctly, and instructed her on how to use the sight to aim at her target.

"The string on the crossbow is shorter and takes more strength to retract, once you pull it back; however, you need to catch it behind this notch on the stock. You will not release the arrow by releasing the string as you did on the longbow; but rather, you will use this trigger release like you did on the rifle."

She listened carefully to his instructions, and she now understood why he insisted on her using the rifle last night. Holding the crossbow felt more like holding a rifle than a bow. She followed his instructions and released the first arrow and missed the target completely. She dropped her arms and sighed. She felt like she was back to square one.

He saw her disappointment when she missed the target. "Don't despair, little warrior. This weapon is completely different. It combines elements of what you learned on the longbow and the rifle, and yet, it is different from both. Concentrate. Focus on what you learned from each, and take your time."

She loaded another arrow in the bow and took aim. She took more time, shifting the weight of the crossbow and trying to lift it higher to compensate for the downward direction her last arrow took. She controlled her breathing, just as he had taught her. She felt her heartbeat. She secured her aim then held her breath and pulled the trigger. The arrow hit the target, but not in the center.

Luca cheered her on, "Good, very good. Now, do it again. Watch the trajectory of the arrow, feel the direction of the wind, compensate, correct. It will come, little warrior, it will come."

He let her practice for several hours, until he could tell she was having difficulty holding the weight of the bow, and then called it a night. She was consistently hitting the target, but she had yet to hit a bull's eye. He was more than pleased with her progress.

Luca praised her results, but she couldn't help but feel a little defeated, like starting all over. The crossbow felt awkward and heavy in her hands. She knew it would take time to master. She rolled her shoulders when he took the weapon from her hands, and turned her neck from side to side, her muscles tight from holding the weight of the bow.

"So, we're done for the night?"

"All done," he told her. "I suggest you take a really hot shower, your neck and shoulders will thank you."

She followed his advice and headed back to the bedroom and into the shower where she turned the hot water on as hot as she could tolerate, and let it soothe the tired muscles in her shoulders and back. She stood under the water, her mind quiet, and wished she could tell Shade. She hated she was hiding this from him. She wanted his approval. She wanted to share what she'd done, and have him be proud of her. He wanted to train her, but look at how much time this had taken. She had spent every night with Luca, working for eight to ten hours, for months now. She would have never had that kind of time with Shade. They were lucky to have a few uninterrupted days. Still, she knew he'd feel disappointment and now she didn't know how to tell him. And she'd only placed Luca in the middle, again. *How do we always manage to make things so complicated?*

She finished up in the shower, stepped out, grabbed a towel to wrap around her hair, and another to rub down her body. The water was so hot her skin was pink all over. She dried her hair and slipped into a gown, then climbed into their bed to read and wait for him.

* * *

Shade had spent the night, once again, sitting on his ass, looking at grids, and recording the damn few kills that came in. He felt he was fucking useless here lately. The rogue activity on the streets had damn near stopped, and he still had no fucking clue who this ass wipe, Angel was. Hearing the heavy booted walk of a warrior approaching, he swung his legs down from the desk and looked up to see Tomas come in, a little later than usual. "Tomas, my brother, taking in a little fun before heading to work?"

Shade grinned as Tomas slid into the chair opposite him. He could tell Tomas was equally bored. He and Skelk were the only ones in this fucked up gang of Alec's crew that were actual warriors, and showed both skill and discipline.

Tomas answered, "Business is business, brother. I just show up and do my job. Looks like your ass could use some time off. I can handle this if you need some time with the mate." He gave Shade a wink. "I know if my woman was home all night waiting for me, the last place I'd want to be is stuck in this shit hole."

Shade laughed. "You know lately, she's been saying the same thing. I promised her I'd be home more, once things settled. It wouldn't take me long to get here if we had a problem. And let's face it, this little gang war we got going on is not happening at the moment. I know you can handle it, brother. I have been toying with the idea of sending a few of my boys back to Florence, letting them have some downtime, and bringing in a few replacements. I've been discussing it with my Second-in-Command in Florence. Give me your thoughts."

That's it, warrior, eat from the palm of my hand. Plant the seed, and it grows inside that warrior's head. "I have no problems handling any of this. Simple to handle. But I do want it made clear to your warriors. They need to understand, when you aren't here, I am Second in your absence. I need to know they won't argue with my orders. As for replacements, now is a good time. Everything is slow. New warriors would have time to get settled. No problem to get you here if things begin to speed up again. And shit, let's hope that doesn't happen soon."

Shade nodded. Tomas was a skilled mercenary, he commanded a hefty fee, and Shade understood that life. If he didn't give him some responsibilities, he would just move on to someone who would. Right now, Shade needed him here. He had been a reliable Second-In-Command.

"Let me put a few things into place and see where I stand. I have no problems with you as Second, and whatever I say goes with Alec. This is my show, brother, and if I say you are in charge, it's the fucking law." As Shade stood, they clasped hands.

Tomas gripped his hand firmly. "Done, brother. I'm going into the southeast grid tonight, check on some of the activity and check in with the warriors out there. Let me know what you decide and when you're ready. You know where to find me, Shade."

Shade nodded as Tomas turned to leave. Tomas already knew how this would end and the smile spread across his face as he teleported out. Now he had two masters making plans, and one was for a battle that would land on the other's doorstep, taking out that mortal ass he loved so much. That 'eternity' would end shortly, and so would Shade. This had been a good night, definitely one good fucking night!

44

Once again, it was time to head into the damn Dead House, organize and wait for... nothing. Every night, it was getting harder and harder to leave her, to see her try not to show her disappointment and her desire for him to stay. Every night, he walked away from her and that ate at him, the hole becoming a cavern inside his heart. He had promised to spend more time with her, and he needed to make that happen.

As he stood, the softest arms surrounded him, arms he longed for every second of his life. Her hair lay along his back as she cuddled him from behind, and his heart screamed in agony, because he had to go. It was his duty. Shade slid his hands along her arms.

"They love that fire pit, *mi amore*. It's good for them. Gives them a place to meet outside, to talk, share stories of home."

He pulled her in front of him and together, they looked out the window as the flames from the fire pit reached for the skies. They knew what the other felt and thought, what they both missed, what they both wanted. He didn't miss the irony of a man who lived for eternity wishing for time, time to spend with her. Nipping the side of her neck, he whispered in her ear, "*Ti amo, mi amore*, but I must go, the warriors wait. But you know I shall return to you."

She turned in his arms and kissed him good-bye. He grabbed his leather coat on the way out the door, looking over his shoulder at her and in sign language, told her he loved her.

Kate made a heart with her hands and held it up for him. No words were spoken between them, and yet, everything that was important had been said.

He reluctantly left her and got his warriors into D.C. Once everyone was out on the streets, it was time to give Alec a call and let him know things were winding down. Tomas was ready to take on Second-in-Command, and Shade was thinking of spending a few nights away from this damn place. Alec didn't take the news well, but Shade really didn't give a fuck.

Laughing to himself, Shade knew Alec was fucked without him and he damn well knew it. Shade rather liked it that way. He sat there making some notes of a few things he needed to get done in the short term. First of all, he wanted to switch out a few of his own warriors, give some of the other young pups from Florence some street experience while things were slow, and send a few of this crew back home for a break. He had already talked to Marco, who thought it was a good idea. Surprisingly enough, he seemed too damn happy about it, for some odd reason. Marco would send him a few replacements to stay a while and the others would return. He was hoping this chaos would not last much longer.

The next thing on the list was this double-date with Luca and Shannon. He would make his assessment of her, and decide whether he could trust letting her inside their coven. And besides, he'd get to break out the Harley and ride. Just the thought of *bel* on the back of that bike made his cock lurch. *Cazzo!* He needed to move that damn task to the top of the list.

Shade heard the light footfall of boot heels on the floor. He rolled his eyes to the door as Raven walked in, hair flying behind him, dressed in leather pants and a satin shirt with a cape. Why was he not surprised? "What the hell are you doing back here? I cannot wait to hear this explanation."

"Well, I could ask the same of you, master! What the fuck are you doing here?" Flinging his hair back, he flopped down on a chair. "Give me a smoke, *si*? I need a fucking smoke!"

Watching him, Shade laughed. Pulling out the pack of cigarettes, he flung them across the table and watched Raven's ringed fingers pull out a lighter and fire one up.

Shade shook his head. "How in fucking hell do you fight with all that shit on your fingers, brother? You know the rules, not that you ever pay attention to them. If you didn't have that lightning speed, your ass would not be sitting here right now. So, while you sit here giving me hell, why don't you explain to me why you and your jewelry box are not out there doing your job."

Raven took a few drags before answering and smiled at him. Raven knew he pushed Shade's buttons, but he also knew Master liked him, and had allowed him to get away with more than most and it amused him.

"You know that other world crossbow warrior, he's just some kind of fucked up! He does this challenging thing with Marcello." Raven threw his hands up in the air, all drama. "He can hit a target, but he smells. And you think I look bad? This is fashion, bro. Camel dung, that's what Skelk smells like. I had to help Marcello, Skelk broke my sword. So, I had to come back and find another weapon. I can't be on the streets without a weapon, is this not a rule? One of those things I never pay attention to, you know... rules?"

Shade sat there watching the performance. The kid always had a fucking answer for everything, the smart ass. Watching him gesture and fling that mop of hair around, Shade began to think the kid picked the wrong damn career and should have been in the movies.

"So, let me get this clear, you broke your sword defending one of my best from one of our own? And what is that fucking get up you are wearing? Get off your ass warrior, get a new weapon and go back to doing what the fuck I pay you for... killing. You do remember that, do you not? And give me back my fucking smokes. Move!"

Raven grinned and slipped a fresh cigarette behind his ear before sliding the pack across the table. He grabbed a new sword and headed out.

Shade just shook his head. *One of these days I am going to beat the living shit out of that kid.*

* * *

Kate waited until she heard Shade leave. She knew he was torn between his desire to be with her, and his responsibilities to Alec and his warriors. She felt their life would always be this balancing act. When she heard him leave with the warriors, she sought out Luca and they began their nightly routine.

Luca had them well into their ten-mile loop and she hadn't peppered him with questions. He finally looked at her and asked, "What's wrong? You're usually talking my ear off during this run."

Kate was pulled from her thoughts. "What? Oh... sorry. I guess my mind is someplace else tonight."

"You okay?"

"Yes, I'm fine. I just miss him, you know? It's very isolating... this life. I mean, before him, I was at work every day, around a lot of people, people who I'd become friends with."

"Like Shannon?"

"Yes, exactly. And after work, we'd all go hang out somewhere together, have dinner or just go for drinks. People came to my house. On weekends, we'd go to clubs or parties or movies. I gave all that up for him... and he's worth it, he's totally worth it. But when he's busy like this, I just see so little of him. You know? I mean, we have maybe an hour or so before his death slumber, unless he gets home a little early, and then maybe a half hour together when he wakes. I sleep in his arms, and it feels like my most precious time, and I'm not even sure he feels me in his death slumber."

"Well, I can answer that for you. I promise he feels you during that time."

"But I mean really feel me. Does he feel me lying beside him, does he feel—"

Luca cut her off mid-sentence, "Kate. He feels everything. He feels your breath on his skin and the beat of your heart. He feels the warmth of your touch. If you hold him, he feels your arms. If you kiss him, he feels your lips. Don't let his lack of response during his death slumber ever lull you into thinking or feeling he's not aware. A vampire is always aware. If you leave his bed, he is aware."

"Really? That's soothing to know, because I love sleeping beside him, and I know he loves me there with him. I just didn't think he was as aware of me as I was of him."

"I think I can safely say he is more aware of you than you are of him." He watched as a smile spread across her face.

"Good. Good. I like knowing that."

Luca gave her a sideways glance. "You can ask him these things yourself, you know?"

"Yes, but we never have time. I just want his time and it's the thing I have the least of. I'm looking forward to this weekend, though. Aren't you?"

"Uh yes... but I'm also nervous."

Kate giggled. "About Shade and the third degree?"

Luca laughed nervously. "Yeah, that too. But also, Shannon. I've never been on a date. You know? And she's mortal, so I'm not sure how to act."

"How to act? Just be yourself. Relax, have fun! Riding the bikes will be fun. I've never ridden with Shade. And we'll be going into town. Maybe we'll go out for dinner, so you know, you and Shade will have to do that thing where you look like you're eating. But there are shops, and art galleries, and they'll have a band playing outside. She'll love it, so just go with the flow. Let it happen naturally, don't force it. Shannon isn't a shy girl, trust me. Her signals will be loud and clear."

"You worry about Shade, I worry about Shannon. What did you call it, 'getting the shit kicked out of you by love'?"

"Yeah... pretty great, huh?"

Luca laughed. "I'll let you know."

They were wrapping up their run and he had her do her free weights, push-ups, and sit-ups while he set up more targets for her. When she was done, they started practicing with the crossbow. Her aim was improving and she got a few bull's eye shots, but not dead center. Still, better than the previous night. After a few hours practice, he could see the weight of the crossbow was taking its toll, so they ended the practice.

"Head to the showers, little warrior."

45

Leaving her car for the parking attendant, Rissa grabbed the small file of photographs she had chosen for their engagement announcement. Placing it inside her briefcase, she began the walk to the elite photography studio she used for her client's weddings and other private events.

Rissa didn't mind the walk. Parking was ridiculous in downtown D.C., so it was almost impossible to park anywhere close to your desired destination. Besides, it was beginning to stay lighter longer in the day. This day had been beautiful, and she always preferred to walk if she could, even though Alec had told her it was a dangerous thing to do these days, but she had yet to have a problem with any of these rogues. She would be finished before dark.

She took the assortment of her favorite photographs of her and Alec together, to her friend to create a collage that could be submitted to the newspapers. Rissa and her photographer friend talked and laughed, going over the photos and choosing the perfect shots, depicting her and Alec as a power couple on the way up. This photo and wedding announcement would be seen all over the country, and she would make sure it hit a few of the international papers as well. Alec's Harvard alumni press agent had agreed to work on writing the announcement. With Alec, things had to be perfect to craft his image for his very public persona.

Rissa's business would boom after this announcement, and the paparazzi would be on them both 24/7 once it hit the press. She wrapped up her business and began to walk back to the parking garage. The air was warm, and even though the sun had started to set, the light was beautiful in the evening in Washington. She loved this city, the hustle and bustle of it, and it was rare she had time alone, without something or someone needing her attention.

She passed one of the many coffee shops and the strong aroma of an expensive coffee hit her nostrils. She sighed, remembering what it used to taste like. What she wouldn't pay to be able to have just one sip. After wrestling with herself, she decided to buy one. Taking a sip or two would not make her sick.

She walked to the coffee house where many of the outside tables were filled with couples, sharing private time. It made her miss spending time out with Alec, being anonymous and unknown, just the two of them together. Now, when they went out, it was for show, perfectly scripted for the entire world to see. After all, they were the royal couple of Washington. Weaving her way around the tables, she was immediately assaulted by the smell of vampire, and her guard went up. All her senses kicked in and her eyes scanned the many people sitting and milling about.

She saw him sitting at one of the tables, dressed in a stylish and expensive suit. He seemed rather anxious, as if he was waiting for someone who was late. Perhaps it was a lady, for in his hand, he held a beautiful bouquet of roses. His eyes rose up to lock with Rissa and her heart raced. He smiled and quickly looked down before lifting his head to look around and locked eyes with her, once again. He nodded and smiled at her. At first, Rissa was taken aback. His scent told her he was definitely a vampire. His hair lay in curls to his shoulders, his look rough yet stylish, but his fidgeting told her he was not used to being in a suit. She looked at his hands and found them roughened, knuckles skinned and callouses on his thumbs... he was a warrior. He didn't make a move toward her, but stood and walked away from her, unfazed.

She began to understand very clearly, there were eyes on her all the time.

Grabbing a small elixir of coffee, she walked on toward the parking garage and hastened her pace. It was beginning to get dark and she wanted to be home. She took two small sips of the coffee and sighed. Being vampire, nothing tasted the same as when she was mortal. As the parking attendant brought her car around, she tipped him handsomely and slid into the seat. She took the lid off her coffee and let the aroma fill the car as she drove back to G-town, wondering and waiting for Max to call again. She knew he would call, he would know of the engagement by now. He was always watching her, and he seemed to know everything. She had to get her brain working on a scheme to get that potion without his knowledge, and she'd do it.

46

After one long ass night, Shade completed his rounds at Alec's and found nothing... again. He teleported home with the warriors and found *bel* asleep. He hated not to wake her, but it was close to sunrise and they had a big night tomorrow with the date with Luca and his woman. It may be best if they both got some sleep.

After a deep slumber, as the sun was setting, he could feel her stir beside him. She was wide awake now and raring to go. He lay there in the last few minutes of his slumber, not wanting to move, enjoying the comfort of their bed with her next to him. He didn't have to go to the Dead House and tonight would be enjoyable for them both. He pretended to still be locked in his death slumber to see what response he would get from her.

Kate slid her hands over him but got no response. She knew he was awake, and yet, he played with her, ignoring her hands as they slid over him. Tonight, he was staying with her. She couldn't wait to get their evening started. She slid her nude body across him, as she climbed over him to get out his side of the bed. She grabbed the sheets and pulled them off behind her, leaving him lying there naked without any covers. She watched as he started to laugh.

She shouted a dare at him, "If I beat you to the shower, then I drive the bike."

He dashed past her so fast and was in the shower ahead of her, hot water streaming over him. She was laughing as she joined him, and they quickly showered, dressed and headed downstairs. Shannon was planning on meeting them here and they were already running late.

Luca had been dressed and ready for an hour, just waiting for Shade and Kate. He left his suite and went to the living room to wait for them. He was hoping they didn't get distracted with an early evening lovemaking session, but it was way too quiet up there for that. He paced the floor, watching the time. Shannon should be here any minute. He wiped his sweaty palms over his jeans. *What is taking them so long?*

Walking into the living room, holding Kate's hand, Shade chuckled as he saw Luca fidgeting. "Luca, you need to stop pacing, you'll wear a hole in my damn floor. *Bel* will have a say about that! Anything you want to say before she gets here? Any questions you need to ask me?"

Luca looked up as they entered the room. "Questions? Uh, yes, I was wondering what I should call you. Both of you? I mean, she doesn't know I'm a vamp, or you're a vamp, so if I call you master and my lady... what? Tell me what to do."

"Call us Shade and Kate. But I ever hear you calling her Kate when not with Shannon, you will have to answer to me for that."

Luca gave him a nervous grin, when Shade heard the doorbell and Gi was already at the door. Shade gave Luca a brotherly hug and whispered in his ear, "Relax, just be yourself. Show her respect, be honorable, be a Medici warrior and you won't have a problem." Shade watched as *bel* scurried to the door to greet her friend.

As Gi opened the door, Kate was already there to greet her. "Shannon! I'm so happy to see you. I'm so excited about this, this... date."

Shannon grabbed Kate in a hug. She had missed having Kate in her life. "I just wore jeans since Luca said we were going on the bikes. Is this okay? Do I look okay? Is Luca here? And Shade, do I finally get to spend time with the mysterious Shade?"

Kate laughed. "Yes, you will meet Shade, and Luca is pacing a hole in the floor, so please, let's go put him out of his misery."

They both giggled as Kate grabbed her hand and led her into the living room. Kate watched Luca's face as he took her in, seeing her for the first time since her previous visit. She could see how nervous he was, but his eyes lit up when he saw her. Kate looked over at Shannon and her eyes were already locked on him. Kate squeezed her hand as she led Shannon over to formally introduce her to Shade. "Shannon, you remember Shade Medici."

Kate watched as she looked away from Luca and shifted her gaze to Shade. Kate saw her face as she took him in, catching first his eyes, then dropping her gaze down the full length of him, and slowly back up to his face. "Wow, no wonder I haven't seen you for six months."

Kate jerked at her hand and stifled a laugh. "Shade, this is my best friend, Shannon. You met briefly once before."

As *bel* introduced her, Shade watched as her eyes took full stock of him, taking his full measure. She was a bold one, and nothing like his sweet *bel*, nothing at all. He smiled and took her hand in his and kissed it softly, rolling his eyes straight up to her and locking her in his gaze. *Hello sweet mortal, mess with my boy and you mess with me.* "Welcome back to our home, Shannon. I am honored. It is a great joy to see Kate so happy and having her friends in our home. Please, may we offer you a drink and sit for a few moments before we go?"

Shannon wondered how long she had been standing with her mouth open and closed it suddenly. *Wow, what is it with these Italian men?* He stood even taller than Luca, and was uniquely handsome. He poured on the charm, but there was an air of danger about him too. Something that warned her, 'don't cross me, little girl.' He intimidated without even trying. Or was it intentional? She was usually good at reading men, but not this one. She bet Kate had her hands full with this one! She remembered how hesitant Kate had been with him in the beginning. How Shannon had to push her to even get his number. But she got it now. He did overwhelm.

"Thank you for having me. I can't tell you how much I've been looking forward to this. I love bikes! I love the speed and the element of danger, so I can't wait to get this party started. I think I'll hold off on the drink for now, but thank you for asking."

Shade smiled. "You are most welcome, *dolce amica*. Anything you need, please ask." He turned to Luca. "Please bring your lady to the living room and we shall talk a bit, get to know one another before we ride." He slid his hand around Kate. "And you, *mi amore*, what do you wish to drink?"

"Nothing for me, lover. I think I'll just wait until we're in town."

"Ah, you are more than ready to straddle that Harley, *si*?"

Shade led Kate into the living room where they took a seat on the love seat, waiting for Luca to follow.

Luca had not been able to take his eyes off Shannon since she entered the room. After the introductions, he reached out to take her hand, but she caught him by surprise as she slid her hand around his waist and leaned her head against his shoulder for just a second, before she looked up at him. He swallowed hard as he looked back at her, and led her to the living room where they sat down on the sofa across from Shade and Kate. He felt Shannon's hand on his knee, and he had to catch his breath.

Shade captured her in his gaze. "So, Shannon, I am curious to know about you, if you don't mind me probing. Luca is an important family member to Kate and me. Beyond that, you are one of Kate's oldest friends, and that pleases me to see her so happy."

Shannon didn't have a shy bone in her body, so she spoke with confidence when answering his questions. "Kate and I worked for the same company in marketing and advertising, the Brunswick Agency in D.C. We were there together for years before you stole her away. In our job, we traveled all over the world together, throughout Europe and Asia. Do you know her favorite city is Paris? Good Lord, I thought I'd never get her out of Paris! Before that, we were in college together at Georgetown. We were both Marketing majors, and we were dorm mates a few years. I'm a Virginia girl. Born here, all my family is here. How about you? How long have you been living in the States?"

Shade nodded. "Oh, I know quite well how much she loves Paris. I have taken her there a few times. As for me, I have not lived in the States long. I'm also a world traveler, for my business, of course. I have vineyards abroad and have acquired this property in Virginia, as well as one in California. But this home belongs to Kate, it is our main residence. My main estate, where Luca and I grew up, is in Florence. I have known Luca most of his life and I rather like that he has joined me here. I do believe," sliding his hand through Kate's hair and kissing her on the side of her cheek, "I will be staying here in the States with my fiancée. Any future plans, *dolce amica*?"

"Plans?" Shannon laughed softly. "Not really. I'm not one of those women climbing the corporate ladder. I like my job, and I like the travel, so I really just take it a day at a time, you know? I want to leave myself open. I want the freedom to move or change, or go where I want, depending on what life presents to me. Maybe that sounds a little aimless, but I feel like you only live once, and I want to be open to experience it."

Shade could tell she spoke her mind, held nothing back and she amused him. She was quite stunning to look at. Her enthusiasm was contagious, and he wondered if Luca knew what he was getting in to. "I know what you mean. Leaving yourself open for change is good. But have some caution, before you know it, the years pass and you have nothing to show for your time. Speaking of time, I suggest we ride into town and see what the evening holds for us." Helping Kate up as he stood, he asked, "Shall we haul ass, *mi amore*?"

Luca had been holding his breath while his master was questioning her. He had no idea what to expect, and he couldn't read his expression. Did Shade like her? He could barely think with her hand on his knee, and as she talked to Shade, she slowly slid her hand up his leg and ran it back and forth across his thigh. *Cazzo!*

When Shade stood up to lead them all out to the garage, Luca reached down to take Shannon's hand. She stood up next to him, leaned against his chest and whispered in his ear, "So good to see you again."

As she pulled back from his ear, her face was only inches from his and he could feel her breath on his face. "I have thought of little else, *mia bellezza.*"

Shade called out to them as they lagged behind, "All right you two lovebirds, move it! I got a hot bike and a hot woman ready to roll"

Heading into the garage, the new dirt bikes were lined up on one side and all the road bikes on the other. He led Kate to the Harley he was taking tonight. He nodded to Luca. "Make sure Shannon has a helmet. We don't ride without them." Grabbing a smaller helmet, he tossed it to *bel* before grabbing his. Kate pulled the helmet on and secured the strap under her chin.

Luca took the Harley that master had indicated he would be riding. He handed a helmet to Shannon and watched her strap it on, as he put on his own. He straddled the bike, kicked the bike stand and walked it to the front of the garage. Shannon walked alongside as she watched Shade maneuver his bike into place. They were both ready to go. Luca stood up and kick-started the bike and listened to the roar of the engine as it filled the garage. He sat back down, straddling the bike and balancing it with his feet, turned and nodded at Shannon to climb on. She slid on the seat behind him, pressing her breasts into his back and slid her arms around his waist. He could feel her chin resting on his shoulder, as he looked back at her and smiled. "Ready, *mia bellezza*?"

She yelled back over the roar of the engine, "So ready!"

Kate watched Shade in his tight jeans, as he straddled the bike and walked it just outside the garage. He was wearing his heavy boots and leather jacket, his hair hanging beneath his helmet. He kick-started the bike and she could feel the rumble of the engine in her chest. She climbed on the back of the bike, arms tight around his waist, her legs straddling him, feeling the vibrations of the engine as they rolled through her body. She knew how he drove those cars–like a bat out of hell–and she had no doubt this ride would be as wild. She squeezed him tight to let him know she was ready.

Revving the engine, Shade looked over at Luca and the damn stupid grin on his face told him all he needed to know. ***"Mi amore*, move your arms down just a bit, I have a chest harness on with a gun. I always wear it when I go out."** Nodding to Luca, he rolled out and down the long drive, with Luca trailing close behind. Once they got to the road, he turned right and let her rip hard, the engine roared and he could feel Kate tighten her grip around his waist. Looking in the mirror, he saw Luca right on his ass and then Luca pulled up beside him, one hand on his knee the other on the handlebars, and Shade watched him raise his hand to the bar and kick it up a gear and blast him in the dust. "Little fucker! Hang on, *bel*!"

Luca could hear Shannon's laughter, and he laughed out loud himself. But if he knew Shade, he would be on his ass in sixty seconds.

Shade looked over his shoulder, shouting loudly, "Hang the fuck on, I have a plan!"

Kicking the bike up to speed again, he took a shortcut across an unpaved road. It was a little rough and narrow, but it would cut a few miles off the trip and he would teach that little shit a lesson. He had no intentions of letting Luca beat him.

Coming into town ahead of them, he knew Luca was still about a mile out yet. He pulled into the parking lot off Water Street near the open-air mall and parked the bike. That will teach him. **"Where the hell are you, speed racer? We're waiting, for fuck sake!"**

Kate shook her head at him. "Boys and their toys."

* * *

Luca watched him in his rearview mirror as he veered off the main road. *What the fuck is he up to?* There was no point trying to second guess him. He felt Shannon's hands slip down on his hips and onto his thighs. He looked over his shoulder at her and she smiled back at him, her hair blowing wildly in the wind beneath the helmet, and she took his breath away. He could tell she had been on the back of a bike before. She molded her body to his, leaned into the curves with him, as if she were born to ride. They drove the thirty miles into the city and made their way to the downtown mall. He could hear Shade's 'speed racer' taunt in his head, as they pulled into the parking lot.

Shade already had the kickstand down, helmet off, was leaning against the bike with his arms crossed over his chest, and a shit eating grin on his face, like 'what took you so long?' Luca pulled up beside him, pulled off his helmet and gave him a sideways glance. Nothing could spoil this night for him, nothing. He had the most beautiful girl in the world sitting on this bike behind him, with her arms and legs wrapped around him. **"Bring it, Master."**

Shade chuckled. **"Don't worry, I can bring it."**

Turning to *bel*, Shade kissed her long and hard, his arms wrapped tight around her waist. "So, are you going to lead me around for a tour?"

Shannon had slid off the bike and Luca took her helmet and strapped it down on the seat, then reached for her hand, their eyes locked and he had the shyest smile she had ever seen. She was so used to having to push guys off of her that this was a welcome change.

"Follow me." Kate said and grabbed Shade's hand. She led him in the direction of the open-air mall, with Luca and Shannon following behind them.

They walked a few steps behind Shade and Kate. Shade was so much taller than her. She thought it was an odd pairing, but she saw that they were mad-crazy in love. Shannon looked over at Luca. "They look really happy together, don't they?"

Luca looked at her as she asked the question, and she had a smile on her face, as if it really pleased her to see Kate and Shade so happy. "They are. They are happy."

"I'm glad for her, for both of them. Everybody deserves that, right? Finding that special someone?"

"Have you found your special someone, *mia bellezza*? I hope I'm not too late." Luca looked over at her and winked.

Oh my god, he did not just say that to me! She smiled back at him. "Why no, Luca, I think you're just in time." She squeezed his hand and leaned over to kiss his cheek. He turned to her and returned the kiss with a gentle touch of his lips to hers. And she was just gone!

Kate was leading Shade into the mall area, which used to be the main street of downtown Charlottesville, but had been bricked over and was closed to all traffic. The mall was lined with little shops, art galleries, and restaurants. Most offered outdoor seating, so you could watch the crowds as you ate. She watched as the women shoppers all turned as they passed by, to take in both Shade and Luca. She looked back over her shoulder at Shannon. She was holding Luca's hand and they were both so wrapped up in each other, they hardly saw anything that was going on around them. Kate caught her eye and Shannon just beamed at her.

Kate slid her arm around Shade's waist. "It's going really well back there, in case you're wondering."

"Well, I didn't have to turn around to know that *bel*. Luca's dick is telling him he's in heaven and he hasn't even done anything." Chuckling, he slapped her ass softly. Taking in the scenery, he liked the brick pavement, and the sound of their feet on the surface. No traffic, just rustic charm. Trees provided shade, and water fountains provided the ambient sound. He was aware he caught the gaze of women passing by, but he was used to it and paid it no mind. He kept his senses alert for anything out of the ordinary. "Is that a jewelry shop over there?"

"It is, lover. Good eyes. Come on, let's go in. You know a girl can never have enough jewelry."

Kate moved in front of him and grabbed both of his hands, walking backward, leading him to the jewelry store. "Hey, Shannon! We're going to the jewelry store."

Shannon heard Kate shouting about the jewelry store and looked up to see her dragging Shade in the direction of Angelo's, and it made her laugh. She felt Luca slide his arm around her waist and pull her against his side, as they followed them into the shop.

Shannon and Kate were both huddled over the jewelry cases, looking at the display of unique artisan pieces, all produced by local artists. All of it was beautiful, but Shannon saw a piece that really caught her eye. It was an elaborate sterling silver 'S' hanging from a chain. She stopped and pointed.

Kate remarked, "It's so you, Shannon. Get it!"

"Should I?" She asked the clerk if she could see the piece. He removed it from the case and placed it on top of the counter. It was the most unusual piece of monogram jewelry she'd ever seen and she loved it. Then she looked at the price tag. *Yikes $400!* "Oh, okay... thank you for showing it to me."

Kate nudged her. "What, you didn't get it?"

"Did you see the price on it? I can't drop that kind of money right now. Come on... we need to find a cheaper store." Shannon pushed her out of the store, as Shade followed after them laughing.

Luca watched as she admired the jewelry and then pushed it away because she couldn't afford it. Before the clerk could put the piece back in the case, Luca slipped the money across the counter and tucked the piece in his pocket. The clerk asked if he needed a bag and he shook his head no and then caught up with Shade.

Outside once more, Kate turned to Shade, taking his hand and watching as Shannon waited for Luca to catch up to her. They all walked arm in arm along the mall. There was a band at the far end that had started to play, and the music filled the night air.

There was an ice cream store across the mall and Shannon pointed it out and said, "There, that I can afford!"

Kate laughed at her as they headed toward Chap's ice cream store.

Luca held Shannon's hand. He asked her what flavor she liked. She turned to look at him and they locked eyes, again. "I don't know. What flavor are you?" She leaned in and kissed him, tasted him, sliding her tongue into his mouth and felt him slide his arm around her waist to pull her hard against him. As she broke the kiss, she had to take a deep breath. "Right, Italian Ice. Strawberry, I think."

Luca wasn't prepared for the flirting, this game play, the teasing. He wanted to pull her down to the ground, now, here, when she broke away. He could see the heat in her eyes and knew she felt the same thing he did. He looked at the clerk and ordered her Italian Ice. As she turned to face the young man serving up the ice cream, he slid the necklace from his pocket. Standing behind her, he reached around and placed the necklace on her. He lifted her thick brown hair, so he could hook it and placed a kiss on her neck, while her neck was exposed, running his tongue along that sweet vein. He could feel his cock harden as he got a taste of her. He had to drop her hair quickly and step back.

Shannon reached up and touched the necklace with her hand. It was the 'S' she had seen in the store. She was about to turn to him when she felt his lips on her neck and the goose-bumps stood up on every inch of her, as her knees felt weak. She felt him step back from her suddenly and she turned to face him. "Luca! You didn't have to. This is so special, thank you." She reached out and he took her hand. She couldn't remove her eyes from his gaze.

"It looks beautiful on you, *mia bellezza*."

Shade had been watching this drama unfold. Luca just stepped neck deep into mortal women, and what a fucking way to start out. She knew what she wanted, and she wasn't subtle about it. She was an aggressive little wild one. Shade looked at *bel* and she was all smiles, she liked what she saw, but she did not see what he saw. Luca's beast was just under the surface and he was losing control. Then the damn fool went right for the neck! Shade held his breath and got ready to grab him, but Luca stepped back, regaining some control.

Taking Kate's hand, Shade whispered in her ear, "*Bel*, I need Luca to get some air. This is moving way too fast. I need to speak with him. Can you get Shannon's attention, walk together down the mall?"

Kate gave him a questioning look. She loved how things were unfolding between the two of them, but she would do as he asked. "Okay, I'll keep her occupied, but I think you're being an overprotective dad right now." Kate got her ice cream cone from the vendor and reached out to grab Shannon's hand. "Come on, girl. Let's go sit over there on the bench while the guys go for a smoke." Shannon followed her reluctantly. Kate just shrugged and dragged Shannon away with her.

As the women walked away, Shade grabbed Luca across the shoulders, pounded him hard across the back, leading him across the mall. Pulling out a pack of smokes, he handed him one. "You need to cool off. Mighty fine piece you got, and I am just making sure you got this under control. So, tell me, how sweet is it?"

Luca lit up and took a deep draw on the cigarette. "Do you remember when we first talked? When I told you about meeting her and I thought I might love her?"

Shade looked down and shuffled his feet, then looked back up to Luca and stared. "*Si.*"

"Yeah, well, it's not a question anymore. I love her, Shade. And I'm not going to do anything that would hurt her or put her at risk. Or put any of us at risk. She still doesn't know. What I am, I mean. Do you think I want to fuck that up?"

"Relax. I'm concerned. You might know what you want, but that beast in your gut has no damn clue what you want, nor does he care. He's got his eyes on the prize, brother. And you have no damn idea about love, you don't know her. I'm not saying she isn't the one, but look at this from my point of view. She's not a feeder. You have no idea what you're walking into here. Just keep it under control, you stepped away, but you went there. I know this is not easy. But I want you to think about it. I find out you fed from her, you won't be dealing with me or her anymore, understood? Take your time."

Luca looked at him incredulously, "What? I can't believe you'd say that to me. I wouldn't even call her until I talked to you. I didn't ask her out until you said it was okay. Do you think I'd feed from her before I even talked to you about it? I mean, for all I know, she'll run in the other direction when she finds out what I am. I thought you knew me better than that."

"I do know you, I *was* you, once. But what I don't know is your beast. I've seen him when he kills, but not when he lusts. I have to trust you to make the right decisions." Turning away, Shade walked back toward *bel*.

"Maybe I've learned to control my beast better than you think," Luca said to Shade's back as he walked away. He followed him back toward the girls. "Just because I haven't been with anyone other than feeders, doesn't mean I haven't felt lust before."

"Then do what you need to do, Luca. Like I said, I trust you. I don't want to see you get hurt. I'm trying to save you from what I've been through, that's all. I love you, brother. *Bel* and I are walking on ahead. Enjoy your time with her."

As he took Kate's hand and led her up the mall, he could tell she was angry.

Kate glared at him. "Now what? What did you say to him? Are you mad at Luca?"

Stopping in mid-step, Shade sighed in exasperation. "*Bel*, I don't want to see him make a mistake."

"Lover, falling in love is never a mistake. Even if she is not the girl, he needs to start somewhere. Maybe they'll work out. Or maybe she'll break his heart, or he'll break hers. It's out of your hands. Let it play out however it plays. Let him find his own path and make his own mistakes. Besides, everybody needs to be kicked around by love a little bit, don't they?"

"*Si*. Both of us have seen our share. And we knew love when we found it. I'm torn is all, she is mortal. She could cause a lot of harm. *Cazzo*! I have to trust him, let him do what he wants right now. And I don't want this to ruin our night, *si*? I think I recall something about a dance?"

"No, let's not let this spoil our night. We have so little time together. I'm always ready for a dance."

Picking her up in his arms, straight off her feet, he kissed her and spun her around in the middle of the mall. He heard gasps as the onlookers walked past them and he truly couldn't care less. "Just never stop loving me, *mi amore*. Never."

"That would be impossible, lover, totally, completely impossible."

* * *

Luca walked back toward Shannon and watched as Shade led Kate away, and he felt even more confused. As he took Shannon's hand, she looked at his face with concern.

She asked, "Is everything okay?"

He nodded. "Yeah, sure. Let's walk."

He led her down the mall. He watched Shade with Kate, walking ahead and saw him stop to listen to her speak. The next thing he knew, Shade had lifted her up and was spinning her around in circles, her red hair flying out behind her. Her laughter could be heard above the noise of the crowd. Luca smiled to himself. Whatever bug he had up his ass, Luca could count on Kate to get through to him.

They had stopped in front of another shop window and it didn't take long before he and Shannon had caught up with them. It was a small art gallery. As they stepped up next to them, Kate turned to Luca and grabbed his arm and said, "Come on, we're going in!" She said it like they were getting ready to storm the beaches of Normandy, and he had to laugh out loud. The four of them made a noisy entrance into the quiet and subdued atmosphere of the gallery. Kate and Shannon were both trying to stifle their giggles. Here was what Luca was observing about mortals, they laughed, a lot. They didn't seem to take life so seriously. They lived more in the moment, maybe because they didn't have an eternity. Whatever it was, it was contagious, and it felt good.

Kate was running from canvas to canvas. "Wow! What a cool gallery. Look at this painting. Luca, look at this. Oh my god, come look at this one..."

Luca watched as Kate ran from one painting to another, pointing things out, barely stopping before she rushed off to another one. He looked at Shannon. "Was she always like this?"

"Oh my god, are you kidding? Always! Get her in a big art museum sometime. Let her drag you through the Metropolitan in New York, or the Louvre in Paris."

Shannon watched as that big hunk of man she was engaged to, just smiled at Kate and shook his head. Shannon moved a little closer to Shade and caught his attention as he turned those piercing blue eyes on her. "I'm really glad she has found someone who finally 'gets her', someone who really appreciates who she is. She waited a long time for you, mister. I always thought Kate was too trusting. She was quick to give her heart, and she paid a big price for that. Men took advantage of her. She had a vision of you, you know? I don't mean like an actual vision floating before her eyes, but she had this idea. This ideal man, I told her didn't exist and she needed to get over it. She didn't listen to me, thankfully, because well, here you are. Exactly what she wanted and waited for. I really can't remember when I have ever seen her this happy."

He held her gaze for a few seconds and then responded in a deep, quiet voice, "*Grazie, dolce amica*, for telling me that."

But the next sound they all heard was Kate screaming out, "Luca! Come look at this one," at the top of her lungs and they all burst out laughing.

Kate heard them laughing, as the three of them found her in an alcove in the gallery and stopped to admire the painting she had singled out. "You know, Luca, this stuff is good, but they don't compare to the stuff you create. You really need to display your art here. Seriously! I mean it."

Shade nodded his head, "*Si,* you should listen to her. You have great talent."

Luca shook his head. "No. I just paint for myself. It's personal to me. It only means something to me, or for the person I paint it for. It feels too private to share."

Kate mocked him, shoved into him with her shoulder. "Wow! Spoken like a true tortured artist. But I'm going to keep bugging you about it."

Shannon spoke up, "I hope you'll share it with me? Is it too personal to share it with me?"

He gave her a smoldering look. "For you, *mia bellezza*? No, it's not too personal for you. I'll be happy to show you my art."

Kate teased him, "Oh god, seriously? That was the classic 'Let me show you my etchings line', you've got to do better than that, Luca."

Shannon and Kate started laughing, and Shade and Luca just looked at each other. Shade shrugged his shoulders and gave Luca a look that said, 'don't look at me, brother'. They finished walking through the gallery and headed back outside on the mall where the band was still playing, and the crowd was getting larger. Kate felt Shade step in close behind her and slide his arms around her as they rocked and swayed to the beat of the music.

Luca slid his hand into Shannon's, as they exited the gallery and walked out into the crowd, pushing their way through the people, getting separated from Shade and Kate. The music filled the night. It was early spring and there was still a chill in the air. He slid his leather jacket off and put it on Shannon, she was clearly getting cold. It was too big for her, but he loved how she looked in it. He stood close behind her, his arms around her, and he felt her lean back, resting her head on his chest. The band started to sing the song from Boys II Men, *I'll Make Love to You*, and Shannon turned in his arms until she was facing him, her arms around his neck, her eyes boring into his, as they moved to the music.

Shannon kissed him lightly and pulled back again to look at him, as they both listened to the lyrics. They came together in a kiss that left no doubt what was on their minds. His mouth was open to hers, his tongue slowly probed as they swayed to the music.

He tasted like sex, he smelled like sex, and she could feel his cock pressing hard against her, as their hips moved in the slow sway of the beat. The heat from him was burning through her skin. She slid her hand into his hair and gripped him tightly, pulling his head harder into her lips. She felt his hands on her back as they slipped under the jacket and he pulled her tight against his chest. She felt her knees buckle and she moaned into his mouth. He broke away from the kiss and dropped his head back, eyes closed, and taking deep breaths. Shannon watched him fight for control. And she got it, she so got it. Her head was spinning, and she felt out of her mind with her desire for him. She was no stranger to men, but Holy Mother of God, this man! He dropped his hands from her back and stepped back from her. She looked at him confused. "Did I do something wrong?"

Luca had been pulled into the kiss, unlike any kiss he had ever felt in his lifetime. He realized the difference with the feeders. They perform, but there was no emotion. There was desire, but not passion. What he was feeling was passion and it overwhelmed him. It took every fiber of his being to control his beast. He had to break the kiss and back away, when backing away was the last thing he wanted to do. Shade was right, the beast was in control. He had never had to fight him back like this. She looked at him in confusion and asked her question. "Nothing, *mia bellezza*, you did nothing wrong, I just need... a minute."

She watched him trying to compose himself, still breathless, and listened to his answer. She had been with enough men to know the look of lust in their eyes, and she smiled at him. "Yeah, I think we could both use a minute, or we'll get arrested soon."

Luca bent over slightly, his hands resting on his knees and took some deep breaths, clearing his head, letting the beast retreat. He looked back up at her. "Sorry... I... you..."

"Oh baby, no apology necessary. Trust me, I felt it and if you hadn't been holding me up, I would have dropped to my knees."

Shade had said mortal women were dangerous, and it never made sense to him, until now. It seemed danger came in a very attractive package, and Luca was so going there.

47

As the music started to slow down, Shade took *bel* into his arms. He let his one hand tangle in her hair, while his other caressed her hip. She laid her head on his chest and his hand wandered to the curve of her ass, and he squeezed it firmly. "Having a good time, *mi amore?*"

"Lover, you have no idea how much I have missed this. Missed us."

Shade slid his hand up her back, and gripped her hair with both hands with ease as he pulled her head back from his chest. He leaned down to her, just a breath away from her mouth. "I have missed you, my minx."

Kissing her deeply, he ground his hips into her and swayed back and forth. The area set aside for dancing was crowded with many couples, so there wasn't much room to move, but he liked this slow, close dance. "I do believe Luca is having a good time as well, *si?*"

"What could be better than slow dancing under the stars? I like being crushed in the crowd. It forces you to hold me tight. And Luca? I think Luca and Shannon are both over the moon right now. So, what are your thoughts? I know you have concerns."

With a wicked grin, he put his hands on her waist and lifted her to his face as her legs wrapped around his hips and her arms went around his neck. He cradled her ass in his hands and kept dancing. "Ah, much better, *si?* I can see you and hear you now."

Letting the smile leave his face, he took a long sigh. "I know I have to make a decision about Luca and Shannon. I have concerns, *mi amore*. But, in all reality, I have to have faith that all the things I've taught Luca will be remembered and put to use. I have to trust him in the mortal world. I've held onto him for my own selfish reasons, not letting him live among mortals, and I have to let go and let him experience first-hand the lessons I've taught him. She is beautiful, *mi amore*, aggressive, humorous and very intelligent. I see her as a good match for him. They complete each other. I am his master, not the ruler of his life and I need to learn to step back. I give my approval."

She looked into his eyes as he spoke. She knew this was a hard decision that had been heavy on his mind, but she was happy with the conclusion he'd come to. "Lover, I know there's still much I struggle to understand about your world, but I feel in my heart, this is the right path."

She kissed him, a deep kiss that drew the stares of the people dancing around them and she heard someone shout out 'get a room' and she chuckled into his mouth before she could break the kiss.

Shade looked over to see Luca and Shannon in an embrace as well and he could feel Luca's beast beating on his door, but it was time to trust him to be able to control the beast among mortals.

"Look to the left, *mi amore*. Luca's beast is rattling him hard, and I know he won't hurt her, but leaving them alone together without her knowledge of what or who he is, is dangerous. I want you to invite her to stay at the house tonight when we return, but you need to speak with her about our world. If she chooses to leave, then it will be better for Luca now than later. He is falling fast. I don't want her to be scared of him if she sees anything. He is hanging by a thread."

"Of course, I wouldn't want Shannon driving back that distance this late at night anyway, and I'll talk to her, somehow. I know Rissa told me, and I didn't believe her. But this is different. I'll make her understand."

Pulling her head to his shoulder, Shade kept his hand on the back of her head, wrapped in that crimson silk and leaned his head on top of hers.

"She needs to understand, *mi amore*, I can't bear to have him hurt. I know he needs to learn that, but he doesn't deserve to be deceived. He is like family. I have been responsible for him for so long, and I'm not ready to expose him to the pain of being rejected. Make sure her intentions are pure as well."

"I'll tell Shannon everything. I'll make her understand. And you might have noticed, she's not as easily intimidated as I was." Kate laughed. "Shannon was always the bold one. She won't be scared off easily."

The music stopped, and the announcement was made that the band was done for the night, and Shade looked up at the moon. It was almost midnight and he sighed. *Damn*, he thought, *this night was way too short.*

"Then let's hope she is game, *mi amore*, because we will have one sore assed vampire warrior on our hands, if she heads for the hills and never returns. We need to head on home ourselves, so let's make our way to them and get back home, *si?*"

Kissing her nose, he smiled and set her feet down on the bricks.

She slid her arms around his waist as they pushed through the crowd toward Luca and Shannon.

Coming up on Shannon and Luca, they found them smiling at each other and his hands remained on her hips, almost in defiance of Shade's warning and he just shook his head and grinned. "I think we should get these two beauties back home safe and sound, *si*, brother?"

"Of course, mas... uh, Shade. We're ready when you are. Lead the way."

Kate tugged at his hand. "There's one more thing before we go." She dragged him over to the First Amendment wall on the mall, a freestanding double-sided chalkboard in the center of the mall space. She found a piece of chalk and wrote 'Shade loves *Bel Rosso*.' Shade looked at her entry among the many chalk drawings and inscriptions on the wall. "*Si*, indeed he does, *bel*."

As she was finishing her entry, Luca picked up another piece of chalk and wrote, 'Luca loves Shannon.' He put the chalk down, brushing his hands together to remove the chalk dust, as he turned and looked at Shannon. He caught her eye and held her gaze, waiting for her response when he was rewarded with a smile as she extended her hand to him.

Grabbing Kate by the hand, Shade swung it back and forth, high in the air as they walked back toward the parking lot. "You ready to roll, momma?"

"Take me home, daddy!"

Kate was laughing out loud as he called her momma, like she was some biker chick. She could hear Luca and Shannon laughing and running behind them.

Shade strapped on her helmet, kissed her quick and lifted her like a feather over the back of the bike onto the seat and turned to Shannon and winked. "That's how you put your woman on a bike!"

Shannon watched the interplay between Shade and Kate, catching the sly wink. Luca was already seated on their bike. Shannon straddled the seat, slid up as close to Luca as she could, slowly letting her hands glide around his waist and down his thighs before shouting back, "And this is how a woman rides with her man."

Shade raised his eyebrows at her and laughed like hell. He knew he had made the right decision. "Well then, you better hang on, *dolce amica*, that boy has a lot of power between those thighs!" Winking at Luca, he straddled the bike, and revved the engine. "Luca!" Luca looked up in quick response to Shade's call, and Shade saw Shannon snap her head to him as well. "The answer is yes!"

Luca heard his master's response. Yes. *Good thing, master. Not sure I would be able to turn back at this point.*

 Patting *bel's* thigh, Shade yelled over the bikes' motor, "Let's roll!"

Kicking the bike in gear, they rolled out slow and easy, as Shade felt her hands gripping his waist, balancing the bike with one hand, he reached down and entwined his leather gloved hand in hers.

Kate loved being on the bike with him, feeling the wind blowing through her hair, her arms wrapped around him, her legs straddling him. She turned her head to the side and laid it against his back. He picked up speed as they left the town and got back on the highway, and the air felt cold as it whipped past them. She squeezed her arms tight around his waist then dropped them to his thighs. **"I'll show you how a woman rides with her man, lover."** She slid her hands up his thighs and into his crotch, cupping his balls in her hands before she slid them up his cock.

"*Cazzo*, you trying to kill us, *mi amore*? Don't stop!"   Revving the bike, he kicked it up another gear and hit about eighty on the open road, and moaned as she kept stroking.

She felt his cock harden beneath her hands, and unzipped his jeans, sliding her hand inside the stiff denim, freeing his cock, as she stroked the full length of him.

Her actions caught him off guard. His sweet *bel* was breaking out his bad ass beast, while they were rocking it hard down the highway. He revved it harder and they were now hitting a hundred, he was concentrating on keeping the bike steady and in one fucking lane. **"Woman! Killing me here."** *He slid* forward on the seat, leaning back just enough to give his cock the room she needed.

Kate leaned into his back, feeling the tension in his muscles as she stroked his member, and he increased the speed of the bike. She used both hands, gripping his dick, and sliding her fingers up his engorged shaft, rolling the palm of her hand over the head of his cock, and wishing she had him in her mouth. She slid one hand under the crotch of his jeans, and lightly squeezed his balls, and let the vibrations of the engine tease them both. **"I want to straddle you like this bike, lover. Can I make you cum?"**

Moaning, he could barely concentrate on keeping this bike on the road, let alone trying to get home. He wanted to stop and bend her over this bike and fuck her right here, make them both cum so hard they'd start a fire, but he couldn't. Luca and Shannon weren't that far behind them. He slowed down to a controllable speed, feeling her stroke faster and harder and he thought he was going to lose his damn mind. **"Yes, *mi amore*, cazzo!"**

He held the bike steady and climaxed in her hand, his moan was loud and the roar unmistakably his. She was in for it when they got home. He was going to ravish her ass hard and sweet. Feeling his body relax after that awesome orgasm, he still couldn't believe she had done that while he was ripping it down the highway. **"You are going to be punished later tonight, my minx, don't even think you are getting away with this. Now, get my fucking cock back in my jeans, we are less than a damn mile from the house."**

She slid his cock back inside his jeans and watched as he squirmed to adjust himself. She laughed and licked her fingers, making sure he knew what she was doing. She heard his 'threat' of punishment and kissed him on the neck, running her tongue along that sweet vein. **"Punishment... my favorite... I can't wait."**

Shaking his head and laughing, he rolled down the long lane to home and went straight to the garage. Keeping watch in his rearview mirror, he had yet to see Luca making the turn into the lane, but knew they weren't far behind. The garage doors were still open, and he drove right inside and shut down the engine. Jumping off the bike, he ripped off his helmet and kissed *bel* hard on the lips. He didn't let up as he probed and sucked at her, driving his tongue deep into her throat. He covered her mouth fully until she melted into him and couldn't breathe. "That will teach you."

She winked at him, "Yes, it will. It will teach me to be bad more often."

The headlights of Luca's bike appeared on the long drive up to the house and they pulled into the garage, Shannon clinging tight around Luca's waist, and Luca beaming.

Laughing together, they all strolled into the house, coming home to a blazing fire in the fireplace Gi had made for them. Turning to Shannon, Shade said, "*Dolce amica*, it would be a good idea, since the hour is late, that you stay here with us for the night. I'm sure Kate wouldn't mind having you here longer, if that's acceptable to you, *si*?"

Shannon looked relieved. "That would be great, if it's no trouble. I was planning to just stay in town tonight because I didn't want to make the drive back to D.C. Maybe Luca could help me get my suitcase out of my car?"

Luca looked from Shade to Shannon as his master invited her to stay the night. *Fuck! This is good news... and bad news.* He wasn't ready to say goodnight to her, but holy fuck, she would be sleeping under the same roof. "Of course, I'll get that for you now."

Kate shouted out to him, "Luca, just bring the suitcase upstairs. Shannon, come on up with me, I'll show you your room."

Shade had to stifle a laugh when he saw Luca's face as he found out his little vixen was spending the night in the same house. *Oh, you want her Luca, fine and dandy, but the beast will test this control you have.* Watching as the girls headed up the staircase, full of giggles and girlish whispers, he smiled. Damn if he didn't love seeing *bel* so happy.

Kate led Shannon up the stairs to a guest bedroom. "This way, you're right down the hall from us."

She gave her a quick tour of the room and her bathroom, at which point, Luca came bursting through the door like a rocket with her suitcase. He stopped short and locked eyes with Kate.

Kate looked back at him. "I'm going to talk to Shannon for a while, so maybe you and Shade can find something to do?"

He looked at her and she saw a momentary flash of fear in his eyes. He knew Kate was about to tell Shannon everything.

"'Yeah, sure... no problem."

He glanced quickly at Shannon and she flashed that megawatt smile his way. He melted under her gaze. He set her suitcase down and seemed hesitant to leave, knowing if this conversation didn't go well, this could be the last time he saw her. He walked over to her and slid one arm around her waist and gave her a gentle kiss before he turned and walked out. He closed the door behind him. As he left, Shannon looked at Kate and did a face-palm slap to her forehead.

"Fuck me! He is unbelievable, Kate."

Kate laughed at her. "See, that's what I always like about you, Shannon. You're such a fine example of a Southern lady."

They both laughed as Kate patted the bed and indicated she wanted Shannon to join her. As Shannon climbed into the middle of the bed, sitting cross-legged in front of her, Kate wondered how many nights they had sat up talking like this, probably too many nights to even count.

Shannon gave her a quizzical look. "Okay... so, what's this about? I can read you like a book, Kate Reese. Something's on your mind. You have managed to get us here together, all private and cozy. So, what is it you want to talk about?"

Kate hesitated, unsure of where to start. "I... wow... I guess I just want to know what your thoughts are, about Luca."

Shannon looked at her with wide eyes. "Really? You have to ask? I want to whack you for not calling me sooner."

Kate whacked at her instead and they both laughed. "No, seriously Shannon... because, well, there's stuff you need to know, but if you don't think this is going anywhere, then I don't even want to bring it up. And not only that, if you don't think it's going to go anywhere, if this is just a fling for you... then I want to ask you to back off."

Shannon stopped short. "Wait! What? Back off? Are you kidding me?"

Kate pushed. "If you don't think it will go anywhere... that's what I said and I mean it. I don't want him hurt. Shade doesn't want to see that either. I know you can't predict the outcome of a relationship, but I'm asking, what is this to you. Right now, what does it mean to you?"

"Wow! Okay, I wasn't ready for a discussion this heavy, but okay, I can go there. I really like him. I mean I really like him, a lot. The chemistry is off the chain. And he's just... so... Luca. What can I say? If you're asking me if I could love him, then yes, the answer is yes. I want to see him again, and often. I want to learn everything there is to know about him. So, no, to answer your question, this isn't a fling. At least, not for me. I hope he's feeling the same."

Kate assured her, "Oh, I can promise you it's not a fling for Luca. He is, wow, he's just so undone already."

Shannon looked giddy. "Really? Are you sure? Because, I mean, you know what's out there. You'd practically given up on finding anybody. And just because I stayed in the game doesn't mean I was finding anybody worth my time. But him, I... wow... when am I ever at a loss for words? He's just... perfect."

Kate slid off the bed and walked over to the window, her back to Shannon. "Okay then, well, first I need a promise, as my friend, that what we say in this room stays in this room." Kate turned around and faced her. "I mean it, Shannon. You may be okay with what I have to say, or you may be freaked out by it, but whatever your reaction, it stays here, understood?"

Shannon looked startled. "What the fuck, Kate?"

Kate gave her a stern look and practically shouted at her, "Promise!"

"Yes! Okay, I promise. When have I ever repeated our secret gab sessions? You know you can trust me, but I have to say, I'm getting a little freaked out already."

Kate put her hands together like a prayer. "I know, I'm sorry. And you have always been a trusted friend. But I'm about to take you on a wild ride, sister. So, I need your assurance."

Shannon frowned. "Oh god, are you going to tell me they're like, in the mafia or something? They're rich. They're from Italy. That's it, isn't it?"

Kate shrugged. "What if that was it? Just asking... what if it was? What would you do?"

Shannon leaned back against the headboard and thought about the question, and then she thought about Luca. "Well, I think I'd probably stay."

Kate probed, "Probably?"

"Well, some of this will depend on Luca, you know? I mean, how he treats me. Is he faithful to me? So, if you're asking me a theoretical, and I assume you are, then if he loved me, and I felt that love from him, and he was true to me, then yes, I would stay. It would take some adjustments, you know, to their lifestyle. So, is that it? Is he in the mafia?"

Kate shook her head. "No. Not the mafia. That would be too simple. But your answer told me what I needed to know. Hang on. You're going to need a drink for this."

Kate went to the door and called down to Gi. Theresa came out of her bedroom and asked if she could help. Kate asked her to bring them a bottle of wine, not Midnight, and two glasses. Theresa ran off, passing Gi on the stairs and letting him know she had it handled. She returned in minutes, the cork already removed from the bottle, and two wine glasses. Kate thanked her as she left the room and Kate poured the glasses full to the rim. She handed one glass to Shannon and then held her glass up to hers. Shannon clinked her glass against Kate's, as Kate told her, "Drink it down... the whole thing."

Shannon gave her a wary look but downed the glass, as Kate chugged hers. She refilled their empty glasses and looked at her. "Ready?"

Shannon looked skeptical. "Uh... you are seriously scaring the hell out of me right now. I mean, the things rushing through my head..."

"Yeah, well, I'm pretty sure what I'm about to tell you is not one of the things in your head."

How did she say it other than to just say it? They were both seated in the center of the bed. Kate held her hand out to her, little finger extended. "Pinky swear, Shannon."

Shannon held up her hand and hooked her little finger around Kate's. "Pinky swear."

Kate took a deep breath and said, "Luca is a vampire."

Shannon heard her say he was a vampire and she gave Kate a blank stare, as she waited for her to say something else, but Kate just sat and looked at her. *A joke?* Shannon burst out laughing, and fell back on the bed, spilling her wine. She rolled onto her side, holding her stomach she was laughing so hard, and then she rolled onto her back and tried to sit up again and noticed Kate was not laughing. Kate was not smiling. Kate was staring at her. She was deadly serious. *Fuck! Fuck!*

"Okay..." She pulled herself together. "Okay, clearly, you weren't joking. But, okay... can I ask some questions?"

Kate answered quietly, "You can ask me anything you want."

"So, if he's a vampire, why does he live here with you?" Shannon started giggling again. "Sorry, sorry... I'm trying to be serious."

Kate responded, "Actually, I live here with them. They're all vampires. Shade, Luca, Gi, Theresa, Reynaldo, and a few more out back you haven't met."

"You're fucking serious, aren't you?"

"Shannon, you have no idea, because I put them all at risk by telling you. This is why I disappeared from work. Why I told everyone I took a job overseas. Once I learned about Shade, and made the decision to be with him, I had to separate myself from everyone I ever knew to protect their secret. That's why it took so long for Luca to call you, to see you. Shade is his... master. He had to approve Luca even seeing you. In fact, that was the reason for the double-date. So Shade could make a judgment call. Mortals still represent a huge risk to them. You passed, by the way."

Shannon looked stunned. "Wait... are you?"

Kate shook her head. "No. But I will be. At some point, Shade will turn me."

"Oh my god! That is fucking awesome! You're a fang-banger just like on True Blood? Holy fuck! I mean, fuck! If this turns out to be a joke, Kate Reese, I will fucking kill you."

"It's no joke, I promise you. But I had to tell you, before, you know, anything happened between you and Luca. And after watching the two of you together tonight, I knew we needed to have this conversation pretty fast."

Shannon set her wine glass down on the nightstand. "Oh my god, I have a million questions in my head. Does Luca know you're telling me?"

"Yes, he asked me to tell you. He thought you would be less afraid, if I told you. He's terrified you would bolt and run when you found out."

Shannon looked back at her. "Do I need to be scared?"

"Of Luca? Are you kidding me? Is there anyone sweeter than Luca?"

Shannon slapped Kate on the knee. "So, you have a vampire for a personal trainer. How awesome is that?"

"Oh... well, he is not actually my personal trainer. I just couldn't think of what to call him the day you were here. He's my protector."

Shannon looked confused. "Protector? What? You just told me I didn't need to be scared and now you're telling me he's your protector?"

Kate shrugged. "Long story for another day. For now, all you need to know is you have nothing to fear from Luca, or Shade, or anyone in this house. Okay? Oh, there is this issue of the beast? But trust me, you'll love him. I'll let Luca give you the details... if you decide to go there."

Shannon responded enthusiastically, "Oh, I'm going there. I am so going there!"

Kate started to slide off the bed, "Okay, well, if you'll excuse me, my vampire is waiting for me. And he is usually working at night, so I'm going to go take advantage of him being home. Oh, that reminds me, Luca is a day-walker. That means he can go out during daylight and doesn't have to go into a death slumber during the day. All the staff are day-walkers. The only one who has to sleep during the day is Shade. So, sleep tight... or not. Luca's suite is at the bottom of the stairs, go left down the hall. His door is right at the end of the corridor. Just tap, pretty sure he is wide awake and waiting." Kate leaned over and kissed her cheek. "Welcome, sister. And just hang on is all I can say."

Kate started to leave the room. Shannon's head was spinning from the wine and the unexpected information. "Wait! One more question. Would you do it again? If you were back at square one today, knowing everything you know, would you make the same choice? Would you choose him? Shade? Would you choose him again?

Kate looked her dead in the eyes. "Abso-fucking-lutely!"

She closed the door behind her as she left, and she could hear Shannon giggle. Kate walked down the hall to their bedroom. **"Oh, lover, I'm ready for my punishment!"**

48

Shannon was sitting in the middle of the bed, holding what was left of her glass of wine. Her head was spinning, and her heart was racing. *Fuck! I forgot to ask her if they do that neck biting thing.* She poured the rest of the wine into her glass and sat there trying to process what Kate had told her. How the hell did Kate end up with a vampire? Good lord, she had so many questions she wanted to ask her. She sipped the wine and let thoughts of Luca drift into her head. Would he come to her? No, Kate said he knew she was telling her about him. He would wait to see if Shannon went to him. He wouldn't push her. She already knew him well enough to know that. However this played out, he would make sure it was her decision. She would have to go to him. He was waiting for her to make the choice. *Fuckity, fuck, fuck! Okay, Shannon, get it together.* She downed the last of the wine in the glass and headed to the bathroom, climbing into the shower.

* * *

Luca went back to his suite as soon as he delivered the suitcase to her room. He had passed Shade on the way down, who asked if he wanted a drink. He shook his head no and headed for his room, closed the door and sat down. He had all his senses tuned to that room upstairs. Trying to feel her, hear her, trying to second guess what her response would be. He heard Kate yell down the stairs for Gi, and then he heard Theresa run down the stairs, the clinking of glass, as she ran back up. *Drinks? They're having something to drink.* He heard Shannon burst out laughing, and then silence. Was that good? Bad? He could hear them talking, but not their words. *That's a good sign, right?*

He heard Kate leave the room, and the door closed behind her, and he listened to the one set of footsteps to Shade's bed. Then there was nothing but silence, a long silence. He heard the sound of the water running. She was in the shower. He had thought she would come to him. His elbows rested on his knees, and he put his head in his hands.

He shouldn't have let his hopes get so high. At least she wasn't so freaked out she left the house. He stood up and stripped off his own clothes and walked to the shower, washing away the dirt from the road and any hopes of being with her. He was soothed by the thought that she stood beneath the running water upstairs and their actions mirrored each other. *Cut it out, Luca. Let it go. Quit torturing yourself.* He stood under the hot water for a long time, letting it clear his head. He got out of the shower and dried off, running a towel through his hair and slipping on the loose white linen draw-string pants he wore in his room.

When Shannon climbed out of the shower, her mind was made up. She dried her hair, put on some perfume and slid a nightgown over her head. She grabbed the empty wine glass, it would be her excuse, just in case.

She opened the door of her room and stood quietly. The house was silent. She walked barefoot down the hall to the stairs and paused a second before she descended. As she reached the bottom of the stairs, she looked about. The lights were still on in the house, but there was no one about. Kate had said turn left at the bottom of the stairs, so she walked down the long corridor to the closed door. She stood still and closed her eyes, taking a deep breath. *He's just a man, Shannon, he's just a man.*

Pushing past her last bit of reservation, she tapped on his door. She heard him moving behind the door, and then it opened. He was standing there, his hair still damp, hanging in loose ringlets around his face, his hazel eyes, heavy-lidded and sexy. His chest was bare and his skin a deep bronzed olive tone, in sharp contrast to the white linen pants that hang loose on his hips and puddled at his bare feet. He took her breath away. Her mouth felt dry. She held out her glass.

He had been ready to climb into bed when he heard a light tap on his door and his heart stopped. He opened the door to find her standing there, her brown hair freshly washed and brushed, falling over her shoulders. Her blue eyes large and round in her face, showing a hint of uncertainty. She was wearing a soft sheer nightgown, and she smelled like heaven. Her skin was pink and warm from her shower, and she was wearing that perfume again. The same perfume she wore the first day he met her. Exotic, heady, and he just inhaled her. He could only stand and stare at her. She came to his door. She came willingly to his door.

"Hi. I, uh, seem to be out of wine."

Luca reached out to take the glass from her hand and his fingers covered hers. His eyes were locked on hers, and they just stared. No words. Time passed slowly, as they both took each other in. He finally opened the door wider and stepped back, allowing her to enter as he took the wine glass from her hand. "Do you want more wine, Shannon?"

"I... uh... will you join me? Do you drink wine?"

"I'll get us something. Have a seat."

He left his suite and headed to the kitchen only to encounter Reynaldo who had already set out another bottle of red wine for her and a bottle of Midnight for him, and fresh glasses. Reynaldo just raised his eyebrows as Luca took the bottles and glasses off the counter.

Reynaldo nodded and said, "Good luck, my friend."

"Thanks," he responded, "I may need it."

He went back to his suite. Shannon was walking around the room, exploring the books on the shelf, looking at the easel and some of the stacked canvases. She turned around suddenly as he entered.

"Oh! I was just looking at your things. Sorry. You have a lot of books. I'm surprised... I mean... I guess I don't think about a vampire reading books."

He set the bottles down and removed the corks, poured wine for both of them. He laughed at her comment. "What exactly do you think vampires do?" He handed her a glass of wine, sat on the sofa and patted the spot beside him.

She took the glass from him and then sat beside him. Their knees were touching as they were turned to face each other. "Well, don't take offense, but I can't say I've ever spent a lot of time wondering about what vampires do. I only know what I see in movies." She watched as that shy smile appeared.

"Movies, okay then. Well, let's fast forward through some of that. Kate thought we wore capes and turned into bats. No to that. And no coffins, we don't sleep in coffins. We're not the walking dead. Our hearts beat, and our hearts break. We live a lot like you."

She responded hesitantly, "Well... the blood thing."

"Yeah... the blood thing. That part is true."

She looked up at him with her large doe eyes. "Will you... uh..."

"Shannon, why are you here?"

She seemed taken aback, "What? What do you mean why am I here?"

Luca's voice was stern, "Am I just a curiosity to you?"

"No! Oh god, no. Did I say something wrong? I'm just... I'm just trying to find my way here. I mean, I'm still trying to process this, but my feelings for you, they're real. I hope you know they're real."

He could feel her turmoil and her genuine emotion. He brushed her hair back from her face. "Shh, *mia bellezza*. I didn't mean to offend. I've never been with a mortal. Shade says there are mortals who seek us out for mere curiosity. My feelings for you are too strong to just be your toy. I'm not here to play, *mia bellezza*. I want to understand what you expect. What you want."

"Luca, I have wanted to be with you since the moment I first saw you. And I knew the feeling was mutual. I could feel that from you. And then you didn't call me for days and it was making me crazy. I called Kate and she said how busy you were, but I thought that was just an excuse, that maybe I'd misread you. And then you called. And tonight. I can't remember when I've had this much fun with a man on a first date. I was immediately at ease with you. All I could think about as we were riding home, was how fast it went by and I didn't want to say goodbye to you. And then Kate told me... you're a vamp, you're all vamps. I realized it didn't matter to me, but that doesn't mean I don't have questions, or I know what to do next. It's just a little confusing, you know?"

"Confusing, *si*. Very confusing, *mia bellezza*, for me as well. And I know much more of your world than you know of mine." He finished off the glass of Midnight and set the glass down, then removed the glass from her hand. "But what Kate said, about being busy, you need to hear that. My time is not my own. Shade is my master. I work for him. It is not a '9 to 5' as you mortals say. I live here, and for the rest of my life, I will live here, or wherever it is Shade chooses to live. I protect Kate when he is away, and I do other things for him when he's home. I'm free when he says I'm free. Shade is a master, and a warrior, and I was raised a warrior in service to him. Shade puts Kate first, above all things. But I cannot give you that. My station in life dictates my allegiance to him first, and then to her. If you choose to be with me, then you must know this." He took both her hands in his. "You'll have my love, *mia bellezza*, my undying love. You'll have my heart, and I'll remain true to you and you alone. But my responsibilities as a vampire demand I place him first, and my first obligation to him is protecting her. If you come to me, you'll always be first in my heart, but understand my obligation. It was why Shade was so reluctant to grant permission. The conflict. I need to know if you can live with that."

"Wow, Luca! That sounds like you're a slave to him."

Luca shook his head. "No. It couldn't be farther from it. Don't confuse the meaning of the word master. Yes, he can command me, and I must show my allegiance to him, but he's also like my father, my brother. To serve him is my honor. To be chosen as protector to his mate, chosen from all his warriors, it is the highest honor. And while I would die to protect you, I would also lay down my life for him, or for Kate. It's essential you understand these things. This is what dictates my life. Don't come to me, unless you can accept these terms, for they're not negotiable."

Shannon asked, "Do you ever get to leave here without him?"

"Of course, my free time is mine to do with as I please."

"If we were to... be together, stay together... would we ever be able to live together? Be married? Have children? I mean, I know that's really jumping ahead, but it sounds like its 'all cards on the table' time."

Luca took her hands. "There are many hurdles to overcome, but yes to all of your questions."

"Well then, it sounds to me like every mortal guy I ever dated. You have a job that takes up a lot of your time and your job comes first. Maybe a little more complicated than that, but I get it, I think."

"But can you live with it, *mia bellezza*?"

She looked at him, with his dark hair and bronze skin, those hazel eyes, his chest smooth and muscled, his relaxed pose on the sofa, his voice deep and soothing. She recalled his laugh, his attentiveness, his touch, and his kiss... That kiss on the mall. She reached up and touched the necklace he placed around her neck earlier. She watched as his eyes followed her hand before returning to lock on hers. "I can live with it, Luca. If the pot of gold at rainbow's end is you, then I can live with it."

Luca ran the back of his fingers across her sweet face and brushed back her hair. "It won't be easy. Mortal and immortal. I've watched Shade and Kate every day. Their love is deep, and yet, they struggle, they fight. But in the end, they always find their way back to each other."

Shannon put her hand on his knee. "Because they have something worth fighting for."

"*Si*. They have something worth fighting for."

"Can we have that, Luca? You and me? Can we have something worth fighting for?"

"*Si, mia bellezza*. I promise you a love worth fighting for."

Shannon leaned in to kiss him, and his arms opened to receive her. She felt his lips close around hers as she lay against his chest and he leaned back on the sofa. She felt his hands as they glided down her back. She felt his tongue as it probed her mouth. She slid her hands up his muscular arms and shoulders, and up his neck and into his hair. Gripping his hair tight in her hands as she slid her breasts across his bare chest, their skin separated by the sheer fabric of her gown. She heard him moan into her mouth. She sat upright suddenly and watched as his eyes snapped open and he looked at her in surprise. She pulled the gown over her head and tossed it to the floor. "I want to feel you. I want to feel your skin against mine."

He was looking at her bare breasts, her nipples pink and erect, and he heard the beast growl deep in his chest. He dropped his head back onto the sofa, taking a deep breath and fighting for control. He felt her straddle his hips as she laid her breasts against his bare chest and purred, "Much better." She leaned over him and her hair fell forward like a curtain, and her perfume overwhelmed. Her mouth was on his again, her tongue deep in his mouth. He slid his hands to her hips and onto her ass as she started to grind her hips into his. He squeezed her ass hard, and the beast growled louder. *Stop, you have to stop!*

He lifted her off him and sat her on the couch as he stood, all in one quick motion. He rubbed his hands across his face as he took a deep breath and he paced the floor. He looked at her, her mouth open, her hair hanging in her face.

"What's wrong? Did I do something wrong?"

Luca was panting, speaking between breaths, "Not you. Me. We'll have to go slow, Shan." He picked up her gown from the floor and handed it back to her. She looked puzzled, but took it from his hands and held it to cover her breasts.

She felt confused. *Go slow?* "Wow... never had a man tell me that before."

Luca chuckled. "Yeah, it's a new one for me too." Pacing, he ran his hands through his hair. "My strength, I need to be careful, Shannon, and there is something else. At the core of me, I am more beast than human. When I'm not being controlled by emotions, by anger or passion... I can control the beast, I'm hardly aware of him. But when my emotions run strong, he takes over. As a warrior, I depend on him, his power and his strength help me to conquer and slay any opponent. I've only had sex with immortals, so if he emerges, they're able to meet his strength. But a mortal..."

Shannon looked at him slyly. "The beast? Kate told me I would meet the beast. She said I'd love him."

"What? Kate said you'd love the beast? What did she tell you?"

"Nothing really, other than that. She said you would explain the beast, but not to worry because I would love him. So, explain the beast."

"Shannon, I don't want to fuck this up. I wanted you to get to know me before I ever exposed you to that. I don't want to scare you away, and I really don't want to hurt you."

"Oh, come on Luca, give me some credit. Do you like, turn into some kind of monster or something?"

"Yeah, actually, I do."

She sat up straighter. "Really? Well, this just got interesting. Can you just bring him out?"

"No, I can't just 'bring him out,'" he answered in an exasperated tone.

Shannon dropped the gown to the floor and stood up wearing only her thong panties. She slipped her thumbs into the side strings over each hip and did a slow rotation of her hips, pulling at the strings on the thong. "But I can tempt him out?"

"Fuck! This is no joke, Shan."

She flipped her head back, tossing her hair, as she walked slowly toward him, inching the strings on the thong down her hips. "Oh, I'm not joking, Luca."

As she stood in front of him, she put both hands on his chest and did a slow hip swerving 'drop it like it's hot' squat, dragging her hands down his chest, until her mouth was at the low-slung waist of those linen pants held in place by a drawstring. She took the string in her mouth and pulled it loose and watched as the linen pants dropped to the floor, around his feet. *Talk about a beast!*

She was looking at the most glorious cock she had ever laid eyes on, and she had seen a few. Her hands glided down his thighs as she slid her mouth over his member and listened to his low, deep growling moan. She felt his hands slip into her hair as she took him deep into her throat. As she slid her mouth slowly up and down the long shaft of him, he gripped her hair tighter and pulled her head more forcefully into him, as she felt his hips thrust to meet the rhythm of her mouth. She slid her hands around to his ass and gripped him tightly. As she sank her nails into his skin, she heard a roar and she looked up at him, his cock still deep in her throat. *Fuck! He has fangs!* His fangs dripped hot saliva down on her and his eyes were glowing red. *He is so fucking hot! He thought I would run from this?*

He untangled his hands from her hair and reached under her arms, lifting her and throwing her onto the bed. Luca saw the expression on her face move from shock to lust, as she smiled back at him, and said, "Oh baby... bring it!"

Upstairs, Kate lay in Shade's arms, when they both heard the loud growl of the beast, as the house shuddered like the aftermath of the clap of loud thunder. Shade sat up quickly in the bed and started to swing his legs to the side, ready to bolt downstairs. Kate grabbed him by the arm and pulled him back down.

"Relax, lover, a mortal girl is about to conquer another beast."

49

Kate felt someone gently nudging her shoulder and woke to find Theresa leaning over her.

"My lady, you asked me to wake you when Miss Shannon was up and about."

"Oh, yes... thank you, Theresa. What time is it?"

"Almost 10 a.m.," she answered as she left the room.

Kate kissed Shade on the cheek as he remained deep in his death slumber, and slid from their bed. She pulled on jeans and a sweater and walked to the guest bedroom. She could tell Shannon never slept in that bed, but her clothes were scattered about. She caught her as she stepped from the bathroom, dressed and her make-up fresh. "Well, good morning, sunshine."

Shannon greeted her with a giant grin on her face. She looked at Kate and the only thing that came out of her mouth was, "Oh. My. God."

Kate started laughing at her. "Yeah...tell me about it. Or actually, you don't need to. I heard most of it firsthand."

Shannon issued a loud guffaw. "Is that... was that... normal? I mean, can I expect that every time we have sex? Holy Mother of God, will it be like that all the time? Or was that just because it was the first time? Kate... he was... we were... Oh. My. God."

Kate leaped across the bed, landing in a belly flop and she couldn't stop laughing at her. "Oh, I think I can safely say it gets better."

"Better? No fucking way... I'm… I'm… I'm…" Shannon climbed across the bed and lay beside her. "No, seriously? Better? How is that even possible? Jesus Christ, no wonder I haven't seen you for six months."

Kate was still laughing at her. "Well, you did meet the beast. He will learn to control the beast as he has more experience. Shade gets really freaked out about the whole beast thing."

"Control the beast? Oh, I hope not. I loved the beast. But yeah, Luca seemed very worried about the beast as well. The beast didn't appear every time we made love last night, just the first time."

"Oh, trust me, he'll be back. But as best as I can understand, when the beast is out, they have to fight for control. In a battle with another vampire, they can let him go, let the beast rule, but with mortals... I don't know, Shade is always afraid I will be hurt by the beast. So, I take it you plan to see him again?"

"Oh my gosh, yes. We talked a long while before... he seemed really serious about my intent. Isn't *that* a role reversal? I mean, I'm usually trying to figure out if a guy is just using me, but he wanted to make sure I wasn't there out of curiosity, that I wanted something more, something long-term."

"You're his first mortal. Actually, Shannon, you're his first relationship."

"First relationship? What do you mean? There's no way that guy was a virgin."

Kate laughed at her. "No, I don't mean it's the first time he's had sex, I mean the first time... wow, how do I explain this? You know they feed right?"

"Yeah, the blood thing. He acknowledged that, but we didn't really talk about it."

"Well, when they are not in a relationship, or not bound to a mate, they go to a breed of vampires called feeders. The feeding is very sexual, and they will typically have sex when they feed, so all of Luca's experience has been with feeders, which, according to Shade, is not unusual among warriors."

"So... almost like a hooker?"

"They don't see it that way. Feeders are not looked down upon. It is just their role in the vampire hierarchy. But trust me, I had the same reaction. The point is, you are the first female, mortal or immortal, that Luca has been drawn to, or at least, drawn to enough to act on it, outside of the feeder community. Choosing a mortal is a big deal, especially for him. He and Shade are old-world vamps from Europe. They tend to stick to their kind and partnering with a mortal is pretty rare and not looked upon with much grace. Shade says it's a more common practice here for the vamps in the States."

"Luca said Shade was his master. Does that mean Shade is the one who turned him?"

"No, both Shade and Luca were born vamps, but Shade practically raised Luca. His parents died when he was young. There is this whole hierarchy in their world. You are pretty much born into your station in life. I'm still struggling to understand it. Shade is a master because his father was a master... and royalty, which I still don't fully understand. But Shade is also a warrior. He trains other warriors. Even though vamps are born to be warriors, they still go through all kinds of training. Then they have this level I call 'worker bees'. The people like Theresa and Gi and Reynaldo. But they are everywhere... doctors, lawyers, not just servants."

"So, any children you have with Shade will be masters?"

"Yes, the males anyway, I think that's how it works. Oh, and speaking of children, be sure you are on birth control. I really screwed up. I just assumed all vamps came from mortals who had been turned. I didn't know they were also born."

"What do you mean, you screwed up?"

"I got pregnant. But, apparently, pregnancies that are the result of mortal and immortal pairings are very high risk. It was a nightmare. At first, Shade was really angry with me that I had gotten pregnant. But then he really wanted the baby. We both wanted the baby. We tried really hard to make it work, to try to keep the baby, but... in the end..."

"Oh my god. When did this happen? Oh, Kate, I'm so sorry."

"It was about three months ago and thank you for caring. You're the first mortal that I've even told that to." Shannon grabbed Kate in a big hug.

"Oh, good Lord! Look at the time. I told Luca I was getting dressed and then coming back down, and now we've been up here just gabbing away. Help me shove all my stuff back in my suitcase and come downstairs with me."

They slid off the bed together, gathered her scattered clothes and jammed them into the suitcase and set it by the door. Kate asked, "Hungry?"

Shannon grabbed her stomach. "Yes. I'm starving. Does anyone in the house ever eat?"

Kate laughed, "Only me, but I have a full-time chef at my disposal, so come on, I'll have him fix us a big brunch."

They headed down the stairs together. As they reached the bottom of the stairs, Luca was just coming out of his room. His eyes lit up when he saw Shannon. Kate extended him an invite. "Luca, come sit with us in the kitchen. I'm going to have Reynaldo fix us something."

Kate watched as the two of them attached at the hip like magnets, and Luca slid his arm around her waist.

"We have this great dining room," Kate pointed it out to Shannon as they passed it by, "but I usually just eat at the counter in the kitchen, so I can talk to Reynaldo."

Emily Bex

When they entered the kitchen, Reynaldo was already banging pots and pans. He served up a feast of omelets, bacon, fresh fruit, and coffee. Shannon and Kate shoveled down the food while both men just watched.

Shannon was cleaning her plate. "This is so good. I was starving. Reynaldo, how can you cook when you never eat? How do you know what it tastes like?"

Reynaldo bowed his head in acknowledgment of her compliment. "Well, I was trained as a chef when I was mortal, and I have a degree in culinary arts."

Kate nearly shouted, "You were mortal?"

"*Si,* my lady, I was not born vampire but turned. My master was killed, and I went to work for the Medici family, and I've been with them for years now."

Shannon spit a mouthful of her omelet across the counter as she started laughing and choking on her food. "My lady! He called you my lady, hahaha... oh my goodness, I can't stop laughing."

Kate whacked her on the back as she watched Luca biting his lip to keep from laughing. "I know, right? Shade insists they all call me that. It drives me nuts. We had to have a talk with him before the double date to get him to agree that Luca wouldn't have to call me that while we were out."

Shannon started laughing so hard she slid off the stool and onto the floor. "Luca calls you my lady? Oh, I am so calling you my lady from now on. Hahahahahahahahaha..."

"Yeah? Well, call me my lady at your own risk, Shannon O'Connor." Kate watched as Luca helped her up off the floor and Shannon climbed back on the barstool, still giggling.

Once she was settled, Luca looked at her. "Shannon O'Connor. I am just hearing your last name. Beautiful name, *mia bellezza.*"

"Thanks. It's Irish... of course. But I am pretty partial to *mia bellezza* right now."

She watched as he looked down and a shy smile appeared. She was already seriously in love with his face. "And your last name? Good lord, I can't even believe we didn't ask these questions."

"Masters have last names, like Shade. He is from the Medici family, and all the vampires in his coven are called Medici. So, it's not really like a last name, it just identifies my coven and my master."

Kate looked astounded. "Wow, really? I didn't know that."

"You never asked, my lady."

Shannon collapsed into a laughing heap again, joined shortly by Kate, Reynaldo, and Luca.

Shannon finally composed herself and checked the time on her cell phone. *Crap. It's already after noon.* "Guys, I hate to break this up, but I really have to get on the road. Is Shade coming down?"

Kate shook her head. "No. He'll sleep until sunset, so you won't see him again before you leave."

Shannon took a minute to let that sink in. "Wow... reality check."

"Yeah, I know. It's hard sometimes. But you lucked out with a day-walker."

Shannon grabbed Luca by the shirt and pulled him in for a kiss. "Oh, I lucked out all right." Luca's arms slid around her waist.

Kate cleared her throat. "Okay, before you two get started again, let me say goodbye, and then Luca can walk you to your car." Kate hugged Shannon tightly. "Love you, Shannon. I'm so glad this is working out."

"Yeah, somehow, I think you're probably not as happy as I am that it has worked out. I'll text you when I get home, okay?"

She watched as Kate headed back up the stairs to be with Shade, then turned to Luca and took his hand. "And now just us..."

Luca lifted her hand to his lips and kissed her palm. "Just us, *mia bellezza*. Do you have your things ready for the car?"

"My suitcase is by the door of the bedroom I never slept in."

They both laughed as Luca headed up the stairs to retrieve her suitcase. When he returned, they walked outside to her car. He loaded the suitcase in the trunk and then opened the driver's side door for her. They stood together in a full embrace.

"When will I see you again, Luca?"

"Soon, *mia bellezza*. You remember our talk, *si*? My schedule is not my own. But as soon as I have free time, I'll come to you."

"I wish we didn't live so far apart. That two-hour drive is time we could spend together... well, four hours round trip."

"That is why, next time, I come to you. I have no need to drive. I'll just teleport."

"Tele-what? Like 'Beam me up, Scottie' on Star Trek?"

"I don't know Star Trek, *mia bellezza*, so I don't know to what you refer, but I'm able to transport myself to you in seconds."

Shannon stood with her mouth hanging open and couldn't seem to close it. "Really? Are you for real?"

Luca smiled at her. "For real."

"Wow. Just wow. That will be awesome." She kissed him again and this time the kiss stretched out as they both lingered. "I hate to leave you, Luca. I think I just had the best time of my life."

"And I hate leaving you, but I promise you there will be many more best times."

He kissed her one last time before she slipped into the driver's seat and he closed the door. She placed her hand against the glass, and he did the same on his side of the door. She started the engine, and as she pulled away, she blew him a kiss, which he caught. Master said he still had much to learn about life, and about women, and he planned to learn it all with her. His cell phone rang and as he pulled it from his pocket, he saw Shannon's face and number on his screen. He smiled.

"Hello, *mia bellezza*."

"I forgot something, Luca."

"And what did you forget?"

"I forgot to tell you how much I love you."

"And I, you, Shan. I miss you already."

Kate had returned to their bedroom, dropped her clothes on the floor and climbed back into their bed, sliding in next to Shade. He lay on his back in his death slumber. She laid her head on his shoulder as she felt his arm encircle her and heard a soft sigh from his lips. "I am back, lover."

She wrapped one arm across his strong chest and tossed her leg across his thighs, and quickly fell asleep beside him.

50

Another night had passed and only a few rogues were spotted here and there. Shade was trying to decide if this attack was winding down or gearing up to go in another direction. After the night out with Luca and his woman, and spending the entire night with *bel*, it was time to put Tomas in charge and be done with these nightly escapades until something happened, one way or another. Shade had a few of his own warriors ready to go back home to Florence for a few weeks, and a few fresh recruits coming in. Walking into one of the empty rooms of the Dead House, looking for the tools to fix a damn door, he found Marcello sitting on a crate looking as bored as Shade felt. Shade leaned against the wall not far from Marcello.

Shade nodded in his direction. "How's that arm? Salve work out? And don't look at me like that. I know there is not a fucking thing to do."

Marcello chuckled to himself. He had watched Shade wandering around here night after night. A master caged was a dangerous thing, but at least he had an outlet with his mate. Marcello held out his arm, twisted it around above his head and grinned back at him. "Fine. Medici warriors recover quickly and never stay out of the battle for long." Marcello watched him as he wandered around, looking for anything to keep his hands busy. "You look like you've been out of battle for a damn long time, master."

"Yeah, well, I hate these lulls in the battle. Whoever was behind these attacks is either over it and has moved on or is waiting in the shadows, strategizing before striking again. Whoever this Angel motherfucker is, his ranks are much depleted with Medici on the streets. So, for now, we have to maintain our presence on the streets, until we can figure out their next move if there is one. It bothers me they never made their objective clear. Makes me think they will be back."

Marcello kicked his boot through the dust on the floor. "I heard a few of the warriors are going back to Florence. They need a break, going back to the old country. Get some rest, have some time with their families and feeders."

Shade looked back at him for any sign of displeasure in his decision not to send Marcello home this round.

"Marcello, I chose you to stay here for a reason. You are more experienced, you're a leader, and I need you here. Although Tomas is Second, he was hired by Alec, a mercenary, so he could bolt at any time. I keep Tomas as my Second, so Alec feels he has some hand in this bullshit. But if I had my choice, it would be you. You have proven yourself to me here. Don't think I didn't notice."

Marcello loosened his boot laces and pulled out the knife he kept stuck inside his boot at all times and twirled it around. "I know you noticed, master, I don't take this opportunity for granted. The only thing I don't like is using feeders only. Some of us need to break out of this pattern. I know you're not around us as much as Marco, but you need to trust us and what you've taught us. Let us break away from the feeders and find something a bit more to our tastes."

Shade had to chuckle at his youthful brashness. "Is that so? Well, I'm not sure if it's the feeders as much as it's the thrill of the hunt and seduction. I have come to realize, I need to trust my warriors more with their judgment and life skills. Luca is teaching me that lesson real damn quick."

Marcello wiped the blade of the knife across his thigh, sighing as he returned it to his boot. "Luca's girl, she's beautiful, I saw her. Hell, we all saw her. And Luca is one lucky bastard to be banging that sweet piece."

"Watch it, Marcello! Luca came to me, talked to me, sought my permission before going to her, so don't go getting any fucking ideas. Besides, Luca doesn't seek her out as an outlet to feed. I'm not going to let all of you wild fuckers have women coming into the quarters. Out of the damn question. But here is what I will put on the table. You need more than what I can offer you with the feeders, go out and feed on your own. You fuck up... you are done. Easy rules. You've been around the block a few times, Marcello, women are no strangers to you, especially mortals. Think on it and think damn hard, warrior. I do not tolerate mistakes with mortal women, nor will I allow anyone to feed from you. If you need to hunt and can control that beast, if you can handle that, then we will see."

Marcello looked him straight in the eyes. He got the message loud and clear. Shade was going to let him break out and set the standard for the others. If he messed this up, none of them would ever have a night out of this place for anything more than the feeder compound again. "I agree. I know the rules, I can handle them. Let me prove it."

Shade stared him down. He wanted him to know that leniency with this rule didn't mean leniency with all rules, "Good. I will let you prove it. But keep it on the down-low. I don't want too much rivalry in the ranks. This is a test, warrior. Now get your ass out on the streets and do some damn work!"

51

Max had followed Tomas' recommendations about pulling their warriors off the street, so Shade and his warriors would get bored and let their guard down. Tomas had called and wanted to give Max an update. Max set out the Midnight because he knew that would be the first thing he wanted when he got here.

Tomas arrived at Max's condo and found the door ajar. He walked in to see Max waiting. Going straight to the table, he poured himself a large Midnight, gulped it down in one swig and then poured another. Walking to one of the chairs, he sat down casually, spinning the fine glass of dark sweetness in his hand and smiled. "I told you my plan would work."

Max smirked. "Some details would be nice, brother. Have they pulled their warriors off the street?"

"Not completely. But Shade took the bait I planted in his head. Knew he would. Took the night off, but also took his protector with him, left me in charge. I'll always be in charge when he's not there, Max. But there's more."

Taking a long swallow of the Midnight, Tomas let him wait. He loved the power information gave him, and the few opportunities he had when he could hold it over a master's head.

Max sighed. He was one damn fucking expensive mercenary, and worth every penny, but his games played on his nerves. Max swallowed down the desire to snap at him. "And do you have any plans to share that information with me anytime soon? Or do you charge extra for that, brother."

Tomas rolled his eyes to him and laughed. "For a master, you have no damn patience, Maximus. Shade is sending some of his warriors back home, bringing in replacements. They're bored, nothing to occupy their time out here. Even Shade is bored. Whatever your plans, you should be getting them in place and quickly. It won't be long before he has decided he's done with this and won't be coming into that hell hole every night. Alec, well, he's way too busy with his Washington lawmakers to give a good damn, which makes him a very stupid master indeed. But I have no concern for Alec's whereabouts, he's no warrior. Keeping up with Alec is your business. But mark my words and be ready when I give you the signal. We're almost there with Shade. I can feel it."

"That's good to hear, Tomas. And I have twenty of my best warriors on standby. They're all ready to go at a moment's notice."

Tomas stood up and walked to the window. His body yearned to be outside now that the darkness had arrived. "Shade is no average warrior or master. He will need to be confused and outnumbered. And Shade's protector has a new hobby, a mortal piece of ass that has caught his fancy. Saw all of them in Charlottesville the other night. I have a feeling getting the protector out of the way will be an easier task than I thought. If Shade is home, his mortal is with him, and the protector... he'll go seek his own little bit of heaven between her legs. You couldn't have asked for more, Max, everything is falling into place, just as I said it would."

"I'll rely on you to tell me how many of my warriors to drop in. My thought was five at first, knowing he could take five. He'd still be confident. He'll leave the house to defend her, keep them away from her. Once he's outside and isolated, fighting the five, drop in the other fifteen. You know he'll call back the protector, but that buys us some time. And I have just the predator to take out the mortal. He fucking loves to kill mortals. I have to rein him in all the time, so he'll be foaming at the mouth to get the assignment to take out Shade's mortal mate."

Tomas stood with his back to Max and smiled. *You may have this under control, brother, but you have not yet told me the blonde vampire bitch is ready to come along for the ride.* "So, we have a plan in place. My end of the bargain is ready, but I'm not so sure about your end, brother. Saw your blonde vixen in town the other night. It's a dangerous thing to be walking alone like that, with no protection, no escort, all alone for the taking. Saw that damn rock on her finger. So, is the purpose of this whole mission backing out on you?"

Max's beast had had it with his insolence and as he grabbed Tomas, his eyes flared red and his fangs bared. He easily lifted him from his feet and pushed him backward until his back was against the wall. His face only inches from Tomas. "You get paid regardless of the outcome, warrior, so my fucking motives are of no concern to you. You let me handle her, and you take care of what you're being paid to do."

Tomas wasn't afraid. Max wouldn't get rid of him, he needed him, and he knew it. Tomas' eyes blazed and his fangs dropped as he growled, eye to eye with Max. "I don't do this to be fucked over, Maximus, make sure you are fucking ready."

Pushing Max off of him, he strolled to the door, adjusting his shirt as he left, leaving Max to figure out how to get that fucking whore of his ready to roll. He wouldn't chase down pussy for him, not in his fucking job description.

Max picked up the bottle of Midnight and threw it at the door. It smashed against the closing door as Tomas exited. If he didn't fucking need him, he would rip his throat out. *Fucking mercenaries, they're loyal only to the dollar and no respect for masters. He better never lose his skills as a warrior.*

52

Driving around, Rissa couldn't keep her mind focused on anything. Her head was spinning with details of cathedrals, dresses, flowers, and all the other minutiae for the wedding of the century. Looking down at her left hand, she still couldn't believe Alec had proposed to her in a proper manner and everyone would be watching them take their vows together. Before she realized where she was going, she found herself at his condo on the Potomac waterfront. Like fate, his call reached her somehow, she could feel him thinking of her, and she knew she had to face him. He would know about the ring by now, just as he knew everything that happened to her.

After parking the car, she glanced quickly around then teleported directly to his door. Finding it open, she was, at first, hesitant to enter, but then she remembered why she was there.

Crossing the threshold she stepped on something that crunched under her foot. Looking down, she saw broken glass and Midnight spilled on the carpet and her heart sped up. Concerned now, she spoke, ready and alert for anything that might come at her. "Max? Are you here? It's Rissie."

Max was grabbing a handful of towels and a vacuum to clean up the glass when he heard her come in. "Rissie, sorry, just step over that mess. Just a little misunderstanding with one of my warriors. Come in, I wasn't expecting you."

Her eyes widened. She lifted her skirt unnecessarily high as she stepped over the broken glass and soaked carpet to show her gartered stockings to whet his appetite. "Max, where is the potion? I need it immediately. I can't take any chances with Alec. Where is it? You can clean that up, and I'll get the potion myself. Just tell me where it is. I don't do clean up."

Max was in no mood for demands tonight. He was already at the end of his rope when she strutted in full of attitude. He dropped the towels at her feet and handed her the vacuum. "You don't do clean up, my angel? Well, besides running from my bed to Alec's, exactly what else do you do?" He grabbed her hair and yanked her to her knees. "If you want the potion, then I highly suggest you learn to do clean-up if you don't want Alec to smell me all over you."

Her plans to distract him while she retrieved the potion were quickly sidetracked, as her words fired his beast. She had momentarily forgotten that quick temper and how easily his beast could surface. Her fangs ripped and she locked eyes with him, growling her response. "You rile my beast, and this will be over before it begins. Is this how you want to greet me? Commanding me, on my knees?" Looking down, her tears began to flow, leaving a trail of red. "I thought it would be… you seem to be able to make me cry easily, please, don't do this."

He released the grip he had on her hair and reached out for her hand. "Take my hand, angel. I'm sorry I forced you to your knees, at least, for this purpose anyway. Let's start over. I'm afraid you caught me at a bad moment. Come, let's sit in the living room. I'll fix us both a drink."

That's it Max, relax. I need you to be calm, make us those drinks, show me where that potion is. Taking his hand, she quickly swiped away her tears with her other hand. Bringing his hand to her lips, she kissed his rough palm. "I was in the area, and I thought I'd just stop in. I can't stay long, but I wanted to see you."

He nodded. "I'm glad you did. You know we need to talk."

He led her into the living room and she took a seat. He went to the bar and pulled out another bottle of Midnight and two glasses. He opened the drawer and removed two vials of the potion, pouring one in each glass then adding the Midnight, swirling the concoction as he walked back to her. "Drink up, angel, and explain to me that big rock on your hand. Does this mean you have made your decision?"

Rissa watched his every move, discovering where he kept the potion, and how much was needed. This could not be more perfect. Pulling her legs up under her, throwing her arm casually over the back of the couch, she took the glass he offered and downed it quickly, closing her eyes and letting it run through her system. "Thank you. Look, there's no decision. What did you expect me to do? Expose everything to Alec? He would have killed me, and you know that. This ring means nothing to him, he doesn't care about marriage, and neither do I. It just means a lot of work for me. This is all about him. It's a charade, the Senator Canton show. He wants the mortal world to view him as a young and happily married man, with a beautiful successful wife on his arm. It's a side-show for the Presidency. Do you think I'd be sitting here with you if I cared about this charade, or this meant anything to me? Give me some credit, Max!"

"Smart girl. I've told you all along, he's just using you. I can bring him down, my angel. I can remove all the obstacles for us, and I will. It'll be just a matter of time before it's my bed you occupy."

She pushed a stray lock of his beautiful long curls behind his ear and let her hand glide over that ruggedly handsome face and looked him in the eyes. "I know what you can do, Max, but I also have to get to the point of leaving him. It won't be easy, and when it's time, you'll know." Sighing, she leaned in and kissed him. "I want to go away with you for a day, a whole day, and not in this damn city. I want to go someplace far away, the beach, the mountains, anywhere but here. Once this circus show goes public, I won't be able to breathe. Please, take me away somewhere." Laying her head on his chest, she clung to him.

He buried his nose in her hair and ran his hand down her back. "It will be a freak show, my angel, and you'll be in the middle of it. Where would you like to go? You name it, and I'll take us there."

Pulling back from him, she kissed him quickly. "The beach. I want to be in the warm sun, in the water, someplace no one knows me. I want to be free to play and make love to you. Imagine, running naked in the sun and water. Promise me!"

Kissing him all over his face, she knew she had him. She could arrange for someone to steal the potion while they were gone for the day, and she promised herself it would be her last time with him. It had to be, but her heart was still unsure. If she went away with him, would she want to come back? "Max, I have to go. I have a meeting and I can't stay. I just wanted to make sure you understood about the ring. I'll call you with the date I'll be free for us to get away. I promise it won't be long." She stood to leave.

"I understand, angel. And the next time we're together, I'll make sure you never want to leave me again. We'll have that day on the beach. I'll take us to my private island, and you'll be treated like a queen. Now go, before I'm tempted to drag you off to my bed."

He watched as she left, stepping over the broken glass and the pile of towels, and closing the door behind her. And damn if she didn't get out of cleaning up that mess! *Well, my angel, I guess you don't do clean up after all.* He could only laugh and shake his head as he vacuumed up the broken glass and blotted up the wine from the carpet. *Women... can't live with them, can't live without them.*

53

After a weekend of having him all to herself, they were back to their routine. Shade arrived home from D.C. as the sun was about to rise, then they shared their short time together before his death slumber when she slept beside him. It had been easy for her to flip her schedule upside down. She had always been a night person anyway, so staying up all night and sleeping with him during the day felt perfectly natural to her. With the electronic blinds in the house, the room remained pitch black anyway. He said things were slowing down in D.C., and she hoped so. She hoped that meant he would be home more often, that they would have more time together.

After he left, yet again, for the Dead House, she prepared to meet Luca. She never imagined when he came here as her protector that such a friendship would blossom.

* * *

Luca felt she was getting close to mastering the crossbow. That had been her original goal, and the timing couldn't have been better. Now with things slowing down in D.C., Shade didn't take all the warriors in with him every night. The ones who stayed behind spent most of the evening hanging out at the fire pit. He couldn't risk taking her out for weapons training and having one of the warriors see them. He had a reward for her, for all her hard work and he'd give it to her tonight. He heard her as she approached his door, and he met her and led her outside. She did her warm-up and they started to run.

Kate thought he seemed quiet as they began their run. "Is there something on your mind, Luca? You seem preoccupied."

"The warriors. Shade has things pretty much under control in D.C., so he's no longer taking all eight of them in with him. He rotates their schedule and usually leaves three or four here. And thanks to you and that nice fire pit, they spend their nights outside drinking Midnight. I don't want to risk them seeing me train you. The running is fine. That's easily explained. But the weapons, that's a whole different issue. And I would especially hate for Shade to hear about it from one them.

You're close to mastering the crossbow. I think we should wrap that up soon, like real soon. Then I think we need to come clean. I think we need to tell him. I don't like keeping secrets from him, Kate."

She nodded in agreement. "No, neither do I. It's just, at the time... I felt like it was my only way to climb out of the darkness. He was in so much of his own pain, it was almost impossible for us to help each other. And then, the longer it went on, the harder it was to tell him. I hate that he doesn't know, Luca, and I hate that I've put you in this position as well. You're right. We do need to tell him. Can we finish, please? Finish up whatever it is you have planned for me to do? And then we just need to find the right time. I know he won't be happy. There's no way around that, I'm afraid."

Luca thought to himself, *not happy is an understatement*. He knew Shade had wanted to train her himself. "Let's just say it's a conversation I'm looking forward to, but I think we have to face it head-on."

Kate reached out to him. "You're right. I know you're right. But let me pick the time, okay? When I can maybe feel like he'll be less volatile?"

"Oh, trust me, I have no problem with that. The less volatile, the better."

As they completed the loop and got back to the house, Luca could hear some of the warriors down by the fire pit. He told her they were going to skip the weight bench tonight, and just have her focus on the crossbow. He moved deeper into the woods, away from the house and away from view, and set up targets for her. He handed her the quiver and she easily slid it over her shoulder. He liked the ease with which she moved. She was comfortable with the longbow and the crossbow. He handed her the crossbow and she began her routine of target shooting. She hit one bulls-eye after another. She was a natural at this. He wished Shade could see her. As she was deep in concentration, he could still hear the warriors at the fire pit and it made him nervous. He let her shoot a few more rounds and then he called it a night. "Let's wrap it up. Follow me back to the house, I have something for you. A surprise."

"For me? You have something for me? What? What is it?"

"Do you not understand the meaning of the word surprise?" He laughed at her. "You'll see when we get back to the house."

They entered the house from the rear patio. He asked her to stand in the corridor outside his suite with her back turned to his door while he retrieved the gift. He picked up the package and returned to the corridor. "Okay, you can turn around now."

When she turned around, he was holding out a large package wrapped in brown paper, and he handed it over to her.

"Can I open it now?"

He nodded his head yes, and she ripped through the paper to find a suit of leathers. She held the garments up to admire them, and she was speechless.

"Every warrior needs leathers, and you have earned yours. I had Cory hand tool these just for you. Go try them on."

She was jumping up and down with excitement. She gave him a big hug then ran up the stairs to the bedroom to try on the leathers. The leather was a matte black, soft, and supple, and conformed to her body. There was even a hood and face guard. She put them on and came back down the stairs for him to see.

He looked up to see her on the stairs. With her red hair hidden from view, her face partially covered, only her small size gave her away, but she looked like the warrior she'd worked so hard to become. She wasn't field-tested, and after the deer incident, he wondered if she'd ever kill. She had the skills, but did she have the will? She acted from her heart, not her head, and his instincts told him she'd fight to defend what she loved. "Good job, little warrior. You deserve it."

As she modeled the leathers, Luca suddenly felt Shade close by. He felt his presence with the other warriors. Fuck! Good thing they wrapped up early. "Shade is here. Get upstairs and get that off... now! Be sure to put it somewhere he won't find it."

She ran back up the stairs, removing the leathers as she went. When she got to the bedroom, she put her jeans and sweater back on and stuffed the leathers in a dresser drawer. She had no idea when she would ever wear them, but she would figure out a better place to store them later.

54

It was only 3 a.m. and nothing, not a damn fucking thing, was going down. Shade knew he had warriors out there who were bored, and a bored warrior was less attentive. That was never a good thing. He knew they were all a trustworthy group. Well, with the exception of one, perhaps, and who the hell knew what Raven was doing? Shade decided to check in. Shadowing himself, he sniffed him out and found him sitting on a rooftop in his assigned quadrant, wearing a leather jacket, a kilt, combat boots, and lighting up a cigarette.

Cazzo! I swear to fucking hell this kid is going to put me in my grave permanently. He should have sent Raven's ass back to Florence with the others, but for some odd reason, he couldn't do it. If things decided to bust loose here again, Shade needed Raven's speed. Despite his smaller size and disregard for the rules, Shade had to admit, Raven was among his best warriors. And if Shade was totally honest with himself, he knew he cut Raven a lot of slack because he was amused by him.

"If you got paid for all the time you fuck off smoking, I would be broke, sure as hell, Raven."

Raven didn't startle at the sudden and unexpected appearance of his master. Rather, he held up his pack of cigarettes to Shade, offering him one. *Busted. Like I give a rat's ass.*

"Nice of you to show up, boss man. If there was something to do besides smoke, maybe I'd be doing it. Let's get real here, shall we? I see the situation like this." Turning his head from left to right slowly, his waist-long black hair swung from side to side. Raven held his arms out to his sides, spreading them wide. "Do you see any rogues, any threat? Do you see anything that would prompt me to not light one up? If you do, master, please inform me and enlighten my weary, bored, awesome warrior ass."

Shade tried not to laugh. He wouldn't accept such insolence from others, but he shook his head and crouched down beside Raven. Reaching over, he took the damn butt out of Raven's mouth. "What the fuck is going down, Rave? This is ridiculous. I'm the fucking master warrior and all I do is sit behind the desk. I have to admit, my ass is weary and bored as well."

As he took the cigarette out of his mouth, Shade's fingers brushed his lips, and Raven's heart skipped a beat, and it crossed his mind that, if Shade ever needed to feed, his ass would be first in line.

Marcello had suggested he take leave and go back to Florence since things were slow here. Raven thought he must be fucking nuts to think he would leave this place. He liked it here. Besides, he was close to master, got to swing a few heads to the ground from time to time, maybe make a good impression. All of Shade's warriors knew he rewarded those who delivered, and Raven was looking for a way up. Not to mention, freedom was a glorious thing, and Raven had his sights set on busting loose. The vampire culture in the States didn't seem quite as formal as Europe, and he'd like the chance to explore.

"At least you're honest about it, master. But seriously, you could be home doing the little mate, or riding the Harley, getting drunk and playing poker. Think about it, you may decide this gig is done and we should seriously go home for some uninhibited fun."

Growling, Shade grabbed a fistful of Raven's hair and pulled his face to his and ground out his words, "You fucking little runt, watch your mouth! I am just in the mood to whale on someone and you fit the bill. She is my lady to you. And you will address her as such. We clear? Don't you ever forget who is master here and where you came from. Your ass can go back real quick."

Shade knew he joked, but sometimes, this one pushed the envelope too far. Releasing his hair, Shade pushed him over.

Raven knew deep in his gut Shade would never hurt him, not intentionally, just not how the big man rolled. "Sorry. I was just trying to lighten the mood. Guess it didn't work."

Sitting back up, Raven smiled at him and Shade punched him in the shoulder.

"Well, at least I know you paid attention to half the shit Marco and I tried to teach you. You can't always learn the things you need to know in the classroom, or even on the field. The true warrior comes out when the cards are on the table, the way your beast rips it up inside you, the way your blood pumps through your veins, not something I can teach, but something you feel and grasp and own. Now, if I could just control that damn flapping jaw of yours, we might make you a warrior someday. *Cazzo*, you are something else, you crazy little bastard."

Raven turned his head toward Shade, letting his hair fall across his face and proceeded to bat his lashes at him furiously while grinning. "Oh master, when I grow up, I want to be a warrior just like you."

As they both laughed, Raven watched him shake his head as the wind blew those dark curls around his handsome face. He liked hearing him laugh, having him sit so near. "But will you get off the damn fence and let us go home already."

Standing up, Shade laughed at him again. If nothing else, Raven did make him laugh, almost as much as *bel*, and that was saying something. "Come on, you half-grown speed demon, let's go home. I got new warriors coming in at sunrise, and I could use some downtime to relax. Besides, there is a crimson-haired goddess calling my ass home."

When Shade and Raven teleported in, the warriors were gathered around the fire pit, sucking up the Midnight.

"Listen up! I am missing my woman, so let's bring my lady down from her turret in the castle."

As they huddled arm in arm in a circle around the fire, Shade put the song into their heads, and on his count, he instructed them to sing as loudly as they could. "One, two, three…" They broke out in song, singing Van Morrison's song, *Tupelo Honey* loudly enough to rattle the stars.

Kate was in their bedroom, stuffing the leathers in the bottom drawer when she heard a chorus of male voices from the fire pit. She laughed out loud as some were dreadfully off-key, but she recognized Shade's call to her. Pulling on her boots she headed out the door and walked through the gardens to the path that led toward the staff quarters. She paused when she was close enough to see the group of slightly intoxicated warriors arm in arm around the fire pit, singing at the top of their lungs. She waited for them to finish their serenade, and then she called to him, "Looking for me, lover?"

Shade watched the sway of her hips as she approached, with her glorious crimson hair flowing behind her in the night breeze. The smile on her face was so beautiful it almost dropped him to his knees. She slid her arms under his jacket and around his waist. He bent into her neck, kissing her softly. He wrapped his jacket around the both of them, crushing her to his chest. "*Si, mi amore*, I was. Your warrior is home early. You are pleased, *si*?"

"Pleased? Come with me, and I'll show you just how pleased I am."

He growled softly. "You would have me leave my brave strong warriors to come with you? Mmm, master has to think on this, *mi amore*." He kissed her deep and long to the sound of whistles and catcalls from his warriors.

Luca heard the ruckus coming from the fire pit, and left his suite to see what was going on. "Don't leave me out of the party."

Shade looked over his warriors. "Looks like the gang is all here. Feels a bit like home, *si*?"

Kate watched his warriors over the top of his shoulder, their ease with each other, their laughter, their camaraderie, their affection. She was glad they all felt at home here. She gave Shade a squeeze around the waist. They really were all brothers.

Shade shouted out to them, "Listen up, you heathens! The lovely lady of the house and her vampire are going to the castle. Keep watch, if that's possible. And for Hell's sake, try to keep the noise down."

Looking down, Shade saw the moon sparkling in Kate's dark eyes and her smile was so inviting. Lifting her with ease into his arms, his eyes never left hers as he began the trek back to the house.

He heard the whistles and Raven yelled, "We have to be loud, so we can hear ourselves think over your noise, master."

The laughter only got louder, but he paid them no mind. He had one thing on his mind right now and she was in his arms. He heard them roar in unison, "*Per sempre*, Medici," and his heart soared. Before he got inside the door of the house, he heard the war cry song for his warriors, Nickelback's *Burn it to the Ground*, and it fired his blood. Master was home tonight and he would spend it with his *bel rosso*. "*Ti amo, mi amore, per sempre*."

55

Alec was on the phone, arguing with the Minority Whip over the Immigration Reform bill when his administrative assistant, Jenny walked in and held up a note for him to read. 'Larissa is here.' He nodded to her and waved his hand to send her in. Jenny was the only vampire on his staff. She worked much too closely with him, and for such long hours, he couldn't risk hiring a mortal for that position.

Rissa took a seat and waited while he wrapped up his conversation. Leaning back in his chair, his feet on the desk, crossed at the ankle, Alec listened to the same lame argument he'd heard on the nightly news. This conversation was going nowhere fast, so he wrapped up the call and turned his attention to Rissa. "What do you have for me, darling. Good news, I hope?"

Rissa had picked up the photos for the press release and was pleased with how they'd turned out. She reached for her briefcase, removing the photos and spreading them across his desk. "I brought the photos I had the studio work up for us. She did an excellent job, but I'll let you decide which ones to release."

Alec flipped through the photos. "These look great. They did do a good job. I'm happy with any of these, so whichever ones you pick will be okay with me."

She smiled; happy he was pleased. "I'm partial to this one. We look... professional, in love and ready to take on the world." Glancing at the photo, she ran her finger around the edges, remembering that evening on the town. "Oh, and something else. Did you know that the First Lady is planning a Rose Garden Tea Party? And guess who she asked to assist the White House staff with planning it."

Alec mulled that over in his head. The annual Rose Garden Tea Party, how very convenient for him. Alec knew the President had had his eyes on Rissa, and Alec would love to see what he could do to make sparks fly. "That's wonderful, darling, what a great opportunity for you, for both of us, actually."

"Well, I'll only be a consultant, the White House has their own staff for organizing these events, and the First Lady didn't call me directly. I was contacted through her administrative personnel. But, if I can, I'll try to manage a brief meeting, one on one, with her." Rissa slid her hand down his sleeve, "I wanted to ask you something about the wedding planning... if you have time?"

Alec checked his watch and he had a few minutes before he had to be back on the Senate floor. "Of course, what do you need?"

Rissa bit her lip coyly. *Play it up, Rissa. You need to make this sound believable.* "While I'm here, I wanted to meet with your assistant about your schedule. I have a designer in New York for my dress. There are several completed sketches he has ready for my review, and some fabrics I would like to look over. It would be a long day trip, and perhaps, I could manage a few other wedding shopping errands while there. So, if I could coordinate it with your schedule, a day and evening you're going to be busy here, so I wouldn't be missed... would you agree?"

Alec was already gathering files and his laptop to take with him back to the Capitol. "Not a problem. You know how important it is to me that you find the perfect dress. Just remember, I want final approval. Other than that, just go over my calendar with Jenny. Let me know what day you plan to be gone. Do you want my driver? Or the private plane?"

"No, I'll reserve a hotel in advance and just teleport. I can manage. I was thinking of taking Anna with me, my friend from the flower studio. We need to do some planning for a few other events and finish choosing flowers for the wedding. If she jumps at the idea, I'll take her along. Kill two birds with one stone."

Jenny entered after a quick knock and told him he was needed on the floor. As Alec stood to leave, Rissa prayed he would show her some sign of affection in front of Jenny.

He answered her in a distracted tone, "That's great, whatever you think." Alec grabbed the latest version of the bill and leaned over to give her a quick but discreet kiss on the lips before rushing out the door. He turned to Jenny and told her to show Rissa his calendar as he headed down the hall.

It wasn't the display of affection she'd hoped for, but then, Alec rarely displayed his affection in public. But Rissa didn't mind. She had her cover story in place for her day away with Max. Mission accomplished.

56

Coming home early had definitely been worth every moment. After the warriors and their hijinks at the bonfire, Shade spent the rest of the night with Kate in his arms. Waking early from his death slumber, he turned his head to see her sleeping soundly. He smiled at the memories of their blissfully long sexy night together. Her hair tumbled around her face and spread across the white pillows. Sitting up, he brushed the crimson from her eyes, but she remained sound asleep.

Getting up, he padded naked to the shower. He needed to get ready a bit earlier than usual this evening. The new warriors should arrive from Florence soon, and he wanted to get over to the staff quarters and greet them and see who Marco had chosen to send. He had released four of the warriors to go back to Florence but asked Marco to only replace two at this time. With the lull in activity in D.C., he didn't have enough work for all of them as it was.

Kate felt him as he slipped from their bed and she nestled into his pillow. She could hear the water running in the shower and she struggled to wake up. As he came back into the bedroom, hair wet and a towel at his waist, she sat up in their bed. "Lover, you're leaving early?"

"Ah, *mi amore*, you are awake. *Si*, I have new warriors arriving and they should be here soon. I want to get over to the staff quarters, see who Marco sent me. I left it up to his discretion who to send over this time. He knows what I need."

Walking to his dresser, he stood with his back to her as he pulled open the drawers, looking for fresh leathers.

She slipped from their bed and went to him, sliding her arms around his waist and released the towel so it dropped to the floor. "Maybe you don't have to leave quite so early?"

"You tempt me, *mi amore*. But I must go to the new warriors, welcome them in." Leaning down, he kissed her softly, pulling her body into his, their naked skin warm against the other. "Why don't you come along? It will give us more time together, and you can meet them at the same time."

"Yes, of course. Just give me a few minutes to get dressed."

She ran to the bathroom to freshen up, put on a little make-up and run a brush through her hair. She pulled on jeans and a red cashmere sweater that fell over one shoulder and put on her red boots. "Okay, I'm ready."

"You look ravishing, *mi amore*, as always." He raised his eyebrows. "Red boots? Planning to ride, are you?" He threw back his head laughing.

"You never know, lover. I need to be prepared for whatever opportunity presents itself." She crossed the room to him and slid her arms around his waist.

Shade ran his hands through her hair, and smiled down at her, touching his nose to hers. "Maybe I should stay home again and make use of those pretty red boots."

No sooner had the words left his mouth than he heard whooping and hollering over at the staff quarters. "Well, it sounds like the natives are restless, which means the new brothers have arrived." He held out his arm to her. "Shall we make an appearance, *mi amore*?"

"I look forward to meeting your new warriors, although, other than Marcello, I really never saw or spoke to the others very much. I saw Raven with Marcello a few times, but I wouldn't have known there were others here except that I heard them tramping through the house sometimes. Shade, since I have your attention, there's something I've wanted to ask you."

"*Bel*, you always have my attention. Ask away. Damn, it is beautiful this evening, *si*?"

She looked up into the night sky. "Yes, I love this time of year, the warmer nights, and everything starting to bloom and grow again. And we have so much property here, and not all the fields have been converted to vineyards. I was wondering if you wouldn't mind, I would really like to own some horses. You mentioned it once. We would have to build a stable. But what do you think, lover?"

Stopping short, he furrowed his brow. "You ride, *mi amore*?"

"I used to ride. When I was younger I went to a riding school and I loved it. I always wanted horses but never lived anywhere that could accommodate them, until now. So, what do you think?"

Taking her hand, he continued to walk toward the staff quarters, the noise becoming louder the closer they got. "I never knew that you could ride. I would love to have stables here. I will bring over some of my horses from Florence."

Suddenly, the wind changed, and he picked up a scent. Female vampire... *Don't tell me those damn warriors brought females into the compound. I will fucking kill them!* "*Mi amore*, maybe this is not such a great idea, let me walk you back to the house, and I will just attend to the warriors myself."

"No, I'm fine. Is something wrong?"

He remembered the last two female vamps she encountered and was hesitant to take her into the staff quarters. There was definitely a female inside that fucking house and he couldn't exactly blurt it out without sounding like he couldn't trust her. *Cazzo!* When he found out which one of those bastards brought one home, he would rip him a new ass and send him back to wherever the fuck he came from.

"No, *mi amore*, I just thought... maybe this would be boring for you."

"It's not boring, and you know I always want whoever you bring here from Florence to feel welcome."

"As you wish, *mi amore*." As they arrived at the entrance of the staff quarters, Shade heard laughter, there was music and talking and he could distinguish Raven and Marcello's voices. Opening the door, he took *bel's* hand and entered the large, open family room and found the males all around, but the scent of a female was strong. Then he spotted her. *Holy fucking hell! Marco sent me a female warrior! I will kill him! He knows this is not going to go over well. Oh, he is going to pay for this damn joke! Cazzo!*

Shade shouted out above the laughter, "Master and his lady are in the house!" Giving a loud whistle, all talking stopped, and everyone turned in their direction. Olivia's eyes immediately went to Shade and she stood, nodding her head respectfully. "Olivia, you have come to join us, I see. Please, come forward."

Shade gripped Kate's hand tightly, waiting for her to take flight or attack. He had no idea how this was going to go down, but he knew it wouldn't be good.

Kate was caught off guard when she saw the young brunette stand up as they entered. Her hair was long, a soft brown color, her skin was gently bronzed, and her pale blue-grey eyes peered out at him. She was tall, like all the vampire females, and she was clearly toned, but she exuded softness about her too. *Who the fuck is that? Olivia... he knows her!* She was poured into leathers that clung to her shapely, statuesque form. No wonder all the male warriors were so rowdy. Kate could feel her back stiffen as she watched the female warrior make eye contact with him.

Kate slid her arm around his waist and stepped in closer to him. *Forget the warm welcome. You'll be headed back to Florence before you can unpack your bags, bitch.*

Shade felt Kate bristle and he took a deep breath. This was going to cost Marco. As her arm went around his waist, he could feel her anger boiling.

As Olivia approached, he nodded at her. "Olivia, may I present to you my mate, Katherine. You will address her as my lady and show her the same respect as you do your master."

Watching as she bowed her head and looked down to the floor, she slowly raised her eyes to him and said simply, "Master."

"*Bel rosso*, this is Olivia, she is one of my female warriors, and yes, I do have a few. She is quite adept at being a warrior. I have known Olivia since she was just a teenager. She came to us, along with her brother, who is also one of my warriors."

Olivia could feel my lady's jealousy and hate, and yet, she had done nothing disrespectful. She bowed her head to her as was expected. "I'm honored to meet you, my lady."

Kate was confused. There were a million questions in her head. *Did he ask for this woman to be sent here? Why didn't he tell me she was coming? Has he slept with her like Sabine? Like Adriana? She won't be staying long.* "And I'm honored as well, Olivia. Welcome to Bel Rosso." *You're on my turf now, and don't let the fact that I'm mortal make you the least bit comfortable.*

"*Grazie*, my lady." Nodding to her, Olivia sensed the undercurrent of tension, and turned slightly to master and nodded again before stepping back in the ranks.

Shade could feel Kate's anger, but so far, she was playing it cool. Then he heard laughter from another female coming from behind him and he closed his eyes. *Oh, no you did not send her, Marco! Not Fiamma! You are fucking dead, Marco!*

Shade turned to see Fiamma and Marcello come rolling in from the other room, both of them laughing and shoving each other and then she stopped dead in her tracks and looked directly at Shade, her red hair tumbling across her shoulders and a huge grin spread across her face. Shade nodded at her. "Fiamma."

Fee glanced at the female standing with her master. So, this was the mortal mate she had heard so much about.

"Master Shade!" Walking boldly toward him, she stopped in front of him and nodded, lowering her eyes in respect and felt the blistering hot glare of the mortal on his side.

Kate watched as the tall, sleek redhead sauntered up to him... she knew him and well. Kate could see it by the look in her eyes. It was a look that implied physical familiarity and her heart was pounding as she fought to restrain herself.

Shade could feel Kate's agitation and spoke to her telepathically. **"*Mi amore*, she is Medici warrior. And I had nothing to do with this. Do you honestly think I would bring them under your roof, without discussing it with you first? Get control! She means no harm."** "Fiamma, I would like to introduce you to my mate, Katherine. You will show her respect and call her my lady. I expect much more respect than you typically show to me, understood?"

"*Bel,* this is Fiamma. She is another warrior in my ranks. We have known each other for a long time. Fiamma has fought by my side in many battles, and I respect her." Shade watched as Fiamma smiled at Kate, and prayed Fiamma behaved.

Fiamma bowed her head. "I'm most honored to meet the woman who has stolen our master's heart. He's a highly honored warrior. And, with all due respect, my lady, I'm glad to see he has chosen a redhead for his mate. We thank you for your gracious accommodations. It's quite beautiful, this countryside."

Turning to her master, she smiled at him. "I'm honored to be called to duty here, master, to serve you in any way you see fit."

As Fee finished her greeting, she felt Marcello's arms go around her as he snuggled into her neck, whispering for her to step back. Fee felt the less than warm welcome from the mortal and realized she wasn't expecting them, nor was master. *Oh dear, Marco, what have you dropped us into?*

Kate watched the interplay between her and Marcello but didn't respond to the female's greeting. **"Get me out of here, Shade... Now!"** What she had to say needed to be said in private, not in front of his warriors.

Shade issued a final word to the new arrivals. "Welcome, warriors. Marcello will get you settled. *Bel* and I are returning to the house. Prepare to leave for D.C. within two hours. Be ready."

Grabbing *bel's* hand, he walked out the door quickly, and then grabbed her to his chest and teleported inside the house to the foyer.

As they stood facing each other, she unloaded all the anger she had been holding back. "I don't want to discuss this, and I don't care how unreasonable this sounds, but I want them gone. Now!" She lowered her voice and spoke through gritted teeth, "And I especially don't want to know the details between you and the redhead. Her eyes said all I need to know."

He had never seen her this fired up and ready to rip ass. Her words inflamed him and the more she spoke, the hotter he got. "Oh, I think you want to know it all, to be honest."

Kate clenched her fists to her side. "Are you defending her? Do you want her here? You may not have known she was coming, but you seemed damned pleased to see her, and she sure as hell was pleased to see you. And I think you want me to know. Are you throwing her in my face, Shade Medici?"

His beast surfaced and stalked her as he talked, "Oh yes, let me throw every woman I have ever laid eyes on in the face of the woman who is my mate. The woman I love and would give up my life for. What in hell is wrong with you, Kate? You assume every woman who crosses my path I am fucking or have fucked? *Cazzo!*"

Slamming his hand against the wall, he spun on her and growled, "So, this is how you show your trust to me, with demands, rage, and jealousy? You never fucking trusted me and apparently, you never will. I am so damn done with this bullshit from you, Kate. Done!" Walking to her, he bared his fangs and growled, "Done."

Her voice still defiant, she spat back, "Done? You're done with me? Just like that? I've always trusted you. Always. But I've never trusted them. You can't deny the parade of women in your past, and I accept that. But I don't need them flaunted in my face either."

He went nose to nose with her. "Oh yes, let me just flaunt them right in front of you! You fucking do not get it, do you? You just cut me to the bone." Reaching into his boot, he whipped out the knife before she could blink and slapped it hard into the palm of her hand. She let it slide from her hand, and its metallic clang echoed through the foyer. "Why don't you just fucking kill me now? I have one long past and you better get over this right now! I am not going to have this damn discussion every time a female crosses our path. So, get it the fuck out of your system or kill me now. I am not doing this with you again. There are female warriors in my ranks and if you think I will just wave my hand and have them all disappear, then you are dead wrong. They are my sisters-in-arms. I take care of them, *familia, familia*! Do you have any concept of that damn word? No."

"I understand family. I left my entire family to be with you. I walked away from everyone and everything to be with you. Apparently, that's not something you're willing to do for me. So, tell me now, look at me when you answer me, did you sleep with either of them?"

Her anger only fueled his, as they both spiraled out of control. "I am not willing to do this for you? All the things I have done for you and you say this to me? Fine! Let's play this little game, Kate."

He walked her across the floor until her back slammed against the wall and he towered over her, like a beast ready to kill. He slammed his hands against the wall on either side of her head. His eyes were blazing red as he stared straight into her, not blinking or flinching. "Oh yes, Kate, I fucked Fiamma until she screamed my name to the heavens. I drank her blood, letting it fuel my desire. She rode me like the wind, fucked me so hard, with her fangs bared and that red hair flying as I slammed my cock deep and hard. Oh, *si*, Kate, I fuck them all, I am master, and I can't wait to jump that warrior bitch right now. Can you feel how much I want her? How I crave to feel her lips suck my cock down that deep throat?"

His words ripped through her. Kate placed her hands over her ears, but there was no way to block what he said. She slid down the wall and crawled across the floor to pick up the knife. Standing, she reached up and cut a lock of her hair. Yanking his arm up, she placed the lock in his hand.   "Then you better decide which redhead stays, because one of us is leaving." She turned and started up the stairs, a part of her hoping he would follow, take back his words, and end this madness.

"Hold! I said hold, damn you, woman."

She faltered on the steps, pausing to hear what he would say, when he answered in a low, deadly tone, "That is what you wanted to hear, is it not? What you believe, Kate? What you will always believe? If you ever loved me, you would feel inside I have no desire to be with either of them. But you can't feel me. Think about that, very hard. You are so consumed with jealousy. You could not feel the truth of me in your heart. Perhaps, I am a fool to love, to want no other but you."

Reaching in his pocket, he took out the small, red, heart-shaped rubies he carried with him wherever he went and laid them on the small table by the door along with the lock of her hair. "All I wanted was to love you and be loved in return. I was wrong to think it possible. I'm sorry."

Turning, he stalked to the door. He felt the need to be far away, while his heart broke into a million pieces.

She watched as he vanished. Then she sat down on the steps and put her head in her hands, too angry to cry. She heard Luca's door open and the sound of his boots as he approached. He had heard every word of this very private, but very loud conversation held just outside his door. "Kate, are you okay?"

She lifted her face to him. "Okay? Do I look okay? He walked away. Again. I am exhausted by this game. I can be his doormat, and agree to his terms, whatever they are, regardless of my feelings, or we play this game. Luca, he knows I can't follow him, and he just leaves. If I pack up some things, would you drive me into town, please?"

He looked at her with astonishment. "Pack? Wait. Don't make a decision in anger, Kate. Let's talk about this."

* * *

Fiamma was outside waiting with the other warriors for Master to take them to the Dead House when they all heard the fight between him and his mate. She knew this was serious and she asked Marcello to come with her. Perhaps if she talked to his mate, she could help somehow. She heard the lies he told her, and damn if she wanted Kate to believe that of her. Knocking on the door, Luca answered. "Luca, please, will you ask my lady if she will speak with me?"

Luca realized Fiamma and all the other warriors had overheard the argument. He didn't know why Shade chose to tell Kate he had been with Fiamma. They all knew he had not. But Kate believed his words, so they needed to move carefully.

"Come in, but tread lightly, Fee."

Fiamma nodded. "Understood." Walking in, she bowed her head to Kate, who was still sitting on the stairs, and spoke softly. Fee could see she was hurt. "My lady, will you please grant me some time to speak with you? Explain some things to you. Please may I?"

Kate took a deep breath before she answered. "Say what you have come here to say."

Fiamma sat down on one of the steps below her, so she could see her face to face. "Thank you, my lady. I know I'm the last person you want to see. I've never been mortal, but I've been in love. At its core, it's a lot of work. Throw in all the confusion of our world and I imagine it's much worse. I come in peace. Master Shade didn't tell you the truth." She held up her hands. "Please, I know you don't believe me, but you can ask Luca,

Marcello, or any of the other. They know. I'm a sister here, not a rival or a threat to anyone, including you."

Fiamma shook her head. "Trying to understand any man is hell, and master, that's a whole other issue. I don't know why he would say those things to you. I've never been with Master Shade. I'm a Medici warrior. I respect and honor him, and those he loves. If any of my sisters in the camp were to behave as he said, we would no longer be warriors, but outcasts. Believe me, when I tell you, I love master very much, but not in the way you think. We all love him. He is my brother, my father, my master, and my friend. Is there anything I can say to help you?"

Kate buried her face in her hands and the tears flowed. She looked up at Fiamma again. "I'm sorry for thinking badly of you, but I asked him outright, and you heard his words. He shared his past before, and I let it get to me. He thinks I don't trust him, but that's not true. You understand what I mean when I try to tell him it's women I don't trust, not him. I see how other women respond to him. Thank you for coming to me. That took a lot of courage."

"My lady... do you hate being called that? It sounds so formal to me. Everyone calls me Fee. Please feel free to call me that. He'd kill me for speaking so informally to you. I trust few women, but I trust my Medici sisters-in-arms. We have to, for our very survival. But I understand your distrust of women in general. When they want something, they think nothing of taking it. It disgusts me to the roots of my red hair to admit that of my own sex. It's not courage that brought me here, but heart. I care about my family and master is my family, as are you. Can I ask you to do something?"

Kate felt the sincerity of her words. "Please, call me Kate, although Shade will hate it. And you can ask me anything."

"Don't turn your back on him, you love him and he loves you. That's obvious to all of us. I know you can't teleport to him, but you need to find him, don't let him walk away from this. I know if you concentrate, focus on him, you'll find he's not far at all. I'm able to sense things, see things, not an exact location but clues to where someone is, like I can see through their eyes. See what they see. Sometimes, I get a random thought from them. Does *dormire guerriero* mean anything to you?"

"*Dormire guerriero*? Is that Italian? I don't speak Italian. What does that mean?"

"*Dormire guerriero* means sleeping warrior."

"Sleeping warrior?" Kate paused as she ran the words through her head. "Oh. He's with our baby?"

Fiamma blinked a few times and let out a deep breath. "Baby?" She recalled the rumors they'd heard in Florence. "Oh, Kate, I didn't mean to bring you pain. But, yes, he's with the sleeping warrior. He feels something there, something in connection with you, which now I understand. He feels lost. Go to him, chase him down, make him face this."

Fiamma took Kate's hand in hers. "There is a warrior inside you, I can feel that. Marcello and I will gather the others and head into the city. You work it out. Don't give up on him, please. He is male, he does some stupid things, but he does them all from love. It's his way. Will you go to him?"

Kate locked eyes with her. "You don't need to apologize. Of course, I'll go. Thank you. And welcome. You're welcome here. I want you to feel it's your home."

Standing, they walked back down the stairs and Kate continued on out the door, toward the garden pathway that led to the angel marking the grave of their baby.

* * *

Shade sat on the bench, staring at the garden statue that marked his son's grave, as he faced the idea of losing her. He had blown it. He blew it far beyond anything he could imagine, and he had felt her need to leave him. Why couldn't she understand his relationship with the warriors? How was it she had the power to push his temper over the edge so quickly? He knew it was because he loved her beyond reason. He knew loving a mortal would be hard. How did he make her understand his life and how it was ruled by his responsibility to his coven? Then there were the women, it always came back to the women. He thought she would love him enough to understand, to feel him so deeply and know, without a doubt, he never wanted to go back to that life again. Maybe he had been wrong, from the very beginning, to think their love could bridge two very different worlds.

He had teleported out in anger and he blocked her still. He bent over his knees, running his hands through his hair. His life was in chaos, and last night, everything had seemed in place. How in the hell had this gone so damn wrong in a blink of an eye? He wanted to go to Florence and rip Marco's throat out, but that would do him no good whatsoever. He needed Marco and fucking loved him, but this was a cruel thing to do to them both, and he wouldn't soon forgive him for it.

Reaching out, he touched the angelic statue, and his heart broke once again. She had no idea what he had sacrificed for her. He had taken their son, their firstborn, to save her. He never wanted to protect anyone more in his life, and yet, he was losing her slowly, he could feel it. He had no idea where to go from here. What to say or do that would make her reach out for him and, once again, be his *bel rosso. I am a damn warrior, the best there is, but I have no idea how to fight this.*

* * *

Kate walked down the darkened path to the section of the garden that she had come to think of as The Baby's Garden. Fee's image could have no other meaning. She knew she would find him here. As she rounded the final curve, she saw him seated on the bench, his head in his hands. *Oh lover, I know your pain.*

She approached him quietly and he didn't look up. *Is he blocking me? Or ignoring me? I won't let him walk away this time.* In a quiet voice, she spoke to him. "How can we love each other so deeply, and then inflict so much hurt and pain? I'm so sorry. Please tell me we're not too broken to fix. Please tell me you'll fight for me, because I won't stop fighting for you."

Looking up, Shade could see the pain she was in and he hoped she could feel he was in the same place. "Kate, my sweet Kate. I can fight anything, at least I thought I could, but this pain that is ripping us apart is something I have no weapons to fight. Just my heart and soul, and they belong to you."

She knelt before him on the bench, laying her head on his thigh and letting her tears flow quietly. "You give me no reason to be jealous. None. But I'm fighting your history and my past. All I ever heard about you from Rissa was what a player you were, how you would leave me and move on to the next woman. You've been very forthcoming about the women in your life. You spoke of Adriana and Sabine, both warriors. I wasn't expecting to see women warriors here tonight. When I did, I'm sorry, it angered me, and things just spun out of control so fast. I know if I had asked you calmly about those women, you would have answered me. But we both go off like ticking time bombs. I don't know how to fix that, but I know I don't want to lose you."

His hand lay softly on her head. "My whole life is about being a warrior, Kate, there is nothing else I understand. I took for granted you knew I had women warriors in my coven. It never crossed my mind that you would think I wouldn't have women within my ranks. My past is long gone, Kate. What we have is our future. You need to let go of whatever past you hold, because it hampers you from moving forward with me. I don't know what has happened to you, and that is something only you can decide when to share with me. But I know it formed you into the woman you are now, just as my past formed me. Lessons to be learned, it is your choice to learn them and not repeat them and leave them in the past. It needs to be done. Do you understand what I am trying to say?"

She looked up at him. "Oh, I learned from my past, but the repeating part was out of my hands. Shannon said I trusted men too quickly, but in any case, in every relationship, the men would be unfaithful. I came to expect it. I decided that real love didn't exist, and men didn't commit. I told myself I wouldn't fall in love again, so I'd never be hurt like that again. Then there you were. And all I heard from others were warnings, but I was drawn to you anyway. I tried to resist you, tried to avoid you. But everywhere I went, we ran into each other and my heart won out. So, I came to you broken. I came to you expecting to be hurt and abandoned because it's all I've ever known. I want to tell you I can put jealousy behind me, but I'm not sure I can. I can only tell you that I'll try."

Listening to her, Shade realized she'd been waiting for him to abandon her and it gave him a new perspective. He also realized that storming off when he was angry was just about the worst thing he could do to her. "Then you have never really felt the love of a man. We are both broken, and if we do not mend together, we will go on the same. I don't want that. I don't want to be broken anymore. I love being loved by you. I love being yours."

Reaching down, Shade pulled her into his lap and tucked her into his chest. "My whole life has been structured around finding my mate. Once found, I could never abandon her. I am genetically programmed to find my mate, my eternity, and I finally found you. Believe in that. Believe that long before the stars aligned in the skies, this was deemed our fate. Our souls finally crashed into one another and damn if I didn't feel the explosion, but what a glorious one it was. I am going nowhere. I don't want to be anywhere but in your arms. You are my home, *bel*, my home. I have lived, fought and struggled to be right here. It was one hell of a journey and I'll be damned if I am giving it up now. I am not those men. I am not like mortal men. I do not think like them, I do not love like them. I do not live like them. I have asked much of you, to become part of this. I want you here, but only if you want to be here. I know you do, I know so deeply how much you love me, I just hope you can reach inside and feel that in me as well."

"I feel the depth of your love every day. I have never doubted it, and I have never doubted you. My jealousy is directed toward the women, it's the women I don't trust. You have never given me a reason not to trust you. It's my temper and your temper. I don't know how to turn that off. Every time it happens, I think I'll control it next time. But then, when we are in the middle of it, we just spiral out of control. Saying words we don't mean, inflicting pain we both regret. We both get so angry, it scares me. And when you leave, when you are able to just disappear, I feel like... you've given up on me. If I ever say I'm leaving, I need you to grab me and say no! We'll fight until we work this out because we're worth fighting for. But when you leave... you just disappear and I can't follow. I only found you tonight because Fee came to me. Don't leave me, lover, don't ever leave me. I don't care how loud we scream or how many walls get smashed, I want us to always figure out how to find our way back. I love you, Shade, I want to spend all of eternity with you."

Taking her face into his hands, he kissed her hard, so hard it rattled them both, and he didn't stop, he kept on kissing her like his life depended on it. Breaking the kiss, he leaned his forehead against hers and spoke softly, breathy, and desperate for her. "*Mi amore*, when you feel that jealousy, you need to stop and feel me inside you. It will tell you everything you need to know, and once you do that, you will see I feel nothing for them. Nothing. I belong to you. I am bonded to the females among my warriors, just as I am bonded to the males. I love them all, as my coven, my *familia*. I will try not to walk away, *mi amore*, but it scares me to think of the damage I could do to us when I get that angry, so I walk away to protect us both. It is wrong, I see that now, I understand now, how you see it, so I too will try to stay and control the beast."

Standing up, he cuddled her ever closer to him and felt her cling to him as they walked back to the house. He stopped as the lights in the windows of their home came into view.

"Look, just look at that. It is our home, *mi amore*, ours. What do you say we go home?"

"I love that word... our home, our bed, and someday, our children. Our life together, bound as one. Will you carry me?"

"I will carry you to the god damned moon if you ask me to. I love you, Kate Reese. I love your past, your present and our future."

He lifted her up and felt her wrapping her legs around his waist, her arms around his neck. "Come along, woman. You are mine!"

Kate clung to him as he ran to the house and they were both laughing. They were like a pendulum, swinging from one extreme to another. She would like to think it was over, these extreme mood changes from both of them, but she knew better. It was the essence of who they were. This wild roller coaster ride he had taken her on just meant she better strap in and hang on.

Once to the house, he kicked open the door with a crashing sound and Luca responded like a bat out of hell. Shade looked at him and grinned as *bel* clung to him, her hair tossed from his run. "I won't be going anywhere tonight. Don't you have a woman of your own to see?"

Luca smiled as Shade brushed passed him. Entering the bedroom, he rolled her off him onto the bed. He unzipped her tight-fitting jeans and she wiggled out of them and kicked them off.

The only thing in his way now, was a pair of black lace panties, which he quickly removed. He gripped her ankles and slowly rolled her over onto her stomach, then slid his hands over her smooth rounded ass. He bit her ass gently letting the stubble on his chin graze across her smooth skin, before nipping her tender skin harder.

They giggled like school kids on a first date. She squealed and squirmed away, partly in pain, partly in pleasure, sometimes it was hard to tell the difference. The pendulum was swinging from anger to ecstasy. The harder she squirmed, the harder he bit, and then he delivered a sharp slap that left a pink handprint on her ass cheek. She lifted her head from the bed, her hair falling across her face and looked over her shoulder at him through red locks and started to crawl across the bed away from him, but he captured her ankles and pulled her back down on the bed, laughing at her efforts to escape.

"And where do you think you're going, my walking sin?"

He spread her legs apart and slid his fingers deep inside her. Her hips began to ride his fingers and she moaned, telling him all he needed to know.

He leaned down and licked the pink handprint he had left on her lily-white skin. He pulled his fingers from her in one swift move, and sliding his arm under her tummy, he lifted her upright so her back was against his chest and slid his honey-soaked fingers across her lips. She sucked them into her mouth and he growled in her ear. "Fuck me, *mi amore*..."

He wanted her body against his, he wanted her to feel his heat, feel his heart racing for her, feel his need to be buried inside the heaven only she could give him. Sliding his fingers deep inside her, he thrust hard until she begged, and when she was ready to cum, he removed his fingers and pushed her face down on the bed. Spreading her legs with his hand, he straddled her from behind and gripped his cock, stroking himself a few times then sliding his cock against her ass, feeling his cock as it glided over those tight ass cheeks, listening to her erotic moans. He couldn't take much more. Sliding his cock between her legs in one hard motion, he pushed deep and hard and felt her accommodate his girth and length.

Throwing back his head, he growled, and his fangs punched through as the beast was loose.

Kate felt the presence of the beast. This was not making love, this was the beast releasing all the anger, confusion, and frustration they had both felt. She pushed her hips back into him, receiving him and those punishing blows, gripping the sheets, wanting more.

He grabbed a fistful of her hair with one hand and yanked her head back so she was lifted from supporting herself on her elbows to supporting herself on her hands. He delivered another stinging blow to her ass with the flat of his hand as he continued to use his cock as a battering ram. All she could whisper was, "Harder."

His beast did not let up and she took what he delivered, and it felt good letting him loose, watching her passion and seeing her need. Lifting her to his chest in one swift motion, he pushed her hair away from the side of her neck and growled, "Cum for your beast, *bel*!"

Sinking his fangs deep into her neck, he held her to him, her back against his chest, his cock buried deep as it spilled inside her, her glorious honey coating his pulsing cock and draining him, as her blood sang into his veins.

Feeling the flash of heat between her legs as he drank from her, she thrashed her head back, exposing her neck fully to him. Neck arched, back arched, ass pushing hard into his thrusting hips, she began the free fall into the orgasm only he could give. Wave after wave of spasms pulled him deeper with each thrust. She felt him release inside her, thick hot cum was filling her, running down her thighs. She reached between her legs, sliding her fingers around the base of his cock, capturing his dripping cum on her fingers then she drew her hand up her body, across her breasts, and to her lips to taste that musky male concoction. As her orgasm faded, she relaxed back into him, letting him hold her, support her. "Don't let go, lover...don't ever let go."

Feeling her body relax, he laid her on the bed and crawled in beside her, his arms around her, letting her know her Shade was back and the beast had retreated. "*Mi amore*, I love you so much, I could not let go even if I wanted too, and I never want to." Sliding his fingers along her neck, he kissed her vein softly and licked the wound for the healing to begin. "Hungry?"

She turned her face to him and locked onto those blue eyes. Their hearts were still pounding, their breath ragged. She nuzzled into his neck and inhaled him, he smelled like the night air and sex, and something uniquely male, and her mouth watered.

She licked at his neck, starting at the base near his shoulder, and let her tongue glide over his skin to his ear as she felt him lean into her. She bit him hard and without hesitation, closing her lips around the wound and sucking the blood into her mouth. Its effect was instantaneous. She felt her back arch as she reached around him, gripping his muscled back, sinking her nails into his skin.

His breathing became ragged as he wrapped her silky crimson around his hand and held her head in place as she fed. *Fuck, she smells so damn good!*

Sliding his other hand down her side, he gently laid it on her hip, his fingers making small circles over her soft white skin. "Take what you need, *mi amore*. I am yours." When he felt her unlatch, he moaned.

Rolling onto his back and pulling her onto his chest, he closed his eyes and sighed. Chuckling, he wrapped her tight in his arms. "You are one greedy vixen, you know that? There is something I need to ask you... It has been on my mind, and I need to know."

"Ask me anything."

"First of all, control that crimson temper. I... Damn, I don't know how to say this to you. Are you using birth control?"

"Yes, of course, as soon as I lost the baby, I went back on the pill. I had a prescription, but I hadn't been seeing anyone for a while, so I had stopped taking them. When I met you, I assumed I didn't need them. I still feel so guilty about that. So much heartbreak could have been avoided, if only—"

"Shh, *mi amore*, we talk no more of this. It is part of our history now. We have learned from our mistake, we move forward, but neither of us will forget him." He rubbed her back, burying his face into her hair. "I love you both. I will always love you both. There will be another son, *mi amore*. I promise you. Sleep *bel*, rest."

She laid her head on his chest and listened to his deep voice as he talked about the son he saw in their future. "And a daughter, lover," she mumbled back to him as she felt her eyes grow heavy, "you will have a daughter to spoil as well. Her name will be Sophia. I dreamt it."

As his death slumber took him, he heard her speak of a daughter. How had she known? He had dreamt of her once as well. Sophia.

57

Kate woke before him and looked at the glowing numbers on the clock. The sun would set soon, and he would wake from his death slumber and the blinds would open to the darkening sky. She stretched out to her full length beside him. Her body felt deliciously sore from the rough pounding his beast had delivered. He had not planned to be home last night, so she guessed their fights were good for something, anyway. She felt him stir and she rolled over onto his chest and kissed his lips before he could even open his eyes. She felt his arms slide around her as he returned the kiss, then he slid from their bed laughing. "Don't get me started, *mi amore*. I have already missed one night from my duties."

She turned on the lamp beside the bed and watched him as he walked nude on his way to the shower, staring at his muscled back, that ass. She shouted at him, "You could just be late, you know?"

He looked over his shoulder at her, that dark hair hanging in his eyes. "Somehow, *mi amore*, your late turns into never. Now behave yourself."

She rolled into his vacated spot in the bed, pulling the sheets to her face to inhale his scent. "That's easier said than done, lover," she shouted over the sound of the running water, and she heard him laugh. When he returned to the room, he wore only a towel tied low on his hips.

"Now who needs to behave?" she asked him, and he looked at her with fake innocence before he broke into a smile and dropped the towel and started pulling on his leathers.

"Give you something to look forward to, *mi amore*," he said as he crawled across the bed and gave her a kiss goodbye.

"Hmm, yes, because the memory of last night is already fading."

He gave her a devilish look and a wicked smile as he responded, "Really? Well, maybe this will refresh your memory." He delivered a sharp smack across her ass. He gave her one more kiss before he left their room, winking at her as he passed through the door.

She stayed in their room as she heard the warriors walking through their house, the voices of the women joking with the men. She couldn't imagine the life of the female warriors. But Fee, she had really misjudged her. She liked her. She hoped Shade would allow her to spend time with her. Kate got dressed when she heard them all leave for the night and then headed downstairs to find Luca. She tapped at his door and waited. That was strange. He usually had the door open before she finished knocking. She tapped again, a little louder and waited. Maybe he was outside already?

Before she headed outside, she slowly opened his door and his room was dark. The light from the hall spilled in and she could see him lying face down on his pillow. Her heart skipped a beat and she moved quickly to his bed and shook his shoulder. "Luca! Are you all right?"

Luca felt someone at his shoulder and he pulled himself from a deep sleep. *Fuck! It's Kate! Fuck! How long have I been asleep?* He sat up quickly in the bed, rubbing his hands across his face, shaking his head.

"Kate... sorry, I just laid down for a minute. I guess I fell asleep."

Kate started laughing as she realized he'd spent his free night with Shannon. "What is it with you big bad vampires and mortal women? Are we too much for you?" She watched as his face turned red.

Luca looked worn out. "Uh... that woman... she barely let me come up for air. Shade was worried about my beast being too much for Shannon. He should have been worried about Shannon being too much for my beast!"

Kate was laughing so hard she couldn't respond to him.

Luca looked at her laughing. "Yeah... you're really not helping right now. I'm going to go take a shower. A really long shower, and if it's okay with you, I think we'll skip training tonight."

She watched as he headed for the shower, looking like he'd been rode hard and hung up wet, and she couldn't stop laughing as she left his room, closing the door behind her. Well, now what? She had the whole night ahead of her with nothing to do. She pulled out her cell phone and called the responsible party.

Shannon answered on the first ring. "Hello?"

Kate walked into the living room and curled up on the couch. "Uh, hey girl. What did you do to my protector?"

Shannon giggled, "Well, it might be a shorter list if you asked what I didn't do. Oh my god, Kate, he's just delicious. Why, is there a problem? Is he upset?"

Laughing Kate said, "Upset? No, I don't think upset would be my choice of words to describe him. I think exhausted might fit the bill, though. Let's just say it's a good thing my ass isn't in any danger tonight, okay? I think he may have to start some endurance training if he's going to stick with you."

She laughed. "Well, he has such a quick recovery, it just seems wrong to let that beautiful cock go to waste."

Kate covered her eyes with her hand. "Oh god, Shannon... TMI." She laughed at her complete lack of filters. Shannon never had them, and she didn't expect her to start now.

Shannon responded, "You held out on me, though."

"Me? What are you talking about?"

Shannon lowered her voice, "The feeding. You didn't tell me how fucking hot that was!"

Kate felt her face get hot, remembering that first experience with Shade. "He fed from you?"

"Well, only after the fifth time I fucked him. He said he needed the strength, but Holy Mother of God, that sent me through the roof!"

"Wait, what? The fifth time? Dare I even ask how many times after the feeding?"

Shannon laughed. "Oh girl, I totally lost count. All I know is, I was three hours late for work today and I got nothing else done because I was totally useless, but it was so worth it."

"Shannon... you didn't... Did you feed from him?"

"No, I didn't. He wouldn't let me, but I really wanted to. After he fed from me, I really wanted to."

Kate sighed with relief. *Oh god, Shade would kill her himself!* "Okay, well, then we need to have a talk. Seriously... because you can't feed from him unless he invites you. Understood? This is important, Shannon!"

Shannon shrugged with her response, "Yeah, okay... I hear you. But what's the big deal? Isn't it just part of the sex?"

"Not for them. They can feed from anybody, mortal or immortal. And they have to feed. But if they let someone feed from them, then that person is bound to them for life. It's hard for me to explain. But it's not something they take lightly. I'm the first person to feed from Shade. Get it? It's reserved for the person they choose to be their mate for eternity, and we're talking real eternity."

Shannon sounded confused. "So... that's not what turns you?"

"It's part of it. It's a gradual process. Apparently, the process of turning someone takes a toll on the mortal, so they must build up their strength by feeding from their mate over an extended period of time. Shade says he'll know when I'm ready, but I have no idea what signs he's looking for. But the point is, don't do it! That's something Luca has to decide, understand?"

"Okay, well that's good to know. But I hope you understand I wouldn't do anything that would jeopardize this. I mean, I really love him, Kate... a lot. And you know me, I don't fall easily."

"I know, and I'm really happy for both of you. But try not to kill him, okay? I've grown rather fond of him myself."

Shannon laughed. "No promises there, girlfriend. Gotta run now. Call me later?"

Kate shook her head. *Poor Luca, his first mortal and I threw him to a shark.* "Yeah, later Shannon. Love you."

She walked through the house, looking for something to do that would take up this night. "Gi?"

He appeared out of nowhere. "Yes, my lady?"

"Guess what? Shade said I could have horses, and he said he has horses in Florence that need to be brought over. We're going to need to build stables... and add fencing."

58

Max was waiting in his condo for Tomas and that freak show named Cuerpo. He was the scariest fucking vampire Max had ever seen and one evil warrior. He sported a full-body tattoo of a skeleton that included his face, as well as a shitload of body piercings. The overall effect was unnerving, to say the least.

Cuerpo loved to kill mortals. He took great pleasure in it. Max planned to use him to take out Shade's mate. But right now, they needed to make sure they were all on the same page with this ambush. Max had the Midnight flowing, and they should be here any minute.

Tomas rapped on the condo door then proceeded inside and went straight for the Midnight. Tomas had decided to arrive before Cuerpo. That vampire had a rep and it was a nasty one. One thing about Max, when he wanted something done, he got the best, and if your objective was torturing and killing mortals, well, Cuerpo was your vampire.

Tomas turned to Max. "So your creature is not here yet? Figures, I'm hoping this doesn't take long, Maximus. I need to be on duty. You wouldn't want me to miss any information, now, would you?"

Max answered, "This shouldn't take long. We'll only have one chance at this. If this ambush on Shade's personal quarters fails, he'll have so many warriors protecting the place in the future, we won't get a second chance. Where is Cuerpo? Didn't he come with you?"

Tomas rolled his eyes to him and took another long swig of Midnight. "Hell no. I don't associate with that creature. Dangerous thing to be seen with the wrong element, Max, you should know that. Mercenaries have rules, and believe it or not, scruples. There aren't many masters who would be seen with him, especially Shade."

Tomas was hit suddenly with the strangest scent, it assaulted his senses, and he shook his head. "He's close. I can smell that fucker five miles away."

Max nodded. "Oh, Shade knows him, knows him well. I doubt there are any masters out there who aren't aware of Cuerpo's rep."

* * *

Cuerpo hung in the shadows, his head laid back. Mortals, he loved the taste of their fear. So sweet! He loved to hear them scream, feel their fear, and watch their useless struggle to survive. That was his drug. He had an appointment with Max who had a tasty mortal for him, but he would pay, and he would pay up front. Cuerpo did no deed, even the delicious ones, without money to feed his lifestyle. He could see everything crystal clear in the dark, but no one saw him until he wished them to. Tasty humans, crunchy bones and ear-shattering screams, and their fear was like erotic foreplay, he loved their fear most of all.

Teleporting to Max's door, he found it open and paused to listen to the conversation. The mercenary Tomas was with him, they were discussing an ambush. Walking in, Cuerpo stood and stared from one to the other then grunted at Maximus.

Max looked up to see the freak show standing in his doorway. *Hell, he scares the fuck out of me. I can only imagine the effect he has on mortals.* He was wearing a suit and tie so all that showed of his tattoo was his face and hands. He looked like a walking anatomical model come to life and it only enhanced the creep factor. "Cuerpo, glad you could join us. Come in, fix yourself a drink and have a seat. We're just getting ready to discuss the details of this job."

Cuerpo adjusted his tie. "No thanks. I only drink mortal blood."

Tomas was grateful the circus freak's shades wrapped around his eyes. That fucking bastard was one spooked out motherfucker with eyes that could blaze a hole in your fucking soul. Tomas looked at Max and shook his head as Max offered him Midnight.

Max settled into his seat across from the two warriors. "Cuerpo, let me fill you in on our little operation here. I'm trying to topple Alec, but he has hired Shade to get his warriors in shape, and in the meantime, Shade has brought his own warriors in, pretty much shutting us down. There's no way I'm going to be able to bring Alec down without bringing Shade down, and there's no fucking way my warriors are going to be able to bring Shade down. But I know we can break him if we kill his mate, and that's where you come in. She's mortal."

Cuerpo sat without moving, the dark glasses obscuring his eyes, so Max couldn't tell if he was looking at him or not. He responded with an evil hiss in his voice.

 "The Medici, that's impressive, but also very serious. And a mortal mate?" Licking his lips as he said mortal, he pulled his glasses off and stared long and hard at Maximus. "I want a visual of the mortal."

Max said, "I've not seen her myself, but I've heard she's on the small side, even for a mortal, so she won't present any problems. Tomas has been conducting some surveillance, so I think he can help you with what she looks like."

Tomas watched Cuerpo sit up and take the bait, and he decided to give him a tempting description before throwing the picture of her on the table. "Her name is Kate. She has flaming red hair. She's petite and meek as a mouse. Shade rarely lets her leave the house, if ever, and she's never alone. Be very aware of that. She has a protector, but Max will explain that matter clearly. This should tempt your palate." Tomas threw him the photo he had a fellow day-walker take.

Cuerpo said nothing. He didn't even look at Tomas. He picked up the photo from the table and stared. She made his mouth water and he wiped at his lips. She was a beautiful redhead, slender and delicate, with soft white skin. He imagined her trembling in his hands. Would she scream in fear, or be immobilized by it? Would she fight and struggle for her life? Or succumb to the inevitable? It was part of the extreme pleasure for him, observing their reaction to the knowledge they were going to die. He could imagine her with her eyes open wide, and her heart pounding. Her heart, the very thought of it made his mouth water again. It would be so tasty and sweet, as he bit into it while it still pumped in his hand. She was small, and he could snap her bones, crunchy, crackling bones, as he gripped her arms behind her and broke them. He felt himself becoming erect thinking of the snapping sound of her bones breaking under the pressure of his hands, while he sucked her sweet body dry. Chuckling deep and low, he said with a hiss, "Sweet mortal, weak and mine." He licked the spittle from his lips.

Max actually felt unnerved by the freak's enthusiasm for this job. "Here's what has to happen. We have Tomas inside Alec's operation. They have no clue he's working for me. And with Alec's rag-tag bunch, it was pretty easy to figure out Shade would gravitate to Tomas, as the warrior from Alec's crew to develop for Second-In-Command. We've purposely pulled back, slowed things down so Shade will show up less frequently at the command center. They call it the Dead House. Shade took off a night last weekend and then didn't show up again last night. He sent her protector away for the night as well. That's what we're waiting for, the next night he takes off and hopefully sends her protector away.

"Tomas, you have to make sure all of his warriors are on duty. We can't have any that stayed back at his house. Get them all on the streets. We can create enough activity to keep them there, so they won't be coming back to the Dead House. As soon as we know Shade is isolated, I want you to call me. I'll drop in five of my warriors. Shade can take five, but that will draw him outside. He'll leave the house to draw the rogues away from her. And that's what we want, Shade outside fighting, and his mortal mate inside.

"Tomas has floor plans of his house. Based on our surveillance, he usually sends her to their bedroom when he wants her separated from his own warriors, so we can assume he'll send her there when he goes outside to fight. There is a second-floor window on the back of the house with a balcony, right into their room. You need to get in position as soon as Shade is drawn outside. I'll have about fifteen more warriors teleport in. Now, I know he'll summon the protector back home, but it buys us some time. Not even Shade Medici can fight off twenty warriors, so the protector will be drawn out as well.

"That is when you make your move. Go in through the window and take out the mortal. And here's the thing. I don't just want her killed. I want her violated, raped, tortured, so feel free to do whatever it is you do to mortals. Shade has to crack when he finds her dead. I want him to see what her last minutes were like, and to have to live with that image in his head. That's what will break him. You got a problem with that?"

Tomas watched Cuerpo salivate at the photo. *Yeah, knew that would tempt your freaky ass.* Tomas wondered what planet the eccentric bastard was from. When Max started yapping about his ambush plan, he was about to bust a fucking fang just hearing about it. Max would have no hand in it whatsoever, just sit back and reap in the blonde pussy. Tomas nodded to Max, affirming his plan, and waited for the freak to speak and take the bait. He could see the wheels turning inside that bastard's head.

Cuerpo listened intently to the plan, staring deeply into the picture of the mortal. *Medici woman, last thing you see and hear will be your mate's wails over your death. I will make sure he sees your last breath, that last look, pleading for his help.* He looks up at the warrior and nods and then turns his head to Max. "One hundred grand. Now."

Max walked over to the desk and pulled out the wad of new bills, secured by a band and tossed them in his lap. *Best money I ever spent.*

"Just remember what I want. Nothing quick and easy, leave your mark. It won't take him long to figure out it was you, and the last face his mortal mate looked at was yours. You make him crack, there's another hundred grand where this came from."

Cuerpo grunted as he stood. "She dies at my hand, my way. She'll bear not only my mark but my seed inside her. You know where to find Cuerpo."

Sliding on his glasses, he teleported out as he came in, back into the night, the shadows and the mortal blood that fed his need.

Max shivered. "What a fucking freak!" He downed a glass of Midnight and turned to Tomas. "I never thought I would work with that guy. Said I never would, but this is the only way I know to bring Shade down."

Max had an image of Cuerpo with Rissa that flashed across his brain and it sent another wave of shivers down his spine. He knew it would break him to find Rissa dead and know that Cuerpo was the force that brought her down. Cuerpo loved to torture. He fed off the mortal's fear. He lived to inflict pain. "You got any questions? Any issues before we put this in motion?"

Tomas was laughing to himself as he watched Max down the Midnight. *You fucking fool. Just threw a hundred grand at some freak to kill a damn weak-ass mortal, the mate of the Medici warrior, and for what? I know what you are paying me, and I'm collecting from two pockets, more yours than the Senator, all for some woman. That damn cunt must be gilded in gold is all I can figure*! "All I can say, Max, is your ass best be heading far from here with your little blonde bombshell, and well hidden, 'cause if Shade ever fucking finds out you were behind the death of his mate, you'll think that thing that just waltzed out of here is the tamest freak you ever met. He'll never stop until whoever took her out is found. He may not survive long without her, but his warriors will never forget. If you're ready to move, I got this, brother, it's all in place. I need to get my ass back to the Dead House, make sure we have everything ready. Give the word, we roll."

Downing the remaining Midnight, Tomas turned and headed toward the door.

"Okay, brother, stay close to your phone, because I think this will go down soon."

Max watched him as he moved his massive hulk through the door, his words still ringing in his ears. He was right about one thing, if Shade ever figured out who killed his mate he would spend his last breath seeking revenge. Max had seen Cuerpo's 'work' before, and even in the world of vampires, he was considered off the charts extreme. It wouldn't be a pretty sight. Those images flashed through his brain again and he pushed down any second thoughts about carrying out this plan. After all, it was the only way he could get to Rissie. He pulled out his cell phone and called.

Rissa felt her phone buzz and wondered what time it was. Glancing up at the clock, it was after 9:00 p.m. Looking down at her phone, she saw it was Max. Smiling, she let her voice go low and sexy. "Hello, handsome. Miss me, do you?"

Max was soothed by the sound of her voice. "Angel, I was thinking about you. You okay? I miss you in my bed, Rissie."

"Of course, I'm fine, Max. Why would you think otherwise? I miss you too. I can't stop thinking about our day out. I need to get away. Alec is about ready to release the engagement news to the press. I want out before this news straps me to the walls." She heaved a fake sigh. "Not like he cares."

"My angel, you just tell me the day. A moment's notice is all I need, and I'll have you on the beach."

"Oh Max, I crave a day to play in the sun. I want to be naked in the sand and the waves, with you." Grinning to herself, she had him right where she wanted him.

"My angel, I'll take you to my private island where you can run naked all day. I'll fuck you under those crashing waves."

Rissa whispered to him in her sexy voice, "Max, you're making me wet. I have everything planned, and it won't be long. Alec has a very busy day coming up. He thinks I'm going to New York to see a dress designer and taking a friend."

"I promise you a day you will remember, Rissie."

"And I promise to make it worth your while, my sweet."

"Just ask and it's yours."

"I'll call you with the date. It'll be soon, and don't forget that potion. I miss you so much."

Max prepared to end the call. "Until then, angel."

"Say it!" Rissa demanded.

"Do you want me to declare my love for you, Rissie? Is that what you need to hear? I love you, my angel. And it'll be in my bed where you spend eternity, not his."

Rissa cooed. "I just needed to hear you say it, Max. I'll always need you."

Hanging up, she grinned to herself. He had never stopped loving her. She wondered if he ever would. Spinning the phone in her hand, she tried to remember the last time Alec called her to say he loved her. It was years ago. A wicked thought crossed her mind. *Oh, I do believe daddy should get a nice engagement present from his baby girl... and a few of her friends!*

59

Shade gathered up the warriors, including the two females, and they all headed into the Dead House. Everyone was on duty tonight as they were all getting a bit lazy for his taste, himself included. As they got inside, he formally introduced his new warriors to Alec's bag of tricks and he got some strange looks. Giving them a hard stare, he decided he had better lay down the law as he heard a few growls from his own male warriors in defense of the females.

"Settle the fuck down, all of you! I run this fucking show and whoever I bring in here, you will fight alongside. Just because they are beautiful and sleek does not mean they are anything less than Medici warriors. If any of you have balls enough to challenge them, I am sure they would be more than happy to accommodate your sorry asses and show you a thing or two. The roster is posted with your quadrants and partners, get your asses out there and bring home some rogue blood tonight. The man paying the bills needs proof his money is working. Move it."

As they gathered their weapons and coupled up, Shade watched as Fee and Olivia stood back, waiting patiently to see where they were assigned.

"Fee, come here please."

Fee had watched this bunch of circus monkeys and held her tongue. Who the hell was supposed to fight with this lot? She caught Marcello's eye and he winked and mouthed to her, "It will be fine." She laughed to herself as Olivia's eyes were almost as big as her head. Olivia was uneasy and Fee hoped Shade had partnered her with one of their own her first night out. Hearing him bark, she told Olivia she'd be right back. Shade pulled out a chair and pointed to it. Sliding into the chair, she put her elbows on the table. "So, what is the plan, and please tell me you have one?"

Shade glared at her. "Welcome to you too, Fee. Christ, you haven't changed much, but I didn't expect anything less." Bending down close so the others couldn't hear him, he spoke to her. "Olivia looks like a fucking deer in the headlights. Help me here, Fee, what's the deal?"

Fee leaned back in the chair, crossing her arms over her chest. "The deal? You intimidate the living hell out of her. She thinks you're the devil himself come to save the day. Tell me you've never noticed, Shade Medici. I know you, and no mate will change your past." Laughing, she watched as his face contorted in anger. She knew she'd hit a nerve. *Oh yeah, Master, you used me to piss off your mate and make her cry. And I like her, so I will goad you when I can!*

He gritted his teeth. "Watch your mouth! And leave my mate out of this. Is that clear, warrior?"

Fee fired back, "Well, let's examine this, shall we? You flew outta the house after screaming like a wild bull with his balls cut off. You act like a damn spoiled brat and just poof from sight. Poor baby, did she piss you off? You didn't go far, though, now, did you? Shade, she loves you with all she has. Let her in, for hell's sake. You'll be much better off."

"Christ, Fee! You know, sometimes, I want to take your ass out! You have more balls than some of these men. And I know *bel* talked to you. *Cazzo!*" He slammed his fist down on the table. "What the hell did you tell her?"

She leaned in close. "Oh, I didn't tell her much. Just that you can be a true bastard at times, and sometimes, you think with your dick, not your head."

He knew she was teasing but he felt his temper flaring up. *Damn it!* "Warrior, I should remind you who is master by challenging you to a sword battle, but you would like that way too much. Now tell me what the hell to do with Olivia. Damn it, we have work to do, Fee."

"Oh yes, I'd love a sword battle, but your mate might have a thing or two to say when you got home bruised and battered by another redhead! She wanted to rip my eyes from their sockets when she saw what Marco sent you. As for Olivia, send her with one of our own. Let her learn the territory with a proper mentor because the rest of this lot is useless. Send her with Marcello, she and Raven will just get into more trouble than it's worth. I need to learn this city before I can take her along and I think it best if we're separated, show these monkeys that we fight just like the rest, no difference, we just look better."

"Good point. Sometimes, you make sense to me, but not too damn often." As she stood and punched him in the arm, he laughed. "Go with Raven, I will send her with Marcello and let him handle her. He seems to have a way with women. Now, get moving. Bring it home, sister."

"I always do, master. I always do."

Sauntering off, she turned before leaving to look at him. She had never seen him like this before. He was contented. He had found what he had searched the whole world for, his destined mate. And, Satan help him, she already had him wrapped around her finger, using nothing but those big brown eyes and her flaming red hair.

Tomas looked on as Shade introduced the two female warriors. Tomas let Shade know he wouldn't be back until the night was over then broke out into the night alone, leaving Shade in the command center. He found a nice dark alley and dialed Max's cell. *Hope to fuck he's not with that blonde. He needs to get his fucking head in this ambush.*

Max was looking at copies of the grid maps from the Dead House when his cell rang. Looking at the caller ID, he saw it is Tomas. *What the fuck? Are we ready for the ambush?* He grabbed up the phone. "Max here."

"You alone?"

Max grunted. "Unfortunately, yes, I'm quite alone. What's on your mind?"

Tomas chuckled. "That damn Shade brought in pussy-ass warriors. If you see tits and ass out here running around looking like they are ready for an apocalypse, it's his women. He just keeps making this easier, Max. He can say they are warriors, but I'll be damned if I ever met one that could fight as well as a male. Easy as leading the sheep to slaughter."

Max paused a moment before answering. "I wouldn't be so quick to judge, if I were you. True, there are women warriors out there that may not be as strong as our male warriors. But I've seen some of the women trained as Medici warriors. I even knew one personally. Sabine. Haven't seen her in a long time, but she stayed in Europe mostly, as do most of his warriors. They were equal to any man, and in some cases, even more effective because they would use their sex to lure the men in, give them a false sense of security. Be careful with that."

Tomas snorted. *Seriously, Max, you need to get the fuck away from blondes for a while.* "Yeah, okay, whatever you think, Max, but they don't look too formidable to me. The one looks like if you say boo to her she will shrivel up and shit her lace panties. Just calling to let you know. I'll keep an eye on them tonight. He's letting them get familiar with the territory. Once that happens, after a night or two, he'll be heading home to his meek little mate. Soon, Max. Be ready."

Ending the call, Tomas slid the phone inside his leathers and thought about this Sabine bitch. She sounded interesting. Europe... Well, maybe he should take a quick trip there after this was over and have a rest. Look up some warrior ass and see if she rode his sword as well as she wielded one.

60

It was a productive night at the Dead House. The women were getting acclimated to the city and would soon be up to full speed. Shade was glad they were in a lull. He had some doubts about Olivia. A hesitant warrior was a dead warrior and he wasn't sure how she'd do under full assault. Hopefully, Fee could help move her along. Maybe he would talk to Marco about her.

Alec's warriors were none too pleased to see women in their ranks, but they'd get over it. They all headed for home and Shade made a brief stop at the fire pit where his warriors were all laughing and talking, before turning to walk back to the house. He had barely set foot in the house when he ran into Gi who was looking frazzled and a little worse for wear. *What the fuck?* "You okay, Gi?"

"Master, everything is okay. My lady is ready to bring the horses here. She said you approved, *si*?"

"*Si,* I approved."

"My lady had a long list of things, the horses transported here from Florence, stables to be built, fenced areas for them to run. Saddles, bridles, feed, hay... *si*, very long list. I have been working on it all night. She is very excited, well, you know how she gets when she is excited. We love her, master, you know we all love her, but that woman can talk your ears off when she gets wound up. Unless you need something from me, I have a lot to do."

The old one shuffled his feet and held the crinkled checklist in his hand, eager to finish all the tasks on his list from Kate.

Shade had to bite his lip to keep from laughing, his hair was standing on end and his ever-fastidious manservant had his bowtie askew. Poor Gi, *bel* had run him ragged tonight. "Well, let me help you out, old friend. I'll see if I can keep her busy for the next several hours, *si*?"

"Thank you, master."

Shade watched as he rushed off and laughed to himself. That little redhead had everyone jumping tonight. He took the stairs two at a time and bounded into their bedroom. "Woman!"

She stepped from the bathroom, fresh from the shower, the fragrance of her rose-scented bath gel hanging in the air, wearing a red silk robe tied loosely at the waist. It swung in the breeze behind her as she walked toward him, the lily-white skin of her legs contrasted against the red color of the robe as her legs were exposed with each step she took.

"Lover?" she answered, and reached for the ties that held the robe together at her narrow waist, releasing them and letting the robe slide off her shoulders and drop to the floor. She walked right into his arms, all soft skin, and sweet curves, her red hair shining, her lips slightly open and inviting. "Am I the woman you're looking for?"

"*Si.* You are just the woman I was looking for."

He picked her up and tossed her on their bed, and quickly stripped off his leathers before crawling into bed beside her. He rode her straight to heaven, and fell into his death slumber, holding her in his arms.

* * *

It was always the same. If he received a vision in his slumber, it always appeared early in his slumber. Shade could feel himself slipping deeper and deeper into the death slumber until it wrapped its claws around him and dragged him under.

> *He could almost feel her, he picked up her scent, but it was faint. He couldn't find her. Was he searching for his bel rosso? Something was wrong. He could feel her concern, like a stab in the heart, and his mind was racing. He tore through the city, searching for her. He couldn't pinpoint her location, and she wasn't answering him, as if she was too frightened to call for him. The images in his head were blurry, as though hidden in a fog. He kept searching and finally, he screamed out for her. His heart filled with dread that something was wrong, and he couldn't understand why she didn't answer him. What was happening to his bel?*
>
> *Then he heard a tiny voice, soft and clear. "I'm right here."*
>
> *He strained his eyes and following the voice, came to a clearing in the deep fog of this unfamiliar place. "Bel?"*
>
> *Her scent was stronger, and he kept moving toward the clearing until he saw a small child. She looked like bel and even sounded a little like bel. He stood still, staring at the face that was so familiar to him. But this was not his bel.*

Her sweet voice floated to him across the fog. "Daddy, you seem lost too. It's me, Sophia. I've lost my way. Can you take me home?"

His heart lurched. Sophia, their daughter yet to come. Sophia! He had dreamt of her before.

"Where is your madre?" He stared at her, her voice so much like bel's, and yet, his feet refused to move. He could only observe her from where he stood, unable to reach her.

He knew he was dreaming, but was unsure if this was just a regular dream or a premonition of what was to come.

Her tiny voice answered him, "Mommy is with the animals. I came out to hunt with her, and I got lost. I'm not afraid. I can kill just as you taught me. I know they're coming. You taught me to be brave, and not be afraid and take care of our family."

He listened and wondered what she was trying to tell him. "Sophia, listen to padre. Who is coming? Tell me." He was finally able to break free and he walked to her, crouching down to her level. He needed her to tell him everything.

"Daddy, you're so silly. The rogues... They're coming, and we must be prepared. I've been practicing my hunting with Mommy. I want to find Mommy and go home. Can you take me home?"

Rogues? No! No rogues.

Lurching for the small child, fear took hold of him and just as his arms encircled her, she disappeared into dust. He screamed, "Bel!"

Kate was sleeping soundly, her head on his chest, his arm around her when she awoke to him screaming out her name. She sat up and turned to him, her hand on his cheek. "Shade! Wake up! You're dreaming. Wake up."

Waking, he felt her touching him as he rose from the fog of his slumber. *"Bel!"* He wrapped his arms around her, crushing her to his chest. *"Bel*, you are here." He had broken out in a cold sweat and felt his heart racing out of control.

Luca had heard master scream out her name in fear. While he didn't feel any threat, he teleported to their room and found him clutching Kate to his chest. "Master?"

Kate brushed his hair from his face. "Lover, it was just a bad dream. Shh. Everything is fine. We're fine."

"Luca, Rogues!" He swung to the side of the bed, his feet hitting the floor, ready to protect her, before sitting back down, realizing he woke from a dream, and trying to sort reality and illusion.

Kate rubbed his back. "You had a bad dream." She nodded to Luca to let him know they were fine and he left the room.

"Lie down next to me. Calm yourself. Everything is fine." She pulled him back down on the bed, ran her hand over his cheek before curling up next to him, her head on his chest. "Just a bad dream, lover."

Was it a dream, or a premonition? Shade held her, felt her in his arms. "*Si, si, ti amo...*"

His death slumber came swiftly, the darkness consumed him, and he knew he would meet her again.

"Soon, Sophia. *Nostra figlia.*"

61

Waking slowly, he felt as though he had fought a war in his sleep. Reaching for *bel*, she was gone and he sat straight up in bed. *Cazzo! What time is it?* "Bel?"

From the bathroom where she was dressing, she heard him stir and call her name. "I'm right here. Are you okay? You woke during the night with a bad dream."

He looked disgruntled. "I'm fine. I don't like waking up without feeling you in this bed. What time is it? Fuck!"

Jumping out of bed, he tossed his clothing from the armoire looking for fresh leathers and a shirt. "Why can't I find anything when I am in a hurry? Do you and Gi have a plan to drive me mad?" Whipping his head around, he smiled at her and winked.

"Lover, you aren't late. I just woke before you and was getting dressed. And I don't think Gi would ever drive you mad. However, I think I may have pushed him over the edge. He has helped me with the house, and then the staff quarters, and the gardens, and now, I have him working on the horses. He seems a bit frazzled. You have plenty of time. You don't need to be in a rush. Your warriors haven't trampled through the house yet."

He laughed. "Yeah, when I came home, I ran into Gi. He was more than frazzled. I think you are pushing his limits, *mi amore*. Cut the old geezer some slack! And, for your information, I like to be ready before my warriors trample through here. Why don't you come down with me? Can you tie back my hair for me? Been a little warm at night and the Dead House is like an oven lately."

He pulled a black t-shirt from the drawer, pulling it over his head and sat at the window, waiting.

Kate stood behind him and ran her fingers through his hair. Closing his eyes, he relaxed and enjoyed the feel of her fingers. Pulling his thick locks back to the nape of his neck, she created a loose ponytail which she secured with a leather tie. She leaned over and kissed the top of his head, before kissing his ear and his neck.

"You taste good enough to eat. And I'd be happy to come downstairs and see the warriors."

He growled, saying, "You keep that up, I will definitely be late."

Standing, he pulled her into his arms and kissed her softly. "I hate leaving you. But this fiasco won't go on forever. Nothing is moving out there, and I'll call Alec tonight, tell him we're backing off. We'll see what the hell he has to say.

Now, I need to get downstairs, I hear them already. *Cazzo*, they are one loud pack of demons. Climb on if you are going with me."

She jumped on his back piggy-back style and he slid his arms under her knees as she hung on around his neck. "Ready?"

They headed down the stairs, both of them laughing. As they entered the main hallway, all heads turned to look at them.

The whole troop went quiet at the spectacle except Fee couldn't help but laugh out loud. Shade certainly had changed since leaving Florence. He had always been so damn serious and now his laughter rang out so easily, Fee thought Kate was good for him.

"Riding him like a true red."

Kate laughed at Fee as the other warriors stared with open mouths. "You know only a redhead could break in this stallion."

"You know it, sister."

Shade slid her off his back. As Kate's feet touched the floor, she went over to Fee and Olivia and the small talk began while Shade and the others left to retrieve more weapons from the bunker. As they returned, Shade winked at Fee, and she nodded back.

Shade liked that Kate was chatting and laughing with the female warriors. It made him happy. Fee seemed to get along well with her and maybe she could help *bel* understand he had never had sex with the female warriors from his own coven. They were like his family. Walking up to them, he wrapped his arms around *bel* and put his chin on her shoulder, licking at her neck and whispered, "I need a kiss before I go, *mi amore*."

Kate turned in his arms and he lifted her up as she slid her legs around his waist and covered his mouth in a kiss. "Go, warrior. The sooner you go, the sooner you'll come back to me."

"I always come home to you, always. And this night will be no different." He leaned his forehead against hers. "Be good, *mi amore*, while I am gone. Luca is here, call if you need me. *Ti amo*."

"And I love you." She watched as they all left through the front door, his small army of warriors.

* * *

As he gathered his warriors in the Dead House, he got out the grid maps. He had doubled the size of the territory for each team of two warrior scouts. The activity level had dropped off and they basically just needed to keep watch. It was easy and boring, and he was just about done with this. As they all headed out, Shade saw Tomas hanging back and he wondered what was on his mind. "You need something, Tomas? Talk."

"No Shade, just grabbing a few knives I left here last night. Forgot them. I'll be heading out now. Damn boring detail. You should be home with your mate. Sounds like you have a lot of property out there to deal with, vineyards and all that business. Heard some of your boys talking." Tomas watched his face closely as he planted the seed. "I can handle all this. Nothing going on here."

Shade nodded his head to agree. "I'm only here to settle in the new warriors and that is about done. I'm calling Alec tonight, letting him know we're going to pull back. We have gone long nights with no activity. Whoever this son of a bitch is, he has either given up or is pulling back to re-strategize. Either way, we'll keep enough out there to monitor the situation, but let our warriors rest, in case they return."

Tomas realized he'd need to stir up some rogues tonight, keep the bait dangling just enough to make sure Shade kept sending his warriors to the Dead House. "Good plan, just don't take them all out. I can manage things fine, and you can come in from time to time and check the situation. It doesn't take you long to get here if the situation changes. Just a thought."

Shade let his words run through his head. "True, and besides that, I want my new warriors to get a taste of the streets. I'll see what Alec thinks, raid his brain box, and see how it goes. See you later, brother. Be careful on the streets."

Watching as Tomas headed out, Shade flopped down in the chair and looked at his phone. It was time to ring up the Senator and see where his fucking head was. Hitting speed dial, he waited.

Alec was in his study, going over legislation when the cell rang. He checked the ID before answering. "Shade... What's going on, brother?"

"Not a hell of a lot. We need to talk. This town is dead of any activity; been like this for a week. This master may have given up, or he may just have pulled back his crew to regroup, re-strategize. If that is the case, they will strike again, but the question is when. Here's the deal, brother. We're going to take advantage of this break. Keep a small crew on watch. Let our warriors get some rest. Let me get some rest. I'll leave Tomas in charge. He's good, one of the best out there, and I won't be far. I can be here in the blink of an eye, but I need some damn downtime. Give me your thoughts. You or Rissa had any problems? Anything I need to know about?"

Alec yawned, "Nothing here. Rissa's been quiet. She's out every day. Hangs at the gym. And she's had no problems, either. I do need a presence on the streets, though. I need to keep my warriors out there just because it sends a message, but I have no problems with scaling back. And I agree with you, of my crew, Tomas is the most solid."

Shade grinned. "Sounds like a plan to me. If you need me, you know where I am. I'll be in and out of here a few nights a week, but I am going to see how this rolls without me here and Tomas in the lead. Made him SIC and tested it out. He did well, knows how to handle the warriors, get things done. He knows what I expect. I will keep a few of my crew out here as well but scaling down so they will have some off time. I still want them to get the experience. I have a few new females in from Florence, giving them a little street experience here."

Alec scratched his head. *Female warriors? That can't be a good idea.* "Female, huh? Well, that should keep you occupied on those long slow nights." *I knew he would get bored with that mortal.*

Shade shook his head, squeezed the phone and growled. "Alec, they are female warriors, not concubines! Some of us are faithful to our mates. Damn it, brother, they are my *familia,* not some damn piece of meat. *Cazzo,* you are a sick motherfucker."

Alec laughed. "Hey, they might be family, but they're not blood family, so everything is fair game, brother. But to each his own."

Shade felt his anger rise. "I need to go, brother." Hanging up, he tossed his phone down. *Cazzo!* He actually felt sorry for Rissa sometimes.

Settling in, he thought about riding horses with *bel.* He needed to work on getting some of his horses transported over from Florence. He'd check into that. Just as he was about ready to call them in and head for home, Marcello and Olivia strolled in and that fucking grin on his face told Shade he either got laid or had a kill. "What's going on, brother?"

Marcello said, "Had two in Quad 4. We split it up and each took one. Simple as fuck, master. No problem. They were definitely trying to hide. Neither had tats like some of the others. And I have no idea if they belong to this Aries coven, but I could smell them, so could Olivia. They're dead now, cleaned up, and if that's all they've got to throw out there, piece of cake!"

Shade chuckled. "It sounds like they are running low on rogues and are scraping the bottom of the barrel now. I am keeping some of you on the streets for a while but leaving Tomas in charge. I got way too much to take care of at home. You up to helping out Tomas?"

"Hey, I got me a kill, always a reason to smile, master. Sure, I have this, leave it to me. Go on home. There's nothing else out there tonight. We can definitely handle this."

As Shade stood up, Marcello fist-bumped him before he teleported out, leaving the Dead House in the hands of Marcello and Tomas.

62

When Shade left with the warriors, Kate went to the kitchen to eat the meal Reynaldo had prepared for her before heading off to find Luca. While she was eating, Gi came in with blueprints for her to look over. The builder had been hired and the paperwork to transport the horses from Florence was done. Kate needed to choose which plans to use for the barn and stables so the builders could get started. After careful consideration, she chose one and Gi hurried off to notify the builder.

She looked at Reynaldo. "Well, at least his hair isn't standing on end today."

Reynaldo just smiled and said, "Give him time, it is early yet, and you haven't been up long."

They both laughed and after thanking him for the meal, Kate headed off to Luca's suite where she tapped on the door. He answered immediately and stepped out into the hallway. Kate bowed to him with a sweeping hand gesture.

"So glad you have recovered and can join me tonight, Don Juan."

Luca knew he would never hear the end of this. He playfully punched her in the arm as they headed outside, and she began to warm up.

"No wonder Shade was worried about me hooking up with mortal women. You know, with the feeders, it's always one and done. But you mortals, you are like a marathon. I'll be ready next time."

Kate laughed. "Just think how much she'll improve your stamina and endurance, warrior. Much more challenging than this ten-mile run."

As they headed out for their run, it occurred to Kate they were winding down their training and she realized how much she would miss it. Maybe they could continue with this part at least.

Luca gave her a sideways glance as they ran. "So, the female warriors. You are good now?"

"Yeah, I think so. I really like Fee. Olivia is quiet, so I don't really know much about her. It's just very hard for me to get used to. Not just the female warriors, but females in general. I mean, I know there were so many, so every time I meet a female who has been a part of his life, I always wonder. I try to turn that off, but I'm not very good at it."

"But that's all in the past, Kate. Whatever happened before is of no consequence. You know he is totally devoted to you. He was single, not committed to any one female. He was just sowing wild oats."

Kate looked back at him and nodded. "But five hundred years, that's a lot of oats. Just sayin'. And I know you're right, he's totally devoted, and I've never doubted him. I just need to get over wondering who's 'on the list' every time I meet another woman from his past. I mean, he's never even inquired about my past, not that it compares."

"He doesn't inquire because he knows it's irrelevant now. You're his now. And he is yours. He knows he doesn't have to compete for your affections. That's one thing in our world that I find very different from the mortal world. Our commitment is for eternity, not so much among the mortals. There's no such thing as divorce among the immortals. We don't trade in our mates when things get rough."

Kate looked at him with a question in her eyes. "But what if you choose the wrong mate? How can you be so sure?"

Luca looked at her seriously. "The beast helps decide. The beast will recognize our mate regardless of whether they're mortal or immortal. It's not a decision any of us take lightly."

"But Alec... I know he's not faithful to Rissa, and Shade has confirmed as much."

Luca sighed. "Master Alec doesn't live as one of us. He has chosen to reject much that is our culture and heritage. There are others who do the same, but you shouldn't judge us by his choices."

"But, you said choice. So, fidelity to a mate is still a choice, not unlike mortals."

"That's true, Kate. But there are very strong cultural influences that drive our decisions. Strong covens protect their legacy. It's complicated because of the feeding, just as Shade had to seek out an alternative to feeding when you were with child. Immortal mates accept this and don't view it as infidelity because there is no deception and it's required for survival, so it's not as black and white as your mortal point of view. And even those vampires, like Master Alec, who have chosen to live an alternative lifestyle don't hide their actions from their mate. Alec's beast knows he has chosen this path. His beast would not be drawn to a mate who demands fidelity. There is no deception. Rissa is aware of his indiscretions and she is still his eternal mate. He may seek out others, but he'll always return to her, unless..." Luca trailed off.

"Unless?"

"We're still a patriarchal society. The male is dominant and rules in all things. Even those who have chosen an alternative to our values will not accept betrayal from their mate."

"I don't understand, Luca. An indiscretion is not betrayal? It feels like a betrayal to me."

"Aside from the feeding, it does to me as well, and to Shade, I assure you. But to those who have chosen an alternative, the betrayal comes with hidden actions, those not disclosed to your mate, for it implies a divided loyalty."

"I'm not sure your explanation is making me feel better."

"You don't need to concern yourself with the alternative lifestyles. It's not something Shade will ever choose again. He has explored enough to know what he values."

She stopped running. "Again? You said again."

Luca stopped short. "Kate, I've said too much."

"Or perhaps you've not said enough."

Luca sighed heavily. "There was the time with Sabine. It was very dark, and we all worried for him. But he wasn't mated to her, wouldn't mate her, and ultimately, rejected all that she offered. His old-world values are ingrained in him, in all of us raised in the Medici coven. In the end, he knew what he wanted, and what he wanted was to remain true to the values and traditions of our culture. To have for himself a mate that was as dedicated to him as he would be to her, not unlike his *madre* and *padre*."

They wrapped up their loop and she began her cool down while Luca set up the weight bench. Her head was filled with their conversation and she wondered if she would ever fully grasp their culture. He put her through her routine of free weights, push-ups, sit-ups, and she let her mind go blank as she counted out the repetitions.

"Ready for the bow?"

"Ready!" As he set up the targets, she pulled the quiver across her shoulders and picked up the crossbow.

He walked back toward her and looked at the old wooden bow in her hands. It was time for an upgrade. "Hold on one second while I run inside."

Luca went back to the weapons bunker and removed the high-tech steel bow from the wall and carried it out to her.

"Here, little warrior, it's time for the big leagues."

He handed her the crossbow that she had chosen from the weapons room on the first night they trained. It was sleek, painted a matte black and included a night laser scope. It was lighter weight than the old bow, but she understood Luca's methods now. He was building strength and technique before letting her take shortcuts with technology. She ran her hands over the sleek surface.

Luca chuckled. "Now that is a warrior move, caressing your weapon. Everything I taught you on the old bow still applies, but you have a scope that will help with the accuracy of your aim. Use the crosshairs in the scope, and the laser beam to line up your target. You still need to compensate for wind and distance. That doesn't change."

He stood behind her as he gave her instructions again. "Slow your breathing, slow your heart rate. Feel the wind direction. Feel your enemy... hear him, smell him. Calm your mind. Focus on the target. Block out everything and focus on the target. When you are ready, hold your breath and fire between heartbeats."

She released the arrow and it hit dead center in the bull's-eye.

"Excellent, little warrior. Now do it again."

He watched as she lined up her shot, paused, took a breath and held it, then released the second arrow. It cleanly split the first arrow.

Kate jumped up and down. "Oh my god! Did you see that?"

She dropped the crossbow in her excitement and Luca grabbed it before it hit the ground.

"Did you see that?"

He laughed at her enthusiasm. "I did see that, little warrior. Quite impressive, however, since you could have more than one enemy, I suggest you not throw down your weapon to celebrate so quickly." He handed the crossbow back to her. "Keep practicing."

He observed closely as she kept every shot tight inside the bull's eye, shredding the target until there was nothing left. He replaced the target and had her continue to shoot. She split the arrow several more times before the night ended. It was another one of those times Luca wished master could see her. He had never regretted training her. Not once had he questioned that decision, but he hated that it was hidden from Shade. As they wrapped up for the night, she turned to hand him the crossbow.

"No, little warrior, that is yours now. You earned it. Put it somewhere safe with the quiver and arrows. A warrior is never without a weapon."

She looked at him in surprise. "Luca, I am... this is mine? To keep?"

"Be careful with it. And keep it hidden, but yes, yours to keep. Now go, before the sun comes up and we both get in trouble."

She kissed him on the cheek before leaving, as she carried the crossbow back to the house. When she got to their bedroom, she looked around. This thing was too big for the drawers, plus Shade was always rummaging through drawers. There was no place to hide it in the closet. She finally pushed the crossbow and the quiver filled with arrows under the bed. *Wow. What's that feeling? Pride! I feel like I won something really huge. Oh wait, I did. I won Luca's respect. Now I just wish I could tell Shade. Why do I have the feeling he won't be as happy?*

63

Marcello was itching to get out on the dirt bikes. It had been so damn slow at the Dead House, master had decided to cut back and give them some downtime. Hell, none of them complained. They had been split into two teams and were assigned to the Dead House on alternate nights. Tomas was in charge when master stayed home with my lady, and Marcello helped them both out as much as possible. Not like there were any problems. Marcello was happy to see his cousin Luca join them for a night on the bikes. Since Marcello had been here in the States, they had spent little time together. One or the other was always on duty.

Tonight, the two of them decided to head out together. They watched as the others revved up their bikes and took off for the rolling hills. The sky was just beginning to darken, and this was going to be a whole night of bikes and warriors, mud and hell-raising.

Revving his bike, he yelled to Luca, "Your woman has you walking like an old cripple, cousin! You should be able to ride that thing like a pro by now. Catch me if you can!"

Slapping down the visor on his helmet, Marcello took off on the dirt bike, spewing mud and gravel, as he followed the others into the dusky spring evening.

Luca laughed at Marcello's challenge and jumped on his own dirt bike and charged after him. Luca could hear the angry roar of the other bikes as they headed up the mountain trails, and he quickly caught up to Marcello, passing him, spinning out in front of him, covering Marcello in a spray of dust and dirt.

Marcello laughed loud enough to be heard over the roar of engines as he watched his cousin pass him. He thought to himself, *Bring it, brother!* It had been raining a lot as the spring weather moved in, leaving the trails soft. He cut through the trees and came out ahead of Luca and laid it down slow, making the spew of mud and water cover him from head to foot. He kept the throttle full out and hoped Luca could keep up. He could hear Luca behind him, but he kept up the speed and took the turns, laying the bike close to the ground, hugging the dirt and it felt damn good to have this machine under his ass pushing the limits.

Luca looked down at his leathers to see them covered in mud. "Fuck!"

Marcello had returned the favor by spattering him in mud and water as he moved down the bike path near the creek bed where the ground was still wet. His wheels caught all mud and he felt the bike lose traction as it started to slide out from under him, and before he knew it, he was flat on his back, with the bike still running on its side. "Fuck! I'll never hear the end of this wipeout."

Marcello looked back in time to see Luca wipeout in the muddy creek bed and he threw back his head, laughing. "Yeah, she's in your head, brother. Thinking about her instead of the machine under your ass."

Doing a figure eight in the mud, he drove back to Luca, put the kickstand down and took off his helmet, still sitting on the bike and stared at Luca's muddy ass sprawled in the mud. "Sometimes, I wonder about your ability to be my lady's protector, you damn runt." He laughed at his cousin.

Luca glared at him. "Don't you worry about my lady. I can protect her just fine." He stood up and tried to brush some of the mud off his leathers.

Marcello lifted an eyebrow. "You seem a bit touchy about her. I see the way you two look at each other. I've been hearing some things about that, cousin. Just a warning. You best be real damn careful about where you're stepping there. If Shade finds out you got anything going on with his mate, your head will be the last fucking thing I ever see."

Luca stalked over to Marcello, pulling off his helmet as he walked and got in his face. "What the fuck, man? There is nothing going on with my lady. You know me better than that, what kind of crap are you hearing? Fuck. That's the last thing I need, for Shade to hear something like that."

Marcello held up his hands. "Back the fuck down, brother."

Swinging his leg over the bike, Marcello let the bike drop to the ground as he pushed Luca out of his face. "Luca, I meant nothing by it, just a warning. Raven said some of the warriors have seen you two out running. Look, I'm trying to be helpful here. Don't be getting in my damn face!"

"Fuck, cousin! That's my job. I go where she goes. If she wants to run, then I run with her. And Shade expects that of me. If she goes into town, which doesn't happen often, then I go with her. None of you have ever been protectors. If Shade isn't here, I'm her shadow. If she sleeps and he's not here, then I'm stationed outside her door. You guys don't have a fucking clue. I know your job on the streets. I've worked the streets. But you don't have a clue about mine, so back off."

Marcello looked hard at Luca. Damn protective of her all right, fucking mortals will screw with your head for sure. Marcello held up his hand.

"I understand, Luca, seriously. I'm not saying it's a bad thing, just finding out how it rolls with you. I like it here, I want to stay around, but that's up to Shade. I guess you're here for the long haul, and besides that..." he paused, taking out a cigarette and lighting it up then passing the pack to him. "Sounds to me like you got something holding you here now. I've seen your woman, brother. She's one sweet looking thing. And I have ears as well. Nailed that like a Medici."

Luca took a cigarette from the pack and lit up. Exhaling, he handed back the pack. It gave him time to cool off before answering. "You know this gig is for life. I'll be here, or wherever Shade goes, for as long as I live. And I've got ears too. I know you and the others think this is a cush job, but it's more complicated than you think. I must stay so close to her it's impossible not to be aware of every detail of their lives together. What they do, what gets said, what doesn't get said, and it leaves me in the middle. Not an easy place to be, between a master and his lady. And yes, I do have something here. Not sure where it will go, I think it's too early for me to think too far ahead about it. It confuses me. You know I've only been with feeders before, this whole relationship stuff... just trying to find my way."

Marcello chuckled and smacked him on the back. "Oh, don't worry, females not only fuck your body but your mind. I hear you, brother. She will tell you in her own way what she wants, and when she wants it. And because she and my lady are both mortals, they'll tell each other everything. Not like the feeders, Luca. They never speak to each other about their clients. That's expulsion from their kind, right there. I know one thing; I wouldn't want your job. I know it's the biggest honor, and I think master chose well picking you, but for me, no way in hell. I like being a warrior on the streets. On a serious note, I'm here if you need anything. Just to talk, whatever. Does this woman of yours have any friends who like vampires? Master gave me permission to hunt, and I miss the thrill of the seduction."

Luca took a deep drag on the cigarette. "Yeah, I wasn't really happy with the feeders here myself, but I never planned on this relationship with a mortal, either. It's getting real serious real fast. She just found out I'm a vamp, so we really haven't talked about her friends. I met her through Ka—my lady. She's friends with my lady."

Marcello heard the slip and ignored it, but it was as he thought. *Luca was getting close to my lady. As her protector, that's a natural thing, especially in this case, since master was gone so much of the time.* But still, it made Marcello uneasy that Luca had allowed himself to get so familiar.

"Just take it slow, brother. In general, women are women no matter what country you're in. But these American women have attitude, tell you upfront just how it will be, and they mean it. Not like at home, that is for sure!"

Luca shook his head. "Dude, I can't talk about Shannon with you like that. She's not just some chick I bang. I know you go from girl to girl without getting attached, but I really like this girl. It's too personal for me."

"You can't be serious? Come on, Luca. What the fuck? You haven't even been out there on the damn playing field. You got a taste of women and you think this is serious? Amateur."

"Hey, I didn't plan it... it just happened. I mean, from the first time I saw her. I'm trying to take it slow, but she's a challenge, that's for damn sure."

Marcello lifted his helmet to put it back on as he laughed and winked. "Hell, brother, all women are a challenge. Let's see what the other nut-bags are up to. Surprised they haven't rolled in here already looking for us. Let's go show them a thing or two about riding."

Luca watched as his cousin took off and he pulled the helmet back on and lifted the bike from the mud. He jumped back on the bike and followed Marcello up the trail. *All women are complicated... No shit!*

Marcello was taking it slow up the mountain. He could hear the whoops of his brothers and the revving of bikes. Once they peaked the mountain, he saw what all the noise was about and he pulled in line behind the others with Luca right behind him. Warriors were brave. They had no damn fear and mortals would cringe at the shit they did, because they could heal. Revving the bike as fast as it would go, it was Marcello's turn, and he hit it hard as the bike shot off the edge of the cliff and he jumped to the other side of the cliff. It was like flying on the back of an eagle as he hit the other side road down the mountain, and back up again.

Luca was behind him, and the warriors lined up for another round. This time, they went one right after the other, pulling handstands in midair, using their strength and the speed of the bike to catapult them through the air. Each warrior was trying to outdo the other and like all males, competitive as hell. Too bad master wasn't with them. He would love this fucking hellfire they had going down. Several hours went by before they all decided to head on home. My lady had built an awesome fire pit and there was enough Midnight to drown in. The moon was beginning its journey to the horizon and it was time the warriors headed back home and ended this night around the fire as they waited for their brothers on the streets to bring it on home to Medici. Yeah, Marcello liked it here.

64

After some thought, Rissa had decided she wanted to give Alec an engagement present neither of them would ever forget. Calling around to a few local covens, she carefully chose a beautiful immortal woman that would fit his tastes. After all, she was his mate and she knew what his beast liked, what sparked their unusual sexual appetites and pleased them both.

Having checked with his assistant, 'Miss Jenny Know It All', Rissa knew he would have some free time this evening. Rissa made the arrangements for the other woman to come to the house, and had all the fun toys lined up and the perfect lingerie laid out. She had everything ready and waiting, now she just needed to spark his curiosity and bring that beast home. She knew, once Alec got home, the beast would roll out with little provocation. Alec was not the romantic type, but she knew other ways that pleased them both.

Grabbing her phone, she sent him a text message:

Your darling has a very special engagement present waiting for you, so please come home when you can, you won't be disappointed. Come straight up to the bedroom.

Grinning wickedly, she ran to take a luxurious bath, drying off and covering her body in lotion that left her skin smooth as silk.

Alec had his cell phone silenced, but he felt the vibration in his jacket pocket and pulled it out to see a text from Rissa. It was an invitation to join her in their bedroom for an engagement present. He checked his watch and it was time to leave anyway. He texted her back:

Give me 20, I'm on my way.

Grinning as she read his message, Rissa instructed the other woman to get into position. They would be ready for daddy when he arrived. After thirty minutes of intense girl play, she felt him enter the house.

When Alec walked in, Santos met him at the door to take his suit jacket and handed him a glass of Midnight. Alec looked at him quizzically and Santos just shrugged his shoulders and rolled his eyes to the stairs. Alec downed the glass and handed it back to Santos and smiled, wondering what the fuck she was up to now. As he walked up the stairs, loosening his tie, he could already hear the moans of pleasure echo down the hall and picked up the strong scent of two females, one was Rissa... and the other?

He walked into their bedroom and saw Rissa seated in a tall bar chair, her legs spread wide and wrapped around the hips of a dark-haired vixen who tossed her hair and looked over her shoulder at him, fangs already bared, as she hissed at him. Alec released his beast and ripped his tie from around his neck, grabbing the front of his shirt, the buttons flew as he yanked it from his body. He roared back at her as his cock went to full staff. He slid his belt from the belt loops in his suit pants and used it as a whip to snap it across the vixen's ass and watched as the red welt appeared and she roared back.

The vixen turned to Rissa and took one pink nipple in her mouth, and Rissa arched her back to lift her breast to her mouth. Alec stepped behind the vixen and growled in her ear, "Fuck her with your fingers..." and watched as the vixen slid her slender fingers deep into Rissa's sex, already hot, wet, and waiting.

He pressed his cock into the ass of the vixen, squeezing her between him and Rissa, as he leaned over the vixen's shoulder and kissed Rissa's mouth, shoving his tongue deep into her throat and feeling the ripple effect of Rissa's body writhing against the vixen. He probed the puckered opening of the vixen's ass with his fingers and she growled again. Without prepping her further for the assault, he slammed his cock hard into her ass as she turned her head and snapped at him.

"What's the matter, vixen? Didn't my Rissa tell you I like inflicting pain?"

He fucked her hard, pushing her hard into Rissa, driving the vixen's fingers deep inside his baby girl, as he gripped the chair with one hand and the back of Rissa's head with the other, pushing his tongue to unexplored depths in her throat.

Rissa felt her juices flow and she wanted to cum, feeling the vixen's body slam into hers as he fucked the vixen from behind. He ripped at Rissa's hair and slammed her head against the wall and she wanted to moan, but his tongue was deep in her throat, making it hard to breathe. Rissa scraped her nails up the vixen's back and ripped through her skin, from the shoulder blades down, feeling the blood flow between her fingers. The smell of blood overwhelmed, hot and sweet. The vixen felt the pain and retaliated by ramming her fist deep into Rissa's sex, bringing its own pain and Rissa exploded with an orgasm.

The smell of the blood triggered Alec's beast just as he felt her orgasm. He bit down hard on her neck right at the base of her shoulder, sinking his fangs deep into the muscle and drinking deep from her. He fucked the vixen harder as she squirmed and tried to pull away from him, but she was trapped between his relentless pounding hips from the back and Rissa's writhing body in front. She tried to reach behind her, clawing at Alec, fangs bared, hissing. He came in her, throwing back his head, eyes glowing red and growling until the windows rattled in the house. After he came, he picked her up and tossed her to the bed, and then picked up Rissa and carried her to the bed. He looked from one to the other.

"Who's next?" he growled.

Leaning over the vixen, Rissa flipped her over onto her stomach and licked at the claw marks left on her back, licking away the trickles of blood and growling deep in her throat. Rissa straddled her, sliding down the vixen's body until she reached her beautiful full ass. She raised her hand and slapped it hard and the vixen responded by raising her ass in the air. Rissa nipped hard with her fangs, bringing a stinging sharp pain. The vixen raised her head and snapped at her, and Rissa quickly grabbed that long mane and yanked her head back and kissed her long and deep, feeling her own juices flow.

Alec watched the action between the two females, then walked to the edge of the bed and grabbed Rissa by her long hair and dragged her to the floor on her knees before him. With his free hand, he stroked his cock and rubbed it across her cheek, circling her mouth. He growled at her to get on all fours and she quickly complied. **"Good girl."**

He growled at the vixen to get behind Rissa, to bury her tongue deep inside that sweet heaven, and watched as she scrambled to the floor, sliding her hands over Rissa's ass before she began exploring with her tongue. He listened to Rissa's moans as he slid his cock into her throat, still gripping her hair, holding her head firm while he thrust into her. **"You want the beast to come play, baby girl? Be careful what you ask for."**

He reached under the bed and grabbed a riding crop, and snapped it hard against Rissa's ass, watching as she flinched in a combination of pleasure and pain, and the vixen looked up in surprise. He locked eyes with the vixen and growled at her. "Don't you dare stop again. I want to hear you eating pussy."

Rissa moaned with the sweet pleasure of his cock down her throat. He fucked her mouth hard, yanking her hair to go deeper and she took all of him. She flinched with the streaking pain that vibrated through her from the riding crop, as the vixen's tongue brought pleasure. She felt another orgasm coming hard and fast again and she struggled to hold on, but the vixen's face was buried between her legs and she was working her clit like a pro and Rissa knew she had to beg the beast to let her cum. **"Please daddy, please."**

Alec heard her begging for release. He snapped the riding crop down hard a second time and pushed his cock deep in her throat, growling, "Cum baby girl," as he released into her throat, knowing his cock was so deep he was cutting off her air.

Rissa bucked hard and felt her orgasm explode like a volcano and once again, he lashed out with the riding crop, and she could feel the welts rise on her soft flesh. Everything connected with perfect timing and her body ignited on every level, taking her to the deepest, blackest edge and she collapsed on the floor before him.

She was gasping for the air she'd been denied. He'd be angry if she passed out in front of this nothing bitch. She rose up on her knees before him, his obedient baby girl, and waited for his command. She could feel the vixen's eyes on her, terrified of what would come next.

Alec was done with this simpering vixen who flinched at the very sound of the riding crop. He walked behind her and struck her ass hard and watched as she howled and hissed at him. He beat her and drove her into the corner and told her to stay there. He turned back to Rissa. "Face down, ass up baby girl. I'll give you what you've been waiting for." She complied immediately.

He walked back to her, running the riding crop gently across her face and over the top of her head, dragging it slowly down her spine as he walked behind her. He slid the tip around her ass cheeks as he dropped to his knees behind her and slid the fingers of his free hand deep into her sex as he used his wrist to deliver another sharp snap of the riding crop across her ass cheeks. He heard her low moan as he leaned over her, his lips only inches from her ears as he whispered in a deep growl. "Now, tell me what you want, baby girl..."

"Please daddy, please fuck me hard, make me scream and cum. Make me your good obedient baby girl!"

He pulled his fingers from deep inside her and grabbed one of the slippery tender petals around her sex and pinched hard, before sliding his hand, coated in her juices along his cock. He ran the head of his cock up and down her clit, teasing, probing, but never penetrating. He watched as she moved her hips back toward him, trying to push her hips into his cock. But he continued to deny her what she so desperately wanted. "Now tell me how bad you want it, baby girl."

"Please daddy, fuck me hard! Take me, show me who I belong to! Make me yours and fuck me till I scream!"

Her fangs elongated, and she roared loud, her body shaking with want for him and she felt him plunge deep.

He exposed his own fangs and growled until the room rumbled. He grabbed her hips in both hands and rammed his cock into her hard, pushing the full length of his sword deep into her. He bent over her back, grabbing her hair and lifting her head back, biting her neck once more and drinking deep. She reached out with both hands, steadying herself against the bed frame and pushing her ass hard against him, her hips matching the rhythm of his thrust, eager to receive all of him. He pounded her hard, jarring her with each thrust, watching as her breasts and hair swayed with the rhythm, her eyes closed, her mouth open.

"Cum with your daddy, baby girl," he growled at her, as he released the last load of cum deep inside her, filling her, watching as it spilled from her, ran down her thighs onto the floor, and listened as she screamed, "Daddy!" while gripping the bed frame.

She collapsed to the floor. He slid his arm beneath her and lifted her up, laying her on the bed and kissing her lips gently. He turned to see the vixen cowering in the corner where he'd left her. He picked up the riding crop and walked toward her. She curled into a ball as he struck her again and again. She started to crawl away, and he struck at her ass, watching as the welts rose on her skin. He reached down and grabbed her hair, lifting her to her feet and dragged her to the door. "You have a lot to learn about pleasing a master, vixen."

He tossed her out the door and yelled to Santos. "Santos... Get rid of this."

He returned to their bed and crawled in from the bottom on all fours, like a predator stalking prey, and crawled to the pillow where she laid her head. He ran his tongue from her shoulder to the full length of her neck. He lay down beside her and pulled her in close and whispered, "Baby girl, thanks for my present," before slipping into a deep sleep.

"I love you, daddy." She closed her eyes, her heart full.

65

Shade stood at the window, looking out at the night. It was good to be home. It was only a home because of *bel* and for that, he could never repay her. She had given up so much to be with him and accepted his coven and his warriors as her own. He watched from the window high above as the warriors came back in on the dirt bikes, and he smiled. They were covered in mud, back-slapping and happy, joking around, and ribbing each other and Luca was in his element. Shade sometimes wished he could be as carefree as the warriors, with no responsibilities, and to have *bel* at his side constantly. But that was not his path in life. Hopefully, though, as things began to fall into place with Alec, he thought they could get life under control and have more time together.

He felt he owed Kate a better life, far more than the one he had shown her so far, and that played heavily on his mind. She deserved babies, to be turned, to learn to be vampire and also, how to drive a damn stick shift! Smiling, he stared out and looked far beyond the rolling fields and mountains. It was all theirs.

Kate entered their bedroom to find him standing, looking out the window. She could hear the laughter of the warriors as they gathered outside the staff quarters. Did he wish to join them? She went to him, slid her arms around his waist and laid her head against his back. "A penny for your thoughts, lover?"

Smiling as he felt her arms wrap around him, he slid his hands behind him and around her. "My thoughts are wandering, *mi amore*. I can see so far on this clear moonlit night. I want to just..." Leaning his head on the window pane, he didn't finish his thought.

She waited as his words hung in mid-air. His words unsettled her and drew on the fear she would never be enough for him. "Just what? Are we enough? You feel at peace tonight, but wistful. I can feel when you are edgy and eager to get on the streets. I understand the pull the night has on you, and I wonder, am I enough? Is our life too small for you, too mortal, or too common? It's much more than I hoped for. More than I could have dreamed of, but I do wonder with all you've experienced, with all you have lived, will I be enough?"

Turning to face her, he looked deeply into those dark eyes. "You, Kate, are everything. The night pulls me simply because I have been cooped up inside the Dead House, and watching the warriors, I sometimes want to run free, but run with you."

He gathered her in his arms and turned to the window, so they could both see out. "Look out there, *mi amore*, this is ours. Do you ever wish to explore it together? It is a beautiful night, come with me. Let's have no plan, just go."

"Shade, you know I'll follow you anywhere, just tell me what to wear."

"You are fine just as you are, *mi amore*. Now keep your eyes open. We are going to teleport low over the grounds. I want us to see it together."

She clung tight to him as he prepared to teleport them into the night sky. "Then lead the way, lover."

Grinning, he kissed her and glided into the night, feeling her arms around his neck, her body tight against his. She was never afraid to teleport with him, she knew he'd never let her fall. As they zoomed over the vineyards, he made a turn and spoke to her telepathically. **"Show me where the horse stables will be, *mi amore.*"**

She pointed in the direction of the field where the barn was under construction, nearly complete, and the fencing was going up for the grazing fields.

Swooping down closer, he hovered over the barn and kissed her softly, then took off over a mountaintop, seeing the trails from the bikes, the hiking paths and all the animals hunkering down for the night. He needed to be out here tonight with her. Then he spotted what he was looking for and gave out a loud call, swooping low and landing them on the edge of the mountain lagoon. He set her down on her feet and saw her eyes register surprise. He'd known it was here. He'd seen it several times at night when he'd teleported home from D.C.

"Want to take a dip with me?"

She stood in the dark on the edge of a waterhole set deep in the mountains with water cascading down the rocks. It was beautiful and peaceful, and the sound of the trickling water soothed and calmed. She could hear the high chirp of the tree frogs, and the deep baritone of the bullfrogs creating the music for this night. He wanted to take a dip, and her first thought was how deep it was? Did it even have a bottom? But she knew he would hold her, and protect her. She pulled her shirt over her head and started removing her jeans. "Lead the way."

"That's my *bel*."

He stripped off his clothes and dove in without her. He heard her laughter as he resurfaced. He swam over to the edge of the lagoon and looked up at her. She was so beautiful standing naked in the moonlight. "The water is warm, *mi amore*. Jump! I will catch you!"

He ran his hands through his hair, pushing it back off his face. Even in the dark, she could see the blue of his eyes in the reflected moonlight. He yelled for her to jump, and she leaped into his outstretched arms. Screaming as she hit the ice-cold water from the mountain streams. He laughed at her as she sputtered, and he pulled her against his chest. "This water is *so* not warm!"

Laughing at her, he kissed her shivering lips. "You just need to get used to it. Hold on!"

He clung tight to her and dunked them both under the water and straight back up again, laughing as she sputtered and smacked him on the back. He kissed her hard to take her mind off the cold.

"I'm sorry, *mi amore*, I should have waited until the summer months to do this, but I wanted to be here with you. Savage lover and his *bel rosso*, I miss them."

She clung to him in the cold water, feeling the heat from his body. "I miss them too. You've been gone so much lately, I understand why, but it doesn't make me miss you any less."

Swirling them around in the water, he held her tight and felt her body adjust to the temperature as she relaxed in his arms and he looked deep into her eyes.

"*Mi amore*, I have been dreaming; seeing visions. I do that sometimes. They are usually a puzzle, something I must solve, but I can't figure this one out. I dreamt of our daughter, Sophia. You told me you had dreamt of her as well. I wonder if what I'm seeing is somehow coming from you because I dream-walk with you every night. Tell me what you have seen."

She looked at his face, lit by the moon and the reflections of the water. "I have dreamt of her. She has fair skin and red hair, and a temper, heaven help us. But she has your eyes... your ice blue eyes. She is small, delicate, but not timid. She's a handful."

He smiled down at her, her hair pushed back from her face, her pale skin reflecting in the moonlight. "Like her *madre*. Just like her *madre*. What does it mean, *mi amore*, that we dream of our child? Is she coming soon?"

She answered him, "I don't know what it means, lover, except she already lives in my heart. She's in our future, somewhere, waiting for us. But she'll be there when we're ready. I feel her impatience. She says, 'Don't wait too long!'"

Kate laughed at the vision that appeared in her head of their redheaded daughter with her brow furrowed, her lips pouting, her red curls swaying. "She stomped her foot when she said that. As I said, she is a handful."

He chuckled at the image she described. "She is so like you, *bel*. I feel that. Do you think she will be first?"

"Lover, as impatient as Sophia is, I don't think she comes first. I know our lost baby was a boy, he told me when I carried him, and he told me he'd be back. But he doesn't speak to me now. He hasn't come to me in my dreams. But I do feel him. Has he come to you?"

"No, *mi amore*, he has not. Perhaps he won't. I do not control the visions, I cannot call them forth. They randomly come to me. Now let us speak of other things, the night belongs to us. Hold on."

Teleporting them up out of the water, he landed them on the ledge high above the lagoon. "Hang on tight, let's take a dive. Trust me?"

He felt her shiver from head to toe and knew he would need to get her back home to the warmth of their bed soon.

"I'm ready, lover."

Holding her close, he felt her legs tighten around his waist and her arms grip his neck. He took a running leap off the ledge and into the lagoon. The moonlight streamed through the surrounding trees, making it a paradise for two lovers to enjoy. They hit the water with a splash, gliding deep beneath the surface until he felt his feet hit the cavernous bottom and he pushed them back up. As they broke the surface, he kissed her as she should be kissed, long and soft and deep.

He held her close to him as they floated on the surface, drifting gently in the current and churn of the waterfall.

"Shade, we never talk of this, but I know you have thoughts about it, about when you think you'll turn me. Do you know when that will be?"

He leaned his forehead against hers, the water trickled between them. "I wish it were done, *mi amore*. Your body is toned and strong now, from all the running and exercising you have been doing. It will help you immensely. I want all this business in D.C. under control first, so I can take you back to Florence. Since you are mortal, the Council will not recognize you as my mate until you are turned, and you are accepted by the vampire community as my mate and become my queen. You become mine for all eternity, no turning back. Are you ready?"

"Lover, I'm ready. I don't know what's involved. You've only alluded to it. You'd mentioned some kind of ceremony that would take place there. But whatever is involved, I'm ready. You seem concerned still. Do you have questions about my desire to be with you? Do you think I'll regret my choice? Because I promise you, this is what I want."

He cupped her face in his hands and moaned softly. "Oh Kate, I have no doubts about your love, or your willingness to become mine for all eternity. I worry mostly about the pain and the fight you will need, to overcome it." Lifting her in his arms, he climbed out of the water and walked with her under a small alcove of overhanging rock. "Let me make us a fire, *si*? I will tell you about it."

She saw the concern in his eyes. It was there every time they spoke of this, and he usually changed the subject. "Please, I want to know everything."

She sat down, pulling her shirt around her shoulders as he gathered fallen sticks and branches, stacking them and building a blazing fire. The crackling and popping of the damp wood was a sound he loved in the night under the stars. They sat together cuddled before the fire.

He knew he needed to give her more information about the turning. He had put it off far too long.

"*Mi amore*, try to curb your questions and listen to what I have to say. I have not told you much. I did not want to scare you, make you change your mind. I wanted to make sure you could handle it, and you truly wanted to be with me forever. I procrastinated in giving you much information, do you forgive me?"

"There is nothing to forgive. You said you'd not turn me until you thought I was ready. I knew you were waiting for something. And whatever it is, I won't change my mind. I know you'll be with me and you'll get me through it."

"I'll do everything I can, *bel*, but much of it falls on you." Facing the fire, he laid his head atop hers. "Let me see if I can explain this to you. We will be inside a royal chamber, which sits underground at Medici Castello. I'll be with you, *mi amore*, through the entire thing. You will never be alone. I'll drain you of your blood, to the last moment of death. That part is not painful, but very erotic. You must remember to not fight it. Don't let the feelings of your own body weakening make you fight me or be scared."

She was processing the information. *A chamber? Underneath Castello?* "I understand that part. It will be like when you feed from me, only you don't stop."

"*Si.* You will not feed from me during this first step, this draining. You will feel the urge to feed, but you must fight it, and if you attempt to feed from me, I will forcefully stop you. The more I drain you, the weaker you will become. I am draining your life from you into me, understand, *si?*"

"I understand."

"When you are at the moment of death, I will know, *mi amore,* trust me. I'll score my wrist, and only then will you drink. You must take from me then and not before. It will not be a lot, and you will not need a great deal. Your mortal body will start to die, and my blood will slowly flow through your veins. With it will come pain and transformation, and it will feel like fire and ice. It is painful, and you will wish to die. Believe me, you will have to fight like nothing before in your life. The darkness will want you, the darkness will call to you, but you must not let it win. You will need to fight to come back to me. Concentrate not on the pain and the call of the demons, but on my voice, my body. You must feel me, hear me, and it will take all you have. Your body will be in great pain to try and distract you from me. It is hard to explain, but my blood will transform you to vampire, and we merge as it is my life inside you. I take your soul when I drain your blood from you, and when I give it back, our souls have been combined, we are bonded, blood, body, and soul, for all time.

"I won't leave you, but you won't always be aware of me. You will be gone from me then. In this stage, you choose to fight to be with me, or the darkness takes you, and you die with your mortal body. I cannot help you here, *mi amore.* It will be up to you to come back to me. Your love for me must be strong enough for you to fight your way back. Can you do that?"

"Lover, I'll have no trouble coming back to you. I promise you."

"Our love is like no other I have ever felt, but it takes more than wanting to get through it and I have much faith in you. This process will take hours. This is where your beast grows and crawls inside you, where your fangs emerge and grow, where you receive your gift. Your outward appearance does not change much, just all the internal changes of being immortal, your telepathy, fangs, and your special skills. If you do not wake within twelve hours, I will begin to call to you, out loud and within your mind, calling you home to your maker, your master. I will know then if you made it through, for if you do not come to me, I have lost you."

"You won't lose me. There's nothing that can keep me from you. And you'll pull me back. I'm not afraid."

Kissing her neck softly, he said, "I know you are not afraid. This is why I have waited for my blood to transform you. You will recognize the call of my body to yours, hear my voice calling to you. I needed you strong and your heart and soul already making connections to mine. Once you awaken, you will be mine for all eternity. You cannot go back, ever. Then you will feed from me, and you'll be starved for blood. A wild bloodlust, newborns, as we call them, are always hungry. That is the part I cannot wait for, "he said with a chuckle. "That is the part I crave to feel, your fangs in me. It is the ultimate pleasure, two immortals, feeding from each other, and your immortality is complete. After we feed, I will give you some time to adjust to your new senses. Everything will seem much more vivid to you, your sight, your sense of hearing, your sense of smell. Then you must be presented to the coven. My warriors will dress in full regalia. We will be seated in the Throne Room, and they will all kneel before you separately and pledge their loyalty to their new Queen of Medici. They will pledge their life to you, their protection and honor."

"Queen? You have always said royalty. When you called me your queen, I thought it was a term of endearment."

"*Si*. I am a king and master of the Medici coven. I am the sole heir. When I turn you as my mate, make you immortal, you take the title of queen. They will address you as such."

She laughed at the title, "So I guess I'm stuck with that 'My Lady' title for sure now." She nuzzled into his neck and kissed him. "When will you turn me?"

He smiled down at her joyous response. She wasn't afraid. "You are ready, *mi amore*. I am wrapping up details with Alec. Once I'm sure nothing else big is going down, then we go." Kissing her neck and then her lips, he broke the kiss. With lips still touching, he growled softly, saying, "And then we will have *bambinos*, it will be safe."

She laughed. "Maybe Sophia will stop stomping her foot then." She kissed his lips, little kisses, soft, tender, again and again.

"There is something you must know, *mi amore*, about the *bambinos*. And it will be important."

"What is it?"

"You remember immortals don't carry their children for nine months, more like six. They will need to be born in Florence. There will be no mistaking their birthright. They will be crowned there, immediately, as

Prince or Princess Medici and their birth witnessed by the Council, recorded for history. No one can ever dispute their birthright. These are important steps to secure their legacy, understand?"

"Yes, of course, the babies will be born in Florence."

"You will know their sex before I do. They will talk to you, in their own way, as they grow inside your body."

"Lover, they speak to me already. At least, Sophia speaks to me, and she is going to be a nonstop talker, I fear. Will I have to stay in Florence for the whole pregnancy? Or can we teleport as we near the time of the birth?"

"We will go to Florence when you are close to your time. My coven will crowd into the town. The bells will toll at the *bambino*'s birth, and there will be celebrations like none you have ever seen! I will take the *bambino,* and we will walk out onto the parapet to face the coven and hold our prince or princess high to them. It is my gift to our coven, *mi amore*, my heir, my covenant fulfilled. It assures that our bloodline goes on, that they are protected and cared for through the next generation. It is sacred to me, important to me that we continue this tradition. Theresa will be with you as you give birth. She is a midwife, and she too bears witness that our Queen gives birth to the next Medici Prince or Princess."

She listened intently as he described the events of her turning, and the birth of their children. "Shade, I've never asked you. We've spent so much time creating our home here, I think I just assumed, but is this where you want to live? Your home is in Florence. It's where you were born and grew up, and it's where the memories of your parents reside. I never asked if you preferred to live there."

He sighed and smiled at her. "There are memories there, but my people are used to me not being there. I make appearances to them, to assure them I am healthy, strong and still their master. But I want to live here. We will come to a point when our son must be trained as a warrior, and he must follow in my footsteps and when that time comes, well, let us not jump too far ahead. I want to be here, *mi amore*, build an empire for our *bambinos*, an empire to rival all masters, to ensure the Medici legacy will not topple again."

She shivered in his arms despite the fire and the warmth of his body. The night air chilled her.

"*Mi amore*, put your clothes back on and I will take us home."

He stood and started to dress as she gathered her remaining things, her head racing with everything he had shared about the turning, the ceremony, their babies, and an empire. She pinched herself to see if it was real and she heard him chuckle as he wrapped his arm around her and teleported them back to their home.

"It is real, *mi amore*, it is very real."

66

Getting ready to head out to the Dead House, Shade quickly showered. From the bathroom doorway, he watched Kate scurrying about the bedroom, trying to get dressed and eat at the same time, grabbing a few bites of food from a tray on the bed each time she walked passed. Chuckling, he grabbed her around the waist and kissed her softly.

"*Mi amore*, I'll be gone for about an hour. I'm just touching base with the warriors and checking in with Tomas, then coming right back home." Slapping her ass, he smiled. "So, don't get into anything that occupies your time, your warrior will return shortly."

"You're coming right back home? That's great! The stables are finished, and the horses are here from Florence. I can't wait to see them. I was going to head down to the stables, so why don't you join me there as soon as you can."

"*Si.* Stay away from the big black stallion, *mi amore*! I mean what I tell you. I am heading out now. The sooner I go, the quicker I can get back to you."

"Okay, I have a lot to check on in the stables. Gi has staff that he brought in from Florence to manage the stables and the horses. I need to meet them, so I'll be busy until you get back. We can look at the horses together."

Kissing her once more, he rushed out the door, wanting desperately to get the hell back here.

She pulled on jeans and riding boots and grabbed the last bit of fruit from the breakfast tray and walked down to the new stables. It looked fabulous, even at night, and she couldn't wait for Shade to see it. She had walked down earlier in the daylight when it was almost done, but the horses had not arrived yet. Gi said they were all here now and survived the transport beautifully.

Kate missed her nightly runs with Luca, so she walked briskly down the road that led to the stables. The stables were all stone and timber, which would age beautifully, and the design of the building complemented the other buildings on the property. The new fencing for the grazing fields was in place and painted white. The spring night still had a bit of chill in the air, and there was a low mist that hung near the ground. The full moon illuminated the landscape. She loved this place, their home, this land, and these people. She loved their life here. But mostly, she loved him.

As she entered the stables, she was hit with the smell of fresh hay and horses. The stalls were being prepped to receive the horses, which were still in horse trailers. There were stalls for twenty horses. She had no idea how many horses Shade owned, or how many he had planned to bring here from Florence.

Gi ran to greet her, looking completely out of place in his waistcoat, white shirt, and bow tie and she had to bite her lip not to giggle.

"My lady, the horses are all here and we have brought in staff from Florence who will manage them. You should meet the stable master. He will oversee everything when it comes to the horses, their feeding, grooming, and training. Anything you need, you work through Angelo. Angelo worked with Shade to train all of these horses, so the animals know him, will respond to him, *si*?"

Gi led her through the stables to meet Angelo, already covered in sweat and smelling of the fresh hay he had loaded into the stalls. He stopped what he was doing to acknowledge her, "My lady."

All Kate could think of was she hadn't prepared a room for him. *Where will he live?* As if reading her thoughts, Gi spoke up and said, "All of the stable hands have rooms over the stables. I included them in the plans, my lady."

* * *

Shade wrapped up quickly at the Dead House, handing out assignments before heading back home, teleporting himself outside the stables. They looked good but were smaller than the stables in Tuscany. Stepping inside, he could hear Gi and Angelo and he knew *bel* was here with them, he could detect her rose scent. "*Mi amore!*"

Kate heard him call and looked up as he entered. "Shade! Don't you love it? Come, welcome Angelo to his new home. And show me the horses!"

He grinned at *bel*. "*Si,* it is beautiful. Come, give your warrior a welcome home kiss."

Kate ran and jumped, legs locked around his waist as she kissed his lips and face, smothering him in kisses. "I'm so glad you're home early."

"As am I, *mi amore.*"

Setting her back down, he walked to Angelo and they hugged like brothers. "Welcome, Angelo!"

They talked a bit about how he wanted to approach bringing in the horses, speaking in Italian so *bel* didn't understand all the things he had in store for her. As Angelo went to carry out his orders, Shade turned and took her hand as they watched several of the horses being brought in, one by one. Angelo led each horse by their reins to their stalls, speaking gently to them. Each horse raised its head and sniffed the air as they passed and whinnied their greeting, pawing at the floor of their new home.

"*Bel*, these are just a few of the horses I have in Florence. I intend to purchase new horses here as well, strengthen the bloodlines. Luca also rides. So, if you wish to ride in the daylight, he can accompany you. What do you think so far?"

"They're all beautiful. I can't wait to ride them, and to ride with you."

"Come, I have something special to show you." Taking her hand, he led her to the stall farthest from them. Shade stepped up to the auburn stallion with a white star on his forehead and held out his hand to the horse, waiting until the horse caught his scent and recognized him.

"*Mi amore*, this is a very special horse... Bravado. He was bred in Florence, and Angelo and I have trained him well. He is gentle but very strong of heart. He belongs to you now."

She clung to his hand as they approached to see a beautiful red stallion with a white star on his forehead. His coat shined like glass, and she could only imagine him in the sunlight, grazing in the fields. She approached the horse slowly, holding out her hand, caressing his nose, letting him get her scent. "He is beautiful. Bravado. That's brave, right? Oh lover, thank you."

Shade stepped behind her, sliding his arms around her waist. She leaned back into him and felt him kiss the top of her head.

"*Si*, brave. You need to stroke him, talk to him, *mi amore*. Let him know he belongs to you. Go on, he will not hurt you. Just go slow."

Looking at the horse, Shade raised his voice a bit. "Bravado." The horse turned his head and stared at him. "Good boy, I know you are nervous from the trip, but this is your new home, and this, is my *bel*. Relax, boy."

She walked alongside the large stallion and ran her hand down his strong neck, through his thick mane and across his back and haunches, speaking softly to him, repeating his name, letting him get used to her touch and the sound of her voice. She slipped her hand into her jeans pocket and pulled out a few sugar cubes and held them under his nose, palm flat, so he could take them from her.

"He's so gentle, so calm after being transported and in new surroundings. He'll be a great horse for me."

"Oh *si*, I chose Bravado because of such. He is ready to ride as well, but when you go out the first time, it is best you go with Angelo or me. He will be calmer with us until he is used to his territory and to you in the saddle. We'll also need to choose a saddle for you."

Suddenly, he heard snorting and pawing and heard Angelo yelling, "Master, he is ready, and I think you best get down here! He can hear you and is restless as fu—restless. Sorry, my lady."

Grabbing *bel*'s hand, Shade walked at a brisk pace down the stables. "I want you to meet someone very special, *bel*."

"Someone special?"

"*Si, mi amore*, very special."

As they came to the far end of the stables, Shade stopped and watched as Angelo led in a horse that stood twice the size of the others. "*Mi amore*, stand back against the wall. He can be unpredictable with strangers."

Shade kept an eye on the huge horse as the Friesian bucked his head up and down and pawed the ground beneath his feet. In his mouth, he held a red rose.

"Impavido, come! I see you are as charming as your master, bringing my lady a gift, *si*."

He took the rose from the horse's mouth, as the horse bowed his head down to greet him and nuzzle into Shade's own long dark mane. He stroked the horse gently before turning to *bel*, holding out the rose.

"This is my stallion, Impavido. Apparently, he has brought you a gift of gratitude for his new home. But I will warn you, *mi amore*, he does not take well to women."

She was amazed by his size and beauty. He was the most striking horse she'd ever seen. He was black as the night sky and his coat shone. His mane was long, much longer than normal.

"And yet, he brings me a red rose. Seems to me you gave me the same warning about your beast and look how well that turned out. I'll give Impavido his space, but I think we'll get along fine."

He laughed at her comment. "You do seem to have a way with big beasts, *mi amore*."

Impavido shook his shaggy head up and down in agreement and Shade laughed harder. Impavido tilted his head down eyeing Kate.

"*Si,* she is my mate, boy. She is beautiful and strong and has a fighting heart. She takes good care of me, so you need to behave with her. Come, *mi amore,* come say hello."

Kate thought the horse had the most soulful eyes she'd ever seen and she stared at the massive animal as she approached him. He bowed his head down low and she placed her hand on his nose and stroked him. "Impavido, you're one beautiful beast. And a perfect match for Shade."

She leaned her head against the horse's bowed head as she stroked his ears and mane. The horse chuffed and nuzzled into her.

Shade remained ready at any moment to handle Impavido and settle him down. The horse had never reacted well to women before, and he was astounded at how quickly he seemed to accept her as if he knew her heart already.

"That's a good boy. *Cazzo, mi amore,* he never does this. He is a warhorse! I swear you bring every warrior I have to his knees. I am surprised I get them to do anything around you."

Walking over to the bucket of apples on a nearby shelf, he grabbed one and walked back and placed it in *bel's* hands.

"No sugar for Impavido, but he is allowed to have carrots and apples. Apples are his favorite, but I don't think it much matters what you give him, he will take anything from you."

Impavido started chuffing as he picked up the scent. She held the apple out to him and he gently took it from her hand, his tongue hot against her palm. "Impavido, what does that mean?"

Shade watched the horse go straight for the apple and he just shook his head. "It means fearless, *mi amore,* but he does not look so at this moment. What have you done to my horse? He looks gentle as a pony."

"He is fearless, lover. Don't worry, he is still your warrior, and just like you, he'll fight when he needs to fight. I feel what's in his heart."

Taking her in his arms, he hugged her tight and kissed her deeply and heard Impavido snort and try to nuzzle between them, breaking the kiss. Shade laughed. "*Cazzo,* Impavido, she belongs to me. Now, *mi amore,* if you will walk with me, I have one more thing I wish to show you." He held out his hand to her.

Kate laughed at the antics of the horse and took his hand as he led her through the stables. "What other surprises do you have up your sleeve?"

"Just one more, *mi amore.*" Stopping short of the back gate, he instructed, "Now, wait here."

He walked to the gate and opened it slowly, reaching in and grabbing the reins, he walked an Arabian out in front of her.

"*Mi amore*, this is Miele. She is a prize Arabian and she was born at Castello. She comes from a line of horses bred by my mother's family. *Madre* owned an ancestor of Miele. I wish to give you the same. Miele is young and very gentle. Come, say hello."

Kate looked at the young Arabian horse. She could tell she wasn't yet full-grown and probably hadn't been ridden much, if at all. She would need to be trained. She looked a bit skittish in her new surroundings, but she was a beauty, an ivory coat with a white mane. "She is beautiful. I love her color. And her name? Miele?"

He grinned softly. "Miele. It means honey."

Kate laughed softly. "Perfect name."

As Antonio came to take the reins from him, Shade grabbed up *bel* and felt her body wrap around his. "What say you, *mi amore*? Ready to make a memory?"

As she giggled, he spun her around in his arms in the middle of stables and heard the snorting and whinnying of the horses in agreement.

67

As the night approached, Shade stretched from his death slumber, looking over at his beautiful *bel*, still asleep beside him, and smiled. Feeling her nuzzle into the pillows, he knew she was almost awake, and he got up from the bed and quietly walked to the window. The warriors were outside, and the sun was just going down... *damn*. He turned and looked at her once more and decided, tonight, this house was going to be empty, with the exception of the two of them. He had enjoyed the few nights he had been with *bel*, the time that belonged to them alone and she deserved this.

Luca needed some downtime too, so he would send his ass to his woman, send all the warriors to the Dead House and give Tomas a call and let him know he wanted them out there all night. Grinning to himself, he liked the sound of that. A night alone with *bel*, and maybe they could take a ride together on the horses. He heard her moan in her sleep and turned to see her feeling around for him in the bed.

"Wake up, sleepyhead."

She looked at him, her hair a tangled mess. The memories of last night flashed through her mind and she smiled up at him. "Is our sleep over already, lover? Is there any way to entice you back into this bed?"

Still naked, he walked to the foot of the bed and crawled to her, up and over her body until he reached her face and kissed her long and hard, sucking her tongue and biting her sweet lips.

"Mmm, *si*! I am staying home tonight, I have a plan. Do you want to hear it?" He pushed her tangled hair behind her ear as he crouched over top of her, her body soft against his hard one.

"A plan? Id love to hear this plan, especially if it includes me." She slid her arms around his neck.

He licked her neck with a long slide of his tongue, hot, slow, and wet, as he felt her body respond. *Cazzo, she makes my blood boil!* He delivered light, soft kisses around her ear, leaving a trail of kisses across her cheek, raising his eyes to hers and winking. "Your warrior is staying home tonight. I'm sending Luca to his woman, sending the warriors to the Dead House and their asses are staying there all night, time they earned their keep. I have already given Gi, Reynaldo, and Theresa the night off, and maybe…" Nipping her chin delicately, he whispered, "If you are a good girl…" Sliding his tongue along the edges of her lips, he said into her mouth, "I will make you some dinner, and then take you for a ride on the horses. What say you, *mi amore*?" He kissed each of her cheeks and nuzzled into her neck.

"Lover, I can't even remember the last time we were in this house alone. I say yes!"

He loved the sound of happiness in her voice. "Well then, I need you to get your gorgeous ass up and dressed. I am going to head down to Luca, give him the details and make a call or two and get these apes on their way. If you give me about thirty minutes, I will return to make you dinner. Afterward, we can ride, or something." Grinning, he kissed her lips. "Deal?"

"Deal. I'll take a quick shower and get dressed while you take care of that, and I'll be ready when you get back." She jumped out of bed and headed for the shower, grabbing her rose-scented bath gel.

He grabbed a pair of jeans and slid them on, leaving them zipped but unbuttoned and hanging low on his hips. He headed downstairs to seek out Luca and get this band of badass warriors on their night journey.

Heading into his office, he grabbed his cell phone and headed to Luca's quarters, but he was nowhere to be seen... *Where the fuck?* Then he saw the door to the basement winery opened slightly and knew he was in the weapon's bunker. Heading down, he found Luca with a few weapons laid out on the table, as he sat restringing a bow. "You intend to hunt to feed now?"

Luca was so intent on restringing the bow, he hadn't heard Shade come in. He turned in surprise. "Uh… No, this one was just, it uh, needed to be restrung. The string was stretched."

Scrunching up his eyebrows, Shade crossed his arms over his chest and grunted. "Well, I haven't seen anyone around here even bother with picking up a bow lately, been a while for myself."

"Just part of my job, master. Some of these weapons, especially the old ones, need maintenance."

Shade gazed over the weapons mounted on the wall, all in impeccable condition. "So, how is that relationship with the sweet mortal going?" Shade sat down in a chair across from him, crossing his leg over his knee.

Luca kept restringing the bow, avoiding Shade's eyes. "It's going great. I think you know how I feel about her. She said she loves me, and I think I love her. I've never been in love. Kate says it's love."

Shade turned his head sharply as he heard Luca call her Kate. *Kate? Oh, this is not good!* He felt his beast rise right up and he had to fight with all he had not to let him loose on one of his own. Growling, Shade looked him dead in the eyes. "Kate?"

"Master?" *Fuck! Did I just call her Kate? I didn't even realize it, it comes so naturally.* "Master, I'm sorry, but I've been referring to her as Kate around Shannon, and that's what Shannon calls her. You know I have the utmost respect for my lady." He bowed his head, hoping he would be satisfied with this answer.

"You are one brave-ass warrior standing in a room full of high caliber weapons with a master who could beat your ass straight to hell and back. Luca, I know you need to bond with her, but you will not show her disrespect in any form." Standing up, he paced a bit, regaining control of his anger. "Tonight, I'm not leaving this house to go into town. Go outside and get the warriors off to the Dead House, all of them. I want no one left behind. As for you, get your ass to your woman and don't come back here until the sun is almost up."

Walking back to the door, he grabbed the doorknob and flung it open and stopped. He did not turn around and look at him but took a few deep breaths. "Luca, I thank you for protecting her. I am grateful beyond words for your love for her. But she will be your queen soon. Don't ever call her Kate again." Walking out, he headed to his office. It was time to call Tomas.

"Yes, master." *Fuck, fuck, fuck! I can't believe I did that. I can't fucking believe I did that!* He set the bow aside to finish another time and went outside to dispatch the warriors for the night then headed to his room to call Shannon and let her know he was coming.

* * *

Sitting in his office, Shade got control of his anger. Damn, it got under his skin how 'Kate' just rolled off his tongue like nothing. Laying his head back, he closed his eyes and took a few deep breaths. He didn't want this night to be ruined with anger. He needed to let it go. Dialing up Tomas, he heard him answer almost immediately.

"Brother, Shade here. I got some plans for the night. Sending in all my crew, do me a favor and keep their asses busy, and don't send them back here till that damn sun is up!"

Tomas laughed and asked if he and the little mate were planning a long night. "Oh, you can bet your ass, brother, just the two of us."

Tomas grunted, telling Shade he was jealous, but he had everything under control and to enjoy himself. Tomas asked where he was taking his mate for the evening.

"Oh hell, we are staying here for the night. I've been stuck in that fucking Dead House twiddling my thumbs too long. I've got my horses here now, might take a ride later, but hell brother, just being here alone with her is enough."

Tomas agreed, and Shade could hear the ruckus of the warriors in the background and knew Luca had sent them and they had arrived ready for the night.

"You're in control tonight. Have a good one." Shade heard Tomas bark out a few orders before he ended the call. Hanging up, Shade headed to the kitchen to see if *bel* was ready to have her warrior cook up a storm.

* * *

Tomas hung up and knew the plan was ready and tonight could not be more perfect. Shade had that house emptied, and the little mouse was alone with him. No fucking protector. He barked out orders and got his whole crew partnered up and ready to send them into the night. Max knew where to send small bands of rogues to keep them occupied. Tomas made it damn clear to them they answered to him this night and no one else. He got no guff from any of them and watched as they left. If they only knew, in a few hours, they would have no master and the Medici Empire would fall. And if they got lucky, a few of his warriors would go down on the streets tonight as well. Walking outside, making sure the Dead House was emptied, Tomas dialed Max and waited.

Max was pacing the floor. Rissa wanted time off for the two of them. She asked for a day at the beach, but she hadn't given him a date as to when they could go, and he was fucking stir crazy cooped up in this temporary rental. His cell rang and it was Tomas. Max made a grab for it. "Brother... good news please."

Tomas needed to say only one thing. *"Bel Rosso!"* Hanging up, he headed back into the Dead House and loaded up on weapons. He might do a little killing himself this night.

For Max, this was the call he'd been waiting for. He called Cuerpo, who had the twenty mercenaries on call and ready to ambush. He picked up on the first ring.

"Cuerpo, it's time. There's no one home but Shade and the mortal. Give him about an hour to get good and comfortable, then get your ass over there, bring in five rogues with you. Make sure you draw him out, and once you do, drop in the other fifteen. You know what I want from you. Don't disappoint."

All he heard from him was a grunt in acknowledgment followed by a loud slurping sound. Fucking freak.

* * *

Walking into the kitchen, Shade opened the fridge and checked out what ingredients he had to work with, poured some Midnight and lit some candles. *Where the hell is my woman?* "Woman! Get that sweet ass down here! Your warrior is cooking, and I don't mean food."

Laughing, he willed on the music and Van Morrison's *Into the Mystic* filtered into the kitchen. Maybe a pasta dish would be a good thing to fix for *bel.*

Kate heard him call her from the kitchen. She finished her makeup and rubbed the rose-scented lotion from head to toe, and then added a few spritzes of the perfume. She grabbed her robe to put on over her lacy underwear and ran barefoot down the steps. Something told her this wasn't an occasion that called for a lot of clothes. "Coming!"

Shade fixed her a mixed green salad, angel hair pasta in a pesto sauce, set out some fresh Italian bread and opened a bottle of Conundrum, her favorite white wine. He set a bottle of Midnight on the table for himself and willed all the candles on. He heard her soft footfalls on the stairs, just as he set the huge dish of steaming pasta onto the bar.

He looked up as she came in, the robe partially open, her legs exposed, her feet bare and he growled. *Fuck me! Why the hell am I slaving in the kitchen, when my mouth is watering looking at this tempting morsel?*

"*Cazzo*, you smell incredible. Good enough to devour." Walking to her, he held out his hand. "May I have a dance before dinner, *mi amore*? I would be honored."

She took his hand and stepped into his arms as they danced to their favorite song, *Into the Mystic.*

His hands slid over her hips as she swayed slowly to the soothing ballad. He changed the music to a more up-tempo song, Justin Timberlake singing, *Rock Your Body.* He let one hand slide over her cheek, as he nuzzled into her crimson and whispered, "*Ti amo, mi amore.*" His other hand went from her hip to her ass, and pulled her to him, feeling her hardened nipples through the thin silk across his bare chest as he ground his hips against her.

She smiled up at him mischievously. "You want to rock my body, lover?" She pushed back against his hips. "I hope you can keep up tonight." She nipped at his neck.

"Oh *si*, rocking—"

He stopped mid-sentence as he picked up their scent. They were close and there was more than one. *Rogues!* Instantly, he willed off the music and snuffed the candles and pulled her close against his chest and stopped moving.

"*Mi amore*, hush! Listen to me. There are rogues close to the house. I need to go outside, take them out. I am calling Luca to come home. Go to the bedroom, lock yourself in, and don't fucking come out for anything. Go, now!"

Kissing the top of her head, he shoved her toward the stairs and his fangs punched through. His eyes lit up as he instantly teleported to the bunker.

Kate ran up the stairs and slammed the door behind her, locking it. She flipped on the light and looked around the empty room, feeling vulnerable in her robe. She quickly pulled on a pair of jeans and a top and climbed onto their bed... Waiting.

Shade could feel them, they were too damn close, and he looked to the security monitors as he rolled out of the bunker. He saw nothing yet, but they were fucking there. **"Luca, rogues! More than one, attacking the house. Get to *bel*, now!"**

Teleporting outside, he felt them coming in, more than one, less than ten, and he knew he could take these bastards out. Raising his sword high in the air, he screamed and felt the rumble of the call, and unleashed the beast within. "Medici!"

Luca had been with Shannon for less than an hour when he heard Shade call to him. **"Master, I'm on my way!"**

He turned to Shannon and just said, "Gotta go," and teleported out, seeing the look of surprise on her face. There was no time to explain this now and she'd better get used to it. He teleported directly into their bedroom. He found Kate sitting on the bed, her knees drawn up to her chin and her eyes large as saucers.

Kate issued a small sigh of relief when Luca appeared. "Luca! What's going on? Is Shade safe? Is he okay?"

"Rogue vampires, from that coven in D.C., I imagine. Not sure how many, but they're attacking the house." They both looked toward the door as the sound of the clashing swords got louder. He watched as she backed against the headboard, making herself even smaller.

With a tremble in her voice, she asked him, "What about him?"

* * *

The rogues heard Shade's call and they didn't back down, five of them hit him all at once, and they were out for blood. They came to own him and take him out, but they messed with the wrong master. Two came at him with swords drawn and he was slashing his way through. He felt Luca and knew he was with *bel* and suddenly, he had his beast one-hundred percent focused on taking these fucking bastards straight to their grave.

As one rogue made a wrong move, his head rolled, but there was another that took his place and Shade had both hands swinging blades. *Yes! This fucking feels like home now!*

Kate could hear Shade fighting, the sound of swords. She recognized the sound from her practice with Luca. The sounds were getting louder because they were closer to the house. She and Luca could both hear the horses neighing and bucking in their stalls in a frenzy. Kate looked at Luca. "Do something! Help him! I'm fine here! Go help him, please!"

Luca shook his head. "My job is to protect you, to stay with you."

She was staring him down, and he was watching her face getting red and saw her temper building and she started to come off the bed. He put his hand out and stopped her. "Okay! I'll go check the monitors, see what's going on. But you don't leave this room. Got it?"

She nodded. "I got it. Now go help him!"

Luca closed the door behind him as he left her in the bedroom and took the steps three at a time as he ran to Shade's office to see the security cameras. There were five rogues, one already down. Shade had his hands full. These were not the untrained rogues he had told him about in D.C. but trained warriors. Still, Shade had it under control. Luca watched him as he held off the four, biding his time to strike down another one.

* * *

Cuerpo watched from a distance as the Medici quickly took out one of the warriors and had the other four in a standoff. The protector was back, just as they expected. Now it was time to make things interesting. Cuerpo sent in another fifteen rogues.

He hissed out, "Okay warrior... let's see how good you are at handling nineteen at once, while I fuck your tender mortal, and you feel my blade slice through her tender skin."

* * *

Shade was leaping over the heads of the rogues and moving quickly, he took another one down, but they keep him tied in one place. Not able to move freely, he was on defense, and it was taking all his concentration to avoid their blades. Fucking bastards had been trained. *Only three more to go. I will fucking kill this Angel motherfucker when I get through with this damn lot!*

As another rogue swiped at his arm, Shade quickly dropkicked him and stabbed another right through the heart. He turned to take out the final rogue when he smelled them rolling in, seething with bloodlust and realized his situation just got real fucking serious. He could feel *bel*'s fear and his only hope was he could take these bastards out before they got to her.

"Luca! More coming. Blitz attack! They are trying to take the house. Stay with her. Don't leave her. Don't fucking leave her!"

He was swamped with more rogues than he could count. They had him trapped and pinned down. *I will die right here if I have to, but you slime motherfuckers will never get to her.* The image of Sophia's dream flashed through his head and hit him dead in the heart. She had said the rogues were coming, she was alone... she was afraid but said she was brave... protecting her family. She was not speaking about herself, she was speaking about *bel*!

He started flinging shuriken's one after the other and took out another rogue. He let the shuriken's fly, it was his only way out of this standstill. **"I can't fucking move, Luca. They have me pinned down. Bastards!"**

Luca was watching on the monitors as more rogues teleported in, and he counted fifteen. *Fuck!* He heard his master's directions to stay with her and watched as they circled him until they had him surrounded. Luca knew if the rogues broke past Shade, he wouldn't be able to hold them off. The only option was to leave the house and go help him fight them where they stood. If Shade fell, then Luca would surely fall, and then his *bel rosso* would be lost for sure. Luca checked the blade in his boot, and grabbed his own swords and teleported outside, landing next to him. Luca stood against Shade's back so neither of them could be taken by surprise.

Shade felt Luca swoop in and slide against his back and he realized she was alone. He couldn't understand why in the fucking hell he would leave her, but between the two of them, none of these bastards were going to get near her. Shade and Luca connected their thoughts and their beasts locked souls and took over, and nothing could stop them. They were indestructible. They raised their swords, touched tips and fire blazed from them as they went to work, screaming, *"Medici per sempre!"*

* * *

Kate had climbed back up on the bed to wait for Luca to return with information on Shade, but now there was more noise, more clanging of swords. Not just louder but... more. Then she heard them, as they yelled in unison, 'Medici *per sempre*.' Luca was with him. She was relieved and frightened at the same time. Relieved that Luca had joined him, but frightened to know that whatever was going on, Luca felt he needed to go. *How many? How many rogues?* It suddenly struck her she was alone in the house. After months of being shadowed by Shade or Luca and sometimes yearning for freedom, she now felt the vulnerability of being alone in their world. Her heart was pounding, and she slid to the floor and took the crossbow from under the bed, pulled the quiver out and climbed back up on the bed, just in case. **"Fight hard, my savage lover!"**

* * *

The blades blazed and they were in their element, fighting back to back, taking the rogues out slowly but diligently. There was a method to their fighting, and Luca didn't disappoint. Shade never doubted his skills, but why the hell was she alone? He tried to concentrate on the hell that he was in the middle of and his beast was going wild. He wanted to get to *bel* and her voice filled his head and he knew she was okay, but her heart was pounding. She felt him deep and knew he was pushed hard at this moment. He kept his wits about him as Luca sliced and diced, and Shade damn near fucking fell as a head rolled under his feet. **"I am coming for you, *mi amore*. I will not let anything happen. *Ti amo!*"**

As the thought left his head, he felt a sharp pain in his thigh. Feeling the sting he knew one of those fucking Aries bastards had struck him with their blade and he rose up against the rogue and lopped off one arm and then the other, as more swords came swinging at him. *To get to her, they will fucking have to kill my ass first!*

* * *

Kate was crouched on the bed, hugging her knees to her chest when she heard Shade speak to her. *He'll come for me*. She was focused on listening to the sounds of the swords, the battle cries from the rogues. She could feel Shade's energy as the adrenaline flowed through him. Sitting there, she thought she heard a scratching sound on the wall outside the window, faint, indistinct. The sound was almost drowned out by the louder sounds of the war raging in front of the house.

Nothing, it's nothing, she told herself. She focused again on listening for Shade, the sound his sword made. She could pick it out distinctly. And then she heard it again, that scratching, almost clawing sound. It sounded familiar to her and she searched her mind. *What is it?* She turned her attention to that sound, blocking out everything else. Concentrate. Focus. There it was again. Climbing, it was the sound of climbing. It was the sound she made when scaling the mountain cliff, and now she heard that same sound outside her window. Hand over hand, scratching for a spot to grip, feet seeking a toe hold in the stone. Her heart pounded even harder and her breath quickened, her first instinct was to run. *Where? Outside? Into the fray? Think Kate, think!*

Luca's words rang in her ears... *slow your heart rate, calm your breath.* Easy to do when you are shooting at a tree! She dropped to the floor, so she was kneeling by the bed and picked up the bow, the bed between her and the window. She pulled an arrow from the quiver and loaded it, and taking aim at the window, flipping on the laser scope. She rested her elbows on the bed to steady her arms. She fought to slow her heart, she fought to calm her breath... and she listened.

The scratching was louder, climbing the two stories to the balcony window which was open to the warm spring night. **"Shade, please!"** She waited in silence, her mouth dry as sand. She could feel evil as it entered the room before him, as thick as a physical presence. **"Lover, please!"** She watched in horror as he rose over the balcony wall. Was he vampire, or something else? He looked like a living, breathing skeleton, and then he lifted his head and looked into the room. His eyes were glowing red, and he hissed, exposing his fangs. Vampire.

His appearance made her weak with fear and she wanted to slither under the bed, but she knew she couldn't hide from him. She knew she couldn't outrun him. She knew she only had one option, and that was to stay and fight, and to hopefully, take him by surprise. To do what Luca had trained her to do. The thing dropped over the balcony and started to climb through the window. She wanted to pull the trigger on the crossbow, but her training kicked in. *Wait, wait, not yet.* Her throat was closing shut with fear, but she knew she would only have one shot before he reacted. As his feet hit the floor, he stood his full height and locked eyes with her. She centered the laser on his heart. She held her breath, listened to her heartbeat, and fired the arrow, seeing the look of surprise on his face as the arrow pierced his chest, just before his body collapsed to the floor.

* * *

Shade and Luca were methodically taking them out, but too fucking slowly. His leg was getting weaker, and then like a steel beam slamming into him a wave of her fear hit him. *Something is after her!* He felt her call, he felt her fear and knew she was terrified out of her mind and he couldn't get out. *I can't lose her. No, Kate, no!*

At that moment Shade realized this attack was a diversion, so whoever or whatever could get to her. Something in him snapped and his beast went somewhere he'd never gone before. The beast emerged raw, in pain and fear. He ripped with his teeth and clawed through the bodies of anything in his way. The beast used the swords as he slashed, grinding rogue vampire flesh into ground-up meat. The blood flowed like a river under his feet and everything he saw was blood red. Shade worked his way free of the carnage and cared not what was behind him. Luca would have his back. **"Kate, Kate, Kate!"**

He saw another rogue in front of him and Shade grabbed his sword with his bare hands and screamed into the night, as he shoved his hand straight through the rogue's chest and ripped his heart from his body, crushing the still pumping organ in his hand, as the rogue dropped at his feet. **"Kate, mi *amore!*"**

She didn't answer him, and he suddenly felt nothing from her... nothing. She wasn't dead, he would know without doubt, but something had happened, and she wasn't responding to him. He ran like the fires of hell toward the house and stumbled, falling to his knees, screaming in agony and fear. "Kate! *Mi amore!*"

* * *

Luca felt Shade's fear spike and his scream for Kate. Something had happened to Kate. Luca had failed him. Luca had failed her. He watched as Shade's beast went mad with rage and ripped through the remaining warriors in his path, with his bare hands, grabbing their swords and ripping limbs from their bodies as the blood flowed. When Shade raced to the house, Luca looked around the grounds, double-checking to see if there were any rogue warriors left before following him into the house. His heart was in his throat at what they would find.

* * *

Shade teleported inside the house and landed in their bedroom. His eyes scanned the room. "*Bel*? *Mi amore*?"

- 388 -

His heart was pounding, and he was ready to attack anything that had her or wanted her. He saw a body lying limp on the floor under the window, a pool of blood spreading across the floor. He crouched and crawled in the direction of the body and saw the arrow straight through the heart. An arrow? He could smell her, but where the hell was she?

He looked more closely at the body and recognized Cuerpo. He was one deadly fucker, and his heart again gripped in fear for *bel*. Angel is Cuerpo? *Cazzo!*

From his position, he scanned the room until he saw the shadow of a body crouching on the other side of the bed. Kate! "*Mi amore*, please. It's me."

He closed the distance between them in one jump. Kate crouched on the floor clutching a crossbow in her arms, dead still, her eyes wide open. *She has a damn bow? She killed Cuerpo? What the fucking hell is going on?*

She didn't move when he laid his hand on her shoulder. He spoke more softly, "*Mi amore*, it's Shade, my sweet *bel*."

She remained unresponsive and he carefully removed the crossbow from her white-knuckled grip. He lifted her in his arms and sat on the edge of the bed holding her like a small child. She didn't respond, and he could feel Luca as he entered the room behind him.

Luca saw Cuerpo lying on the floor in a heap, a kill shot to the heart. He recognized the arrow. *Fucking Cuerpo!* He was shunned by almost every coven. His mind was racing with the image of Cuerpo climbing through that window, and Kate facing him alone, and he knew that was the fear Shade felt. That was what sent his beast into a rage. She was in shock, but that would pass. **"That will pass, little warrior. But steel yourself, we will have another battle now."**

There was no hiding anymore, the crossbow and the kill shot. He would figure it all out in minutes, if he hadn't already. Luca stood ready to take all his anger for leaving her, and for training her. But right now, he could only sigh in relief, Kate was safe.

* * *

Shade sat with his mate in his arms, alive. He had much to do, but right now, she was all he cared about. He felt Luca's presence and knew he had trained her. They didn't just run, he had trained her as a damn warrior, preparing her for the change. All this time, they hid this from him, right under his nose, under his own roof. He couldn't think of anything except the thoughts of the fear she had felt. She defended herself while he was trying to get to her. It should never have happened, but he was torn. He should kill Luca where he stood for what he'd done behind his back, for leaving her alone as her protector, and for defying a direct order. But without what he'd taught her, she would now be dead in his arms.

His voice was soft and emotionless, as he spoke in a monotone. He didn't look at him but looked straight ahead as *bel* lay in his arms. "Take Cuerpo's body to the bunker. I want it in the dark. Remove the head, I need it. Call them home. I need all the warriors home. No one leaves this house. No one comes into this room until I emerge. Do as you are told, warrior. You left her alone."

"Yes, master."

Luca picked up the limp body of Cuerpo and started to carry him from the room. As he stood in the door, he turned back toward Shade. "If I have brought shame on you, master, if I have failed you, I'll stand down from my post."

"Get out, warrior."

Shade heard him leave and the house was deadly still. His tears finally fell, and he could not stop them. Laying his head on top of hers, he rocked her in his arms like a baby. "Kate, I'm here. I need you right now. I need you to show me you hear me. I am right here, *mi amore*." He nuzzled deep into her neck, whispering, "Feel me, *mi amore*, smell me, I am right here with you. I have you, *bel*. I have you."

She had felt him take the crossbow from her hands and lift her in his arms. *He came for me.* He held her in his lap, tight against his chest, rocking her, his head on top of hers. She heard his voice. It sounded far away, like an echo. She felt him snuggling into her neck. She raised her hand and ran it through his hair, wet with his sweat and sticky with blood. "I feel you, lover, I feel you."

"That's my *bel*. *Ti amo.* God, how I love you. Are you hurt? I'll always come for you. Nothing will stop me, nothing. It's okay, everyone is okay, Kate." She wrapped her arms around his neck and cried and they held each other, and he knew she was coming back to him, feeling safe at last.

He was soaked in blood, but she only wanted to feel him against her. "I love you, Shade. I stayed strong for you. I fought for you. I knew you would come for me."

She let her tears flow as he gripped her tightly, and she felt safe in his arms. She kissed his neck and kissed his face as his blood tears mixed with her own salty tears.

He slid his hands up and down her back. "Shh, *mi amore*. I know you fought for me, as I did for you. You are my brave, sweet *bel*, so brave. It's over, all over."

Standing, he carried her to the shower. "Let's clean up, and we'll sleep in the guest room tonight. Nothing else is out there *bel*, it's over now. We'll talk later, just let me hold you."

As she snuggled into his neck, he knew she'd be okay. She had Medici blood in her veins, and like it or not, she was a warrior. They were still alive, his beautiful mortal and her savage beast, and eternity was before them still. Tomorrow, they would talk, for there was much he needed to know, but tonight, he would hold her.

68

Shade knew it was going to be another long night. There was still much to do since the attack the previous night. After cleaning both he and Kate up, he had carried her to a spare bedroom, farther away from the carnage, where he held her close through the night. He encouraged her to feed, to help her heal and regain her sense of power. They spoke of nothing. Even as nightfall approached, he slept little, waking often from his death slumber out of concern for her, to make sure she was still in his arms, cradled tight to his chest. His sweet *bel* had slept soundly, retreating into sleep to escape reality.

He slipped silently from the bed they shared, careful not to wake her, and walked down the hall to the now spotless master bedroom. He pulled on a pair of jeans and a t-shirt and found his boots.

As he was lacing his boots, Theresa popped in and looked shocked to see him. Her face reflected her concern, as she asked of my lady and he assured her she was fine. He told her there were a few things he needed to take care of and to please call him immediately if *bel* awoke and was frightened. *Bel* was over the worst of the shock, but only time would tell how long it would take her to truly recover. He knew one thing, she sure as hell had never killed a damn thing in her life before, but she took out Cuerpo with a single kill shot to the heart. That first kill is always the one that makes or breaks the warrior.

He headed down to his office, to call Alec and let him know they took down Angel, but first, Shade wanted to watch the security video. He wanted to be able to give Alec as much detail as possible on the events of the previous night, as well as see for himself what went down. He stopped in the middle of the floor and listened, Luca was not in the house, but he was close enough. Shade could sense him on the property. It really didn't matter at the moment, he would deal with that issue once *bel* was awake and he felt she could handle the conversation. She had clung to him the entire night and he was pretty sure she wasn't letting him out of her sight for long this night either, and that was damn fine with him.

Replaying the video, Shade noticed one rogue had taken off just as he had turned to run into the house. The rogue ran deep into the wooded mountainside, but Shade wouldn't let him get too far. He would find him and kill him but letting the rogue live long enough to spread the word that Cuerpo was dead was not a bad idea. Leaving the office, he sought out Marcello in the staff quarters to ask for details of how the evening had started off in D.C.

Luca had called them all home after the ambush and they came running, and according to Marcello, most weren't in the mood to face him. They felt like hell that they'd not been called home sooner to help him and Luca fight the rogues. It taught Shade a damn good lesson. They would have the security of warriors at Bel Rosso now on a permanent basis. As he listened, Marcello gave him more information about what happened in town last night, and Shade felt certain that Cuerpo was the elusive Angel.

He and Marcello returned to his study and together watched the security feed of the ambush, comparing the time stamps on the video with Marcello's accounting of the rogue attacks that had kept his warriors busy. Shade was certain it was a setup. It was a clever war plan, cut off the head of the snake, or better yet, take out his mate and the show was over. This still had something to do with Alec, he didn't doubt that. But Cuerpo knew who was responsible for killing the rogues on the streets, and he damn sure knew Shade.

While comparing the two timelines they realized that as soon as Cuerpo was dead and Luca had recalled their warriors, all rogue activity in D.C. stopped.

If Angel is dead, is this over? He couldn't be sure. If his followers were loyal, they might seek revenge. Shade told Marcello to send a few warriors to the Dead House for the night just to keep an eye on the area and let him know if they found anything. He knew Tomas would already have informed Alec's men about what went down, and he would keep them on watch tonight as well.

As Marcello was leaving to carry out his orders, he mentioned that Luca had spent the night in the staff quarters and didn't seem himself. Shade grunted and told him he was pretty damn sure he didn't feel like himself. He would deal with Luca later. As for now, Shade wanted warriors patrolling the perimeter of their property routinely through the night from now on. He would call a meeting in a few nights and discuss what his plans were for them. Those warriors not on duty at the Dead House would be here, guarding the master and his mate. They all needed to rest, but first things first, he pulled out his cell phone and lit up a cigarette.

Leaving the house he made his way down the path through the garden, the cigarette smoke trailing behind him. He wanted to be sure he was far enough away that *bel* would not overhear him. He followed the path to the grave of their lost *bambino*... his son. Holding the cell in his hand, he looked at the little angel that marked his grave. "You know, *dormire guerriero*, your *madre* is one brave ass redhead! She made me so proud last night." Hitting speed dial for Alec, he waited.

Alec was stretched out in the family room of his Georgetown home, reading, drinking a Midnight, and enjoying a rare weekend with no speaking engagements. Rissa was at the gym again, so he had a quiet house to himself. He had received a call earlier from Tomas. Seemed they took out Angel, so that was one big fucking load off his shoulders. Now he could focus on what was really important without worrying that his true identity would be exposed. His cell vibrated on the table and picking it up he saw it was Shade. He had been expecting him to call as soon as this was wrapped up.

"Brother, it sounds like you solved my problems."

Shade shook his head. *Yeah, solved your problems all right, brother, but created a shit load of my own on top of it, but don't worry, you will pay, you bastard!* "There is a head in my weapons bunker you need to see. And it seems this Angel was someone we knew all along."

Alec took a sip of the Midnight. "You gonna tell me who it is? Or you want me to drag my ass all the way out there to that piece of backwater property you accepted for this job?"

Shade grinned to himself. *Oh you stupid fuck, you haven't been here since my bel got a hold of this place. No longer a backwater property but a palace on a mountain and all mine!* "Well, fucking forbid you need to leave your comfy city life, but you will come out here and see it. You know the rules, brother. Master to master, heads need to be seen to seal the deal, no doubts. And your Angel is, or was, Cuerpo."

Alec sat straight up on the sofa. "Fuck! No way you took out that fucking bastard! Yeah, this I've got to see. Okay, let me call Alto, he can drive me down there. Should be there in about two to three hours depending on traffic."

Shade shook his head again and stifled the laugh that wanted to roll out of him. "Get the fuck over here now! I got things to do, Alec.

Important shit. This fucking house was ambushed last night, and I don't have time to play your fucking games. Now!"

Hanging up, he let out the laugh, that fucking bastard might wrinkle his suit and muss his hair getting here, but by fucking hell, he would teleport his ass this time.

Alec stood up, ran his fingers through his hair. "Fuck! I fucking hate to teleport! But I might as well get this over with." He gulped down the remaining Midnight and teleported out of the house.

Hope I remember where the fuck this dump is.

* * *

He landed on the property using the coordinates he remembered and looked around. *This can't be the place!*

Shade had headed back into the house and was just about to sit down when he saw Alec teleport in. Shade watched him through the window for a minute, enjoying Alec's confused expression, before he teleported about a foot from Alec and stood with his hands open to his sides. "Welcome to my backwoods shithole."

"Fuck! You startled me! You know I fucking hate to teleport. I live in a world of mortals. I have to stifle every impulse. But what the fuck, Shade? This place? This looks nothing like the property you took for this deal."

"Well, what the hell did you think I was going to do, Alec? Plow the fucking fields and live in a barn? *Cazzo!*"

Pointing and gesturing, he gave Alec a layout of the land. "The vineyards are over there, about eight-hundred acres and I have some special stock coming out of here, I will send you over a case. Over here, Kate has renovated and expanded that old building into staff quarters, where the warriors bunk down. And over there, Kate just finished overseeing the construction of the horse stables. Fencing still needs some work, but won't take us long. I brought over some fine horseflesh from Florence, if you need horses or boarding, let me know. I have intentions of breeding them here. And this behind me... this is Bel Rosso Palazzo. So, come on in, side entrance is over here just through the wine cellar and down into the weapons bunker."

Alec took in all that had been done with the property. It had to be worth ten times its original value now. Not a bad investment. Still, it wasn't a lifestyle for him and this land had been of no value to him except as a bargaining chip, not to mention it was in the middle of Max's territory. He followed Shade into the house. He was impressed by what he could see. Clearly, the entire house had been renovated. He followed

Shade down the stairs into the wine cellar and through a heavy door to a modern, well-equipped bunker. There it was, on the table, in the center of the room. No mistaking that face.

Shade grabbed a bottle of Midnight and two glasses and watched Alec's face as he saw Cuerpo's head sitting in the middle of the table. That was one crazy-ass lethal vampire. Uncorking the bottle, he poured them each a glass and handed one to Alec before he plopped down in a chair and put his feet up on the table, crossed at the ankles.

"Sit down, Alec, before you fall down. So, there it is... Angel. I haven't seen nor heard about Cuerpo in a long damn time. So, wherever he was hiding, he was hatching this plan. He have a grudge against you or something?"

Alec took the glass he was offered and sat down at the table, eyeing the grotesque head of Cuerpo. "Who didn't have a grudge with Cuerpo? I didn't know he had warriors. I always thought he worked solo. But that explains the rag-tag bunch of rogues and some of his tactics at turning mortals and just letting them loose. Motherfucker loved to kill mortals. But why target me specifically? I have no idea. One thing for sure, the vampire community will shed no tears for him. Whoever killed this fucker will have one hell of a rep among the covens. They will be legendary. So, who was it? You?"

Shade threw his feet on the floor, he looked to the wall and saw the hidden video camera and the green light was definitely on, and at some point, *bel* was going to love watching this.

"Well, here is the skinny in short form. I had planned to spend the evening alone with Kate, my mate, in case you have conveniently forgotten her name again. I sent her protector off for the night, sent all the warriors into the Dead House under Tomas, and gave my staff the night off as well. Next thing I know, five rogues dropped in at once, easy pickings for me, so I went out after them, called back the protector for Kate. Meantime, small rogue attacks were going down in D.C. last night that kept my warriors busy. Very well planned.

"Cuerpo's strategy was to take out the master, his mate to boot, and this war is over, he wins. But he forgot who the fuck I am, apparently. While I was taking out the five, I was ambushed with another fifteen. They had me tied down heavy. My protector came out to help me get rid of the bastards, and these were no ordinary rogues, these were trained warriors. Cuerpo saved his best for last. While we were slicing and dicing out front, Cuerpo attacked from the rear of the house, going after Kate.

Only three people in this house last night, Alec. Shouldn't take you long to figure out who took out this fucker. One clean shot straight through the heart, with a precision high-powered crossbow."

Shade sat back and grinned from ear to ear and waited for the reaction.

Alec listened to the retelling of the story and he had a clear visual. It was no surprise that Cuerpo went for the mortal. But what was he saying? "Okay, I don't get your drift. You? Luca? Which one of you took him out?"

"Damn Alec, that teleporting got to your brain. Kate took him out! Cuerpo scaled the wall and went in through the bedroom balcony after her. Yeah, Alec, believe it. I got nineteen well-trained rogues against me and my best warrior, and you think I had time to shoot that bastard with a crossbow? I'm good, but fuck me, brother, I'm not that damn good."

Alec set the glass down on the table and ran his hands through his hair. *Is this a fucking joke? That weak sniveling mortal killed Cuerpo? Or have I misjudged her all along?* He remembered Rissa telling him how she attacked the feeder, a mortal attacking a vamp with her bare hands. And now Shade was telling him she took out Cuerpo?

"So, you have trained her like your warriors. You trained her on a crossbow?"

Shade just stared him down. He wasn't ready to go down that road. "Doesn't matter who or when or how, she protected herself, her home and her family. And she is still mortal. So, that leaves one more task, Alec, you owe her, but I don't want money. Something else is high on my list as a reward. And you will reward her just as you would any warrior of my coven." Shade leaned down into his face. "You will reward her, Alec. That was the deal."

"Yes, fuck yes. That was the deal. Besides, Cuerpo dead is good for both of us. But if not money, what? What are you looking for as a reward?"

He twirled the wine glass in his hand and then drained the Midnight and set it down carefully on the table, raising his eyes to Alec. "You once told me you had a building in Paris, you ever do anything with that? I know you told me you wanted it for Rissa, so she had someplace to stay when she went shopping."

Alec creased his brow. "Not just any building, Shade. It's right on the Champs Elysees. Prime real estate."

"Not what I asked you, brother."

"Yes... I still own it. Renting it out now, but I was holding it for Rissa. A wedding present for our mortal wedding."

Shade held up his hand. "I don't want to know your fucking plans. But how damn romantic of you, brother. I don't have time to play rock, paper, scissors with your ass tonight, I got shit to do. I want that building for Kate."

Alec stood up and paced the floor. *A deal's a deal... Fuck! That place is worth millions. But I'll never get another warrior to work for me again if I break the code. Good fucking thing I never told Rissa I was planning to give her that property, she would shit a solid gold brick.* "Okay, okay, yeah, all right... it's yours. It needs work, but hell, that doesn't look like it will be a problem for you. So yes, take it. I have to get the renters out. Some rich bitch Greek aristocracy, so I'll need to give them notice. So, thirty days?"

"Thanks, brother. Seriously. Important to me. Important to her as well." Standing up, he shook hands with him. "Look, I'm still keeping my warriors at the Dead House along with yours, but I expect things will slow down with Cuerpo gone, and we can go back to using a smaller squadron. I know you usually have your driver and bodyguard with you, so if you need an escort out of here, I can easily accommodate you with one of my warriors, make sure you get home safely." *I know just the warrior for this job.*

Alec shook his hand. "If you don't mind, I'll take you up on that. I know this issue may be behind us, but believe it or not, I have made more than a few enemies, in both the mortal and immortal world. So a warrior escort would be appreciated."

"No problem, brother, after all this fucked up mess, I won't think anything of it." **"Marcello, send Raven over to the bunker now!"**

"He will be here—"

Before Shade got out the words, Raven came in like a bolt of lightning, just as Shade had hoped for and watched as he went down on one knee, wearing a kilt, his hair flying like a fucking black sail in the wind.

"At your service, master."

"Raven, this is Master Alec, his territory is the one you have been protecting in town. He will need a bodyguard and escort home, and I expect your best service to Senator Canton."

Shade looked at Alec and it took more power than he'd ever mustered to not laugh out loud at the look on his face.

"Alec, this is Raven, one of my finest. Rogue killer extraordinaire. Don't let his size or his flair for the dramatic bother you, warrior has the speed of a damned bullet."

Alec scanned Raven from head to toe. He wasn't very tall for a vampire; very slender build, hair to his waist, androgynous. If he added some lipstick and heels and got rid of his facial hair, he could easily pass for a bitch.

"Yeah, okay... can we just get back to civilization, please? And the faster the better."

Raven stood and bowed to Alec. "Let's rock and roll, brother."

Shade roared, laughing as Alec growled at him and the two of them took off. *Yeah, Alec, this will be the longest fucking trip you ever took back home!* Still laughing, Shade headed back to *bel*. It was time to wake up his mate and see how she faired this night.

69

Kate awoke slowly, turned on the light and was momentarily confused as she looked around the guest room. Then memories from last night washed over her. Shade was gone from their bed, but she remembered he held her close all day. She had felt him stroking her hair and her back, even as she slept. She remembered that he had cleaned himself up in the shower first and then, ever so gently, he stripped her of the clothes she had worn and carried her into the shower where he proceeded to bathe her, wash her hair, and dry her off, then he carried her here. He had come for her, and found her crouching on the floor, after that... that thing climbed through the window. And he'd sent Luca away. She'd heard the cold emotionless tone in his voice when he spoke to Luca. She sat up in bed. He knew now. He'd figured it out and this was not how she'd wanted him to learn about all the training. They should have told him sooner, on their own terms. She needed to tell him, explain to him. She knew Luca would shoulder all the blame when the fault really lay with her. It was time to find Shade and put an end to the secrets.

Shade stood outside the door listening until he was sure she was awake. He had no idea what condition she would be in, but if he felt she was strong enough to talk to him, he needed answers to how, why, and when. Pushing the door open slowly, he stuck his head in and smiled. "*Buonasera, mi amore.*"

She looked up as he entered, his voice warm and gentle, his smile soft, and he melted her heart. "Lover, I'm always a little confused when I wake and find you have left our bed. But I felt you holding me as I slept, I felt you keeping me safe."

He sat on the bed and she curled up in his arms. "I will always keep you safe, at least, give it all I have, I will give my life for you." He sighed. "I'm sorry, *mi amore*, for last night, so very sorry. I never expected an ambush, and for that matter, never did I expect Luca to leave you. I need to go speak with him, and it cannot wait until later, this needs to be done now. Will you be all right until I am done?"

"Shade, I need to ask you, please. This conversation with Luca. There is much that needs to be said, much you need to hear, but I ask that you hear it from both of us. Please."

He stood and walked to the window. He wasn't sure if she should hear what needed to be said to Luca. He wanted to handle them separately. Turning, he looked at her and his face showed concern. "*Bel*, are you up for that? What I'm going to say to him you may not want to hear. This is an extremely serious matter."

"Shade, I feel your anger with him, your disappointment, and I know him. He'll shoulder the blame, and accept it all to protect me. But he doesn't own the blame, and he'd never tell you that. I carry the blame. You need to hear it all. I have lived with these secrets long enough."

Growling, he looked at her. "Secrets? Then *si*, you will come as well."

His mind began to spin, and he wasn't sure, after her words, what he was facing, but he worked to control his temper as it rose fast. *Secrets, they have secrets now! Oh, this will be another night I won't soon forget!* "You need to get dressed. I will call Luca to come to the house. It is time both of you faced the music and let me in on your... secrets."

She left the bed and walked to him. He was angry already and they hadn't even started this conversation, but she'd been prepared for that. "Lover, I just ask that you listen. Hear what we have to say. Know that I found the only path that would lead me out of the darkness after the baby died. Please, find Luca, and I'll get dressed, then we will talk, all of us."

He looked down at her, heard her plea and knew she was right. "I'll give you both that chance, *mi amore*. Go, I will send for Luca."

"That's all I ask of you."

She left the room and walked back to their bedroom. The door was closed, and she opened it slowly, stepping inside and looking around. It was spotless as if nothing had happened here last night. That thing was gone. The blood was gone. Theresa and Gi had worked their magic as usual. She quickly got dressed and headed down the stairs. She could hear Luca and Shade in the living room. When she walked in the tension could be cut with a knife.

Shade turned as she came into the room and watched as she stared at Luca and he just stared back. This wasn't going to be easy for any of them.

"Please sit down. I have a few things to say before we begin. I agreed to have this conversation with *bel* included, not exactly what I was planning, but it is what it is. First of all..." He locked eyes with Luca and didn't let him look away. "You did two things that broke the rules of a protector. One, you left her alone. Two, you disobeyed my direct order.

As your master, I could kill you. I could take your position from you, send your ass packing back home, dishonored and banished from my coven, and your family as well. I hope you fully understand the impact of that. No other master would ever have a thing to do with you. But I am a fair master, I have always been so, do you agree, Luca?"

Luca bowed his head. "Yes, master, you have always been fair, and I accept complete responsibility for my actions. As I said last night, if it is your wish for me to step down from my position, I will accept that decision and the dishonor that goes with it."

Shade nodded his head. "Good, I have not yet decided on your punishment." His eyes went to *bel*. "*Mi amore*, I know you need to trust Luca as your protector, you need complete trust in his abilities and skills, but when you tell me you have secrets between you, my mind goes places that are dark and deep and extremely evil. I have heard and consented to your plea to explain to me, your master and eternal mate, the events that led to last evening. Do you agree to divulge the truth about everything that is going on in my own house?"

She looked at him with solemn eyes. "Yes, I'll tell you everything. And it's my burden, not Luca's. It started after we lost the baby. I was so lost. We were both so lost. You had your own pain and I had mine. I couldn't lay my pain at your feet when you were carrying so much of your own, and you needed me to be okay. So, I pretended I was okay. When you were home, I wouldn't speak of our baby. But as soon as you would leave the house, I would retreat to the nursery, lie on the nanny's bed and sleep, because my dreams were the only place where I could see him, my little warrior.

"I went there for weeks. I couldn't even remember what it felt like to not feel broken. And you, lover, you hid your pain from me as well. You came home covered in blood. You started showering in Luca's suite before you came to me so I wouldn't see. I felt trapped with nowhere to put all this pain. But Luca came to me every day, made me talk, slowly pulling me back. And every day, when I walked past that nursery, I felt its pull. It called to me, and I knew it had to go. So, Luca and the rest of the staff helped me to remove everything from the nursery and it was carried out to the fields. Luca poured the gasoline, and I lit the match and I watched it all burn.

"It was our baby's future... his life and I had to let go. I had to release its pull on me. But the anger, I was so angry at losing him. I felt so helpless, and it was my fault. Getting pregnant, not understanding. I wanted to hit something. Kick something. I had such rage inside and nowhere to put that, and I asked Luca to train me. He didn't want to do it. It wasn't his idea. I really had no idea what the training would involve. I just knew it would be physical, that it might provide an outlet for the anger. I really never expected to learn all that I learned. And one more thing... He calls me Kate because I insisted. So please, your anger needs to reside with me, not him. And last night? When he left me? He left because I asked him to. I threatened to leave the room and go to you, so he agreed to go check the monitors. Me, Shade. It was all me. Not Luca."

As he listened, he fought back the tears that burned his eyes. Her pain was visible as she spoke and it all came back to him, that death, those nights, her suffering. He listened as though living it through her eyes and his heart ached that she suffered so deeply. *How could I have not known this?* In the meantime, she had turned to Luca instead of him. He should have seen it. He should have been the one she came to for comfort, but he had been so lost in his own grief and his own secrets, that he couldn't see she needed him more than he ever could have imagined.

"*Bel*, none of this is your fault. I have only myself to blame for putting you in that position. I drove you to Luca because I was lost in my own selfish agony over our son's death. I too was lost, and I will never forgive myself for being absent from your pain. Not being able to help you through. As for Luca, he is a warrior and although he knows to take orders from you, he also answers to me. I gave a direct order. Luca knows how to say no very easily, *mi amore*."

Swinging his eyes to Luca, he nodded his head. "Anything you want or need to add to this? Here is your chance, lay it on the table, Luca. I'm listening."

Luca locked eyes with him, he wouldn't look away. "Yes, master. She tries to carry the full burden, but I understand my role all too well. Everything she speaks of about the baby is true, the nursery, the burning, and the training. I was reluctant to start her training, but I understood why she was asking, and I also saw something else. She has a warrior's heart, but not a warrior's head. I watched as she attacked that feeder, with no regard for the fact that she was mortal and the feeder immortal. She attacked with raw emotion and no skill, but she showed me, at that moment, her warrior's heart. It played a part in my decision to train her because I knew then that, if she was threatened, if those she loved were threatened, she would stand and fight, and with no skills, it would mean her certain death.

"I told her when we started this was no game. If she wanted to train, we would train, but I would take no shortcuts, and if she was going to learn these skills, she was going to work like she never worked before. I thought she would tire of it, but she didn't. Your blood, and her spirit, master, they have made a very powerful combination. You should know she has mastered swords, she couldn't hold her own against a vamp with a sword because she doesn't yet possess the strength, but once she is turned, it will be another story. She mastered the longbow, but her goal was the crossbow. And I think you saw for yourself her skill level.

"And another thing... her gift? Even she doesn't know this, master, as I haven't discussed it with her. I think it will be animalism. I've never seen it in my lifetime. Perhaps you've seen it in yours. It's the rarest of gifts among vampires, and I've only read about it. She killed a large ten-point buck with a single shot to the heart, but it broke her. She marked her face with his blood and called upon his spirit. I questioned then whether she would ever be able to kill. Now the animals speak to her, are calmed by her. Once she is turned, she will calm the wildest beast, and have them do her bidding. When you heard the horses last night? It was she they were responding to, her fear. Had they not been stabled, they would have come to her. Impavido, Bravado and Meile, Angelo said they kicked out the walls of their stalls and tried to break free of the barn.

"As for last night, my intention was to check the monitors and then return to her, let her know you were okay. But while I was there, the additional rogues dropped in. You were fighting nineteen. I knew you could take out the four with no problem, but the nineteen had you surrounded. My thought was, if they took you down, there would be no way I could hold them off and protect her. And the best way to protect her was to help you. It was my lack of experience, master. I assumed you were their target. I know now she was their target all along, and everything else was just a diversion. That's my failing. And there's nothing my lady can say that lifts the burden from my shoulders. I stand ready to accept your judgment."

Shade listened as Luca answered him from the heart. He knew this was no ordinary warrior in his ranks, but his Luca. And both of them were vital in his life. So, this situation lay on his head, as much as theirs. He could put no blame on either of them. It had been all judgment calls and blind faith... also, love. He saw a lot of love and pain that pushed them beyond their limits, to help each other survive as a family.

"I am not punishing you, Luca, in any way, but you must learn from this ambush. You never know the true goal of your enemy. I asked you to stay with her, and you left her for me. Remember that, because you may need to let me die the next time if that is what it takes to save her. I understand why you did what you did. I am honored that you took *bel*, taught her the skills you have been taught in the ways of my *familia*. And I know as well, she has the heart of a warrior. She has proven that, beyond any doubt, to all of us. My intention was to train her personally, once turned. It is my responsibility as her master, and her maker. I'm only angry with myself now because I understand the reasons behind it."

He beckoned for *bel* to sit on his lap. He waited while she curled into him then gently caressed her hair.

"So, you now have warrior skills, and you have made two kills, one of them distinctly more important than the other. Cuerpo is the warrior you killed, and he was one of the deadliest of the immortal world, *mi amore*. I had made a deal with Alec, as masters do, whoever took out this so-called "Angel", he or she would be rewarded. Alec has seen the head, agreed to pay you and he will do that in time. Your first kill... the deer... you felt his spirit? You are showing your gift already? Very unique indeed, *bel*. I have one thing to ask you. I leave this decision entirely up to you. Do you still wish for Luca to be your protector? Whatever your decision, it will be mine as well, *si*?"

With her head against his chest, she lifted her eyes to him. "Lover... we are family. We are bonded like family, and I trust him completely. I want him to stay. He is loyal to both of us, and I'm afraid I've placed him in compromising positions when my requests did not always align with yours. He tries to please you, and he tries to please me. He has been caught in the middle. Please don't send him away. Besides, then I'd have to break in a brand-new protector and who knows what trouble I'd get into."

He laughed out loud and hugged her tight. "*Si,* none of us truly knows what may fire up in that crimson head of yours, but I would have you no other way, *mi amore*. No other way. Luca, speak to me, are you torn between us? Do you wish to stay as Kate's protector? I must say, I am impressed with what you tell me so far in her training. Do you still wish to protect the love of my life, my eternity... your Queen?"

He stood from the chair and bowed on one knee. "Master, there is no greater honor. I have already pledged my life for her, and nothing has changed. I would die for this *familia*."

Watching as he honored them both, Shade whispered softly in Kate's ear, "You need to go to your protector and raise him from his knees. It is the proper thing to do and he won't move until you do so. Go."

Kate slid from Shade's lap and went to Luca. She had known her requests had put him in a difficult position but she hadn't understood just how difficult. She placed her hand on his shoulder and asked him to rise. Doing so, he towered over her. She stood on tiptoe and kissed each cheek. "You are like a brother to me, Luca."

Watching, he saw their bond and Shade knew deep in his heart, these two would never be separated. "*Mi amore*, there is a black box in that armoire behind the books, will you please take it out and hand it to me?"

She looked at him questioningly but went to the armoire and pushed the books aside to find the box he referred to and brought it back to him.

Taking the box from her hand, he held it and looked to Luca. "Luca, I have held on to this a very long time. I was waiting for the right moment to present it to you, but I can think of no better time than this. I'm grateful beyond words for the things you have given me; your life, your skills, your loyalty, and your love. You have made me proud, made Kate proud as well, and I know we both would be at a great loss without you." He handed the box back to *bel* and asked her to give it to Luca. "I hope you will accept this gift of appreciation from me to you, for what you have given me. Accept this from us both in appreciation for her protection that rivals my own."

Kate presented him with the box then returned to Shade's lap, curious to know what was in the box.

Luca accepted the box from her, his face as puzzled as hers. He opened the box to find official documents with seals. They were old and yellowed, so he lifted them gently from the box. It was a deed to his father's land, his father's house. It had all been lost when he died. *What does this mean?* He looked up at his master. "Master, I don't understand."

Shade nodded to him. "It's very simple, Luca. Your *padre* owed much on your family lands and home, and it was forfeited to pay off his debt when he died. I retrieved it, and have maintained it since recovering it. I've held it for you for a long time. You were too young when I obtained it to appreciate its meaning and worth, but now you are a grown man, a warrior your *padre* would be proud of. The debt has been paid and your family name honored and in good standing with the Council, and you being his only heir, now own that property. It is yours, Luca, that deed bears your name now, not my own."

Luca bowed his head to him, to honor Shade and to hide his tears. His family had lost everything, and master had honored his commitment to Luca's father to raise him, to make him a warrior. And now he had restored all that was his father's legacy. There was no way to repay him for all he'd done for him, other than to serve him for all eternity. With his head still bowed, he answered him.

"Master, I remain." His emotions overcame him, and he had to pause, take a breath. "I remain your humble servant. I have no means to repay you for a gift of this magnitude. You have restored my family's name, and you have bestowed on me the greatest honor. I will gratefully remain in service to you and yours until my death."

Shade knew he had chosen the right time to present him with this. He was old enough now to understand the immense responsibility of owning property, property that would continue to provide him tremendous wealth. Kissing *bel* on the cheek, he shifted her off his lap and walked to Luca, taking him in his arms, hugging him tightly, pounding his fist against Luca's back.

"You have already repaid me, Luca. We will soon travel to Florence for *bel*'s turning and when we do, you will come with us, there you will officially become protector to the Queen. Now, were you with your woman when I called you back last evening?"

"Thank you, master, and yes, I was with Shannon."

"Well then, I think you should return to her for this evening, don't come back, stay for a few days and nights if you need to. This is over, and I will be home with Kate for several days. I know Shannon is probably more than a bit worried, or at least pissed off." Chuckling, he said, "*Ti amo*, brother, *per sempre*. Now go, enjoy your Shannon."

Luca hadn't even called Shannon since he'd left her so suddenly the night before. After the battle with the rogues, he wasn't sure he'd be allowed to stay here, fully recognizing Shade could have chosen to send him back to Florence. He would have a lot of explaining to do.

"Thank you, master." He backed out of the room, bowing to him one last time as he left.

Watching him leave, Shade's heart was light, and he knew things were now fine with all of them. He turned toward *bel*, picking her up and spinning her around. "Now, as for you, woman. What is this gift of animals, hmm? You have my horses breaking down their new stables trying to get to you. Shall we go out and see how they fair, let them see that you are well and then you can tell me all about this adventure you have been having without me. *Si*?"

"Shade, that was the kindest thing you did for Luca. Just when I think I couldn't love you more." She gently kissed his lips. "You are full of surprises yourself. Yes, let's go check on the horses. But don't ask me about this gift with animals. I have no idea what Luca is talking about."

He set her down and took her hand, and they walked together out to the stables.

70

Entering the stables, Shade glanced around noting which horses had been moved to other stalls. In their panic, they'd caused the stalls to be splintered and shattered. It made him angry that such craftsmanship was ruined as a result of some damn rogue attack. He held *bel*'s hand as she walked with him. They approached Impavido and Shade watched as the massive horse nodded his head up and down, snorting his welcome.

"It's okay boy, calm down, just a small change. We will get your big stall fixed quickly, you deserve it." Shade chuckled as the horse totally ignored him and went to the stall door, leaning his head over trying to get *bel*'s attention.

"Well, I am just mincemeat now, I see." He turned to *bel*. "Mind explaining to me how you have a hold over this stallion when he doesn't like women and was the meanest beast on four legs?"

"Lover, I have no idea. I heard Luca explain to you I had the gift of animalism, but I honestly don't know what that means."

"Well, *mi amore*, every vampire has a gift, some of them are normal vampire traits, but amplified. Then others have extraordinary gifts, mine is dream-walking. Apparently, you have the gift of speaking to the animal spirit. You can calm them or enrage them. You can talk to them telepathically. They know you mean them no harm. They feel you, in a way, like I feel you. It is a rare gift, and there have only been a few who were born vampire to have this gift. You are not yet turned, so I do not understand it myself."

"Luca told you about the deer I killed. A few nights after that while we were out for our run a coyote approached the running path and I felt him as if he'd called to me or something. I knew I could go to him and he wouldn't fear me. He knew I wouldn't harm him. I was able to pet him, and then he turned and walked away."

Shade stood with his arms crossed over his chest and listened to her, and then heard Impavido snort and kick the stall gate.

"All right, already! Damn, boy! *Mi amore*, if you don't come over here and touch him he is going to break down this gate to make sure you are all right! I can't believe you have this power so strong already and not even turned, but I promise you, once turned, we will work on that skill.

It is your gift and could be very useful. Now, come pet my damn stallion before he bites me."

She stepped up on the rail, so she could reach the huge horse, running her hand over his massive head, speaking to him in a soft voice. "Look at him, lover, calm as a kitten."

"Go ahead, rub it in, you damn vixen." Slapping her ass, he laughed and grabbed her by the waist, lifting her off the gate and setting her back down on the floor. "Let's go check on Bravado, shall we? Where the hell is he? You know the oddest thing made me laugh tonight. Alec came by to do some business, wrap things up and he told me something I thought was funny at first, but now, it has me thinking.

"Alec was here? What did you discuss that has you thinking?"

Shade laughed. "Well, it was rather humorous. He didn't recognize the place. The prancy fucker thought he was lost. Anyway, he told me he and Rissa are having a mortal wedding. Did you know about this?"

"A wedding? No, I hadn't heard anything about it. I haven't talked to Rissa since... wow, I think she called right after I lost the baby. That was the last time I spoke to her."

Bravado snorted and bobbed his head up and down ferociously as Kate and Shade approached him. She reached up and with one gentle touch, she calmed him.

Shade shook his head. "*Cazzo*, if you can do that with animals, I hope you can do that with all beasts. Well, apparently, this wedding is some type of charade for the mortals, but it never occurred to me until now that perhaps you would wish for a true wedding. The turning ceremony is more or less a wedding ceremony to me, to my kind. But for you, perhaps you wish to have something more traditional in your world."

She stroked Bravado and felt him nudge against her, snorting, as she listened to Shade talk about a wedding. She thought about what he was asking her and looked over her shoulder.

"Lover, I think I have left so much of the mortal world behind; my family, all of my friends, except Shannon. The turning is our wedding. A mortal wedding for us would feel false, somehow. Mortals take vows they don't honor, and half of them end up divorced. I think what we have, what you plan, that is our path."

He would give her whatever she wanted, but her answer pleased him. There was no commitment ceremony with stronger bonds than the blood covenant and the turning. He leaned on the gate and looked at her and other thoughts began to churn in his head. "Luca calls you Kate, doesn't he?"

Her impulse was to look away, but she knew she had to face this one head-on, she owed that much to Luca. "Yes, he calls me Kate, but he does so at my insistence. I haven't asked that of the others. Theresa, Gi, and Reynaldo all call me my lady. Though it is not my preference, I will honor your request. But Luca feels more like family, the title feels too formal, too distant, and I unloaded a lot of crap on him after the baby died. A lot! But if this is something you can't live with, then I'll do as you ask."

Flexing his hand as it hung over the gate, he reached out and slid it through Bravado's mane. "It's fine that he calls you Kate if it is what you want, but I ask when he is amongst my warriors, family, and others, he refers to you as is proper. I understand what he has done for you has helped you to overcome the grief. Sometimes, I can be lenient, *mi amore*, but not always. I want you to be close to Luca, but I also need him to show respect before others. They would think less of him if he did not, and of me as well. Do you understand?"

"I understand, lover, and that is a fair compromise." She leaned over and kissed his neck as he continued to stroke the horse. She whispered in his ear, "I wonder if the animal gift thing works on your beast?"

Growling, he said, "Well, it's working right now!" Picking her up, he threw her over his shoulder and slapped her ass hard. Hearing her yelp the horses grew restless. "Oh, calm down. I love this woman. I was going to take you out riding, but since you think you can tame this beast, I think you should prove it."

Laughing, he ran to the house with *bel* draped over his shoulder, her crimson hair flying, beating his back, and laughing along with him.

71

Returning from the gym, Rissa was surprised to find Alec wasn't at home. That seemed odd since she had spent much longer at the gym than anticipated, and he was usually home by now. His car was parked outside. *Don't tell me he... No, he wouldn't teleport!* Maybe something was going on with the warriors. Without another thought to the matter, she took a nice long hot shower, scrubbing herself clean, drying her hair, and lay on the bed for a while, thinking.

She had already set up the plan to steal the potion. She had made arrangements with someone reliable to get into Max's condo while they were out together. Rissa had given them all the details, and when she called, they would go to Max's and get the potion. Hopefully, once she took this trip to the beach with him it would be the last she saw of Max. She would miss him, though, she would miss... *No Rissa, don't go there! Just get that potion for Alec.* Maybe Max wouldn't even notice it was missing. Who knew how much was stored in there, and besides, he probably never kept count. She only needed a few vials for Alec to have tested and figure out its ingredients. Speaking of which, where the hell was Alec? It was getting really late.

* * *

Raven remained at Alec's side, as they teleported back to Georgetown, and landed with him at his front door. Raven gave him a sly grin. "Need me to take you inside?"

Alec snorted. "That will be all warrior." He listened as the warrior laughed when he teleported away. The teleport had given him time to think though. Who the fuck would have guessed Shade could turn that property into such a revenue center so fast? The vineyards were already there when he signed over the property, but they had been untended. Alec had no interest in developing and managing vineyards when he had owned the property. He could only assume Shade had done the same with the California property. And now he was taking his building in Paris? Not a bad payday. Fuck, if he got these rogue vamps off his ass, it was worth every penny. He just had to make sure Rissa never learned about the Paris deal. He entered the house and immediately poured himself a Midnight and took a look at the glass of deep red liquid, and realized with every sip, he put more money in Shade's pocket. He had to give him credit. The fucker knew how to make money. He walked upstairs to Rissa. At least she would be safer now with this Angel out of the picture. He walked into their bedroom to find her sprawled, half-naked, across their bed.

"There you are, my darling. Sorry to be so late tonight, had some business to attend to."

She knew the moment he teleported in and wondered what kind of mood he'd be in since he abhorred teleporting. "I'm glad you're home. Want to share why you were out so late?" She bit her lower lip. "I know you teleported, and you never do that."

Alec started undressing as he talked. "I went to see Shade at his place in Virginia. Had no idea what he had done to it, so that was a surprise. But it seems our little battle with the rogues is over, my darling, he slew the dragon, so to speak. I told him from the beginning I wanted the head of the dragon as proof, so that's what I went to see, the head of my unseen enemy in this little battle for D.C. This 'Angel', he's dead now, and I saw his head on a platter to prove it. I still want you to be careful. I'm sure whoever remains from his coven will try to exact revenge before they move on, but this will blow over soon."

Rissa sat up as he spoke and her heart skipped a beat. *The warrior killed Angel? No! Not Max! Max is dead?* She clutched her chest and tried to control her rapid breathing, blocking her thoughts from him. Her mind was spinning. There's no way his warrior could kill Max! He was a master, and a warrior, one of the best! Besides, she'd not felt anything. She was sure she'd have felt it if he'd been killed. Still, he could have blocked her somehow. Her mind was filled with questions and doubt.

"So, you saw the head?" Her hands began to shake slightly and she curled them into fists at her side, her eyes were wide.

Alec tossed his shirt onto a chair. "Oh, and that's not the best part. You'll never guess who killed him!"

Her head was hurting and she felt like someone had ripped her heart straight from her chest. She was so lost in her thoughts. She heard Alec speaking but didn't comprehend. She looked up at him. "What Alec? Who? Who was it? Did you know them?"

Alec chuckled. "Oh I know them, as do you, my darling. And I'm afraid I may have to start thinking a little differently about this individual. Apparently, this Angel staged an ambush on Shade's estate and was going to take out his mate, your old friend Kate. In case you aren't aware, the best way to defeat a master is to remove his mate. Not unlike a game of chess, the queen always protects the king. Take out the queen, and the king falls, checkmate. Who knew the mortal was prepared and took out Angel with a fucking crossbow. A crossbow! She took him out with a single kill shot right through the heart. Now that's something I'd have paid to see. The expression on his face when he realized he'd been bested by a mortal! Priceless! Maybe I should have Shade's warriors train you? Think about it. Anyway, I have some things to wrap up before morning, and this wasn't how I'd planned to spend my evening, so I need to get back to the study. I'll be up to bed in a while."

He slipped on a robe as he prepared to return downstairs to the study.

Looking at him, Rissa realized her mouth was hanging open. Kate killed Max? With a bow? She couldn't lift her damn hand the last time Rissa saw her. How dare that bitch kill Max! Rissa would have her head. This couldn't be happening. "Alec, wait, please. Just hug me. I feel like this is a victory for you, but none of it makes sense to me, Kate and a crossbow, an ambush?"

Alec was surprised by her response. She seemed more upset than he'd anticipated. Maybe she'd been putting on a brave front and had been more afraid than she'd let on. He sat on the side of the bed and slid his arms around her. "You're fine, my darling. I'll still have Shade's warriors watching over you for a while yet. You know I won't let any harm come to you."

She clung to him. She felt the tears build but pushed them back. "I know you'll always protect me, Alec, nothing will ever happen as long as I have you to take care of me. I'm sorry, I didn't mean to show weakness, I'm just a little surprised by this. Go, finish your work and come back to me." Kissing him softly on his neck, she sat back and straightened his robe as she smiled up at him. "I'll be fine, I'm your strong baby girl, remember?"

He creased his brow as he looked at her. This wasn't the response he expected from Rissa and she seemed oddly shaken by this news. He listened as she reassured him she was strong. *Not so sure, baby girl, not so sure.*

"Rissa, it'll be fine. Trust me. It turned out as expected. I haven't lived this many years without facing many challenges from rival masters. I overcome them all. Always."

She put on a brave face. "Well, of course, you do, Mr. President. Who better to lead all of us in conquering the world? Now go on, I have some calls to make. Damn foreign dressmakers have the oddest times!" Blowing him a kiss, she gave him a smile she didn't feel.

Alec left her and returned to the study. *Women, mortal or immortal, there is no figuring them out. Seven-hundred and fifty years and they still baffle me.* He poured himself another glass of Midnight and downed it in one gulp. Some things never changed.

Rissa waited a bit for Alec to get settled downstairs and she could hear the shuffle of papers, the click of his keyboard and knew he was deep in his work. Her hands shook as she picked up her cell. She rushed into the bathroom and locked the door, still blocking all her thoughts from Alec, not that he much noticed once his nose was in his damn work. He was oblivious to her. She bit her lip and looked at his number. *Oh please, Max!* She didn't expect to get an answer as she slid down the wall, sitting on the floor, and hit call.

Max heard his cell ring, again. *Now what?* If he got one more call from Tomas tonight, with any more bad news, he would fucking go on a rampage! He grabbed it up and answered without looking to see who the caller was, and barked into the phone, "What now?"

Her face lit up, her heart skipped a beat. *Max was alive!* Not expecting to hear his voice again, she was now shaking all over. He was alive! "Max, oh Max! You're alive!"

Max leaned back on the sofa, happy to hear her voice. "Rissie! Angel, of course, I'm alive. Why would you think otherwise?"

She answered breathlessly, "Alec just went off about an ambush and his warrior having the head of Angel, and oh Max, just tell me you're okay, this is all some stupid mistake!"

Max threw his head back laughing. "Oh Rissie, you've given me the first good news of the night. They think Cuerpo was Angel? That's perfect, just perfect. It was Cuerpo who lost his head, my angel, not me. Do you think I'd insert myself in the middle of an ambush when I have warriors to carry out those details? I'm fine, my angel, more than fine. But I could be better. You can make it better by telling me when you plan to go away with me. A promise is a promise, my angel, and I think I've been patient enough."

Smiling and hugging her knees, she said, "Oh Max, I knew it couldn't be true! I just knew it! You'd never be so weak as to let some warrior take you down." She laughed along with him. "Tomorrow... oh please, Max, say tomorrow we can be together." She had received a call late this afternoon from that cow Jenny letting her know Alec had added more appointments to his calendar for tomorrow that would keep him busy well into the evening. "It's all set. I'm leaving my car at the gym. Can you meet me there? Or tell me where to teleport to meet you? I don't want to come to the condo Max. It's too dangerous, especially after this! Please, Max, say yes."

He smiled and relaxed for the first time all evening. "Whatever you wish for is yours, my angel. Tomorrow is perfect. I'll make it a perfect day for you. I'll meet you at the gym. We'll leave from there. I can't wait to be with you again. I hope you feel the same."

"Of course, Max, I've just been waiting for the perfect time. Alec thinks I'm heading into New York City for a fitting for the wedding dress. How ridiculous is this affair? He thinks I'll be gone day and evening, he won't notice my absence. He'll be too busy, but we must be careful, Max. He still has those baboon warriors watching me. I never see them, but I know they're there. So, meeting me at the gym is perfect, that is a normal place for my car to be seen. Oh, Max, I'm so excited to just be free of all this and be with you."

"I have so much to show you, my angel. Until tomorrow then. I love you, Rissie. I hope you know how much I love you, and what I can give you he can't. Sleep well, dream of me. And I'll dream of you."

"Yes Max, sweet dreams, until tomorrow."

Hanging up with Max, she quickly dialed another number and set the plans in motion for the potion to be stolen tomorrow. It had been an hour since Alec had gone down to his office. It was time to work her magic on him.

Knocking as she opened the door, Rissa approached his desk. "Alec, I don't wish to interrupt, but I'd like to go to New York City tomorrow. I just finished talking to the designer. He has sketches and fabrics ready for my approval and I need to check them to have the dress ready in time. May I please go tomorrow, Daddy? Baby girl wants to be beautiful for you on our wedding day."

Alec cringed as she called him 'daddy'; it was a name he only expected to hear when she was on her knees with her ass in the air. He suppressed his anger as he growled back at her, "Go. By all means, go"

She cringed at his tone. *Oh, don't you think I won't!* "Thank you, Alec."

She fumed off to bed. *Oh, I will definitely have the time of my life tomorrow, in the sun, sand, and water, and anything else I damn well please.*

72

As the sun came up, Max teleported into the gym parking garage, ready to meet Rissa. With any luck, this would be a one-way trip and he'd keep her with him forever. He saw her in her car, waiting for him as he touched down. He walked to the driver's side window and tapped lightly. "Ready, my angel?"

Rissa had been waiting impatiently, wishing he would hurry. She was so anxious to be away from everything here, including Alec. The tapping on the window made her jump slightly. Turning her head, she saw Max, gorgeous, rugged, the opposite of Alec in every way. Jumping out of the car, her eyes scanned the parking garage before she answered him. "More than ready, Max. Do you have the potion? I can't take chances."

"My angel, I'm not in the habit of carrying a glass of Midnight everywhere I go. As soon as we get to my island, you can drink, and you'll be safe. I assure you. Now hang on to me, and let me show you what can be yours."

She grabbed Max around the neck and cuddled into him. She couldn't remember ever teleporting much with Alec. She reveled in being in Max's strong arms as they surrounded and protected her. She could feel how much he loved her. His body felt so warm against hers. "Let's go, Max. Please take me."

Max chuckled. "Oh I intend to take you, my angel, in more ways than one." He teleported them from the garage and out of the hustle and bustle of D.C.'s traffic and honking horns, and away from the throngs of tourists. It didn't take long before they were out over the Chesapeake Bay, then across the Atlantic and straight to the Caribbean and his own private island.

"Look down, my angel. That's mine. It can be yours as well, to visit, to live there, whatever you wish."

As they sailed easily over the Caribbean, she looked across the sky and its smog-free splendor, the dolphins jumping in the waves below, and wondered what the hell she ever saw in D.C. Looking down to where Max pointed, she took in the lush tropical vegetation and the white sand beaches surrounded by pure blue waters so clear she could see the coral reefs beneath the surface.

"That's yours, Max? Put us down! I want to run in the sand!" Laughing, she kissed him.

"Patience, my angel, we have all day, or the rest of our lives, your choice." He landed outside his home. It was an ultra-modern design, all steel and glass, so there was a view of the ocean from every room.

"And this, my angel, could be your home, one of many, of course. I wouldn't subject you to the schedules of Congress. We could go where we want, whenever we want. Do you like it? If not, I'll tear it down and build whatever you want."

Her eyes took in the luxury. She saw nothing but beautiful skies and ocean in every direction. She heard nothing but the songs of tropical birds and the waves crashing on the beach. She turned to look at him. "Max, tell me I'm not dreaming?"

"Come inside. See your home. It's all for you, my angel. This is the living room. You can open the window wall, just slide it, and you will always feel the ocean breeze in your hair. You'll have staff to wait on your every need."

The room was all white and reflected back the beauty of the light, and the floor to ceiling windows allowed the ocean view to take center stage. As she took in the view, he poured them both a glass of Midnight and added the potion. He joined her at the window and handed her a glass.

He clinked the edge of the glass in a toast. "To us, my angel. To an eternity of us." He watched as she smiled and drank down the glass of wine and potion.

She quickly swallowed down the wine then slid the massive doors open, leaning out and breathing in the sweet, ocean air and feeling it blow through her hair. Closing her eyes, she imagined being here forever and her heart sang. Spinning on her heels, she ran to him and wrapped her legs around his waist, kissing him deep and long. "Max, I love it here! I love it."

He relished her happiness. It was what he'd been waiting for. Hell, he could have saved himself that nightmare of battle in D.C. and just brought her here in the first place.

"Come with me. Let me show you our bedroom, where we'll sleep and make love, when I'm not making love to you on the beach." In the bedroom, where the window wall was already open, the sheer white canopy danced in the breeze that blew across the bed.

Alec never took her anywhere like this. He never did anything romantic. Sitting on the edge of the bed, she stared out at the ocean and felt as though her life choice had been the worst decision she'd ever made. She had left Max a long time ago, and perhaps that was the biggest mistake of her life, walking away from him. He truly loved her, always had and now she thought of all the years she wasted when she could have been as happy as she was in this moment. "Max, when did you do all of this?"

"I did this for you, angel. When I knew I'd made a mistake by letting you go. I know you don't understand, but turning, it's not to be taken lightly. I've never turned a mortal. It's an awesome responsibility, and the mortal doesn't always survive the turning. In hindsight, I can see my error. But at the time, I felt it better to let you go. But make no mistake. I never stopped loving you. I thought you'd leave my world... find a mortal husband. But then, when you went to Alec, it almost destroyed me. I've regretted the decision every day, and I can't go forward without you. Not another day, my angel." He took her hand and led her out onto the open balcony. "Look, right outside your window, we step out into our own paradise."

His words mimicked her thoughts and she wondered if they truly were meant to be together. She tried desperately not to think of what could happen if she chose Max over Alec. But Max would never make this an easy choice for her, and there were things that pulled her to Alec. That blood bond couldn't be broken, even in death, and she had bonded herself to both of them. Max offered her everything Alec couldn't, the gentleness and the romance her heart craved. He would hold her and love her, and expect nothing in return. But would he still allow her independence?

No master ever let their mate have complete independence, but Alec gave her more than most. She didn't think Max would be so generous. He would insist on having her around, knowing her whereabouts. Squeezing his hand, she turned and laid her head on his chest and sighed.

"Max, I never knew it could be like this. I knew you loved me, but when you refused to turn me, I thought you didn't love me enough."

He led her back inside the house and through the bedroom.

"I've always loved you. I know the position I've placed you in. I just hope that, in your heart, you know where your true happiness lies." He was well aware of her inner conflict.

"I love being in your arms, Max, they make me feel safe. I love how I feel right now as if nothing bad could ever touch me and I'm just happy and free. I want to feel like this every day."

"Every day, my angel, I'll protect you above all others. Now change. I assume you brought a swimsuit? If not, no worries, there is no one here to see you other than me."

Kissing him, she stepped inside the bathroom and quickly slipped into a black bikini. Strolling out, she saw him staring out at the ocean. He was her strong, rugged, warrior master, the ultimate dream for any immortal woman. "Your angel is ready."

Max turned and took her in. She was his now. This would be their life. This is what a warrior fought for. He reached out to her and she walked to him. Max lifted her in his arms and carried her outside to the beach that lay at their doorstep. "Your own private paradise."

He set her down gently on the sand. "I have more to show you, my angel. Before you go running off into the surf." But the words were hardly out of his mouth before she ran for the water and lay down in the surf line, letting the waves crash over her. He laughed with joy at her happiness.

As he approached, she stood in the surf and splashed him then took off running, throwing her head up to the glorious sun, laughing as if she'd just found her wings.

Max chased after her, letting her run ahead, watching her hair fly and listening to her laughter. He caught up to her, reached out and grabbed her arm, spinning her around so she faced him. He placed his hands on either side of her face, her blue eyes gleamed in the sunlight, and he lowered his mouth to hers, kissing her as she deserved to be kissed. Not with savagery, but with love and passion.

She felt the kiss from Max in her heart. She returned the kiss and it made her body sing, ache for him. She remembered the long nights of making love, how sweet and gentle he was with her, how he adored just touching her, and she loved him. She never thought she'd love another.

"Max, I love you. I forgot what this felt like, to be kissed for no reason, to be loved for being me."

She said the words he'd been waiting to hear. He knew she'd not forgotten how it was with them. He picked her up and she wrapped her legs around his waist as he walked with her into the ocean, letting the waves wash over them, and feeling the heat of the sun on their shoulders.

"And I love you, my angel. This will be our life every day. This will be our life."

She was lost in the moment, lost in him, thinking of a life she craved, and she pushed Alec and D.C. far from her mind. She didn't care about tomorrow; she just wanted this, right now, here with Max. She fought the pull of her heart that told her this was wrong, and was a betrayal to her mate, her maker. Max was here and now.

"Max, I wish this had happened before, this feeling I have now, I wish I had known we could be like this, that you loved me like this, but I didn't know."

She leaned back into the water with her legs still wrapped around his waist. She untied her bikini top as he watched, feeling his eyes burn into her, but it was Alec she felt in her veins.

Max watched as she let her body float on the surface with the soft rise and fall of the waves. He watched as she tossed her bikini top aside. He felt himself grow hard for her, and he slid his hands up her back, supporting her body as her hair fanned out in the water. She slowly lifted herself upright and wrapped her arms around his neck. He carried her back toward the seaside cabana he'd built just for her, where they would make love for the first of many times today.

With her lips at his throat, her tongue slid across the soft pulsing of the veins in his neck, running her hands in his long wet curls, tugging softly on his hair. Her breasts were wet and slippery against his chest as the sun beat down on her back, firing her body.

"Show me what's in my future, Max. Show me what every day will be like."

Max carried her up the steps of the cabana and into the small bedroom. He slid off his wet clothes and she pulled the small thong bikini down her hips and let it drop to the floor. "I'll show you, my angel."

He picked her up and laid her on the bed as he crawled over her, his hair hanging down around her face. "I'll show you everything."

He leaned down and kissed her, feeling her arms slip around his neck as her legs went around his hips, pulling him down. He felt her hunger, her desire. "You'll never want again, my angel. You'll know you're loved every day."

He was so unlike Alec and she remembered how it once was, how she spent every moment wanting him, needing him and he gave her back everything she needed except eternity. She wanted him to show her again, this was for her, and he wasn't using her to gain more territory or power, not some ulterior motive like molding his public persona.

She pulled him to her, her hands stroking his wide muscular back, his arms so hard with muscle. His abdomen was toned and sleek, and his face was rugged beauty. His dark curls hung down and dripped droplets of water on her face, and she licked the drops as they fell. His male musky scent was animalistic, and his skin was sun-kissed. Letting her nails slide up his chest, she drew a heart with her nail over his left nipple and then slid her tongue in the heart shape her finger just etched and felt him growl softly, passionately.

Max closed his eyes and took a deep breath, willing himself to go slowly, but she made it difficult. With his weight on his elbows, he lowered himself on top of her, ran his hands through her hair, letting her feel the hard steel between his legs as it pressed against her soft belly. He lowered his head to hers, and kissed her lips again, soft kisses, biting at her, drawing her bottom lip into his mouth, licking at her lips, teasing both of them as he drew out the moment.

She could feel him hard against her. She was already wet and ached to have him buried deep inside her. She wasn't used to this foreplay and she struggled to control the urge to go faster. She wiggled beneath him, pushing her hips upward to him in agonizing want and need. "Max, please. Such sweetness and I need you."

He felt her body move beneath him, and he slid one hand from beside her face and let it trail over her shoulder, and across her breast, her slender waist and her rounded hip, where he squeezed hard, but not enough to cause pain. She wouldn't feel pain from him, but he squeezed hard enough to claim her. Hard enough to communicate, this is mine now. He rolled off of her and moved his mouth from her lips to her breast, where he sucked her sweet nipple into his mouth, rolling his tongue over it, feeling her arch her back. He slid his hand between her legs, to find her wet and waiting, and he slipped his fingers inside her and listened to the moan that escaped her lips. "Angel, my angel. Tell me what you want."

For Rissa, the pleasure he gave her was in some ways more painful than what Alec inflicted on her. The sweetness of it melted her. His lips and soft beard felt like heaven against her breasts, it tickled and tantalized her even more. She knew he wanted her, to be inside her and he was holding back. She wanted to feel him pounding her hard and sweet, showing her how much he wanted her.

"Take me, Max, show me. I want to remember..." Grabbing his ass, she sank her nails deep while she bit into his shoulder hard enough to draw blood. She licked the small beads of blood that rose to the surface of his bronzed skin and her body felt electric as his blood hit her tongue and she moaned so loud the walls seemed to echo with her need. Taking his blood was the ultimate betrayal. Alec might be convinced to forgive her for the sex, but he'd never forgive her for taking his blood, and eternally bonding herself to Max. "Max!"

He lifted himself over her, pushing her thighs farther apart with his knees as he slid his hand under her waist, lifting her hips up to him as he sank his cock deep inside her with a single stroke. He heard her gasp, and he moaned with the pleasure of that sweet tight grip around his cock. His head thrown back, his eyes closed, he focused on the feel of her as he began to rock his hips against hers. She matched his rhythm, slow at first, letting his cock glide its full length in and out of her. He felt her hands slide down his back and grip his ass, her nails biting into his skin. She wanted to be ridden and ridden hard. He pulled at her thighs until she wrapped them around his hips. He slid both arms beneath her and crushed her to his chest as he thrust hard into her. He lowered his head so it was beside her face and growled deep from his chest. "I love you, my angel. Stay with me. Cum with me. You're mine now. Mine."

He knew how to pleasure her. She gripped a fistful of his curls and pulled him to her neck as she came hard with him buried inside her. She screamed loud, holding nothing back.

She was lost, for she could no longer feel where she belonged, or who she belonged to. Her heart splintered into pieces. She knew she would lose one of them as her body shook from the violence of the orgasm. Rissa pulled him to her neck, turning her head to the side, giving him full access to all of her. It was the final betrayal of Alec, letting Max drink her blood, that sacred union of one mate to another.

Max sank his fangs deep into her and drew deep, tasting Alec and taking in the power of a rival masters' blood, swallowing the blood as his cock responded and throbbed deep inside her, releasing into her, filling her, as he rode her harder. He unlatched and threw his head back and growled as he heard her screams, and every bird on the island took flight. The cabana rocked with the motion of their lovemaking, and his cock emptied completely into her. He collapsed forward, kissing her gently before rolling off of her, lying beside her, his heart pounding, and gasping for breath. He ran his finger down her forehead and nose, and across her lips, to her chin. "My Rissie. It's just like it was before, and how it will be again."

She rolled to face him her hand slid over his cheek and whispered softly, "Max... all for love." She curled into him as his arms surrounded her and she fell in love with him all over again.

He lay next to her and imagined an eternity of her next to him. There was so much to share, so much he could give her. "Come, my angel. There are things I want to show you. I don't want us to miss any of this day."

"More? There's more?" Giggling, she climbed on top of him and straddled his hard-muscled body and kissed him softly. "I can't go out without a swimsuit. I seem to have lost mine." Displaying a mock modesty,, she threw her arms over her breasts. "I need a suit, Max." She bit her lower lip, making a coy, sexy face.

"My angel, you look ravishing just as you are. But this cabana was made for you and I have plenty of swimwear, beach towels—whatever you might need."

He slid his long muscular body from their bed and walked to a dresser, pulling fresh clothes out for both of them. He turned and handed her a bikini in the softest color pink. "Wear this one, angel. I love you in pink."

The color complemented her skin perfectly and she wiggled into it as she turned her back to him. "Max, will you tie the string for me please? I never knew you loved me in pink!" She could feel his hands on her back. "Where are we going?"

He took her hand and led her from the cabana as they walked down the beach. "Patience, my angel."

They walked along the surf line, letting the waves break over their feet and watching as the surf ebbed and flowed, the sandpipers running at the edge of the surf line, and listening to the seagulls call out to them. Her skin glowed in the sun and the breeze tossed her blonde hair. He squeezed her hand as he smiled down at her, his beautiful angel.

"Just up here, Rissie, our own private alcove on our own private island. Come, swim with me."

As they walked hand in hand in the sun, she enjoyed every second. Then she saw the alcove filled with the bluest of water and a huge waterfall. "Max! Oh Max!" Yanking on his hand, she ran headlong for the alcove, her hair whipping behind her as he followed. She looked back at him, laughing. "You're getting old and slow. Come on!"

He listened to her laughter. He remembered how easily she used to laugh. He watched her as she ran, her ass tight and toned, her legs long and lean, that hair flying. It was a sight to behold. As he caught up with her, he slid his arms around her waist and jumped with her into the deep waters of the alcove. She squealed with delight and he swam away from her, dunking under the water, and came up behind her, his hands on her shoulders, his lips on her neck.

"Come angel, swim with me under the waterfall."

She squealed with laughter as he went underwater and she shook her wet hair, running her hands through it when she felt his hands on her shoulders behind her. The water felt cooling to their skin, hot from the sun. His lips sought out her neck and she craved to feel him feed from her again.

She swam with him, paddling her feet, her arms spread in front of her, heading straight to the thundering waterfall.

The water crashed over them, and created a churn in the water that spun them in a slow circle. He reached for her and she grabbed his shoulders, wrapping her legs around his waist once more as they allowed the current of the undertow to carry them in a circle, around and around, like a cork floating in the ocean. And with each turn, they were taken under the falls to create a pattern of being in a curtain of water, then clear of it, then under it again, and clear of it, and he kissed her softly, waiting for that next curtain of water to fall over them again. With each rotation, the kisses became more passionate, hungrier, and needier. He had gone without her for so long. He'd been tormented by the thoughts of her with Alec, lying with him, feeding from him, fucking him. But that would all end soon. This woman was his now.

She felt that pull to him, this was what she'd always wanted, to be loved like this once more. As they went around again, she laid her head on his shoulder, feeling the water break over them, bringing such a feeling of contentment. She could stay here all day like this, his arms around her. She could make his life so wonderful. She let her lips barely touch his neck and she moaned with the smell of him, the feel of him, and the call of his blood. She snaked her tongue out and licked the beads of water from his skin and she felt him wanting her to feed. His hands entangled in her hair, his cock hard as it rested between her legs, pressed against her sex.

He felt her lips at his neck and he sensed her hunger. Alec withheld from her. Max knew him well. It was all about control with Alec. He ran his hand through her hair and pulled her to his neck, turning his head. "Drink, my angel. Drink your fill."

"Max, I'll never forget this day." As her fangs elongated, she sank them deep and felt the rumble of his body vibrate through her own and she shivered from the pure ecstasy of that feeling. No mortal could ever understand the eroticism of feeding from a vampire. She drew slowly and moaned, tasting that musky all male taste of him, master and beast combined in gentle love and giving. She kept feeding slowly, as her arm went around his neck, the other laying on his chest. She crossed her ankles at his back and squeezed against him, fitting him like a glove. Taking one last long draw, she unlatched and threw her head back, his blood running down her chin as she licked it slowly, lashing her tongue out to capture it all.

He covered her mouth with his, tasting his own blood on her lips, and kissed her passionately. He broke the kiss and swam, pulling her beside him to the side of the lagoon where he helped her out. "Come, my angel. Let's get back in the sun. Walk with me. Our day is passing way too fast."

He helped her from the water, leading her away from the lagoon as she moaned softly, looking over her shoulder at the paradise they were leaving. His stride was long and covered much distance compared to her. He finally slowed down, and they began to walk, hand in hand once again. "Max, what would you say if I wanted to keep my business? I love my work and what I do. Would you object to that?"

Max turned and looked at her, pulled her down onto the white sand where they both stretched out side by side. "Rissie, our life can be whatever you want it to be. It's ours to create. What do you envision? What do you desire? I have the means to make it so. Do you want to work? If that's your choice, then by all means, I would want you to work. But this island is just one of many homes. I have homes all over the world, in the most exotic places. From Bangkok to Paris, my angel, and all points in between. I have another island in Greece. Do you want to ski? Then we go to Switzerland. Gamble? We're off to Monte Carlo. The world is at your feet. You have only to tell me how you wish to live, and you shall have it."

* * *

Lying on the sand next to him, she heard him give her the world. She could get whatever material things she desired from Alec, but what she wanted was something money couldn't buy. She sat up and wrapped her arms around her knees, staring at the water, waves, and white sands for miles.

"I can have all those things now, Max. I like working, it's who I am. It gives me a great sense of accomplishment to succeed and make my own money, develop my own friends and contacts worldwide. I enjoy being tired at the end of the day from doing something I love. I'm not a possession, something to be put on a pedestal and admired. That's not who I am anymore."

He listened to her speak. This Rissa was much changed from the young girl he once knew. She was more confident, more independent, but it was a change that suited her.

"Rissie, if working is what you want, then I'm more than happy to accommodate you. My coven is Virginia, Maryland, and Delaware. I literally surround D.C., so there would be no need for us to move. No reason for you to give up your business. I have an estate in Virginia, a large house on the James River. If it's not to your liking, we can sell it, and you can pick where we live. It matters not to me as long as you're there."

She watched as he stood and faced the ocean waves, the soft breeze catching those long curls. His body was rock hard and that face, she could drown in its ruggedness. As her eyes fed on him, she knew Alec could give her something Max would never be able to give. Alec was her master, he would hear her call forever, care for her in his wicked loving way. There was no breaking the blood covenant, and the crack inside her heart for Max suddenly sealed closed. Alec had ambition. With Alec, she climbed with him, fought with him, decided with him, they did it together. She would be walking away from something she loved doing with Alec, helping him climb to the top. It fed her lonely soul. Alec would always be her maker, her master, who delivered his own brand of love.

Max pointed out onto the blue horizon. "Look out there, my love, the yacht, see it? It's 'The Angel'. And we can sail away any day, to anywhere you want. You decide our future."

As he pointed out to the water, she focused her sight onto the huge yacht. "Max! You named a boat after me?" Laughing, she looked up at him. "Max, why? Why all of this? Why now?"

He sat down on the sand next to her side by side at ocean's edge. "I told you, angel. I made a mistake and I can never apologize enough for it. I made a mistake when I let you go. I knew, immediately, it was the wrong choice, but you went straight to him. I thought I'd get over you in time, but I can't. I can't get over you. And I won't stop until you're mine."

Laying her head on his shoulder, she looked out and knew this day would be locked in her heart forever. "My sweet, Max, you're so handsome, so gentle with my heart. I'd have much to wrap up before I could leave. I know you're impatient, but I can't just leave on a dime. My business is vital to me. I'd have to plan carefully. And I'm scared. You know what he can and will do to me."

She turned in his arms, her hands slid down his back, his muscles taut and well defined, strong and tanned. He spent much time in the sun and she loved the color of his dark tan against the comparative paleness of her skin. They were like night and day, his dark hair, long curls, and her blonde locks. She snuggled into his neck and breathed him in so deep. "Just hold me tight, Max, hold me."

He lay back on the sand and pulled her over on top of him. "My angel, I have waited all this time, I can wait for you to get your affairs in order so you can come to me. I know he'll try to follow, and I'll handle it. Now come make love to me one last time before this day ends."

Rissa knew Max would not let her go easily, and the potion was already as good as in her possession. She was ready. He would never touch Alec. Sliding on top of him, she kissed him long and deep, her hair cascading over his face and then she slid down his body, leaving small nips as she went. Reaching his trunks, she yanked them down and tossed them into the waves behind her. She cupped his balls, squeezing them slightly. She flicked her tongue back and forth playfully over the head of his bulging cock as it stood at complete attention. She swirled her tongue around the head, sliding her tongue over top to catch that tasty bead of cum and moaned. Grasping his steel in her hand, she pulled it from her mouth. "I've learned a few tricks since we were last together."

Lowering her head, she flung her hair back and then took him deep into her throat in one gulp, and began to stroke him in and out of her mouth.

Fuck! This woman will drive me mad! He lifted her up, disengaging his cock from her mouth most reluctantly. "Save it, my angel. Come with me. I have one last surprise for you."

He walked with her into the ocean and swam out past the surf line to where the water was calmer and took her to a bed suspended on a platform, floating in the water. He climbed up the platform and reached down to grab her hand, lifting her up. He carried her to the bed, lay her down and stretched out on his back beside her. "Now, where were we before I so rudely interrupted? Ah yes, my cock in your mouth, please, resume your pleasure and mine, my angel."

She looked at him with slight annoyance. He interrupted her, and now he expected her to proceed? Men! She stared at him long and hard, and then leaned down and nipped the inside of his thigh hard.

"You tease me! You taunt me, and drag me away from my most pleasurable treat?" She slid her hands up under his ass, sinking her nails deep into the hardened muscles of his ass cheeks. "And then you wish for me to resume as if nothing happened?"

She bent over him and sucked him down hard and deep, sliding him in and out of her mouth several times, feeling him respond and she let go of his cock. "You have teased me unfairly, Max."

Sliding up his body, latching her mouth to his, he rolled her over onto her back. The sun was starting to set. He knelt between her legs and ripped the bikini bottom from her body, lifting her knees to her chest, sliding his hands up her calves until her ankles were on either side of her face and her sex was exposed to him. He drilled her hard, slamming his cock into her, feeling the bed rock with the motion.

She screamed out as he pierced her, pounding hard into her. "Rough sex, my angel? We can play that too." He was hunched over her, thrusting hard, holding her legs up, gripping her ankles tightly, as her hips rose to meet every thrust. He pounded her with such ferocity, he watched as her breasts bounced to the rhythm, her head thrown back, her mouth open, eyes closed. He pulled out and released her legs and flipped her over in one swift move, lifting her hips so she was on her knees as he pushed her head down so her ass was in the air. He took her from behind, gripping her hips and slamming into her, the bed rocking and riding the waves, as she gripped the sheets in both hands and growled with pleasure. He slapped her ass hard and she groaned and pushed her hips into him. He slapped her again, harder this time. "Don't think I don't remember, Rissie... don't think I don't remember who taught you to first love the sensation of pleasure mixed with pain." His cock throbbed deep inside of her and his body screamed for relief. He reached beneath her and rubbed her clit, pinching her, tugging at her, sending signals screaming through her body. "Cum for me, baby girl. Cum hard for Daddy."

She gasped with such sweet pain and pleasure as his fingers pinched her clit bringing her close to orgasm. She could feel her beast calling to his. Then she heard those words, 'baby girl' and 'daddy', but the voice was not her Alec, not her daddy! She was not his baby girl!

She snapped as her beast reared up in anger beyond anything she had ever felt. Reaching up behind her, gripping Max and flinging him over her head and watched his body slam into the water. She crouched and then stood tall and roared like a beast gone wild. Her eyes were glaring like the fires of hell and her fangs dripped. "How dare you call me that! You don't own me! I'm not yours! My master is the only beast allowed to call me that, and you're not my master!" She snarled at him like she could eat him alive.

Max's beast exploded, and he leapt back to the bed and picked her up by the neck and teleported them back to the beach where he dropped her in the sand, kicking and screaming, her fangs bared as she hissed at him. He walked around her slowly and growled out his words.

"You toy with me, Rissa? You toy with my heart? Was this a fun little game for you? Was this a little diversion in your life of boredom? A life where your master ignores you? Where your master makes you beg for affection? I've sorely misjudged. You don't love me, you never loved me. The only person Rissa loves is Rissa. Get out! Leave! And rest assured, you self-centered bitch, you'll pay for this betrayal!"

She leapt into the air but hovered before she teleported away to shout at him, "You can't buy this mate from her master. He will reign over me and I gladly let him. Thank you for showing me my master gives me so much more than you can ever imagine. You threw me away! Now pay the price for your stupid error!"

Disappearing into the air, he didn't follow, and she knew he was done with her. He wouldn't follow or return to her again. Her heart sang, for she was finally sure of her purpose, the only thing she ever needed or wanted... Alec.

Max stood on the shore as she teleported herself away from him. Wise move, because he was ready to strangle the life out of her. He heard her scream her words back at him, and then she was gone. His fists were clenched, and he screamed with rage into the night air as the sun started to sink below the horizon. "That bitch! She played me! She played me all along."

He teleported nude back to the condo in D.C. and walked to his bedroom and got dressed. He was pacing the floor in anger, his beast wouldn't recede, and he would take to the streets himself this night to vent this rage. He walked to the bar to pour himself a healthy glass of Midnight when he noticed the cabinet door was open and he picked up the scent of another vampire. He ripped the door from the hinges as he leaned in and looked at the box that contained the vials of the potion. There were two missing vials. "Fuck! Fuck you, Rissa! Fuck you to hell."

He teleported out into the city and landed in Georgetown. *You think it's over? It's over when I say it's over!*

He knew the area was still being monitored by Shade's warriors so he struck fast, killing mortals and moving on, slashing, gutting, removing limbs, removing heads. He struck, and struck, and struck again, until he was covered in their blood, and he could feel Shade's army of warriors behind him. He teleported back to the condo and climbed into the shower, watching as the water turned red as it ran down the drain, and still, he felt no relief, because the source of his anger still walked, still taunted him.

"Rissa. My angel. This time tomorrow, you will be dead."

73

Teleporting to her car in the gym garage, Rissa sped home. Her anger was receding, but her fear of what Max would do continued to grow. Once he found out the potion was missing he might link it to her, but she highly doubted it. At least, that's what she tried to convince herself. After all, he must have tons of enemies, what master didn't?

She knew Alec wasn't at home, he'd been scheduled for the entire evening and she knew he'd be late. Once inside the house she ran for the shower, scrubbing herself raw, cleaning the sandy grit from her hair and covering herself in a luxurious lotion to further mask the scent of sun and sand and Max. Curling up in her bed, she lay there and thought about the day, and dreamt of tomorrow when she met her liaison and get those vials. Alec would be so impressed, now she just had to come up with a believable story of how she got them.

* * *

Max slept little, tossing and turning, waking often to see her face. How could she betray him in this way? Why lead him on? Why make him think they could be together again? Why? It was all too clear why. To distract him so she could get the potion for her Alec. *Well, my sweet angel, if I can't have you, no one will.*

Max had tried to crumble Alec's empire and expose him to the mortal community by trying to force him out in the open with all the rogue attacks, make him weak in her eyes and have her return to him. He tried to lure her away with a lifestyle he knew she craved, and it had all come to nothing, except his humiliation and failure. There was only one way to get her out of his mind, and that would be to end her life. Max was sending one of his best warriors, the only one to escape the ambush at Bel Rosso, the Butcher. He would be loaded with the potion, so she and any protectors would not detect his scent. The Butcher would take her down. The Butcher would wait for her at the gym. *It will be so easy, my Rissa. You make it so easy with your predictable schedule. This ends tonight.*

* * *

Alec returned home later than usual, and Rissa pretended to be asleep. He didn't attempt to wake her, apparently oblivious to the events of the day. He woke early, dressed and gave her a quick kiss, telling her he'd see her tonight. She waited until he was gone before getting up and dressing. After working all day in her office it was finally time to head to the gym. This felt like the longest day of her life and she worked out like a fiend, releasing her anger and pain. At the agreed upon time, she made her way to the locker room to meet her contact and exchanged a large wad of bills for the vials. When Rissa was sure she was alone again she pulled a vial out and examined it. They were made of very hard plastic, perfect for toting around. Stuffing them in her purse, she grabbed up the rest of her things and headed to the nearly empty garage. It was late and most people in G-town were tucked into their expensive homes by now.

* * *

From her position crouched low outside of the gym, Fiamma kept her eyes peeled for anything unusual. Last night's raid on the city brought many careless mortal deaths, the work of a single rogue warrior. Master had hoped this was over, but clearly, something was still going on out here. Shade sent them all back on duty tonight to keep things under control, and she was assigned to following Master Alec's mate. Since dusk all she had done was exercise at that damn gym. Fee saw a hooded figure approach and enter the gym garage. Rissa was finally leaving the gym so Fee moved in closer to the garage entrance but didn't enter. She was better off staying out here where she could monitor both the inside and outside of the garage. If there was a problem she could be on it in no time.

The Butcher was confident the female warrior wouldn't pick up his scent as he strolled into the dark parking garage. He chose a pillar near the entrance to the gym where he could be hidden, and yet, had a clear view of anyone who came into the garage. He watched as Rissa pushed open the door, completely distracted, balancing a large gym bag and a purse. She was looking for her car keys, oblivious to her surroundings when he slipped up behind her. Why make this quick when she was such an easy target and he could have some fun with it. He stepped up right behind her, whispering in her ear. "Greetings from Max, my angel."

Rissa felt his hot breath and the deadly voice sank deep into her soul. Trying to focus, she concentrated all her skills and zeroed in on him. Swinging her leg, she kicked it hard into his crotch and saw him crouch over in pain as she did a backflip over his head. He rose up, fangs bared and eyes blazing and the sight before her was terrifying. He was definitely here on a mission and if his words did not cut her to the bone, his looks did He was ferocious, muscled and raging, and she knew she was out of her league.

The Butcher sprang forward and grabbed her around the throat with both hands, squeezing hard enough to block her air, but not hard enough to snap her neck, yet. She dropped her purse to the ground as she clawed at his hands, trying to pull them away from her throat. Her feet kicking against the pavement as he lifted her just slightly off the floor, just high enough to make her feel she didn't have sure footing. Just high enough to let her know she wasn't going anywhere. He watched as her mouth opened and closed, gasping for air that wasn't there, her eyes wide with fear. Then he squeezed, just a little tighter. Rissa's heart was slamming inside her chest, her beast couldn't fight this.

"Alec! Help me! Master, please!"

Fee heard scuffling feet and teleported immediately behind them. She saw he had Rissa by the throat, and Fee hoped the bitch had been smart enough to call her own damn master, but she could have some fun in the meantime. She taunted the rival warrior.

"Pick on someone your own size. She isn't meaty enough for your taste!"

Rissa went down hard, gasping for air when he let go and turned to Fee. Clutching her throat, gasping and coughing, she looked up to see a red-headed Amazon woman in leather taking on this insanity. **"Alec, please!"**

Leaping and spinning in the air, Fee took the opportunity to catch him when he was still off guard. She grabbed him by the collar and slung him over the hood of the car.

Pushing herself backward and out of the way, Rissa saw the vials rolling out of her purse. She scrambled to retrieve them then crawled further back into the darkness, terrified beyond anything in her life. She watched in horror as the rogue sprang from the hood of the car and attacked the female warrior in red.

* * *

Alec was home reading through a fuck load of legislation when he heard her scream his name, and he felt the power of her fear. He teleported to the gym parking garage where Rissa was on the garage floor, gasping and choking. He saw two other vamps in a struggle. One was male and the other a female, a red-head all in leather. She had to be one of Shade's. No time for a conversation, he could only hope he made the right choice.

He lifted the male up with one hand and pulled him backward crushing him to his chest and with his other hand he twisted his head until he heard it snap. The body went limp in his hands and Alec let him drop to the floor. He looked over the female standing before him. Definitely one of Shade's.

Fee nodded her head at him. "Thanks for the assist."

Alec turned to Rissa who was still crouched on the floor, clutching her purse. He squatted down in front of her, put his hand under her chin and lifted her face to him, her eyes still wide.

"It's okay, Rissa. Come on, let me help you up. We're going home now." He lifted her into his arms and teleported out, nodding to the red-head as he left.

Rissa knew he had saved her from certain death. She clung to him, head buried deep into his neck as she felt them teleport back home.

* * *

At home, Alec carried her to their bedroom. Shade's warrior bought Alec time to get to her. Clearly, the rogue was toying with her, because if he'd moved more quickly, attacked from behind... Alec pushed the thought from his head. He laid her on the bed and tugged at the purse she still clutched to her chest. "Rissa, let go of your purse. You're safe now."

He stroked her hair and he could feel her tremble. Her neck already showed evidence of the attack. He leaned in and whispered, "Rissa, it's Alec. Look at me. You're safe now. I want you to drink from me. Do you understand? Drink from me, and it will heal you."

She felt the softness of the bed against her back and his voice broke through her black panic as she tried to steady her breathing. The vials rolled from her clenched fist as she struggled to reach him, her voice scratchy and weak as she whispered, "Master."

He turned his neck to her and felt the sting of her bite as she began to drink. He saw the two vials roll from her hand onto the bed. Picking them up, he turned them in his hand before placing them on the bedside table. He cradled her head to his neck, letting her drink her fill, healing the red scars around her neck, calming her fears as his blood filled her, making her strong again. Her hands gripped his shoulders, her lips suckled at his neck, as she fed. He knew she drank more from fear than injury. This would be a reality check for his Rissa. For the first time in her immortal life, she had faced an enemy vamp with the intent to kill.

"You're safe now, my darling." As she unlatched, he kissed away the blood on her lips and brushed the hair away from her face. He lay down beside her and pulled her back against his chest before pulling the blanket up.

"Rest. Sleep. Heal, my darling."

* * *

Fee quickly moved the dead rogue to a prime spot where the early morning sun could do its work before anyone noticed the body. Pulling out her cell, she called Shade and wasn't surprised when he answered immediately. He was at the Dead House waiting for any news. She updated him with the details of the attack on Alec's mate then headed out to find Marcello and see if there was any activity showing on his grid.

Cazzo! Good fucking thing I had them out there tonight. After last night, he'd known instinctively that it wasn't over yet. Attacking Kate and now Rissa, this bastard meant business. Cuerpo must have had a small band of followers who were looking to avenge his death. He knew at least one rogue had fled from the scene of the ambush on Bel Rosso. Shade needed to know if Alec had any ideas what this attack might be about. Dialing him up, he waited, unsure if Alec would be able to answer if he was attending to Rissa.

Alec was lying quietly in bed next to Rissa as he stared at the ceiling. She had finally fallen into a deep healing sleep. Her neck would heal quickly, but her psyche would take a little longer. He heard his cell phone ringing in the study. He slipped from their bed and moved quickly to the study to check the phone. He was expecting this call. "Brother..."

"Alec, how's Rissa? Fee just called, gave me the details. Is Rissa okay?"

"She'll be fine, thanks to that red-head in leather. She bought me enough time to respond. Whoever that rogue was, he was just toying with her, planned to take her out slowly. If he'd moved faster, I'm pretty sure we'd be looking at a different outcome. So, what the fuck, brother? First, your mate and now mine? Whatever the fuck this is, it sure isn't over. Rissa doesn't know it yet, but her ass will be grounded here for a while until this gets sorted out. I can't stay here all day, so I'll need you to assign someone to watch the house. And you know Rissa, she'll be looking for any way out."

Shade nodded. "When I watched the security video, I told you one got away. I think that may be the one you just took out, bro. I agree, Rissa needs to stay put. I'll think about who would be a good protector for her. I think a female might work out better for Rissa. If you need anything else, you know where to find me. Take care of your mate, and I'll send over someone to provide permanent protection tomorrow evening. You need final approval?"

Alec grunted. "You chose, I'm sure I'll be happy with her. Rissa, that's another story."

* * *

Max grabbed his cell phone on the first ring expecting it to be the Butcher. Looking down he recognized Tomas' number. What the fuck was going down now? Tomas broke the news that the Butcher was dead, and that fucking bitch was safe. One of Shade's warriors interrupted the attack and Alec got to her and the Butcher. Max threw the phone across the room. *Fuck! Everything failed! It was all for her and she threw it in my face.* He teleported out of the condo where he had made love to her, and out of this fucking town where she walked the streets. He teleported to the island where they had spent the day, and he set it on fire. He stood silently and watched as it burned to the ground, the house and the cabana, gone. When the flames started to ebb, he teleported to his home in Bangkok, as far away from her as he could get. His hatred for her matched the love he had once felt, and it burned out of control. *Someday, my angel... someday.*

74

Shade hung around the Dead House waiting for everyone to get back and give their morning reports. When Marcello and Fiamma walked in, Shade shook his head. Fee looked like she walked straight out of some damn club and not someone who just tackled a deadly rogue vampire. Aside from the attack on Rissa, there had been no other rogue activity in any of the other districts tonight but he knew they'd need to remain vigilant. For the time being they would continue to monitor the city.

"Are you two done slapping backs? I need to speak with Fee. Alone."

Fee's night had been made even better by the fact she was the only one who saw any action tonight. Unfortunately, she had to defer to the master to take the kill, typical male vampire. Alec's method was too easy for her taste, snapping a neck, clean and done. Fee preferred a bit more blood and a battle with the blades to challenge her skills. As a woman, she always had to be a bit better than the boys. Shade sat down at his desk, papers strewn everywhere. Fee could tell he was bored out of his head, and restless to get back to Kate. She chuckled to herself. Kate surely had her master handled, and the kill she chalked up with Cuerpo was the stuff of legend. Damn, that girl was going to make a hell of a Medici Queen. She closed the door behind her and approached the desk. "What did I do now?"

Shade rolled his eyes at her. "You didn't do anything, just sit down. I have a dilemma and I need a female perspective. What we talk about stays between us, Fee, I'm in no mood to play games, this is serious business. *Si*?"

"Of course, master. I'm listening. What's the problem?"

"Well, tonight, you got a look at Rissa. You also got a close-up view of him. They are no normal vampire couple. They live a high-profile lifestyle in the public eye, as mortals. The rogue attack spooked her. He is happy with your performance, but did you have to wear the damn red leather?"

Letting a slow grin build on her face, she stared at him. "What? Are you now enforcing a dress code? Because if you are, I have a few complaints about Raven. I had Cory custom design these for me, and in my defense, I need to be a lure as well as battle, to draw out any vamps that might be looking for a bite or two."

He shook his head at her. "Sometimes I worry about you, warrior! Now listen up. Alec wants me to send a protector for Rissa. He will keep her ass in the house for a while, and I don't have to tell you, she is one bitch on wheels. No one is going to tie her fancy ass down inside that house for long. She has a business to run, so she won't sit still. Rissa is no skilled warrior and this was her first experience encountering a hostile. Alec has never used a protector before, she wouldn't have it, but now he has no choice." Shade ran his hands through his hair. "He has never taught her how to do a damn thing to defend herself."

Fee crossed her arms over her chest and thought to herself, *Hit too close to home, did it?* Shade continued. "I need a female for this job with Rissa and they will need to be a day-walker. I need someone with excellent skills, a solid rep, someone who can outwit Rissa. And that's saying something. Her protector will not be able to stick out in social situations, she needs to blend into the background when necessary and not look out of place. So I am asking you, who the hell can I bring into this? I thought of you, Fee, but you aren't a day-walker, and Olivia is too inexperienced. I need someone with damn good experience with weapons, especially guns. She can't be toting a fucking sword in crowds around here."

Fee ran the list of needed skills through her head, trying to match them up with the other female warriors she knew. "So you need someone with style and class, but solid with a weapon, someone used to working closely with masters. Why are you specifically looking for a female? Just curious."

Shade laughed. "Well, I have a score to settle with Rissa, and she won't be expecting a female. You have someone in mind?"

Fee flipped her hair back. "There's only one female warrior I can think of that suits this job perfectly, and that's Jacqueline." She watched his face and waited for the dawning of recognition come back to him. Fee was pretty sure he hadn't seen her for a very long time nor would he have any idea where she was and what she was doing these days, but Fee did.

Shade looked back at her in confusion until the memory of Jacqueline surfaced. "You mean Jacks!"

Fee sat back in the chair. "Yes, Jacks. She's perfect for this job. She would fit in with the social elite, not a problem. She's independent, needs no backup and she can dress up like a damn movie star if need be. Bitch can talk her way out of anything, but she's an artist with any firearm. And she's day-walker."

"*Cazzo*! I haven't seen her since she left camp. That was forever ago. I completely lost track of her. I know she only came to train at Medici for a while. She is fucking perfect for this gig. Do you know where she is?"

"She's close, New England somewhere the last I heard. You know she's going to cost you. She only takes top dollar clientele, masters only, and only the most powerful. She wasn't at Medici long. If you remember, she was sent there by another master who wanted her trained in firearms. I've stayed in contact with her, as I do with all my sisters. If I'm not mistaken, Jacks may even know Master Alec. Isn't he from that area? Jacks is gorgeous, sleek, turns heads and you know as well as I do, it will take something extraordinary to deal with that blonde I saw tonight. She reeked of major diva attitude."

Shade threw back his head, laughing. "Oh, Jacks could show Rissa a lot of things. Damn Fee, Jacks would be perfect for this job. Can you contact her for me? Ask if she's interested. Alec has more fucking money than brains, so price is no obstacle. If she can meet me at the house early tomorrow night, I would make myself available. We weren't close, she stuck close to camp and had her nose to the grindstone the whole time, but she isn't a female you forget easily, and I can only imagine what she has become now."

Fee chuckled. "Oh, you have no idea what she's like now. But I'll give her a call. I can fill her in a little before she makes the trip, if she's available. But under one condition."

He shook his head. "There is always a condition with you. Name it, warrior."

"You tell your mate there's a female coming this time. No surprises for her!"

He growled, "For your damn information and short-lived memory, I would have told her the last time, but I didn't know. Fucking Marco played that card and I still have a score to settle with him on that. So, rest assured, she will be informed. She can attend this meeting if she so chooses. I am hiding nothing from her."

Standing up, she put her hands on her hips. "Great. I'm out of here then, I'll let you know what she says." Teleporting home to the staff quarters, Fee couldn't wait to give Jacks the details on this job. *Damn, I hope she'll take the job. It would be great to see my sister, it's been too damn long!* Realizing the place had emptied out, Shade slid into his leather jacket and prepared to teleport back home to *bel*.

Jacks! Imagine that.

* * *

75

She awoke slowly, Shade still asleep beside her. She heard the soft whir of the electronic blinds as they opened, signaling the sunset. He had been at the Dead House the last two nights after some rampage on the streets, and then last night, he said Rissa had been attacked. In addition to having Luca at her elbow every second he was away, he had also posted extra warriors to guard the perimeter of the house now. She thought about calling Rissa, she knew how she must be feeling. She must be feeling vulnerable just like Kate was. She still had flashes of that thing, that face. It sent shivers through her, and she snuggled in closer to Shade and felt him stir. "Lover, are you awake?"

Hearing her voice, he yawned and stretched. Wrapping her in his arms, their legs entangled and her crimson askew, he loved waking up with her like this.

"*Si, mi amore*, very awake now. How are you this evening? Talk to me. We didn't get much time together before the slumber took me."

She looked up at him through her tangled hair. "I thought it was over, all the stuff going on in D.C. I thought I'd have you home more, and now this, the attack on Rissa. It scares me."

Sliding his hand across her cheek, he kissed her gently, tucking a few strands of crimson behind her ear, wanting to see her eyes clearly. "*Bel*, listen to me. Everything is okay. Don't be scared, I am here and when I can't be, you have Luca. He will keep you safe. Hell, you can keep yourself safe if you have that crossbow around. Rissa was attacked by a rogue that fled from here. I saw him on the security videos I watched after the attack. He is dead now. Alec heard her cries and took him out. Fee was there in Alec's territory and responded to the attack. Then Alec arrived. Rissa is scared, I'm sure, but she'll get over it and now Alec wants me to get her a protector of sorts."

Kate nuzzled into his chest. "But that's good, right? She should have a protector. I was surprised when she said she didn't have one."

"Yes, it's a good thing. She's not going to like it, but I don't think Alec is giving her a choice. Kate, I want to spend more time with you, show you the life I want to share with you, and not be running all the time, taking care of business. I have decided to keep a full camp of warriors here, permanently. I'm thinking about doing so in California as well. I want to stay in this area, build a life here. We have made a great start, but there is so much I need to attend to. This incident with Cuerpo has shown me I need to guard Bel Rosso as I guard Castello, and perhaps, it will allow me to have more time at home. What do you think about that?"

"You know I leave those decisions to you. I love our home here, I love everything about it, so do whatever you have to do. If you bring more warriors, we'll need to add more quarters for them. I have them in the staff quarters now, and Theresa has had to sacrifice her own room. I'll work with Gi and Luca. I'm sure they'll know what we need in order to accommodate more warriors on a permanent basis. Do you have an idea of how many I should prepare for?"

He listened as she went straight into planning mode to take care of his warriors. She gave him so much and took whatever happened in stride. How the hell did he get this lucky? He would never deserve her, even with an eternity to try.

"You sure you don't mind? I want to get things started; eventually making it a full working camp just like in Florence, training new recruits, making an army and establishing my name here. I want Marcello in on this too, *mi amore*. I think I want him to oversee training here, be my Second-in-Command over the warriors. I think if we start out with about fifteen to twenty at first, then recruit from here in the States, it will grow. *Padre* built the original camp, but I made it what it is today, and I want that for our sons. I want them to have a strong legacy, one we built together."

"One thing we have is plenty of land. So, I will work on that. I'll let Marcello and Luca lead the project. Don't worry about it. I'll take care of the quarters for the warriors, and a training facility. You have enough to worry about. And if you want the facilities duplicated in California, I can manage that as well."

"Let's just do one at a time, get this one done, see how it functions. We will build here first. Figure out what works, what doesn't work or needs to be improved once we get moving and then we take on the West Coast and duplicate, *si*? I'm thinking Raven could handle California pretty damn well. He damn sure acts like he is from another coast."

Kate laughed. "Raven. Now I bet he has stories to tell. Lover, is that your phone?"

"*Cazzo*! Where is my damn phone?" Reaching beside the bed, he scrambled to get the phone out of his leathers' pocket.

"Fee, yeah, what's the deal?" Fee told him Jacks was up for a meeting, and she was willing to meet tonight.

"Great job, Fee! Go ahead and set it up and let me know the time."

Kate looked at him with concern. "Are you going to the Dead House again?"

"No, it was Fiamma. I have a female coming to the house for a meeting tonight. She is from Italy. She is a warrior and one Fee and I hope will take on the job of Rissa's protector. Can you handle that? You are more than welcome to come meet her, sit in on the meeting. You know Rissa, and you may be of some help convincing Jacks to take the job."

As soon as he mentioned he was bringing a female here, Kate's back stiffened. She felt her anger rising and she had to fight the automatic response. She reminded herself of her experience with Fee. Kate wondered if the day would ever come when her first response to any female around him wasn't one of jealousy and rage. She took a deep breath and calmed herself.

"I... yes. I would like to be at this meeting. Will Fee be there as well, or just Jacks?"

He had felt her temper rise and saw her struggling to gain control.

"*Bel,* relax and listen, please? Fee won't be there. This is a job interview. The protector's name is Jacks, actually Jacqueline, everyone calls her Jacks. I would like you to be with me. This is part of my world, and soon to be your world as well. Meet her before you decide if you like her or not. You hated Fee the moment she walked in, and now you are friends. Do this for me, *si*?"

Kate lowered her eyes because he read her like a book. She didn't want these feelings, she hated these feelings, but they came automatically, and he did nothing to deserve it. She knew it wasn't him. It was her own lack of self-esteem, her own fear that she wouldn't be enough. "I know, lover. I'll try not to pre-judge her."

Kissing her softly, he pulled her into his arms and snuggled into her neck. "*Mi amore,* I have never been with Jacks. She was at the camp a very long time ago. Her master sent her there to learn from Medici, but she works as a mercenary now. Fee suggested her to me after I asked if she knew anyone that would suit this position. I didn't even remember Jacks until Fee mentioned her. I know what you are thinking. I am yours, I want no other."

Kate let him enfold her, reassure her. She sighed in relief as he told her he hadn't been with Jacks, unlike Adriana and Sabine. She let the anger go and prepared to meet this new warrior. What a complicated world he lived in, and one she still struggled to navigate.

"Then let's meet her."

He whispered softly into her ear, "That's my *bel*. You make me proud. Now, let's get up out of this bed and begin our night."

76

Waking, Rissa was startled by the images in her head and she clutched her throat, frantically looking around, trying to orient herself. She was home, safe. *Where's Alec? Did he leave me alone?*

"Alec!" She sat straight up in bed and tried to feel him.**" Oh Alec, please, where are you?"**

Alec was on his way back upstairs when he felt her fear and heard her call to him. Entering the bedroom, he found her sitting upright in the bed. He sat beside her.

"What is it, my darling? Bad dream? I imagine you'll be plagued with them for a while. Very normal, but it'll pass with time." He stroked the side of her face. "Now lie down, you really need to rest. It's important for your healing."

As soon as he appeared her heartbeat slowed to normal. Bad dream, yes. It was just a bad dream. Lying back down, she grabbed his hand and clung to it. "Please don't leave me, Alec. Sit with me until I go back to sleep. Please?"

"I'm right here. Not going anywhere right now. You know I'll have to go into work eventually, though, so I've been talking to Shade. I think it best he assigns a warrior to you for a while. I don't want to hear any arguments, Rissa. The decision is made. Not a full-time protector. This won't be a permanent assignment like a protector and they won't live here, but they'll guard the house and follow at a discreet distance when you're out. It's a temporary precaution and I'm telling you now, I expect your cooperation."

"Yes, Alec, no arguments. I'll listen."

No arguments? Who the hell is this woman in my bed and what did they do with Rissa? Whoever she is, I don't expect it to last once she has her feet under her again. "I'm not kidding, Rissa. I'm not sure you realize the magnitude of this event. If Shade's warrior had not been there, I wouldn't have reached you in time. If this rogue had taken you out on sight, even Shade's warrior would have been no help." He leaned in until they were nose to nose to make his point. "You were this close, my darling. This close to your eternal sleep."

If keeping her scared kept her in line, then he would keep her scared for a while.

Her eyes widened at his implications. Her voice was shaking and barely audible. "I'll do what you ask, Alec."

"Quiet now. I want you to rest, and I'll lie here beside you. But what's this, Rissa?" He reached for the vials on the bedside table. "What are these vials? You had them clutched in your hand last night."

He picked up the vials from the bedside table and held them out to her.

Her brain clicked into gear as she sat up to offer an explanation. She quickly settled on a lie that would explain how she came to have them in her possession. Looking down, she wrung her hands. "The rogue, they fell from his jacket. I didn't know what they were, but I grabbed them from the floor. I was frightened but I thought they might be of use to you in identifying him." She turned her head and looked at him through her disheveled blonde hair with an innocent expression in her eyes.

Alec raised an eyebrow. "They were on the vamp that attacked you? Interesting. Maybe this is the potion they spoke of, the one that eliminates their scent. Good job, my darling. I'll have this sent to a lab to see if they can analyze it and figure out what's in it. This could be quite useful. Perhaps I could even use it as payment for some of Shade's services. This would be a mighty weapon in his arsenal, and maybe I wouldn't have to give him so much fucking property."

He tucked the vials in his pockets and gently pushed her back onto the bed. "And now, I believe I said lie down and rest." He stretched out beside her so she'd calm down and get some sleep.

She took his hand. She didn't want him to leave again. She was tired but she needed to feel him and couldn't fall asleep unless she felt him touching her. His presence calmed her, and it wasn't long before her eyes felt heavy and she drifted into a dark sleep.

77

Kate and Shade sat in the study going over some plans and rough sketches for the warriors' camp that would include barracks, a gym, a training center, a dedicated weapons bunker, and a large practice field. Since there were mortals who pulled onto the property to see the vineyards, the exterior design of the new buildings would mimic the Tuscan architecture of the house and be enclosed by a high stone wall. The plan would use roughly eight hundred acres of property, which was still much smaller than the warrior camp in Florence. Kate was excited to work on this project. She'd seen the camp in Florence briefly but didn't yet have the experience to know exactly what was needed. Shade would be involved in the planning but would leave Luca and Marcello to provide oversight. Shade was explaining how the facilities would be used when Gi announced that Jacqueline had arrived.

"Give me five minutes, Gi, then send her in." Looking at *bel*, he could already feel her bristling.

"Take a breath and relax. It's Jacks... warrior, assassin, mercenary, and spy. She just happens to be female."

Kate hated that her reaction was so visible, but she took a deep breath and mentally prepared to meet her. "I'm ready, lover."

"Good, *mi amore!*" Standing, he kissed her softly. "Business, remember?"

He could feel Jacks in the house. He turned as Gi announced her and she walked into his office. At first Shade didn't recognize her. It had been a long time since he'd last seen her and she had grown from a young girl into a woman.

"Welcome, Jacqueline. I am honored you have agreed to meet and discuss this assignment to see if you would be interested."

As she entered the room, Jacks took note of the mortal. Not typical of Shade, based on what Jacks knew to be his taste in women. Jacks had heard the rumors he had mated and she was curious about this female. She nodded to him.

"Master Medici. It's been a long time since we last met. You've done well, as have I."

Jacks was tall, and beautiful, as typical of vampire females. At five-foot-eleven, she almost stood eye to eye with him. Her long brown hair cascaded over her shoulders. Her dark eyes smoldered.

Kate eyed the newcomer and recognized immediately that Jacks had been born a vampire. Women who were born vampires were generally taller, but it was their presence that really set them apart. Kate knew that the turning would make her immortal and more powerful, but it wouldn't give her that extra something. For a moment, Kate wondered if she'd have to fight this insecurity for eternity. *Fuck it, Kate. Quit questioning yourself! He picked you!*

Kate stood to meet her, stepping around the desk with her hand extended. "Hello, my name is Kate. Welcome to our home."

As she introduced herself, Jacks saw she was small and determined, but her eyes gave away her momentary insecurity. Kate was definitely making sure Jacks knew Shade belonged to her. Whoever held the Medici heart *should* feel possessive. Taking her hand, Jacks nodded and shook it with one firm shake, noticing that Kate never broke eye contact with her. Shade had picked a feisty one.

Shade gestured toward a chair. "Please, Jacqueline, have a seat."

Kate watched as Jacks sat down, crossing long leather-clad legs which ended in four-inch heeled boots. She wasn't overtly coming on to Shade, but her very presence oozed sexuality and Kate's sense of inferiority made her mistrust the warrior. She'd try to keep an open mind, but she'd keep an eye on this one.

Shade took a seat across from her and Kate sat down next to him, as Shade addressed her. "I know that Fee briefed you on the situation, but I wished to give you more details before going into this meeting with the master who wishes to hire you. Excuse my manners, can I offer you a drink?"

Jacks held up her hand to Shade. "Thank you for the offer, but no. A warrior's body is her temple, and she must treat it as such."

Kate laughed out loud. "A warrior's body is a temple? Someone forgot to tell that to that pack of wild things living in the staff quarters who guzzle down Midnight after every shift."

Jacks chuckled, amused by her observation and looked at Shade.

"I learned my weapons skills at the Medici camp, but I've trained with others as well who teach purity of body to maintain strength. I don't smoke, or drink, and feed as often as possible from master's who will allow it. Their blood gives me power beyond that of the regular warrior.

I never forget that I'm a female in a world dominated by males, and I need every edge I can get. Above all, you taught me to never forget there's always a warrior out there better than me, ready to take me out." Smiling at him. "I haven't forgotten my lessons."

Shade nodded. She'd made a name for herself in the assassins' world. He knew she learned something from him and he was proud to have been part of her training. She had some Medici skills and that alone could take her far.

"I see that. And I'm proud of you, Jacks. Let's get down to business, shall we? Master Canton lives in D.C. The bastard is eccentric and into mortal politics. He is a tough one but doesn't get his hands dirty. He has some old-fashioned views about female warriors, so you'll need to be on your toes. His mate Larissa was attacked by a rogue. She is one high profile bitch. She was spooked by the attack, and is still unsettled. Master Canton is looking for a temporary protector, a short-term contract, not a lifetime assignment. Rissa is a handful... you can't tie her down. I don't know exactly what he has in mind. He's down with the D.C. goons most of the time, he has no time to watch her and keep her ass in line. And let me tell you, she will test you to the limits."

Jacks made mental notes of the information he shared. The real reason she was here was that the job was for Master Canton. She didn't usually take on protector jobs, but she'd waited a long time to even the score with Alec and she was well aware of his old-fashioned views.

"Master Canton, yes, I know of his mate, they call her Rissa, the Darling of G-town. I understand he has high ambitions in the mortal arena. I've heard they're about to announce their engagement, so she'll require high-profile coverage. This is a dangerous place. Master Maximus, Master Canton and now the Medici, that's a lot of big egos in a small space. This will cost you, Shade, I do nothing cheap and my skills are worth a pretty price. And if you're not willing to pay, then someone else will."

Shade laughed. "I have no intention of paying one dime in this deal. This is Alec's gig. Name your price to him. Make him pay, warrior!"

Jacks had a wicked grin on her face, and thought, *Don't worry, he will pay!* "Good to know. I might have cut you a deal on the price since I trained with the Medici, but for Master Canton, I may raise my price. I ask only one thing of you—don't tell him who you're sending. I'd like for my presence to catch him off-guard. It gives me an edge." Jacks gave

Kate a smile as she asked, "So, may I ask you, my lady, who is your protector?"

Kate had watched the exchange between Shade and Jacks and was surprised that Jacks came off somewhat cold and calculating. She looked up quickly when Jacks addressed her. "My protector? My protector is Luca."

Jacks' face reflected her surprise. "Luca. Little Luca?" She glanced at Shade. "Impressive."

Shade nodded to Jacks. "Yes, it is the same Luca you are thinking of. You would not recognize him. Like you, he has matured into a fierce warrior. There is no one who can top him, only the best for my *bel*." Taking Kate's hand, he brought it to his lips and kissed it gently before looking back at Jacks. "So, I make one call, you meet with Alec. Are you in?"

Jacks had the impression Shade treated his mate more as an equal than a subordinate; very unusual for an old-world European master. She wondered if Kate knew that when the rumor of his mating made the rounds, many females around the world wished her dead. He was the catch of the vampire realm. "Make the call."

Standing, Jacks walked to Shade and kissed him on each cheek, then turning to Kate, she took both of her hands in hers.

"I'm more than honored to have met you. Please give my regards to Luca, although, he may not recall me." Turning again to Shade, she smiled at him. "It's good to see you again. I'll meet with Master Canton and see what his wishes are and if he's willing to pay my price. I don't usually accept contracts for protector positions, but this could be interesting, to say the least. She was Master Maximus' lover before Alec stole her away from him." Chuckling, she shook her head. "Masters and their ladies, always an interesting adventure."

Kate heard the reference to someone named Master Maximus. Could that be Max? That guy Rissa chased when they were in college together? She'd have to ask Shade about that.

She spoke to Jacks as she prepared to leave. "Jacqueline, I hope you'll join us here again sometime if you decide to take this job. You're always welcome here."

Shade added, "Yes, if you need anything, you know where I am. I'll call Alec and you can head on over there. Any problems, I'll let you know."

Jacks bowed her head. "Thank you both for your gracious hospitality. I've enjoyed seeing you again, Shade, and meeting you, my lady. I'm sure we'll see each other again soon."

Gi appeared at the door to escort Jacks out and Shade took Kate into his arms. As soon as Kate was sure she was gone, she turned to him. "Who is Maximus?"

He laughed at her. "Oh, so for once you are not going to ask me a million questions about the female? Maximus is the Master of Virginia. And yes, we live in his territory. He is a warrior and owns property all over the world. I took this property over from Alec as part of the deal to come here and help him, with no intention of living here permanently. But then I met you, and now I am not budging. So, long story for another time, but I need to get a territory agreement from Maximus. As for Rissa, that was a long time ago. She had a thing with Max, but I don't think it was serious. I don't pay much attention to those things unless a master gets mated, then you look a bit deeper. A mate may bring territory with her, increasing her master's power. There were some rumors, at the time, that Alec stole her from Max, but I don't recall the details. I had much better things to do than worry about masters and their women. Not long after, Rissa became Alec's mate. Since she had been mortal that basically meant she was not a threat in the vampire world. She doesn't bring him more power. Don't take that in a bad way, I only mean that masters selecting mortals as mates is rare. Mates for a master can extend their territory and increase the size of their coven and their power."

She looked up at him as he towered over her. "And yet, you selected me?"

"*Si, mi amore*. I have spent my life gaining power and territory. I assumed my mate would be immortal, the daughter of a master, probably royalty, and bring with them their own dowry of sorts in the form of more power and territory. It was what was expected of me. But until you, I never found anyone who spoke to my heart. I chose my mate for love, not power."

Kate pondered his words. What did she bring to the table as his mate? She knew her vulnerability was part of his attraction to her, his need to protect her and take care of her. "Okay, so you own this land? But it's in the middle of another master's territory?"

"*Si.*"

"And Rissa, clearly, I don't know her as well as I thought, but Rissa was with this Maximus guy before Alec? She dated a guy in college called

Max. We never saw him much, but I never imagined he was a vampire. But then again, I never imagined Alec was, either. But now, you work for Alec, and we live in the middle of Max's territory?"

Shade sat down, pulling her down next to him. "*Mi amore*, come, we need to talk."

"Lover, I know there's much I don't understand about your world, but if you don't mind me saying so, it sounds like we're in the middle of a hornets' nest here."

Not wanting to scare her more, he had to tell her how it was, no more secrets. She needed to know his world.

"*Bel*, I don't like telling you these things. You've just had a bad experience. I don't want to frighten you more, but I made a promise to keep you safe and protected and that means I need to explain more to you about what is going on around you. I have every intention of keeping this property. I will try to negotiate with Max and reach some sort of agreement, as Alec did. But if the negotiations fail, I will fight. That is why I need this warrior camp up quickly. Maximus is also a warrior, and a good one. If I have to fight him for this, it will be master against master, and I will win. I always win. I want this for our sons and daughters. This is for us, *bel*, not just me. I do this for us, our *bambinos*, for Medici. Trust me when I tell you I win what I want."

She looked at him. "If you don't fight him... then this, all of this, our home, the vineyards, the farm, it's all at risk, isn't it?"

"*Si*, very much so. The rules here in the States are different from Europe. In Europe, we don't give up territory in deals. We fought too hard to get it, and we don't give it away. But here, the masters seem to deal out bits and pieces to gain something they want. I used that as a bargaining chip with Alec so I had a place to base the warriors, a place for me to stay, and the vineyards. But I never saw you coming, *mi amore*, and when I did, it changed everything."

She had always known that accepting a life with him meant accepting the warriors and his lifestyle. One that involved more violence than she wanted to acknowledge. Her own life had been threatened twice, and he came home covered in blood more nights than she could count. It was the price she paid to have him in her life.

"Then just promise me, lover, that you position yourself to win every battle. You know I'll stand beside you."

Shade leaned his forehead against hers. "I always position myself to win. I haven't made my legacy of creating warriors that rival any in the world by not knowing such. But if you don't stand beside me, I have no reason to fight, for I do this for you, for the *bambinos* that will grow inside you, to give them wealth and stability in my world. So, I suggest we make those plans to travel to Florence. I have made up my mind. I will turn you within the month. Once I get things organized here, delve out responsibilities, we will go. We'll stay for a short while. As my queen, you need to meet my people and see where you reign. I will also be taking Theresa, Gi, and Luca with us. We will arrange a temporary Lady in Waiting there at Castello for you. I want Theresa to have some time for her and Marco."

His plans to turn her both excited and scared her, but it was the path she must follow to stay with him. "I'm ready whenever you are, and I'll find a way to bring value to your coven."

He kissed her deeply, letting his tongue play with hers, sucking her lip and letting his hands play along her back, and in the crimson fire he adored. "Then I suggest you get your sweet ass cracking on those details. I need to call Alec and check on the repair work in the stables. I want that to be done before we head to Florence. You will inform Theresa for me? I think she will like hearing it from you."

Kate smiled at him. "Theresa will be glad to go to Florence and see Marco and to have her own room back once the warrior camp is built, so that's news I'll be happy to deliver."

Shade buried his nose in her hair. "Do you have any idea," he said, letting his hand slide along her cheek, "any idea at all how much I love you, *mi amore*?"

She angled his chin so she could look into those ice-blue eyes rimmed with long black lashes and ran her hand through his dark locks. "As a matter of fact, I do."

"Do you, *mi amore*? I swear to you now, I will love you this much every second of my life. I promise you a beautiful life. We will rise as Medici, live happily, and see our own children bring forth their own into this world, then guide them with love and respect. You claimed me hard and swift. It knocked this warrior off his feet but made him rise to conquer all that he could for you... and it is as it shall be."

78

Luca paced in his room as he called Shannon to let her know he was okay and to see if he was still welcome after his sudden exit. She was full of questions, and he asked if he could explain everything to her in person. She responded, "Of course," and in moments, he teleported to her condo in Alexandria. Still holding her phone, she was startled by his sudden appearance, but then she laughed.

"I'm sorry, *mia belleza* for our interrupted date, but it's as I told you... my time is not my own."

Shannon looked at him. "What happened? Can you tell me what happened?"

"It's complicated and has to do with the job Shade has taken with a master in the D.C. area."

"There is a master vampire in D.C.? Seriously? Who is it?"

Realizing he'd already said more than he should, he needed to get her off this topic. Master Alec demanded anonymity. "No one you would know, and vampires prefer to remain anonymous to the mortal community, so please, don't ask me questions I can't answer."

"No, I understand that. But what happened at home that you were called away? Can you talk about that?"

"I'm sure Kate will tell you everything, so yes, I can talk about that. There was an ambush on the house. Five rogue vampires attacked to draw Shade outside to fight, leaving Kate alone in the house. That's when Shade called to me to return. That's my job, as I explained to you. Protecting her. Once I was with Kate, another fifteen rogues teleported in and had Shade surrounded. I made the choice to leave Kate's side and join Shade in the fight. It was a judgment call on my behalf because my orders from Shade were not to leave her side. Unbeknownst to us at the time, the ambush was all a ruse to draw us out so Kate would be isolated. She was the target all along. A lone assassin climbed the outside wall to their bedroom and climbed over the balcony, entering through the bedroom window. Fortunately for all of us, Kate was ready and waiting for him and killed him with a single shot to the heart with a crossbow."

Shannon stood looking at him while the story sank in. "Okay, Luca, that will go in my diary as the most original excuse ever for why a guy ended a date suddenly. Now what really happened?"

Luca shook his head as he looked at the floor, understanding how preposterous this must sound to her, and yet, how common it was in his world. He raised his head and looked at her.

"That's what happened. We talked the first night we were together. I told you what I could in a short period of time, but Shannon, we live in very different worlds. This is why Kate has a protector. She's mated to a master, and a master will always be a target, their children will be targets. The masters battle each other for power, for territory. Shade is both master and warrior. So, I'll ask you again, can you live with this? I told you the first night we were together, I would commit my heart to you, but my loyalty to Shade is unbreakable. What he commands of me, I'll always deliver. I told you my time wasn't my own. And now you've seen that firsthand. So, tell me now, I beg you. Are you in? Or are you out? If this isn't something you can live with, then please tell me now, because I'm in love with you, and I fall more in love with you every day. If this lifestyle is not something you can accommodate, then let's end this now before my love for you grows even greater, and the thought of losing you crushes me."

Shannon's head was spinning with the realization that his story was true. Kate had given her some information, and he'd told her more, but it was a lot to take in. "First of all, and most importantly, I'm in. But be patient with me, okay, because I feel like I just stepped into an episode of *Game of Thrones*. So, this will take some adjusting."

Luca smiled at her. "Patience is something I have plenty of, *mia belleza*. But game of thrones? I'm not familiar with this game."

Shannon laughed. "It's not a game, Luca, it's a TV show."

"Ah, like Buffy."

"What?"

"Never mind, the important thing is, we both want to continue in this relationship, and I believe we were about to begin our second date when I was called away, yes?"

"As a matter of fact, we *were* about to begin our second date before you were so rudely called away." She began to unbutton her blouse.

His eyes followed her hands as she slowly unbuttoned her top, teasing him. She opened one button, pulled at her blouse, exposing the top of her breast, and then opened another, and another. He felt his palms grow moist as his mouth went dry. "Was there, uh, someplace you had in mind that you wanted to go?"

Shannon maintained eye contact with him, although his eyes flicked from her eyes to following the actions of her hands. She unbuttoned the last button and slipped the blouse from her shoulders, letting it drop to the floor.

"Oh, I had someplace in mind, all right, and given that Shade might zap you out of here at any moment, let's just skip over all that 'dinner and a movie part' and get right to what we both want in the first place." She turned her back to him and walked to her bedroom.

Luca stood mesmerized as he watched the sway of her hips as she walked away from him and listened to her clear invitation to follow. "I like the way you think, Shannon O'Connor."

She tossed her hair and looked over her shoulder at him as he followed her to the bed. "I knew you would, Luca... I knew you would."

79

Before leaving for the meeting with Alec, Jacks changed clothes, choosing a fitted dress instead of pants and a leather jacket. It had been a long time since she and Alec had seen each other. He was the only reason she was here. *Your head will turn this time, Master Alec, and you will sit up and beg. Jacks is back in your life, and you need me this time.*

Driving to his home, she saw it was a very classic Federal style house, in an upscale neighborhood, nestled among the mortals. Alec always hated certain aspects of his immortality, so she wasn't surprised to find him here. But she knew his sexual appetites were far from anything his mortal neighbors would call vanilla.

Alec heard the knock at the door and heard Santos as he answered and escorted her to his study, informing her she was expected. Jacks chuckled to herself knowing he'd be expecting a male warrior.

She walked in gracefully and waited to see the expression on Alec's face.

Alec stood up to greet the warrior. *Fuck! He sent a woman? Wait, I know her. It's been a few years, but I... Fuck! It's Jacks! Well, this could get interesting real fast.*

He took her in, head to toe and back again, locking eyes with her and giving her a slow smile. He walked toward her, extending his hand. "Jacks... Have to say, you were the last person I was expecting tonight, but not an unpleasant surprise. Please, sit down. Can I pour you a drink?"

Taking his outstretched hand, Jacks shook it firmly. "Good to see you, Master Canton, you've come a long way since last we met. Unfortunately, unpleasant circumstances have brought us back together, it seems." Sitting down, she crossed her legs slowly, letting her long elegant legs and strong smooth calves take his attention for a moment. She declined his offer of a drink. "Nothing for me. My body is my temple, but thank you for the offer."

Alec chuckled. "Your body is your temple, yes, as I recall, it was quite a temple, and appears to be even more so." He poured himself a glass of Midnight and sat down across from her. He took a cigarette from the box and lit it, inhaled deeply then dropped his head back to exhale before locking eyes with her again. "So, I guess that means no to an offer of a cigarette. Anything else? Any other vices you're swearing off I need to know about?"

She watched as he smoked the cigarette, already seducing her with his eyes. Long ago, she'd been attracted to him and tried to snare him, but his sights were set on bigger things and he rejected her. Now she was powerful in her own right.

"Alec, I didn't come here to have a reunion, but to talk business. As for my vices, there were more than you could imagine, but I'm past all of the old vices. They bore me now."

He chuckled at her response. "Oh don't underestimate the power of my imagination, Jacks. I'm pretty sure I could think of a few you haven't tried. But yes, we're here to discuss business. As Shade explained to you, Rissa was attacked. We've had some conflict in the district, some master named Angel no one's even heard of. He's dead now, but, apparently, there're still some of his rogues on the street. At any rate, they went after Rissa. One of Shade's warriors responded, some red-head in red leather, she bought me enough time to get to Rissa and take out the rogue. Rissa's pretty traumatized. This is the first time she's been attacked. As Shade may have explained, I live in the mortal world, and my position makes me high profile to the press, which makes Rissa high profile to the press. Add to that the fact we plan to marry soon, and she'll be hounded. That'll make her an easy target for some rogue hiding in a throng of reporters and paparazzi. She needs protection, Jacks. She has her own business, she's out a lot. I'm at work, so she's often alone."

Alec swallowed down more Midnight as his eyes traveled over her bare legs, the short skirt, and the form-fitting dress that left little to the imagination and he made a split-second decision.

"You'll need to move in here. You'll have your own room, of course, own bath. Our house staff will be at your disposal, whatever you need. I'm not sure how long this assignment will last, but at least through the wedding, which should be in six months."

Uncrossing her legs, she stared at him, taking in his conditions. It sounded like an easy enough assignment. "So, you want around the clock protection. That's more than Shade described. I don't normally take live-in positions, but I'll adjust my schedule to accommodate you. It will, of course, cost you. I'm a mercenary, assassin, warrior to the masters but I can adapt to your mortal lifestyle and hers as well. I'm quite used to working in professional environments. I'll need her to heed my commands, for her own safety, and I'll have it no other way. She must take my commands seriously. I'll give her as much freedom as is safe and practical, but she must understand her lifestyle in the public is changing. Is that agreeable to you, Alec?"

He downed the remnants of the Midnight and set the glass on the table. "Oh, it's more than okay with me, Jacks. Now, Rissa, that'll be another story. Currently, she'll be compliant because, as I said, she's feeling vulnerable. But once she gets her feet under her again, I'm afraid you'll have a challenge on your hands. Rissa is not good at following orders, so you'll have to use a strong hand. Don't worry, I'll talk to her. I'll make myself clear as to what I expect, but I'm a realist when it comes to Rissa. Her cooperation will only extend so far. So, let's just say, it's in your best interest to keep her scared."

She chuckled and cocked her eyebrow. "Oh, don't worry. I always use a firm hand. I take no bitching from anyone, Alec.

When would you like for this assignment to begin?" Leaning forward she placed her hand on his knee. "This will cost you dearly, Alec, this isn't normally a case I'd consider."

He was acutely aware of her hand on his knee, and he was sure it was a very measured and intentional move on her part. "As to the when, Jacks, the answer is as soon as possible. Just let me know when you can move in. And money is no object, but I do expect to get my money's worth." He stared hard into her eyes.

She held his gaze with a look that let him know, if he chose to play, he would pay.

Alec smiled back at her. "Now, what do you say I bring Rissa down to meet you?"

She nodded. "Please, let us meet."

He stood and walked out of the room, going to the bottom of the stairs and calling up to her. "Rissa! Come downstairs, my darling. Your protector is here. You need to meet."

* * *

Rissa had barely left their bedroom since the rogue attack. She heard when their visitor arrived and sat up in their bed, brushing out her hair and trying to look presentable. She knew he'd be returning to work soon, and she wasn't sure she could stand being alone. Hearing his call, she walked to the top of the stairs, nodded to Alec and walked down slowly.

He watched as she came down the stairs a little tentatively, still in her pajamas, no make-up and he took her hand. "Come with me to the study, darling, and meet Jacks." He led her into the study where Jacks stood to meet her.

Rissa gripped his hand hard. Jacks stood on black stilettos, her designer dress elegantly styled to show every damn well-toned muscle. Her breasts were plump and bulged over the top of the dress. She was beautiful. She had exotic eyes with long lashes, defined cheekbones and a black mane that just screamed for a man to grip it and take what he wanted. Her lips were plump, full, and bee-stung in a natural pout, and Rissa's heart sank. He chose Jacks not for her but for himself. She locked eyes with Jacks and didn't budge. Who the hell did she think she was? This was a bitch that meant business, and he chose this for her? She wanted to run screaming at her, rip every hair from her head. Rissa locked eyes with her, immortal to immortal, this was a blatant challenge of wills! Then Rissa slowly closed her eyes, as her fear trumped her jealousy. *I must listen to Alec, I need her more than I could imagine.*

Alec watched with curiosity as the two she-cats sized each other up and was surprised to see Rissa capitulate so easily. "Rissa, this is Jacks, it's short for Jacqueline, but I think she prefers Jacks as I recall. I asked Shade to send me the best, and he selected Jacks for you. I think she'll be the perfect choice."

Rissa shook her hand. "I'm Larissa Benneteau. Welcome, and thank you for your service. I'm sure if Alec has chosen you, you're more than capable."

"Now sit down, darling." He led her to the couch where they sat together across from Jacks. "We need to go over the ground rules."

Jacks took her measure. She was slightly shorter than her, although tall for a mortal female, a good body, but clearly pampered. Jacks couldn't imagine that well-manicured hand had ever touched anything more deadly than a dinner knife.

Alec turned to Rissa, who was unusually quiet and moved to take advantage of her current state of cooperation. "I've decided since I'm away so much, it'll be best if Jacks lives in. I'll have Santos get one of the guest bedrooms ready for her. That way, you'll have twenty-four-seven protection, my darling, as you deserve. Now let me make this clear, Rissa, and this isn't open for discussion. When you leave this house for any reason, Jacks must accompany you. If someone comes to the door, Jacks and Santos will handle it. And whatever instructions Jacks gives you, you'll follow. Do you understand?"

"Yes, Alec, whatever you say."

He leaned in close to her, his lips to her ear and whispered, "That's my good baby girl."

Alec turned to Jacks. "Do you have anything you want to add before we finalize our business transaction."

Jacks looked at Alec and slowly crossed her legs and leaned back in the chair, gliding her arms along the armchair.

"I do believe you've covered everything, Alec. I'll plan to move in tomorrow for however long you wish Rissa to be protected."

"Perfect. Why don't you just run back upstairs, darling? I'm going to wrap up the financial details with Jacks, and there's no need for you to trouble yourself over that."

Rissa stood and let her hand slide over his arm and walked out of the room as elegantly as if she were wearing a ball gown and not pajamas, dismissing Jacks just as he dismissed her.

As Rissa left the room, he turned to Jacks. "So, tomorrow is perfect. And your fee? You didn't say."

Standing, she walked around the room, her hand gliding slowly across the pieces of furniture. "She is scared of her own shadow, Alec. She'll make easy prey since she's so vulnerable. As I previously stated, I'm not usually a live-in, so that'll take away my freedom." Turning slowly, she stood tall, squared her shoulders. "One million for the six-month period. If it goes longer, the fee will be renegotiated. I do have one condition."

He raised an eyebrow. "A condition? Now, why am I not surprised?" He chuckled at her. "I'll meet your price, Jacks, but don't expect Rissa to remain that timid. She'll get past this and when she does, you'll have your hands full. But what's your condition?"

She moved fast, leaning over the chair where he sat, her hands on the armchair, and went nose to nose with him. "I get the full amount whether I'm here two months or six. Half upfront, the balance when the job ends. Any kills," she hissed softly, "go on my record, not yours, whether they are master or rogue. Deal?"

"That's it? Those are easy conditions to meet, vixen warrior. You forgot to ask if *I* have any conditions." He reached out and brushed her hair back from her face.

She grabbed his wrist and squeezed. "Careful, Alec, you might excite me and then who knows what might happen. You have already made your conditions quite clear." Leaning in, she felt her heart race. She loved a challenge and keeping one step ahead of him would be the race of her life, one she had waited for a long time. She leaned her full plump red lips against his and spoke, "Seal the deal, master."

He nipped at her full pouting lower lip, drawing it into his mouth, before kissing her, sliding his tongue deep into her throat. "Sealed with a kiss, vixen. If you need more than a kiss to seal this deal, then I'll need to take you elsewhere for the evening... you were quite the screamer, as I recall."

Throwing back her head and laughing loud, she made sure the princess heard the laughter upstairs. "Oh, I no longer scream, I just howl like the wild female beast I've become. I'll arrive at 8:00 a.m., have my money, one-hundred-dollar bills, crisp and new."

Walking to the door, she turned and lay her hand on her hip. "Don't worry, I'll take care of your precious darling, Alec. Oh, and another thing, I belong to no master."

Alec smirked, already enjoying the game. "I'll have your money ready, and you don't need to belong to me, Jacks, to enjoy me. I come with no strings attached. See you tomorrow."

She strutted out his study door and saw the house ape open the front door for her. *He always did prefer some good ass over anything else, and mine could easily accommodate him better than the simpering little blonde afraid of her own shadow and too weak to even defend her right to stand next to him.*

Alec poured himself another Midnight. *Damn, Shade what a perfect choice. This warrior will be hell on wheels and keep me entertained while Rissa gets back on her feet. Don't tell me it's not a fucking harem. Maybe your mate buys that bullshit, but I know better.* He grabbed his cell phone off the desk and hit speed dial for Shade. "Brother, I'm just calling to express my sincere gratitude."

Shade was in the stables with Kate when he heard his cell phone. He grabbed it out of his jeans pocket and heard Alec's voice. "No problem, brother, she rip your bank account good?"

"What? Oh yeah, the money's no problem. Jacks, she's prime ass, brother. Did you know we had some history?"

Shade held out his phone and looked at it, then raised his eyes to Kate as she turned and smiled at him. Shade grinned back then turned his back to her and walked away, trying to put a little distance between them so she wouldn't hear the call.

"What the fuck? You and Jacks? No fucking way in hell! "

Alec chuckled. "Oh, it was years ago, but I remember her well. I assumed that was why you picked her. We had a thing, she chased me for a while, but she wasn't in my league, so I left her behind. Looks like she filled out nicely, though."

Shade shook his head, "Alec, I picked her because she is among the best there is. She is a warrior. She's not one of my warriors, but my referral, so keep your sick ass sexual preferences and my name out of it!"

Alec laughed at him. "Shade, you're so fucking old school. Let's just say I owe you one, and I plan to get my money's worth. I'm beginning to see why you're so taken with those female warriors, brother. All those females living right under your roof? Like I said, you have your own harem."

"If I wasn't so damn busy building a life with my mate, I would come over there and give you a fucking piece of my mind. I don't give a rat's fucking ass what deal you made with Jacks, no interest. Go tend to your own fucking mate, will you! Good fucking luck!" Hanging up, he wondered when the fuck he would ever outlive this damn reputation he had.

Alec laughed as he ended the call, *Ah Shade, I think thee doth protest too much, my brother.*

80

Alec wondered how Rissa had done on this her first full day with him gone. Jacks had arrived this morning and moved her things into the guest room Santos had readied for her. Two women under his roof was not a situation Rissa would normally accept, but hell, if Shade could pull it off, then surely, he was up for the challenge. Santos greeted him as he walked in and informed him the women were each in their own rooms. Tossing his suit jacket to Santos, he took the stairs two at a time and headed toward the guest bedroom. The door wasn't shut so he tapped lightly to announce his presence.

"I hope you've found everything to your liking?"

Jacks heard a light tap at her door and looked up to see Alec. "This works fine for me. I have what I need to do the job. Thank you for asking."

Alec stepped into the room. "I want you to feel at home here, Jacks. You are, by no means, confined to this room. Santos will be happy to show you where everything is. I'm frequently gone during the day, but I'm home most evenings. I spend a lot of time in the study, but feel free to join me. I'd appreciate the company. Once Rissa is herself again, she'll work during the day. She has an office here in the house, but she's frequently out with clients. A lot of her events are staged in the evenings, and if she isn't working, she's at the gym. So, you can see... I'm often alone in the evenings."

Jacks almost laughed out loud at his blatant offer. "Really, Alec, in case you've forgotten, I'm her protector, not yours, so if she's out, I'll be as well. Every step she takes, I'll be there, that *is* what you're paying me for or have I got that wrong?"

Looking up at him, she stood with her thumbs through the belt loops in her low-rise jeans, letting him get a look at her exposed abdomen below her crop top. Walking to the window, she stared out at the rain. "For someone whose mate is too terrified to leave her room, you don't seem too interested in how her day went."

Alec followed her to the window, standing close behind her, placing his arms on either side of the windowsill, capturing her inside his arms as he looked over her shoulder at the rain, his lips close to her ear.

"I know you're here, Jacks, so why would I have any worries? I knew you'd have everything well in hand. And I know, all too well, what I'm paying for. I expect you to shadow Rissa. I'm just trying to give you a sense of our home, what our patterns are... In case you need to find me to talk. Or you need company. Don't you ever need company, Jacks?"

Ah, the old, I'm informing you of our patterns of living excuse. She hid her wicked smile. Still, his closeness made her a bit flustered, her heart rate accelerated, and she calmed it with ease. His scent was intoxicating and would spin most immortal females off their feet. Turning her head slowly, her lips mere inches from his ruggedly handsome face, she lowered her voice. "Company is something I never experience a lack of."

Her words rejected him, but her tone didn't. She teased and taunted, and he liked her games. His cock responded to her nearness, and he stepped closer, pressing his rod of steel against her shapely ass.

Her hands moved quickly, and she removed the dagger from her jeans pocket and held it up in front of her face. "Do you remember... the taste of another? Does it call to you sometimes? Or does the taste of your mate inhibit that desire for the intoxicating rush to have my blood again?"

Licking her lips, she slid her tongue along the edge of the sharpened dagger as her blood trickled slowly down the blade, as she licked the blood from her lips. "Blood is a powerful and intoxicating tool, don't you agree?"

"Do I remember? Of course I remember the taste of you, Jacks." He nuzzled his face into her neck, pushing aside that thick mane of hair and licked her neck. The smell of her blood made him insane with desire. He grabbed her hips and squeezed them hard, pulling her against him where he ground his cock into her. "A thousand years couldn't erase that taste from my memory."

He breathed his hot breath against her neck and nipped her skin just enough to draw her blood, licking it away with a flick of his tongue. She was like fire in his blood.

His touch was as she remembered, but softer. His hands were soft from never lifting anything heavier than Rissa's ass. He liked his sex rough, he liked to be the dominant, but she no longer played that game.

"Careful, Alec, your mate lies across the hall, and she can smell blood quite easily. Perhaps she doesn't care about you taking my blood? Don't you love her? Or is the thought of my red lips wrapped tightly around your cock creating a distraction from the main purpose of my being here?"

She reached up, gripping his hair hard and yanking his head back, as she turned to face him. Lowering her head to his protruding Adam's apple, she nipped it hard while holding the knife to the side of his throat. "Master Canton, letting your guard down, dangerous thing with a warrior in your home. But then again," she breathed, licking at the wound she created, "the call of your blood is an enticing one."

He was aroused by her aggressiveness. "Oh, I love Rissa, make no mistake. But I don't subscribe to those archaic rules of fidelity, vixen. I'm not offering you an eternity, but I'm going to fuck your brains out. Now, go ahead, use that blade, or your teeth, whatever pleasures you and take my blood."

He scooped her up in his arms and carried her to bed, dropping her down hard on the mattress.

She let him manhandle her. She could fight him, but that's exactly what he wanted. As soon as her back hit the mattress, she rolled off the bed, landing on the opposite side from him.

"You want it, earn it. But I have one question." Letting her fangs punch out, she slid her tongue over them. "Do you remember what it's like to fuck a warrior?"

His beast emerged, and he was crouched on the bed. He ripped his shirt and pants from his body as he growled at her. "You want to play cat and mouse, little vixen? We can play that game. But rest assured, I'm the cat and you're the mouse. And yes, I most assuredly do remember what it's like to fuck a warrior. Do you remember what it's like to fuck a master?"

She wanted his beast out and raring to go long before she began to play. She pulled the crop top over her head, and stepped out of her jeans, and purred like a cat. "I remember all too well. This body was made for a master to pleasure and feed."

Standing naked before him, she crawled back onto the bed. She ran her hands down his shoulders, and sank her fangs deep into his neck and drew deep. They both felt that first flash of memory of their shared past pleasures, and her body felt the power of a master's blood in her veins.

His beast roared as he threw his head back and the windows rattled with the sound. He grabbed her shoulders and flipped her onto her back. He crawled over her, crouched on all fours, licking her face, her neck. He felt her lift her legs and lock them around his hips, her strength was crushing. He lowered his mouth to hers and pushed his tongue deep into her throat. Reaching beneath her, he lifted her hips to him, sliding his cock along her wet, hot clit and feeling her arch her back to receive him. He growled into her mouth as he slid his cock deep inside her and listened to her moan in return.

Jacks reveled in her conquest. That weak little mate of his couldn't come close to what she'd give a true master like Alec. She could no longer hold back the intensity of the long-awaited need to feel him inside her again, but this time, she took back, and she clenched her muscles hard and heard him gasp as she squeezed his huge cock like a vice grip, pulsing the muscles of her sex, gripping and releasing. She grabbed handfuls of his hair on both sides of his face and yanked his head back, licking his fangs, sucking one into her mouth.

Alec moaned deep in his chest. His beast roared as his eyes glowed red and he gripped her hips with both hands, slamming his cock into her. The headboard slammed against the wall as the plaster cracked, and he pounded her harder, thrusting with all his strength, holding back nothing. The wood of the headboard began to splinter as it slammed against the wall with each thrust. She gripped him even harder with those thighs, pulling him deeper inside her as he felt her hips respond, thrusting up to meet him. He watched as she dropped her head back, mouth open and fangs bared, as he felt his cock throbbing for release. "Cum with me, vixen."

Jacks knew he was close and she'd pushed him to the edge, and she loved it. Feeling her body rejoice in the thickness of his cock and how deep he pushed into her, he brought her to the edge and he wanted release. *One more little thing, Alec...just one more.* Her fangs were aching, but she controlled her need and snapped her head up, glaring deep into his eyes. Turning her head to the side, exposing her neck, she invited him to feed. "Feed and cum together! Take it, Alec..."

Slamming her hips upward hard, she clenched his cock as hard as she could, locking it in a grip she knew he'd never felt before. "Take me!"

His beast growled at her as she challenged him, but he sank his teeth deep into her neck, and drew deep from her, swallowing mouthfuls of her, as he felt her do the same. His body rocked with the electricity of her blood through his veins, and he could hold back no longer. His hips thrust hard and his cock released, filling her, spilling out of her, as he rode her hard, growling into her neck, still drinking, lapping away the last drops of her. He felt her respond, her body arching, thrusting, taking all he had to give and begging for more. The crack in the plaster extended with each thrust and reached the ceiling, as the chandelier swung above them. He felt his cock empty into her. He had given her everything. As he dropped forward, unlatching, at last, letting his body lay against hers, he supported his weight on his elbows, heart pounding. He raised his head and looked at her, licking his blood from her lips.

"Now that, my vixen, is how you seal a deal." He rolled off her, lying beside her, still breathing heavily, his body covered in a light sheen of sweat.

Jacks smiled to herself. Feeding only from masters was how she maintained her incredible strength, how she remained strong, sleek and at the top of her game. Not all masters were willing to let her feed, but she'd learned the art of seduction and found that most would succumb, even the ones who were mated. She was her own woman, and yet, the bounty of the masters' skills and blood filled her full and made her strong.

Laughing, she sat up and strutted to the bathroom. "When you can walk and breathe again, you might want to explain this little episode to your mate. Goodnight, Alec."

Closing the door to the bathroom, she turned on the shower and stepped inside, washing away his scent.

Alec turned on his side and watched that ass as she walked to the bathroom and closed the door. He smiled at her comments about walking and breathing. She was always hell on wheels, but she had upped her game for sure. He might have to reconsider the length of this assignment. Suddenly, six months seemed much too short.

Looking around the room, he made a note to have Santos replace the bed and make whatever repairs were needed, and to keep a crew on standby. He picked up his shirt and slid his pants back on, not bothering to zip them, but letting them hang loose on his hips. He looked about for his shoes, but they were nowhere to be found. He left her room and walked to their bedroom to check on Rissa.

81

The day had been a long one. Rissa tried to work from home, but every time she tried to get on the laptop or make calls, she found it difficult to concentrate. She was tired of sleeping, restless yet lethargic. Maybe it was all this change so quickly.

She could hear the Amazon bitch Alec hired moving about the guest bedroom. She didn't want to be alone, but not having Alec in the house made her whole body ache with unease. She'd heard the bitch come to check on her every hour, standing outside her closed and locked door. She wasn't getting in here, not if Rissa could stop her.

Finally, Rissa felt him. *Alec is home!* Her heart raced and she sat on the bed listening, waiting, knowing he'd come to her immediately, making sure she was okay, and giving her comfort. She heard him running up the steps and she smiled, but he didn't come, and he didn't come.

She heard his voice. He had stopped at her room. Of course, he'd talk to her, make sure Rissa had been okay, and then he'd rush in and check on her.

As she waited for him, his emotions rolled over her, and they were filled with sexual intensity. *No!* He wouldn't do this to her, knowing how she was right now, needing him. Rissa felt his pleasure rise in intensity. His roar went straight through her heart, and she couldn't take it! His sexual pleasure washed over her, and she knew for certain he'd hired Jacks for himself. He didn't care about her at all. She was nothing to him. He'd never been faithful and had never promised to be, but he'd never flaunted his infidelity before.

She didn't know whether to cry or scream. Picking the laptop off the bed, she threw it across the room, watching it hit the wall, electronic pieces exploding across the floor. She felt the moment when he orgasmed, and his body was awash in sexual pleasure, and her heart broke in two. The noise of the two of them together was killing her, and she couldn't escape it. Suddenly, it was quiet, and still, he didn't come to her. She buried her face in her hands, feeling lost.

As Alec entered the bedroom, he saw her laptop on the floor, shattered, and Rissa seated on their bed. He tossed his torn shirt across a chair, dropped his dress pants and pulled a pair of jeans from the closet.

He slipped on a t-shirt and decided to stay barefoot. He picked up what remained of the laptop.

"Are you having technical problems, darling? I know it's frustrating, but you know you can call Santos and he'd have a technician here for you in minutes. I'll let him know you'll need a new one."

Desperately trying to keep herself together, Rissa kept her head bowed because she couldn't stand the sight of him at the moment. "I'm not helpless. I can get my own."

"Rissa, I know you're not helpless. But you're still reeling from the attack. Did you try to go out today?"

As he moved around the room, he reeked from the smell of her, and she wanted to gag. Why was she suddenly so jealous of some warrior whore? And damn Shade, he would pay for this little deed.

"No, why don't you shower then get back to the study. There are some papers you may want to see. Santos brought them to me earlier, but I asked him to take them to your study." Still not looking at him, she moved to sit at her make-up table and couldn't look at herself in the mirror, pulling open drawers, rambling through them, pretending to be busy.

He looked at her. She was still jealous after all these years. "Rissa, do we need to talk? Because I don't plan on watching you sulk around the house for the next six months. You know I take what I want. No apologies. But you're my mate. You're the one I choose to stay with, to have at my side for eternity. The others are just toys. I play with them and toss them away. Now, why don't you join me in the shower, my darling? And stop all this foolishness."

She spun on the chair and stood facing him. "Just take your shower and get that bitches' smell off you and get out of this room. Leave me alone! Foolishness? Oh, I'm a fool, alright."

Walking to the door, she stalked out and ran down the stairs, no idea where she was going but feeling the need to put some distance between them. She just wanted to be alone. She felt like her world was spinning off its axis.

Alec sighed heavily as he stood with his hands on his hips, counting to ten. If she thought they were going to go through this every time he fucked someone, she better think again. He stepped into the hallway and called out to her. "Rissa! Get your ass back up here! Now!"

Rissa ran into the study and grabbed the stack of worldwide newspapers, most of them with their picture and wedding announcement splashed across the front page. She headed back up the stairs and watched his fuming face as she dropped the stack of papers at his feet and locked eyes with him. "As you wish, master."

He'd had enough of her insolence and attitude. He gripped her strongly by the neck and pushed her back against the wall, and spoke his words through gritted teeth, his beast just under the surface. "Don't pull this shit with me, baby girl. I'm not amused. Do you need to be fucked too? Is that your problem? Because I can take care of that real quick."

Rissa couldn't breathe and her heart beat so fast it felt like it would explode in her chest. In her mind, she saw the rogue attack and felt herself gasping for air. She shook with fear as her knees went weak.

He saw the level of her fear return and realized she was remembering the rogue. *Fuck!* He released her neck so she could breathe freely, and slid his hand behind her head, pulling her to his chest. "You're safe here. I've got you. Nothing's going to happen to you, Rissa. I'll protect you." He kissed the top of her head.

She laid her head on his chest and tried to control the emotions that kept seizing her. "I'm sorry, Alec, I feel so out of control."

He scooped her up in his arms and carried her to their bed, laying her down gently, and lying down beside her. He brushed her hair back from her face.

"Shhhhh, baby girl. You're okay. But I want you to start fighting this fear. You're in a safe place. Nothing can get to you here. Nothing can harm you here. Now calm down."

She curled up into a ball and lay there staring, She knew if Max really wanted to kill her, she couldn't stop him but if she kept letting her fear stop her from even leaving the house, he'd won. She would never let him win without a fight.

"I'll be fine. I know you hate this, so just go, Alec. Tell her I'm going out in the morning. Just tell her. "

He rose up on one elbow and looked at her, her defiance returning. "Rissa, what I hate is watching you hide in fear. That's not the Rissa I know. I want to see you get your confidence back, to a point. This attack was a wakeup call. All my lecturing was going in one ear and out the other. I hate the bloodlust and violence of my world, and I've tried to separate myself from it as much as possible by seeking a power base among mortals. That has isolated us from many in the vampire community, but they're never gone. This is your first experience with it, but I doubt it will be your last. I'll protect you to every extent possible, and that's also why you have a protector. I know you. I know you'll try to test this situation to see how far you can push it. How much you can get away with. But let me make myself clear. This is not a game. And you need to get used to this idea right now. Her name is Jacks. *You* will speak with her, and you will coordinate your schedule with her. I'm not your fucking secretary, and furthermore, you'll follow her commands. She knows what to do, how to protect you when I'm not here. Do you understand what I'm saying? Because this is my fucking house, and we're not going to have this drama every day over your protector. Understood?"

She closed her eyes and heard his demanding voice. Biting her lip, trying not to fall apart, she curled up tighter. "Yes, Alec. Your house, your rules, my protector, be strong, be tough. Yes, I understand."

"Don't be contrite, Rissa. It's not an attractive trait on you. Now tell me what you need from me. How can I help you?"

She pulled out of her ball and stared at him. "I don't need anything from you. You've given me all I need. So please don't worry, I'll go out tomorrow and pretend everything is fine. I won't give anyone a sign that anything is wrong. After all, I'm the Darling of G-town."

She sat up and threw her legs over the side of the bed and walked to the closet. Taking out a robe, she slipped it on and went to her writing desk. She grabbed some of her personal stationery and her schedule book, holding it up in the air.

"See, fine, giving Jacks my itinerary for the day and evening. Go to work, don't worry. Rissa is fine, your house, your mate, making your world perfection."

Setting the book down, she began to write with speed and precision the details of her day tomorrow. *Bitch wants my schedule, she'll get it. And I'll smile and pretend all is well for master.*

He smirked as she strutted from the bed, grabbed up her schedule book and started to scratch away. A little of that old Rissa attitude was returning. She was still angry, he could feel it, but she'd get over it. She always did. She knew the rules. "Now you want to explain all those newspapers you threw at my feet?"

Keeping her head down, she continued to write. "The big news. The whole world is about to experience Mr. and Mrs. Canton. Go on, go look. I'm fine, Alec. I'll be doing this for a while."

He walked to her chair, standing behind her. He pulled her hair aside and leaned down to her ear and whispered, "You're not fooling me, baby girl." He licked at her ear and neck. "I can feel your anger from across the room. Did I spoil our big day? I wasn't aware the announcement would come out today. I'll make it up to you, my darling."

He turned to leave the room, heading to the study. There would be no pleasing her tonight. He needed to give her space to get over her anger.

Turning in her chair, she called out to him. "Alec... wait."

She went to him as he stopped in the doorway. Standing on tiptoe, she kissed him on the lips, softly yet longingly. "Thank you for everything you do for me. For making me feel safe. I love you. Now go," winking, "I think you may like a few of those announcements. Sounds like the affair of the year to me."

He smiled down at her and smacked her ass before giving it a hard squeeze. This was his Rissa.

82

Shade had asked her to get ready for Florence, and Kate didn't know where to begin. He said they'd be there several weeks for the turning. Her heart skipped a beat whenever she thought of it. It was what she'd wanted but also feared. She put it out of her head because there was no going back now. She headed for Theresa's room to ask for her help and share the news. Theresa's door was closed so she tapped lightly, and like Luca, Theresa opened it right away.

"Theresa, I have great news for you, and I need your help."

"Of course, my lady, how can I help?"

"Could you come with me back to my bedroom? I have some packing I need help with." They walked together back to the master bedroom.

"You're going on a trip, my lady?"

"More accurately, Theresa, we're going on a trip, me, Shade, Luca, Gi, and you. We're all going to Florence for several weeks. I don't know exactly when we'll depart. Shade has some things he needs to wrap up here. But he said he'd assign someone from the Castello staff to attend to me while we're there, so you'll have some free time for Marco."

Theresa blushed when Kate said his name. She knew Kate had spoken to Shade about Marco, and Kate had encouraged her to hang the paintings Luca painted up in her room.

"My lady understands a woman's heart. Thank you. That's wonderful news. I'll let Marco know right away."

"And the second part of my news is Shade has decided, after that ambush, he should have warriors here full-time, so he wants to add warrior's quarters on the property. That means you'll soon have your own room back."

"My lady, thank you. That's good news as well. I feel like I'm imposing on your private time with master."

Kate had to laugh to herself. As if anything that happened between Shade and her inside this house remained private for very long. The staff was extremely discreet. She'd never heard them gossip, and they kept her private activities to themselves, just as she was sure they did with Shade. But she had no illusions. They knew everything, heard everything, and saw everything.

"Theresa, I hardly know you're here. But I know you must miss having your own things, and your own space."

"Yes, but I did appreciate being able to live here while the warriors were in the staff quarters. So, this trip, what's on the agenda?"

"Well, my turning. What do you pack for a turning?"

"My lady! I don't think we've ever held a turning, and I can't remember the last time those sacred chambers below Castello were used. It's been centuries! Probably Shade's birth was the last event there. But don't worry about the turning. Everything that will be needed is already there, so all you need to pack are your regular clothes. As I recall, there was a considerable wardrobe for you there as well. I do remember a room filled with red dresses scattered about when you couldn't decide."

Laughing as they went through drawers, they placed items in the steamer trunks to be flown over. "Ah yes, Shade said wear red. I remember that day well. I was terrified to meet everyone. It seems so long ago now, doesn't it?"

"My lady, it feels like yesterday to me. Our concept of time is very different, yes?"

Her comment reminded Kate of how much everything about her life was about to change. "Yes... very different."

Shade had informed Luca they'd be going back to Florence for several weeks and he'd have a lot of free time while he was there so he could visit with friends. Luca realized that with Marcello and Raven here, everyone he cared about was already in the States. The feeder in Florence, he thought he might check on her, make sure she was okay, but he had no desire for the feeder again. He'd asked Shade to make sure she was taken care of, but since he'd been separated from her, he no longer felt any attachment.

He'd fed mainly from Shannon since they'd been together. Although he'd not been able to see Shannon frequently enough to make it exclusive, he hoped that would change. He found he didn't care for the feeder encounters after experiencing an emotional bond with someone. As he contemplated this trip, he knew the person he'd miss the most would be Shannon and he wondered if master would allow Shannon to make the trip? They were going to Florence for Kate's turning. He doubted master would agree to bring a mortal to Florence, but he'd ask him.

Luca knew Shade felt an urgency to have Kate turned since the ambush, and he was staying closer to her until that could be done. Best not to wait until the last minute to ask him, in case he needed to think about it. Luca could hear him in the bunker. He'd been in and out of there all night. He headed down the steps and entered the bunker. "Master?"

Shade looked up as Luca entered. "Luca. I was just checking our inventory, seeing if there might be some weapons we should bring back from Florence with us. Is there anything, in particular, you think we need?"

"Uh, other than replacing shuriken's, I can't think of anything else." Luca walked through the room, looking at the weapons that were mounted on the walls.

Shade watched him closely. He was clearly distracted, and his mind wasn't on weapons. "So, give it up, warrior. What's on your mind?"

Luca seemed startled. "What?" He hadn't even organized the thoughts in his head, but Shade already knew he was here with a problem.

"Luca, sit down. You didn't come down here to discuss weapons."

Shade kicked one chair back from the table for him, and pulled a chair out for himself, propping his feet on the table, crossing his arms over his chest.

Luca sat in the chair, leaning forward, resting his elbows on his knees. "I was just thinking about Florence."

"Florence. *Si*. What about it? You miss living there? You are eager to go back?"

"Actually, I don't miss it as much as I thought I would, master. I feel like my family is here now. And with Marcello here, well, everyone I love is here. I'm eager to see my old home, my family home. I haven't seen it since I was ten and went to the warrior's camp." His hands were fidgeting, and he was rambling, talking around everything but Shannon.

Shade sat quietly and listened, waiting for him to get around to what he really wanted to talk about as Luca looked to the floor and twisted the ring on his finger. "So, you don't want to go? You want to go? What is it, Luca?"

Luca looked up at him. "No, I do want to go. It's Kate's turning. She'll be presented to the entire coven as our queen. And I, I'm the protector to the queen. I wouldn't miss that. No, master, I want to go, but I wanted to ask, since you said I'd have free time. I know it's not usual, but would you consider—"

"Luca! *Cazzo*! Spit it out, warrior. I don't have all day."

Luca could feel his palms sweating and he rubbed them on his thighs. "So yes, the question is, master, whether you would consider allowing me to bring Shannon to Florence." He spit the words out quickly and waited for his answer, but all he heard was silence.

Shade turned his head away, creasing his brow. This wasn't what he'd been expecting to hear. It was a highly unusual request. She wouldn't be the first mortal at Medici Castello, but a mortal at the turning? That would set the Council on edge for certain. He rolled Luca's question around in his head. "So this is serious then."

"Yes, master. It's serious. The night you gave me the deed to my father's house, I came back to my room and I was so overcome with emotion. I couldn't wait to go there, to walk in those rooms again. But in my head, I saw her there as well, showing her the home where I grew up. I realized my joy isn't complete unless it's shared with her. I love her, master."

"Luca, I don't doubt your feelings for her. But she is the first non-feeder you have been with. There are many women out there, mortal and immortal. You have experienced none of that, and yet, you choose this path? You are feeding from her, *si*?"

"Yes, I wish to feed from her exclusively, but I haven't been able to see her frequently enough to do that, so I've had to use the feeders on occasion. But it doesn't fill me. It's her blood I want."

Shade gave him a stern look. "Has she fed from you?"

"No, master! I told you I'd not let her feed from me without discussing that with you. But my body craves her to do so. And I know she'd come willingly to me if I were to offer. I know you think this is sudden, and I'm young, and I haven't experienced a lot of women, but I know what my heart wants, master. And my heart wants her."

"It pleases me that she has not fed from you, that you understand the seriousness of the next step, and you will discuss this with me. For here is my decision. Bring Shannon to Florence. She can stay with you at Castello, you can take her to your home, stay there a few days if you like. She can see the coronation ceremony, when Kate becomes queen and is presented to the coven. She will see our world as few mortals ever do. After that, Luca, we will talk again about whether she should feed from you. I suggest you spend some time talking about what that will mean for her. It is not a decision to be made lightly, for either of you."

"Yes, master. We'll talk. Thank you."

"Make sure you understand fully the conflicts of a protector with a mate. Make sure *she* understands the conflicts of a protector with a mate. Make sure this is something you can both live with. *Si*? You would not be the only protector who has ever mated, but it is rare, Luca. Very rare."

"I understand, master. We have talked briefly about this already. But we'll discuss it in detail."

Shade gave him a final look. "Anything else?"

"No, master, that was all."

Shade dropped his feet from the table back to the floor and stood, slapping Luca on the back, a small smile playing at his lips. "Good. Now, let me get back to work before I take to my slumber."

Luca headed back to his suite, checking the time. It was the weekend, so he knew Shannon would be home, but it was still a little early. He decided to teleport to her condo unannounced. It was early morning and the sun was turning the sky pink. He stepped into her bedroom to find her sleeping, her face in profile, her dark hair spread out across the pillow. She slept nude and the blankets had slipped free of her shoulders. He stepped to the bed and knelt beside her, kissing her shoulder softly before pulling the blankets up to cover her. *"Mia belleza?"* He watched as she stirred from sleep, her lips parted, her long lashes fanned out across her cheeks.

She slowly opened her eyes to find him eye level with her across her bed, his arm resting on her bed, his chin on his arm. She smiled at him. *This is how I should wake up every day, looking at that face. That beautiful, handsome face.*

"Buongiorno, mia belleza."

"And good morning to you, Luca." She lifted the blankets in the air, inviting him in. "It's still a little early, don't you think? Why don't you join me?"

Luca stood and stripped from his clothes and slid into the bed next to her. Her body was soft and warm as he drew her into his arms, her head on his chest, their legs entwined.

Shannon ran her fingers through his hair. "Not that you ever need a reason, but to what do I owe the pleasure of this unexpected visit?"

He kissed her nose. "I come with an invitation, *mia belleza*. Shade will be taking the whole family back to Florence soon, for Kate's turning. We'll be there for several weeks, and he has agreed I can take you with me. Now please don't break my heart by telling me you can't go."

"Luca, I'd love to go to Florence! I have vacation time, so yes! Yes, I'll go. Kate and I traveled there... Did I tell you that? Florence was our favorite city in Italy, and Tuscany. Driving through Tuscany. Kate and I stayed in this cottage in an old vineyard in Tuscany once. We got there on a Sunday, and all the stores were closed. All we had to eat were some pears, cheese, fresh bread and wine we'd bought at the farmers market in Florence the day before. We ate that for breakfast, lunch and dinner. Oh my gosh, we had so much fun on that trip. Oh Luca, I can't wait. To have uninterrupted time with you, wow... Now my head is spinning with everything I'll need to get ready. Do you know where we'll be staying?"

Luca smiled to himself at her excitement and he understood the attraction to mortals and why Shade was so captivated by Kate, and he was so enslaved by Shannon. It was their enthusiasm for life, their eagerness about what lay ahead. When your lifetime is an eternity, there is very little you haven't seen, or haven't experienced and it's easy to become jaded. Shannon and Kate made life wondrous again. They made them see the world through new eyes.

"*Mia belleza*, we'll be staying at Medici Castello. It's Shade's ancestral home, where he was raised, and also where he rules. You know he is master, but he's also royalty. He is king, *mia belleza*. Not in the mortal world. His mortal roots in the Medici family lost their bid to royalty centuries ago. But his bloodlines are pure, and he is king in the vampire world. He rules over a very broad territory that includes all of Tuscany. Once Kate is turned, she will be his queen."

Shannon put both hands to her head. "This is blowing my mind. Kate, a queen. Sorry, but this is just so unreal. And we'll watch all this? Her turning?"

"Not her turning. No one is with her during the turning except Shade. It's personal and intimate, performed in private. You'll see her enter the chamber as a mortal, and when they emerge, several days later, she'll be immortal."

"Will she look different?"

"I don't think she'll look different to you, *mia belleza*. She'll have fangs, but as you know, they're not always on display. She'll have a beast that will be untamed and undisciplined. It will be Shade's job to help her learn to control her own beast, which should be an interesting process, given the short fuse he has with his own. She'll no longer be able to consume human food and will feed from Shade only. She'll need to learn to control her thirst, and Shade will teach her that as well. She'll have great strength, not as great as a vampire who is born immortal, but much greater than a mortal. And she'll have a gift. Usually, we don't know what gift the mortal will be given. If you are born vampire, you have your gift from the beginning... Just as I'm a day-walker. But I already know Kate's gift. It's already displayed itself. She'll have the rarest of gifts among vampires, and I've never heard of a turned vampire with this gift, but she will communicate with animals."

Shannon looked at him quizzically. "You mean she'll talk to the animals?"

"Not in words, exactly. She'll connect with them telepathically. She'll be able to direct them to do her bidding. She can call on them in her defense. It's a powerful gift, and it will serve Shade well. He's already a powerful master in his own right, but now his mate will bring him a broader range of power. They'll be very strong together. She's aware she has this gift already, but she doesn't understand its impact. Its full potential will present once she's turned. She'll need to learn to master it."

"Luca, this sounds so...so... Wow, I don't even know how to describe it. What happens after? Once she is turned, when they come out of the chamber?"

"There's a great ceremony where she's officially presented to the coven as their queen and is recognized as Shade's mate for all eternity. She's already mated to him, but since she remains mortal, she's not recognized by many in the vampire community as a true mate. As a mortal, she's free to walk away from him like a divorce. Once she's turned, the blood connection will bond them for all time, they'll never part until death."

"Until death? But aren't they immortal?"

"*Si*. That means we don't die of illness. We do eventually die of old age, but we can live for centuries. Time passes for us, and we age, but at a much slower rate. We can be killed, *mia belleza*, and there's much violence in our world. It's why Kate has a protector, why Shade trains warriors. In our world, there's always a battle for territory, for power."

"Trust me, Luca, there are battles for power and territory among mortals too. I don't think we're that different after all."

"*Si,* my beauty. There's much we share. We love, we have families. And sometimes, our worlds cross paths, and the mortal and immortal find each other, like Shade and Kate."

She smiled at him. "Or like Luca and Shannon?"

"*Si,* like Luca and Shannon. I love you, Shannon. I don't speak those words lightly. I know what lies ahead if you choose to be with me, and it's not a decision you should enter into lightly."

"If I choose? You talk as if you've already decided. As if you've already chosen."

"*Si, mia belleza*, I've chosen. I've chosen you." He ran his fingers down her cheek and under her chin, lifting her face to his, kissing her softly.

Shannon let him lead the kiss and succumbed to him. *Melting. Melting here.* She gave herself up to him and that kiss, letting go of any reservations she might have had about following this man.

84

Shade teleported with *bel* into the grand foyer at Medici Castello. *Bel* was nervous, he could feel it, and he knew it was a combination of her fears about the coronation as well as the actual turning. He knew this must seem surreal to her, but he was trying to make it as easy as possible and make her feel relaxed. There was much that needed to be taken care of, but the staff knew the process, so they'd been faithfully working to arrange everything. It had been centuries since a turning had taken place within the walls of Castello and his coven had waited an extremely long time for him to take a queen. Shade knew Kate had no idea how important this was for him, his *familia*, and all the people he protected and provided for in his coven, but she'd learn, and he had no doubts she'd exceed their expectations.

He leaned down, kissing her. "You can breathe now, *mi amore*."

Gi had arrived ahead of them and the entire staff of close to fifty were lined up and ready to greet them. Shade reassured her, saying, "Relax, it's going to be fine."

It took a minute for Kate to orient herself and regain her balance any time they teleported. She'd forgotten just how big and imposing this castle was. Their footsteps and voices echoed through the halls. The castle was beautiful, ornate and over-the-top grandiose. She tried to imagine Shade as a boy growing up here, and she felt sad. As beautiful as this building was, she couldn't feel a sense of home. She felt his loneliness instead.

The staff was lined up before her, in a castle that wasn't even occupied. That told her a lot about the size and scope of the building, and how much work it took to maintain. She felt like she was in a museum. She was nervous about this trip, and the turning, but she trusted Shade would guide her.

"Lover, I forgot how big it is. I remember I never left our bedroom without someone to escort me because I was afraid I'd get lost. It's hard to imagine you growing up here."

He pulled her into his arms, holding her to his chest and ignoring the stares of the staff. This wasn't his *padre*'s home any longer, and he wasn't his *padre*. His *padre* had always been careful not to show affection to his *madre* when the staff was present. Everything was by the rules, but this was his home now and he'd rule it his way.

"I know it must seem impossible to envision me as a boy living here. It was the only home I'd ever known, and although it was not exactly the most loving at times, it was a good upbringing. They did the best they knew how, *bel*. Now, we have a chance to change all of that and make this place ring with happy laughter. Now, we must greet the staff, and get on with getting settled, *si*?"

"Lead the way."

Gi stepped forward and took Kate's hand, kissing it lightly. Shade said, "You see, *mi amore*, there will be some familiar faces amongst us."

Shade took her arm, threaded it through his and walked down the line of servants as Gi introduced each of them. They bowed at the waist or curtsied, never speaking to her unless she spoke first. He could feel her nervousness and kept his free hand on the small of her back, letting her know he was with her. He knew she hated this pomp and circumstance, but she had to learn this was how it had always been for them. As they got halfway through, Shade saw movement at the end of the line and looked up and smiled. They continued onward, as Gi introduced each by name and title or duty within the castle. Shade stopped to chat with a few of them, asking after their families, as each servant bowed to him with acknowledgment.

The line seemed endless, and Kate marveled that he knew each one by name. No wonder they were all so devoted and loyal to him. She'd seen it with his warriors, that same devotion. She must make the effort, to learn their names, their families. She owed them that much respect for their servitude. She took each hand, and repeated each name, trying hard to remember the faces. She knew GI and Theresa would both be invaluable in helping her to remember them all and learn about them. She didn't want their respect out of some obligation to Shade. She wanted to earn their respect. It was the only way she could make peace with the bowing and the titles.

As they came to the end of the line, Shade watched as Marco was introduced as his Second-in-Command at Medici and he let go of Kate's arm and stepped back. If Marco didn't respect her, there would be a brawl right here in the middle of this hall come hell or high water. Marco must show her respect even though she wasn't yet immortal.

Marco bowed low and Shade watched as he took her hands in his, softly kissing each cheek, as was tradition, and Shade was pleased but still waited to see what words he spoke. The damn devil could roll straight from his tongue at times.

* * *

Marco had been running late as usual, and he snuck in the back and slipped into the end of the line and watched the sleek, red-headed mortal that would be Shade's official mate before the end of the week. Damn place had been a fucking zoo making preparations for all this, but finally, it would be done, and the sooner the better. He'd heard from Terri she was kind, had a huge heart, and he should never misjudge her small stature for weakness. Apparently, his little trick with Fiamma had set her off, and Marco grinned at the thought of it. She'd better get used to it. He had no damn intentions of changing who he was for her, queen or not. She was nothing like Shade's mother, and she'd have much to prove to him.

He intended to show her respect, but he wouldn't go down on one knee to her, she wasn't the queen yet. "My lady, I speak for the Warriors of Medici in welcoming you back to Castello. I am honored to finally have the pleasure of making your acquaintance. If you are in need of my services, please feel free to call for me."

Kate's curiosity was aroused. So this was the man Theresa was in love with. What an unlikely pair they were with her meekness and his boldness. Kate knew Shade's bond to him was strong, but she sensed tension as well. Luca had said there were many who didn't accept her as Shade's mate as yet because she was mortal, and she felt his resistance.

"Marco, I'm so pleased to finally meet you. I recognize you, of course, from the paintings Theresa has of you in her room. I sincerely regret your separation, and I hope we can find a way for the two of you to be together. I know Shade seems oblivious to the love that takes place around him, but I assure you, I'm not. It pains me the two of you are separated."

As she spoke, her voice was soft yet commanding, and she stood her ground with him, and Marco liked it. He might warm up to her in time. Terri adored the fucking ground she walked on, but he wasn't that easy a sell.

"Terri displays the paintings of me there?" Marco chuckled. "My brother knows nothing of love, love of war, perhaps, but I'm sure your beauty and charm have changed him. He returns to us as our master, but I hope you haven't softened him too much."

Kate fired back at him, "Soften him? Quite the contrary. Love doesn't soften you. It gives you something to fight for. Surely, you know that."

Marco nodded to her. "*Si,* my lady. That's very true. But there is a rumor," leaning in close to her ear, "the rumor is you have slain a nemesis of ours named Cuerpo?" Marco heard her intake of breath, followed by Shade's growl.

Kate was taken aback. *Is he taunting me? Trying to provoke Shade? What's his game?* She heard Shade's growl behind her. "Cuerpo, well, that's no rumor, warrior. As I said, love gives you something to fight for. I killed him where he stood with a single arrow through the heart. He expected to find me timid and unprepared, cowering and immobilized by fear. Misjudging me cost him his life. I'm sure you'd never make that mistake."

Shade stifled a laugh as Marco bowed his head. "No, my lady. I stand before you a hardened warrior. My compliments to your skill and patience for that kill."

Standing back, Shade watched them spar and chuckled because Marco had no damn idea what he was up against. He stepped forward and wrapped Marco in a brotherly hug and they beat each other's back with their fists. To Shade, Marco was his true brother. "Old man, brother mine, we have a score to settle later, and you keep that tongue!"

"*Si,* I have heard you were not well pleased with the warriors I sent." Pulling back, they locked eyes and began to laugh like old times. "I shall let you get back to your business, brother. You know where to find me." Turning to Kate, he asked, "My lady, may I inquire if Terri will be arriving soon?"

"She should be here tomorrow. She was wrapping up a few final details in closing down the house in Virginia. But she'll be worth the wait, yes?"

"*Si,* my lady. She's worth waiting for. I bid you a pleasant evening." Bowing to her, then bumping fists with Shade, he turned and retreated, and knowing it would be a long night waiting to have Theresa in his arms again.

Shade turned to Kate and lifted her up in his arms, taking the grand staircase two at a time, yelling, "Master is home and he brings with him his queen!"

Kate was caught off-guard when he swept her off her feet and started running up the stairs, leaving the staff standing with their mouths open in the grand foyer. Clearly, this was not behavior they were used to seeing from him, but it made her laugh out loud. Theresa had already told her their bedroom had been moved. The last time they were here, they were in the bedroom that belonged to Shade; the room he'd previously shared with Adriana and Sabine. As he entered this new room, one of many she'd yet to see in this castle, it took her breath away. "Shade...this room is beautiful!"

This bedroom was easily three times the size of the bedroom they shared when they stayed here before. It was decorated in ivory and soft taupe with accents of gold. A plush round rug covered the cold marble floor. Massive columns created a canopy over a bed that was beyond king-sized.

"Well, it should be, you can thank my *madre* for it. This was my parents' bedroom, *mi amore*. I was conceived in this room. And if I have anything to do with it, so will our son."

Setting her down, he smacked her ass lightly and kissed her long and hard. "Now go, I know you're anxious to explore. This is your home now, where you rule. Make it your own."

Kate walked around the massive room. The headboard had a strange crest at the center, and she ran her hand over it. It was shaped like a shield that was topped by a crown and centered on the shield was a circle of chain. Lying across the chain were three evenly spaced swords. "Lover, what is this?"

"That, *mi amore*, is the Medici crest. You will see it displayed on many things within the house and on the warriors' armor, mine as well. It is rampant here." Chuckling, "*Madre* believed very much in traditions, she was a proud queen." He paused as she explored, and then awkwardly inquired. "Have you refrained from taking the pill, as we discussed? *Mi amore*, I must stress from this point forward, no drugs, not even anything for head pain, *si*? Tell me you are ready, please."

"Yes, I stopped taking my birth control as you instructed. I'm ready.

She stretched out on a luxuriously upholstered chaise lounge situated by a window, looking out on the night sky.

He sat beside her and laid his head in her lap. "I will go mad until this is over. I cannot stand this closeness without ravishing you. *Cazzo*! Hardest thing I have ever done my whole life is abstain from taking you. Tell me, Kate. You have a little time left to change your mind before the turning. I know you are still frightened, and you have reason to be, but you can change your mind, please understand that."

"Lover, I won't lie, it does frighten me. But it's the only way we can be together, and I know you'll take care of me. I'll never change my mind. This is what I want. It's not the castle or the title of queen. It's not money or fast cars. It's you. It's all for you."

"I know that, *mi amore.* But I want you to know, even if you do not want to be immortal, I will never leave you. Do you understand that?"

"Shade, my life is but a moment in time compared to yours. And children, you want a mate who can give you children. I'd age and die, and you would remain young and vital. To see myself aging and knowing I'd have to let go of you at some point, that's not something I could bear. This is our path, lover."

"*Si, mi amore.* You are my life. I was born to be yours and yours alone. Now, if I cannot make love to you, we need to do something else for I will go mad if I lay here like this. I may have to wear fucking armor to bed at this rate."

Laughing at him, she stood up from the chaise lounge and walked through the room. She stood before a huge mirror with an ornate gold frame that was propped against the wall and stood taller than her.

"Was this mirror in your parents' room? Did your mother stand here, and look at her own reflection? Did she put on her beautiful dresses and prepare herself for your father standing before this mirror? Can you feel her here tonight, lover?"

Watching her, he smiled with the memories. "I didn't often come in this room, *mi amore*, it was forbidden. This was their private space. No one bothered them when they were in here together. But as I got older, I remember a few times she was sitting in a chair by this window, and my *padre* would kneel at her feet, slide on her silken slippers, or help her with her laces. Those moments are burned into my brain because they were most tender, it was how I knew he loved her, and when he would be strict with her, I would remember those moments to remind me he truly loved her with all his heart."

Shade slid his hands through his hair. "She is here now, *mi amore*. So is he, they never leave where they were the happiest together. They exist in another realm. And once turned, I have a feeling you will feel them and perhaps see them. Don't be frightened, she means no harm. Embrace her, for she would surely love to have been here to see this and meet you. I sometimes…" feeling his emotions overwhelm him, he walked to Kate.

She turned as she saw him approach her in the reflection in the mirror and opened her arms to him. "I'll welcome her. I wish I could have met her when she was alive. I wish they both could be here, to see our children, watch them grow. To know you have found happiness."

She took his hand and walked with him into a massive octagon-shaped bathroom that was larger than their Virginia bedroom and bathroom put together. The room was so large it echoed. A large chandelier hung from the center of the room and brought a warm glow to the soft ivory and gold marble. There were mirrors on every wall, which expanded the space and a huge tub large enough for two that was on a raised platform.

As he followed her, he felt his *padre*'s presence and saw him standing there. He was watching her. He didn't quite accept she was inside this room as a mortal, but he knew the change was coming. **"She is mine, Padre, and she will rule, embrace her for me. If you do nothing else, embrace her for me. She will not let me down."**

His father disappeared and Shade knew *bel* couldn't see or feel him yet, but she would. He followed her as she explored the massive bathroom. "Well, *mi amore*, most of this was remodeled to accommodate modern water and electric, but my parents used to bathe in the hot springs. The springs are still here, I believe."

"A hot springs? Theresa said there was a room with a hot tub that had water from an underground hot springs. Through this door?"

Kate pushed open the door into a windowless room that looked like a Roman spa, marble floors and walls, large columns surrounded the pool. The pool was round and filled with water that remained in a constant churn as the steam rose to the ceiling.

He laughed as she discovered the hot springs. "Are you sure *Madre* is not talking to you right now? Come on, *mi amore*, let us get naked and soothe our teleporting bones, shall we?"

"Lover," she said, laughing, "there's no way we're getting naked in a hot tub tonight. You're too much of a temptation already. And if I must abstain from making love with you from now until after the turning, let's not make it any harder on ourselves. Come on," she took his hand. "We're both tired from our travels, and the sun will be up soon. Let's sleep together in that giant bed. Tomorrow, Theresa arrives, and Luca and Shannon. You can show me the rest of the castle then. But now, we sleep."

She led him back to the large bedroom. In the short time they were out of the room, someone had entered and laid out a nightgown for her and pulled down their bed. They both stripped down and she slid on the snow-white silk gown and felt the cool silk against her skin. Shade slid between the sheets nude, and she climbed across the massive bed to lie beside him, her head on his shoulder, her arm across his chest. She felt his arm around her, and his kiss on her head. The lights went out, and she recognized the sound of the soft whir of the electronic blinds that would seal out the light of day.

Then she heard his voice, a soft whisper in the dark. "*Ti amo, bel rosso.*"

85

Shannon rushed to finish up some last minute packing. Luca had told her to pack and leave her luggage by the door, and someone would pick it up and have it sent to Florence. He said he'd pick her up and they'd teleport together.

She had everything ready. At least she thought she was ready. She was pacing the floor and checking the clock. Teleporting to Italy! It made her head spin to think about it. She walked to the window and looked out like she might see him flying through the air or something. She turned to resume her pacing and walked right into him. "Oh, good Lord, Luca, you scared me to death!"

Luca laughed. "Sorry, *mia belleza*. I was going to put my arms around you at the window. I didn't expect you to turn so suddenly. Are you ready?"

"I...uh...I guess. Do I do anything? Think happy thoughts? Flap my arms?"

Luca shook his head and ran his hands through his hair. "Happy thoughts? You can think about whatever you please, but no arm flapping."

He pulled her in close to him and kissed her lips. She responded by putting both arms around his neck and leaning in. His tongue slipped between her lips and she sucked gently, sending shivers down his spine. He broke the kiss before it became more than a kiss. He took a deep breath and noted that heavy-lidded look she got when she was aroused.

"Right. We'll have plenty of time for that once we're in Florence. But now, all you need to do is hang on. Tuck your head under my chin, hold on just as you are now, and lean your weight into me. Keep your eyes closed, since this is your first experience with teleporting, you may feel dizzy. It helps if your eyes are closed."

She tucked her head under his chin. "Do you keep your eyes closed?"

Luca chuckled. "Not if we want to end up in Florence, *mia belleza*. Now hang on."

He lifted them out and over the district, and out to the Atlantic. He watched the sun set behind them as they moved into the darkness and he felt the air cooling around them. Her hands were gripping into his shoulders and he leaned down and kissed the top of her head. "You okay, Shan?"

He felt her nod against his chest. The sky turned darker and he saw the white caps of the waves beneath them reflecting in the moonlight. He ran his hand up her back, letting her know she was safe in his arms. He could finally see the coastline of Spain, and knew they were close. They passed over the country and out over the Mediterranean Sea, and he watched as the coastline of Italy appeared. He turned north and followed landmarks to Florence until he saw it, standing like a gem on the river Arno... Castello Medici. He dropped them into the grand foyer, setting her down gently on her feet. "We're here, *mia belleza*."

Shannon had clung to him, her eyes shut tight as she felt the rush of air flowing past them, and then felt him set her down. She opened her eyes and looked around the massive hall with the wide marble staircase, and a ceiling that reached three stories into the air.

"And this is where Luca?"

"Castello Medici. This is Shade's ancestral home."

She shouted, "Are you kidding me?" She heard her own voice echo through the halls and suddenly, there were servants rushing into the hall from all directions. She recognized Gi from Kate's house in Virginia.

Gi bowed to her. "Is there something you need, *Signorina* Shannon?"

"No, I'm so sorry. I didn't mean to yell out like that. I'm fine Gi, thank you."

He nodded his head to her and made eye contact with the other servants who'd appeared, and they all turned and left the hall. Shannon looked up at Luca who was biting his lip to keep from laughing. She spoke to him in a soft voice.

"Sorry, what I meant to say was, are you fucking kidding me? This is a house? People live here?"

Luca finally released the laughter he'd been trying to hold inside. "*Si, mia belleza*, people live here. Shade lives here when he's not in Virginia, although, something tells me Virginia may be his more permanent home from now on and Castello is somewhere he visits. And now Kate will live here... and their children."

She craned her neck to look up at the vaulted ceiling that extended three stories and ended with a ceiling of glass panes.

"You grew up here?"

"I grew up in the warrior camp, which is on the property. I didn't live here in the castle. The warriors didn't typically come inside, although I've been inside on a few occasions. There are about fifty house staff who keep things running, and some of them are allowed to live inside the castle. The others have quarters provided for them. Gi lived here. He's been here the longest. He was the manservant to Shade's parents, and now fills that role for Shade. Theresa will become Kate's Lady in Waiting. These are honored positions, hard earned, and not taken lightly. Do you want me to walk you around? I suggest you not wander out on your own because you'll get lost. The first time Kate was here, she never left her room without an escort. It takes a while to figure it all out."

"I...yes...a tour... Holy Mother of God, I didn't know anyone lived like this."

He took her hand and walked her down wide corridors, with ornate frescoes on the ceilings, hand-painted by the Masters of the Renaissance, and massive gold and crystal chandeliers. They entered room after room, each more grandiose than the last, a formal living room that looked bigger than a bowling alley, a formal dining room that could easily seat a hundred people, a modern home theater room, a library to rival any library in the world, a huge kitchen, for people who don't eat food, go figure. Sitting rooms, reading rooms, parlors, music rooms, ballrooms, bathrooms, and on and on until they ended up back in the hall he called the grand foyer. Gi was standing there as they returned to the foot of the stairs.

Gi nodded to Luca as he and Shannon returned from their tour. "Luca, Master has chosen your permanent room here at Castello for this and all future visits. Your luggage has not yet arrived, but I have had the staff lay out night clothes for *Signorina* Shannon, and in the morning, we will bring up your luggage as soon as it arrives. You will find a tray of hot tea and some finger sandwiches and fruit in the room...some light refreshment for *Signorina* until morning. All your belongings from the warrior camp have been moved to the room as well. You have a large trunk and some other items. The staff did not put these away as they assumed you would prefer to do that yourself. Follow me please." He turned and headed up the marble stairs that curved to a landing, before curving again to the second floor. Luca was already surprised that Gi was leading him upstairs to the family living quarters, and not the staff quarters.

"Thank you, Gi." He took Shannon's hand and followed Gi up the stairs. Shannon would have a sore neck by morning she was whipping her head so fast to see everything, looking left, right and up. They followed Gi down the long second-floor corridor to the bedrooms and he stopped in front of Shade's old bedroom and indicated to Luca this was his room. Luca gave him a puzzled look.

"Gi, this is Shade's bedroom."

"*Si*. This *was* Shade's bedroom. However, master has decided his old room was not adequate for him now that he has a mate. And he has moved to the bedroom his parents once occupied. He requested this room be held for you."

"He wants me to have his room?" Luca was expecting a room like the rest of the house staff in the servants' quarters... not this room, Shade's room. He swallowed hard to hold back his emotions. He looked down at his feet to hide the tears that started to form as he wrestled to get his emotions in check. He felt Gi's hand at his elbow, the lightest touch, he understood.

Luca cleared his throat and looked up again as Gi opened the door for them to enter. He knew Shannon didn't understand the significance or the honor Shade had shown him by giving him this space, but she was still suitably impressed with the beauty of the room. Its massive carved mahogany canopy bed and the rich brocaded fabrics in deep burgundy and ivory colors were opulent. The room did have a masculine feel, as did the bathroom with the large marble tub. Shannon had let go of his hand and was running about the room, grabbing a sandwich on the run. She headed for the bathroom and he could hear her call out to him again.

"Oh my god, seriously? Can I get in this tub? I could swim in here!"

Luca followed her into the bathroom. "*Si, mia belleza*, we can get in the tub if you wish."

He reached over her and turned on the water from the solid gold faucets, and poured the scented bath oils into the water, watching it create rich foam on the surface. As the large tub filled and the steam rose, they both stripped from their clothes. He held her hand, as she stepped into the large tub, and then he stepped in behind her. He sat with his back against one wall of the tub, and she sat down between his legs, her back against his chest, and laid her head back on his shoulder.

"*Mia belleza*, I can't tell you how happy I am you've joined me on this trip. You're only the second mortal to enter these walls in centuries." He ran the tips of his fingers down her arm, dipping his fingers in the water, and drawing them back up her arm again. "Shade has agreed he will allow you to attend the coronation, where Kate is officially crowned as our queen. And I promise you, no mortal has ever witnessed that before, not in this coven or any other."

"Luca, this is all so unreal, I mean, this freakin' castle, and the king and queen thing, and Kate being converted, or whatever you call it."

"The turning... it's the turning. You'll not see the turning, as I mentioned. And both Kate and Shade will be sequestered in chambers that lie beneath the castle for several days."

She looked up at him. "Days?"

"*Si*, several days. The time for the turning will take from one night to the next. It's not an easy transition for a mortal. There are parts of the transition that'll be painful, and it's not without risk. But I don't have concerns. Kate is strong...and stubborn. She'll fight hard."

"Fight? I don't understand, Luca."

"Shade must take her to the very edge of death, one breath away... One heartbeat away. He must drain her mortal life from her and inhale her soul. He'll then feed her a few drops of his blood, but she'll fall away from him while her body undergoes the transformation. It'll be up to her to fight her way back. If Shade drains her too far, he'll lose her. If she's not strong enough to fight her way back from the pull of the darkness, he'll lose her. If she comes back, he returns her soul, now bound with his, and they're one. That will happen on the second night. If it's successful, we'll see the moon turn a bright red in the sky."

"And then they can come out?"

"No, Kate will need to feed from him, a lot, and often. He'll let her feed, but he'll also begin to teach her restraint, because initially, she'll feel none. If she were free to leave the chambers, she'd feed from anyone. Her need would be ravenous and uncontrollable. He keeps her in the chamber to protect her, and others. Once she's stabilized, in a few days, then they'll emerge. And then we'll have the coronation."

"Does Kate know all this? This sounds..."

"Frightening? *Si*, Kate's well aware. Shade has explained it all to her. She's been feeding from him for almost a year now, her body is stronger, and Shade considers her his mate as they only feed from each other. But in the vampire community, until she's turned, until she's immortal, she cannot be officially recognized as his mate, and certainly not recognized as our queen. As a mortal, it's unlikely she could successfully bear his children. And, of course, she'd age, and he wouldn't."

Shannon reached through the sudsy water and grasped his hand. "Oh, she told me about their baby."

"*Si*, not something any of us want to go through again. It almost broke them both. But this is their path, *mia belleza*. They didn't set out to find each other, mortal and immortal. It's a very difficult path to follow. But they're in love, *si*? And if they're to be together, this is their only way. I'm glad you're here to witness this, and you're friends with Kate, because we'll need to decide, my beauty, if this is our path. Don't answer now, please. I want you to watch and consider. I want you to think hard about these choices. As with Shade and Kate, there's no turning back, no undoing. This turning will bond them, blood to blood, soul to soul, for all eternity. And if one is killed, the other may choose to quickly follow, they're that tied to each other."

She tilted her head back so she could look up at him, "But Luca—"

He put his forefinger to her lips. "Shh. *Mia belleza*, I know you think you want to answer now. I ask that you not. Please. I only want your answer when this is all over and you've had time to think. Do that for me, please?"

She looked at his dark hair, hanging in loose strands around his face as the steam rose around him, and his hazel eyes looked pale against his dark skin. "I'll do that for you, Luca."

He picked up the natural sea sponge and poured the thick concoction of oils and sea salts onto the sponge.

"Sit up, my beauty, and I'll wash your back."

As she sat forward in the tub, he washed her porcelain skin with the salt scrub, watching as the heat and the friction turned her unflawed skin pink. She turned in the tub to face him, and straddled him, as he washed her arms and her breasts, his eyes roaming over her, taking in every curve. She took the sponge from his hands and poured more salt scrub onto it and began to bathe him. He watched her face, and those large doe eyes that portrayed innocence, when she was anything but. She dropped the sponge to float on the water as her hands disappeared beneath the surface and he felt her slide her hands up his inner thighs, and he took a sharp intake of breath.

She spoke to him in a breathy voice. "Will we wake the whole house if we make love?"

"*Mia belleza*, there are only vampires in this house. We'll wake no one."

She stood up in the tub with her feet on either side of his legs, facing him, as she let the water run down her body and watched his eyes devour her. "Well, how very convenient for us."

She stepped out of the tub and onto a plush mat, watching as he stood and stepped out of the tub beside her, bronzed and muscled, broad chest and slender hips, his legs lean and defined. He grabbed a thick towel and dried her off, and then snapped the towel hard across her ass. *Oh! Now here's a side of Luca I haven't seen before!* If he was expecting a squeal, he was disappointed, because the moan that escaped her lips betrayed her desire.

He heard the moan, the raw passion, the sexual pleasure she felt in the pain and his cock responded to her immediately. This shouldn't have been a surprise, this from the woman who'd teased and taunted his beast on the first night they made love. He looped the towel around her and pulled her to him, although she needed no encouragement, her body pressed into his, her face raised, eyes closed, and lips seeking. He didn't kiss her but looked at her face... That face had so captivated him. She slowly opened her eyes, locking onto his.

"I love you, *mia belleza*."

In her husky voice, she replied, "And I love you, Luca. But could you please fuck me?"

He laughed out loud at her boldness and picked her up and carried her to the bed, dropping her down hard on the mattress before crawling in bed on top of her, mounting her and riding her hard. She was ready. She was always ready. He pushed her hands above her head and held her wrists tight against the mattress. She wrapped her legs around his hips in a death grip and gave as good as she got. And this was round one of many.

* * *

Shannon woke up slowly, wrapped in his arms, to find him already awake and watching her. She smiled and stretched and looked around the huge room. The sun was bright today, and the room looked even more beautiful as the light bounced off the marble walls.

"What time is it?"

"It's late, *mia belleza*. Maybe ten."

She sat up suddenly in bed. "Ten! Wow, I don't usually sleep that late." She giggled. "But then, I don't usually spend the whole night making love. It's so quiet here. No traffic noise from the city. No alarm clocks going off. This feels glorious." She slid across the large bed and over the side. As her feet hit the floor, she noticed her luggage had been set inside the door.

"My stuff! When did that get here?"

"Early this morning, around seven I think, one of the staff brought it in."

"Seriously? I didn't hear a thing!"

"You were sleeping soundly, my beauty. But the staff has all been trained by Gi to do their jobs in a way that is minimally intrusive. They're not usually seen or heard unless you call upon them."

"Did you sleep, Luca?"

"*Si,* my beauty. I slept. But I'm a day-walker, remember, I can sleep when I need to, day or night, and my body doesn't require as much sleep."

"How do you become a day-walker?" She walked across the room in bare feet, feeling the cold marble floor, and dragged her luggage into the middle of the room and started unpacking her stuff. She pulled out a pair of jeans and a top and stepped into her clothes.

Luca lay on his side in the bed, his head propped up in his hand, and watched her as she walked nude across the room and began unpacking with no sense of modesty or any sense of awareness of her own nudity. She was a woman comfortable in her own skin.

"One doesn't become a day-walker, one is born a day-walker. It's a gift. Every vampire will have a gift when they're born."

"Every vampire has a gift? What is Shade's gift?"

"Shade's a dream-walker. He can enter your dreams, to observe, or shape them, good or bad."

"Wow, that sounds a little creepy. You said Kate will have that animal thing, but will she also be a dream-walker? Since he turns her? Will she inherit the same gift?"

"Sometimes a gift is passed on, but not necessarily. But no, we are only given one gift and I've already seen Kate's gift manifest. She'll have the gift of animalism."

"So, does that mean, if you turned me, I wouldn't necessarily be a day-walker too?

"*Si,* exactly. You may have to hide from the sun and slip into your death slumber. I've never known that existence for myself. But the gift of day-walking seems more and more prevalent among the younger vampires. Whether that's an evolution to modern times, I don't know. But most of the older vampires, like Shade, must avoid the sun. It's a burden, *mia belleza.* Even as a mortal you can choose to go out in the day or to sleep in the day. For those vampires who must avoid the daylight, there is no choosing. And their sleep comes unbidden. They must succumb to it. That's why we call it a death slumber. It takes you. The vampire can arouse himself if threatened, but there's a vulnerability that comes with the death slumber too. Most vampires in a death slumber will have day-walkers around them, who can respond, protect them. Does this frighten you, *mia belleza*? The death slumber?"

She finished putting the last of her clothes away in the drawers and wardrobes, and returned to the bed, sitting on the side, and looking at him stretched out before her, his chest exposed, and his dark skin against the white sheets draped low over his hips.

"Frightened? I wouldn't say it frightens me. It sounds odd to me. So if I... if you turned me... and I had to sleep during the day, you'd protect me?"

Luca frowned. They were back to this. It would always come back to this. He held her in his gaze as he sat upright in the bed and took a deep breath. "Shan, I'll always do my best to protect you, when I'm with you. But my first responsibility—"

"Kate. You'll protect her first."

"*Si,* I'll protect her first."

"Does that seem odd to you, Luca? I mean, if we're married, or mated, or whatever you call it, she'd always come before me?"

"Shannon, you know we've talked about this. And no, it doesn't seem odd to me because it's what I've spent my entire life training for. It's our custom, our world. You're equating my job and my responsibilities as a warrior and a protector to my love for you, and they're two separate things. But I'll tell you, most protectors don't have a mate. There are exceptions, and I've discussed this with Shade. My heart tells me he'll allow this for me... for us... if we choose this path. But you'll need to understand, *mia belleza*, my bond to him as my king and my master, and my bond to her, as my queen, and her chosen protector, these are things that won't change. I'll be with her until her death. These customs in no way reflect my love and devotion to you, and I'll protect you, directly or indirectly. We are Medici. This is a mighty coven, among the largest in the world. There are many warriors, and we're protected by our numbers. We protect our own. There'd always be someone assigned to you in my absence. Do you understand this, *mia belleza*? But further to the point, do you accept this?"

"I do, Luca. I do accept it, I think. It's just a hard concept to wrap my head around. If I think of it in mortal terms, like a bodyguard to a queen, or a Secret Service Agent for the President, then I get it. As a woman, I just have to get past the part where I feel like you're choosing her over me. I mean, I know Kate. She's my best friend. And I can see how much she loves Shade. I know her heart. I know her intent. I'm not jealous in the sense I feel she's trying to steal you away from me, do you understand? But I love you, Luca. And there's a part of me that wants, I don't know… I guess I want to think if I were in trouble, you'd come to me first."

Luca pulled her to his chest, wrapped his arms around her, and buried his nose in her hair. "It's our burden, *mia belleza*. All I can promise you is an eternity of my love, and a commitment to protect you and our family directly or indirectly. It's the same for Shade, my beauty. He cannot always be here for Kate. That's my job. I'll not always be here for you, but someone will be. And you must decide if this is a path you can follow, for there's no compromise, *si*?"

"I do understand, Luca, and I know what my heart wants."

She kissed him and then slid from the bed. "Come on, I'm starving! There must be more food in that huge kitchen!"

She grabbed a pear from the tray Gi left in the room for them last night and took a big bite as Luca climbed from the bed and started to dress.

He opened the large trunk Gi said had been brought here for him and started taking things out. It looked like a bunch of clothes and books.

Curious, she wandered over. "What's this stuff again?"

"Just stuff I left in the barracks when I was chosen as Kate's protector and left for the States. Someone packed it all up."

Shannon noticed a stack draped with a tarp of some sort and she lifted it away to reveal canvases containing his art. Kate said he was a painter. "Can I look at these, Luca?"

He looked up from the trunk to see her with a stack of canvases that were leaning against the wall. He'd completely forgotten about those. "Sure. But I warn you, I'm not very good."

Shannon flipped through the canvases and scanned through landscapes of the castle and surrounding Tuscany, the Florence skyline with the Duomo, a view of Ponte Vecchio, portraits of other warriors, and pictures of warriors fighting. He was wrong, he was very talented. She flipped to the last canvas to see a face, a woman's face, young, beautiful, and revealing a softness in her exposed shoulder, and a sensuality in her expression. "Luca, who's this?"

Luca stopped unpacking the trunk to look over to see which canvas she was holding, it was Alicia, his feeder. Less than a year, and yet, it seemed like another lifetime for him now. He had planned to see her during this trip, and to check on her and her family. The vision of Kate attacking the feeder flashed through his head and he warned himself to tread lightly. He stood upright and walked over to Shannon, took the canvas from her hands to look at it again.

"This is Alicia, *mia belleza*. She was my feeder. I chose to have only one." He handed the canvas back to her and returned to the trunk, bracing himself for her response.

"She's beautiful, Luca. She looks very... What word am I looking for? Vulnerable, maybe? Soft?"

"*Si,* feeders are bred, just as warriors are bred. We all have a role. For a vampire without a mate, a feeder is their soft place."

"Did you love her? You said you chose to only have one."

He sat down on the bed and looked at her. "In my fashion, Shannon. I wouldn't call it love, affection, maybe. A feeder can never belong to you. A feeder can never become your mate. And many vampires sample all the feeders, going from one to the other. But that wasn't my style. I felt a connection with her. I could talk to her. It's not what I feel for you, *mia belleza*, you need to understand that. Feeders are paid for their services, and in the end, it's a business transaction. But I was with her for many years, and I asked Shade to make sure she was taken care of when I left. I did miss her when I first went to the States, and I have to say, I didn't find the feeders in the States to my liking, although not all my brothers in arms have had any problems adapting. Then I met you, my beauty, and everything changed. I had planned to see her while I was here, if you don't object."

She put down the canvas and turned to him. "You want to see her? You'd feed from her?"

He heard the jealousy in her voice. *Tread softly here, Luca.* "I want to see her to make sure she's okay, her family is okay, and no, *mia belleza*, I wouldn't feed from her. I feed from you now." He watched her shoulders relax with his words.

"If I asked you, and I am asking you, to not see her, would you..." She paused. "Luca, I feel like I'm crossing boundaries here. Do I have the right? I don't doubt your love, but if I asked you not to see her..." She wrung her hands and pursed her lips. "What would your answer be?"

"Shan, if it makes you uncomfortable, I can refrain from seeing her. That's not an issue."

Did he tell her he had to supplement his feedings from her with other feeders in the States? He thought this was one of those, what did Shannon call it? An all cards on the table moment?

"But Shannon, you should know this, because I want no secrets between us. I don't see you often enough for the feeding to sustain me. I've had to feed from the feeders in the States since we've been together. I never seek the same feeder. I have no ties, no bond. And I look forward to the day when I'll feed from you only."

He still uses feeders? Well, this sucks, excuse the pun very fucking much! She felt her back stiffen. She hated this feeling, and she hated being jealous, but she was glad he'd told her. She walked to the window and looked out over formal gardens, with hedges trimmed to precision, creating a maze work. In the distance, she could see the tower near the Ufizzi in Florence and the Duomo.

"Does my opinion matter here?"

"*Si,* it matters very much, *mia belleza.*"

She turned and faced him but remained at the window. "I'd like to say it doesn't bother me, that I'm above it all. But I'm not. It hurts me to think of it. I heard what you said. I get it. And Luca, I appreciate that. But I watch when you feed from me. I don't know exactly what you feel, but clearly, it brings pleasure. I know what it makes me feel, to have you feed from me. It's an intimacy that goes beyond sex. So, if I have a say, knowing this now... I..." She sighed and fought back tears. *No fucking tears, Shannon!* "Tell me where we go from here, Luca. When you speak to me, it sounds like you want us to be together forever, and I'll have to come to terms with the fact I share you on some level with Kate. So, I need to know I won't also be sharing you with feeders. What part belongs just to us?"

He stood and went to her, taking her in his arms. "*Mia belleza,* until I knew your feelings for me, I had no right to make demands. I fed from you whenever we were together. In between, I sought out the feeders. If you wish for us to be exclusive, it means you're accessible to me whenever I need you. I didn't know if you were ready for that commitment. This life... It's a paradox. We're charmed in many ways and tortured in others. But if you chose it, I wanted you to choose it freely, understanding the demands, the implications."

"Then I guess my question for you, Luca, is, are *you* ready? Are you ready for a commitment to me?"

"I think I was ready the minute I laid eyes on you, *mia belleza.* But yes, I'm ready. I've been ready."

"Then that's what I want. I want you to feed from me only, be with me only."

"It's done, my beauty."

"And me from you? We haven't talked about that."

He released her from the hug, holding her at arm's length, looking at her. "*Si,* we haven't. One step at a time, Shan. I want us to move slowly. Now, let's get you downstairs so you can eat. Come on."

He led her by the hand as they walked through these halls as he hoped to lead her through their life together.

86

Luca stood in the city where he was born, looking at the Duomo one last time before taking Shannon's hand and heading back to Castello after a day of walking through the streets of Florence. He'd grown up around these treasures, but they were still new to her and her excitement was infectious. She did want to see Kate, though, so they timed their tour to end around sunset. Luca had told Shannon that Kate didn't have to sleep during the day yet, but she chose to sleep then because that was when Shade must sleep. They arrived back at Castello at dusk, ran to their rooms for a quick change and headed back down the stairs.

Shannon turned to him on the stairs. "Where would we find them? Kate and Shade?"

Luca laughed. "They could be anywhere on the property."

Shannon tugged at his hand, "Well, that could take days! Come on...I'm starving. You keep forgetting I'm mortal and I need to eat. Can you get me to the kitchen again?"

He took her hand and led her through the atrium, down the hall of ancestors until they got to the kitchen. He could hear Kate's voice as they entered.

Shannon heard her before she saw her and rushed ahead of Luca into the large kitchen, calling out to Kate. Kate turned and they both ran to each other and hugged.

"I'm so happy you came, Shannon. Gi told me you were here that you got in last night."

Shannon stepped back, still holding onto her. "I've been here a whole day, and this is the first time I've even seen you. When is this turning thing?"

Kate shrugged. "Tomorrow night, I think."

"You think? Aren't you excited? Nervous? Something?"

"Uh... yes, yes, and yes... all of the above. To be honest, I've tried not to dwell on it much."

Luca joined the girls and directed his inquiry to Kate, "Where's Shade?"

"Do you even have to ask? He's in the barracks with Marco. I think there's a little bromance going on."

Luca chuckled. "Yeah, that's been a long-standing bromance. But I'll have him join us. **Master, there is a spontaneous celebration breaking out between these two mortal women... you may want to join us in the kitchen.**"

* * *

Shade had been checking out the warriors, observing with Marco some of the skill sets on display. He was impressed with their development and keeping an eye on a few specific warriors he may want to bring back with him to the new camp in Virginia. They'd need some skilled warriors in the new camp, as they brought in new recruits. He made a mental list and headed down to the end of the barracks to check on Cory. Shade tapped at his door and entered to find him busy as usual. Cory had been working on the ceremonial leathers for all the warriors to wear to the coronation and had gotten behind in his routine orders and repairs. Shade cleared a stack of leathers that had been dropped off for repair from a chair and took a seat as Cory stopped his work and turned to him.

"Master? I heard from the warriors you were here, and you were bringing your mate to be turned. I completed the ceremonial leathers bearing the Medici crest on their chest."

"*Si*. This will be her last night as a mortal, then she will emerge as your queen. All of the warriors, as well as you, will be there to pledge their loyalty."

"My queen?"

"*Si,* you are Medici, are you not?"

Cory absorbed what Shade had said to him. For the first time in his life as a half-breed, he'd found somewhere he felt he belonged, and yet, he was keenly aware he wasn't one of them. While he'd always referred to Shade as master, it was in recognition of his status. Cory felt he worked for Shade, and as a result, enjoyed some protection from him, but didn't know Shade considered him a part of his coven. "Am I? Medici?"

"*Si,* of course. You belong to this coven, you have conducted yourself with honor, earned your way here, earned the respect of the warriors. I came to ask you about moving back to the States."

Cory had a flash of panic. Leave this? Leave the craft of designing and making the leathers for the warriors? This was the only thing he knew. "You're not happy with my work here, master?"

Shade chuckled. "The opposite, son. I am starting a warrior camp on my property in Virginia. It's under construction now and I hope it will be ready to open when I return. I will be recruiting young vampires from the States to the camp, and we will need leathers for all of them. Do you think you can manage that?"

Cory's eyes brightened. This was a chance to stay with master and live in the States. Not just in the States, but on master's property, making leathers for new recruits. He'd never mastered Italian, and even though many of the warriors here spoke English, when speaking to each other, they usually spoke in their native tongue and he felt excluded. "Yes, master! I can manage that. All the warriors here have several full sets of leathers, and I focus on repairs. I could probably still oversee that, and I have their measurements if they need new sets, I can manage both camps for you."

Shade stood and Cory jumped to his feet. Shade gave him a fatherly hug. "Good. We will work out the details after the coronation. You have made me proud, Cory. I gave you an opportunity and you grabbed it with both hands. And that Medici crest needs to be on your leathers as well... warrior or not."

Cory beamed with pride and was always surprised at how much Shade's praise meant to him when he considered he'd spent such little time in his presence. But living in Virginia, working directly for master, he'd have to let his Mom know!

As Shade was wrapping up his good-byes with Cory, he heard Luca tell him about a celebration. Shade thought, before this got out of hand, he better get inside. Shade gave Cory a hug and teleported to the foyer, making his way into the kitchen. Spotting *bel*, he stood back against the wall, legs crossed at the ankles, arms crossed over his chest and waited for her to feel him.

Kate looked up to see him standing in the doorway with a look that smoldered. **"Too bad we have company, or I'd be dragging you upstairs."** "Lover! Come join us... Shannon's here with Luca. I think we should celebrate."

"Don't start me up, *mi amore*, I'm hanging by a thread now, woman. You drive me wild!" Walking past Luca, he gave him a fist bump, but his eyes never left her face. He picked her up in his arms and twirled her around, kissing her deeply, his tongue inside her mouth, tangling with hers, probing, sucking, then biting her lip and slapping her ass. "Mmm, I could eat you alive, *mi amore*. And what are we celebrating?" Smiling at her, he glanced over at Shannon, grinned and winked. "Welcome to my home, Shannon... sorry, I was a bit... distracted."

Shannon gave him a sly grin. "Hey... don't mind me. I love a good X-rated movie. You two just go for it and Luca and I will watch."

Luca grabbed her hand and drug her over close to him. "No... we will *not* watch. Sorry, master."

Shade threw back his head and laughed. "Don't apologize, Luca, you may learn a thing or two on how to please a mortal woman, but," looking deep into *bel*'s eyes, "better make it quick, this mate won't be mortal for long. So, someone tell me what we are celebrating."

Shannon leaned across a massive butcher block island. "We're celebrating Kate's last night as a mortal. Do vampire's drink? You have all these freakin' vineyards, you must drink something!"

"Oh *si*, Shannon, we do drink. Gi, break out the Midnight! Time to celebrate, but tell me, Shannon, what is your mortal poison?"

"Am I limited to one? Let's see, where do I start? Cosmopolitans, Martini's, Margaritas, Pina Coladas, and wine, red or white. If it's in a bottle, I'll drink it. And can we get some food? I'm starving! Luca forgets I still need to eat."

Gi ordered the kitchen staff to enter, servants and cooks appeared and Shade watched the reaction on Shannon's face and chuckled. "Ladies... please put your order in for anything you wish to eat, and it will be prepared... anything you wish to drink... will be made for you... welcome, Shannon, to the world of Medici... the world lies at your feet."

Shannon shook Kate by the shoulders. "Kate, do you realize this may be your last meal?"

"Gee thanks, Shannon. You say that like I'm going to the electric chair or something."

"No, seriously! No more pizza. Doughnuts. Gelato. No more chocolate! Oh my god... pasta, steaks, French fries... macaroni and cheese, strawberry shortcake, coconut cream pie... girl, I think you need to rethink this decision."

Kate responded, "I think we need to pig out on all the things you just named. No salads tonight. The boys can get drunk off their ass and watch. And maybe... Shade can feed me honey one last time?"

"Oh *si*, *mi amore*... honey it is."

Kate looked up, as the cooks started laying out the table with all the foods Shannon had been shouting out, and the two of them dove in, starting with the pizza. "Oh, god... this is so good." Shade and Luca both pulled up a bar stool, propping their feet on the table, pouring themselves tall glasses of Midnight. Kate saw Shade turn to Luca and say, "It's going to be a long night, warrior", and she and Shannon both started laughing...and eating doughnuts.

Shade playfully tried to grab at the pizza slice from Kate's hand.

She smacked at his hand. "Hands off the pizza!"

He laughed as she moved to take a big bite. He grabbed the slice from her hand, and walked backward away from her, holding the pizza in his hand and hit the music. "Want something in your mouth, do you, *mi amore*?"

He started playing Nickleback's *Something in Your Mouth,* as it echoed through the halls of the castle and taunted her with a slice of pizza.

"Oh, I want something in my mouth all right, and it's not pizza." She chased after him as he ran around the counter, and Shannon laughed at their antics.

As she gave chase, Shade kept just ahead of her and watched her getting dizzy chasing him around the island counter. She stopped to regain her equilibrium and he slipped up behind her and stepped on a single pepperoni that had dropped on the floor. He fell flat on his ass, pulling her down with him. Kate squealed as she fell, and Luca was laughing so hard he fell off the chair.

Shannon was laughing, her mouth still full. "Well, that didn't take long. I can drink both of them under the table any day! Come on, sister. There's strawberry shortcake with our name on it. Get off the floor and dig in."

Shannon reached down, stepping over Shade who was still sprawled on the floor, and grabbed Kate's hand. Kate stood up with assistance and joined Shannon at the counter. Shannon handed her a spoon and they both dug in. Speaking through a mouthful of cake, strawberries and fresh whipped cream, Kate asked her, "Aren't you going to help Luca up?"

Shannon looked down at him on the floor. "Luca, honey, do you need help?"

Luca rolled from his side onto his back, "I think it's safer down here. But you could hand me the bottle."

Shannon handed the bottle of Midnight down to Luca who took a big swig while still lying on his back.

Shade laughed. "*Si,* that's a warrior!" Crawling to Luca, he reached for the bottle.

Shade rolled over on his back and taking a huge swig, passed it back to Luca who was trying to sit up and failing miserably.

Kate looked at him sprawled on the floor. She walked over to where he was lying on his back, and stood over him, straddling his chest.

Looking up, Shade had a terrific view up her skirt of her sweet red thong. He slid his hand up the back of her calf and onto her thigh. "Careful, *mi amore*, you tempt me way beyond what I can handle and I... Fuck, woman!" He took a deep breath and tried to shut down his senses, when all he wanted to do was ravish her right here on the floor.

Shannon was laughing through a mouthful of coconut cream pie. "I love that he calls you woman... so cave man. Does he drag you off by your hair too?"

Kate bent at the waist and let her hair sweep across Shade's face. "Not yet, but he does other things with my hair we can't talk about in public."

Shade started groaning. "I can't take this anymore." Before he knew what was happening, Kate was laughing and there was food all over his and Luca's face. *Damn, who the hell did that?* "What the fuck?"

Kate looked around to see Shannon using the big serving spoon like a catapult to fling a big glob of whipped cream right at Luca's face. Luca swiped his hand across his own face and flung the glob to the side, hitting Shade. Kate reached behind her to the counter and grabbed a handful of the strawberry shortcake and smashed it on Shade's face. Shannon grabbed whole platters of food and started slinging it, screaming "Food fight!" The floor was soon covered in food. It was almost impossible to remain upright.

Shade screamed, "This is war!" Slipping and sliding over the floor, he managed to get to his knees, and crawled forward, only to slip again, falling on his face. He looked up to see Gi standing back, and for the first time in about four-hundred years, the old butler was doubled over laughing. Music rang out through the halls and the castle was rocking. Shade saw the house staff appearing, one or two at first, and then the doorways were filled with faces of the staff, laughing as they watched their master uncharacteristically playing. Shade threw a pie at Gi in retribution and watched the old vampire duck.

"Luca!" He watched as Luca started to stand and then did a split in the middle of the floor, trying to get to him. They both hurled themselves to the counter to have something to hang onto and started swinging anything they could at Gi, laughing their asses off.

Kate was trying to walk to Shannon, but her feet were sliding out from under her. She kicked off her shoes and fell just as she got to her, grabbing Shannon to hold on to, but pulling both of them to the floor. Shannon squealed as they went down, hitting the floor hard, but they couldn't stop laughing. Kate rolled off her and found a doughnut.

"Oh look...a doughnut." As she took a big bite, she dropped over with laughter. Shade and Luca were doing some kind of obscene mambo in the middle of the floor in an attempt to pull Gi into the food fight.

Kate was sliding in the goopy mess on the floor and tried to crawl under the table to escape. She saw Shade crawl to join her under the table as Luca and Shannon continued the battle. She wiped the cake and whipped cream from his face, and he pulled a chunk of doughnut out of her hair before they exchanged a wet, sticky, sweet kiss.

"*Ti amo, bel.* I love you so much right now. Holy hell, we need to get the fuck outta here!" Pulling her close, they lay under the table and looked out at the chaos around them. "We need an escape route. I think I can manage to teleport us out of here... you game?"

"I'm game, but we're leaving Luca and Shannon. Can't you send him a message or something?"

He blew his hair out of his eyes and grinned at her. "Every damn warrior for himself. Hold on vixen, let's get outta here."

As she clung to him, he teleported out of the kitchen and landed in the middle of their bedroom. He set her down and chuckled as he looked at her. "What the hell just happened?"

They were both covered in food. Kate hated to move because she didn't want to mess up anything else in the house. It would take the staff forever to clean up that kitchen. "Well, that was unexpected. Make a note, Shannon, Luca, you, me, and alcohol, not a good combination. Can you carry me to the shower, please? I don't know which one of us looks worse."

"Worse? You look beautiful, *mi amore*, like a beautiful dessert just for me. I will carry you to the shower." Picking her up, he carried her to the bathroom where they slowly peeled away their soaked clothing.

She laughed at him with whipped cream on his head. She peeled off the sticky top and watched as a strawberry fell to the floor. Her jeans felt like they were glued on, and she had to wiggle them down an inch at a time until they were free of her hips. She finally sat on the floor and held up her feet to him and asked him to pull the jeans off.

He grabbed her feet and yanked on her jeans until she was free of them.

She crawled to the shower and reached up, turning on the water, letting it wash away the sticky mess. "Get in here, lover." He joined her in the large marble shower stall and into the falling water. She watched as the water poured over his face, his eyes closed. She leaned in and kissed him, the water falling over both their heads. They sat together in the middle of the elaborate mosaic tile floor of the shower, and she grabbed the bar of soap and began to soap him down with her hands. "I sincerely hope your mother isn't watching. Or worse, your father."

He chuckled. "I hope they were watching, *mi amore*. I hope they were laughing with us. My *padre* would have been shocked at such outrageous behavior from the staff, but I can almost hear my *madre* laughing at the fun. She would have loved that little episode. There were no such events when they lived here. There were banquets, of course, but nothing that got out of hand." Closing his eyes, "I wish they were here, *mi amore*, to see you, to see how much I love you, and that I have found you. I wish *madre* could dress you tomorrow night in your gown before the turning. She would have loved that. Would you have liked that?" Taking the soap from her hands, he returned the gesture of lathering her up and letting his hands slide over her white skin.

"I would have, lover. I'd have loved for her to be here to help me. I have to say, this isn't how I expected to spend my last night as a mortal." She felt his hands glide over her, slippery from the soap, as he washed away the last of the stickiness.

"*Mi amore*, it doesn't matter how you spend it, we are together, laughing and in love. We are surrounded by people who love us both, old and new. All that matters... or is there something more you wish?" He softly kissed her neck.

"I have everything I need right in front of me, everything." She stood up and rinsed the soapy lather from her skin and let the water run through her hair. She felt him stand up beside her, his hand running up her leg, her hip, her shoulder, before his lips found hers again. He rinsed off and together, they stepped out of the shower, grabbing oversized plush towels to dry themselves off. She walked into their bedroom and noticed a tray on the table by the bed with jars of honey, and she turned and looked at him.

Shade cocked his head to the side and smiled. "Gi hears everything, *mi amore*." Walking to the bed, he picked her up and laid her down softly.

"Shh... relax, mortal." Picking up the jar, he twisted it open and grinned at her. Walking to the end of the bed, he crawled up slowly and let the honey drizzle from the jar into her belly button and watched her hips arched upwards. "Patience, mortal..."

"It's not patience I need, lover."

"Ask and you shall receive, *mi amore, si*?" Firing up the music, he played Van Morrison's *Tupelo Honey*, he set the honey aside, leaned down and twirled his tongue around her belly button, then dipped his finger into the small pool of sweet stickiness and brought it to her lips and watched as she sucked the honey from his finger. He moaned as her tongue swirled around his finger. Still on all fours, he moved back down her body, straddling her and ran his tongue along her stomach, sucking away the last of the honey, then kept moving down further. Grabbing her thighs, he spread her legs and gazed at the beautiful heaven in front of him He dove into her, his tongue probing her sweet soft paradise, feeling her hands grab his hair and her body respond instantly.

He took her higher, his own beast and cock raging. Teasing her clit with his tongue, he heard her beg and he knew it was time. Pulling from her, he sat up and slid his hands under her arms and raised her to a sitting position and looked into her eyes. "*Mi amore*, I cannot be inside you, it is too risky. But we both need to feed for strength tomorrow. Please, take me in your hand, I will do the same for you, we will feed from each other, and give each other pleasure. "

She felt his hand between her legs and his teeth sinking into her neck. She slid her hand around his cock just as he took the first swallow. She was dizzy with pleasure, as she bit hard into him and felt that bolt of current hit her as his blood touched her tongue. She felt his fingers probing, tasted his blood, and listened to his moans as she stroked him... pushing them both to pleasures edge.

With each draw from her neck, his beast screamed for release, and he was pleasured by the touch of her hand, the sweet hard strokes, how her fingers glided over the tip, teasing him. The erotic sensual pull of her dull teeth on his throat drove him even further and his fingers stroked her, moving them inside her, faster, then slower, repeating and when he could feel they were both almost there, he slid his thumb over her clit and pushed his fingers deep inside her, feeling her cum violently as he spilled his seed into her hand, and threw back his head screaming for the world to know she was his.

She dropped back on the bed and looked up at him, locked eyes with him, before she lifted her hand to her mouth and licked away every last drop of that salty goodness. "Better than honey, lover."

"Wicked vixen!"

Hearing the electronic blinds go down, he knew it was time they slept. The next few nights would be the longest of their lives. He knew this was the last time she slept with him as a mortal. His fears were calmed, she was strong and as prepared as she could be. Somehow, deep inside, he knew she'd fight the darkness and come back to him in the turning. Lying on his back beside her, he pulled her onto his chest, her head resting beneath his chin and let his hand rest in that beautiful crimson he adored.

"This is your last time, *mi amore*, to sleep next to me as a mortal. I want you to know, I want nothing more than for you to become my true mate. It is a marriage of eternity to me. But even at the last second, if you change your mind, please tell me. Rest, for we have a long few nights ahead of us. They will be the most important we ever experience together. Trust in me, believe in me... use everything I have taught you and you will be fine. Just come back to me."

"Shade, as long as you're with me, I'll get through it. I'll come back to you. Nothing will change my mind."

"*Ti amo*. Now sleep, tomorrow night we rise and begin the journey of eternity."

87

The night of the turning came quickly, as Shade stood in one of the many guest chambers of Castello, his thoughts were filled with Kate. Gi helped him get dressed. He didn't need assistance, but it was customary in his royal lineage to do so for such occasions. He wore white, as would she, as she would return to him a virgin of his kind, immortal, and they'd mate and feed as two immortals for the first time.

The house was silent, and Gi remained quiet as he moved about the room. Shade concentrated his mind and spirit on the task that lay ahead of him, for tonight would be the most important night of his life. This night, Kate began the process of becoming his true mate. It was something he'd dreamed of since the moment he first saw her. He'd never turned a mortal, but he'd read enough books on how it was done.

He must perform the turning in the birthing chamber. All Medici royalty were born in these underground chambers of Castello, a chamber created especially for these occasions, providing safety and privacy to carry out their customs. It was the chamber where he'd been born, and his father before him. But this was an event the Medici coven had never seen before, the turning of a mortal and entering the royal bloodline of their people. His mind was heavy with what was to come, and he was well aware of the risks.

There had been a temporary Lady in Waiting to assist Kate here in Florence. Her name was Emma, and she'd been hand-picked by Theresa, so Theresa had free time to stay with Marco. But tonight, Theresa had come to their bedroom to assist Kate in dressing. She brought with her the long flowing white gown Kate was to wear. Kate bathed and washed her hair. Theresa added oils to the water she said were necessary to prepare her body for the turning. After her bath, Theresa dried her skin, rubbing briskly with the plush white towel. Kate sat at a vanity while Theresa dried her hair and brushed it out until it shined. Kate did her make-up and sprayed on her rose scented fragrance as Theresa helped her into the gown.

"It's almost a wedding dress, Theresa."

"*Si,* my lady, it's a wedding, of sorts. I know master drinks only from you and you from him, but until you are immortal, that mating cannot be sealed. There. All done. You look beautiful, my lady."

Theresa stepped back from her and Kate looked at her reflection in the huge mirror, the mirror that belonged to Shade's mother. This dress was beautiful, and she knew Shade loved her hair worn down like this. As she looked at her reflection, she saw a transition taking place, something changed before her eyes. The image of another woman, dressed in clothes from an era past, appeared in the mirror. She had blonde hair, blue eyes, fair skin, and was wearing a heavy velvet gown of deep burgundy. Kate stepped back from the image, looking over her shoulder to see Theresa busy picking up items in the room. *Does she see this?* Kate turned back to the mirror to see the woman looking at her, holding her gaze.

Portia stood regal in her gown and watched Kate prepare. She'd been observing her son's choice for a mate for some time now. She was beautiful, small even by mortal standards, but with strong character and a heart of gold. She'd make him a good mate, a good mother to his children, and give him the life he never allowed himself to dream of. Portia had found her long before her son had, had picked her out for him, and placed her in his path. She knew her son had been reluctant to start this journey, had taken great pains to avoid it, and she understood why. He'd carried the burden of the curse, and it couldn't be avoided, but securing the Medici legacy took precedent over everything else. Portia could tell Kate was frightened by the image of what appeared before her, but this was Portia's only time to speak with her before she became an immortal.

"Do not be frightened, *mia figlia.* I am Portia, Shade's *madre.* Theresa cannot see me, nor hear us. I walk among you silently, giving only you this vision. Do you have questions for me?"

Kate heard the image in the mirror speak to her. *Am I going crazy?* She reached out and touched the mirror, touched her face. She recognized Shade's mother from the large oil painting. She was even more beautiful than the portrait, regal in her bearing, standing straight and proud.

"Tell me you approve. Tell me you see how much I love him, how much I'll sacrifice for him, and that I'd die for him."

"*Si, mia figlia.* I led him to you, you are his destiny. He was born from a love such as you speak, inside my body, he grew and became the warrior of his people... our people. This night, you take my only son to become his true mate. Do not be frightened of what you will see, nor feel, nor hear." Leaning closer, her hand reached through the glass and her long, slim fingers stroked the cheek of her son's mate. "Fight for *mio figlio*. Fight hard! The turning will not be easy, but you become Medici when you return to him."

Kate listened to her words of encouragement. She knew she'd need them for what lay ahead. She could feel Portia's hand as she stroked her cheek. "I'll always fight for him. Always."

"You are his light, his comfort and his strength. You will bear him a son and two daughters who will carry forth our bloodline, so we will walk forever amongst this land he has fought so hard to retain. He would die for you, and he would die without you. So, do not take him from me this night. You must fight to the end. I know him. I know his heart. If you do not return to him, he will follow you in death. Listen for him, *mia figlia*, he will call you. You must listen to his blood singing within your veins. Let it fill your heart and let your soul go to him. He will always love you and no other. He will always give you what you seek. He is the darkness seeking your light. Give it to him, for no other can. You are loved here. Love him in return and he will be the king he dreams of becoming."

Turning, she slowly dissipated into the fog inside the mirror, to return to her eternity and her king. Tonight, her son becomes the king her Christofano always wanted him to be.

Kate stood stunned before the mirror as Portia disappeared. She looked again at Theresa who moved about the room as if nothing had happened.

"Did you hear that, Theresa?"

"Hear what, my lady?"

"Nothing... never mind." *Was she real? Or just my imagination running wild, knowing what lies ahead of me tonight. I hope she was real.*

* * *

As Gi finished dressing Shade, he stared out the window. High above the grounds he looked out, knowing after this night, everything in his life would be different. She'd finally be his for all eternity. Gi advised him Kate was ready and waiting in their bedroom. Shade nodded and walked silently down the long hall to their door. He opened it quietly and walked in to find Theresa. She smiled and told him Kate was ready and waiting, and he watched as she left the room, closing the door behind her.

Shade walked to the middle of the room and the sight of her made his knees weak. Theresa had dressed her in a flowing white gown that was backless. It clung to her bodice then floated away at the hips, trailing behind her on the floor. It was made of the softest silk and delicate Italian lace and she looked stunning. Her hair shone and cascaded down her back like crimson fire and stood out against the white dress and her pale skin. She looked like an angel, and this night, she was going to hell and back for him.

"You look beautiful, *mi amore*, more beautiful than the stars and moon. Are you ready to proceed?" He stood back and didn't approach her. He wanted her to come to him, with an open soul, to join him for all eternity.

She turned to face him. He was also dressed in white. Soft white linen pants, and a loosely constructed white jacket with no shirt. His dark hair was hanging in loose curls, his olive skin looking even darker against the white, and those eyes... always, those eyes. She walked to him, her arms extended to him. "And you, lover... your beauty makes the sunlight pale by comparison."

Taking her in into his arms, he looked deep into her eyes and said nothing. There were no words needed this night. He kissed her deeply and passionately. "Then let us begin our journey, *si*? We must have your death come at a specific hour. We must soon begin. The walk is long, *mi amore*, but I will not teleport. We must walk to the chamber under the castle. From this moment on, I will not leave your side."

Taking her hand, he led her out the door, where Gi waited for him. He held the ancient and most precious book among the Medici treasures. It held the history of matings, births and deaths that recorded their royal bloodline. He'd placed a rose at the page that would bear her name this night, documenting for all future generations, her place in history as his mate.

Shade took the ancient text and handed it to her. "Please, *mi amore*, will you carry this to the chamber? It is my family's ledger of our royal heritage. I will write your name upon the page when you come back to me. The ledger is sealed in a vault and only unlocked and taken out to record these events. You will carry no bouquet for a traditional mortal wedding, but for me, this is far more important."

She took the ancient book from his hands. The pages were crisp and yellowed with age, the leather bindings were cracked, and the single blood red rose was inserted between the pages. They continued to walk through the long halls of the Castello. He had one hand holding hers, and the other placed at the small of her back, guiding her, as he'd always guide her.

As they walked the long halls together, the house staff appeared one by one and stopped whatever they were doing to see them on their way. They didn't speak but nodded as a sign of respect to Shade and his chosen mate, and a silent wish for the safe turning of the beauty on his arm. He held his head proud. She would be his now, nothing would ever take her from him.

As they made their way down the long staircase to the below ground chambers, the stones were old, and the chamber he sought hadn't been used since his birth five-hundred years ago. The walls almost spoke to him of the events that had come before them. It was a blessing, in a way, as their ritual surfaces bled water that trickled downward, and held the memory of their history. He wove his way through the torch-lit archways, carefully making sure *bel* didn't fall or stumble, her beautiful gown trailing behind her. *Madre* would've been so damn proud and would've loved her in this gown. As they finally approached the enclosed chamber, the stone door was closed.

"*Mi amore*, once you go inside this chamber, there is no returning. There is only the two of us far beneath the ground. Do you wish for me to become your master this night, the maker you will forever cherish for the rest of your immortal existence? You will now be bound to me for all eternity. Are you ready to give your soul to me to carry?"

Her heartbeat picked up as he led her to a massive door and stopped. "Lover, I'm already bound to you for all eternity. Just promise me you'll not leave my side. Will I hear you? During the turning, in my head... will I be able to hear you?"

"There will be times, *mi amore*, when you cannot hear me or feel me, but I will never leave your side. When you have turned, when it is time for you to come back to me, you must listen for me, concentrate and feel all of me. You will have to fight hard. The darkness of Hell will call you, the devil wants you and he will fight you for your hand. Do not let him win. You must feel my blood in your veins, make the remnants of your soul seek me, listen for my words. You will not feel them at first. You will only feel the pain of the changes inside you. You must fight! Your body will be an empty shell, open to the devil to inhabit, *mi amore*. He can claim you as his own. Let the beast I have given you come out and fight to return to me. Now, we must enter."

Turning, he laid his hand on a raised stone, carved with the Medici crest and pressed his hand flat against it, speaking in the ancient code he was taught. Watching as a red glow flared beneath his hand, the chamber stone opened, and he willed the candles to come alive, lighting the very chamber where he was born, where his *bel* would be reborn, and all their *bambinos* to follow.

"I will not carry you across this threshold, *mi amore*, but I will carry you out as my mate. Come, my *bel*, it is time to welcome you to my world."

Kate peered inside this cave, this cavern carved in stone, lit only by candles and it was silent as a tomb. She could see a raised platform, and centered in that platform a bed of stone... or an altar? Her mouth felt dry, but she stepped over the threshold and into the chamber. The room was cold as they were so far below ground, and the air was musty. She felt him step in behind her. *The devil will fight for my soul? But Shade fights as well... and I will fight.* She squeezed his hand.

He could feel her fear and that was good, she needed to be deeply aware of all her senses. Taking her hand, he led her up to the dais and sat her down softly upon the bed of stone draped in white silk. Kneeling at her feet, he took off each of her leather slippers and placed them aside, and looked up into her eyes, those beautiful dark pools, open wide and reflecting the candlelight.

"*Mi amore*, relax. I am going to make love to you, right here. I will play music for you as well, and once you are comfortable, I will take your blood, you will feel no pain, just pleasure, a lot of pleasure."

Winking, he stood and slowly stripped for her, standing tall before her, he saw the wicked smile on her face and he knew she'd come back to him. Letting his hands slide up under her gown, he gripped her thighs gently and slid her back to lie down. He took the book from her hands and gave her the blood red rose, picked at its peak from their very own garden.

"Now, keep the rose, *mi amore*, take it with you, it will help you. Kiss me... kiss me like it is the last time you will ever kiss me. Let me feel how much you love me, how much you want to be my mate, how much you want to come back to me."

Still holding the rose, she put her arms around his shoulders and drew him to her, until their lips touched. Their kisses gentle, soft, teasing. And then his lips covered hers, his mouth opened, his tongue probed, and she took him into her mouth, as she would take his blood and his soul before night fell again. And as she kissed him, long and deep, they felt their passion build.

He kissed her lips, her neck, her cheeks, her eyelids. He moaned softly and growled, feeling her come alive under his hands. Gently pulling on her tongue with his teeth, he broke the passionate kiss that lit up both their bodies.

"You cannot feed, *mi amore*, you must hold back. But I will not. You are so beautiful in this candlelight."

Letting his lips slide to her breasts, he teased her nipples through the silken white material and felt her breasts arch up to him. He pulled her gown up around her waist, she was naked beneath the dress and his cock slid along her silken sex. She was wet and aching, and he felt her need to have him deep inside her.

"I love you, *mi amore*, I love you more than my own life."

The moan escaped her lips as his hands pulled at her hips, drawing her to him. She slid her legs around him, the gown draping to the floor.

He felt her desire for him, but the timing must be right for her to feel no pain, just pleasure as he drained the life from her. Sliding his cock in deep, he sank his fangs into her neck, he began to draw deep, experiencing the exquisite sexual pleasure in her blood, gorging himself on her unique taste that was all his. He felt his body respond with her blood rushing inside him. He drew deeper, swallowing more and more of her blood, as his hips thrust harder and harder, wanting her to cum right before she was drained. He didn't let go of her neck, keeping his fangs sunk deep into her soft skin, draining her as her orgasm built and he felt her bucking beneath him, wanting to cum for him. Her body would feel that erotic blend of orgasm and that moment of near death, a dizzying feeling for any mortal. He held her tight and for one second, he felt a burst of panic rush through her, she felt the dizziness taking her, and for a split second, she was scared, her mortal instincts for survival kicking in, but he caressed her hip, pushing inside her deeper, penetrating her like never before as he gulped down the sweetest blood of his life.

* * *

He laid over her, his weight on her, holding her down. She felt the sweet sting of his fangs and the erotic rush that always followed. She felt his cock, plunging deep inside her. He drank deep, much deeper than usual, as his hips pounded against her, thrusting hard, her legs latched tight around him, open to him. He took her, all of her, and she gave herself up to him.

She began to feel dizzy, a light-headedness that she'd not felt before, and she realized he was draining her of all her blood, and she felt a momentary panic. She struggled as she felt his hands caress her and he pushed deeper, pushing her to the edge of orgasm. **"Lover, don't let me go."**

She felt the tension build inside her. It was a deep ache in her belly that sought release, when she felt his cock throb, and his mouth sucked hard and she let herself fall. Falling backward into this abyss, as the orgasm washed over her, wave after wave, and still, he didn't stop. The pleasure overwhelmed... she needed it to stop... but he drank from her still.

* * *

He knew they were close, and then he felt her body respond with pleasure as they both came together and he filled her with his seed. Her body relaxed as he felt her heart take a slow struggled beat, and she dropped away into another world. Her weak heart told him she was near death, but for a short while, she could still hear him in that fog where she resided between the worlds of those who live, and those who don't. Unlatching his fangs, he placed his lips to her mouth and whispered. "I love you, *mi amore*, come back to me. Come back to me..."

Sinking his fangs right above her heart, he took the last drop of blood and felt her heart stop. She was gone. He leaned over her, lifting her limp and lifeless body, his lips close to hers as he used his fingers to open her red lips, their color fading fast. Covering her mouth with his, he slowly inhaled her soul as it rose in a white mist into his mouth. He inhaled deeply, taking her and felt her spirit come to him easily, escaping the dead cage of her body and curling into him, taking refuge inside of him. His body shook as his soul wrapped itself around hers, his beast cradling her spirit, giving her love and protection until she could come back to claim it. He only hoped she'd fight the darkness to come back to him.

He brought his wrist to his mouth and scored it with his fangs and held the gaping wound over her mouth. He held her mouth open with his fingers and watched his blood slowly drip into her mouth. Kissing the top of her head, he massaged her throat with his hand to help her swallow his blood. She must get his blood into her system to make her body turn. His body was spinning with the intake of her blood and her soul and his tears began to flow. He must let her go, for now, she must fight the hand of the devil to return to him. He knew the first thing she'd experience would be the excruciating pain of his blood as it changed her body from mortal to immortal, giving her the gift of eternity. He sat up from her and stared, her blood mixed with his on his body, his face and his hands. His blood tears streaking his face, and all he could do now was wait. He could no longer help her. He must wait in this chamber for the process to run its course. She was dead. He had drained her. And now her battle began.

Kate felt herself dropping away, falling backward into nothingness, surrounded by darkness, and she heard his voice from far away, telling her to come back to him. She watched as, from a distance, his fangs sank into her chest and he drew the last drop of blood from her, and her heart slowed and stopped. She kept falling further from him, and looked back to see her mortal body, still on the stone altar, as he leaned over her, his face close to hers, as he parted her lips and drew her soul into him, and she felt it. She felt her soul as it left her body and entered his. She felt his soul entwine with hers, holding it safe. **"Lover... I am dead."**

She felt herself tumble into a free-fall, out of control, and she struggled to right herself. She looked back into the chamber once more, to see him biting his wrist and dripping his blood into her open mouth. He stroked her throat, and it was the last vision she had of him as she spun and fell further into the darkness, the white gown, now stained with her blood, a tangle around her legs. The single red rose still held tightly in her grip. She could feel the skirt of her gown fluttering around her in the fall.

She felt his blood in her mouth, tasted the salt and the metal. Felt it seep down her throat. Falling still, she looked back. Looked for the chamber, looked for Shade, but saw nothing but darkness and felt nothing but this never-ending sensation of falling. She reached out, tried to grab something, anything, but it was an empty chasm, and she realized in her panic to grab onto something, she had dropped the rose, her last link to him.

* * *

He knelt beside the dais. She lay dead, motionless, her lily-white skin now indistinguishable from the pure white silk gown. Her red lips were colorless, and her crimson hair cascaded over the sides of the ceremonial stone altar. One arm hung over the side of the altar, and in her hand, she held the blood red rose. He watched as the rose dropped from her hand to the floor. He wept like a child. She was gone, and already, he couldn't bear her absence. His body screamed for her, needing her and wanting her, but she wouldn't respond. All he could do now was wait, he laid his head beside hers and let his blood tears flow.

His hand slid through her hair and he cried out, "What have I done?" He kissed her cold dead lips, letting his fingertips trail over her white, colorless cheeks. Her beautiful dark eyes were hidden from him, as her lashes fanned out on her cheeks. She could no longer give him that smile to light his heart, no sparkle, no laughter. He raised his head to the heavens and screamed, "*Bel!* Come back!"

Collapsing over her, he let the music blast loud to comfort her... to reach her. Breaking Benjamin echoed through the cavern with *Anthem of the Angels.* **"I am here, *mi amore*. You are not alone. Just come back to me."**

The falling stopped, but she was nowhere, suspended in space and time. All she could see was darkness, pitch darkness. **"Lover, I'm scared."** Nothingness above her, nothingness below her, suspended in this abyss and this deathly quiet. There was no sound of her breath because she didn't breathe. There was no sound of her heartbeat because her heart was silenced. **"Shade, can you hear me? Can you feel me?"**

She strained to hear his voice in her head, but there was nothing. There was nothingness inside her. And then she heard it, music, faint... soft like an echo.

"I'm alone, lover." She remembered his promise. **"Don't leave me. I'm here, Shade. I'm here in the darkness."** She could faintly hear the lyrics of the song he played, and knew he spoke to her in this song.

Then she was falling again, falling in a pit with no bottom as the song faded away, too far in the distance to hear. She felt herself tumble once more as she went into a roll, an out of control fall, spinning and a part of her wished for an end. **"Pull me back, lover. Pull me back."**

The falling stopped again, and her body floated free, suspended in this darkness. She had no sense of time. How long had she been here? How would she get back? She felt a burning sensation in her fingers and toes. At first, it felt pleasant in this cold darkness, but the intensity of the heat escalated rapidly to pain. She felt it creep slowly up her arms and legs, the burning inside her veins. She threw her head back and screamed, her throat felt raw, and yet, there was no sound. Her mouth was open in silence, and there was no relief from this burning. She drew her body into a ball, suspended in this nothingness, curling up in pain, as it crept slowly, slowly through each vessel, burning its path from the inside out. **"Shade?"** *He's out there. I know he's out there. He wouldn't leave me.*

She opened and closed her hands, shaking them, trying to free them from the grip of this pain, and she felt the pain slide further up her arms.

Her bones ached, a deep crushing ache that joined the chorus of pain that sang in her veins. *Please stop! Stop! Stop!* **"Shade?"**

She pulled her knees to her chest, and wrapped her hands around her knees, making herself smaller, like there was less of her to hurt. She cried but there were no tears on her cheeks and no sound to the sobs that racked her body. Her head was on fire! She shook her head, her hair flying. She released herself from this tight ball and reached her hands to her head, but felt no flames, just this pain, this pain, this unbearable, unending pain searing through her brain, burning in her eyes, her mouth. She ran her tongue across her teeth, and she felt them... fangs. **"Lover, I'm turning."** She was slammed with a pain in her gut that caused her to double over once more, curling into a ball, and screaming out once more that silent scream.

She heard something. **"Shade? Is it over? Is that you?"**

She heard a low growl in the darkness, and she strained her eyes to see something, anything in this pitch black, when the space around her started to glow with a red light. She looked around and saw two eyes glowing red. **"Lover?"** The growl got louder, and the eyes came closer, through the dark and into the red glow. *Not Shade... not Shade... Oh God, what is that? A wolf? Not a wolf? Not logical.*

It crept closer, fangs bared, growling, and saliva dripping. **"He'll kill me. Surely, he'll kill me. You're already dead, Kate. Shade? You didn't tell me this part."** She watched as the wolf crept closer, until she could feel his breath against her face. She closed her eyes against the inevitable attack and then... What? She felt him dissolve into her. She absorbed the wolf and felt him curl up inside, calm and warm. The wolf spoke to her, **"I will protect you and all that you love, but you too must fight."** She opened her eyes again, to only darkness, confused by the wolf, and yet comforted.

* * *

He lay for the longest time, just watching her. He knew it was futile, she wouldn't move a muscle, nor bat those long beautiful lashes. He waited for endless hours, there was no clock, but he felt time as it passed. How ironic, to have to live eternally and feel the moments as they dragged by, second by second, hours never-ending without her. The candles began to drip, getting smaller by the hour, as if to remind him, this was just the beginning of the longest wait of his life. It seemed he'd spent his whole life waiting for her, and he'd wait longer, however long it took for his *bel rosso*, his Kate. He knew she was fighting the pain of the change inside her, turning her from mortal to immortal. It was nothing he'd experienced for himself. He could only go by what had been written, and what other mortals that had made it through the turning had told him. For him, it felt as though there was a sword through his heart, as he could only wait for her now. His beast was curled around her soul, awaiting her return.

"Please come back, *bel*. Fight for us. Fight through the pain, the agony. I promise it will be worth it. Just keep fighting. I'm right here... waiting."

He finally got up and walked the chamber, round and around in circles. Every few turns, he stopped and kissed her dead lips, ran his fingers through her hair in case, somehow, she could feel him, but he knew she couldn't. This was a journey she must take on her own.

* * *

Kate hung suspended, trying to focus on something other than the pain. *That wolf thing, inside me? Is it inside me? That makes no sense, but then, what about this experience does?* She shook her head, like it would clear her thoughts and she became aware that the burning pain was subsiding. It crept back the way it came, slowly leaving her gut, slowly easing back down her arms, back down her legs, until once again, it was concentrated in just her hands and feet, until gradually, it disappeared. The pain was gone. She released her body from the ball, stretched out her arms and legs, and released a silent sigh of relief. She rolled her body over in this darkness, straining her eyes again to see anything, hear anything. There was still nothing, but she was thankful for an end to that searing pain.

The relief was short-lived. She had barely gotten over the searing pain that felt like liquid fire in her veins when she started to feel a tingling sensation again in her fingers and toes. She felt cold, like she'd been standing outside on a winter's night too long, and like the fire, it quickly escalated. A freezing cold that brought pain as it began that slow crawl up her legs and up her arms, and she realized it was just starting, and she'd go through this process of pain all over again. She opened her mouth and screamed, "*Nooooooo!*" But heard nothing. She knew he didn't hear her. He didn't feel her. Whatever connection they had, was broken. She was alone here. The cold crept in and she curled into a ball again, trying to shield herself from the cold, from the pain. But its crawl was relentless, and it took her, all of her, into its icy grip.

* * *

Picking up the faded and aged book, Shade took it across the room to the small writing table and the quill pen. His eyes roamed to her and he closed them, praying to anything that could hear him, that she fought the pain that encompassed her body. Picking up the quill pen, he opened the pages of ancestral history for the Medici and read through the entries slowly and found his own name scrawled across the pages by his *padre* to record his birth. He went to the next page open for entry and his hand shook. Dipping the pen into the inkwell, he carefully wrote each letter with precision... Katherine Reese Medici, Queen of Medici. Alongside it, he inscribed his own name... Shade Medici, King and High Master of Medici. He then wrote the date, and his eyes looked to the edge of the page where there were distinct columns to indicate the event as a mating, a birthing or a death. His eyes flashed back to her as she lay on the altar and he laid the pen down gently, leaving the column blank. Would it be their mating? Or would it be their death? He knew if she didn't return to him, the chamber would become their tomb. If she paid with her life, then he wouldn't go on. **"Come back, Kate. Come back. Fight!"** Suddenly, he felt a presence in the chamber, and he knew it was his *padre*.

Slowly lifting his eyes, he saw a reflection of himself in Christofano. He had forgotten how much he looked like him. He had his *madre*'s eyes, but all his other features, his body type, his hair, his skin tone, his bone structure, he inherited from his *padre*. His father's eyes locked with his and Shade still felt intimidated by his presence, even though Shade was the master now, and his father resided in the spirit realm, He had come to her turning, and Shade was sure, once again, he had failed to live up to his father's expectations. Although he no longer needed to strive for anyone's approval, his father would always remain someone who goaded him to rise above and beyond others.

"*Padre.*"

Christofano had kept himself hidden from Shade's presence and watched as he brought the mortal into the chamber, his intentions clear. She was a mere mortal, a disgrace to their kind, and yet this was who he'd choose to mate. His heart was in turmoil with the absurdity of his son's actions, although Shade had always been hard to train, hard to break and clearly, had a mind of his own. If Portia hadn't been so soft-handed with him, perhaps he would've accepted the arranged marriage and would've mated with a royal-born immortal to keep the royal bloodlines pure, as Christofano would've insisted upon. Shade had accomplished much, but not always in the manner Christofano would've chosen. And now there was the girl... the mortal. Christofano looked at her closely.

She was an exquisite beauty, and her devotion and faithfulness to Shade was without question. She lay cold and lifeless on the altar stone, and he feared she'd never make it through. This journey for a mortal wasn't an easy one, and this was his reason for coming to Shade now. He wouldn't let his son follow her to his death. An American mortal! He snorted in disgust. He understood love, and he understood the call of one's mate, but Shade deserved to have a blue-blooded immortal female whose loins were made for bearing him sons. Their entire lineage and future hung on this one small creature and if she failed her mission, he knew Shade was already planning to follow her into death. Christofano wouldn't let his son make that sacrifice. Letting his presence be known to Shade, they locked eyes. Portia lay inside his son, he was the best of both of them, and their love had made Shade strong. He was a master that few could rival, his body was toned and sculpted, and his sword wielded death like the true Medici he was, and yet, he carried Portia's tenderness of heart. He was king of all he surveyed, a true son of his immortal mating. The pain of Shade's deed this night wracked through his bones and Christofano felt him suffer like no other.

"Shade."

Shade looked up at his father. "Never *figlio*, always Shade... even now, *Padre*?" Shade's eyes glanced at *bel* and back at him. "I have turned her. She is mine now. She will always be mine."

Christofano walked to the altar and the still body of the one Shade had claimed as his mate. "*Si*. In death or in life, she will always be yours now. But your hand hesitates to mark her standing as a Medici within the family history. Mated? Or death? Even you doubt whether the mortal is capable of coming back to you. If you love her as you say, mark it now."

Shade felt his beast arise, but he reined him in. His father wouldn't physically challenge him, even over her, and he knew he was king here now. Christofano stood over Kate and spread his hands across the stone altar and glared at him. "Mark it now, Shade. Mating or death!"

Shade's body shook with anger and he'd never again let his father dictate his actions. Calming himself, he walked to her and sat on the stone dais, his hand stroking her face lightly and raised his eyes to his father, his hands unconsciously playing with the crimson that draped over the side of the altar.

"Whatever your intentions for this night, *Padre*, they go without notice. I am master now, king to the coven. Kate will remain as my queen, whether she returns, or she does not. I need neither book nor marking to know such. *Madre* taught me to mate for love, to seek and find the singular one destined for me, to bring back to Medici the female that would reign eternally beside me, and Kate is the one. I will not reign like you, *Padre*. I live in a world far different than the one you inhabited. I am a man now. I no longer live in a small boy's shell. Open your eyes and see what I see. I will not choose a mate who reigns by standing behind me, or who walks ahead of me, but the one who reigns beside me, fights for my coven, and for me. *Madre* never would have challenged your commands or questioned your words, but Kate does. She makes me see things in a different light, and I respect her for bringing that to me, for it makes me a better man. She is all that I love, and if this night I lose her, then I will lose all that you and I have fought to build, and I will not care." Shade leaned down and kissed her forehead gently. "She is my Portia, *Padre*. Why can't you see that?"

Christofano frowned. Shade's words told him so many things. His heart and soul were already long gone to her. He already saw her as his eternal mate, mortal or immortal, he didn't differentiate. His last words rang to his soul... She was his Portia. Christofano knew the love he held for Portia had not wavered, and had grown stronger, even in their death. There was nothing he wouldn't endure for her. He wanted nothing more than to see Shade have that kind of love in his life, to reign in the glory of love and family. Christofano walked slowly to the dais and the memory of the time he had stepped upon these stones at the birth of his only son crashed through his heart. Placing one hand upon Kate's forehead and the other upon Shade's, the words of his heart rang forth and he called upon the spirits of their ancestors who graced this chamber to bring her back to him.

"Let the Medici blood run strong through your veins, my daughter, and bring you back to us. Let your love lead you home to my son. Return to fulfill your destiny on the throne of eternity, Queen of the Medici."

Feeling the spirits of their ancestors surround her, Christofano knew she now entered the dance with the devil, and all the powers of Medici lay at her feet to use as a weapon. He kissed Shade's cheeks, one at a time as he took his face into his hands. "She will return to you, *mio figlio*." He faded as quickly as he appeared, into the fog, and back to the arms of Portia.

* * *

The pain of the cold crept into every cell. There was no escape. Kate curled up tighter, seeking warmth where there was none. She pulled her knees tight to her chest as ice cut through her veins. **"How much longer, lover? How much?"** She strained to hear him. He said she'd hear him, and yet, she heard nothing... and then a whisper.

"Come with me, daughter."

"Shade?" Her silent lips cried out. **"Is that you?"**

The disembodied voice replied, his voice a cold hiss. "Come with me, daughter, and I will take away the pain."

Kate felt his hands on her, caressing gentle hands. **"Lover, yes. Take away the pain."** He came to her, surrounded her, and she felt his arms embrace her. **"You took so long!"**

The demon replied, "Yes, my daughter. Way too long. Your lover has abandoned you here. He waited and you did not return. He grieves not for you. His cock already seeks solace with another."

No! Not my lover! She pushed his arms away, and the pain pushed back, every motion of her body brought more pain.

The demon circled her like smoke, "Come with me, daughter. Let me put an end to this torture. I can hold you now. I can comfort you now. Let me end this pain. It will be so easy, my daughter... so easy. Just give yourself up to me."

Stop! **"Shade, make him stop!"** She struggled in the darkness, against his unseen arms that grabbed at her, pulled her to his chest, and she could feel the heat of his breath against her face. Heat... warmth... and the coldness started to fade. It was so tempting, so easy to let go.

* * *

The hours passed and Shade paced. The time of his death slumber came and went, and he fought through it. He'd never leave her side, even in his death slumber, to fight this battle alone. He felt the new night arrive, and yet, still, she didn't move. He told her twelve hours, and that time had long gone. It had been close to twenty-four. His heart beating rapidly, his pain and agony a living entity within this chamber of stone. Every hour, he caressed her body as it lay cold and lifeless on the altar. He spoke to her, touched her, kissed her lips, trying to pull her to him, making sure whenever she could hear him or feel him again that she did. He was left here alone to wonder when that time would come... if ever. He didn't feel her inside him, she was dead, her soul lay cold and protected inside him, his beast nestling it with his life. She should have returned to him by now!

His screams of agony became louder and he knocked over anything within the chamber not permanently attached. The candles had burned out one by one, leaving only pools of wax. He built a fire to keep out the chill of the chamber, but nothing could penetrate the chill of his heart, knowing she might have lost the battle to fight the devil and come back to him. He felt the moon rise higher in the sky and still nothing. "*Cazzo*! It has been too long!"

Walking to her, he lifted her in his arms, cradled her and continuously talked to her, speaking to her louder and louder, anything to break through to her, and yet, still nothing. "Fight, *mi amore*. Fight! Come back to me. Do not leave me here. I can't do this without you! Please come back to me, *bel rosso*. Why is this taking so long? Damn it, *bel*, listen to me, listen to my call... feel my blood... Medici!"

* * *

The demon had her in his grip. "Let me take the cold away, my daughter. Let me take away the pain."

As the demon pulled her to him, the pain subsided, and she wanted that relief. Her body cried out for a release from the pain. *Not Shade. Not Shade. I have to fight him!* She pushed hard against him, kicking him away, and felt him let go, and she was falling once again, falling into the darkness, falling further away from Shade. **"Lover... how will I ever get back?"**

The demon followed her in the darkness. "Never. Never. You will never get back."

She heard his voice whispering. She hit the bottom hard and grunted with the sudden and unexpected impact. She felt around in the darkness. Hard smooth floor, four walls, close, very close, like a prison cell. And then she heard them, a thousand voices, all whispering.

"Never get back. He has abandoned you here. Never. Take his hand. Never get back. Alone here. Abandoned. Take his hand. Your salvation. He will save you. Take his hand."

Kate curled up in a ball, covering her ears with her hands. She yelled her silent command, 'Stop! Stop!' **"Shade, make them stop!"**

The voices stopped as quickly as they started and she fell over on her side, crying silent tears. There was no end... no end. **"Lover, please don't abandon me here. Can I come back now? Do you hear me?"** As she lay on the floor, she felt a hand reach out and brush her face. She started to reach for that hand when she felt another, and another, many hands reaching out, touching, grabbing, pulling her, and then the voices returned.

"Take his hand. So easy. Your salvation. Alone now. Take it. Take it. He will save you. So easy, my daughter. I can make it so easy."

Kate curled back into the ball and shouted, "No! Leave me!" She heard her own words echo in the room. Her voice. She could hear her own voice, no longer silent.

The hands and the voices disappeared, and the demon returned. His voice was soft and seductive, and he leaned in close.

The demon stroked her face, his fingers tangled in her hair, "Why have you been so foolish, my daughter? What has you so blinded you cannot see the truth? He is vampire. You think a vampire lives for eternity on your mortal blood? Just *your* blood? That is foolishness, my daughter. He lives for eternity because he steals your soul, and you gave it to him freely. It was all a trick, my daughter. He does not love you, it was your soul he needed. Why would a vampire of royal blood choose a mortal for a mate? How easily he played you. How easily he seduced you. And now he lives on, my daughter, with the strength gained from your blood and your mortal soul and you are trapped here. Let me free you. It will be so easy, so very easy, my daughter. Let me breathe into you. I am your salvation now."

His words hurt her, pierced her, and wounded her. **"Not true. Not true. Please, lover... tell him!"** The demon lifted her up like a rag doll and held her close to his face and she could feel him breathe into her, felt his hot breath filling her lungs, feeling the warmth return to her body. And he was right, it was so easy.

"Stop him. Stop!" She turned her head, pushed at him, his words... not true. But it was so easy, so easy to let go, so hard to fight.

"No! No! He waits for me. I know he waits for me." Kate pushed hard against him. "Not yours. His! Not yours! Get behind me, Satan!" He dropped her hard back onto the floor, and she felt his hand around her neck, squeezing.

The demon hissed at her, spitting out his words, "Take me, daughter, or I will end it here. Take me for all eternity or spend all eternity here in this darkness. They are your only options now. You have no other."

"Lover!" Kate went deep inside herself, closing her eyes and ears to the demon's seductive words. **"Shade, please."** Memories of them flooded through her head. The first time she saw him. The first time she saw those ice blue eyes across a crowded room, those piercing blue eyes. The first time he touched her. She felt his kiss and remembered the taste of him. She recalled the feel of him as he lay next to her in their bed. She heard the sound of his laughter. His love. His love. His love filled her. Must find him. Must get back. Get back. **"Lover, show me the way."** She stood in the small space and felt around the walls. An outlet, there must be an outlet, but she felt nothing but solid walls surrounding her.

The demon watched her struggle. "Take my hand, daughter, I am your salvation."

Kate screamed at him, "Leave me, demon! Leave me now! I'm not yours, I'm his. I'll always be his!" She dropped to her knees and coughed violently, exhaling out the darkness he breathed into her, releasing it all, rejecting it all, and watched as the cloud of dark poisonous vapor poured out of her mouth and drifted above her like smoke. She coughed and choked, spitting out the last of his vile soul. *Shade waits for me. He waits!* Kate felt the wolf inside her rise up, pacing, restless.

The demon roared in anger and the walls around her shook and crumbled. He towered over her and roared, "You cannot escape me, daughter. I will hold you here. You have no soul now. You gave it freely to a vampire. You have only what I will give you."

As the demon stepped forward, she saw him for the first time. He was death, and hate, and evil. He was cruelty and wickedness, corruption and depravity, he was everything foul and malevolent. He was villainy and obscenity. He was an abomination against nature. He was everything she rejected. His grotesque face was ghostly white with cold, dead black eyes, and massive horns that curved above his head like a ram. She cowered in the corner, pulling back from him. *No, no, don't show your fear. You are Medici now! Fight him. Like a Medici. Fight him, like a warrior!*

In her head, she heard him... she finally heard him. Shade called to her... 'Fight, *mi amore*, fight!' She stood upright and faced him, holding out her hand to block him.

"I reject you, demon. I defy you! You have no power here. You have no hold over me!"

He reached for her and she screamed, "No!" as she jumped away from him. She was falling again, but she was falling up. She was being pulled at a rapid speed back in the direction she came.

* * *

The moon rose well past midnight and his fears rose with it. Shade was at his wits end, and he feared the darkness had beaten her spirit. Even the power of his ancestors couldn't help her fight the demon's hand. He'd go with her into death and join her in the spirit realm. He wouldn't live without her. Lying down on the stone altar, it would now become their death bed. The chamber was sealed. He'd stay here with no source for feeding and die with her in his arms. He pulled her onto his chest in the position he always held her when he was in his death slumber. He'd hold her like this now, for all eternity, in love and protection. He was the sole heir to the Medici dynasty. When he was gone, his coven would disperse, joining other covens. His warriors would fight for other masters. This chamber would be sealed for eternity. He held her tight, her body cold and lifeless. He'd die holding her as he held her every night. His death would be slow, but he'd not leave her, and neither of them would rise again. He caressed her hair and spoke to her one last time.

"*Ti amo, mi amore per sempre.* I will never let you go. You will always reside in my soul. My heart cannot go to another. It goes wherever you go. I will die for you, I will die with you, but I will never let you go."

* * *

Kate was falling with increasing speed through the darkness, and suddenly, she was surrounded by a blinding light. She felt its heat, and the brightness was so strong she squeezed her eyes shut, but the light still hurt her eyes with its brightness. She covered her eyes with her hands, and she could see the light through her fingers. The light felt healing and warmed her as she opened herself up to it, embracing it. She passed through the light and felt herself re-enter her body, just as Shade pulled her onto his chest and enveloped her in his arms. It was how he held her every night as they slept. She heard his sweet voice, her head against his chest, '*Ti amo.' Is he real? Is this real?* She raised her head from his chest and looked at him, lifted her hand to his cheek. "Lover, I came back for you."

He felt a movement on his chest, and almost jumped out of his skin when he heard her voice speak softly to him. She came back! He sat up quickly, pushing her back onto the altar, and was enveloped by a tremendous force that lifted his body into the air, spinning him slowly and he felt her soul rise inside him, pure and white and immortal. He let it fill him, taking him higher, making his own soul soar. The beast inside him came alive as her beast slammed into him hard, taking his beast as a mate. His whole body trembled as her love took root in him, filling him, running in his veins. His heart felt like nothing he'd ever felt before as the sound of its beating nearly deafened him and her heart joined his, their rhythm synchronized. He dropped slowly down over her, hovering.

"Medici Queen, arise to your master. Arise to your maker!" He watched as her eyes followed him, their color a beautiful amber as she stared back at him. She was home, and she was now eternally his.

* * *

Luca held Shannon's hand as they walked through the formal gardens of Castello under the full moon. She was pointing out things in the garden, but he was distracted and not responsive. Kate's turning was taking far too long. He knew if the turning was successful, she would have to come back into her body tonight, and if it wasn't, she'd be lost to them forever. Shade didn't speak of it, but Luca knew him. If he lost her, he'd never leave those chambers. He'd lie down beside her and let himself die of starvation, and they'd lose both their king and their queen.

Shannon knew he'd felt distracted since Shade took Kate to the chambers. She could tell his mind was somewhere else as they walked through the gardens. The moon had lit the path for them on this cloudless night when suddenly the sky darkened. She looked up to see the moon had turned a deep red. "Luca! Look at the moon!"

Luca looked up to see the red cast of the blood moon, and he dropped to his knees, and felt his blood tears on his face. Shannon knelt beside him, clutching at his arm.

"What is it? What's wrong?"

"There's nothing wrong, *mia belleza*. Kate is turned. She has returned to Shade from the darkness and she walks as an immortal now." Luca could hear the cheer of the warriors in the camp as they all filed outside, cheering and howling, welcoming the newest immortal to their ranks, welcoming their master's mate, and their queen.

* * *

Marco was glad Terri was finally home where she belonged. He'd spent every moment with her he possibly could and the reunion had been a memorable one. But the whole reason she was here was for the turning of Shade's mate... the mortal. She was soon to be their queen and his mind was still in turmoil over the whole thing. Marco agreed it was damn overdue for her to be turned, but it wasn't a simple procedure and she seemed tiny and frail compared to the immortals. He also knew it wasn't just physical strength that she'd need, but strength of mind and will as well. He and Terri were outside as he felt too restless to be indoors. As she sat under the tree, he paced like a madman, and couldn't shake the relentless thought of her non-survival from his head. If she didn't make it, he was damn sure the old fucker would try to follow her into death and Marco wouldn't let that shit go down. He had a whole fucking camp of warriors, and one way or another, they would bust his ass out of that chamber.

"*Cazzo*! I can't stand this damn waiting!"

Theresa patted the ground beside her. "Marco, sit down next to me, please. Your pacing will not make the process go any faster, and you're making me nervous!"

"You should be nervous. Do you have any idea what the hell he will do if she does not make this turn? She remains in a type of purgatory in there like the fucking dead dancing with the devil. He can't communicate with her. I know him, Terri. He will lay in there and fucking rot with her. I can't bear losing him. I won't!"

Theresa sighed. "I agree with you. If she doesn't return to him, he will seal himself inside that chamber, lie down next to her and die. I see his devotion to her every day, so, of that, I have no doubt. But you've underestimated her. She will battle all the demons of Hell to get back to him, and she'll win. I've watched her this past year. Come to know her. Watched them lose their first child, their ups and downs as mortal and immortal. She stood against a rogue and used what Luca taught her. She'll come back. Her love for him will prevail."

He sat down beside her, laying his head on her shoulder, nuzzling her neck. "You always see the good in people, Terri, but I'm not so sure. I think he should have chosen an immortal. What if the damn Council deems her unfit? He has no heir for Hell's sake. I won't watch him give up everything and suffer because of his choice. I saw the fucking suffering he went through with Adriana. He blamed himself for her death, and still carries that with him. He won't go through that again."

Standing up, too restless to stay put, he looked to the moon and kicked the damn ground and let out some of his frustration with a howling growl. "She should have risen by now, Terri. I am fucking going in! I will not let him die in there. He is my brother!" Turning to head back to the barracks, he intended to gather up some warriors. He wasn't waiting any longer.

Theresa jumped up and chased after him. "Marco! Stop! You can't enter the chamber without putting the turning in jeopardy. Stop! If we don't see the blood moon before sunrise, then I'll agree to let you enter.

I'll even follow you there. But you must not risk this. I know her! Trust me. She'll come back to him."

He stopped in his tracks as she caught up to him. "Terri, I would die for you, and I know he will die for her, but he has so much to lose, so much more than I do. My heart is ripping to shreds thinking of him lying in there holding her, going mad without her. He will take this blame on himself."

"Marco, you're one of the most stubborn men I've ever met. You and Master Shade are two of a kind. I'd swear you were brothers if Gi weren't around to confirm your birth wasn't from Portia. I know how much you love him, and he you. And I hope you know my devotion to him lies as deep as yours. I promise you, if we don't see the blood moon by sunrise, I'll help you to bust down the door. But please, I'm begging you, if you love me at all...give her time. I know her as well. She's small in stature, but she already has the heart of a warrior, a Medici warrior. Even Luca sees it. I know she'll return to him. As sure as I stand here before you, I know she'll return to him. Look at me, I'm not nervous. I don't pace the floor. I have no fear because there's no reason to fear, my love. Look heavenward, Marco... even as I speak... look up."

Marco looked up at the sky and saw the moon turn blood red, the color of the dawn for vampires, a newborn was among them.

She lives! Their queen lives, and now she joins them all. He fell to his knees and covered his face in his hands. He let the blood tears run and then looked to the sky above. "You did it, old man, you did it. Medici!"

He felt Theresa's hands on his shoulders as she stood behind him. He laid his head back, still on his knees and looked up at her as he heard the whooping calls of the warriors in the camp come alive. *We have a queen!*

"The mighty will reign. She is now born into the ranks of royalty. I can't believe he did it. *Cazzo!*" Standing, he grabbed her up and spun her around, their laughter ringing out for all to hear. Once again, they were graced with a Medici immortal couple to rival the ranks of those that came before them. "It is time to celebrate, Terri. And I can only think of one way to do it." Holding her hand, he ran with her to his private quarters,

She laughed as she ran beside him, entering his room. "Correction, my love. You can't believe *she* did it. Even now, you don't give our queen credit. She'll rule with kindness and grace, just as his mother did, but don't ever doubt her power, my love, for she'll be a mighty defender of all that is Medici."

88

Rissa was finishing up the itinerary for that black-haired Amazon wench protector, but couldn't bring herself to give it to her. Alec was buried in the study and would be for a long while. He had a lot of business to take care of and she'd not made things easier for him with the situation with Max and the rogue. But she'd be damned if she'd give Jacks the satisfaction of perceiving her as some meek whimpering mate, handing over her schedule for her approval. If Jacks couldn't figure out how to protect her, that was her issue. Definitely not Rissa's!

She was getting restless being cooped up in the house, but still leery of going out, and her body was suffering from not working out. Throwing on some workout clothes, she sat on the floor of her dressing room and started stretching, followed by the push-ups and sit-ups. It felt good, it felt empowering, but she knew with clarity, Alec was right, she couldn't fight what was out there. If Max was behind it, he wouldn't stop until his goal was reached, so traveling without a protector wasn't an option. Rissa had to learn to be aware of every single thing around her, and that damn bitch better earn her keep, doing something besides fucking her vampire whenever it pleased. She was suddenly aware of her presence and looked up to see Jacks standing at the open door.

Jacks observed for a while, watching her sorry attempt at a workout. *Not bad for a mortal convert who's kept as a house pet, but dear Blondie, you need to do a whole lot more than toning that body to keep whatever is chasing you at bay.* Despite her disdain for this mortal convert, Jacks needed Rissa to trust her, but she could see Blondie was ready to resist. She needed to know, up front, who was boss. Jacks still couldn't see what Alec was attracted to. No turned mortal was as well-toned as a female who was born vamp. She was pretty, with sultry blue eyes, and still had some of that mortal femininity and vulnerability.

Jacks knew Alec abhorred weakness in anyone, even women, but he loved submission, and Blondie had that act down in spades. But one lone rogue had made her crumble, and cracked her spirit. Alec had sheltered her from the immortal life he gave her. He only used his immortal skills when it was convenient for his goals. He'd never been a street fighter.

She wondered if he ever trained Rissa on weapons or if she knew what a weapon looked like. "Rissa, we need to speak at some point."

Rissa's back bristled the moment she heard her voice, but she'd do whatever she had too to please Alec. "I don't have to like you, just listen to you so you can do your job, then get the hell out." Rissa nodded to the list on her desk. "My itinerary for the week is on my desk, if that's what you need. I'm going out tomorrow. Just be ready. I have a business to run. Keep up if you think you can." Turning her back on Jacks, she started to do more stretching, waiting for Jacks to get the damn schedule and leave.

Jacks smiled at her back, she was amused by the brave front. Rissa tried so hard to act brave, but her fear of walking out that door was greater than even she thought. Moving to the desk, Jacks glanced at the schedule.

For Jacks, this would be a piece of cake. This was nothing compared to what she normally dealt with. Walking over to where Rissa stretched on the floor, Jacks sat down beside her and decided it didn't serve her purpose to make herself a threat to Rissa. She'd talk to her and find out as much as she could about this attack. Alec had enemies, but this wasn't some random attack, but something more and Jacks wanted to know everything.

"I don't need you to like me, just listen to my suggestions, and pay attention to my signals. I know you hate this. You've made that obvious. But if you let me do my job, your life will be much easier. And Alec will be pleased, because no matter what you think about me, I know that's your true goal. What's that saying, happy master, happy mate? I'm the best there is at what I do, Rissa. Accept what it is."

Rissa looked at her and wondered what the hell she was up to. She was a bitch, but she had some points that made sense. Rissa couldn't take on Max alone. He wanted her dead. Rissa spit out her words at Jacks, "He's mine. You're nothing but a toy, I'm his mate. You'll not take him from me. Nothing will take him from me."

Jacks' face remained emotionless, "You're wrong about one thing. There's someone out there who wants to take you away from him, and they mean business. I protect the highest masters of this world. Most masters are not warriors, they hire out, to vamps like me. That lone rogue that attacked you was no coincidence. He waited and watched for you and you alone. He didn't mean to scare you, but to take you away from

Alec forever. Yes, I'm a warrior first, but I remain a woman to my core and you don't fool me for a moment."

Rissa's eyes were locked onto her face, she didn't flinch, but Jacks' words cut deep into her soul. *She knows!* Her fear rose so high it almost strangled her. If she knew about Max, she could tell Alec, and then Jacks would have him all to herself. If Alec ever found out, he'd kill her, and it would be a slow torturous death and she realized Jacks held all the cards. In her heart, she knew Jacks didn't want Alec, not for keeps anyway. She played with him as much as he played with her. It was how she manipulated her power as a woman, how she kept her position at the top of the game board.

Standing up, Jacks walked to the door and then paused. "Tell me what to call you in public."

"Miss Benneteau. Rissa is fine in the confines of the house."

Jacks responded, "See you in the morning, Rissa." Jacks walked back to her room, the schedule memorized in her head. *Game, set and match. I'm in charge here, and you'll follow my lead, Blondie.*

89

Kate watched him as she lay on the stone altar and his body rose in the air before her, his back arched as if he were in pain, his head thrown back as he called out to her to arise. She felt her soul re-enter her body. Only it wasn't just her soul now. Their souls... their souls entwined. She was his. And he was hers. Her body lifted of its own accord from the stone altar with the power of their two souls joined, and she felt it flow through her, her own back arching.

The power released her, and she floated back down to the altar stone. She lay quietly, and she could hear the water dripping off the chamber walls, the sound of each drop as it ran across the stone before dripping to the floor with a loud *plop*. The light from the fire was blinding her eyes and she had to turn away. She rolled over on her side, and then onto all fours, the stone feeling rough and hard beneath her skin, every ripple and curve of the stone pressing against her. She heard the scratching of tiny feet and looked sharply to the left, her fangs automatically bared, to see an insect crawling in the corner. She issued a deep growl when she heard footsteps behind her and turned suddenly, crouched and ready to attack, hissing and growling as she saw a dark silhouette approach her.

Shade observed her getting used to her skin. This wouldn't be easy for her. *Cazzo! My whole body aches for her.* He saw her fangs punch through, and he could barely stand still. Fuck, she was so damned beautiful! He could sense her fear and knew she was ready to attack, her beast sat right on the edge, ready to go after any source of food. He kept his voice low so as not to startle her until she recognized him. She needed to see him, hear him.

"*Bel*, relax, *mi amore*. It is me. I will not hurt you. I know you feel strange, you will need time to get used to it. " He could tell by her defensive posture, it wasn't working, she was poised to strike, and she had one thing on her mind, and that was to feed.

She saw him approach, his words a jumble in her head. *Too loud! Too loud!* The fire was behind him and she couldn't see his features. She held up her hand for him to stop and he walked closer still. She crouched further and growled at him, baring her fangs. He took another step and she sprung forward, catapulting herself through the air and hit him square in the chest. He stumbled backward as she latched her arms around his shoulders and dug her nails deep into his skin. He rolled to the ground, his voice...she recognized that voice... but his words were a mass of confusion in her head. Her hunger overwhelmed her, it was all she could feel, fear and hunger, when she savagely sunk her teeth into him, ripping at the skin. His blood hit her tongue and she felt the energy rip through her, lighting up every cell, and she drank whole mouthfuls, gulping down his blood. She knew this taste. It was him. It was Shade. But she couldn't stop the frenzied feeding.

He could feel her fear of him. She clung to him, her fangs bared as she rolled his ass to the floor, sinking nails and fangs all at once. *Fuck me!* He was taken off guard at her speed and agility, the sheer magnitude of what she'd become and then, his whole body lit up with desire. Her fangs went deep, not a clean bite but ripping at his flesh, attacking the vein that was now her only lifeline. The sensation of her fangs in his flesh pushed him over the edge. This was the first time his immortal mate had fed from him, and his body and beast responded. His beast was having a damn field day, clawing for release, wanting her with all he had. Struggling to maintain his beast and his own need, he had to let her feed and still gain some control over her.

He allowed her to take her fill, then gripped her neck and no longer did it gently. He felt her nails sink deeper into his skin. He could feel his blood running down his back from the wound her sharp fangs created in his skin. His own fangs punched through, long and sharp, and they ached with a desire unlike anything he'd ever felt. *Cazzo! I want her! I want all of her!*

He pulled her head back from his neck and felt his flesh tear further, but even the pain felt pleasurable. Gripping her hair like he was taming a wild beast, he pulled her face to his and growled, his fangs in need, dripping with saliva.

"*Cazzo*, woman! Look at me!" He saw her eyes, glowing a bright red, looking back at him and he kept a tight hold on her, not letting her have her way.

Her body began to recognize his, the feel of him beneath her hands, his intoxicating scent, the sound of his voice, and the taste of his blood. All familiar, and yet, enhanced. The muscles in his back strained against her, his arms encircled her, grabbing at her hair, yanking her head back from his neck. His eyes glowed red and his fangs were exposed. His grip was firm and unyielding, holding her face inches from his. She heard his voice, commanding her, and she locked eyes with him, issuing a very low growl as he has pulled her away from the thing she wanted the most right now... His blood.

Shade was well aware her thirst was out of control. He grabbed her arms and held them firmly at her side. She was strong, but he was much stronger. Her growl was threatening, and it tantalized his beast. He wanted a taste of her in the worst way.

Sitting her down on the stone altar, he watched her move like a lithe jaguar, and he ripped away what remained of her gown. Her body glowed in the soft light from the fire. Holding her down with one hand, he got in her face, fangs bared. "Come to your master! Rein in, mate!"

He sank his fangs deep into her upper thigh and he heard her scream and felt her arch her hips. As her blood hit his system, he instantly came, feeling the hot sticky wetness slide down his leg, and her blood electrified him like never before. Every dream he'd ever had of her blasted through him.

Kate felt him holding her in place as he sank his fangs into her thigh. She felt the sharp and delicious sting of his teeth as she arched her back. She felt his cock release against her, his hot cum spilling forth. She was still on her back when she sat up on her elbows, locking eyes with him. The veins in his neck pulsated and drew her attention once more. He held her stare as she hissed out the word, 'master', and ran her tongue slowly and seductively over her fangs. She reached up quickly and grabbed him, pulling him forward on top of her, wrapping her legs around his hips and gripping him like a vice. She saw his beast and knew his beast saw her, and she invited him out to play. She traced the path of his vein with her tongue, starting at the base of his shoulder and running up to his ear. She ran her tongue over his ear and whispered once more, 'master', before she sank her teeth deep into his neck again and felt his cock like hardened steel between her legs.

Her beast aroused him like nothing before and his beast was at full roar when she wrapped those legs around him. She tantalized, and he was instantly hard again, needing to bury himself inside her. Her fangs sank deep and he moaned. He moved his hips back and slipped into her hard, fully engorged and taking it to the hilt. He felt her grip him tight, her muscles stronger now, and it was like a vice grip stroking his cock and he let one hand tangle in that gorgeous screaming red crimson and held her head tight to his neck.

"Feed, *mi amore*. Feed."

His other hand slid to her hip and squeezed her tight as he stroked her fast and hard, her sex hot and dripping wet for him. He let the music play loudly inside the chamber as they listened to Imagine Dragons' *Demons* echo off the walls. He sank his fangs deep into her neck and he was transported. Her body fucked and bucked him, and he kept thrusting, taking them higher as they fed and nourished from each other. He was so lost to her, lost to her for all eternity. She had him... He was complete.

Kate was mad with wanting his blood in her mouth, flowing through her veins. Wanting his cock buried deep inside her. Every sensation enhanced, every need amplified. She drank from him with a need like nothing before, his blood igniting a path of fire in her veins that was pure pleasure. Her new fangs ached with pleasure, sunk deep into his neck. Her mouth latched tight against him, not wanting to lose one drop of his precious blood. She felt his hips pounding into her, her body trapped between him and the unyielding stone altar beneath her. His beast was loose, and she welcomed him. His deep growl vibrated through them both, and she responded with a growl of her own, careful to never break away from his neck and that erotic liquid that filled her. Her hips rose to match the rhythm of his deep thrusts, as her legs gripped him tighter, pulling him deeper. She felt like she couldn't get enough of him, pulling, clawing, grabbing him, deeper, drinking more until her whole body screamed with the pleasure he brought. She finally unlatched from his neck as he took them both over the edge, her head thrown back and fangs bared as she heard the roar of her own beast in the chamber. He slid both hands beneath her hips as he drove deeper, and she felt his cock throbbing and pulsing as he released his cum, filling her, spilling from her. The power of the orgasm shook her to her core as her nails clawed the full length of his back, and she grabbed his ass, nails sunk in tight to pull him deeper. *He is mine... He is mine. For all eternity, he is mine. I feel him in my veins, I feel him in my heartbeat, my soul wrapped around his. I am him, and he is me. We are one.* The orgasm rocked her, wave after wave, until she finally, reluctantly, felt it fade and her body relaxed, yet she held him still. She loosened her grip, but her legs remained wrapped around his hips, her arms at his waist, her face buried in his neck. She turned her head to look up at him. That face, those eyes, his dark tangled curls hanging forward, his bronzed skin glowing in the light from the fire. Her love for him exploded inside her heart.

"Lover. For all eternity... I am yours."

"*Si, mi amore*, all mine... eternity."

Pushing her hair from her face, he kissed her softly, her fangs now retracted, as were his. Her thirst was quenched, for the moment. He had no idea how long it would take her to get it under control, but he'd stay here with her as long as it took.

"Are you all right, *bel*? Tell me you like this new skin you wear. You made it back to me, you came back to me!" Hugging her tight to his body, he held nothing back. "I love you so fucking much, Kate."

Kate's tears came suddenly, unexpectedly, as the emotion overwhelmed her. She had loved him from the beginning, and her love for him grew with each passing day. She couldn't imagine a life without him, and now, an eternity didn't feel like enough time to share it all, or to express to him how deeply she loved him. She'd die for him. She'd kill for him. There was nothing she'd ever let come between them, nothing she'd not do for him. He crushed her to his chest, and she reveled in the feel of him, the scent of him. "Nothing can keep me from you, lover. Nothing."

Lying down on the altar, he pulled her to his chest, letting his hands run through her hair and smiled. "Some things will never change, *mi amore*, we will always sleep like this. I need you to rest. The sun rises soon, and my slumber comes. I won't leave you and you cannot get out. If you need to feed, I'll feel it, *mi amore*, so relax."

He felt her snuggle against him, ready to feed again when the bloodlust hit her. "We have all of eternity now. Patience is needed, *mi amore*, something you may have difficulty adjusting too!" He felt her body as it relaxed, and he drifted slowly into sleep, but he knew it wouldn't be for long.

She felt him slip into his slumber, and she waited for it to take her as well. She felt tired from the turning and slowly slipped into a restful sleep. She slept a few hours and awoke to the dark room. The fire long gone and only embers glowed in the dark. Her eyes adjusted quickly, and she found she could see about the chamber almost as well as if it were daylight. The chamber blocked any natural light, so she had no idea of the time, only that Shade remained in his slumber, and she was awake... And hungry. Was this normal? Was it normal for her to awaken in the daylight? Maybe it's because she was new, and they were sealed away from both the sun and the moon. Or maybe it's because her body needed to feed. He'd told her she might need to feed. She wanted to wait until he awoke, but her need for his blood screamed through her, and she inched her lips forward, brushing his neck and inhaled him. It was too much.

It was too hard to resist him, and she felt her fangs punch through, and the low growl rumbled forth from her chest. She sank her fangs into him and heard his low moan, felt his arm grip more tightly around her, and yet, he slept. She drank from him again, large gulps, her lips covering the wounds in his neck, careful not to lose any of his blood. She felt his blood singing in her veins again. Felt his energy and his strength infuse her, she took and took, unable to stop herself when she felt him stir, arousing from his slumber, growling slightly as he pulled her away from him. Her hands grabbed at him, trying to pull him closer to her mouth, but he gripped her wrists with a power she hadn't felt him use on her before.

"Enough, *mi amore*, enough. You must learn restraint. Patience. *Si*?"

He held her tight against his chest, her arms pinned to her side as he kissed the top of her head, and she felt him slip back into his death slumber, but his grip on her remained tight. She lay with her head against his chest, wide awake, fighting the desire to feed, fighting the desire to find a way out of the chamber and hunt. She lost the battle and tried to sit up from the stone altar, but he held her firmly in place, feeling her struggle, and she heard him.

"Shh. You must fight the impulse, *mi amore*."

"I am fighting, lover. I feel like I've been fighting for a very long time. The pain, the fire and the ice, the demon in the darkness who tried to lure me away from you, and now the hunger. The hunger consumes me. It consumes me. How much longer?"

"Several days, *bel rosso*, I will keep you here for several days, until your hunger is under control. It will pass, *mi amore*, like the fire and ice, it will pass. You will feed from me and learn control. I will not leave you, *bel*. We are safe here. The chamber is sealed, you cannot escape, so do not struggle against me. Sleep, your body needs the sleep."

He gripped her tightly to his chest, making it clear she wouldn't get up, and she'd not feed from him again right now. She felt him slip back into his slumber, and she lay with her head on his chest, listening to the beat of his heart. She was counting the beats and waiting... waiting... until he'd let her feed again.

90

Her hunger wasn't yet under control, and Kate woke him in his slumber to feed. Her hunger was a controlling factor for her now, but he let her feed a little at a time, making her learn control. It was a fight, and a hard one for a newborn. Shade knew she'd conquer it. Holding her down tight against him, restraining her, she hadn't discovered yet she could bite him any damn where and get his blood. Drifting back into his slumber, he tried to catch as much rest as possible. He awoke at some point later and heard an intense growling and opened his eyes to find her snarling at him and struggling against his hold on her, her eyes blazing red and her fangs protruding. "So, this is how you awaken your lover?"

He tried to calm her with his words, but Kate had waited impatiently for him to wake. He'd held her in a tight grip for the remainder of his death slumber, and she'd waited, awake and hungry.

"Please don't deny me. You asked me to be patient and I've been patient." She struggled against his grip, straining to get closer to his neck.

Her hunger had pushed her to the edge, and this was the time to break her a bit more. "You are a wild little vixen when you're hungry, *si*? If I let go of you, will you lay back for me? Come on, *bel*, I will give you what you want, but I refuse to just hand it over, *mi amore*. You need to control this. I know you are tired of fighting, but this is the process, and you can't get out of this chamber until you learn control. Let that be your goal, *si*? Now, lay back. You attack, and I will not let you feed."

He released his grip on her as she lay beside him. "Lover! I've waited already! Will it always feel like this? Will my hunger always consume me?"

"No, *bel*, it won't, the hunger eases with time, but your body is going through a change and the bloodlust consumes you. It never leaves completely, and you will need to control it. I cannot let you out of here if you attack every living creature you see. Once you can control your need, then we can leave. Your hunger will still be strong, but I will feed you on a regular basis. Your body will adjust, and your hunger will become more controlled. You'll be fine. When you feed from me, it will satisfy, but your body will always crave me, need my strength, my energy, and power. You will adjust, *mi amore*. But for now, woman, lay the hell back!"

She sighed in resignation, as her body wanted his blood, but she submitted to his command and lay back on the stone altar.

"Ah, you see, it was not that hard of a fight..." He bit into his wrist, letting the blood slide down his hand and felt her body jump. "You move, you do not feed! Fight it, *bel*!"

He watched as she laid back, her body shaking in need. "Easy, my vixen. Go slow." He held his fingers over her mouth and let the blood drip slowly onto her tongue. "Don't gulp, savor it, taste it. Learn to control and appreciate what I give you. Slide it around in your mouth, feel the power, the energy, the love." Letting his blood drip into her mouth, he saw her slowly gain some control.

Kate's eyes were transfixed as he held his fingers over her lips and let his blood drop slowly into her mouth. She wanted mouthfuls. She wanted a bucketful that she could lift and tip to her mouth and drink her fill. But he trained her with drops. Each drop hit her tongue and the taste of it exploded in her mouth. She savored the taste, and the sensations it brought, the power, the energy, the erotic feelings. She gripped the side of the altar until she heard the stone crack beneath her hands as she resisted the urge to reach up to him, pull him down to her, and sink her fangs deep into his neck. Her want was so intense she needed to cry, but she dared not, as he may take his hand away, and she'd lose even those precious drops. If she behaved, he might let her feed, really feed, and not subsist on the appetizer.

Shade watched her closely and it was working, she understood if she didn't follow his commands, she wouldn't get more. He hated doing this to her, but if he didn't, they would fucking be in this damn place for a month!

"That's it, *mi amore*. You understand. I know it's hard."

Pulling his hand away from her, she growled, and he locked eyes with her, growling back, warning her she wasn't to move. "*Bel*, I don't like doing this any more than you do. Trust me, this hurts me immensely, but you have to learn control. I need you to come back to me as my *bel*, not a beast. Not your fault, but you must fight and learn, *si*? You look beautiful. Now tell me what you see, concentrate on something else. Tell me, are you cold?"

"I am cold, lover. The fire has burned down to embers and I feel warmth only when I'm wrapped in your arms. And I feel my heartbeat. I feel your blood in my veins, the path it takes. I can hear *your* heartbeat, even from where you stand, it calls to me. What else do you want to know? That I can hear the water as it runs in droplets down the walls of the chamber? That I hear the drops as they strike the cavern floor? The feet of the insects as they crawl across the stone? Do you want to see me crush the stone altar in my hands?" She releases her grip on the side of the altar and held out her hand with the pulverized stone. "Tell me what you want, lover."

He smiled down at her, "Tell me three words I crave to hear."

Kate closed her eyes and breathed in, inhaling him, his scent was male, all male, and hers. When she opened her eyes, she looked deep into his, those ice blue eyes that were such a contrast to his dark hair and dark skin. She felt their souls connect as they held each other in their gaze.

"I love you. I love you through all eternity. I loved you in past lives and I will love you in future lives. You, my savage lover... you are my everything. And I'll never fail you."

He was lost in her words, the all-encompassing love she passed to him now that she was immortal. He was so in love with her, lost inside her now, forever and all eternity. He suddenly felt the room blaze with heat and light and looked up to see *Padre* standing at the fireplace, looking over his shoulder. He had built a fire for his *bel*.

Christofano spoke to him, "Let her feed, *mio figlio*. She needs the nourishment and she has been patient enough."

Shade's eyes returned to her, sliding his hand under her head, he lifted her to his neck and cradled her body, and act so intimate and something he shared with her and her alone. His heart was bursting with so much love, and the overpowering need to protect her took hold of him, to never let another have her, or harm her.

"Do not gulp, *mi amore*, it will help to not gulp. Feed normal, draw slowly and swallow, try it." Shade wondered if she could see *Padre* in the room, or if she thought he had been the one who willed forth the fire.

Kate slid her arms around his back and laid her head on his shoulder, her lips brushed his neck and she felt her fangs punch through with a clicking sound. She licked the soft skin of Shade's neck before sinking her fangs into him and feeling his blood hit her tongue. The moan escaped her, and she felt his hands as they caressed the bare skin of her back. She drank slowly, eyes closed, savoring the taste of him. When she opened her eyes, she saw the silhouette of a man standing near the fire, which was now burning brightly once again. She unlatched from him as her heartbeat quickened. They were in this tomb alone, who was this man?

She growled, and he turned his head slowly and looked at Kate over his shoulder. Except for the brown eyes, he looked strikingly like Shade. "Lover? Who is this man?"

"I am Christofano Medici, Shade's *padre*." Bowing slowly, he raised his eyes to her. "Welcome, Queen Medici. You have done well to return to *mio figlio*. You have pleased me greatly."

Kate stared at him, as she did Portia only a few nights earlier as she stood before the mirror. She was suddenly aware of her nudity and leaned in closer to Shade, when his father stepped forward, picked up her torn gown from the floor and slipped it around her. Kate stared at him, his features, his mannerism, his movements, "You are just like him... or, he like you."

His face showed no emotion, and she understood why Shade felt only coldness from him, but there was more there than he liked the world to see. Kate had seen Portia, felt her kindness, and her gentle spirit. She wasn't a woman who'd be drawn to a cold and heartless man. This was a man who kept his feelings deep inside and shared them only with her, in private. To the rest of the world, including Shade, he only shared the warrior.

"I promise you, *Padre*, my life belongs to your son. I'll never dishonor the Medici name. I'll bear his children... your grand-children. And they'll take their place in history to carry on the legacy you started, and that Shade carries forth with pride."

He listened to her words, as she spoke from the heart. She called him '*padre*', and something inside him cracked wide open.

"You will honor Medici by loving *mio figlio*. You have lost a son, but you will never lose another. Love him and he will rise far. Give him *bambinos*, and you will become the most prized treasure of Medici, ensuring our legacy." Walking to her, he kissed each cheek gently. He looked to Shade and slid his hand along his jaw before turning back to Kate. "May I ask that you stand before me, *mia figlia*?"

Kate looked up at Shade and he nodded to her, as she slid her legs over the altar and stood on the dais, clutching the torn white gown to her breasts.

As she stood before him, holding the remnants of the torn gown, he swirled his hand above her head and within it appeared a bright red cloak, made of the finest silk Italy had to offer. He wrapped it around her, covering her body and watched as it draped around her curves and flowed to the floor. He stepped in closer to her and pulled the hood over her red hair.

"Red is the color of deep immortal love. Medici women wear this color with honor for all eternity. Love *mio figlio* as only you can, he deserves a love to rival even my own. It is my dream for him. Give this to him with my blessing."

Christofano softly kissed her forehead and turned and walked away, disappearing into the fog.

Kate turned to Shade as his father disappeared. "And now we have their blessing, lover. It's what you wished for, that they could be here. First your mother, and now your father."

Shade watched his p*adre* fall slowly but surely in love with his *bel* and his heart soared. Shade looked at *bel* and tilted his head to her, "*Madre*? I have not seen *Madre*, nor even felt her. Did she come to you in your turning?"

"No, she came just before the turning, while Theresa was helping me dress. She appeared in her mirror in our bedroom. She said she chose me for you, that she brought us together. She said I was your destiny."

"*Si*, you are, *mi amore*. *Madre* loves me very much and I return that love as well. I have no doubts she chose you for me, for you are perfect as my mate in all things." Standing, he took her hand and led her to the table with the open ledger of Medici history.

"Let us record now, our mating... together." Handing her the quill pen, he held his hand over hers and checked the ledger where he had previously recorded their names as they made the mark under the column for '*Mating*' together. Grabbing her tight to his chest, he kissed her passionately and felt her body rise again to feed and he smiled.

"Greedy!"

91

Rissa woke to a cold empty bed. Her heart raced, and then she remembered she'd felt Alec leave earlier than normal this morning. His schedule was busy, and he didn't wake her to say goodbye. To be honest, she wasn't surprised he'd left before she woke. He knew today would be her first day out since the rogue attacked her, and she was damn sure he didn't want to deal with her drama over that warrior bitch from hell in the next room. Rissa could hear Jacks rummaging about in her room. Despite her dislike for Jacks, she knew she needed a protector and she couldn't deny her trepidation about going out alone.

Although she'd cut herself off from Max completely, she knew him well enough to know he was aware of every breath she took, and no protector was going to get in his way. If he couldn't have her, he'd take her out, or die trying. Shaking her long, tangled mane, Rissa put all thoughts of him and recent events out of her mind. She had to face her clients, keep her business afloat and plan this charade of a wedding. On top of that, she must act as if nothing bothered her, and follow Alec's orders to cooperate with the protector. *Come on Rissa, you can do this!*

Once showered, she scanned her calendar and saw she had a schedule that was booked solid. Often, she took cabs to wherever she went. D.C. was a traffic nightmare even on a good day, and parking was even worse. If she could only teleport everywhere, she could get ten times more done! She dressed in a light spring suit and sat down to slide on her heels. She was going to the office she held in downtown Georgetown. Although she did a lot of work from home, she needed a place outside the house to meet with mortals. Alec and she had agreed, years ago, when they moved in together, having a parade of mortals through the house wasn't a good idea.

She checked once more in the mirror to make sure her make-up was appropriate, and she still looked a little pale. Her lack of energy gave her skin a dull look. Walking into the bedroom to grab her briefcase, she heard an unusual commotion outside, and she went to the window to look out. Her heart went into overdrive. The street in front of the house was littered with press and paparazzi, all of them with cameras aimed at the front door, waiting for her appearance. She'd forgotten the papers had come out with their wedding announcement and the press was clamoring for that perfect shot. Rissa stood staring out the window, looking at the press as they waited for the Darling of G-town to appear when all her fears come screaming back.

* * *

Jacks had been ready a long time, even before Alec had left. This live-in situation wasn't normal for her, but for this chunk of change, she'd gladly put up with it. The press had been outside since sunrise, waiting on Rissa, and Jacks knew Blondie wasn't prepared for the onslaught of craziness that awaited her.

Getting up, Jacks walked to the master bedroom. She tapped on the door lightly and got no response. She slowly opened the door and saw Rissa staring out the window. Jacks walked inside and stood behind her, looking down at the mob.

"Rissa, just give them a smile, let them take a few photos and answer a couple of questions. It gives them something to print, and then they'll leave you alone. I'll drive, and you can sit in the back. Your windows are tinted, but if you don't give them something, they'll hound you all day. I know how to handle these situations, done it many times. I'll be close, but I won't crowd you. Keep your senses alert. Give me eye contact if you feel threatened or sense anything. We have to work together."

Rissa snapped at her, "I know what I'm doing. I deal with press all the time. I can handle myself Jacks, be assured. Just stay the fuck out of my way!"

Turning around, Rissa glared at her. "Now if you're done acting like Zena the Warrior Princess from Hell, can we please leave? I'm busy and have things to do." Grabbing her briefcase, she headed out of the room. "And another thing, you'll wait downstairs for me in the mornings, don't be walking in this room ever. This is our private space and I'll be damned if you'll intrude any further in our lives!"

Jacks chuckled to herself. *I see that Blondie has woken up with an attitude more like the one Master Canton warned me about.* "Don't get your corset in a twist, Cinderella."

Jacks followed her out and watched as Rissa stopped dead in her tracks going down the stairs. Jacks waited to see if that attitude would flare up again. But instead, Rissa stood still and took a few deep breaths, steeling herself for what waited outside the front door. Watching her flip her hair back with her perfectly manicured hands and pushing those shoulders back, she made good use of those overpriced heels and marched her ass right to the door. Jacks smirked. *Glad we got that settled.*

92

Santos met Alec at the door, taking his jacket while Alec loosened his tie, and Santos handed him a glass of Midnight.

"Is Rissa home?"

"Master, she went out this morning with her protector. There were a lot of paparazzi here following the announcement of the wedding, but her protector seemed to have things under control."

Alec swallowed down the glass of Midnight and handed it back to Santos, asking for another as he headed to his office. He'd seen the coverage on CNN of Rissa leaving the house this morning and the paparazzi swarming her. Jacks was with her and kept an appropriate distance, but it was clear to any observer she was there as a bodyguard. Alec was sure Rissa was behind on some of her appointments, as she'd been holed up in the bedroom since the rogue attack. He was glad at least she'd found the confidence to get back out there.

Santos returned with the second glass of Midnight and a stack of newspapers, all turned to the society section, featuring pictures of Rissa taken just this morning. He flipped through them, propping his feet up on the desk. She hadn't called or texted him, so that was a good sign she was holding her own. But still, Rissa and Jacks together were like a keg of dynamite with a short fuse. He had to chuckle to himself as he pulled from his briefcase a few pieces of legislation that were coming up for a vote.

* * *

As they approached home and the car rolled to a stop, Rissa literally ran for the damn door. She couldn't stand Jacks' driving, her constant presence, or anything else about this bitch. She'd managed to keep her composure throughout the day as the damn press had been on her like flies on honey. Jacks was right on her heels.

Rissa let the door slam in her face and headed straight for the Midnight. Santos was there asking her something and she didn't need him getting in her way. Rissa shouted at him, "Get out! Just do whatever it is you do!"

Pouring a Midnight, she slung it back in one gulp and felt Jacks as she entered the room behind her. Rissa spun on her heels and let her have it. "You can back off now, Zena. I'm home now. I don't need you up my ass anymore. And tomorrow, I drive, got that? I'm not helpless. Christ, you are like an old woman driving out there! And another thing," she slammed her glass down on the bar. "When I address the press, you don't have to look as if they're going to tackle me to the ground at any damn moment. I know half of them by their first names. I need them for my business! And stop giving me that fucking look. I can feel if anything is wrong out there."

Growling, Rissa grabbed another Midnight and prepared to sling it back.

Alec heard the outburst from his home office. *Well, so much for a quiet evening at home.* He'd been wondering how long it would take for the powder keg to ignite. He dropped his feet to the floor and tossed the papers on the desk and headed to the family room where he found them in a stand-off. He stood in the doorway, leaning his shoulder against the doorjamb with his arms crossed over his chest, the sarcasm not hidden from his voice.

"Is there a problem in here, ladies?"

Jacks continued to stare her down as she answered, "No problem at all, Master Canton. Cinderella here doesn't approve of my driving skills. No problems I can't handle."

Alec looked from one to the other, locked in their stand-off. If looks could kill, they'd both be dead by now, and he had to fight back a smile at this barely controlled cat-fight. Rissa was fit to be tied, and come to think of it, that might not be a bad idea. He was afraid she'd more than met her match with Jacks, though.

He spoke to them both. "I've got it from here, Jacks. You can leave. And Rissa, you need to calm down. Now! I don't need the drama. You know you need a protector, I think even you can acknowledge that, and I don't plan on coming home to this every day. Understood?"

Rissa smirked when he dismissed Jacks. She poured herself another Midnight and walked past him, pacing the room.

"Calm down? Do you have any idea what it's like to deal with that throng of idiots following me like a pack of bloodhounds all day, then have Zena the Warrior Bitch from Hell up my ass? I know I need her, Alec, but seriously, she needs to stop glaring at everyone around me. I feel like a caged animal, with a trainer. I'm not a child. I can feel danger, and blah, blah, blah, so what, she's a warrior... fine. If she's so damn great, then she doesn't need to be right on top of me. Nothing unforeseen happened. See, still here! And it was my first day out, I just…" Taking a sip of her Midnight, she looked down at the floor. "It was my first day and I feel like my independence is totally gone. It won't happen again."

He remained in the doorway, leaning against the doorjamb listening to her rant. He waited for her to run out of steam. "Finished? Get it out of your system if you haven't. You knew this marriage announcement would blow the roof off of things. You're used to the press, and besides, in the long run, it'll only help your business. So just smile for the cameras, my darling. As for Jacks, she's doing what she's supposed to be doing. Do you ever see pictures of the President? He's always surrounded by Secret Service. And the First Lady is also always surrounded. So get used to it, Rissa. Jacks isn't going anywhere for a while. This is the path I've chosen for my life, and as my mate, the path you'll follow. You may not have independence in the way you've known it in the past. Comes with the territory, so this is just good practice for the future. Is any part of that not clear?"

She jerked her head up and listened to him, her eyes locked onto his. She felt like she wanted to scream, hit him and fight to get Jacks out of her life, but it would do her no good. She bit her lip, holding back the tears. Taking a deep breath, she let her body relax.

"Everything is perfectly clear." Walking to the door, she tried to go past him, to her room, where she could be alone, take a bath, and hear herself think.

He felt her turmoil and saw the defeat in her face. As she walked to the door to leave the room, he reached his arm across the doorjamb, blocking her path.

"Look at me, Rissa."

She closed her eyes and then opened them wide and looked up at him. Alec responded calmly, "I know you're still afraid, and I'm proud of you for going out today. I know how much you hate being on a leash. Do you think I don't know you? This is necessary right now. Just because nothing happened today doesn't mean we're out of the woods. The rogues are still around. We have no idea why you were attacked after Angel was killed. Retribution maybe? But if it happened once, and they failed, they may try again. I can't take that chance with you. For all my harshness, my impatience, you know I love you. You know that, right?"

She watched his face, his eyes looked inside her, and she felt him giving her strength, giving her what she needed. Her voice was soft and emotional as her hand slid softly across his cheek and rested on his shoulder.

"Alec, I know you love me. My trust in you is complete. If you think I need this, then I do. I do this because you ask it of me. Yes, I'm scared. But the fear is abating. I don't have to like her, I just have to get through it, and I will." Smiling, she kissed him softly. "I love you, Alec."

Alec took her in. She was more vulnerable than he could ever remember seeing her before, and Rissa didn't like being vulnerable. He scooped her up in his arms and carried her up the stairs, kissing her forehead and taking her to the bathroom. He willed the tub filled with hot water and sat her down gently on the side of the tub and watched as she removed her clothes and slipped into the water. He rolled up his sleeves and picked up her bath salts, spilling a generous amount into the steamy water, and swirled his hand through the water, creating the frothy bubbles on the surface.

Santos appeared at the door with the request for Midnight that he had sent him. He got up to retrieve the glass and carried it to her, sitting it on the side of the tub. "Enjoy your bath, my darling, and your drink. Just don't get too used to being pampered by me."

He leaned in and kissed her once more before standing to leave. Before closing the door behind him, he stood for a moment and took her in, her head resting back against the tub, the soft hair around her face hanging in damp tendrils, her eyes closed. She was loved.

"Take your time, my darling. I'll be waiting for you in the bedroom."

93

Another few nights had passed, and the death slumber took Shade at each sunrise. He would wake to feed her, and then drift off again. Her control was becoming stronger with each feeding, she was learning each time to slow down, and he knew he needed patience to help her get there. He heard something stirring and he opened his eyes to a fire blazing in the fireplace and a red-cloaked beauty staring wide-eyed at him. Shade could feel her heartbeat, the rhythm in sync with his. She was very close to being over the bloodlust. She no longer begged to feed and had stopped clinging to his neck in her sleep, all very good signs this was almost over.

"Hungry?"

* * *

She woke before him and moved to the embers of the fire. The chamber was cold, and she pulled the red cloak his father wrapped around her over her head and wrapped it around her body. She knelt in front of the embers, looking around for something more to burn. There was wood stacked in the corner that she added to the fire, but the embers had burned too low for the wood to catch. She focused hard on the fire, wishing for warmth in these cold damp chambers, when she saw the flames flicker. *Did I do that?* She concentrated hard on the fire, willing it forward and watched as the flames leapt up, catching the wood, and the blaze grew higher, lighting the chamber and sending out its heat. She looked back at Shade, as she heard him stir on the altar stone.

"For you, lover, I am always hungry for you."

"Mmm. Then come cuddle with me and have something to nourish you, *si*?"

She walked toward him, the fire lighting her pale skin and making it shimmer, as the cloak slipped from her shoulders and fell to the stone floor revealing her body, lithe and strong. She straddled him but didn't go for his neck. Her eyes turned a beautiful red and she sat on his thighs and twirled her finger around one long black curl that hung over his forehead. He observed her feeling the texture of his hair, absorbing every sensation that was now brilliantly enhanced for her. His hands slid up her thighs and softly gripped her hips and he saw her wicked grin. She knew and felt his intentions.

"Ah yes, *mi amore*, you are going to love being an immortal. So, tell me, who made that blaze in the fireplace?"

"I started the fire. I felt chilled in this chamber."

"*Mi amore*, I am so proud of you."

Lifting himself up, he kissed her and felt her fangs punch. Pulling her head down to his neck, he felt her lick his vein and he moaned. Each time with her was more erotic and pleasurable for him than the last, and now that she was taking her time, he felt like he'd go insane. She was so sexy, and he could feel the rush of her sexual desire driving through her body with each heartbeat. "Woman, you will drive me mad with lust!"

Her body felt him in a new way. Every sensation enhanced. His muscles felt more pronounced under her hand, his eyes bluer, the texture of his hair as she tangled it around her fingers. His scent, his maleness, filled her. She breathed him in as she laid her body down against him. She felt her soft breasts against the firm muscles of his chest and listened as her heartbeat synchronized with his. She laid her head on his shoulder, and ran her tongue over his neck, the taste of his skin excited her, and she heard his moan. The sound of his moan vibrated in his throat as it escaped his lips. The same ache she felt in the core of her belly was the same ache she felt in her fangs as they punched through with a click. She wanted him, only him. She sank her teeth into his neck, and felt his body respond. Felt his head drop back, his neck exposed, and the next moan she heard was hers as his blood hit her tongue, and with it, that erotic current of electricity that connected directly to her sex, the heat between her legs exploding outward, as she felt his cock turn to steel beneath her.

His head lolled back, and he felt her body come alive, her love pouring through him, her need, and her want of him like no other in his lifetime. At this moment, he'd kill anything that even blinked at her. Shade shifted her position on top of him, sliding into her already dripping wet heaven and glided in like steel sliding through honey. He could feel her inside his blood, singing with passion, and she felt it now too. No mortal relationship would ever go to the depths of an immortal one. He felt her in his veins, his heart and soul, alive and screaming to him, wanting him, needing and loving him. He held onto her hips and pushed deep inside her as her lips left his throat and she threw back that crimson wave of silk and rode him hard. He felt his cock ready to let go already. She controlled him now, everything about him, and he realized her power was much stronger than he'd imagined. This change would take them to another level and that thought made him cum like a volcano inside her and he screamed her name, his chest heaving with love. She was his forever.

She dropped her head forward, covering him in a curtain of her hair, before collapsing onto his chest. Catching her breath, waiting for their hearts to find that synchronized rhythm again.

He could do this night and day with her. He caressed her back as he caught his breath. They lay quietly together, his hand in her hair as her body relaxed against his, and they lay in the afterglow of their lovemaking.

"Did you rest, *mi amore*?"

"I did rest, lover. I know you've never experienced mortal sleep, so you don't have a comparison. But I was expecting it to be different... the death slumber. I've watched how it takes you, and maybe it takes me in the same way and I'm not aware. But it really feels no different. I don't fall asleep as soon as you do, and I usually wake before you."

"More than likely it is just the turning. Your body is still adjusting, *mi amore*. The bloodlust and thirst overcoming any sleep you need. Do not concern yourself with it. You will be fine in a few more days. Each day will be different for a while. You will see and hear things you never imagined. I will help you, teach you how to teleport and use your powers to your advantage. You are full-blown Medici now." He lifted her face so he could see her, and looked deep into her eyes, "my queen."

She looked back at him, locked in his gaze, and for the first time, the use of the word 'queen' didn't make her wince. The title she thought she'd wear with reluctance now fit. She could feel it in her blood. She was his queen. And he was her king. She'd loved him more than she thought humanly possible before the turning, and now, they were one and the same. Each a part of the other in a way she couldn't have anticipated. She was glad she'd been born mortal. If she'd been born immortal, she'd not have felt this change. She would have taken for granted these feelings. She'd do it all again, to be with him, and she'd destroy anything that ever threatened them, threatened him, or their children. She could see all of the children now, all of them. Should she tell him? Or did he know as well?

"Lover, can you hear my thoughts? Do you know this love I feel?"

"*Si, mi amore*, I have always felt it with you. I knew, long before you did, how I could love and protect you. I wanted for you, this life, and this love. I want those ghosts of past men in your life gone, to show you this is how love is supposed to feel. Tell me you understand now. Let me hear you, *bel*. Tell me you understand that other females hold no appeal to me, you can feel that now, you are the only one I will ever love."

Laughing as she nuzzled against his neck. "Lover, even as a mortal, I never doubted your love, or your fidelity. Your devotion to me was never in question. But I'm still not blind as to how other women respond to you. I guess we won't know my response to that until after we're out of the chamber and I'm faced with it again. You may be stuck with a jealous mate, but I'll try my best."

He chuckled. "*Si, mi amore*, all I can ask for. But I do believe we are almost ready to escape our prison, journey forth into our world. We have a huge ceremony to present you to my coven, letting them pledge their loyalty and protection. Masters who are allies and acknowledge my standing in our world will be present. And Council as well, to prove to the world, you are no longer mortal but immortal, and you are mine. The true Queen of Medici. Are you ready for this? It is the last step, *mi amore*... The last step to get through and then we go home."

She slid her fingers across his cheek, feeling the stubble. She touched his lips and felt him nibble lightly at her fingers before drawing one into his mouth, sucking lightly.

"I'm ready, Shade. You lead, and I'll follow. Tell me some things will never change for us. Tell me our passion doesn't die, this connection we feel, it doesn't end. Tell me immortal love doesn't dwindle and burn out. That you won't tire of me with time. Tell me we'll have an eternity of love, like your mother and father. That's what I want for us, lover. I can feel both of your parents so strongly here."

"*Mi amore*, look in my eyes." Taking her hand, he placed it over his heart. "Feel that, it's beating in complete sync with yours. Immortal love becomes stronger with time. We would die without the other. Our beast will always recognize our mate. We don't always know who it will be. I thought I would never find you, and out of nowhere, you appeared, and I knew right away. Our passion will grow stronger with time. *Madre* and *Padre* made this their home, where they loved each other and made a life for all eternity. They are long gone to another realm, *mi amore*, but as you can see, they are still together. It will be the same for us. Their gifts to me were to teach me about my responsibilities toward my mate, learn to take care of her, protect her, and love her with all I have, above all others. But my home is no longer here, this is my past. This is their home, not mine. Where we begin our life is Bel Rosso. You are now my life. It is complete now for me. I have you for all eternity."

"Shade, your parents, I've seen them both now. Your mother is fair and blonde. Your father, you look just like him. You have your father's intensity, his temper and passion, his warrior spirit, and your mother, you have her compassion."

As she spoke of *Madre* and *Padre*, his heart felt such pain, he thought he would choke, and he saw her rear back as it hit her as well. She would learn that, unless he was blocking her, whenever any extreme emotion came over him, she'd feel it as well, just as he'd feel hers now that she was immortal.

"*Bel*, it's okay, you're just feeling the pain it brings me. You will feel my emotions now, as I do yours. Their death still pains me, even after all this time. But they died together. And I pray to whatever hears me we go the same way, because I will go mad without you."

She felt his pain of loss, his grief, as if it were her own. It comforted her to know that all she felt, all he felt, they'd share, and no burden would ever be carried alone, no joy would go unshared. Everything they tackled going forward, they'd share together. It gave her strength. It gave them a power together she couldn't have foreseen. She still had so much to learn. She put her forefinger on his lips, "Shh, don't speak of death. We'll conquer all, lover."

"All, *mi amore*, all." Pulling her to his chest, he closed his eyes. "Try to rest, there is much to come, much ceremony. We both need our rest to conquer the world that lies before us. One step at a time, *mi amore*. Together. *Ti amo*."

Emily Bex

94

Raven was keeping an eye on this huge estate in Virginia master now called home. He thought it would be boring, but he was finding it was fun. Never a dull moment out here in the middle of bum-fuck nowhere! Having finished up his rounds, looking for any signs of trespassers or illegal entry onto the property, he headed back to the staff quarters and walked in to find Marcello. Marcello tipped his ever-present shades down his nose, looking over his dark glasses at Raven and grinned, asking how his night went. Raven shook his head and laughed.

"To be blunt, bro, riding antlers gets old, but the mountain lions, now that is some major entertainment! I can see your ass has really accomplished a lot. So, what gives, brother? Any news from the master?" Raven walked over to where he sat, took off his shirt, and grabbed a smoke. "Hell, something should have happened by now with my lady."

Marcello lit up with him. "Luca called, my lady made it through the turning. Red Moon rising, brother. So, this means two things. We have a new queen, and a ceremony to attend in Florence, and we better have our asses out there on time. Luca wasn't sure how long it would take for her to get over the bloodlust. Master is locked down in the chamber with her. Also means, master will be sending in temporary replacements for you, me and Fiamma. We'll need to get them up to speed quickly, make sure they're familiar with the property before we leave."

Raven let out a war call. "I knew my lady would make it, she doesn't take shit from anybody, not even the mad-ass devil himself! *Cazzo*, I hate the ceremonial leathers, tedious heavy nonsense. But damn if I don't look fine in my custom rags, bro. I'm one sleek ass warrior, turning it up a notch since Cory came on board." Flopping down on one of the couches, he blew a plume of smoke into the air and watched it rise above him, forming into a heart. "So, we just wait till the relief warriors get here and head home?"

Marcello laughed to himself. One thing Raven never lacked was self-confidence. Watching him take this a little too casually, Marcello sat forward in the chair. "Raven, listen, brother, you need to take this seriously. This is like a mortal marriage for Master Shade, as well as the coronation of our queen. If you don't act like a fucking Medici warrior, he may lop your damn head off where you stand, and if he doesn't, Marco will. You push his fucking buttons as is. The occasion calls for full ceremonial dress leathers, in the Throne Room where my lady will be presented as our queen and all the Medici warriors of rank, as well as prominent masters from other covens will be there. Besides, I heard Cory made new ceremonial leathers for everyone, very sleek, with the Medici crest on the chest, so the old heavy ceremonial garb is out. And one more thing, Rave, Council will be there. So, you best play your ass straight! You got that, bro?"

Raven sat up and looked at him. "Marcello, I've never done anything 'straight' in my life and I'm not about to start now. But I hear you loud and clear, brother. Master will be on his guard, I have to look like a warrior, act like a warrior, bow, be all amped up for my lady. I got it. I won't let master down, and besides that, I like my lady." Sliding his hand through his waist-long hair and looking at Marcello, "Council. I hate those fucks. That's one thing I don't miss from home, those high and mighty bastards strolling around. Relax bro, I got this."

Marcello rolled his eyes and shook his head. "Raven, if you don't honor master and my lady, you aren't going anywhere but six feet under! No idea what master has in mind, but with the development of a damn warrior camp going on here at Bel Rosso, something is about to change big time. A lot has been accomplished in building the warriors' barracks and the training facilities since they've been gone, and when they return here, things will start happening fast. It looks big, and you know master. He's impatient, so he'll be bringing in more warriors, recruiting, and training. It'll be a whole new ballgame, Rave."

Marcello continued, "Our queen is immortal now, so this is going to be a whole new experience for her. Duties are going to be handed out, so if you have any intentions of returning here, I suggest you get your ass in order, act like you have a fucking brain, and don't push him over the edge. Look, brother, master has some big plans for the future here in the States. We're two of the best he has in his ranks. We've already been here a while. Don't fuck this up. If you want to come back here, don't give him cause to have doubts about you. For once in your damn life, Rave, be responsible." Marcello smacked him upside the head lightly, then stood up and headed for his sleeping quarters. "Slumber is yanking me, just be ready for anything. We're Medici, and wherever master commands us to go, we go."

Raven listened to his brother-in-arms, watched his face. He knew Marcello didn't want to return to Florence permanently, he already knew he was going to be something much bigger here in the States than he ever would in Florence, and Raven wanted the same. As he watched Marcello head for the sleeping quarters, Raven lay back on the sofa and thought about where he wanted to go in life. He liked the States, but Virginia wasn't for him. He had no true desire to go back to Florence either. He knew if he could prove himself here, master would give him options, let him stay with Medici and get bigger assignments.

Raven wanted to see more of the world, and he knew if he stayed here for a while, proved himself to master, it would lead to bigger things. He hadn't found a mate here in Virginia, and he'd yet to find someone like himself here. Females! He had no time for their drama. He preferred something a bit harder against his skin when he slept. But if Shade stayed here, expanded his territory in the States, then this was Raven's ticket to the world. Raven was loyal and pledged to him for life. Now he'd be pledged to his queen as well.

Grinning, he thought he better make a good appearance in Florence, make sure he won his way back here. The States suited his style.

95

It had been several days since the Blood Moon, Luca and the rest of Castello were all waiting for Shade to emerge with their new queen, then the real madness of the ceremony would begin. Shannon had enjoyed living in Castello and taking day trips with him into Florence, Siena, and San Gimignano. The staff had been extremely kind and attentive to her, keeping an eye on her each time she left their suite without him, to make sure she didn't get lost. Luca was sure that was Gi's doing and he must remember to thank him. However, he wanted to see his family home. He hadn't seen it since he was ten. He left home to go to the warrior camp after his father died in battle, and he never returned home. His mother had died before his father, and his father thought he could stay alive for Luca. But it was rare, when vampires mate, for one to stay alive if the other died when a true bond existed. Shade kept him at the academy then, took him under his wing, trained him himself, and raised him like a son. Their family home had been lost to his fathers' debt, or so he'd always thought. To have it back now, as a gift from Shade, bought by him and maintained all these years, was overwhelming. He had no idea the condition it was in, but his heart beat faster at the very idea of walking through those rooms again.

Shannon emerged from the bathroom still wrapped in a plush white towel–she loved that huge marble tub–her skin aglow and her long brown hair catching the sunlight.

"*Mia belleza*, I have something special planned for us today. Are you up for an adventure?"

"Luca, every day with you is an adventure. Last week, I was sitting in a cubicle, working on a marketing campaign for a new hand and body lotion, and now I'm living in a castle, waiting for my best friend to emerge as a vampire and be crowned queen of a coven. So, I'm pretty sure I can handle whatever it is you have planned for us."

She dropped her towel, and watched as his hazel eyes washed over her, that shy half-smile appeared, and she knew she could pretty much take this day in any direction she wanted, an adventure in bed, or out of bed? She smiled back at him and proceeded to slide on her bra and panties, spritzing on her perfume.

"What should I wear for this adventure, babe? Am I already over-dressed?"

"You tempt me, *mia belleza*. Every minute of every day, you tempt me. But I think I'll save that for dessert. What I have in mind for the day will require the daylight hours. I want to show you my home, where I grew up. I thought it was lost to me all these years, after the death of my parents. But before we came here to Florence, Shade gave me the deed to the property. He'd bought it years ago and saved it for me. I haven't seen it since I was ten, and I want you to be with me when I see it again."

Shannon slipped into a pair of jeans and a blouse, and stepped into a pair of ballet flats. "Luca! That's... wow, I don't even know what to say! That's fabulous! I'd love to see your home! I'm surprised you waited this long. I think it would've been the first place I visited."

"I needed some time, *mia belleza*. My memories of home are both bitter and sweet. It's where I grew up with my mother and father, but also, it reminds me of their absence in my life. This will be... an emotional journey for me, I think. I needed to, what is that American phrase? Get my head around it?"

"No, of course. I understand that. Oh, Luca. I'm so honored you want me to be with you. Really, I am."

Luca grabbed a light jacket, slid his arm around her slender waist and led her out. "Come on, let's see what car Gi has ready for us to take out today."

Gi had a different car from Shade's fleet of cars, pulled out and ready for them each day. He said Shade insisted he use them while he was here. Every car Luca saw only reminded him of the silver Jaguar that sat in the garage in Virginia, waiting for Kate to learn to drive a stick shift. He made a mental note to move that to the top of his priorities list when they returned. He walked with Shannon to the garage, which was in a separate building from Castello, and had been built years later to accommodate these vehicles. As they entered, the bright red Alfa Romeo Spider was pulled out and ready. The on-duty mechanic approached, handed him the keys, telling him it was gassed up and ready. Luca watched the smile on Shannon's face, as he opened the door for her to climb into yet another sports car. The top was already down on the convertible, so she pulled a scarf from her bag and tied it around her hair and put on her dark glasses. As he walked to the driver's side door, the mechanic opened the door for him and he climbed in, started up the engine, and pulled out into the warm Tuscan sun.

Luca casts sideways glances at Shannon as they drove, her face tilted back to the sun, her smile beaming. The thought entered his head that if he were to turn her, there was no guarantee she'd be a day-walker like him. She may inherit his gift or be given another. He could condemn her to a life lived in darkness. He quickly brushed away the thought.

Shannon laid her head back on the headrest and raised both hands in the air, feeling the wind. The sky was the brightest blue without a cloud to be seen, and the sun seemed to be shining just for them. "What a beautiful day! Luca, this has been an amazing trip. I can't thank you enough for inviting me. And I can't wait to see your home. Where is it? Is it far?"

"Not far, *mia belleza*. My home is just outside Empoli. It's only about twenty kilometers from Florence."

"Luca, I'm American, remember? We don't do metric."

Laughing at her, "*Si,* I remember... about twelve miles, *mia belleza*. But I warn you, my home, it's nothing like Castello. My home is humble. Although we had land, it's not as big as Bel Rosso, and I have no idea what condition it's in. Shade said it was maintained. I take that to mean the property has been cared for. The house will not be falling down around our ears, but it's a very old property, several hundred years old. He would have maintained the land, not let it become overgrown. Land is important to Shade. We had lemon groves there when I was a boy. My father sold the lemons to be made into limoncello, the Italian liqueur.

"Limoncello! Kate and I drank that on our first trip to Italy! It's a dessert liqueur, right?"

"*Si*. I haven't seen it in the States since I've been there. I'm sure it's available, but it doesn't have the same popularity as it does here. My father made his living from the lemon groves. I'm sure they're long gone now."

As they drove through the Tuscan countryside, the rolling hills and the Cypress trees, it wasn't long before they passed through Empoli, and left the main road to go to his family home. As they topped the hill, he saw it and his heart skipped a beat. It was just as he remembered it. The stone house, nestled in the grove of trees, rich green from the spring rains. He stopped the car on this little-used road and looked down at his home, feeling the rush of memories flood through him. He could hear his father's voice, his mother's laughter ringing in his ears. He felt the blood tears well up behind his dark sunglasses.

Shannon rose up in her seat as much as her seat belt allowed. "Is that it? Luca! It looks like a post-card. It's beautiful!"

Luca reached over and squeezed her hand. "*Si, mia belleza.* Beautiful."

He shifted back into first and started the descent down the hill to his home. It had been more than *maintained*, it had been lovingly cared for. He pulled the car up in front of the house and parked, getting out and opening the door for Shannon. He had to stand a second and take it all in, as she took off her scarf and stuffed it back in her handbag, sliding her sunglasses on top of her head, and scanning the house and the surrounding grounds.

"Luca, seriously... this is just breathtaking." She slipped her hand in his as he started to walk toward the house.

Luca stepped up to the main entrance of the stone house, climbing the few steps to the door, framed on either side by faded white shutters. Terracotta pots filled with healthy plants lined the walkway and the porch. He slid his hand into the pocket of his jeans to withdraw the key Shade had given him. He opened the ironwork gate and slipped the key in the ancient wooden door. He closed his eyes and paused before he pushed it open to all the memories of his childhood.

Shannon felt him give her hand a tight squeeze, as he paused at the door. The house was very old but looked picture-perfect. Shannon craned her neck to take it all in. Not quite as big as the house at Bel Rosso, but close. And land... if all this land was his, it was worth a fortune. She could sense his nervousness as he inserted the key in the door, then hesitated. She gave him a kiss on the cheek. "Ready, babe?"

Luca looked to her and her sweet face. She'd just started calling him babe since they'd been in Italy. He liked the sound of it, this term of endearment. No one had ever called him anything other than Luca.

"Ready, *mia belleza.*"

With one last deep breath, he pushed open the door that led into the foyer. The thick stone walls blocked the heat of the sun, and he could immediately feel the temperature drop as he entered the space. Shannon clung to his hand as they stepped under the arched ceiling of the entryway, and everything looked just as it had when he lived here as a boy. The old heavy wooden bench remained in the entry hall, the picture on the wall. The lighting fixture had been updated but was still an antique chandelier that remained true to the original design of the house. He could almost hear his mother's voice calling out to him, 'Don't track in mud, Luca... Kick off those muddy boots by the door!'

Shannon noticed he was lost in his own thoughts and memories, and she could see the emotion on his face. She so loved this man and his gentle heart. She looked about the entry hall with its. stone tile floor. The exterior walls were all stone, while the interior walls were brick covered in a thick plaster, with sections of exposed brick where the plaster had chipped away over the years. She was in love with this place. He pushed the heavy wooden door with its black metal hinges closed behind them, blocking out the heat of the bright sun, as he led her into another room.

Luca took her into the living room with the arched ceilings, expecting to find it empty, but found it furnished instead. Some of the pieces belonged to his family, but the upholstered pieces, the sofas and chairs, had all been replaced. He could literally move in today. *Master, you have done so much more than "maintain" this house, you have kept it my home.*

Shannon let go of his hand as he walked through the room, and she sank down in one of the plush chairs. He was right about one thing, this was nothing like Castello with it's over the top opulence. This was a home. She could imagine him here. It suited him. She watched as he picked up items from the table, from a shelf on the wall, running his hands over each piece. He was quiet, but she saw that slight smile he wore, and knew the memories in his head were happy ones. He replaced a book on the shelf and turned to her, holding out his hand, ready to move on. She stood and took his hand, and they locked eyes.

"Do you like it, *mia belleza*?"

"I love it, Luca. I love it."

"Come, so much more to see." He led her through the dining room with the ancient tapestry mounted on the wall, the table and chairs the same as when he was a boy.

Shannon commented, "I don't get it, the whole dining room thing. I mean, you don't eat. What's up with that?"

Luca laughed at her. "Appearances, *mia belleza*. We live in a world of mortals. It was always important to appear as one of them, still is. Come, you can see the kitchen where we never cook." He smiled at her laughter.

Shannon followed him into the kitchen and had a visual image of herself puttering around this quaint room, making fresh bread or her own pasta from scratch, and then remembered with a jolt, there'd be no one to cook for. This was just another room for appearances only.

He took her through the family room and out to the arboretum, where his mother potted plants for the summer and grew plants during the winter. So many memories of her here, she loved to garden. The arboretum led to the covered back patio. He took Shannon down the back hallway and out to the shaded patio, overlooking the rolling Tuscan hillside, where he once played. Like Shade, he'd been an only child. His mother died young, and his father chose not to seek another mate, as was their custom. He wondered what his life would've been like had they lived. Would he be the warrior he was today had Shade not taken him under his wing? Trained him personally? Would he have traveled to the States? Been protector to their queen? Would he have met this mortal woman who held his heart? These were questions that would forever be unanswered.

Shannon was left breathless by the view from this patio. She could imagine him playing here as a small boy, running through those hills. She could see he was so lost in his memories. "A penny for your thoughts, babe. Or *lira*? A *lira* for your thoughts?"

Luca looked over at her, the light breeze blowing through her hair. "Contemplating my fate, *mia belleza*."

"Wow... heavy thoughts."

"*Si*. But all good, I think. My parents are gone, and yet, I feel them here. Shade did everything my father asked of him and more, so much more. Maybe even giving me a life my father couldn't have provided. I'm weighing that in my head, the outcome. Was my loss also my gain? It's a lot to take in, *bella*."

"Luca..."

"I know you don't completely understand it, *mia belleza*, my devotion to him, and my station. But I owe him everything. Come..." Luca took her hand once more and led her back inside. "I'll show you the bedrooms. There are many. My mother wanted many children, but sadly, that wasn't to be."

He took her back to the foyer entrance where, at the far end, there were stairs leading to the second floor. They climbed the stone steps, the stone worn down in the center by the many feet that had trod here over the years. The stairs opened on a long hallway, his parents' bedroom to the left, and the other six bedrooms, including the one that used to be his, off the long hallway to the right. He turned left, to the bedroom his parents shared. This room held the bed his mother carried him to whenever he had a bad dream, tucking him into their bed, allowing him to sleep safely for the rest of the night between his mother and father. He pushed open the door to their room, and their essence, their spirit overwhelmed him.

The room with the stone walls and arched ceilings looked like his parents could have just stepped out only minutes before. It looked exactly as he remembered it. His father's jacket was hanging on a coat rack, his mother's slippers by the bed, and a book on the nightstand, with a bookmark tucked between the pages. No dust or cobwebs, the room was immaculately cleaned, and yet, Shade wouldn't let them touch any of their things. He felt like he'd stepped back in time and his head spun, as he reached out and touched the wall to steady himself.

Shannon could see his emotions swell as they entered this room, the bedroom his parents shared. She saw him steady himself against the wall. "Luca? Are you okay?"

He regained his composure and walked around the room, running his hand across their bed when he heard his mother's voice in his head.

"This girl, this mortal girl, you love her?"

"Si, Madre, Lei è il mio vero amore."

"Your one true love? And this girl, Luca. Does she love you? Could she love you for all eternity?"

Shannon heard him speaking in Italian and she looked up, looking around the room. "Who are you speaking to, Luca? Me? Because I don't speak Italian."

"No, *mia belleza*, I speak to my mother. She wants to know if you can love me for all eternity. What do I tell her?"

She looked at him, those hazel eyes looking back at her, and she went to him, slid her arms around him and kissed him with gentleness and passion. "You can tell her I said an eternity wouldn't be long enough."

His arms pulled her tight against his chest as his lips sought out hers, and the gentleness was gone, just passion remained. He reluctantly broke the kiss, brushing his hand through that thick brown hair, running the backs of his fingers down her cheek, his eyes drawn to her neck when he must fight the impulse to feed from her.

"Come on, I'll show you my old bedroom."

He took her back into the hallway and to the double doors that led to his bedroom. One of the doors was slightly ajar and he remembered those old wooden doors, worn smooth with age, and how they'd never close all the way. He ran his hand over their surface. This was the best bedroom, his mother used to say. And it had been saved for her oldest son, or as it turned out, her only son. "*Madre*, **how I miss you.**" He pushed against one of the doors and heard the creak of the hinges as he pushed it open and stepped into his old room.

Shannon was entranced by this house, and she could feel its pull on him. He was right, it was bittersweet. She could see it on his face. She followed him as he led her to his old bedroom. She was trying to remember her old bedroom when she lived in her parent's house. She remembered it was covered in posters of Nirvana and Pearl Jam. She thought she and Luca were about the same age, so it would be interesting to see how he'd lived. "Luca, how old are you?"

He stopped in the doorway and turned to her, wondering what prompted this question. "*Mia belleza...* you know we don't age in the same way. If you compare me to a mortal, I'd say probably about thirty. But as a vampire, I've lived one-hundred and fifty years. Still very young."

Shannon knew her mouth was hanging open and she was seriously doing her best to close it, but with no luck. *Did he say one-hundred and fifty? I'm dating a man who is one-hundred and fifty?* "Oh... I... wow. I had no idea. So, if Shade raised you, then he's how old?"

Luca had to chuckle out loud at the expression on her face. "Shade is about five-hundred, I think. So, you see, *mia belleza*, I have a long way to go yet."

"Five-hundred? Seriously? Does Kate know that?"

He threw his head back with laughter. "*Si, mia belleza*, I'm sure she knows. But it means nothing, *si*? Age just means wisdom, experience and a keen sense of survival. We do eventually die, after many centuries Shan, but we can be destroyed, just like any mortal. Come, see my old room with me."

He pushed the door all the way open and stepped back into his past. His bed was placed under the window, exactly as it used to be. The shutters were thrown open and fresh air blew through the room. A small vase holding flowers from his mother's garden sat by his bed. Someone had been here today, maybe even knew they were coming? Gi perhaps? He was sure of it.

Her head still reeling from the knowledge he was one-hundred and fifty. She followed him into his room, no Nirvana posters, or posters of whoever was making music one-hundred and fifty years ago. *Wow, that's like the Civil War period. Like banjo on my knee time. He was alive during the Civil War, only he lived here, not in the States.* She followed him around the room, as he looked through his things and watched as he kept glancing at her.

Luca asked, "You okay, Shan?"

"Yes, yeah sure... it's just... one-hundred and fifty. I mean, I know you're immortal. I understood that, in theory. I never really thought about your age, we seemed so close in age, or I thought we seemed so close in age. But you said if you were mortal you'd be about thirty, right? And I'm twenty-eight. I don't understand, is it like dog years or something? No, forget I said that. Erase, erase, erase!"

He walked over to his bed as she rambled on, his back to her, so she couldn't see his smile. He leaned over the bed so he could look out the window at the view he had looked at so many times as a boy. He lay down on his bed, looking up at the ceiling, and the familiar crack in the plaster. He patted the bed beside him, inviting her to join him.

"What's the matter, *mia belleza*? Are you worried I won't be able to keep up with you?"

She looked at him lying on the bed, one arm behind his head and his feet crossed at the ankles, his free hand patting the empty space beside him, and he made her weak in the knees. *Oh, baby! Two can play this game.* She pulled a straight back chair from against the wall and positioned it at the foot of the bed, straddled the chair and slowly unbuttoned her shirt. She gave him a funny sexy face, sticking out her tongue, and then asked him, "I don't know, old man. You sure you can handle all this?"

She made him laugh out loud with her antics and her playful striptease. "You are a handful, *si*? You may have to take it easy on me, *mia belleza*, in my advanced state of aging. I may only be able to make love to you for ten or twelve hours before I'd need a break, but I'll do my best to keep up."

She made a face of mock surprise, and fanned herself with her hand, making him laugh again.

Shannon spoke to him in an exaggerated Southern accent, giving him her best damsel in distress impression. "Why, sir? Only ten to twelve hours? What's a girl to do with the other twelve hours in the day?"

Luca laughed at her bad acting. "We can always call in reinforcements, *mia belleza*, until I'm able to revive my strength."

She stood up from her chair and slid her jeans off, still speaking in her phony accent, and batting her eyelashes at him. "Reinforcements, indeed, sir. I suppose that's always an option."

As she kicked her feet free from the jeans, she dove across the foot of the bed at him. She saw the startled expression on his face, as she landed on top of him and they both started laughing uncontrollably, until the laughter dissolved into a playful kiss, which turned into a very passionate kiss.

She broke away from the kiss and placed one finger on his lip. "Shush now, sir, while I undress you. You need to preserve all your strength."

She unbuttoned his shirt, never breaking her gaze from those hazel eyes, as he gave her that half-smile that made her so crazy for him. She pulled his shirt free from his waistband and then struggled to get the shirt off his arms. "A little help here, sir, would be nice."

"*Si, mia belleza*, I was preserving my strength as requested." He rose up and pulled the shirt off, while she moved to the button on his jeans and proceeded to unzip them. He continued to play her game. "Now you want me to help with that too, I suppose? If you have any hope of removing these jeans, *bella*, I suggest you take my boots off first."

"Oh! I'm so inexperienced at this, sir. It's so good I have you to guide me." She crawled to the foot of the bed on her hands and knees to remove his boots, leaning down as she untied them, her ass in the air for his full viewing pleasure.

"*Cazzo!*" She had that beautiful ass facing him, her back arched, and he slid his hands up the backs of her thighs and onto her ass cheeks, running his fingers under the lace edge of her panties which were already wet with her juices. The scent of her sex turned his cock to steel and he felt his fangs punch through. She removed each boot and pulled off his socks, when he sat up to help her pull off his jeans. Her ass was tantalizingly close and he ran his tongue across a tight rounded cheek, before snapping the tiny band of elastic that encircled her hips and tossing the torn panties to the floor. He gripped her hips with both hands, as he slid his tongue across her sex, tasting her sweetness, before plunging his tongue deep inside her. She felt her body tense, as she gripped the bedding and her moans filled this long silent room.

His hands, his tongue, pushed every thought from her head and replaced it with this burning need. She gripped the bedspread in her hands and moaned, as she felt his tongue plunge into her. She felt his fingers replace his tongue, as he teased, probed, pinched, and pulled at her sex until she thought she would scream. He grabbed her hips and pulled her down. His cock slid deep inside her with one smooth motion, and she straddled him with her back to him, as she started to slide herself along the full length of his cock. His grip controlled her rhythm, his hips lifting, thrusting. She tried to push her hips back, sit down on him, taking all of him, but his hands held her tight, not letting her have everything she wanted. Her body strained to feel all of him, yet he continued with this tease, sliding his member half in, half out. The sounds she made were more animal than human as he pushed her closer, but never giving up control of the pace he was setting. "Please..." It was the only word in her head. She whispered it again. "Please..."

When he heard her plea, he pulled her hips down hard as he lifted his own, slamming his cock deep inside her, and he heard her groan from deep in her throat, her head thrown back, that thick hair hanging down to her ass, as he released her to ride his penis at her own pace. He watched the rise and fall of her hips, and watched as his cock slid inside her, disappearing each time her ass pounded hard against him. He squeezed her hips hard, waiting for her, as his dick throbbed and begged for release. Her pace quickened, as did the cries from her mouth. He felt her reach her climax, felt the spasms deep inside her as he let his own body respond, filling her with cum, lifting his hips higher, thrusting deep, and holding her there in a vice grip until they both collapsed back on the bed. He pulled her close to him, watched her flushed face with its light sheen, and the rapid rise and fall of her chest as her body slowly returned to normal.

"You like my room, *mia belleza*?"

"What? Your room?" She was still out of breath and he was asking her about his room? "Of course, babe... great room."

He slid from his old bed and picked her up, carrying her from the room. "Good. Not counting my parent's room, there are six bedrooms in this house. That leaves only five more to break in."

"Oh, god help me."

Luca laughed at her as he took her into the next bedroom and tossed her on the bed. "Try to keep up with the old man, *bella*."

He took her from one room to the next, tossing her on each bed, and making love to her in each room. Luca on top, Luca taking her from behind, Luca sitting on the bed with her straddling him, Luca on the bottom, Luca feeding from her, his fangs deep in her neck, Luca with his face between her legs, making her scream to the heavens, until she begged him to stop.

"Perfect timing, *mia belleza*, we have run out of bedrooms anyway." He slapped her ass as he slid from the bed. "Come on, my fair damsel, we need to find our clothes."

"Seriously... I need to just lie here."

He grabbed her ankle and dragged her across the bed, nipping at her leg. "Clothes, *mia belleza*, or I will take you again."

He picked her up and carried her over his shoulder back to his bedroom and set her down in the room where they'd started. Their clothes tossed haphazardly across the floor.

"Remind me to never bring up that age thing again." She flipped her hair back out of her face, to see his eyes with a mischievous glint, and that sly half-smile, as he handed her jeans to her.

"I tore your panties." He picked them up off the floor and held them to his nose, inhaling her, keeping her locked in his gaze. "You'll have to go commando, like me."

Sweet Mother of God... this man! She slid the jeans over her hips and looked for her bra and blouse. He pulled on his own jeans and put his socks and boots back on. Shannon found his shirt, he found her blouse and they traded, laughing, her eyes glued to his. Her legs were literally shaking they'd had so much sex. As he finished dressing, he stepped to her, pushed her hair back from her face, his lips close to her ear, and she felt his hot breath against her skin. "Are you okay, *bella*?"

"Aside from not being able to walk, you mean? Other than that minor detail, I'm fine, babe."

"Keep up, mortal," he teased her and led her back down the stairs. He wanted to look outside. His father had a lot of property here. The soil was rich for planting, but Luca was sure nothing had been grown here in years. As they went through the kitchen to the back of the house again, there was a bottle of Limoncello on the counter, along with an aperitif glass that hadn't been there before. Gi again? He stopped and poured her a glass of the sweet and sour liqueur.

"It looks like someone thinks you may need a little refreshment, *mia belleza*."

He handed her the glass and she took a few sips, *delicious.* She remembered the taste. At first sour as the bite of the lemon hit your tongue, followed quickly by the sweetness. Drinking it on an empty stomach sent the alcohol straight to her head. Great, she was already having trouble walking. He watched as she emptied the glass, and she realized it was a taste he'd probably never savored. "Do you know what it tastes like, Luca?"

"I do not, *mia belleza.*"

"You've never tasted a lemon? Or sugar?" She swirled her finger in the glass and offered it to him, his mouth closing over her finger. She felt the heat from his tongue and her knees buckled. She smiled at the expression on his face, as he registered the initial burst of mouth puckering sourness, followed by the sugary sweetness. She slowly pulled her finger from his mouth, his lips pursed around her finger, applying pressure, holding her there, as they locked eyes again. *I swear, those eyes.*

As her finger left his lips, he licked them, savoring this strange flavor she'd shared with him.

"I think I prefer the taste of you, *bella.*" He gave her a quick kiss as he led her from the kitchen, before they consecrated yet another room. She followed him out the door and onto the open patio that overlooked the land. The sun told him it was late afternoon, as they walked across the courtyard.

As they cleared the courtyard, he saw large terra cotta pots filled with small lemon trees. The smell of the lemons and the sweet blossoms filled the air. It was only a small number compared to the groves that used to be here, but it made him smile to see it, to remember his father tending the fields, overseeing his crops. Even to maintain the lemon trees in pots required attention. Clearly, there was staff here, and not temporary staff. The house and the land were in too good condition for that. Shade had had people here caring for this house, this land, as if someone still lived here every day. It humbled him. He was his master. Luca's life was his to direct. Shade owed him nothing, and yet, gave him everything.

She watched him again as they walked outside, he stopped and stared at the lemon trees planted near the house. A flood of emotions could be read on his face, and she squeezed his hand.

He felt her light squeeze, her acknowledgment, her silence, as she stood beside him allowing him this time to absorb it all.

"Come, walk with me." He led her down the path to where the lemon groves used to grow, and he couldn't believe his eyes. They were still there. More than a hundred years, and they were still there. The lemon groves that supported their family had been restored to their full glory. The bottle of Limoncello in the kitchen was a message to him. This property still produced tons of lemons, sold on the market, producing a substantial income, an income that was now his. He squeezed his eyes shut to block his tears. Shade had done everything to secure his future. His love and generosity had no boundaries. Luca knew, if he were to ask for his independence, to move here, to live here with Shannon, to have his own babies here, he'd grant it. But Luca would never ask it. His loyalty to Shade was now more secure than ever. He looked at Shannon and wondered if she'd ever understand this, the bond Luca had with him. His love for her was never-ending, as was his loyalty to Shade, and he'd find a way to have them both in his life.

"Come, *mia belleza*. The sun is setting. Let's head back to Castello. We never know what night my king and queen will emerge from the chamber, and I want to be there."

96

Alec was working late in his home office, again. Rissa had had a good day. She had gone out again today with Jacks, with apparently less drama, but she was behind in her business as well. She had retreated to her own office upstairs, trying to get caught up. Santos came to the door, tapping lightly.

"Sorry to interrupt, master, but I have a hand-delivered letter for you."

Alec gave him a questioning look and Santos shook his head, indicating he didn't know the sender. Santos brought him the letter and then left the room. Alec slid his fingers under the seal of the heavy ivory colored envelope and pulled out the elaborately hand-written invitation.

High Master Alec Canton and Mate Larissa Benneteau
are cordially invited to the
Coronation of Queen Katherine of Medici.
Mated with Great Honor to King and High Master Shade Medici.
The Coronation will take place at Castello Medici
Florence, Italy
May 24 at Midnight.
RSVP

He flipped the stiff ivory stationary over in his hand. And so it was done. The mortal was now immortal. Well, at least the event was over a weekend, as if not attending was even an option, very bad vampire protocol.

"Rissa! Can you come downstairs, please?"

Rissa heard Alec call to her from downstairs. Rushing out of her room and down the stairs, she found him in his office, walked in and sat across from him. "Alec, I swear I was good today. What's going on? Your voice was booming."

"Was it booming, my darling? Didn't notice." He handed her the invitation. "It seems we have plans for the weekend. We'll leave on Friday, take the private jet. Be there for the coronation on Saturday, then fly home on Sunday. You can have a little time during the day on Saturday to shop if you like. Nothing is open in Italy on Sunday, and I mean nothing, except cathedrals."

As he handed her the elegant linen card, she noticed it was handwritten in beautiful calligraphy. She heard him babbling on and on about what? *A coronation? Is he kidding me?*

"Alec," holding up her hand, "Hold up a moment, did you say coronation? Italy?"

"Yes, a coronation, for your friend. What's her name? Kate? Shade is a king, my darling. His family is royalty. Bloodline goes back for centuries. I'm sure you've heard of the Medici's... the mortal ones. They practically built the city of Florence, financed Michelangelo, Da Vinci, Galileo, among others. Once Shade finally turns her, officially mating her, she becomes queen. I think his coven covers all of Tuscany, some in France and Greece, and if my instincts are right, soon in the U.S. She'll rule with him over every Medici coven."

His words didn't register right away, then it dawned on her, and she rolled her eyes to him in absolute astonishment and jealousy.

"You mean the warrior is royalty? I... wait... Kate? Meek little Kate? Kate is a queen? There has to be some mistake! *The* Medici's?"

She stood up and covered her mouth in disbelief. She paced around the room, trying to comprehend how the hell that bitch landed a king. Spinning on her heels, she looked Alec dead in the eyes. "You never told me he was a king!"

"Yes, well, meek little Kate took out the meanest fucking mercenary vamp when she was still mortal. I mean, she killed the vamp that scares other vamps. So, I've had to rethink my whole impression of her. And Shade... he's a master warrior by profession. It's what he does. He doesn't really flaunt that king title, doesn't need to. Every vamp knows who he is. Excuse me, my darling, I thought I'd mentioned he was royal blood. Every vamp that was born vamp knows who he is. I've been in that fucking castle many times before, though. You should enjoy that. That place is protected like a fortress, and it's not often other vamps not of the Medici coven would ever see inside."

She stood staring at him like she was in some bad dream, make that a nightmare! A castle? She closed her mouth quickly as she discovered it hanging wide open the longer he talked. She was shaking her head back and forth.

"No! I don't believe this." Walking over to him, she bent down and looked him in the eye. "Are you playing a trick on me?"

He laughed out loud, swallowing down the rest of the Midnight. "Darling, I feel the trick is on me. I spent millions in property value to have Shade provide protection, try to work with my warriors, get them in shape, and when that didn't work, had him bring his own warriors here from Florence. And after all that money, who kills Angel? Some scrawny little mortal red-head. And to add insult to injury, I have to pay the bounty we agreed to from the beginning. Whoever brings the head of my enemy can claim their reward, and what does he want for Kate? That fucking building in Paris sits right on the Champs Elysees. No, my darling. I assure you, it's no trick."

All she heard was Champs Elysees and her eyes went wide and she growled, with gritted teeth, her chest heaving in and out.

"You gave her the house in Paris? I wanted that house. Damn it, Alec!"

She spun around and walked to the other side of the room, kicking the elegant solid cherry bookcase as she went by and heard it shatter and splinter. "You didn't think it was important to tell me about him? Then you... Fuck, I can't believe this! The Paris house. It's worth a fortune! I had plans for that. That bitch!"

"Hold on, wildcat. As far as I know, she had nothing to do with that transaction. Shade wanted to surprise her with it, and I had tenants in there that needed notice to move out, so I don't think he has even told her yet. And for the record, my darling, my property that I gained through the centuries is mine to bargain with as I see fit. I don't need to discuss with you any of my business decisions, so be careful where you tread. I gave him the deeds to the Virginia property and the California property. They brought no value to me, but to him, with the vineyards, it was like gold. Besides, that Virginia property is sitting right in the middle of Max's coven. I have no quarrel with Max. We've been allies in the past. But it's never a good idea to own property within another master's coven. Good riddance, as far as I'm concerned. And now Shade will have to deal with Max, and I don't think that will take very long since I hear rumors Shade is building his own warrior camp out there now. I can't imagine Max not seeing that as a direct threat."

She stopped dead in her tracks, her back to him. *Max!* She felt her heart beat rapidly, her blood racing. She swallowed hard and took a deep breath and felt the room spinning. She found her hand suddenly at her throat and she closed her eyes, turning slowly to face him.

"Maximus? The Virginia property is in his territory. Does this mean he'll be at the coronation?" She felt all her hatred and jealousy of Kate slide away as it was replaced with fear.

"I'm not sure, my darling. I'm not privy to his guest list, but it's customary for a coronation to invite any master who'd be considered an ally, and I'd assume since we've not seen a war for territory they perceive each other as allies. So, it's possible. I'll tell you it's very bad form to refuse the invitation. It's considered an insult to that master, so we'll be going. And needless to say, it's formal. So, I'll wear black tie, and you need to find something appropriate from that warehouse you call a closet."

Her mind went into overdrive and she had to come up with some excuse to get out of this invitation! She couldn't face Max! He could easily kill her while there. Walking slowly to Alec, she knelt down in front of him and laid her head on his knee.

"Alec, I'm just getting back out there, I don't even know what I'm supposed to do. What if I make a mistake? Oh hell, do I have to bow to her? I'm not bowing. Not to her! Maybe I should stay here, I have Jacks now, and well, I'm so far behind on my work."

Alec shook his head no. "She's not your queen, so you aren't required to bow. His warriors, all the vamps in his coven, they're her subjects. All other masters and their mates are there as a sign of respect. But you'll go, my darling. My relationship with Shade isn't over. I still have a long-term issue of protection, and he'll provide that, so snubbing him isn't acceptable. You don't have to do anything. You will attend, you will watch. She'll be crowned, and his warriors will pledge to her. The Council will have to confirm her immortal and royal status with her blood. It will be a lot of pageantry. I'd think this would be right up your alley, my darling. You'll not need Jacks. I'll be with you. And the place will be swarming with his warriors. Trust me. There will be no safer place for any vampire to be than at that coronation."

She almost laughed out loud. *That's what you think, Alec.* Her life could be in danger.

"Well, as long as you're with me and don't leave me alone." Standing, she put her hands on her hips. "I suppose I'd best go. If she thinks for one minute this ridiculous coronation is going to outdo my wedding, she has another think coming! As for my warehouse of a closet, maybe you should get a hall pass and come peruse the goods and choose for me if this is that important. I don't want to make one false step." She headed for the door, mumbling as she went, "A damn queen, of all things, and my house! My Paris dream house. That bitch has some nerve trying to get one up on me!"

Alec watched her as she skulked out of the room, mumbling under her breath. That was one pissed off woman. He knew she'd be angry about the Paris house, but Kate becoming queen? Women! If he lived another thousand years, he doubted he'd ever understand them.

Alec went to the bar to pour another drink but found the decanter empty. "Santos! Out of Midnight in here!"

Stomping up the stairs, she tried to wrap her head around all this hell dumped on her tonight. She heard Alec yell at Santos to bring him some more Midnight. Leaning over the railing, she yelled her own command.

"Make that two!"

97

As one more night passed, Kate had finally beaten the worst of the bloodlust, and Shade knew she'd be able to control her hunger for the most part. He would remain with her constantly, while she learned control of her enhanced emotions and new sensory perceptions. He was more than ready to get out of this chamber and back to their life. They must first get through the ceremony for her coronation, to officially claim her as his mate and queen. She'd be presented to all of his coven, his warriors, the Council, and close allies as she assumed this new role, reigning with him over the coven. He watched her walk slowly around the chamber, running her hands along the rough stone walls, she was getting impatient too.

"*Mi amore*, come to me, I want to ask you something."

She walked to him, took his hand. "Yes, lover?"

Shade smiled at her, pulling her into his arms and kissing her softly, gently.

"*Mi amore*, I think it is time we leave this chamber and head to our bedchamber above ground." He took her face in his hands, looked into her eyes. "Are you prepared to leave here? I know you're still afraid of what awaits you out there, and there are many things I still need to teach you, but it's difficult within this chamber, *si*?"

She nodded her head. "I think I'm ready. It scares me a little, but as long as you're with me. There was some ceremony around coming into the chamber, Theresa preparing me in the white gown. What happens when we leave?"

Taking her chin and tilting it up to his face, he looked deep into her eyes. "I will not leave your side, *mi amore*, not for a while. I will be right beside you." He pulled her into his lap and cuddled her into his chest. "I wish to leave here, *bel*, with you in my arms. We walked in together, both dressed in white. You were still a mortal, still pure to the immortal world. We leave officially mated, in red, and I carry you out as my chosen mate, just as in the mortal world it is tradition to carry you across the threshold, is that not right?"

"Yes."

"*Si,* so I shall carry my new immortal bride across the threshold of this chamber, in my arms. I will not teleport but carry you to our bedroom within Castello. Are you ready, *mi amore*? Do you have any questions before we leave this chamber?"

Kate felt anxious. "Will anyone be outside? Will anyone see us?"

He gently caressed her back and snuggled into her neck, feeling her trepidation of what lay beyond that stone door, and who'd be awaiting her. "No one will be directly outside, *mi amore*, but I do believe we may encounter Gi, Theresa perhaps, and I would believe that Luca is impatiently waiting for both of us to emerge. And if Luca is there, I believe Shannon will be there as well. I can summon the rest of the staff to either witness us, or be unseen, what is your choice?"

Her response was immediate, "No! Don't summon the staff, please don't. I know there were many who watched us as we went in. But my senses feel raw. I'm afraid I'll feel overwhelmed. I can hear the water as it runs down the chamber wall. I can hear the drop as it hits the chamber floor. These are sounds I normally wouldn't hear. I'm trying to imagine how all the hustle and bustle of the world will sound to me now. All the smells, the lights, it feels like too much."

He clutched her tighter to his chest, "Shh, *mi amore*, it will be fine, and soon enough, you will learn, on your own, how to tune out all the sounds you don't need to hear, how to zero in on those that are important. Also, how to unblock sounds when you feel danger. It will take time, but learning will be easy enough. No one will be about, I promise you." Kissing the top of her head, he slid her off his lap. "Gi has left a red robe here someplace, have you seen it by chance?"

"In that carved out shelf by the door, there is something red folded there."

"Ah, *si!*" Walking to the shelf, he picked up the folded robe. He shook it out like a huge sheet above his head and twirled it around him, pulling the hood up over his long curls, his blue eyes peering out at her. The robe fell to the floor in a perfect length. She was already wearing the red robe *Padre* had bestowed to her.

"Come, *mi amore*, it is time we leave, my queen."

Queen. She no longer flinched at the word. She stood and went to him, eager to leave, and yet, nervous about what lie ahead, as he lifted her effortlessly in his arms, he telepathically asked Gi to make sure no one was present on their journey.

She settled into him, like it was home for her, and he loved having her there in the protection of his arms, her head so close to his heart. He pressed the stone engraved with the Medici crest and the stone chamber opened.

She heard the massive door swing open and felt the rush of fresh air into this sealed chamber. She could smell the dampness in the air as he began the long walk back through these stone corridors, weaving his way through the tunnels and stairs they originally took that lead them deep underground. It was still night, so he could walk the long expanse of the castle to reach their bedchamber. As soon as they emerged, she could feel the presence of others, but she saw no one. She turned her face to his chest, closed her eyes, blocked out the light from the chandeliers, and the reflection of the light on the gold that trimmed the ceilings. She could already feel the sensory overload, even though it was quiet in these halls. When they reached the grand foyer, he took the stairs, returning them to their bedroom, his parent's old bedroom, where Portia welcomed Kate as her daughter, and told her to fight for him.

As they approached their bedchamber, the door was closed, but Gi waited outside the entrance. Leaning down, Shade whispered in Kate's ear, "*Bel*, Gi is outside our bedchamber door. I need to put you down on your feet, *si*? He will wish to bow to you. It is his duty seeing you for the first time as his queen. Can you manage to open your eyes?"

Kate nodded against his chest, opening her eyes to his blue brilliance, those eyes looking even bluer now they were in the light of the chandeliers that lined every hallway. "Of course, lover."

Smiling down at her, he kissed her nose. "*Ti amo.*" Sitting her down softly on her feet, he watched as Gi nodded to her and then bowed deeply, holding the bow, waiting for her acknowledgment of his presence and the honor and respect he was showing her. Gi kept his eyes lowered until he was spoken to. "**Just speak to him, *mi amore*, acknowledge him and his respectful and honorable gesture.**"

Kate responded humbly, "You honor me, Gi, with your service and your loyalty. I'll work hard to be a worthy queen."

As Gi raised his eyes to her, his smile was wide and broad, and he nodded to Kate and opened the door, telling Shade if there was anything they needed, please let him know. Gi informed him all had been arranged for the ceremony. Shade thanked him, and lifted *bel* into his arms once again, carrying her through the bedchamber doorway, kicking the door closed behind him. "Tough to handle the light and sound and everything you feel, *si*? Are you all right, *bel*?"

The sound of the door slamming closed sounded loud and jarring to her ears, and she flinched slightly at the noise. "I'm all right, Shade. I'm glad we're alone."

"Well, you have a few days to adjust before the ceremony. You'll get used to this. We'll be having the ceremony at midnight in two nights. I know you feel you aren't prepared, but at this stage, you will never feel ready, simply because it is all new. It must feel like you are seeing the world for the first time. By the time we get back to Bel Rosso, you should have this under control. There is much hustle and bustle going on here now, especially with the ceremony coming. Perhaps we should lie down, rest our bodies and our senses, *si*?"

She walked around this room as he talked to her, looking at everything again with new eyes. The colors were more vibrant, and details in the fabrics not visible before stood out to her. She felt texture in the marble floor under her feet, where before it felt smooth. When he spoke to her, she felt the vibrations of his voice through her body. She closed her eyes and inhaled, and his scent was as strong as if he were standing next to her with her nose buried in his neck. She could feel his heartbeat, in rhythm with her own. He was calm, so she was calm. She wondered how far away from him she could be, and still pick up his scent, still feel his heartbeat? She turned to look at him and he took her breath away. The red hood still draped over his head, those eyes following her as she moved about the room.

"Lie down, rest our senses, yes."

98

Bel was re-exploring the bedroom, picking things up and looking at them, her senses on overload, but Shade was pleased with how she was handling the transition. Suddenly, he felt coldness in the air, a shift in the energy and he knew another vampire had entered Castello, a vampire with power.

One of the housemaids came to Gi in a panic. "The Council!" She was repeating it, over and over, "The Council!"

Gi straightened his waistcoat. "What are you jabbering about?"

She blurted out there was a member of the Council at the front gate, wishing to enter. The Council had never come to Castello except for ceremonial occasions and never uninvited. It was not a good sign. Gi rushed to the entrance in the grand foyer and swung open the door to find the green-robed High Council Malachi. He bowed deeply.

"High Council Malachi, please, come in, how might I be of service to you this evening?"

Malachi stepped into the grand foyer, looked at its opulence, and shook his head. *What was he thinking?* "It is imperative I speak to the Medici... in private, please."

Gi bowed his head. "Of course, High Council. Please, follow me to the parlor, and I will return with Master Shade." Gi escorted him to the room and offered him a seat, but Malachi chose to stand. Gi rushed up the stairs and rapped hard at Master Shade's bedroom door.

Shade stood still and closed his eyes, concentrating. *Cazzo! Bel* responded to his change in energy, sensing something was wrong and was on top of him immediately.

"Shh, *mi amore*, it is fine. Relax. Enter!"

Gi opened the door, looking flustered. "Master, so sorry to interrupt, but the High Council Malachi is here. He asks to see you in private. I have taken him to the parlor and he waits for you there."

Shade stared at Gi and wondered what the hell had happened. Council never made personal visits unless it was bad news. "See to his needs immediately, Gi, inform Malachi I will be there directly."

As Gi nodded, Shade could tell this unexpected little visit had his entire household in an uproar. He looked down to see Kate's eyes, round as saucers in her face. Taking her face into his hands, he kissed her softly.

"Listen to me, *bel*, I need to attend to this immediately. I have no idea why a member from Council is here, but I will find out shortly. You are perfectly safe inside this room, but do you wish me to call Luca?"

"I... yes... no. I'm fine, lover. You go. I'll be fine, and Luca is just down the hall. Are we in danger?"

"We are in no immediate danger, but something is wrong. It's not normal for Council to come uninvited, without notice. Malachi is Head Council. He oversees and records matings, births and deaths of any vampire under the realm of the European Council, so I am assuming he is here to see me about our mating. The official announcements have gone out for the ceremony. Perhaps he wants to inquire about details around the coronation." Shade shrugged his shoulders. "I will return immediately when I am done, *si*?"

"Go, I'm sure it is nothing. I'll be waiting here for your return."

He gave her a quick kiss and without another word, teleported immediately outside the parlor. He took a deep breath and entered to find Malachi standing, observing the room, his deep emerald green robe to the floor. Each member of Council wore the color of the crystals that reflected their area of responsibility, and they were named as such. Malachi assumed his name from the deep emerald green malachite, the crystal that represented clearing the heart of past pains, so it was open to receive love.

Shade entered the parlor with pride and honor. He bowed to no one, not even Council. He was well respected within the Council, as was his *padre*. He showed them respect, as they were the ruling body of his species and had kept them from extinction.

"Malachi. Welcome to Castello Medici. Please be seated. I hope Gi has obliged you with anything you need. To what do I owe this honor?"

"Medici. It has been many years since I have stepped inside the walls of Castello. I think the last time was your birth, perhaps? And yes, your man-servant was most solicitous, but I prefer to stand. This is not a social visit. I come to express the grave concerns of the Council. We were notified when you made the journey to the States, and were well aware of your duties there in service to Master Alec, and we approved that move. We were notified of the transfer of property between you and Master Alec, and although we see some potential pitfalls with Master

Maximus, we reluctantly approved that as well. We have been notified of the deed transfer to Luca of Medici, and that has been recorded. A very generous gesture, I might add.

"That is not the reason for my visit, however. We heard of your dalliance with a mortal, but then that is nothing new. The mortals have always been a curiosity for our kind. Then we heard you had chosen her for your mate. Surely, this was wrong, Medici. Surely, we had not heard correctly, but then it was confirmed to us. And now, the turning. I am here on behalf of all in the Council to express to you our deep disappointment. Not once did you approach us with this choice. You are not just High Master, you are royal blood. Our expectations of you are much greater, as I am sure your *padre* shared. We had all assumed you would make your choice for a mate from one of the other royal families, and if not royal, at least the immortal daughter of a master. But a mortal? How do you expect a mortal to uphold the Medici legacy? How can a mortal be expected to rule this coven, and earn the respect of those that follow you? When you breed with her, surely the blood of your off-spring will be diluted. What kind of legacy will you leave? Will your sons even have the power to rule? I expected more from you, Medici. You have lived over five-hundred years, long enough to think with your head and not with your heart."

Shade listened to him go on and said nothing, but his beast reared up, ready to rip something apart. He knew the Council would not be happy with his choice, but how dare they come into his domain and tell him *bel* was nothing.

Growling, Shade glared at him once he was finished speaking. "You step into my domain, my rule, and tell me you are not accepting of my choice of mate? This family has given more funds and more blood than any other family within Europe!" Spreading his arms wide, sweeping the room, "Do you think my *padre* gave his life for you? He gave his life for me! He left this legacy, this coven to me. He rose to power, taking advantage of the times, and I have done much the same. I have achieved much more, as well you know, Malachi. Whom I choose to mate, is my decision. You may not like her nor think she is deemed worthy enough for me, but let me advise you," leaning over the chair, his growl was strong, "my *padre* has accepted her bonding to me, he approves, as does my *madre*. I would suggest you walk lightly in my presence when you reference, with such disdain, the Queen of Medici. You will taste her blood, you will see she is no longer mortal but immortal and mine. And as I rise, you better be prepared to deal with two Medici because she will be at my side, as will my sons!"

Malachi held his own anger at bay. "I assure you, we will be at the ceremony, and I will taste her blood as is protocol, and I have no reason to doubt she is now immortal. We will proclaim her such, and we will recognize her to the realm as your queen. That will be our public position, and no one will hear otherwise from the Council. We owe that to you and your family. But privately, we are still left with doubt this mortal can rise to the duties required. Prove me wrong, Medici. I hope you do, for the protection of the Medici legacy, I sincerely hope you do. The Medici name is the strongest and most respected name in our realm, its bloodline the most pure. It pleases me to know your *padre* and *madre* have visited you, have given their blessing. Although I must say, to hear your *padre* has blessed this union comes as a surprise. But what's done is done, Medici. She is yours now. Try not to embarrass us all with your impetuous choice, *si*?"

Throwing back his head and howling with laughter, Shade laughed in the face of this fool who thought that damn green robe gave him the right to fuck with him. Swinging his head down, he walked closely around and around him. "Don't ever forget that Medici is the strongest and most respected coven Malachi. That would be a grave mistake for the Council. Medici funds pay for many of the luxuries you enjoy, if I were to ever pull my coffers from your greedy grip, all of you would suffer. I have no desire to prove you wrong, none whatsoever. My queen will do that quite well all on her own. Embarrass you? I am sure she will, without a doubt. But not in the way you expect, only to show all of you, she is more than deserving of this title. I have prepared her, as has *Madre,* she guides my queen. Now, if you have no other damn insults to lie at my feet, I will be returning to the States once her coronation is over. I have much to do yet. Master Alec is a businessman, and both of us have fortunes and lands to conquer in the States."

Malachi nodded his head to him, in recognition of his status, but Council did not bow, not even to royalty. "I will deliver your sentiments to the Council, Medici. We will not interfere with your affairs. It is too late at any point, and your path has been chosen. But it sounds as if you plan to make this venture in the States a more permanent one? We have heard of plans for a new warrior camp. You are aware, are you not, that the land you own is in the middle of Master Maximus' territory? We have not heard from him. He has made no formal complaint to the Council in this regard, but surely, you cannot expect this invasion of his turf to go unaddressed. The Council can't help but wonder if the mortal has clouded your judgment. You have everything here. Your coven is established here. Your power is known and goes unchallenged here. These actions in the States are sure to bring discord."

Shade crossed his arms over his chest. "Malachi, as you have stated previously, I am over five-hundred years old, I'm no amateur master. I'm well aware of what I have gotten myself into. I also know Maximus and I will come to an agreement, just as Alec and I have. And yes, there is a warrior camp abroad, expanding the reach of the Medici. 'Go and seek your fortune,' is what my *padre* taught me, and he taught me well. Medici will need to grow to provide for our expanding coven.

"I will not be completely absent from Castello. My children will be born here, as is customary, and I expect their birth to be witnessed by Council. But I have much to accomplish. I have just achieved the only thing that will secure my legacy, a mate who loves me. Her loyalty and dedication to me and my coven has already been shown to my warriors. And if you have a problem with my being in the States, speak with Master Alec. We have no conflict, Malachi, masters do not always go to war to get what they need."

Malachi huffed. "Well, Master Alec is a whole different discussion, Medici. You know him well, he thumbs his nose at the Council, he defies our bylaws, and he lives more as a mortal than an immortal and puts us all in danger with his actions. Your association with him is watched closely by the Council as well, and I would advise you to tread lightly there."

Shade shook his head, chuckling. "Alec plays by his own rules, he always has. He follows his own lead, but as you say that is another matter. I know I'm being watched, well aware, and I'm also aware you will let me know the moment I take a misstep. So, Malachi, if that's all you require of me, I'll ask that you take your leave. I don't want my entire coven in an uproar because of your visit. I have taught them to respect you and Council elders, as they should, and I have tried to set for them a good example. I will see you at the ceremony and please give my regards to the Council for at least pretending to give a good fucking rat's ass about my mating!"

"Medici, I assure you, we mean no disrespect. I will take my leave now, and you will see the Council giving your queen all due respect at the coronation. You have my word."

The Turning: The Medici Warrior Series

* * *

Luca felt the presence of a powerful vampire in Castello, not an enemy, but something wasn't right. He heard Gi as he rushed past his door and knocked hard on Shade's bedroom door, telling him the Council was here. *The Council! The Council doesn't come to you... you go to the Council!* He heard Shade leave, pulling the door closed behind him followed by silence. He must have teleported down. Luca turned to Shannon. "Shan, I need to go to the next room and be with Kate. I need you to stay here."

Shannon looked back at him concerned. "Is everything all right?"

"Everything is fine, *mia belleza*. But Shade has been called away, and Kate is newly turned." He left their bedroom and walked down the hall to the massive suite, now occupied by Shade and Kate. He tapped at the door lightly and waited for her to answer.

Kate opened the door, expecting to see Gi again, but it was Luca. He bowed deeply to her, as soon as she opened the door.

"My Queen."

Kate sighed. "Luca, you honor me. Please, come in. And please tell me we don't have to do that from now on."

Luca smiled at her. "Only if my lady wishes it."

"My lady does not wish it. What's going on? Gi came to get Shade, told him the Council was here. He seemed in a panic, and it's not like Gi to panic."

Luca shrugged. "I'm not sure, Kate. A visit by the Council. Well, first of all, I've never heard of a visit from the Council except for ceremonial events, like your coronation. They'll be there, of course, but an uninvited visit? Unheard of."

Kate sat down on the bed. "But it's probably just about the ceremony, right? I mean, what do they do anyway?"

"They're our ruling body. They oversee all vampire covens in Europe. There's a separate Eastern Council that oversees all Asian countries. There are rules of law in the vampire community that must be followed, and those that break the rules must answer to the Council. The Council knows where every master is. Shade would have informed them of his intent to go to the States, for example. They settle disputes between covens to avoid battles if possible. Each Council member is on the Council for life, and they each have specific areas of responsibility. I heard Gi telling Shade Malachi was here. He oversees all births, deaths and matings. He will record your turning, as well as your ascension to the

Throne of Medici in their records. Your ceremony here at Castello, establishes your reign over the Medici coven, but the Council validates your standing in the vampire community at large."

Kate threw her hands in the air. "So, there. It's nothing then. Just details about the ceremony."

Luca looked closely at her. "And how are you, Kate. Since the turning."

She closed her eyes and took a deep breath. "You mean, besides hungry? Will I always feel this way?"

"The hunger will fade, but it never goes away. Not completely. You learn control with time. When we get back to Bel Rosso, I'll take you out again on a run like before, and you'll see the difference in your senses. You'll be able to hear the animals in the brush miles from us, and detect which animals are near, just from their scent alone. Not right away, we'll need to wait a bit until you have control, to control the urge to hunt. You don't feel it now because Shade is here, you feed from him regularly. I know he is weaning you, but the fact he's accessible to you helps to control the need."

Kate stood up and paced. "I feel like I have so much to learn."

"And he will guide you. He's your master, and your maker, in addition to your mate. I speak from experience when I say there's no master who takes that responsibility more seriously. He'll always guide you."

She looked at him as he spoke of Shade, and his devotion to him was without question. It was something she noticed with all the staff here, all the warriors. They'd follow him right over a cliff, no questions asked. And she'd hold his hand.

"I know he's always guided me. I feel like I've hardly seen you, or Shannon. Why didn't you bring her over?"

Luca looked at the floor. "She is still a mortal... and you... a newborn. Like I said, time and control."

Kate looked at him, creasing her brow. "What? What are you talking about?"

Luca caught her eye. "Your impulse would be to attack. To feed from her. She is weak compared to you. Prey."

Kate's hand went to her throat. "Oh my god, are you kidding me? No wonder he's kept me in this room. I thought, after the chamber, things would just go back to normal. She's my friend! Doesn't that mean anything? I wouldn't attack my friend."

"*Si,* in your heart she's your friend. But right now, your instincts and your beast identify her as prey. All mortals are prey. Another impulse you will learn to control."

"Luca, this ceremony, the other masters, the Council, his warriors, and Shannon, what if I mess this up? Oh god, that's why the Council is here, isn't it? It's not the ceremony. It's me! They're worried about me."

"Stop pacing. He'll guide you. Every step. He'll be right next to you. He'll not let you mess up. Trust him."

"I do trust him, but what you're saying is, I can't trust me."

"Trust him to take care of you. He'll not let his queen fail."

* * *

As Malachi was escorted from Castello, Shade sat back down and stared into space. He wanted to rip his fucking throat out, but he knew better. *Why can't they just accept her?* She was his, and he chose her, but his choice was not good enough for them.

Hanging his head, he sighed deeply and closed his eyes. He wanted so much to give her everything, her status in their community, and the honor and respect she deserved. He wanted to give her babies they would raise together. He wanted her to want for nothing. No matter what he did, he failed someone's expectation of him, someone's dream for him. He slammed his fist down on the table in anger and frustration.

"She is my fucking dream. Damn you all to hell! She is my queen, my mate. Do you hear me? And she will rule as a Medici!"

He heard the servants scurry, and heard the warriors on guard in the courtyard, ready to attack whatever had gotten him into this state and he headed outside for a smoke. His head was still spinning at the nerve and audacity of the Council.

Kate was still talking with Luca when she felt him, felt his anger and frustration, and she wanted to go to him. She saw Luca respond, stand up straighter, listening and she knew he felt Sade too. Kate stood to go to him, but as she reached the door, Luca stepped in front of it, blocking her exit.

"Kate, are you sure? You haven't been out since the turning?"

Kate pleaded with him, "I can feel him. He's angry. Something is wrong. Please, Luca!"

He reluctantly stepped aside, as she opened the door and found her way down the stairs to the grand foyer. She opened herself up to him, letting her instincts lead her to him. She was drawn to the parlor and followed there. The room was empty, but she could feel his presence.

"Shade? Are you okay?" She heard only silence. He had left this room. Shade could feel her frantically looking for him. *"Mi amore,* **come find me, use your senses. I have left the parlor, concentrate,** *bel.* **Come to me."**

Kate left the parlor and wandered further through the grand hallway, the sound of her footsteps echoed in the hall. She heard him call to her. She stopped and listened, feeling him... and let him lead her. She walked to the door that led outside to the back of the estate and into the formal gardens. She stepped outside for the first time since the turning. The scents overwhelmed her as the night air hit her face, and her head spun with dizziness. She reached out and steadied herself against the wall. She stood still, and could pick up his scent, from all the smells that assaulted her. She shut out everything else and followed his scent through the maze of the gardens, to find him standing alone, his back to her.

"Lover?"

"*Ti amo*, my queen. You have found your king. You have done well. Do you wish for your prize? Come closer, *mi amore*. I am pleased you shut out all the things around you, used what I have taught you. You can always find me, Kate, never be afraid you cannot. There will never be another moment for the rest of my life that I won't feel you, hear you, know your heart beats for me and me alone." He remained with his back to her, controlling his anger for Malachi, knowing she felt that and it had upset her greatly.

Kate walked to him, slid her arms around his waist and leaned her head against his strong back. "You are my prize. Now, what has you so upset this night?"

He sighed deeply as he felt her body on his, just her touch ignited him and calmed him all at the same time. She was magic. "Council. And you let me worry about them, no need for you to become agitated as well."

"It's about me, isn't it? They're concerned about me." She felt his heavy sigh and felt their heartbeats as her breasts were pressed against his back, their hearts synchronized, and beating with the same rhythm. "I won't let you down, lover. I promise you."

"I have no doubt." Pulling her around in front of him, he lifted her off her feet and felt her legs wrap around his waist. "I want you to listen to me, *mi amore*. I'm not the one with doubts, no one in this coven, nor do those that protect you doubt you. The Council has a huge problem and it's theirs, not mine. They will attend the ceremony, test your blood for immortality and acknowledge you as my mate and queen. That is all I need from those bastards. I have, in my arms, all I care about."

She'd known he'd always hidden much from her, to protect her, but what he'd never shared was what a gamble he was taking with his decision to choose her as his mate. Being here now, in Castello, with the ceremony looming, she finally appreciated the scope of it. The whole "king and queen" thing, which just seemed so farfetched, was very real. Her mortal status would probably always be something he'd have to deal with, as it related to those who were born immortal. She'd always be an intruder to them. It only made her more determined to prove them all wrong.

"I don't know what you saw in me. What drew you to me from the beginning? I felt the same pull, the same connection. So much so that it scared me. But your mother saw it too. When she came to me before the turning, she said she chose me for you. We were meant to be. Even with all the drama, whatever we have overcome, and whatever lies ahead, we were meant to be."

Pulling her head to his shoulder, he began to walk through the gardens, the moonlight streaming over them, like a beam meant for them. "*Madre* knows me deeper than anyone else. She knew what I needed, what I wanted, she had the ability to go anywhere and seek and find for me the perfect mate." Chuckling softly, laying his head on hers. "I think also she may

have had grand-children on her list of things she wanted. She would always say to me, give me grand-children, my sweet Prince! I would always laugh at her. Tell me you still want them, *mi amore*."

"Of course, lover. Our Sophia speaks to me almost every day. She's in quite a hurry that one."

"Every day? She is so beautiful, *mi amore*, so gorgeous with that hair and those blue eyes. They look straight into my heart. Does she make you feel this way as well?"

"They live in my heart, all of them. I see all of them. Do you?"

He stopped suddenly and pulled back from her. "All of them?" He felt his heart race. "Tell me, is there a *figlio*? Tell me, *mi amore*."

"He comes first, lover. A warrior, our little warrior. His name is Lorenzo, and he'll look like you with your dark skin and dark hair, your blue eyes. He'll make his father proud."

He held her closer. A son, she'd bear him a son. "*Mi amore, ti amo.* Our son, our warrior, the future of Medici."

"He is beautiful and so like you. He'll take pride in his name and his legacy. He yearns to walk in your footsteps, to be just like his father. He'll follow your example. He'll be followed by his most impatient sister, Sophia. She'll not be like him. He's steady and focused. She's impetuous, hot-tempered. She'll be curious and spirited, a handful. I'm warning you now."

He covered her in kisses. "So many *bambinos*, so much life for us to live together."

"Lover, there is more... I see another daughter, Natalia. I don't see the future for our daughters. But Lorenzo, I can see him the clearest, maybe because he is first."

"I say we get started now!" Throwing her over his shoulder, he ran, hearing her squeal as he laughed out loud.

"Where are you taking me?"

Stopping outside the door, he slid her down over his chest onto her feet and took her face into his hands.

"Two daughters? I shall be one jealous *padre* anyone tries to take my girls from me. And a son! Their futures will be bright, *mi amore*, they are coming, and that makes me joyously happy knowing we will raise them together. I want them to live in Virginia, to grow up on the estate, experience life and culture as I did. But most of all, I just want to love them. And I'm taking you back to our bedchamber."

"Making babies, are we, lover?"

"*Si, mi amore*, we are always making babies."

Sample of Book Three:
The Medici Queen

* * *

Alec and Rissa arrived by private jet at the Firenze airport, where Alec had a private car waiting with Alto at the wheel. Rissa had packed half her closet for this trip. She'd dozed on and off through the flight and slept now with her head on his shoulder.

"Rissa, we're here, my darling. The car's waiting to take us to Shade's home."

The flight felt like it took forever, Rissa still had reservations about this trip, but she had no damn choice. Max could easily be here, or he could've sent someone here to come after her. She heard Alec's voice break through her light sleep as she sat up, looking out the jet window.

"Oh good, these long flights are ridiculous. Make sure they don't damage my luggage or leave anything behind. I need everything I've brought."

"Rissa, your luggage will be taken care of and delivered to the castle. Now come, my darling." Alec exited the plane with her, as Alto held the door open to the car. Alec allowed her to enter the car first and then slid into the seat next to her. "Refresh my memory, darling. Have you been to Florence before?"

"Not Florence, Milan, of course. What fashion expert doesn't know Milan? Rome too, but Florence, no. Why do you ask? And how far is this drive?"

"Not too far. Alto has some Midnight for us in the car. Would you like a drink? We'll drive through a little of Tuscany to get to Florence. The Medici Castello is on the far side of Florence. You'll see it as we approach. Just relax and enjoy the countryside. It's quite beautiful, if I do say so. This is all Shade's territory. Pretty much everything you'll see on this trip will be inside Shade's territory. It's been a while since the last time I was here."

She looked out the window and although the landscape was stunning, it did nothing for her, she was a city girl at heart. *He owns all of this? Damn, that bitch! She can't be happy enough with all his property, the bitch has to take my Paris house as well?*

"So, you were here before? I think you mentioned his home and visiting here."

"Yes, I've known Shade for centuries, my darling. Before I lived in the States and presented myself as American, I was British, lived in London mostly. That's where I first met Shade. I believe we met at a Gorean Cult orgy that was held in London." He laughed at the memories. "Let's just say we've found our association to be mutually beneficial through the years. The castle is quite impressive, as I recall. Again, haven't been there in a few years. A little too opulent for my taste, but then again, he inherited it from his father."

Rissa glanced over at him. "I knew you were British, but you've completely lost any accent. I wondered, since we have a bit of a drive, are there things I should know before I get there about any protocol, rules, or customs? I want to make sure I make no mistakes. I already know going into this I'm not well received by the masters."

He lit up a cigarette and cracked the window open to release the smoke. "For our free time, there are no rules. We can do what we want. At the ceremony, you should only speak when spoken to. You shouldn't approach a master or his mate. Their mates will do the same. I may initiate a conversation with another master, or he with me. Other than that, I think you'll be fine. You've never seen a coronation, so I'd think you'd find it interesting."

"I'm sure I will since I've never had the pleasure, nor probably will again, unless, of course, they have brats." Sighing, she threw her head back on the seat. "All of this, she has all of this, and still she gets my damn Paris house. Seriously, Alec, there's something immensely wrong with that!" Leaning over, she kissed him on the cheek. "But I'm sure you'll find me an even better house in Paris. And besides, I get to spend the whole weekend alone with you, without Zena the bitch warrior."

Alec struggled to keep the annoyance out of his voice. "Rissa, first of all, it's my Paris house, not yours, but if it's important to you, although I can't imagine why because neither one of us ever takes vacation time, but if you want a place in Paris, I'll find something. Now please, can we drop the subject? And that warrior bitch? She's there to keep you safe. What has you so disagreeable? Most women would be delighted to have this trip. Are you so jaded already, my darling? Eternity is a long time to be bored."

She laid her head back and looked out the window. "No, Alec. Point taken."

Watching as the Tuscan landscape slid by, she was lost in her thoughts. As they crested a hill, she saw they were approaching a huge estate and it was something to behold. She sat up straighter in her seat and cocked her head. "Is that it? Tell me, it can't be!"

Alec saw the castle ahead. "Hmm, I do believe it is. Welcome to Medici Castello, surrounded by formal gardens, and sitting on the banks of the Arno River."

Alto pulled up to the estate and stopped at the huge gates. He pressed the intercom button. Once he identified himself and provided the password, the gates were opened to him.

Rissa laughed, but an annoyed and jealous laugh. "Well, it's regal."

She watched as Alto pulled into the huge roundabout drive, the buildings and gardens went on forever. Several house staff came out to open doors and Alto held her hand as she exited from the car. She remained quiet and waited for Alec to do whatever he needed to do to get them inside this palace. She intended to remain quiet or she'd never hear the end of it. This was very important for him, and she wanted him to be proud of her and how she presented herself. The staff started removing the mountain of luggage from the trunk. Gi stood at the entrance, overseeing the activity. Alec led Rissa up the steps to the door where Gi bowed deeply.

"Master Alec. It has been too long. It is our pleasure to have you as our guest at Medici Castello once more. And Miss Benneteau, our warmest welcome to you on what I hope will be the first of many visits. My lady has requested we reserve the Gold Room for you. I think you will find it to your satisfaction. And this is Carlos.

He will be your private butler for the duration of your stay. You will also have a personal maid, Miss Benneteau. Carlos will introduce her to you in your suite. I believe she is drawing a bath for you, so you may refresh after your long journey. Now please, come with me."

Alec took Rissa's arm and followed Gi into the grand foyer. *Ah yes, how could I have forgotten this?*

Rissa was already impressed with getting her own personal maid. She should have one of those at home. She made a mental note to work on that. As they were escorted in, she gasped. "My, this is impressive. It's gorgeous!" Her head was on a spring, she couldn't take it all in.

Alec smirked, finally something had impressed her. Alec watched as she tried to take in the over-the-top opulence of this room with the gilded gold bannisters on the marble staircase, and the massive chandeliers.

Carlos stepped up to greet them and bowed greatly . "Master Alec? If you're ready, I can escort you to your room now. I or someone will be stationed at your door twenty-four hours a day. We've been informed you are both day-walkers. If there's anything you wish to see in Castello, please ask and you'll be escorted. Otherwise sir, I'm afraid you'd only get lost. Your car will be kept in the garage, and your driver has been provided with private quarters. You need only let us know if you wish to leave the premises, and your car will be brought around. This way, please."

He led them up the massive staircase and down a long corridor of rooms, behind closed doors. When he reached their suite, he opened the door and stepped aside so they could enter. "If there is anything not to your liking, please let us know and we'll have it changed."

As Rissa walked into their room, she stood with her mouth open. *Is he joking? Not to my liking?* "Alec, this place is immense. This is gold, real gold! Oh my god, look at these roses! There must be seventy roses in this bouquet. This is over the top. I can't imagine Kate living here, living like this, every single day. I'm jealous, I'm beyond jealous, I'm astounded. Now I do need a drink!" Turning to him, she wrapped her arms around him and kissed him on the cheek. "Thank you. Thank you for bringing me here, Alec."

Carlos bowed to her. "Miss Benneteau, my lady has requested you have fresh flowers every day of your stay. If you have a favorite, please let us know. Oh, and this is Rosa. She'll be your personal maid. Just ring and she'll respond, otherwise, you'll not see her."

Rosa curtsied. "Miss Benneteau, I've drawn a hot bath for you, and filled it with fresh rose petals, my lady's favorite. It's ready whenever you are. There's Midnight and crystal for both of you on the table if you wish a drink. My lady requested you have silk robes to wear after your bath and when you're in your room. Please feel free to keep them as my lady's gift to you. Your toiletries have been laid out for you. Please let me know how I can be of service."

Nodding to Rosa, she perused the housemaid's outfit, the traditional black and white, and the Medici crest was everywhere she looked.

"I wish to bathe immediately, and you may assist me with my clothing. I also require all of my garments and shoes be unpacked and put into the wardrobes. Do you have rose-scented bath salts and oils since you have placed rose petals in my bath water?"

Turning to Alec, she smiled. "You won't mind if I smell like roses tonight, will you, Alec? Very romantic, don't you think?"

Alec dared not tell her roses were Kate's signature scent. "Of course, my darling, I'd find it quite romantic."

About the Author

Emily Bex is an avid life-long reader, and a first-time writer of the epic six book Medici Warrior Series. As she says, "Why start small?" She worked for over twenty years in marketing, developing ad campaigns, catalogs, product launches and promotional literature. She figured if she could write creatively about products, then surely she could write something about these characters that were rattling around inside her brain. She currently lives in Virginia, but has used her extensive love of travel, both foreign and domestic, to create the backdrop for her characters to play out their story.

View the Medici Warrior Series Here:

https://www.emilybex.com/books/

Make sure to stalk me!

Instagram:
https://bit.ly/3dAaO5k

Facebook:
http://bit.ly/3k5GHUC

Goodreads:
http://bit.ly/3ukYcVU

Twitter:
https://bit.ly/3s6m3GG

Bookbub:
http://bit.ly/2ZBJ9ZM

Website:
https://www.emilybex.com/

Printed in Great Britain
by Amazon

28494705R00337